Praise for Maeve Binchy

'Oh, the bliss . . . Maeve's back, on top form . . . The heart is the theme, literally and metaphorically, and this is heart-warming stuff – sweet but never cloying' *The Times*

'The book rattles along from one gripping story to another, leaving the reader with a satisfying glow' *Daily Mail*

'Binchy weaves her magic once again in an addictive story about families and people who aren't always quite what they seem' *Woman & Home*

'Warm, witty and with a deep understanding of what makes us tick, it's little wonder that Maeve Binchy's bewitching stories have become world-beaters' *OK!*

'To read it is like being wrapped up in a pink blanket with a hot-water bottle – but, make no mistake, there is magic at work' *Sunday Times*

'Binchy is degrees better than most other novelists, and her storytelling ability is second to none' *Sunday Express*

'A Maeve classic, it'll leave a warm, fuzzy feeling in your tummy' *Company*

'It's always a treat to read one of Maeve Binchy's novels, and this is no exception . . . [She] leaves us caring about [her characters] as if they are our friends' *Bella*

'One of the world's best-loved writers' *Woman's Weekly*

BY MAEVE BINCHY

Fiction

Light a Penny Candle
Echoes
The Lilac Bus
Firefly Summer
Silver Wedding
Circle of Friends
The Copper Beech
The Glass Lake
Evening Class
Tara Road
Scarlet Feather
Quentins
Nights of Rain and Stars
Whitethorn Woods
Heart and Soul
Minding Frankie

Non-fiction

Aches & Pains
The Maeve Binchy Writers' Club

Short Stories

Victoria Line, Central Line
Dublin 4
This Year It Will Be Different
The Return Journey

Maeve Binchy was born in County Dublin and educated at the Holy Child Convent in Killiney and at University College, Dublin. After a spell as a teacher in various girls' schools, she joined the *Irish Times*. Her first novel, *Light a Penny Candle*, was published in 1982, and since then she has written more than a dozen novels and short-story collections, each one of them bestsellers. Several have been adapted for cinema and television, most notably *Circle of Friends* and *Tara Road*. Maeve Binchy was awarded the Lifetime Achievement award at the British Book Awards in 1999 and the Irish PEN/A.T. Cross award in 2007. In 2010 she was also presented with a Lifetime Achievement award by the Romantic Novelists' Association. She is married to the writer and broadcaster Gordon Snell. Visit her website at www.maevebinchy.com.

Minding Frankie

Maeve Binchy

An Orion paperback

First published in Great Britain in 2010
by Orion
This paperback edition published in 2011
by Orion Books Ltd,
Orion House, 5 Upper St Martin's Lane,
London WC2H 9EA

An Hachette UK company

1 3 5 7 9 10 8 6 4 2

A CIP catalogue record for this book
is available from the British Library.

ISBN 978-1-4091-1791-9

Typeset by Deltatype Ltd, Birkenhead, Merseyside

Printed and bound in Great Britain by
Clays Ltd, St Ives plc

The Orion Publishing Group's policy is to use papers that
are natural, renewable and recyclable products and
made from wood grown in sustainable forests. The logging
and manufacturing processes are expected to conform to
the environmental regulations of the country of origin.

www.orionbooks.co.uk

For dear generous Gordon
who makes life great every single day.

CHAPTER ONE

Katie Finglas was coming to the end of a tiring day in the salon. Anything bad that could happen had happened. A woman had not told them about an allergy and had come out with lumps and a rash on her forehead. A bride's mother had thrown a tantrum and said that she looked like a laughing stock. A man who had wanted streaks of blond in his hair became apoplectic when halfway through the process he had enquired what they would cost. Katie's husband Garry had placed both his hands innocently on the shoulders of a sixty-year-old female client who had told him that she was going to sue him for sexual harassment and assault.

She looked at the man standing opposite her, a big priest with sandy hair mixed with grey.

'You're Katie Finglas and I gather you run this establishment,' the priest said, looking around the innocent salon nervously as if it were a high-class brothel.

'That's right, Father,' Katie said with a sigh. What could be happening now?

'It's just that I was talking to some of the girls who work here, down at the centre on the quays, you know, and they were telling me ...'

Katie felt very tired. She employed a couple of school-leavers; she paid them properly, trained them. *What* could they have been complaining about to a priest?

'Yes, Father, what exactly is the problem?' she asked.

'Well, it *is* a bit of a problem. I thought I should come to you directly as it were.' He seemed a little awkward.

'Very right, Father,' Katie said. 'So tell me what it is.'

'It's this woman, Stella Dixon. She's in hospital, you see ...'

'Hospital?'

Katie's head reeled. What *could* this involve? Someone who had inhaled the peroxide?

'I'm sorry to hear that.' She tried for a level voice.

'Yes, but she wants a hairdo.'

'You mean she trusts us again?'

Sometimes life was extraordinary.

'No, I don't think she was ever here before ...' He looked bewildered.

'And your interest in all this, Father?'

'I am Brian Flynn and I am acting chaplain at St Brigid's Hospital at the moment while the real chaplain is in Rome on a pilgrimage. Apart from being asked to bring in cigarettes and drink for the patients, this is the only serious request I've had.'

'You want me to go and do someone's hair in hospital?'

'She's seriously ill. She's dying. I thought she needed a senior person to talk to. Not, of course, that you look very senior. You're only a girl yourself,' the priest said.

'God, weren't you a sad loss to the women of Ireland when you went for the priesthood,' Katie said. 'Give me her details and I'll bring my magic bag of tricks in to see her.'

'Thank you so much, Ms Finglas. I have it all written out here.'

Father Flynn handed her a note.

A middle-aged woman approached the desk. She had glasses on the tip of her nose and an anxious expression.

'I gather you teach people the tricks of hairdressing,' she said.

'Yes, or more the *art* of hairdressing, as we like to call it,' Katie said.

'I have a cousin coming home from America for a few weeks. She mentioned that in America there are places where you could get your hair done for near to nothing cost if you were letting people practise on you.'

'Well, we do have a students' night on Tuesdays; people bring in their own towels and we give them a style. They usually contribute five euros to a charity.'

'Tonight is Tuesday!' the woman cried triumphantly.

'So it is,' Katie said through gritted teeth.

'So, could I book myself in? I'm Josie Lynch.'

'Great, Mrs Lynch, see you after seven o'clock,' Katie said, writing down the name.

Her eyes met the priest's. There was sympathy and understanding there.

It wasn't all champagne and glitter running your own hairdressing salon.

Josie and Charles Lynch had lived in 23 St Jarlath's Crescent since they were married thirty-two years ago. They had seen many changes in the area. The corner shop had become a mini supermarket; the old laundry, where sheets had been ironed and folded, was now a laundromat, where people left big bags bulky with mixed clothes and asked for a service wash. There was now a proper medical practice with four doctors, where once there had been just old Dr Gillespie who had brought everyone into the world and seen them out of it.

During the height of the economic boom, houses in St Jarlath's Crescent had been changing hands for amazing sums of money. Small houses with gardens near the city centre were much in demand. Not any more, of course – the recession had been a great equaliser, but it was still a much more substantial area than it had been three decades ago.

After all, just look at Molly and Paddy Carroll with their son Declan – a doctor – a real, qualified doctor! And just look at Muttie and Lizzie Scarlet's daughter Cathy. She ran a catering company that was hired for top events.

But a lot of things had changed for the worse. There was no community spirit any more. No church processions went up and down the Crescent on the feast of Corpus Christi as they used to three decades ago. Josie and Charles Lynch felt that they were alone in the world, and certainly in St Jarlath's Crescent, in that they kneeled down at night and said the Rosary.

That had always been the way.

When they married, they planned a life based on the maxim that the family that prays together stays together. They had assumed they would have eight or nine children, because God never put a mouth into this world that He didn't feed. But that wasn't to happen. After Noel, Josie had been told there would be no more children. It was hard to accept. They both came from big families; their brothers and sisters had produced big families. But then, perhaps, it was all meant to be this way.

They had always hoped Noel would be a priest. The

fund to educate him for the priesthood was started before he was three. Money was put aside from Josie's wages at the biscuit factory. Every week a little more was added to the Post Office savings account and when Charles got his envelope on a Friday from the hotel where he was a porter, a sum was also put into the Post Office. Noel would get the best of priestly educations when the time came.

So it was with great surprise and a lot of disappointment that Josie and Charles learned that their quiet son had no interest whatsoever in a religious life. The Brothers said that he showed no sign of a vocation and when the matter had been presented to Noel as a possibility at the age of fourteen, he had said if it was the last job on earth he wouldn't go for it.

That had been very definite indeed.

Not so definite, however, was what he actually *would* like to do. Noel was vague about this, except to say he might like to run an office. Not work in an office, but run one. He showed no interest in studying office management or bookkeeping or accounting or in any areas where the careers department tried to direct him. He liked art, he said, but he didn't want to paint. If pushed he would say that he liked looking at paintings and thinking about them. He was good at drawing; he always had a notebook and a pencil with him and he was often to be found curled up in a corner, sketching a face or an animal. This did not, of course, lead to any career path, but Noel had never expected it to. He did his homework at the kitchen table, sighing now and then, but rarely ever excited or enthusiastic. At the parent–teacher meetings Josie and Charles had enquired about this. They wondered, did anything at school fire him up? Anything at all?

The teachers were at a loss. Most boys were unfathomable around fourteen or fifteen but they had usually settled down to do something. Or often to do nothing. Noel Lynch, they said, had just become even more quiet and withdrawn than he already was.

Josie and Charles wondered, could this be right?

Noel was quiet, certainly, and it had been a great relief to them that he hadn't filled the house up with loud young lads thumping each other. But they had thought this was part of his spiritual life, a preparation for a future as a priest. Now it appeared that this was certainly not the case.

Perhaps, Josie suggested, it was only the Brothers' brand of religious life that Noel objected to. In fact, might he have a different kind of vocation and want to become a Jesuit or a missionary?

Apparently not.

And when he was fifteen he said that he didn't really want to join in the family Rosary any more, it was only a ritual of meaningless prayers chanted in repetition. He didn't mind doing good for people, trying to make less fortunate people have a better life, but surely no God could want this fifteen minutes of drone drone drone.

By the time he was sixteen they realised that he didn't go to Sunday Mass any more. Someone had seen him up by the canal when he was meant to have been to the early Mass up in the church on the corner. He told them that there was no point in his staying on at school as there was nothing more he needed to learn from them. They were hiring office staff up at Hall's and they would train him in office routine. He might as well go to work straight away rather than hang about.

The Brothers and the teachers at his school said it was always a pity to see a boy study and leave without a qualification, but still, they shrugged, it was very hard trying to interest the lad in anything at all. He seemed to be sitting and waiting for his schooldays to end. Could even be for the best if he left school now. Get him into Hall's, the big builders' merchants; give him a wage every week and then they might see where, if anywhere, his interest lay.

Josie and Charles thought sadly of the fund that had been growing in the Post Office for years. Money that would never be spent making Noel Lynch into a reverend. A kindly Brother suggested that maybe they should spend it on a holiday for themselves, but Charles and Josie were shocked. This money had been saved for God's work; it would be spent on God's work.

Noel got his place in Hall's. He met his work colleagues but without any great enthusiasm. They would not be his friends and companions any more than his fellow students at the Brothers had become mates. He didn't *want* to be alone all the time but it was often easier.

Over the years Noel had arranged with his mother that he would not join them at meals. He would have his lunch in the middle of the day and he would make a snack for himself in the evening. This way he missed the Rosary, the socialising with pious neighbours and the interrogation about what he had done with his day, which was the natural accompaniment to mealtimes in the Lynch household.

He took to coming home later and later. He also

took to visiting Casey's pub on the journey home – a big barn of a place – both comforting and anonymous at the same time. It was familiar because everyone knew his name.

'I'll drop it down to you, Noel,' the loutish son of the house would say.

Old Man Casey, who said little but noticed everything, would look over his spectacles as he polished the beer glasses with a clean linen cloth.

'Evening, Noel,' he would say, managing to combine the courtesy of being the landlord with the sense of disapproval he had of Noel. He was, after all, an acquaintance of Noel's father. It was as if he was glad that Casey's was getting the price of the pint – or several pints – as the night went on, but he also seemed disappointed that Noel was not spending his wages more wisely. Yet Noel liked the place. It wasn't a trendy pub with fancy prices. It wasn't full of girls giggling and interrupting a man's drinking. People left him alone here.

That was worth a lot.

When he got home, Noel noticed that his mother looked different. He couldn't work out why. She was wearing the red knitted suit that she wore only on special occasions. At the biscuit factory where she worked they wore a uniform, which she said was wonderful because it meant you didn't wear out your good garments. Noel's mother didn't wear make-up so it couldn't be that.

Eventually he realised that it was her hair. His mother had been to a beauty salon.

'You got a new hairdo, Mam!' he said.

Josie Lynch patted her head, pleased. 'They did a

good job, didn't they?' She spoke like someone who frequented hairdressing salons regularly.

'Very nice, Mam,' he said.

'I'll be putting a kettle on if you'd like a cup of tea,' she offered.

'No, Mam, you're all right.'

He was anxious to be out of there, safe in his room. And then Noel remembered that his cousin Emily was coming from America the next day. His mother must be getting ready for her arrival. This Emily was going to stay for a few weeks apparently. It hadn't been decided exactly how many weeks ...

Noel hadn't involved himself greatly in the visit, doing only what he had to, like helping his father to paint her room and clearing out the downstairs box room where they had tiled the walls and put in a new shower. He didn't know much about her; she was an older person, in her fifties maybe, the only daughter of his father's eldest brother Martin. She had been an art teacher but her job had ended unexpectedly and she was using her savings to see the world. She would start with a visit to Dublin from where her father had left many years ago to seek his fortune in America.

It had not been a great fortune, Charles reported. The eldest brother of the family had worked in a bar where he was his own best customer. He had never stayed in touch. Any Christmas cards had been sent by this Emily, who had also written to tell first of her father's death and then her mother's. She sounded remarkably businesslike, and said that when she arrived in Dublin she would expect to pay a contribution to the family expenses, and that since she was letting her own small apartment in New York during her absence, it was only fair. Josie and Charles were also reassured that she seemed sensible and had promised not to be in their way or looking for entertainment. She said she would find plenty to occupy her.

Noel sighed.

It would be one more trivial happening elevated to high drama by his mother and father. The woman wouldn't be in the door before she heard all about his great future at Hall's, about his mother's job at the biscuit factory and his father's role as a senior porter in a very grand hotel. She would be told about the moral decline in Ireland, the lack of attendance at Sunday Mass and that binge drinking kept the emergency departments of hospitals full to overflowing. Emily would be invited to join the family Rosary.

Noel's mother had already spent considerable time debating whether they should put a picture of the Sacred Heart or of Our Lady of Perpetual Succour in the newly painted room. Noel had managed to avoid too much further discussion of this agonising choice by suggesting that they wait until she arrived.

'She taught art in a school, Mam, she might have brought her own pictures,' he had said and amazingly his mother had agreed immediately.

'You're quite right, Noel. I have a tendency to make all the decisions in the world. It will be nice having another woman to share all that with.'

Noel mildly hoped that she was right and that this woman would not disrupt their ways. This was going to be a time of change in their household anyway. His father was going to be retired as porter in a year or two. His mother still had a few more years in the biscuit factory but she thought she might retire also and keep

Charles company with the two of them doing some good works. He hoped that Emily would make their lives less complicated rather than more complicated.

But mainly he gave the matter very little thought.

Noel got along by not thinking too deeply on anything: not about his dead-end job in Hall's; not about the hours and money he spent in Old Man Casey's pub; not about the religious mania of his parents, who thought that the Rosary was the answer to most of the world's problems. Noel would not think about the lack of a steady girlfriend in his life. He just hadn't met anyone, that's all it was. Nor indeed did he worry about the lack of any kind of mates. Some places were easy to find friends. Hall's wasn't one of them. Noel had decided that the very best way to cope with things not being so great was not to think about them at all. It had worked well so far.

Why fix things if they weren't broken?

Charles Lynch had been very silent. He hadn't noticed his wife's new hairdo. He hadn't guessed that his son had drunk four pints on the way home from work. He found it hard to raise any interest in the arrival next morning of his brother Martin's daughter, Emily. Martin had made it clear that he had no interest in the family back home.

Emily had certainly been a courteous correspondent over the years – even to the point of offering to pay her bed and board. That might come in very useful indeed these days. Charles Lynch had been told that morning that his services as hotel porter would no longer be needed. He and another 'older' porter would leave at the end of the month. Charles had been trying to find the words to tell Josie since he got home, but the words weren't there.

He could repeat what the young man in the suit had said to him earlier in the day: a string of sentences about it being no reflection on Charles or his loyalty to the hotel. He had been there, man and boy, resplendent in his uniform and very much part of the old image. But that's exactly what it was – an old image. The new owners were insisting on a new image and who could stand in the way of the march of progress?

Charles had thought he would grow old in that job. That one day there would be a dinner for him where Josie would go and wear a long frock. He would be presented with a gold-plated clock. Now, none of this was going to happen.

He was going to be without a job in two and a half weeks' time.

There were few work opportunities for a man in his sixties who had been let go from the one hotel where he had worked since he was sixteen. Charles Lynch would have liked to have talked to his son about it all, but he and Noel didn't seem to have had a conversation for years now. If ever. The boy was always anxious to get to his room and resisted any questions or discussions. It wouldn't be fair to lay all this on him now.

Charles wouldn't find a sympathetic ear or any font of advice. Just tell Josie and get it over with, he told himself. But she was up to high doh about this woman coming from America. Maybe he should leave it for a couple of days. Charles sighed about the bad timing of it all.

To: Emily
From: Betsy

I wish that you hadn't decided to go to Ireland, I will miss you greatly.

I wish you had let me come and see you off ... but then you were always one for the quick, impulsive decision. Why should I expect you to change now?

I know that I should say that I hope you will find all your heart's desire in Dublin, but in a way I don't want you to. I want you to say it was wonderful for six weeks and then for you to come back home again.

It's not going to be the same without you here. There's an exhibit opening and it's just a block away and I can't bring myself to go to it on my own. I won't go to nearly as many theater matinées as I did with you.

I'll collect your rent every Friday from the student who's renting your apartment. I'll keep an eye open in case she is growing any attitude-changing substances in your window boxes.

You must write and tell me all about the place you are staying – don't leave anything out. I am so glad you will have your laptop with you. There will be no excuse for you not to stay in touch. I'll keep telling you small bits of news about Eric in the suitcase store. He really is interested in you, Emily, whether you believe it or not!

Hope you get your laptop up and running soon and I'll hear all about your arrival in the land of the Shamrock.

Love from your lonely friend,
Betsy

To: Betsy
From: Emily

What makes you think that I would have to wait to get to Ireland to hear from you? I'm at J.F.K. and the machine works.

Nonsense! You won't miss me – you and your fevered imagination! You will have a thousand fantasies. Eric does not fancy me, not even remotely. He is a man of very few words and none of them are small talk. He speaks about me to you because he is too shy to speak to you. Surely you know that?

I'll miss you too, Bets, but this is something I have to do.

I swear that I will keep in touch. You'll probably get twenty-page letters from me every day and wish you hadn't encouraged me!

Love,
Emily

'I wonder, should we have gone out to the airport to meet her?' Josie Lynch said for the fifth time next morning.

'She said she would prefer to make her own way here,' Charles said, as he had said on the previous four occasions.

Noel just drank his mug of tea and said nothing.

'She wrote and said the plane could be in early if they got a good wind behind them.' Josie spoke as if she were a frequent flyer herself.

'So she could be here any time …' Charles said with a heavy heart.

He hated having to go in to the hotel this morning, knowing that his days there were numbered. There would be time enough to tell Josie once this woman had settled in. Martin's daughter! He hoped that she hadn't inherited her father's great thirst.

There was a ring at the doorbell. Josie's face was all alarm. She snatched Noel's mug of tea from him and swept up the empty eggcup and plate from in front of Charles. Patting her new hairdo again, she spoke in a high, false voice.

'Answer the door, please, Noel, and welcome your cousin Emily in.'

Noel opened the door to a small woman, forty-something, with frizzy hair and a cream-coloured rain-coat. She had two neat, red suitcases on wheels. She looked entirely in charge of the situation. Her first time in the country and she had found St Jarlath's Crescent with no difficulty.

'You must be Noel. I hope I'm not too early for the household.'

'No, we were all up. We're about to go to work, you see, and you are very welcome, by the way.'

'Thank you. Well, shall I come in and say hello and goodbye to them?'

Noel realised that he might have left her for ever on the doorstep, but then he was only half awake. It took him until about eleven, when he had his first vodka and Coke, to be fully in control of the day. Noel was absolutely certain that nobody at Hall's knew of his morning injection of alcohol and his mid-afternoon booster. He covered himself very carefully and always allowed a bottle of genuine Diet Coke to peek out of his duffel bag. The vodka was added from a separate source when he was alone.

He brought the small American woman into the

15

kitchen where his mother and father kissed her on the cheek and said this was a great day that Martin Lynch's daughter had come back to the land of her ancestors.

'See you this evening then, Noel,' she called.

'Yes, of course. I might be a bit late. Lots of things to catch up on. But settle in well …'

'I will and thank you for agreeing to share your home with me.'

He left them to it. As he pulled the door to behind him he could hear the pride in his mother's voice as she showed off the newly decorated downstairs bedroom. And he could hear his cousin Emily cry out that it was just perfect.

Noel thought his father was very quiet today and last night. But then he was probably just imagining it. His father didn't have a care in the world, just as long as they made a fuss of him in that hotel and while he was sure there would be the Rosary every evening, an annual visit to Lourdes to see the shrine and talk of going further afield one day, like maybe Rome or the Holy Land. Charles Lynch was lucky enough to be a man who was content with things the way they were. He didn't need to numb himself against the dead weight of days and nights by spending long hours drinking in Old Man Casey's.

Noel walked to the end of the road where he would catch his bus. He walked as he did every morning, nodding to people but seeing nothing, noting no details about his surroundings. He wondered mildly what that busy-looking American woman would make of it all here.

Probably she might stick it for about a week before she gave up in despair.

At the biscuit factory Josie told them all about the arrival of Emily who had found her own way to St Jarlath's Crescent as if she had been born and reared there. Josie said she was an extremely nice person who had offered to make the supper for everyone that night. They were just to tell her what they liked and didn't like and point her to the market. She didn't need to go to bed and rest, apparently, because she had slept overnight on the plane coming over. She had admired everything in the house and said that gardening was her hobby, so she would look out for a few plants when she went shopping. If they didn't mind, of course.

The other women said that Josie should consider herself very lucky. This American could have easily turned out to be very difficult indeed.

At the hotel, Charles was his normal, pleasant self to everyone he met. He carried suitcases in from taxis, he directed tourists out towards the sights of Dublin, he looked up the times of theatre performances, he looked down at the sad face of a little fat King Charles spaniel that had been tied to the hotel railing. Charles knew this little dog: Caesar. It was often attached to Mrs Monty – an eccentric old lady who wore a huge hat and three strands of pearls, a fur coat and nothing else. If anyone angered her, she opened her coat, rendering them speechless.

The fact she had left the dog there meant that she must have been taken into the psychiatric hospital. If the past was anything to go by, she would discharge herself from the hospital after about three days and come to collect Caesar and take him back to his unpredictable life with her.

Charles sighed.

Last time, he had been able to conceal the dog in the hotel until Mrs Monty came back to get him, but things were different now. He would take the dog home at lunchtime. Josie wouldn't like it. Not at all. But St Francis had written the book as far as animals were concerned. If it came to a big, dramatic row Josie wouldn't go against St Francis. He hoped that his brother's daughter didn't have any allergies or attitudes towards dogs. She looked far too sensible.

Emily had spent a busy morning shopping. She was surrounded by food when Charles came in. Immediately, she made him a mug of tea and a cheese sandwich.

Charles was grateful for this. He had thought that he was about to miss lunch altogether. He introduced Emily to Caesar and told her some of the story behind his arrival in St Jarlath's Crescent.

Emily Lynch seemed to think it was the most natural thing in the world.

'I wish I had known he was coming. I could have got him a bone,' she said. 'Still, I met that nice Mr Carroll, your neighbour. He's a butcher. He might get me one.'

She hadn't been here five minutes and she had got to know the neighbours!

Charles looked at her with admiration. 'Well, aren't you a real bundle of energy,' he said. 'You took your retirement very early for someone as fit as you are.'

'Oh no, I didn't choose retirement,' Emily said, as she trimmed the pastry crust around a pie. 'No, indeed, I loved my job. They let me go. Well, they said I *must* go, actually.'

'Why? Why did they do that?' Charles was shocked.

'Because they thought that I was old and cautious and always very much the same. It was a question of my being the old style. The old guard. I would take children to visit galleries and exhibits. They would have a sheet of paper with twenty questions on it and they would spend a morning there trying to find answers. It would give them a great grounding in how to look at a picture or a sculpture. Well, I thought so anyway. Then came this new principal, a child himself with the notion that teaching art was all about free expression. He really wanted recent graduates who knew how to do all this. I didn't, so I had to go.'

'They can't sack you for being mature, surely?'

Charles was sympathetic. His own case was different. He was the public face of the hotel, they had told him, and these times meant the hotel's face must be a young face. That was logical in a cruel sort of way. But this Emily wasn't old. She wasn't fifty yet. They must have laws against that kind of discrimination.

'No, they didn't actually say I was dismissed. They just kept me in the background doing filing, away from the children, out of the art studio. It was unbearable, so I left. But they had forced me to go.'

'Were you upset?' Charles was very sympathetic.

'Oh yes, at the start. I was very upset indeed. It kind of made nothing of all the work I had done for years. I had got accustomed to meeting people at art galleries who often said, "Miss Lynch, you started off my whole interest in art," and so I thought it was all written off when they let me go. Like saying I had contributed nothing.'

Charles felt tears in his eyes. She was describing

exactly his own years as porter in the hotel. Written off. That's what he felt.

Emily had cheered up. She put twirly bits of pastry on top of the pie and cleared the kitchen table swiftly.

'But my friend Betsy told me that I was mad to sit sulking in my corner. I should resign at once and set about doing what I had really wanted to. Begin the rest of my life, she called it.'

'And did you?' Charles asked.

Wasn't America a wonderful place! *He* wouldn't be able to do that here – not in a million years.

'Yes, I did. I sat down and made a list of what I wanted to do. Betsy was right. If I had gotten a post in some other school maybe the same thing would have happened. I had a small savings account so I could afford to be without paid work for a while. Trouble was, I didn't know exactly what I wanted to do, so I did several things.

'First I did a cookery course. Tra-la-la. That's why I can make a chicken pie so quickly. And then I went on an intensive course and learned to use computers and the internet properly so I could get a job in any office if I wanted to. Then I went to this garden centre where they had window-box and planter classes. So now that I am full of skills, I decided to go and see the world.'

'And Betsy? Did she do that too?'

'No. She already understood the internet and she doesn't want to cook because she's always on a diet, but she did share the window-box addiction with me.'

'And suppose they asked you back to your old job? Would you go?'

'No. I can't now, even if they *did* ask. No, these days I'm much too busy,' Emily said.

'I see,' Charles nodded. He seemed about to say something else but stopped himself. He fussed about, getting more milk for the tea.

Emily knew he wanted to say something; she knew how to listen. He would say it eventually.

'The thing is,' he said slowly and with great pain, 'the real thing is that these new brooms that are meant to be sweeping clean, they sweep away a lot of what was valuable and important as well as sweeping out cobwebs or whatever ...'

Emily saw it then. This would have to be handled carefully. She looked at him sympathetically.

'Have another mug of tea, Uncle Charles.'

'No, I have to get back,' he said.

'Do you? I mean, think about it for a moment, Uncle Charles. Do you have to? What more can they do to you? I mean, that they haven't done already ...'

He gave her a long, level look.

She understood.

This woman he had never met until this morning realised, without having to be told, exactly what had happened to Charles Lynch. Something that his own wife and son hadn't seen at all.

The chicken pie that evening was a great success. Emily had made a salad as well. They talked easily, all three of them, and Emily introduced the subject of her own retirement.

'It's just amazing, the very thing you most dread can turn out to be a huge blessing in disguise! I never realised until it was over that I spent so much of my life on trains and cross-town buses. No wonder there were no hours left to learn the internet and small-scale gardening.'

Charles watched in admiration. Without ever appearing to have done so, she was making his path very smooth. He would tell Josie tomorrow, but maybe he might tell her now, this very minute.

It was much easier than he would ever have believed possible. He explained slowly that he had been thinking for a long time about leaving the hotel. The matter had come up recently in conversation and, amazingly, it turned out that it would suit the hotel too and so the departure would be by mutual agreement. All he had to do now was make sure that he was going to get some kind of reasonable compensation.

He said that for the whole afternoon his head had been bursting with ideas for what he would like to do.

Josie was taken aback. She looked at Charles anxiously in case this was just a front. Perhaps he was only blustering when inside he was very upset. But in as much as she could see, he seemed to be speaking from the heart.

'I suppose it's what Our Lord wants for you,' she said piously.

'Yes and I'm grabbing it with both hands.'

Charles Lynch was indeed telling the truth. He had not felt so liberated for a long time. Since talking to Emily today at lunchtime, he had begun to feel that there was a whole world out there.

Emily moved in and out clearing dishes, bringing in some dessert, and from time to time she entered the conversation easily. When her uncle said he had to walk Mrs Monty's dog until she was released from wherever she was, Emily suggested that Charles could mind other people's dogs as well.

'That nice man Paddy Carroll, the butcher, had a huge dog called Dimples that needs to lose at least ten pounds' weight,' she said enthusiastically.

'I couldn't ask Paddy for money,' Charles protested.

Josie agreed with him. 'You see, Emily, Paddy and Molly Carroll are neighbours. It would be odd to ask them to pay Charles to walk that big, foolish dog. It would sound very grasping.'

'I see that, of course, and you wouldn't want to be grasping, but then again he might see a way to giving you some lamb chops or best ground beef from time to time.'

Emily was a great believer in barter and Charles seemed to think that this was completely possible.

'But would there be a real job, Emily, you know, a *profession*, a life like Charles had in the hotel? Where he was a person who mattered?'

'I wouldn't survive just with dog walking alone, but maybe I could get a job in a kennels, I'd really love that,' Charles said.

'And if there was anything else that you had both *really* wanted to do?' Emily was gentle. 'You know, I so enjoyed looking up all my roots and making a family tree. Not that I'm suggesting that to you, of course.'

'Well, do you know what we always wanted to do ... ?' Josie began tentatively.

'No. What was that?' Emily was interested in everything so she was easy to talk to.

Josie continued, 'We always thought that it was a pity that St Jarlath was never properly celebrated in this neighbourhood. I mean, our street is called after him, but nobody you'd meet knows a thing about him. Charles and I were thinking we might raise money to erect a statue to his memory.'

'A statue to St Jarlath! Imagine!' Emily was surprised. Perhaps she had been wrong to have encouraged them to be free thinkers. 'Wasn't he rather a long time ago?' She was careful not to throw any cold water on Josie's plan, especially when she saw Charles light up with enthusiasm.

Josie waved this objection away. 'Oh, that's no problem. If he's a saint does it matter if he died only a few years back or in the sixth century?' Josie said.

'The *sixth* century?' This was even worse than Emily had feared.

'Yes, he died around AD 520 and his Feast Day is 6 June.'

'And that would be a very suitable time of the year for a little procession to his shrine.' Charles was busy planning it all already.

'And was he from around these parts?' Emily asked.

Apparently not. Jarlath was from the other side of the country, the Atlantic coast. He had set up the first Archdiocese of Tuam. He had taught other great holy men, even other saints: St Brendan of Clonfert and St Colman of Coyne. Places that were miles away.

'But there was always a devotion to him here,' Charles explained.

'Why would they have named the street after him otherwise?' Josie wanted to know.

Emily wondered what would have happened if her father Martin Lynch had stayed here. Would he have been a simple, easily pleased person like Charles and Josie, instead of the discontented drunk that he had turned into in New York? But all this business about the saint who had died miles away, hundreds of years ago, was a fantasy, surely?

'Of course, the problem would be raising the money for this campaign about the statue *and* actually earning a living at the same time,' Emily said.

That was apparently no problem at all. They had saved money for years, hoping to put it towards the education of Noel as a priest. To give a son to God. But it hadn't taken. They always intended that those savings be given to God in some way, and now this was the perfect opportunity.

Emily Lynch told herself that she must not try to change the world. No time now to consider all the good causes that that money could have gone towards – many of them even run by the Catholic Church. Emily would have preferred to see it all going to look after Josie and Charles, and give them a little comfort after a life of working long, hard hours for little reward. They had to endure what to them must have been a tragedy – their son's vocation 'hadn't taken', to use their own words. But there were some irresistible forces that could never be fought with logic and practicality. Emily Lynch knew this for certain.

Noel had been through a long, bad day. Mr Hall had asked him twice if he was all right. There was something behind the question, something menacing. When he asked for the third time, Noel enquired politely why he was asking.

'There was an empty bottle, which appears to have contained gin before it was empty,' Mr Hall had said.

'And what has that to do with me and whether I'm

all right or not?' Noel had asked. He was confident now, emboldened even.

Mr Hall looked at him long and sternly under his bushy eyebrows.

'That's as may be, Noel. There's many a fellow taking the plane to some faraway part of the world who would be happy to do the job you are meant to be doing.'

He had moved on and Noel had seen other workers look away.

Noel had never known Mr Hall like this, usually there was a kindly remark, some kind of encouragement about continuing in this work of matching dockets to sales slips, of looking through ledgers and invoices, and doing the most lowly clerk duties imaginable.

Mr Hall seemed to think that Noel could do better and had made many positive suggestions in earlier days. Times when there was some hope. But not now. This was more than a reprimand, it was a warning. It had shaken him and on the way home he found his feet taking him into Casey's big, comforting pub. He vaguely recalled having had one too many the last time he'd been there but he hesitated only for a moment before going in.

Mossy, the son of Old Man Casey, looked nervous. 'Ah, Noel, it's yourself.'

'Could I have a pint, please, Mossy?'

'Ah now, that's not such a good idea, Noel. You know you're barred. My father said—'

'Your father says a lot of things in the heat of the moment. That barring order is long over now.'

'No, it's not, Noel. I'm sorry, but there it is.'

Noel felt a tic in his forehead. He must be careful now.

'Well, that's his decision and yours. As it happens, I

have given up drink and what I was actually asking for was a pint of lemonade.'

Mossy looked at him open-mouthed. Noel Lynch off the liquor? Wait till his father heard this!

'But if I'm not welcome in Casey's, then I'll have to take my custom elsewhere. Give my best to your father.'

Noel made as if to leave.

'When did you give up the gargle?' Mossy asked.

'Oh, Mossy, that's not any of your concern these days. You must go ahead serving alcohol to folks here. Am I interfering with your right to do this? I am most definitely not.'

'Wait a minute, Noel,' Mossy called out to him.

Noel said he was sorry but he had to go now. And he walked, head high, out of the place where he had spent so much of his leisure time.

There was a cold wind blowing down the street as Noel leaned against the wall and thought over what he had just said. He had only spoken in order to annoy Mossy, a foolish, mumbling mouthpiece for his father's decisions. Now he had to live with his words. He could never drink in Casey's again.

He would have to go to that place where Declan Carroll's father went with his huge bear of a dog. The place where nobody had 'friends' or 'mates' or 'people' they met there. They called them 'Associates'. Muttie Scarlet was always about to confer with his Associates over the likely outcome of a big race or a soccer match. Not a place that Noel had enjoyed up to now.

Wouldn't it be much easier if he really *had* given up drink? Then Mr Hall could find whatever bottles he liked. Mr Casey would be regretful and apologetic, which would be a pleasure to see. Noel himself would

27

have all the time in the world to go back to doing the things he really wanted. He might go back and get a business certificate so as to qualify for a promotion. Maybe even move out of St Jarlath's Crescent.

Noel went for a long, thoughtful walk around Dublin, up the canal, down through the Georgian squares. He looked into restaurants where people of his own age were sitting across tables from girls. Noel wasn't a social outcast, he was just in a world of his own making where that kind of woman was never available. And why was this? Because Noel was too busy with his snout in the trough.

It would not be like this any more. He was going to give himself the twin gifts of sobriety and time: much more time. He checked his watch before letting himself into number 23 St Jarlath's Crescent. They would all be safely in bed by now. This was such an earth-shaking decision, he didn't want to muddy it all up with conversation.

He was wrong. They were all up, awake and alert at the kitchen table. Apparently his father was going to leave the hotel where he had worked all his life. They appeared to have adopted a tiny King Charles spaniel called Caesar, with enormous eyes and a soulful expression. His mother was planning to work fewer hours at the biscuit factory. His cousin Emily had met most of the people in the neighbourhood and become firm friends with them all. And, most alarming of all, they were about to start a campaign to build a statue to some saint who, if he had ever existed, had died fifteen hundred years ago.

They had all been normal when he left the house this morning. What could have happened?

He wasn't able to manage his usual manoeuvre of sliding into his room and retrieving a bottle from the box labelled 'Art Supplies', which contained mainly un-used paintbrushes and unopened bottles of gin or wine.

Not, of course, that he was ever going to drink them again.

He had forgotten this. A sudden heavy gloom settled over him as he sat there, trying to comprehend the bizarre changes that were about to take place in his home. There would be no comforting oblivion afterwards, instead a night of trying to avoid the art-supplies box or maybe even pouring the contents down the handbasin in his room.

He struggled to make out what his father was talking about: walking dogs, minding pets, raising money, re-storing St Jarlath to his rightful place. In all his years of drinking, Noel had not come across anything as surreal and unexpected as this scene. And all this on a night when he was totally sober.

Noel shifted in his seat slightly and tried to catch the glance of his cousin Emily.

She must be responsible for all this sudden change of heart: the idea that today was the first day of every-body's life. Mad, dangerous stuff in a household that had known no change for decades.

In the middle of the night Noel woke up and decided that giving up drink was something that should not be taken lightly or casually. He would do it next week when the world had settled down. But when he reached for the bottle in the box he felt, with a clarity that he had not often known, that somehow next week would never come. So he poured the contents of two bottles of gin down his sink, followed by two bottles of red wine.

He went back to bed and tossed and turned until he heard his alarm clock next morning.

In her bedroom, Emily opened her laptop and sent a message to Betsy:

I feel that I have lived here for several years and yet I have not spent one night in the country!

I have arrived at a time of amazing change. Everyone in this household has begun some kind of journey. My father's brother was fired from his job as a hotel porter and is now going to go into a dog-walking business, his wife is hoping to reduce her hours at her place of employment and set up a petition to get a statue erected to a saint who has been dead for – wait for it – fifteen hundred years!

The son of the house, who is some kind of recluse, has chosen this, of all days, to give up his love affair with alcohol. I can hear him flushing bottles of the stuff down the drain in his bedroom.

Why did I think it would be peaceful and quiet here, Betsy? Have I discovered anything *about life or am I condemned to wander the earth learning little and understanding nothing?*

Don't answer this question. It's not really a question, more a speculation. I miss you.

Love,
Emily

CHAPTER TWO

Father Brian Flynn could not sleep in his small apartment in the heart of Dublin. He had just heard that day that he had only three weeks to find a new place to stay. He hadn't many possessions, so moving would not be a nightmare. But neither had he any money to speak of. He couldn't afford a smart place to live.

He hated leaving this little flat. His pal Johnny had found him this entirely satisfactory place to live only minutes from his work in the immigrant centre, and only seconds from one of the best pubs in Ireland. He knew everyone in the area. It was worrying to have to move.

'Couldn't the archbishop find you a place?'

Johnny was unsympathetic. He himself was going to move into his girlfriend's place. This wasn't a solution open to a middle-aged Catholic priest. Johnny was in the habit of saying to anyone who would listen that a man must be certifiably mad to be a priest in this day and age, and the least the Archbishop of Dublin could do was provide lodgings for all these poor eejits who had given up anything that mattered in life and went around doing good day and night.

'Ah, it's not really the archbishop's job. He has more important things to do,' Brian Flynn said, 'but it should be no trouble to find a place.'

It was proving more troublesome than he had thought possible. And there were only twenty days to go.

Brian Flynn could not believe the amounts people were asking as rent. Surely they could never get sums like that? In the middle of a recession as well!

Other things kept him awake too. The appalling priest who had broken his leg in Rome falling down the Spanish Steps was *still* out there, eating grapes in an Italian hospital. Father Flynn was therefore *still* acting chaplain in St Brigid's Hospital with all the many complications that this added to his life.

He kept hearing reports from his old parish in Rossmore. His mother, who was already fairly confused and in a home for the elderly, was thought to have seen a vision, but it turned out she was talking about the television and everyone in the old people's home was greatly disappointed.

He found himself increasingly brooding about the meaning of life now that he had to see so much of the end of life in St Brigid's. That poor girl Stella who seemed to like him just because he had arranged for a hairdresser to come in and visit her. She was pregnant as well as dying. She had lived a short and vaguely unsatisfactory life but then she told him that almost everyone else did as well. She seemed not even marginally interested in preparing to meet her Maker, and Father Flynn was always very firm about this, unless the patients brought the matter up themselves, it wasn't mentioned. They knew what his job description was, for heaven's sake. If they wanted intervention made, prayers said or sins forgiven, then he would do that, otherwise he wouldn't mention the topic.

He and Stella had many good conversations about

single malt whiskey, about the quarter-finals in the soccer World Cup, about the unequal division of wealth in the world. She said that she had one more thing to do before she was off to the next world, whatever it might bring. Just one thing. But she had a sort of hope that it was all going to work out all right. And could Father Flynn kindly ask that nice hairdresser to come again fairly soon. She needed to look well when she did this one last thing.

Father Flynn paced his small apartment with the football posters nailed to the wall to cover the damp patches. Maybe he would ask Stella, did she know anywhere for him to live. It might be tactless since he *was* going to live and she wasn't, but it would be better than looking into her ravaged face and haunted eyes and trying to make sense of it all.

In St Jarlath's Crescent, Josie and Charles Lynch whispered long and happily into the night. Imagine – this time last night they hadn't even met Emily and now their lives had been turned right around. They had a dog, they had a lodger and, for the first time in months, Noel had sat and talked to them. They had begun a campaign to have St Jarlath recognised properly.

Things were better on every front.

And, amazingly, things continued well on every front.

A message came to the hotel from the psychiatric hospital, saying that Caesar's mother, a titled, if eccentric, lady, was unavoidably detained there and that she hoped Caesar was being adequately looked after. The hotel manager, bewildered by this, was relieved to know that the matter was all in hand and somewhat embarrassed to learn that the rescuer had been that old porter he had just made redundant. Charles Lynch seemed to bear him no ill-will but let slip the fact that he was looking forward to some kind of retirement ceremony. The manager made a note to remind himself or someone else to organise something for the fellow.

At the biscuit factory they were surprised to hear that Josie was going to reduce her hours and raise money for a statue to St Jarlath. Most of the others who worked with her were desperate to hold on to their jobs at any cost.

'We'll have to give you a great send-off when you finally retire, Josie,' one of the women said.

'I'd really prefer a contribution to St Jarlath's statue fund,' Josie said. And there was a silence not normally known in the biscuit factory.

Noel Lynch found the days endless in Hall's builders' merchants. The mornings were hard to endure without the injection of a strong shot of alcohol that he would swallow in the men's room. The nice fuzzy afternoons were gone and replaced now by hours of mind-numbing checking of delivery dockets against sales slips. His only pleasure was leaving a glass of mineral water on his desk and watching from a distance as Mr Hall either smelled it or tasted it.

Noel could see only too well that his job could easily be done by a not very bright twelve-year-old. It was hard to know how the company had survived as long as it had. But in spite of everything he stuck to it and before too long he was able to chalk up a full week without alcohol.

Matters were much helped by Emily's presence at

number 23. Every evening there was a well-cooked meal served at seven o'clock and, with no long evenings to spend in Casey's bar, Noel found himself sitting at the kitchen table eating with his parents and cousin.

They fell into an easy routine: Josie set the table and prepared the vegetables, Charles built up the fire and helped Noel to wash up. Emily had even managed to put off the Rosary on the grounds that they all needed this joint time to plan their various crusades, such as what strategy they should use to get the fund-raising started for St Jarlath's statue, and how Emily could go out and earn a living for herself, and where they would find dogs for Charles to walk, and if Noel should do night classes in business or accountancy in order to advance himself at Hall's.

Emily had, in one week, managed to get more information out of Noel about the nature of his work than his parents had learned in years. She had even been able to collect brochures, which she used to go over with Noel. This course looked good, but rather too general, the other looked more specific, but might not be relevant to his work at Hall's.

Little by little, she had learned of the mundane, clerical-officer-type work Noel did all day – the matching of invoices, paying of suppliers and gathering expenditure data from departments at the end of the month. She discovered that there were young fellows in the company who had 'qualifications', who had a degree or a diploma, and they climbed up what passed for a corporate ladder in the old-fashioned builders' merchants that was Hall's.

Emily spent no time regretting time wasted in the past or wrong decisions or Noel's wish to leave school and not continue with his education. When they were alone she would sometimes say to him that the whole business of beating a dependency on alcohol was often a question of having adequate support.

'Did I ever tell you that I was battling against alcohol?' Noel had asked her once.

'You don't need to, Noel. I'm the daughter of an alcoholic. I know the territory. Your uncle Martin thought he could do it on his own. We lived through that one.'

'Maybe he didn't choose AA. Maybe he wasn't a social man. He could have been a bit like me and didn't want a lot of other people knowing his business,' Noel said in his late uncle's defence.

'He wasn't nearly as good a man as you are, Noel. He had a very closed mind.'

'Oh, I think I have a closed mind too.'

'No, you don't. You'll get help if you need it. I know you will.'

'It's just I don't go along with this thing. "I'm Noel. I'm an alcoholic" and then they all say, "Ho, Noel," and I'm meant to feel better.'

'People have felt better for it,' Emily said mildly. 'AA have a great success rate.'

'It's all a matter of "me and my illness", it's making it so dramatic for them all as if they are heroes of some kind of thing that's working itself out on stage.'

Emily shrugged. 'Right, so, they don't do it for you. Fine. One day you might need them. The AA will still be there, that's for sure. Now let's have a look at these courses. I know what CPA means, but what are ACA and ACCA? Tell me the difference between them and what they mean.'

And Noel would feel his shoulders relaxing. She wasn't going to nag him. That was the main thing. She had moved on and was asking his advice on other matters. Where could she get timber to make window boxes? Would his father be able to make them? Where might Emily get some regular paid work? She could run an office easily. Would it be a good idea to get a washing machine for the household in number 23 as they were all going to be so busy raising money for St Jarlath's statue?

'Emily, you don't think that will really happen – the statue business, do you?'

'I was never more sure of anything in my life,' Emily said.

Katie Finglas went to the hospital again. Stella Dixon looked worse than before: her face thin, her arms bony and her little, round stomach more noticeable.

'This has got to be a really good hairdo, Katie,' Stella said, as she inhaled the cigarette down to her toes. As usual the other patients kept watch in case a nurse or hospital official should come by and catch Stella in the act.

'Have you your eye set on someone?' Katie asked.

She wished that she could take a group of her more difficult clients into this ward so they could see the skin-and-bone woman who knew nothing ahead of her except the certainty that she would die shortly when they did the Caesarean section to remove her baby. It made their problems so trivial in comparison.

Stella considered the question.

'It's a bit late for me to have my eye on anyone at this stage,' she said. 'But I *am* asking someone to do me

37

a favour, so I have to look normal, you know, not mad or anything. That's why I thought a more settled type of hairstyle would be good.'

'Right, we'll make you look settled,' Katie said, taking out the plastic tray that she would put over the handbasin to wash Stella's thin, frail-looking head with its Pre-Raphaelite mass of red, curly hair. She had styled it already, but the curls kept coming back as if they had decided not to take any notice of the diagnosis that the rest of her body was having to cope with.

'What kind of a favour is it?' she asked, just to keep the conversation going.

'It's the biggest thing you could ever ask anyone to do,' Stella said.

Katie looked at her sharply. The tone had changed. Suddenly the fire and life had gone out of the girl who had entertained the ward and made people smuggle her in packets of cigarettes and do sentry duty so that she would not be discovered.

'Call for you, Noel,' Mr Hall said.

Nobody ever telephoned Noel at work. The few calls he got came in through his cellphone. He went to Mr Hall's office nervously. This was a time he would normally have had a drink; it was the low time of morning and he always liked a drink to help him cope with an unexpected event.

'Noel? Do you remember me, Stella Dixon? We met at the line-dancing night last year.'

'I do, indeed,' he said, pleased.

A lively redhead who could match him drink for drink. She had been good fun. Not someone he would want to meet now, though. Too interested in the gargle for him to meet up with her these days.

'Yes, I remember you well,' he said.

'We sort of drifted away from each other back then,' she said.

It had been a while back. Nearly a year. Or was it six months? It was so hard to remember everything.

'That's right,' Noel said evasively. Almost every friendship he had sort of drifted away from him, so there was nothing new about this.

'I need to see you, Noel,' she said.

'I'm afraid I don't go out too much these days, Stella,' he began. 'Not into the old line dancing, I'm afraid.'

'Me neither. I'm in the oncology ward of St Brigid's, so in fact I don't go out at all.'

He focused on trying to remember her: feisty, jokey, always playing it for a laugh. This was shocking news indeed.

'So would you like me to come and see you sometime? Is that it?'

'Please, Noel, today. At seven.'

'Today …?'

'I wouldn't ask unless it was important.'

He saw Mr Hall hovering. He must not be seen to dither.

'See you then, Stella,' he said and wondered what on earth she wanted to see him about. But, even more urgently, he wondered how he could approach a cancer ward to visit a woman he barely remembered. *And* approach her without a drink.

It was more than any man could bear.

*

The corridors of St Brigid's were crowded with visitors at seven o'clock. Noel threaded his way among them. He saw Declan Carroll, who lived up the road from Noel, walking ahead of him, and ran to catch him up.

'Do you know where the female oncology ward is, Declan?'

'This lift over here will take you to the wing. Second floor.'

Declan didn't ask who Noel was visiting and why.

'I didn't know there were so many sick people,' Noel said, looking at the crowds.

'Still, there's lots that can be done for them these times compared to when our parents were young.' Declan was always one for the positive view.

'I suppose that's the way to look at it, all right,' Noel agreed.

Declan thought he seemed a bit down, but then Noel was never a barrel of laughs.

'Right, Noel, maybe I'll see you for a pint later? In Casey's, on our way home?'

'No. As a matter of fact I don't drink any more,' Noel said in a tight little voice.

'Good man, yourself.'

'And, anyway, I was actually barred from Casey's.'

'Oh well, to hell with them then. Big barn of a place anyway.'

Declan was being supportive, but he had a lot on his mind. Their first baby was due in the next few weeks, and Fiona was up to high doh over everything, and his mother had knitted enough tiny garments for a multiple birth even though they knew they were going to have only one baby.

He could have done with a nice, undemanding

pint with Noel. But that was obviously not on the cards now. He sighed and went purposefully towards a patient who was busy making plans to come out of hospital soon and wanted Declan to try and hurry up the process. The man's diagnosis said that he would never leave the hospital, sooner or later, and would die there within weeks. It was hard to rearrange your face to see something optimistic in this, but somehow Declan managed it.

It went with the territory.

There were six women in the ward. None of them had great, tumbling, red, curly hair.

One very thin woman in the corner bed was waving at him.

'Noel, Noel, it's Stella! Don't tell me I've changed *that* much!'

He was dismayed. She was skin and bone. She had clearly made a huge effort: her hair was freshly washed and blow-dried, she had a trace of lipstick and she wore a white, Victorian nightdress with a high neck and cuffs. He remembered her smile, but that was all.

'Stella. Good to see you,' he mumbled.

She swung her thin legs out of the covers and gestured for him to pull the curtains around the bed.

'Any ciggies?' she whispered hopefully.

'In *here*, Stella?' He was shocked.

'Particularly in here. Well, you obviously didn't bring me any, so reach me my sponge bag there. The other girls will keep watch.'

He looked on, horrified, as she pulled a cigarette from behind her toothpaste, lit it expertly and made a temporary ashtray out of an old envelope.

'How have you been?' he asked and instantly wished he hadn't. Of course she hadn't been well, otherwise why was she wasting away in front of his eyes in a cancer ward? 'I mean, how are things?' he asked, even more foolishly.

'Things have been better, Noel, to be honest.'

He tried to imagine what Emily might have said in the circumstances. She had a habit of asking questions that required you to think.

'What's the very worst thing about it all, Stella?'

She paused to think, as he had known she would.

'I think the very worst thing is that you won't believe me,' she said.

'Try me,' he said.

She stood up and paced the tiny cubicle. It was then he realised that she was pregnant. Very pregnant. And at exactly that moment she spoke to him.

'I was hoping not to have to bother you about this, Noel, but you're the father. This is your baby.'

'Ah no, Stella, this is a mistake. This didn't happen.'

'I know I'm not *very* memorable, but you must remember that weekend.'

'We were wasted that weekend, both of us.'

'Not too drunk to create a new life, apparently.'

'I swear it can't be me. Honestly, Stella, if it were, I would accept … I wouldn't run away or anything … but … but …'

'But what, exactly?'

'There must have been lots of other people.'

'Thanks a lot for that, Noel.'

'You know what I mean. An attractive woman like you must have had lots of partners.'

'I'm the one who knows. Do you honestly think I

would pick *you* out of a list of candidates? That I'd phone you, a drunk in that mausoleum where you work, in some useless job? You live with your parents, for God's sake! Why would I ask *you*, of all people, to be the father of my child if it wasn't true?'

'Well, as you said yourself, thanks a lot for that.'

He looked hurt.

'So you asked me what would be the worst thing. I told you and now the worst *has* happened. You don't believe me.' She had a defeated look.

'It's a fantasy. It didn't happen. I'd remember. I haven't slept with that many women in my life and what good would I be to you anyway? I am, as you say, a useless drunk with a non-job in Hall's, living with my mother and father. I'd be no support to you. You'll be able to bring this child up fine, give him some guts, fight his battles for him, more than I would ever do. Do it yourself, Stella, and if you think I should make some contribution, and I don't want you to be short, I could give you something – not admitting anything – just to help you out.'

Her eyes blazed at him.

'You are such a fool, Noel Lynch. Such a stupid fool. I won't bloody well be here to bring her up. I'm going to die in three or four weeks' time. I won't survive the operation. And the baby is not a boy, by the way, she's a girl, she's a daughter, her name is Frankie. That's what she's going to be called: Frances Stella.'

'This is only a fantasy, Stella. This illness has made you very unhinged.'

'Ask any of them in the ward. Ask any of the nurses. Wake up to the real world, Noel. This is happening. We have to do something about it.'

'I can't raise a child, Stella. You've already listed all the things against it. Whatever chance she's going to have, it can't be with me.'

'You're going to *have* to,' Stella said. 'Otherwise she'll have to go into care. And I'm not having that.'

'But that would be the very best for her. There are families out there who are dying to have children of their own ...' he began, blustering slightly.

'Yes, and some other families, like the ones I met when I was in care, where the fathers and the uncles love to have a little plaything in the house. I've been through it all and Frankie's not going to have to cope with it just because she will have no mother.'

'What are you asking me to do?'

'To mind your daughter, to give her a home and a secure childhood, to tell her that her mother wasn't all that bad. Fight her battles. The usual things.'

'I can't do it.' He stood up from his chair.

'There's so much to discuss—' Stella began.

'It's not going to happen. I'm so sorry. And I'm really sorry to know how bad your illness is, but I think you're painting too black a picture. Cancer can be cured these days. Truly it can, Stella.'

'Goodbye, Noel,' she said.

No matter how often he said her name she would not turn towards him.

He walked to the door and looked back once more. She seemed to have shrivelled even further. She looked tiny as she sat there on her bed. He fancied that the other women in the ward had heard most of their conversation. They gazed at him with hostility.

*

On the bus home Noel realised that there was no way he could force himself to sit at the kitchen table eating a supper that Emily would have kept warm for him. Tonight was not a time to sit and talk about saints and statues and fund-raising and accountancy and business-management classes. Tonight was a night to have three pints in some pub and forget everything. He headed for the pub where Paddy Carroll, Declan's father, took his huge Labrador dog every night. With any luck at this time of night he might get away without being spotted.

The beer felt terrific. Like an old friend.

He had lowered four pints before he realised it.

Noel had hoped that he might have lost the taste for it, but that hadn't happened. He just felt a great sense of irritation and annoyance with himself that he had denied himself this familiar and friendly relaxation. Already he was feeling better. His hand had stopped shaking, his heart wasn't pounding as it had been.

He *must* stay clear and focused.

He would have to go back to St Jarlath's Crescent and take up some semblance of ordinary life. Emily would, of course, see through him at once, but he could tell her later. Much later. No need to announce everything to everyone all at once. Or maybe no need to announce anything at all. It was, after all, some terrible mistake. Noel would *know* if he had fathered a child with that girl.

He would *know* it.

It had to have come from her mind having been affected by this cancer. Anybody normal would not have selected Noel, of all people, as the father of their child. Poor Stella was far from normal and he pitied her, but this was ludicrous.

It could not be his child.

He waved away the suggestion of a fifth pint and moved purposefully towards the door.

He didn't see Declan Carroll having a drink with his father but looking curiously at the man who had claimed to have given up alcohol but who had just downed four pints of beer at racing speed.

Declan sighed.

Whatever Noel had heard at the hospital, whoever he had visited, it had not made him happy.

Paddy Carroll patted his son's hand.

'In a couple of weeks it will all be behind you. You'll have a great little one and the waiting bit will be forgotten.'

'Yes, Dad. Tell me what it was like when Mam was expecting me.'

'I don't know how I survived it,' Declan's father said and told the old, familiar story again from the point of view of the father of the baby.

The mother's role in the birth had been merely minimal, apparently.

Noel had only opened the door when Emily looked up at him sharply. It was as if she had called the meeting to order.

'We're all tired now, it's late. Not a good time to discuss the running of a thrift shop.'

'A what?'

Noel shook his head as if that would somehow settle the collection of thoughts and ideas that were nestling in it. His parents looked disappointed. They were being carried along by the enthusiasm of Emily's planning and they were sorry to see it being cut short.

But Emily was adamant. She had the whole household ready for bed in no time.

'Noel, I kept you some Italian meatballs.'

'They were just delicious,' Josie said. 'Emily can turn her hand to anything.'

'I don't think I really want anything. I stopped on the way home, you see …' Noel began.

'I did see,' Emily said, 'but these are good for you, Noel. Go on into your room and I'll bring a tray in to you in five minutes.'

There was no escape.

He sat there waiting for her and the storm that would follow. Oddly there was no storm. She never mentioned the fact that he had taken up drinking again. And Emily had been right, he *did* feel better when he had something to eat. She was clearing up and about to go when she asked sympathetically if it had been a bad day.

'The worst ever,' he said.

'Mr Hall?'

'No, he was fine. Just something mad and upsetting happened later on in the day. That's why I went back to the pints.'

'And did they help?' She seemed genuinely interested.

'At first they did a bit. It's not working now and I'm just annoyed with myself for staying off it for all those days and nights and running straight back when I get a bit of an upset.'

'Did you sort out the upset?'

She was completely non-judgmental. She looked at him, inviting him to share whatever it was, but she would have left if there was no information to hear.

'Please sit down, Emily,' Noel begged and he told the whole story, haltingly and with a lot of repetition.

47

Mainly he said that he could not have fathered a child without remembering it.

'I have so little sex, Emily, that I'm not likely to forget the little bit I *do* have.'

She was very still as she sat and listened to him. Her face changed from time to time. It was concerned and distressed when she listened to how gaunt and painful Stella's face had become. She inclined her head to show sympathy as Noel told how Stella had said that if she were to choose a father from anyone in the world, he would be the very last choice – a drunk who was a loser and still lived with his parents.

It was only when Noel came to the end of his tale, when he got to the part where he had walked away from Stella, the hospital and the problem, that Emily's face became confused.

'Why did you do that?' she asked.

'Well, what else could I do?' Noel was surprised. 'It has nothing to do with *me*. There's no point in my being there, it's adding to the whole charade. The girl's head is unhinged.'

'You walked out and left her there?'

'I *had* to, Emily. You know what a tightrope I'm walking. Things are quite bad enough already without inviting the Lord knows what kind of fantasies in on top of me.'

'You say that things are bad enough with you, Noel? Right?'

'Well, they *are* bad.' He sounded defensive.

'Like you have terminal cancer?' she asked him. 'Like you were abused when you were in care? Like you are going to be dead a month from now before you see the only child you will ever have? No, indeed, Noel, none

48

of these things have happened to you, yet you just said things are very bad for *you*.'

He was stricken.

'That's all you think. You think how things are for *you*, Noel. Shame on you,' she said, her face full of scorn.

This was the nearest he had come to having a best friend and now she was turning against him.

'Emily, please sit down. You asked me what was wrong, so I told you.'

'Yes, you did, Noel.' She made no movement to sit down.

'So? Won't you stay and discuss it?'

'No. Why should I join in this charade, as you call it? Don't pull faces at me, Noel. These are your words. Why should I not think of the perilous tightrope that *I* am walking in my life? I'm sorry, but everyone in all this is becoming ... what did you call it – "unhinged in the head"? Why should I let people surround me in their fantasies?' She was almost at the door.

'But they're not fantasies, Emily. It's what happened.'

'That's right. They're not fantasies. It's what actually happened. But hey, what the hell? It's got nothing to do with *you*, Noel. Goodnight. I'm sorry, but that is all I feel capable of saying.'

And she was gone.

He had thought that this day just couldn't get any worse. That's why he had told her. In a few short hours two women had turned away from him in disgust.

And somehow it had made the day worse than ever.

Betsy,
There is a drama unfolding here which we would

49

*have considered compelling when we were kids and
we went to the movies on Saturday afternoons. But
oddly it's too sad to talk about just now. I will tell
you how it turns out.*

*Of course you should go out with Eric! I told you a
hundred times he is not interested in me. He just said
that as a devious way of getting to know you better.*

*I know! I know! But the longer I live, the more
crazy I think everyone is.*

Love,
Emily

Katie Finglas was locking up the hair salon. It had been
a long day and she was tired. It was Garry's night out.
Once a week he and a group of the lads kicked a ball
around a pitch and planned strategy for the year.

Katie would have loved to have gone home and had
a long bath while he made them some French onion
soup. Then they could have sat by the fire and talked
about the big decision they had to make. People thought
that Katie and Garry had plenty of time to talk to each
other all day since they worked together in the salon.
Little did people know how rarely they had a chance
to snatch a five-minute coffee together. And then there
were always people within earshot and it was impossible for Katie and Garry to talk about their plans.

So she was looking forward to a proper discussion.
One where they would put all the arguments on one
side and then the other. They would list the reasons
why they *must* take over the lease on the flat over their
salon: they needed to expand, they had no storage
place, they had no proper staff areas. They would be
able to install little manicure stations and could fit in

tables and mirrors for at least six more customers. They would be able to compete on equal ground with the successful health and beauty salons in Dublin.

Then they might examine the possibility that only the totally insane would spend serious money on a property that so badly needed renovation. It was too much to take on. Too big and spread out, so they would use only half the space upstairs.

And just suppose they *did* do it, then they would have to do up some of the rooms and let them in order to try and get some return on their money.

And just suppose that they did let them – what kind of people would they get? Suppose they turned out to be the tenants from hell, making a lot of noise and leaving litter, making nonsense of all Katie and Garry's hard work?

Katie sighed as she set the alarm outside her premises.

Across the street she saw Father Flynn, that cheerful priest from the centre down the road, the one who had introduced her to poor Stella Dixon up in St Brigid's.

Stella had said that she didn't normally have a lot to say for the clergy, but Brian Flynn was a very decent fellow and didn't go on about sin and redemption and things. He did what a priest should do, he brought her cigarettes and did little jobs for people.

Katie called out to him and was delighted when he suggested they go for a coffee in a small Italian place on the corner.

Father Flynn spoke briefly and testily about his friend the priest who had fallen down the Spanish Steps and was still malingering in Rome. He also spoke about his greedy landlord who had evicted him and how it was impossible for a man of simple lifestyle, like himself, to discover any kind of budget accommodation.

'I'm such an undemanding person, really,' Brian Flynn said, full of self-pity. 'If people only *knew* how little I want in terms of style or comfort.'

Katie looked at him thoughtfully across her cappuccino. 'Exactly *how* undemanding?' she asked.

She suddenly saw a solution to everything.

Father Flynn would be the perfect tenant.

'Finish up your coffee there and come with me,' she said, draining her cup and heading back to the salon that she had just locked up.

By the end of the month, he had moved into his new home. His friend Johnny had put up a few bookshelves for him and Katie's husband Garry had found him a second-hand fridge where he could keep his milk, butter and the odd can of beer. His only duty was to make sure that he locked the salon properly and put on the burglar alarm whenever he left the premises after hours. It suited everyone perfectly.

CHAPTER THREE

Noel couldn't believe that Emily, who had become part of his every waking moment at St Jarlath's Crescent, now seemed to have disappeared completely.

'Where is she?' he asked his mother on the morning after Emily had left his room in scorn and disgust. 'It's not like Emily to miss breakfast.'

'Oh, she's gone to find premises for the charity shop,' Josie Lynch replied, confident that Emily would have one before the day was out. There was nothing that woman couldn't do.

'She took Caesar with her. She's going to make enquiries for me about dog-walking opportunities as well.' Charles was pleased too. 'She said she'd have more credibility if she was accompanied by a dog herself when she went looking for business.'

'She'll be back at lunchtime, Noel, if you wanted her for anything,' Josie said. 'She's going out this evening, apparently, but she said she'd leave a supper for us. What *did* we do before she came to stay?'

'Where's she going this evening?'

Noel hadn't known Emily to be out of the house for two meals in one day. Not since she had arrived. There was only one explanation. She was avoiding him.

He did try to stay off drink when he was at work, but the sharp pain of Stella's situation and Emily's

53

shocked revulsion kept coming back to him as the day crawled along. When it came to mid-afternoon he could bear it no more and made an excuse to go out and get some more stationery supplies. He bought a half-bottle of vodka and decanted it into a bottle that already had a fizzy orange drink in it. As he drank mug after mug of it he felt the strength coming back to him and the pain receding. The familiar blur came down like a thick, comforting shawl.

Noel now felt able to face the afternoon again; but what didn't go away was the feeling that he was a loser who had let down three people: the dying Stella, his strong cousin Emily and an unborn child called Frankie, who could not possibly be his daughter.

But he should have handled it very differently.

Emily was in the launderette with Molly Carroll. She had brought towels for a service wash but actually she was there on a mission. On a previous visit she had noticed two outhouses that were not in use. They might form the basis of the new thrift shop that would help raise money for the statue of St Jarlath. She had to take it one step at a time; find out who actually owned the premises first.

It had turned out to be much simpler than she had feared. Molly and Paddy Carroll had bought the premises some years back when the owner had had some gambling debts that were pressing and was anxious for a quick sale. They had never needed the unused part of the premises but had been loath to sell it in case someone built a noisy takeaway food outlet.

Molly thought that a thrift shop would be perfect. She and Emily toured the place and decided to put shelves here and clothes rails there. They would have a second-hand book section and Emily said she could grow a few plants from seed and sell them too.

Together they made a list of people to approach, those who might give a few hours every week to working in the charity shop. Molly knew a man who had the unlikely name of Dingo. He was a decent skin and would help them with his van, collecting things or stacking them. Emily had met several women who said they would be happy to help, but were a little anxious in case they wouldn't be able to manage the till properly. Emily said she would check what permits they might need and if they had to apply for a change of use of premises; she promised she would deliver a fully planted window box to the laundromat the following week to celebrate the whole deal.

Molly said her husband Paddy's friend had a lot of Associates in the pub who would do the refurbishments.

They decided to call the place St Jarlath's Thrift Shop and Molly said it would be great to be partly in charge because if a nice jacket came in she could get first crack at it. Emily left with the air of someone who had completed a difficult and complicated assignment.

She stopped at a fishmonger and bought some smoked cod for tomorrow. Charles and Josie had not been great fish lovers or salad eaters when she arrived but, little by little, she was changing their ways. It was a pity that she couldn't do anything to direct Noel, but the boy had built a shield about himself and came home later and later each evening. It was obvious that he was avoiding her.

*

'Is there anything I can get you, Stella?' Father Flynn had brought her the usual pack of cigarettes.

'Not much, Brian, but thanks all the same.'

She looked very down, not her usual gutsy self.

He hesitated asking any more. The future was bleak for her. What helpful words could he find?

'Any visitors?' he asked.

Stella's eyes were dull. 'No visitors to speak of,' she said and as he looked at her with sympathy and the realisation he had no comfort to give, he saw for the first time a tear in her eye.

'I'm no good with words, Stella,' he began.

'You're fine with words, Brian, and with getting me fags and a hairdresser – for all the bloody use it was.'

'Your hair looks very nice,' he said hopelessly.

'Not nice enough to make that no-hoper believe me.'

'Believe you about what exactly?' Brian was confused.

'That he was the father of my child. He said he couldn't remember having sex with me. That was nice, wasn't it?'

'Ah, God, Stella, I'm so sorry.' There was real compassion in his face.

'It was probably my own fault. I told him all wrong. He's a bit drinky, as I was indeed myself, and he couldn't face it. He ran out of here. *Ran*, I tell you.'

'Maybe he'll come back when he sees sense.'

'He won't, he literally doesn't remember. He's not making it up.'

She sounded resigned, defeated.

'Could you get a DNA test to prove he's the father?'

'No. I thought about it, but if he doesn't remember being there at her conception, there's no point in asking him to be a father to her. No, she'll have to take her chances like the rest of us.'

'Would it help if I had a word with him?'

Brian Flynn felt that he should offer anyway.

'No, Brian, thanks, but no. If he ran when I told him, he would go into orbit if I sent a priest after him.'

For a moment, there was a flash of the old Stella.

That night in St Jarlath's Crescent Emily was busy explaining her day's negotiations with Molly Carroll. Charles and Josie were drinking in every word.

Charles had news too. There would be a goodbye celebration for him in a few weeks' time at the hotel – finger food, wine and beer, and a presentation. And would you believe who wanted to come to it, but Mrs Monty – who was really Lady Something. The woman who wore only a fur coat, a big hat and pearls and nothing else: the hotel manager was very nervous about letting her in.

Mrs Monty was now going into a residential home where sadly Caesar would not be welcome; and since Charles had agreed to take him, she wanted to thank the kind employee who had given the little spaniel such a good home. She was also going to make a donation to a charity of his choice. It would be a wonderful start to the fund-raising.

Charles was being allowed to bring a small number of family and friends. As well as Josie, Emily and Noel, he thought he would invite Paddy and Molly Carroll and the Scarlets, Muttie and Lizzie.

'Will Noel be able to come, do you think?' Emily's voice was slightly tart.

'Well, here he comes now – we can ask him!' Josie cried out happily.

Noel listened carefully, arranging his face in various receptive expressions as the excitement of the goodbye celebrations was revealed.

Emily knew the technique: she recognised it from her father. It was a matter of saying as little as possible and therefore cutting down on the possibility of being discovered to be drunk.

Eventually he had to speak. Slowly and carefully he said that he would be privileged to be part of the ceremony.

'It would be great to be there when they are honouring you,' he said to his father.

Emily bit her lip. At least he had been able to respond adequately. He had managed not to rain on his father's parade.

'There's some lamb stew left, Noel. I'll heat it and bring it up to you,' she said, giving him permission to leave before his mask of sobriety collapsed.

'Thank you, Emily, I'd love that,' he said and fled to his room after shooting a grateful look in her direction.

When she went in with the tray, he was sitting in his chair with tears streaming down his face.

'Oh Lord, Noel, what is it?' she asked, alarmed.

'I'm utterly *useless*, Emily. I've let everyone down. What's the use of my going on, waking in the morning and going to bed at night? What good does it serve?'

'Have your supper, Noel. I brought you a pot of coffee as well. We have to talk.'

'I thought you didn't talk to me any more,' he said with a great sniff and wiping his eyes.

'I thought that *you* were avoiding *me*,' she said.

'I didn't want to come home and have you being cold and distant. I don't have any friends, Emily. I have no one at all to turn to …'

His voice sounded lost and frightened.

'Eat your supper, Noel. I'll be here,' she said.

And she was there while he told her how despairing he was and what a hopeless father he would be to any child.

She listened and then said simply, 'I hear all that and you may well be right. But then again it might be the making of you, *and* Frankie. She might make you into the kind of person you want to be.'

'They'd never let me keep her … the Social Welfare people …'

'You'll need to show them what you're made of.'

'It's better they don't know,' Noel said.

'Please, Noel, no self-pity. Think – think what you should do next. A lot of lives will be affected by it.'

'I couldn't bring the child here,' he said.

'It was time for you to move on anyway.'

Emily was as calm as if they were discussing what to have for lunch tomorrow, rather than Noel's future.

Next morning, Stella looked up from the magazine she was reading as a shadow fell on her bed. It was Noel carrying a small bunch of flowers.

'Well, hello!' she said. 'How did you get in? It isn't visiting time.'

'Am I interrupting you?' he asked.

'Yes, I'm reading about how to put more zing back in my marriage, as if I knew what either zing or marriage were!'

'I came here to ask you to marry me,' he said.

'Oh Christ, Noel, don't be such an eejit. Why would I marry you? I'll be dead in a few weeks' time!'

'You wouldn't say the baby was mine if it wasn't. I would be honoured to try and bring her up.'

'Listen, marriage was never part of it.' Stella was at a complete loss.

'I thought that's what you wanted!' He was perplexed now.

'No. I wanted you to look after her, to be a dad for her, to keep her out of the lottery of the care system.'

'So will we get married, then?'

'No, Noel, of course we won't, but if you *do* want to talk about looking after her, tell me why and how.'

'I'm going to change, Stella.'

'Right.'

'No, I am. I was up all night planning it. I'm going to go to AA today, admit I have a drink problem, and then I'm going to enrol to do an evening business course at a college, and then I'm going to find a flat where I can bring up the baby.'

'This is all so sudden. So spur-of-the-moment. Why aren't you at work today anyway?'

'My cousin Emily has gone to Hall's to say I have a personal crisis today and that I will make up the time next week by going in one hour earlier and staying one hour later every day.'

'Does Emily know about all this?'

'Yes. I had to tell someone. She was very cross with me for walking out on you.'

'You didn't walk, Noel. You ran.'

'I am so sorry. Believe me. I *am* sorry.'

'So what has changed?' She wasn't hostile, just interested.

'I want to amount to something. To do something for someone before I die. I'll be thirty soon. I've done nothing except dream and wish and drink. I want to change that.'

She listened in silence.

'So tell me what you'd like if you don't want us to get married?'

'I don't know, Noel. I'd like things to have been different.'

'So do most people walking around. They all wish things had been different,' he said sadly.

'Then I'd like you to meet Moira Tierney, my social worker, tomorrow evening. She's coming in to discuss what she calls "the future" with me. A fairly short discussion.'

'Could I bring Emily in? She said she'd like to come and talk to you anyway.'

'But is she going to be a nanny figure? Always there hovering, making all the decisions?'

'No, she'll be going back to America soon, I think, but she *has* made me see things more clearly.'

'Bring her in then. Is she dishy? Could you marry *her* maybe?' Stella was mischievous again.

'No! She's as old as the hills. Well, fifty or forty-five or something, anyway.'

'Bring her in then,' Stella said, 'and she's going to have to talk well to deal with Moira.'

He leaned over and put the flowers in a glass.

'Noel?'

'Yes?'

'Thanks, anyway, about the marriage proposal and all. It wasn't what I had in mind but it was decent of you.'

'You might still change your mind,' he said.

'I have a tame priest in here. A very nice fellow. He could do it if we were pushed, but actually I'd prefer not to.'

'Whatever you think,' he said, and touched her gently on the shoulder.

'Before you go, one thing … How *did* you get in outside visiting hours?'

'I asked Declan Carroll. He lives on my road. I said I needed a favour, so he made a phone call.'

'He and his wife are having a baby at the same time as I am,' Stella said. 'I always thought the children might be friends.'

'Well, they might easily be friends,' Noel said.

When he looked back from the door he saw she was lying back in her bed, but she was smiling and seemed more relaxed than before.

He set out then to face what was going to be the most challenging day of his life.

It was hard to go into the building where the lunchtime AA meeting was taking place. Noel stood for ten minutes in the corridor, watching men and women of every type walking down to the door at the end.

Eventually he could put it off no longer and followed them in.

It was still very unreal to him but, as he had said to Emily, he had to get his head around the fact that he was a father and an alcoholic.

He had faced the first and he could still recall the glow on Stella's face this morning. *She* hadn't thought he was a loser and a hopeless father for her baby.

Now he had to face the drinking.

There were about thirty people in the room. A man sat at a desk near the door. He had a tired, lined face and sandy hair. He didn't look like a person who was a heavy drinker. Maybe he was just part of the staff.

'I would actually like to join,' Noel said to him, hearing, as he spoke, his own voice echoing in his ears.

'And your name?' the man asked.

'Noel Lynch.'

'Right, Noel. Who referred you here?'

'I'm sorry? Referred?'

'I mean, are you coming here because of a treatment centre?'

'Oh heavens, no. I haven't been having any treatment or anything. I just drink too much and I want to cut it down.'

'We try to encourage each other to cut it out completely. Are you aware of that?'

'Yes, if that were possible, I would be happy to try.'

'My name is Malachy. Come on in,' the man said. 'We're about to begin.'

Later in the day Noel had to face his third confrontation.

Emily had made an appointment for him with the College Admissions Supervisor. He was going to sign up for the Business Diploma, which included marketing and finance, sales and advertising. The fees, which would have been well beyond him, were going to be paid by Emily. She said it was an interest-free loan. He would repay it when he could.

She had assured him that this was exactly what she wanted to do with her savings. She saw it as an investment. One day when he was a rich, successful man, he would always remember her with gratitude and look after her in her old age.

The Admissions Supervisor confirmed that the fees had been paid and that the lectures would start the following week. Apart from the lectures on three evenings, Noel would be expected to study on his own for at least twelve hours a week.

'Are you married?' the Supervisor asked.

'No, indeed,' and then almost as an afterthought Noel said, 'but I'll be having a baby in a couple of weeks.'

'Congratulations, but you had better get a good bit of the groundwork in before the child arrives,' said the Admissions Supervisor, a man who seemed to know what he was talking about.

That evening at supper Josie was eager to discuss the thrift shop and its possible date of opening. She was excited and alive.

Charles was in high good form too. He wasn't going to have to give Caesar back to Mrs Monty, he was going to have this big celebration at the hotel, he had more plans for dog walking and dog exercising, and he had been to a local kennels.

But before the conversation could go down either route – thrift shop or dog walking – Emily spoke firmly.

'Noel has something important to talk to us about, perhaps before we make any more plans.'

Noel looked around him, trapped.

He had known that this was coming. Emily said they could not live in a shadowy world of lies and deception.

Still, he had to tell his parents that they were about to become grandparents, that there was no marriage included in the plans and that he would be moving into a place of his own.

It was not news he was going to find easy to break. Emily had suggested that he might pause before using the same opportunity to tell them that he was joining Alcoholics Anonymous and that he was registering as a student at the college.

She wondered whether it might not be too much for them.

But when he began his tale, sparing nothing but telling it all as it had unfolded, he felt it was easier and fairer to tell them everything.

He went through it as if he were talking about someone else and he never once caught their eye as the story went on.

First he told of the message from the hospital: his two meetings with Stella, her news – which he had refused to believe at first – but realised that it must be true. His arrangements to meet the social worker and plan for the future of the baby girl whose birth would also involve her mother's death.

He told them how he had tried to give up drinking on his own and had not succeeded, that he now had a sponsor in AA called Malachy, and would attend a meeting every day.

He told them that his job in Hall's had been depressing and that he was constantly passed over while younger and less experienced staff were appreciated because they had diplomas or degrees.

At this point he realised his parents had been very silent, so he raised his eyes to look at them.

Their faces were frozen with horror at the story he was telling.

Everything they had feared might happen in a god-less world *had* happened.

Their son had enjoyed sex outside marriage and a child had resulted, and he was admitting a dependency on alcohol even to the point of getting help from Alcoholics Anonymous!

But he would not be put off. He struggled on with the explanations and his plans to get out of the situations he had brought on himself.

He accepted that it was all his own fault.

He blamed no outside circumstances.

'I feel ashamed telling you all this, Mam and Da. You have lived such good lives. You wouldn't even begin to understand, but I got myself into this and I'm going to get myself out of it.'

They were still silent so he dared to look at them again.

To his amazement they both had some sympathy in their faces.

His mother's eyes were full of tears, but there were no recriminations. No mention of sex before marriage, only concern.

'Why did you never tell us this, son?' His father's voice was full of emotion.

'What could you have said? That I was a fool to have left school so early? Or that I should put up with it? You were happy at work, Da. You were respected. That's not the way it is at Hall's.'

'And the baby?' Josie said. 'You had no idea this Stella was expecting your child?'

'None in the wide world, Ma,' Noel said. And there was something so bleak and honest in his tone that everyone believed him.

'But the drink thing, Noel … are you sure that it's bad enough for you to be going to the AA?'

'It is, Da, believe me.'

'I never noticed you drunk. Not once. And I'm well used to dealing with drunken people up at the hotel,' his father said, shaking his head.

'That's because you're normal, Da. You don't expect people to come back from work half cut, having spent two hours in Casey's.'

'That man has a lot to answer for.' Charles shook his head with disapproval for Old Man Casey.

'He didn't exactly open my mouth and force it down,' Noel said.

Emily spoke for the first time.

'So, we are up to speed on Noel's plans now. It's going to be up to us to give him all the support we can.'

'You *knew* all this?' Josie Lynch was shocked and not best pleased.

'I only knew because I could recognise a drunk at fifty feet. I've had a lifetime of knowing when people are drunk. We don't talk about it much, I know, but my father was one very unhappy man and he was miles from home with no one to help him or advise him when he had made one wrong decision that wrecked his life.'

'What decision was that?' Charles asked.

This evening was full of shocks.

Since Emily's arrival there had been no mention of the late Martin Lynch's drinking.

'The decision to leave Ireland. He regretted it every day of his life.'

'But that can't be right. He lost total interest in us. He never came home.' Charles was astonished.

'He never came home, that's true, but he never lost

interest. He was probing it like it was a sore tooth. Talking about all he *could* have done if only he had stayed here. All of it fantasy, of course, but still, if he'd had someone to talk to …' Her voice trailed away.

'Your mother?' Josie asked tentatively.

'No joy there, I'm afraid. She never understood what a hold drink had on him. She just told him to stay away from it as if it was a simple thing to do.'

'Could you not talk to him? You're great at talking to people,' Charles said admiringly.

'No, I couldn't. You see, my father didn't have the basic decency that Noel here has. He could not accept that in the end it was all down to him. He wasn't half the man Noel is.'

Josie, who had in the last half-hour been facing the whole range of disgrace, mortal sin and shame, found some small comfort in this praise.

'You think that Noel will be able to do all this?' she asked Emily pitifully, as if Noel were not even there.

'It's up to us to help him, Josie,' Emily said as calmly as if they were discussing the menu for tomorrow's supper.

And even to Noel it didn't seem quite as impossible as it had when he had begun his explanation.

'Stella, I'm Emily, Noel's cousin. Noel's gone to get you some cigarettes. I came a little early in case there's anything I should know before the social worker comes.'

Stella looked at the businesslike woman with the frizzy hair and the smart raincoat. Americans always dressed properly for the Irish weather. Irish people themselves were constantly being drenched with rain.

'I'm pleased to meet you, Emily. Noel says you are a rock of sense.'

'I don't know that I am.' Emily seemed doubtful. 'I came over on a whim to learn about my late father's background. Now I seem to be up to my neck in organising a statue for some saint who has been dead for centuries. Hardly a rock of sense ...'

'You're very good to take all this on as well.' Stella looked down somewhat ruefully at the bump in her stomach.

'You have enough problems to think about,' Emily said, her voice warm and sympathetic.

'Well, this social worker is a bit of a madam. You know, interested in everything, believing nothing, always trying to trip you up.'

'I suppose they have to be a bit like that on behalf of the child,' Emily murmured.

'Yes, but not like the secret police. You see, I sort of implied that Noel and I were more of an item than we are. You know, in terms of seeing each other and everything.'

'Sure.' Emily nodded approvingly. It made sense.

There was no point in Stella telling a social worker that she hardly knew the least thing about the father of the child she was about to have.

It wouldn't look well from the start.

'I'll help to fill you in on all that,' Emily said.

At that moment Noel came in, closely followed by Moira Tierney.

She was in her early thirties with dark hair swept back with a red ribbon. If it had not been for the frown of concentration, she would have been considered attractive. But Moira was too busy to consider looking attractive.

'You are Noel Lynch?' she said briskly and without much enthusiasm.

He began to shuffle and appear defensive.

Emily moved in quickly. 'Give me your parcels, Noel. I know you want to say hello to Stella properly,' and she nudged him towards the bed.

Stella held up her thin arms to give him an awkward combination of a hug and a peck on the cheek.

Moira watched suspiciously.

'You and Stella don't share a home, Mr Lynch?' Moira said.

'No, not at the moment,' he agreed, apologetically.

'But there are active plans going ahead so that Noel can get a place of his own to raise Frankie,' Emily said.

'And you are … ?' Moira looked at Emily enquiringly.

'Emily Lynch. Noel's cousin.'

'Are you the only family he has?' Moira checked her notes.

'Lord, no! He has a mother and father, Josie and Charles …' Emily began, making sure that Stella could hear the names as well.

'And they are … ?' Moira had an irritating habit of asking a question the wrong way round as if she were making some kind of disapproving statement.

'They are at home organising a fund to erect a statue to St Jarlath in their street.'

'St *Jarlath*?' Moira was bewildered.

'I know! Aren't they wonderful? Well, you'll meet them yourself. They'll be in tomorrow to see Stella.'

'They will?' Stella was startled.

'Of course they will.' Emily sounded more confident than she felt.

Josie would take a lot of convincing before she arrived to see the girl who was no better than she should be. But Emily was working on it and the important thing just now was to let the social worker see that there was strong family support.

Moira absorbed it all as she was meant to.

'And where do you intend to live, Mr Lynch, if you *are* given custody of the child?'

'Well, of course he will have custody of the child,' Stella snapped, 'he's the child's father. We are all agreed on that!'

'There may be circumstances that might challenge this.' Moira was prim.

'What kind of circumstances?' Stella was angry now.

'A background of alcohol abuse, for one thing,' Moira said.

'Not from me, Noel,' Stella said, apologetically.

'Naturally, we make enquiries,' Moira said.

'But that is all under control now,' Emily said.

'Well, that will be looked into,' Moira said in a clipped voice. 'What kind of accommodation were you thinking of, Mr Lynch?'

Emily spoke again. 'Noel's family have been discussing nothing else but accommodation. We are looking at this apartment in Chestnut Court. It's a small block of flats not far away from where he lives.'

'Would it not be preferable to start the child off living with a ready-made family in, er ... St Jarlath's Crescent?'

'Well, you see—' Noel began.

'You see, Moira, you are very welcome to come and

visit Noel's home at any time, but you will realise that it's entirely unsuited for a baby. The places in Chestnut Court are much more child-friendly. The one we are all interested in is on the ground floor. Would you like to see a picture of it here ...'

Moira didn't seem as interested as she might have been. She was looking at Noel and seemed to spot the surprise on his face.

'What do *you* think of this as a place to move to?' she asked him directly.

Stella and Emily waited anxiously.

'As Emily said, we have talked through so many ideas and this one seems to be the most suitable so far.'

Moira nodded as if in agreement and if she heard the breath of relief from the two women, she gave no sign.

There were questions then about the rent that would be paid and the babysitting support that would be available, seeing that Noel would be at work all day.

And soon it was over.

Emily made one last statement to show how reliable her cousin Noel was.

'I don't know whether you realise that Noel is very anxious to marry Stella. He has proposed to her, but Stella would prefer not to. This is the attitude of a committed person, someone who would be reliable and responsible.'

'As I said, Ms Lynch, there are some formalities that have to be gone through. I will have to talk about it with my team and then the last word will be with the supervisor.'

'But the first and most influential word will be from *you*, Moira,' Emily said.

Moira gave one of her brisk little nods and was gone.

Stella waited till she was out of the ward before she started to celebrate. With a flick of her wrist she pulled the curtains and produced the cigarettes.

'Well done to the pair of you,' she said, looking from Noel to Emily and back. 'We have Madam Moira on the run!'

'We still have a way to go,' Emily said and they settled down to discuss further strategies.

And they continued to do this for the next few weeks. Every aspect of the effort to turn Noel into a father was discussed.

Josie and Charles were introduced to Stella and, after some awkward shuffling at the start, they found an astonishing amount of common ground. Both Noel's parents and Stella herself seemed entirely convinced that shortly Stella would be going to a better place. There was no pretence that perhaps she might recover.

Josie talked wistfully of Stella going to meet Our Lord fairly soon and Charles said that if Stella were to meet St Jarlath, she could pass on the news that the statue would indeed be erected but it might take a little longer than they had once believed possible. They had helped by paying a deposit on the flat in Chestnut Court. St Jarlath's image might have to wait a little, but it would happen.

'Wouldn't he be able to see that already?' Stella asked.

'Yes, I imagine he would,' Charles agreed. 'But it would be no harm to give him a personal message, seeing that you'll be seeing him there.'

Noel felt ashamed that his parents took this whole idea of an afterlife so casually.

They really and truly saw heaven as some kind of a big park where they would meet everyone. And what's more, they expected that Stella would be there shortly.

Stella rolled her eyes a bit at the whole notion, but she didn't seem put out by it either. She was game to take a message to any old saint just to keep the show on the road.

But they also made plans on a more practical level.

Chestnut Court was only a seven-minute walk from St Jarlath's Crescent.

Noel could wheel the baby around to his parents' home before work each morning; Josie and Charles would look after Frankie until lunchtime. Then she would go for the afternoon either to Molly Carroll's house or to this couple called Aidan and Signora, who looked after their own grandchild; to Dr Hat, who had retired recently and found time hanging heavy on his hands, or to Muttie and Lizzie Scarlet, who, quite apart from their own children, had raised twins who were no blood relation to them at all.

The three evenings a week when Noel would be at his evening classes at college would be covered as well.

For a while Emily would go to the new apartment in Chestnut Court and do her paperwork. Noel would return after his lectures and she would cook him a meal. He had started getting lessons from the district nurse on what he would need in the new flat to welcome the baby and had been shown how to prepare a feed and the importance of sterilising bottles. Declan Carroll's wife Fiona had sent a message to say that she had already received a baby's layette that would be enough for sextuplets. Stella and Noel *must* help her out and get the garments worn; their babies would arrive at around the same time. What could be more luck?

Noel was swept along in the whirl of activity of it all.

The thrift shop was up and running; he and his father had painted it to Emily and Josie's satisfaction, and already people had begun to donate items to be sold. Some of these would be useful for Noel's new flat, but Emily was adamant: a fair price must be paid for them. The money was for St Jarlath, not to build a comfortable lifestyle for Noel.

'Everyone is being very generous,' he said, stepping over another box of books as Josie and Emily sorted through piles of clothing and bric-a-brac.

Josie was looking doubtfully at a small collapsible baby buggy; it might do for when the baby was a bit older, but they needed something a bit sturdier for an infant. Something might turn up, and she resolved to say an extra prayer to St Jarlath.

Emily had had other ideas: she had already printed off a flyer which Dingo had put through local letter-boxes saying that he would collect unwanted baby items in his van. Days later, he went to pick up an old Silver Cross pram; it was huge but it was beautiful and it had been well looked after. It would be perfect for the new baby.

Noel had little time alone with Stella. There were so many practicalities to be sorted out. Did Stella want the child to be brought up as a Catholic?

Stella shrugged. The child could abandon the faith once she was old enough. Possibly to please Josie and Charles, there should be a baptism and First Holy Communion and all, but nothing too 'Holy Joe'.

Were there *any* relations on Stella's side that she might want to involve?

'None whatsoever.' She was clipped and firm.

'Or anyone at all from the various foster homes from the past?'

'No, Noel, don't go there!'

'Right. It's just that when you're gone, I'll have no one to ask.'

Her face softened. 'I know. Sorry for snapping at you. I'll write her a letter, telling her a bit about myself, and about you and how good you've been.'

'Where will you leave the letter?' Noel asked.

'With you, of course!'

'I mean, if you wanted to leave it in a bank or something …' Noel offered.

'Do I look to you like someone who has a bank account, Noel? Please …'

'I wish you weren't going to leave, Stella,' he said, covering her thin hand with his.

'Thanks, Noel. I don't want to go either,' she said.

And they sat there like that until Father Flynn came in for a visit. He took in the scene and the hand-holding, but made no comment.

'I was just passing,' he said foolishly.

'Well, I was on my way anyway, Father.' Noel stood up to leave.

'Maybe you could stay a minute, Noel. I wanted Stella to tell me what, if anything, she wanted for her funeral.'

The question didn't faze Stella at all.

'Listen, Brian, ask Noel's family what *they* want. I won't be here. Let them have whatever is easiest.'

'A hymn or two?' Brian Flynn asked.

'Sure, why not. I'd like a happy-clappy one. You know, like a gospel choir, if possible.'

'No problem,' Father Flynn said. 'And burial or cremation or body to science?'

'Don't think my body would tell anyone anything they didn't know already.' Stella considered it. 'I mean, if you smoke four packs a day, you get cancer of the lung. If you drink as much as I did, then you get cirrhosis of the liver. There isn't a part of me sound enough for a transplant, but what the hell ... It could be an awful warning.'

Her eyes were very bright.

Brian Flynn swallowed.

'We don't talk about this sort of thing much, Stella, but do you want a requiem Mass?'

'That's the one with all the bells and whistles, isn't it?'

'It gives a lot of people comfort,' Father Flynn said, diplomatically.

'Bring it on then, Brian,' she said good-humouredly.

CHAPTER FOUR

Lisa Kelly had been very bright at school; she had been good at everything. Her English teacher encouraged her to do a degree in English Literature and aim for a post in the university. Her sports teacher said that with her height – by the age of fourteen she was already nearly six feet tall – she was a natural and she could play tennis or hockey, or both, for Ireland. But when it came to it, Lisa decided to go for art. Specifically for graphic art.

She graduated from that, first in her year, and was instantly offered a position in one of the big design firms in Dublin. It was at that point that she should have left the family home.

Her younger sister Katie had gone three years previously, but Katie was very different. No child genius, only barely able to keep up with the class, Katie had taken a holiday job in a hairdresser's and found her life's calling. She had married Garry Finglas and together they set up a smart salon, which had gone from strength to strength. She loved to practise on Lisa's long honey-coloured hair, blow-drying it and then styling it into elegant chignons and pleats.

Their mother Di had been very scornful about it all. 'Touching people's dirty heads!' she had exclaimed in horror.

Their father Jack Kelly barely commented on Katie's career, any more than he had on Lisa's work.

Katie had begged Lisa to leave home.

'It's not like that out in the real world, not awful silences like Mum and Dad have. Other people don't shrug at each other the way *they* do, they *talk*.'

But Lisa had waved this away. Katie had always been over-sensitive about the atmosphere at home. When Katie went out to friends' houses, she returned wistfully talking about happy meals at kitchen tables, places where mothers and fathers talked and laughed and argued with their children and their friends. Not like their home where meals were eaten in silence and accompanied by a series of shrugs. And anyway, Katie had always been easily affected by people's moods. Lisa was different. If Mum was distant, then *let* her be distant. If Dad was secretive, then what of it? It was just his way.

Dad worked in a bank where, apparently, he had been passed over for promotion; he didn't know the *right* people. No wonder he was withdrawn and didn't want to make idle chit-chat. Lisa could never interest him in anything she did; if ever she showed him one of her drawings from school, he'd shrug, as if to say, 'So what?'

Her mother was discontented, but she had reason to be. She worked in a very upmarket boutique, where rich, middle-aged women went to buy several outfits a year. She herself would have looked well in those kinds of clothes, but she could never have afforded them; so instead she helped to fit plumper women into them and arranged for seams to be let out and for zip fasteners to be lengthened. Even with a very generous staff discount, the clothes were way out of her league. No wonder she looked at Dad with disappointment. When she had married him at the age of eighteen he had looked like a man who was going somewhere. Now he went nowhere except to work every morning.

Lisa went to her office and worked hard all day. She had lunch with colleagues at places that were high in style and low in calories. But it was at a private lunch for a client that Lisa met Anton Moran: it was one of those moments that was frozen for ever in her mind.

Lisa saw this man crossing the room, pausing at each table and talking easily with everyone. He was slight and wore his hair quite long. He looked confident and pleasant without being arrogant.

'Who's *he*?' she gasped to Miranda, who knew everyone.

'Oh, that's Anton Moran. He's the chef. He's been here for a year, but he's leaving soon. Going to open his own place, apparently. He'll do well.'

'He's gorgeous,' Lisa said.

'Get to the end of the line!' Miranda laughed. 'There's a list as long as my arm waiting for Anton.'

Lisa could see why. Anton had style such as she had never seen before. He didn't hurry, yet he moved on from table to table. Soon he was at theirs.

'The lovely Miranda!' he exclaimed.

'The even lovelier Anton!' Miranda said, archly. 'This is my friend Lisa Kelly.'

'Well, hello, Lisa,' he said, as if he had been waiting all his life to meet her.

'How do you do?' Lisa said and felt awkward. Normally she knew what to say, but not this time.

'I'll be opening my own place shortly,' Anton said.

'Tonight is my last night here. I'm going round giving my cellphone number to everyone and I'll expect you all to be there. No excuses now.'

He handed a card to Miranda and then gave one to Lisa.

'Give me a couple of weeks and I'll give you the details. They'll all know I must be doing *something* right if you two gorgeous girls turn up there,' he said, looking from one to the other. It was an easy patter. He might be going to say something similar at the next table.

But Lisa knew that he had meant it. He wanted to see her again.

'I work in a graphic design studio,' Lisa said suddenly, 'in case you ever need a logo or any designs?'

'I'm sure I will,' Anton said. 'I'm certain I will, actually.'

And then he was gone.

Lisa remembered nothing about the rest of the meal. She yearned to go to Miranda's flat and talk about him all night, check that he wasn't married, that he didn't have a partner. But Lisa had survived life so far by remaining a little aloof. She didn't go to stay with friends as she didn't want to invite them home to her house. She didn't want to wear her heart on her sleeve and confide to someone gossipy like Miranda about Anton. She would get to know him herself in her own time. She would design him a logo that would be the talk of the town.

The important thing was not to rush it; not to make any sudden moves.

She thought about him way into the night. He wasn't conventionally handsome but he had a face that you wouldn't forget. Intense, dark eyes and a marvellous smile. He had a grace you'd expect in an athlete or a dancer.

He must be spoken for. A man like that wouldn't be available. Surely?

She was taken aback when he telephoned her the next day.

'Good. I found you,' he said, sounding pleased to hear her voice.

'How many places did you try?'

'This is the third. Will you have lunch with me?'

'Today?'

'Well, yes, if you're free ...'

And he named Quentins, one of the most highly regarded restaurants in Dublin.

Lisa had been going to have lunch with her sister Katie.

'I'm free,' she said simply. Katie would understand. Eventually.

Lisa went to her boss Kevin.

'I'm going to have lunch with a very good contact. A man who is about to open his own business and I was wondering—'

'—if you can take him to an expensive restaurant, is that it?'

Kevin had seen it all, heard it all.

'No. Certainly not. *He's* paying. I thought I might offer him a glass of champagne and that I might go an hour early so that I can get my hair done and present a good image of the agency.'

'Nothing wrong with your hair,' Kevin grumbled.

'No, but better to make a good impression than a sort of half-hearted one.'

'All right – do we have to pay for the hairdo as well?'

'No way, Kevin. I'm not greedy!' Lisa said and ran off before he could think about this.

She raced out to buy a large potted plant for Katie and turned up at the salon.

'So this is a consolation prize. You're cancelling lunch!'

'Katie, *please* understand.'

'Is it a man?' Katie asked.

'A man? No, of course not. Well, he is a man, but it's a business lunch and I can't get out of it. Kevin is on his knees to me. He even let me have time off so that I could have my hair done.'

'What do you want done? Apart from bypassing the line of people who actually made bookings?'

'I beg you, Katie …'

Katie called to an assistant, 'Could you take Madam to a basin and use our special shampoo. I'll be with you in a moment.'

'You're too good—' Lisa began.

'I know I am. It's always been my little weakness, being too good for this world. I wish it *were* for a man, you know, Lisa. I'd have done something special.'

'Let's pretend it *is* for a man,' Lisa begged.

'If it was a man who would get you out of that house, I'd do it for nothing!' Katie said and Lisa smiled to herself.

She yearned to tell her sister, but a lifetime of keeping her own counsel intervened.

'You look very elegant,' Anton said as he stood up to greet Lisa at Quentins.

'Thank you, Anton. You don't look as if you made too late a night of it yourself.'

83

'No, indeed. I just gave my phone number to everyone in the restaurant and then went home to my cup of cocoa and my narrow, little bed.'

He smiled his infectious smile, which would always manage to get a return smile. Lisa didn't know what she was smiling at – cocoa, the narrow, little bed, or an early night ... But it must mean that he was giving her signals that he was available.

Should she send back a similar signal or was it too early? Too early, definitely.

'I told my boss I was coming here for lunch with a man who was going into business on his own and he said that I should offer you a glass of champagne on the company.'

'What a civilised boss,' Anton said admiringly as Brenda Brennan, the proprietor, came over.

She knew Anton Moran already. He had worked in her restaurant a while ago. He introduced Lisa to Brenda.

'Lisa's company is buying us a glass of champagne each, Brenda, so could we have your delightful house sparkling to start us off, with a receipt for that to Lisa, and the rest of the meal is on me.'

Brenda smiled. Her look said she had seen Anton here with several ladies before.

Lisa felt a stab of hurt, which surprised her. In her twenty-five years she had never known such a feeling. It was envy, jealousy and resentment all rolled into one. This was completely ludicrous.

It wasn't as if she was a starry-eyed teenager. Lisa had had many boyfriends, and some of them had been lovers. She had never felt a really strong attraction to any of these men. But Anton was different.

His hair looked soft and silky and she longed to reach across the table and run her hands through it. She had the most absurd wish to have his head on her shoulder while she stroked his face. She must shake herself out of this pretty sharpish and get back to the business of designing a look and styling a logo for his new company.

'What will you call the new place?' she asked, surprised that she could keep so calm.

'Well, I know it's a bit of an ego trip, but I was thinking of calling it Anton's,' he said. 'But let's order first. They have a really good cheese soufflé here. I should know, I made enough of them in my time!'

'That would be perfect,' Lisa said.

This could not be happening. She was falling in love for the very first time.

Back at the office Kevin asked her, 'Any luck with Golden Boy?'

'He's very personable, certainly.'

'Did you give him any outline and our rates?'

Kevin was anxious there would be no grey areas.

'No – that will come later.'

Lisa was almost dreamy as she thought of Anton and how he had kissed her cheek when they parted.

'Yeah, well, as long as he understands it doesn't come free because he's a pretty boy,' Kevin said.

'How do you know that he's a pretty boy?' Lisa asked.

'You just said that he was personable and I think he was the guy that my niece had a nervous breakdown over.'

'Your niece?'

'Yes. My brother's daughter. She went out with a

chef called Anton Moran once. Nothing but tears and tantrums, then she drops out of college, *then* she goes to face him down about it all and he's gone off cooking on a cruise ship.'

Lisa's heart felt like lead. Anton had told her of his wonderful year on board a luxury liner.

'I don't think it could have been the same person.' Lisa's tone was cold.

'No, maybe not ... probably not ...' Kevin was anxious for the least trouble possible. 'Just as long as he knows he's getting nothing on tick from us.'

Lisa knew with a terrible certainty that there would be a lot of trouble ahead. Anton had barely the money to cover the deposit on his premises. He was relying on outstanding restaurant reviews to meet the mortgage payments and the expenses of doing the place up. He had given no thought whatsoever to the cost of a graphic artist and a campaign.

The site for the restaurant was perfect: it was in a small lane just a few yards off a main road, near to the railway station, a tram route and a taxi rank. He had suggested a picnic. Lisa brought cheese and grapes, Anton a bottle of wine.

They sat on packing cases and he described his great plans. She hardly took in any of them as she watched his face. His sense of excitement was entirely infectious.

By the time they had finished the cheese and grapes, she knew that she would leave Kevin and set up on her own. Perhaps she could move in with Anton; work with him – they could build the place together, but she must not rush her fences. However hard it was, she mustn't look over-eager.

Anton had mentioned very little about his private life.

His mother lived abroad, his father lived in the country and his sister lived in London. He spoke well of everyone and badly of no one.

She *mustn't* ask him about Kevin's niece. She must hassle him about nothing. She knew that he was totally right – this place was going to be a huge success and she wanted to be part of it and in at the very start.

She gave a sigh of pure pleasure.

'It's good, that wine, isn't it?' he said.

It might as well have been turpentine. She couldn't taste it. But she mustn't let him know at this early stage that she was sighing with pleasure at the thought of a future with him.

It would be lovely to have someone to tell – someone who would listen and ask, what did you do then, what did he say to that? But Lisa had few close friends.

She couldn't tell anyone at work, that was for sure. When she left Kevin's studio she wanted no one to suspect why. Kevin might become difficult and say she had met Anton on *his* time and that he had stood them the glasses of champagne that had clinched the deal.

Once or twice he had asked her if 'Anton pretty boy' had got any further along the line in his decision-making. Lisa shrugged. It was impossible to know, she had said vaguely. You couldn't rush people.

Kevin agreed. 'Just so long as he's not getting anything for free,' he warned several times.

'Free? You *must* be joking!' Lisa said, outraged at the very idea.

Kevin would have been astonished had he known just how long Lisa spent with Anton and how many drawings she had shown him to establish a logo for his new venture. At that moment she had concentrated on the colours of the French flag, and the A of Anton was a big, curly, showy letter. It could not be mistaken for anything else. She had done drawings and projections, shown him how this image would appear on a restaurant sign, on business cards, menus, table napkins and even china.

For the last eighteen days she had spent every single evening with Anton – sometimes sitting on the packing cases, sometimes in small restaurants around Dublin, where he was busy seeing what worked and what didn't.

One night, he did a shift at Quentins to help them out and invited Lisa to have a meal there at a staff discount. She sat proudly, looking out from her booth. Three weeks ago she had never met this man and now he was quite simply the centre of her whole life. She had definitely decided to leave Kevin's office and set up business on her own.

She would shortly leave the cold, friendless home where she lived now, but would wait until Anton suggested that she move in with him. He would ask her soon.

The whole business had been brought up for discussion. As early as their fifth date he had made the first move.

'It's a great pity to go back alone to my narrow bed …' he had said, his voice full of meaning as he ran his hands through her long hair.

'I know, but what are the alternatives?' Lisa had asked playfully.

'I suppose you could invite me home to *your* narrow bed?' he offered as a solution.

'Ah, but I live with my parents, you see. That kind of thing couldn't happen,' she said.

'Unless you were to get your own place, of course,' he grumbled.

'Or we were to explore *your* place?' Lisa said.

But he didn't go down that road. Yet.

When he brought the matter up again it was in connection with a hotel. A place thirty miles from Dublin where they might have dinner, steal some ideas for the new restaurant and stay the night.

Lisa saw nothing wrong with this plan and it all worked out perfectly. As she lay in Anton's arms she knew she was the luckiest girl in the whole world. Soon she was going to be living with and working with the man she loved. Wasn't this what every woman in the world wanted?

And it was going to happen to her, Lisa Kelly.

'I always knew you would fly the coop one day,' Kevin said. 'And you have been restless for the last couple of weeks. I guessed you were planning something.'

'I was very happy here,' Lisa said.

'Of course you were. You're very good. You'll be good anywhere. Have you decided where to go yet?'

'On my own,' Lisa said, simply.

'Not a good idea in this economic climate, Lisa,' Kevin advised her.

'*You* took the risk, Kevin, and look how it paid off for you ...'

'It was different. I had a rich father and a load of contacts.'

'I'll make the contacts,' Lisa said.

'You will in time. Have you an office?'

'I'll start from home.'

'The very best of luck to you, Lisa,' he said and she managed to get out before he asked her was there any news of Anton.

Kevin, however, knew all about the place Anton had in Lisa's life and the reason for her move. He had spent a weekend in Holly's Hotel in County Wicklow, and Miss Holly, forever anxious to give her customers news of each other, mentioned that one of his colleagues, Ms Kelly, had stayed there the previous night.

'With a very attractive young man. Most knowledgeable about food, he was out in the kitchens talking to the chef.'

'Was his name Anton Moran?' Kevin asked.

'That's the very man.' Miss Holly clapped her hands. 'He even asked us for the recipe for our special orange sauce that the chef makes with Cointreau and walnuts. Normally Chef won't tell anyone, but he told Mr Moran because he was going to cook it for his parents.'

'I'll bet he was,' Kevin had said grimly. 'And did they share a room?'

Miss Holly sighed. 'Of course they did, Kevin. But that's today for you. If you tried to apply any standards these days you'd be laughed out of business!'

Kevin thought of his niece who was still in fragile health and he shivered a little for what might lie ahead for Lisa Kelly, one of the brightest designers he had ever come across.

Lisa wondered were there other homes in Dublin like hers where the communication was minimal, the conversation limited and the goodwill non-existent. Her parents talked to each other in heavy sighs and to her hardly at all.

Every Friday, Lisa left her rent on the kitchen dresser. This entitled her to her room and to help herself to tea and coffee. No meals were served to her unless she were to buy them herself.

Lisa wasn't looking forward to telling her parents that shortly there would be no salary coming in, therefore the rent would be hard to pay. She was even less enthusiastic about telling them that she would be using her bedroom as an office. In theory, they might offer her the formal dining room, which was never used and which would have made a perfectly presentable business surrounding. But she knew not to push things too far.

Her father would say they weren't made of money. Her mother would shrug and say they didn't want strangers traipsing in and out of the place. Better do it little by little. Tell them about the job first, then gradually introduce the need to bring clients to the house as they got used to the first situation.

She wished over and over that Anton was less adamant about their living arrangements. He said that she was lovely, the loveliest thing that had ever happened to him. If this was so, why would he not let her come and live with him?

He had these endless excuses: it was a lads' place – he just had a room there, he didn't pay for it, instead he cooked for the lads once a week and that was his rent, he couldn't abuse their hospitality by bringing in someone else. Anyway, it would change the whole atmosphere of the place if a woman were to come into it.

He had sounded a little impatient. Lisa didn't

mention it again. There was no way she could afford a place to live. There were new clothes, picnic meals and the two occasions she pretended to have got hotel vouchers in order to spirit him off for a night of luxury. All this cost money.

Once or twice she wondered whether Anton might possibly be mean. A bit *careful* with money, anyway? But no, he was endearingly honest.

'Lisa, my love, I'm a total parasite at the moment. Every euro I earn doing shifts I have to put away towards the cost of setting the place up. I'm a professional beggar just now, but in time I'll make it up to you. When you and I are sitting in the restaurant toasting our first Michelin star, *then* you'll think it was all worthwhile.'

They sat together in the new kitchen, which was coming to life under their eyes. Ovens, refrigerators and hotplates were springing up around them. Soon the work would begin on the dining room. They had agreed the logo and it was being worked into the rugs that would be scattered around the wooden floors. The place was going to be a dream and Lisa was part of it.

Anton was only mildly surprised that she had left Kevin. He had always assumed that she would one day. He was less enthusiastic, however, about the notion that she might move into one of the spare rooms in the new building.

'I could make a bedsitter out of *this* room and my office out of *that* one.' Lisa pointed out two rooms down the corridor off the new kitchen.

'This one's the cold room and that's for linen and china,' he said impatiently.

'Well, eventually, but I have to have *somewhere* to work and we agreed that I should help with the marketing as well …' she began, but he started to look cross again so she dropped it.

It had to be home.

The reception was more glacial than she had expected.

'Lisa, you are twenty-five years of age. You have been well educated – expensively educated. Why can't you find a place to live and work like other girls do? Girls with none of your advantages and privileges …'

Her father spoke to her as if she were a vagrant who had come into his bank and asked to sleep behind the counter.

'Even poor Katie, and Lord knows she never achieved much, she's at least able to look after herself.' Lisa's mother spoke witheringly of her other daughter.

'I thought you'd be pleased that I was going out on my own,' Lisa said. 'I'm even thinking of taking some classes, on starting your own business and the like. I'm showing initiative.'

'Mad is more like it. These days anyone who has a job holds on to it instead of throwing it up on a whim,' her father said.

'And no rent for the foreseeable future,' her mother sighed. '*And* you'll want the heating on during the day when there's no one else at home. *And* you want business people filing in and out of this house. No, Lisa, it's not on.'

'If we were to let your room to a stranger, we could get a proper rent for it,' her father added.

'What about the dining room? I could put shelves and a filing system into it—' Lisa began.

'And ruin the lovely dining room? I think not,' her mother said.

'Why don't you forget the whole idea and stay where you are … in the agency,' her father suggested, his tone slightly kinder as he saw her distressed face. 'Do that, like a good girl, and we'll say no more about any of this.'

Lisa didn't trust herself to speak any more. She walked quickly to the front door and left the house.

She didn't *care* about money. She didn't *mind* working hard and even though she hated self-pity she did begin to feel that the world was conspiring against her. Her own family were so unsupportive and her boyfriend impervious to any signals and hints. He *was* her boyfriend, wasn't he? They had been together every evening. He had mentioned no other woman and he had said she was lovely. Admittedly, he hadn't said he loved her, but being lovely was the same thing.

Lisa caught sight of herself in a shop window: she looked hunched and defeated.

This would never do. She brushed her hair, put on more make-up and held her shoulders back, and strode confidently along to Anton's, to the place where a great restaurant was about to rise from the rubble and confusion that was currently there.

Later, she would think about where to live and where to work. Tonight she would just drop into the gourmet shop and buy some smoked salmon and cream cheese. She wouldn't weary him with her problems. She would hate to see that impatient frown again on his handsome face.

To her great annoyance there were eight people there already, including her friend Miranda, who had been the one to introduce her to Anton in the first place. They were sitting around eating very gooey-looking pizza.

'Lisa!' Anton managed to sound delighted, welcoming and surprised at the same time, as if Lisa didn't come there every evening.

'Come on in, Lisa, and have some pizza. Isn't Miranda clever? She found *exactly* what we all wanted.'

'Very clever,' Lisa said through her teeth.

Miranda, who looked as slim as a greyhound but who ate like a hungry horse, was sitting on the ground in her skinny jeans, wolfing down pizza as if she had known no other food. Some of the men were people who shared Anton's flat. The other girls were glamorous and suntanned. They looked as if they were auditioning for a musical.

None of them was broke, in debt, with nowhere to live and nowhere to work. Lisa wanted to run away and go and cry somewhere, big heaving sobs. But where could she go? She had nowhere and this, after all, was where she wanted to be.

She slipped the smoked salmon and cream cheese into one of the fridges and came to join them.

'Anton has been singing your praises,' Miranda said when she looked up momentarily from the huge pizza she was devouring. 'He says you are a genius.'

'That's going a bit far.' Lisa smiled.

'No, it's the truth,' Anton assured her. 'I was telling them all about your ideas. They said I was very lucky to get you.'

These were the words she had wanted to hear for so long. Why did it not seem as real and wonderful as she had hoped?

Then he said, 'Everyone is here to give some ideas about marketing, so let's start straight away. Lisa, you first …'

Lisa didn't want to share her ideas with this cast. She didn't want their approval or their dismissal.

'I'm last in – let's hear what everyone else has to say.' She gave the group a huge smile.

'Sly little fox,' Miranda whispered, but loudly enough to be heard.

Anton didn't seem disturbed. 'Right, Eddie, what do you think?' he began.

Eddie, a big, bluff, rugby player, was full of ideas, most of them useless.

'You need to make this place a focus for the rugby set, somewhere people would lunch on the days of an International.'

'That's about four days a year,' Lisa heard herself say.

'Well, yes, but you could host fund-raisers for various rugby clubs,' he said.

'Anton wants to *make* money, not give it away at this stage,' Lisa said. She knew she sounded like someone's nanny or mother, but honestly ...

A girl called April said that Anton could have wine-appreciation classes there, followed by a dinner serving some of the most popular choices of the evening. It was so ludicrous as a moneymaker that Lisa hardly believed anyone would take it seriously, yet they were all eager and excited.

'Where's the profit?' she asked, icily.

'Well, the wine manufacturers would sponsor it,' April said, annoyed.

'Not until the place is up and running, they won't,' Lisa said.

'Anton could have fashion shows here,' Miranda suggested.

Everyone looked at Lisa to see how she would knock this one down, but she was careful. She had been too snide already.

'That's a good idea, Miranda. Have you any designers in mind?'

'No, but we could think up a few,' Miranda said.

'I think it would take from the meal itself,' Anton said.

'Yes, maybe you're right.'

Miranda didn't care, she was only there for the laughs and the pizza anyway.

'What do *you* think, Lisa? Do you have a background in marketing and business as well as graphic art?'

'No, I don't, April. In fact, I've just decided to do an evening course in management and marketing. The term starts next week, so at the moment all I have is my instinct.'

'Which says ... ?' April was obviously keen.

'Just as Anton says, that the food is going to be extraordinary and everything else is second to that.'

Lisa even managed a smile. She had surprised herself with her announcement. She'd had the vague notion that such a course would be a good idea, especially now that she was going freelance, but being challenged by April had made her mind up. She was going to do it. She'd show them.

'You didn't tell me you were going back to college,' Anton said when the others had all left.

It had been touch and go as to whether April would *ever* leave, but somehow she realised that Lisa would outstay her and she did go grudgingly.

'Ah, there's lots of things I don't tell you, Anton,'

she said, scooping away the glutinous pizza and paper plates into a refuse bag.

'Not too many, I hope,' he said.

'No, not *too* many,' Lisa agreed.

This was the way it had to be played. She knew that now.

She signed on for the business diploma the next day. They were very helpful in the college and she gave them the cheque that was the very last of her savings.

'How will you support yourself?' the tutor asked her.

'It will be hard, but I'll manage,' she said with a bright smile. 'I have one client already, so that's a start.'

'Good. That will keep you solvent,' the tutor said, pleased.

Lisa wondered what he would say if he knew that the one client wasn't going to pay a cent for the job she was doing and that he was costing her a fortune because he liked a woman to smell of expensive perfume and have lacy underwear, but because he was putting everything he had into the business he was unable to buy her any of these things.

At her first lecture, she sat beside a quiet man called Noel Lynch who seemed very worried about it all.

'Do you think it will help us, all this?' he asked her.

'God, I don't know,' Lisa said. 'You always hear successful people saying that qualifications don't matter, but I think they do because they give you confidence.'

'Yes. I know. That's why I'm doing it too. But my cousin is paying my fees and I wouldn't want her to think it was a waste ...'

He was a gentle sort of fellow. Nothing smart and lively and vibrant like Anton's friends, but restful.

'Will we go and have a drink afterwards?' she asked him.

'No, if you don't mind. I'm actually a recovering alcoholic and I don't find myself at ease in a pub,' he said.

'Well, coffee, then?' Lisa said.

'I'd like that,' Noel said with a smile.

Lisa went back to the bleak, terraced house that she had called home for so long. *Why* was Anton so against her moving into his premises? It made absolute sense for her to be there and once settled there she could persuade him to give up his ludicrous bachelor existence with the others. After all, they were still on the prowl, while he had everything sorted: his own restaurant, his own girlfriend. What *was* the point in keeping up the charade of all being men about town?

If she could have gone back to the restaurant now and told him about the introductory lecture, it would have been great.

Mother was out somewhere and Father was watching television. He barely looked up as she came in.

'It went very well,' she said to him.

'What did?' He looked up, startled.

'My first lecture at the college.'

'You have qualifications already: a career, a job. This is just some kind of a *figario* you are taking.' He went back to the television.

Lisa felt very, very lonely. Everyone in that lecture hall tonight had someone to talk to about it. Everyone except her.

Anton was out tonight. He and the flatmates were going to some reception, not that he would have been *very* interested, but he would have listened for a little bit anyway.

Katie would have cared, but Katie and Garry had gone away on a long weekend to Istanbul. It seemed too far to go just for three nights, but they were highly excited about it and regarded it as one of the great explorations of all time.

There were no other friends. None who cared.

What the hell? She would call Anton. Nothing heavy, nothing clinging, just to make contact. He answered immediately.

There was a lot of noise in the background and he had to shout.

'*Lisa*, great. Where are you?'

'I'm at home.'

'Oh, I thought you'd be here,' he said and he actually sounded disappointed.

Lisa brightened a little. 'No, no, I was at my first lecture tonight.'

'Oh, that's right. Well, why don't you come along now?'

'What is it exactly?'

'No idea, Lisa, just lots of fun people. Everyone's here.'

'You must know what it is.'

She could hear him frown. Even over the phone.

'Love, I don't know who's running it, some magazine company, I think. April invited us. She said there was unlimited champagne and unlimited chances to meet people and she was right.'

'April asked you.'

'Yes, she's part of the PR for it all. I was expecting you to be here too ...'

'No, honestly, I have to dash,' she said and just got off the phone before she began to weep as if she was never going to stop crying ever again.

Katie came back from Istanbul and called Lisa to say she had a present for her.

'How was it at the college?' she asked.

'You remembered?' Lisa was amazed. Nobody else had asked.

'I got you a terrific present at the bazaar,' Katie said. 'You'll love it!'

Lisa felt a prickling behind her nose and eyes. She never remembered getting Katie a present from anywhere.

'That's lovely,' she said in a small voice.

'Will you come over this evening? Garry and I will bore you to death about all we saw.'

Normally Lisa might have said that she'd have loved to but she had a million things to do. But she surprised both herself and her sister by saying that there was nothing she would like better.

'Brian might come as well, but he's no trouble.'

'Brian?'

'Our tenant. We gave him the two rooms upstairs. I told you about him.'

'Oh yes, of course you did.'

Lisa felt guilty. Katie had indeed been wittering on about someone coming to live upstairs. She wished she had thought of asking for the rooms herself, but as usual the timing had been all wrong.

'You're not trying to set me up with this Brian, are you?' she asked.

'Hardly! He's a priest and he's nearly a hundred!'

'No!'

'Well, fifty anyway. Not about to break his vows. Anyway, don't you *have* a fellow?'

'Not really,' Lisa said, admitting it for the first time to herself.

'Of course you do,' Katie said briskly. 'Anyway, I'm glad you're free tonight – come around seven-thirty.'

Lisa was free that night. She had been free the night before, and the night before that. It was three days since Anton had gone to April's party. Lisa was waiting for him to contact her.

Waiting and waiting.

Brian Flynn turned out to be a very decent man and great company. He told them about his mother who had dementia but seemed quite content and happy in whatever world she lived in. How his sister Judy had married a man called Skunk, how his brother had left one wife and fled from one girlfriend.

He told them about a holy well that he didn't rate very highly, and about the immigrant centre where he worked now and had a lot of respect for the people there.

Occasionally, he asked Katie and Lisa about their family. They both made excuses to get on to other subjects, so he either gave up or realised this was not an area where they were comfortable.

Garry talked cheerfully about his parents and how his father had originally said that being a hairdresser was only a job for 'nancy' boys, but had slightly softened in his view over the years.

He told them about the time he had gone to the zoo on his birthday when he was seven and his parents had told the elephant that he was the best boy in the country, and they told him that the elephant would never forget this because elephants don't forget. And to this day Garry always thought that the elephant remembered.

They smiled at the notion.

Lisa wondered why she had ever thought Garry plodding. He was just decent. And romantic, too. He showed them pictures on his phone of Katie with her hair blowing as they went for a cruise on the Bosphorus and another of her with minarets in the background. But he hardly saw anything except her face.

'Katie looks so happy,' he said over and over.

'And do you have a young man of your own?' Brian Flynn asked Lisa unexpectedly.

'Sort of,' Lisa answered him truthfully. 'There is a man I fancy a lot, but I don't think he is as serious as I am about it.'

'Oh, men are fools, believe me,' Brian Flynn said with the voice of authority. 'They have no idea what they want. They are much simpler than women think, but more confused as well.'

'Did you ever love anyone? I mean before you joined up ...' Lisa asked.

'No, nor after either. I'd have been a useless husband anyway. By the time they end this celibacy thing for priests, I'll be too old to get involved with anyone and that's probably all for the best.'

'Is it lonely?'

'No more than any other life,' he said.

As Lisa walked home from Katie's house she took a detour that brought her past Anton's. There were lights on upstairs in the room he was going to have as his office. She yearned to go in, but was too afraid of what she might find. Probably April with her legs stretched out on his desk, Miranda sitting on the floor and any number of others.

She went home in the dark and let herself into the house where there were no lights and no hints as to whether anyone was at home or not.

Just silence.

Next morning, she got a text from Anton: *Where ARE you? I am lost without you to advise me and set me on target again. I'm like a jellyfish with no backbone. Where did you go, lovely Lisa? A totally abandoned Anton.*

She forced herself to wait two hours before replying, then she wrote: *I went nowhere. I am always here. Love Lisa.*

Then he wrote: *Dinner here? 8 p.m.? Do say yes.*

Again, she forced herself not to reply at once. It was so silly, all this game playing, yet it appeared to work. Eventually she texted: *Dinner at 8 sounds lovely.*

She made no offer to bring cheese or salmon or artichoke hearts. She couldn't afford them for one thing and for another he was inviting *her*, she must remember that.

He had, of course, expected she would bring something to eat. She realised that when he went to the freezer to thaw out some frozen Mexican dishes, but she sat and sipped her wine, smiling, and asked him all about the business. She didn't mention the reception that April had invited him to. She only asked, had he made any new contacts to help him with the launch?

He seemed slightly abstracted as he prepared the meal. He was his usual efficient self, expertly slicing avocado, deseeding chillies and squeezing limes over prawns as a starter, but his mind was somewhere else. Eventually he got around to what he wanted to say.

'Have I annoyed you, Lisa?' he asked.

'No, of course not.'

'Are you sure?'

'Well, obviously I am. Why do you think you had?'

'I don't know. You're different. You don't call me. You didn't bring anything for dinner. I didn't know if you were trying to say something to me ...'

'Like what?'

'Like you're pissed off with me or something?'

'But why should I be? You invited me to dinner and I'm here. I'm having a lovely time.'

'Oh good. It's just a feeling I had ...'

He seemed totally satisfied.

'Fine. So that's that out of the way,' she said cheerfully.

'I mean, I value you, Lisa. We're not joined at the hip or anything, but I really do appreciate all you've done to help me get started ...'

He paused.

She looked at him expectantly, not helping him out.

'So, I suppose I was afraid that there had been a misunderstanding between us, you know.'

'No, I don't know. What kind of a misunderstanding?'

'Well, that you might be reading more into it than there is.'

'Into what, Anton? You're talking in code.'

'Into ... well, into our relationship,' he said eventually.

She felt the ground slip away from her and had to struggle hard to sound normal.

'It's fine, isn't it?' Lisa said, hearing her own voice as if from very far away.

'Sure. It's just me being silly. I mean, it's not a commitment or anything … exclusive like that.'

'We sleep together,' Lisa said bluntly.

'Yes, we have, of course, and will again, but I don't ask you about who you meet after lectures or anything at your college …'

'No, of course not.'

'And you don't ask me about where I go and who I meet …'

'Not if you don't want me to.'

'Oh, Lisa, don't take an attitude.'

He was definitely frowning now.

The food tasted like lumps of cardboard. Lisa could barely swallow it.

'Will I make you a margarita? You're only nibbling at your food.' Anton feigned concern.

Lisa shook her head.

'So cheer up then, and let's talk about the launch. April has all her people working on it.'

'So what's left to talk about, then?' She knew she sounded childish and mutinous but she couldn't help it.

'Oh, Lisa, don't turn into one of those whining women. *Please*, Lisa …'

'Does this relationship, as you call it, mean anything to you? Anything at all?'

'Of course it does. It's just that I've taken a huge risk, I'm scared shitless that I'm going to fall on my face in this new venture, juggling a dozen balls in the air, just ahead of the posse in terms of debt, and I haven't the *time* to think of anything seriously yet like ... you know ... permanent things.'

He looked lost and confused.

She hesitated. 'You're right. I'm just tired and intense because I'm doing too much. I think I *would* like a margarita. Will you put salt around the rim of the glass?'

He brightened up at once.

Maybe that priest who lived over Katie and Garry was right: men *were* simple. And to please them, you had to be equally simple in return. She beat down her feeling of panic and was rewarded with one of Anton's great smiles.

The evening classes at college were going well. Lisa was actually much more interested than she had expected to be. She *was* quick, she realised.

Noel told her that she was the first in the group to understand any concept. He felt slow and tempted to give up, but life in his job was so dreary and dull and he had no qualifications, and this would give him the confidence and clout he needed.

She learned about him during their coffee breaks. He said the classes and his AA meetings were his only social outings of the week.

He was a placid person and didn't ask many questions about Lisa's life. Because of this, she told him that her parents had always seemed to dislike each other greatly and that she couldn't understand why they stayed together.

'Probably for fear of finding a worse life,' Noel said glumly and Lisa agreed that this might well be true.

He asked her once, did she have a fellow, and she had replied truthfully that she loved someone but it was a bit problematical. He didn't want to be tied down so she didn't really know where she was.

'I expect it will sort itself out,' Noel said and somehow it was fairly comforting.

And Noel was right, in a way. It sort of sorted itself out.

Lisa never called around to Anton without letting him know she was on her way. She took an interest in all he was doing and made no more remarks about April's involvement in anything. Instead, she concentrated on making the cleverest and most eye-catching invitations to the pre-launch party.

There was no question of her getting anything new to wear. There wasn't any money to pay for an outfit. She confided this to Noel.

'Does it matter all that much?' he asked.

'It does a bit because if I thought I looked well I'd behave well and I know this sounds silly, but a lot of the people who will be there sort of judge you by what you wear.'

'They must be mad,' Noel said. 'How could they not take notice of you? You look amazing, with your height and your looks – that hair ...'

Lisa looked at him sharply, but he was clearly speaking sincerely, not just trying to flatter her.

'Some of them are mad, I'm sure, but I'm being very honest with you. It's a real pain that I can't get anything new.'

'I don't like to suggest this but what about a thrift shop? My cousin sometimes works in one. She says she often gets designer clothes in there.'

'Lead me to it,' Lisa said with a faint feeling of hope.

Molly Carroll had the perfect dress for her. It was scarlet with a blue ribbon threaded around the hem. The colours of Anton's restaurant and the logo she had designed.

Molly said the dress could have been designed just for her.

'I'm not very up-to-date in fashion,' she said, 'but you'll certainly stop them in their tracks in this one.'

Lisa smiled with pleasure. It *did* look good.

Katie treated her to a wash and blow-dry and she set out for the party in high good spirits. April was there in a very official capacity welcoming people in.

'Great dress,' April said to Lisa.

'Thanks,' Lisa said, 'it's vintage,' and went to find Anton.

'You look absolutely beautiful,' he said when he caught sight of her.

'It's *your* night. How's it going?' Lisa asked.

'Well, I've been working for two days on all these canapés but you wouldn't think it was my night. April believes it's hers. She's insisting on being in every picture.'

Just then a photographer approached them.

'And who's this?' he asked, nodding at Lisa.

'My brilliant designer and stylist, Lisa Kelly,' responded Anton instantly.

The photographer wrote it down and out of the corner of her eye Lisa could see April's disapproval. She smiled all the more broadly.

'You're really gorgeous, you know.' Anton was admiring Lisa openly. 'And you wore my colours too.'

She savoured the praise. She knew there would be times when she would play this scene over and over again in her mind. But she mustn't dwell on herself and her dress.

Lisa blessed Noel and Molly Carroll. She had paid so little for this outfit and she was one of the most elegant women in the room. More photographers were approaching her. She must try to look as though she wanted to deflect attention from herself.

'There's a great crowd here,' Lisa said. 'Did all the people you wanted turn up?' Across the room she saw that April had a face like a sour lemon. 'But I mustn't monopolise you,' she added as she slipped away and knew that his eyes were on her as she went to mingle with the other guests.

Miranda was slightly drunk.

'I think it's game, set and match to you, Lisa,' she said, unsteadily.

'What do you mean?' Lisa asked innocently.

'Oh, I think you've knocked April into Also Ran ...'

'What?'

'It's a saying, you know, in a horse race. There's the winner and there's Also Ran, meaning the ones that didn't win.'

'I know what it *means*,' Lisa said, 'but what do *you* mean?'

'I think you have the single, undivided attention of Anton Moran,' Miranda said. It was a complicated phrase to finish and she sat down after the effort.

Lisa smiled. What should she do now? Try to outstay April or leave early? Hard though it was to do, she decided to leave early.

His disappointment was honey to her soul.

'You're never going? I thought you were going to sit down with me afterwards and have a real post-mortem.'

'Nonsense! You'll have lots of people. April, for example.'

'Oh God, no. Lisa, rescue me. She'll be talking of column inches of coverage and her biological clock.'

Lisa laughed aloud.

'No, Anton, of course she won't. See you soon. Call me and tell me how it all went.'

And she was gone.

There was a bus at the end of the lane and she ran to catch it. It was full of tired people going home late from work. She felt like a glorious butterfly in her smart dress and high heels, while they all looked drab and colourless. She had drunk two cocktails, the man she loved had told her that she was gorgeous and he wanted her to stay.

It was only nine o'clock at night. She was a lucky, lucky girl. She must never forget this.

CHAPTER FIVE

For Stella Dixon the time just flew by: there was so much to see to every day. There was a lawyer to talk to, a nurse from the health authorities, another nurse – this time from the operating theatre – who tried to explain the procedure (though Stella was having none of it, she was far too busy, she said). Once she got her anaesthetic, that would be curtains for her. While she was still here she had to try to deal with everything.

Her doctor, Declan Carroll, came in to see her regularly. She asked after his wife.

'Maybe the babies will get to know each other,' Stella had said wistfully one day.

'Maybe. We'll have to work on it.'

He was a very pleasant young man.

'You mean *you* will have to work on it,' she said with a smile that broke his heart.

For Noel there weren't enough hours in the day either. He had AA meetings every day, since the thought that most things could be sorted out by several pints and three whiskeys was always with him. Any time that he was not slaving in Hall's, going to Twelve Step meetings or catching up on his studies, he spent surfing the net for advice on how to cope with a new baby. He had moved into his new place in Chestnut Court and was busy making preparations for the arrival of a newborn.

He began to wonder how he had ever found time to drink.

'Maybe I'm nearly over it,' he said hopefully to Malachy, his sponsor at AA.

'I don't want to be downbeat, but we all feel this in the early days,' Malachy warned him.

'It's not really early days. I haven't had a drink for three weeks,' Noel said proudly.

'Fair play to you, but I am four years dry and yet if something went seriously wrong in my life I know only too well where I would *want* to find a solution. It would solve everything for a couple of hours and then I'd have to start all over again … as hard as the first time, only worse …'

For Brian Flynn the time flew by as well. He adapted perfectly to his new living quarters and began to think that he had always lived over a busy hair salon. Every month, Garry was going to cut his hair for him and tame the red-grey tangle into a reasonable shape. They said he was better than any security firm and that he was a deterrent to intruders.

He left each morning for the immigrant centre where he worked; as he passed through the salon he encountered many ladies in varying degrees of disarray and marvelled to himself how they endured so much in the cause of beauty. He would greet them pleasantly and Katie always introduced him as the Reverend Lodger Upstairs.

'You could hear confessions here, Brian, but I think you'd be electrified by what they'd tell you,' Katie said cheerfully.

She had discovered that, in the middle of a recession, women were more anxious than ever to have their hair done. It kept them sane, somehow, and feeling in control.

For Lisa Kelly the time crawled by.

She was finding it difficult to get decisions made about her designs for Anton's restaurant, as a decision meant money being spent. Although the restaurant was open and full to bursting every night, there was still no verdict on whether to use her new logos and style on the tableware. Instead, she was concentrating on her college work and giving Noel a hand.

Noel had undergone some amazing conversion; at first Lisa had thought his plan to take on a baby was a fantasy. She had felt sure he would never be able to cope with a job, a college course and a newborn: it was too much to ask from one person, especially someone who was weak and shy like Noel. Now, however, she had begun to change her mind.

Noel had surprised her and in a way she almost envied him. He was so dedicated to all that he was doing. Everything was new for him. He had a whole new life ahead while Lisa felt that it was for ever more of the same. Of course it was all still theoretical; the baby wasn't even born yet. But he was preparing as much as he could to be a father. His notes always had lists scribbled in the margins: *nappy-rash cream, baby wipes, cotton wool*, they would say. *Four bottles, bottle brush, teats, steriliser* ...

Her parents still went on living in their icy, uncaring way, sharing a roof but not a bedroom, not a dining table, not any leisure time. They had no interest in Lisa or her life, any more than they cared how Katie fared with Garry in the salon. It was just casual indifference, not outright hostility, that existed between them as a couple. One had only to come into a room for the other to leave it.

Lisa had never been able to pin Anton down: there was *this* conference and *that* sales meeting and *this* television appearance and *that* radio interview. Weeks had gone by and she had never seen him alone. The pictures of her and Anton together at the launch had given way to shots of him with any number of beautiful girls, though she would have heard if he had any new real girlfriend. It would have been in the Sunday papers. That's the way Anton attracted publicity – he gave free drinks to columnists and photographers, and they always snapped him with several beautiful women, giving the impression that he was busy making up his mind between them all.

And it wasn't as if he had abandoned her or was ignoring her, Lisa reminded herself. A day didn't pass without a text message from Anton. Life was so busy, he would text. They had a rock band in last night, they were going to do a society wedding, a charity auction, a new tasting menu, a week of Breton specialities. Nowhere any mention of Lisa or her designs and plans.

Then, just as she was about to face the fact that he had left her, he wrote about this simply beautiful restaurant he had heard of in Honfleur where the seafood and shellfish were to die for. They *must* sneak away there for a weekend of self-indulgence soon. No date was fixed – just the word 'soon', and when she was starting to think that it meant 'never' he said that there was a trade fair next month in Paris, which they could both go to to fish for ideas and *then* run off to Honfleur. They might even dream up a whole Normandy season for the restaurant while they were there.

It was an unsettling life, to say the least.

Lisa couldn't seem to get on with other work. She kept changing or improving the outlines she had done for Anton. Ideas that had never been discussed or even acknowledged.

She was doing all right at college. Nothing like Noel, of course. *That* man was like something possessed. He said that he made do with four and a half hours' sleep. He laughed it off, saying that he would probably get less when the new baby arrived. He was so calm and accepting about it all.

'Did you love her, this Stella?' Lisa had asked.

'I think love is too strong a word. I like her a lot,' he'd replied, struggling to be honest.

'She must have loved you, then, to leave you in charge,' Lisa said.

'No, I don't think she did. I think she trusted me. That's all.'

'Well, that's a big part of life. If you trust someone, you're halfway there,' Lisa had said.

'Do you trust this Anton you talk about?'

'Not really,' Lisa said, with a face that closed the door on any further conversation about the topic.

Noel had shrugged. He was off anyway up to the hospital. It was all too soon before Stella had the Caesarean operation, which, by all accounts, she was unlikely to survive.

Three days later, Declan Carroll was in the delivery room, holding Fiona's hand as she groaned and whimpered.

'Great, girl. Just three more ... Just three ...'

'How do you know it's only three?' gasped Fiona, red-faced, her hair damp and stuck to her forehead.

'Trust me, I'm a doctor,' Declan said.

'You're not a woman, though,' Fiona said, teeth gritted and preparing for another push.

But he had been right – there were only three more. Then the head of his son appeared and he began to cry with relief and happiness.

'He's here,' he said, placing the baby in her arms. He took a photograph of them both and a nurse took a picture of all three of them.

'He'll hate this when he grows up,' Fiona said.

The baby, John Patrick Carroll, let out a wail in agreement.

'Only for a while and then he'll love it,' said Declan, who had his fair share of a mother who showed pictures of him to total strangers at the launderette where she worked.

Declan left the delivery ward of St Brigid's and headed for oncology. He knew what time Stella was going down for surgery and he wanted to be there as moral support.

They were just putting her on the trolley.

'Declan!' she said, pleased.

'Had to come and wish you well,' he said.

'You know Noel. And this is his cousin Emily.'

Stella was totally at ease, as if she were at a party instead of about to make the last journey of her life.

Declan knew Emily already as she came regularly to the group practice where he worked. She filled in at the desk as a receptionist or made the coffee or cleaned the place. It was never defined exactly what she did except that everyone knew the place would close down without her. She also helped his own mother in the launderette from time to time. No job seemed too menial for her even though she had a degree in Art History.

He tried to think about her as they stood in a little tableau, waiting for Stella to be wheeled to the operating theatre. It helped to concentrate on the living rather than on Stella, who would not be in their number for much longer.

'Any news of *your* baby yet, Declan?' Stella asked.

Declan decided against telling her of his great happiness with his brand-new son. It would make things even worse for the woman who would never see her own child.

'No, not a sign,' he lied.

'Remember, they are to be friends,' Stella urged him.

'Oh, that's a promise,' said Declan.

Just at that moment the ward sister came in. She smiled when she saw Declan.

'Congratulations, Doctor, we hear you've had a beautiful baby boy!'

He looked like something trapped in the headlights of an approaching car. He could not deny his son, nor could he pretend to be surprised when it would be known that he was there for the birth.

He had to face it.

'Sorry, Stella, I didn't want to be gloating.'

'No, you wouldn't ever do that,' she said. 'A boy! Imagine!'

'Yes, we didn't know. Not until he was born.'

'And is he perfect?'

'Thank God.'

And then she was wheeled out of the ward, leaving Noel, Emily and Declan behind.

Frances Stella Dixon Lynch was delivered by Caesarean section on 9 October at 7 p.m. She was tiny, but perfect. Ten tiny, perfect fingers, ten tiny, perfect toes and a shock of hair on her tiny, perfect head. She frowned at the world around her and wrinkled her tiny nose before opening her mouth and wailing as if it was already all too much.

Her mother died twenty minutes later.

The first person Noel telephoned was Malachy, his sponsor in AA.

'I can't live through this night without a drink,' he told him.

Malachy said he would come straight to the hospital. Noel was not to move until he arrived.

The women in the ward were full of sympathy. They arranged that he get tea and biscuits, which tasted like sawdust.

There was a small bundle of papers in an elastic band on Stella's locker. The word 'Noel' was on the outside.

He read them through with blurred eyes. One was an envelope with 'Frankie' written on it. The others were factual: her instructions about the funeral; her wishes that Frankie be raised in the Roman Catholic faith for as long as it seemed sensible to her. And a note dated last night:

Noel, tell Frankie that I wasn't all bad and that once I knew she was on the way I did the very best for her. Tell her that I had courage at the end and I didn't cry my eyes out or anything. And tell her that if things

had been different you and I would both have been
there to look after her. Oh – and that I'll be looking
out for her from up there. Who knows? Maybe I will.
  Thanks again,
  Stella

Noel looked down at the tiny baby with tears in his
eyes.

'Your mam didn't want to leave you, little pet,' he
whispered. 'She wanted to stay with you, but she had to
go away. It's just you and me now. I don't know how
we're going to do it, but we'll manage. We've got to
look after each other.'

The baby looked at him solemnly as though concentrating on his words as if she wanted to commit them
to memory.

Baby Frances was pronounced healthy. A collection of
people came to visit her as she lay there in her little cot:
Noel came every day; Moira Tierney, the social worker;
Emily, who brought Charles and Josie Lynch to see
their grandchild – and who visibly melted at the sight
of the baby. They seemed to have completely forgotten
their earlier condemnation of sex without marriage,
and Josie was even seen to lift the child in her arms and
pat the baby's back.

Lisa Kelly came a couple of times, as did Malachy.
Mr Hall came from Noel's workplace, even Old Man
Casey came and said that Noel was a sad loss to his
bar. Young Dr Declan Carroll came in, carrying his
own son, and introduced the babies formally to each
other.

Father Brian Flynn came in and brought Father Kevin

Kenny with him. Father Kenny, still on one crutch, was eager to take up his role as hospital chaplain again. He seemed slightly put out that Father Flynn had been so warmly accepted as his replacement. Many people seemed to know him and called him Brian in what Father Kenny thought of as a slightly overfamiliar way. He had obviously been involved in every stage of this unfortunate woman's pregnancy and the motherless baby who lay there looking up at them.

Father Kenny assumed that they were there to arrange a baptism, and started to clear his throat and talk about the technicalities.

But no, Father Flynn had brushed that away swiftly. The baby's grandparents were extraordinarily devout people and they would discuss all that sort of thing at a later time.

Charles and Josie Lynch's neighbour, Muttie Scarlet, came to pay his respects to the child. He was in the hospital anyway, he said, on business, and he thought he would take advantage of the occasion to visit the baby.

And eventually Noel was told that he could take his baby daughter home to his new apartment. It was a terrifying moment. Noel realised that he was about to stop being a visitor and become entirely responsible for this tiny human being. How was he going to remember all the things that needed to be done? Supposing he dropped her? Poisoned her? He couldn't do it, he couldn't be responsible for this baby, it was ludicrous to ask him. Stella had been mad, she was ill, she didn't know what she was doing. Someone else would have to take over, they'd have to find someone else to look after her baby – *her* baby, nothing to do with him at all.

He had a sudden urge to flee, to run down the corridor and out into the street, and to keep on running until the hospital and Stella and Frankie and all of them were just a memory.

Just as his feet were starting to turn towards the doorway, the nurse arrived with Frankie, wrapped in a big pink shawl.

She looked up at him trustingly, and suddenly, from nowhere, Noel felt a wave of protectiveness almost overwhelm him. This poor, helpless baby had no one else in the world. Stella had trusted him with the most precious thing she ever had, the child she knew she wouldn't live to see.

Nervously, almost shyly, he took the baby from the nurse.

'Little Frankie,' he said. 'Let's go home.'

Emily had said she would come and stay with him for a while to tide him over the most frightening bits. There were three bedrooms in the apartment, two reasonably sized and one small one, which would eventually be Frankie's, so she would be perfectly comfortable. The health visitor came every couple of days, but even so, there were so many questions.

Was that horrible-coloured mess in the baby's nappy normal, or did she have something wrong with her? How could anyone so very small need to be changed ten times a day? Was that breathing normal? Did he dare go to sleep in case she stopped?

How on earth did anyone manage to get all those poppers on a baby's sleepsuit in the right places? Was one blanket too much or too little? He knew she mustn't be allowed to get too cold, but the pamphlets were full of terrible warnings about the dangers of overheating.

Bathtimes were a nightmare. He knew to test the temperature of the water with his elbow, but would a mother's elbow signal a different temperature to his? Emily needed to come and test the water as well.

She was kept busy: she would do the laundry and help him prepare the bottles, and they could read the hospital notes and the baby books and consult the internet together. They would take the baby's temperature and make sure they had supplies of nappies, wipes, newborn formula. So much of it and so expensive. How did anyone cope with all this?

How did anyone learn to identify what kind of crying meant hunger, discomfort or pain? To Noel all crying sounded the same: piercing, jagged, shrill, drilling through the deepest, most exhausted sleep. No one ever told you how tiring it was to be up three, four times every night, night after night. After three days he was near to weeping with fatigue; as he walked up and down with his daughter, trying to wind her after her third feed of the night, he found himself stumbling against furniture, almost incapable of remaining upright.

Emily found him asleep in an armchair.

'Don't forget you have to go to the centre every week.'

'They're not taking any chances on me,' Noel said.

'It's the same for everyone. They call it the Mothers' and Babies' Group, but more and more it can be Fathers and Babies.' Emily was practical.

'It's not just that they think I'm a bit of a risk – past history of drinking and all that?' Noel asked.

'No. Don't be paranoid. And aren't you a shining example of what people can achieve?'

'I'm terrified, Emily.'

'Of course you are. So am I but we'll manage.'

'You won't go back to America and leave me here all on my own ...'

'No plans to do that, but I think you should set up some kind of a system for yourself from the very start. Like going to your mother and father for lunch on a Sunday every week.'

'I don't know ... *Every* week?'

'Oh, at least ... and in time you should offer to take Declan and Fiona's baby one evening a week to give them a night off. They'll do the same for you.'

'You definitely sound as if you're going to jump ship and you're just building me up some support to keep me going,' Noel said.

'Nonsense, Noel. But you have to learn to do it without me. You'll be on your own soon.'

Emily had no plans to go back to New York for a while; but she must be practical and get this show properly launched and on the road.

Father Flynn found a gospel choir, who sang at the funeral Mass, down at his church at the welcome centre for immigrants. Muttie Scarlet's grandchildren, twins called Maud and Simon, prepared a light lunch in the hall next door. There were no eulogies or speeches. Declan and Fiona sat next to Charles and Josie; Emily had the bag of baby essentials, while Noel held Frankie wrapped in a warm blanket.

Father Flynn spoke simply and movingly about Stella's short and troubled life. She had died, he said, leaving behind a very precious legacy. Everyone who had come to know and care for Stella would support Noel as he provided a home for their little daughter …

Katie was there with her husband Garry and her sister Lisa. She had only recently found out that Lisa was on the same course as Noel, they had begun at the same time. They knew each other, had coffee together once or twice; Lisa knew the story. Katie had hoped that Lisa would learn something from Noel – like that it was totally possible to get up and leave the safety of the family home. Home was not a healthy place to be, Katie thought, but there was no talking to Lisa, beautiful and restless as she had always been.

Katie noticed that Lisa, for once, was not being distant and withdrawn as she so often was. Instead she was being helpful, offering to pass plates of food or pour coffee. She was talking to Noel in terms of practicalities.

'I'll help you whenever I can. If you have to miss any lectures I'll give you the notes,' she offered.

'People are being very kind,' Noel said. 'Kinder than I ever expected.'

'There's something about a baby,' Lisa said.

'There is indeed. She's so very small. I don't know if I'll be able … I mean, I'm pretty clumsy.'

'All new parents are clumsy,' Lisa reassured him.

'That's the social worker over there. Moira,' he indicated.

'She's got a very uptight little face,' Lisa said.

'It's a very uptight job. She's always coming across losers like me.'

'I don't think you're a loser, I think you're bloody heroic,' Lisa said.

Moira Tierney had always wanted to be a social worker. When she was very young she had thought she might be a nun, but somehow that idea had changed over the years. Well, nuns had changed for one thing. They didn't live in big, quiet convents chanting hymns at dawn and dusk any more. There were no bells ringing and cloisters with shadows. Nuns, more or less, *were* social workers these days without any of the lovely ritual and ceremony.

Moira was from the West of Ireland, but now she lived alone in a small apartment. When she first came to Dublin, she went home to see her parents every month. They sighed a lot because she hadn't married. They sighed over the fact that she was working among the poor and ruffians instead of bettering herself.

They sighed a great deal.

After her mother died, her visits became less frequent. Now she would go just once or twice a year back to the ramshackle farmhouse she had once called home.

She wished that her block of flats had a garden but the other residents had all voted for more car parking, so it was just yards of concrete outside. Still, democracy ruled, she thought, and made do with window boxes, which were the envy of her neighbours. She liked her work, but it was rarely, if ever, straightforward.

This man, Noel Lynch, was someone who puzzled her. It appeared he had known nothing of the child he had fathered until a few short weeks before the baby arrived. He had lost touch with the mother. And then, suddenly, he had almost overnight changed his lifestyle totally, joined a Twelve Steps Programme, taken up his education again and approached his job in Hall's seriously. Any one of these things would have been life-changing, but to take them all on while looking after an infant child seemed to be ludicrous.

Moira had read too many concerned and outraged articles about social workers who didn't do their jobs properly to feel in any way at ease. She knew what they would write. They would say that all the signs were staring everyone in the face. This was a dangerous situation. What were the social workers *doing*? She didn't know why she was so certain about this, but it was a feeling that wouldn't go away. Every box had been ticked, all the relevant authorities had been contacted, yet she was completely convinced that there was something out of place here.

This Noel Lynch was an accident waiting to happen. A bomb about to explode.

Lisa Kelly was thinking about Noel at the same time.

She had once said to her sister Katie that if she was a betting woman she would give him one week before he went back on the drink and two weeks before he gave up his lectures. And as regards minding an infant – the social workers would be in before you could say 'foster home'!

Just as well she hadn't found a betting shop.

Lisa had done a job for a garden centre but her heart wasn't in it. All the time that she toyed with images of floral baskets, watering cans and sunflowers in full bloom, she thought of Anton's restaurant. She found herself drawing a bride throwing a bouquet – and then the thought came to her.

Anton could specialise in weddings.

Real society weddings. People would have to fight

to get a date there. They had an underused courtyard where people often escaped for a furtive cigarette. It could be transformed into a permanent, mirror-lined marquee for weddings.

He didn't open for Saturday lunch so that was the time to do it, and the guests would have to leave by six o'clock. There was a singing pub called Irish Eyes nearby and they could make an arrangement with the pub that there would be a welcoming pint or cocktail, and the scene would move seamlessly onwards. The bride's father would be relieved that he wasn't paying for champagne all night and the restaurant could get straight into 'serving dinner' mode. There would be only fifty Anton Brides a year, so there would be huge competition to know who they would be.

It was too good an idea to keep to herself.

Anton had sounded fretful in his recent texts. Of course he couldn't fix a date for their trip to Normandy. Not now, not in the middle of a recession. Business was so up and down. No groups of estate agents and auctioneers celebrating another sale as they had every day during the property boom. No leisurely business lunches. Times were tough.

So Lisa knew that he would love this idea. But when to tell him?

If only she had her own place. It would have been totally different: Anton could have popped around in the afternoon or the early evening. Or, better, he could have come to visit late in the evening when he could unwind and stay the night. When she did spend time with Anton it was always at a conference hotel or on a visit to a speciality restaurant where they would over-night at a nearby inn. This hope of Honfleur was what had kept her going for weeks and now it looked as if it wasn't definite, but when he saw all the work she had done on the concept of Anton Brides, he would be so pleased. Yet again she would have rescued him and he would be so grateful.

She just couldn't wait any longer. She would tell him tonight. She would go to his restaurant tonight, straight after her lectures. She would go home and change first. She wanted to look her very best when she told him about this news, which would turn his fortunes around and change their lives.

At home, Lisa went to her room and held two dresses up to the light. The first, a red and black dress with black-lace trimming, the other a light wool rose-coloured dress with a wide belt. The black and red was sexy, the pink more elegant. The black and red was a little tarty but the pink would attract every stain going and would need to be dry-cleaned.

She had a quick shower and put on the black and red dress and a lot of make-up.

Teddy, the maître d', was surprised to see her when she arrived at the restaurant.

'You're a stranger round here, Lisa,' he said with his professional smile.

'Too busy thinking up marvellous ideas for this place, that's why.'

She laughed. In her own ears her laughter sounded brittle and false; she didn't much care for Teddy. Tonight, though, she was going to establish her place in this restaurant. Anton would see how brilliant her scheme was; she wasn't even remotely nervous of meeting him and explaining her new plan.

'And are you dining here, Lisa?'

Teddy was unfailingly polite but very focused. There was no room for vagueness in Teddy's life.

'Yes. I hoped you could squeeze me in. I need to talk to him about something.'

'Alas, full tonight.' Teddy smiled regretfully. 'Not a table left in the place.'

They were having a special event, he explained, a four-for-the-price-of-two night in order to get the word out about Anton's. Of course it had been April's idea.

'The place is packed out this evening,' Teddy said. 'There's a wait-list for cancellations.'

This was not what she had come to hear. She had come to give him news about how to change the downward spiral.

'But I really need to talk to him,' she insisted. 'I've got a great idea for bringing in new business. Look, Teddy,' she continued, becoming aware that the shrillness in her voice was starting to attract attention. 'He's really going to want to hear my ideas, he's going to be very angry if you don't let me see him.'

'I'm sorry, Lisa,' he said firmly. 'That's just not going to be possible. You see how busy we are.'

'I'll just go back into the kitchen and see what Anton has to say about that ...' Lisa began.

'I think not,' said Teddy firmly, stepping smoothly to one side and gripping her elbow. 'Why don't you telephone tomorrow and make an appointment? Or better still, make a reservation. We'd love to see you here again, and I will certainly tell Anton you called in.'

As he spoke, he was guiding her firmly towards the door.

Before she knew what had happened, Lisa found herself outside on the street, looking back at the diners who were staring at her as if hypnotised.

She needed to get away quickly; turning on her heels, she fled as quickly as her too-tight skirt would allow her.

When she was able to draw breath, she pulled out her cellphone to call a taxi and found, to her annoyance, that she had let the battery run down. The night was going from bad to worse.

It started to rain.

The house was quiet when she let herself in but that didn't make it any different to usual. Here there was no conversation, unless Katie had come on one of her infrequent visits. Lisa hoped that no one was going to be there tonight. She was in luck. As she reached the bottom of the stairs, there was just silence about the house, as if it were holding its breath.

And that's when it happened. Lisa saw what the newspapers would have called 'a partially clothed woman' come out of the bathroom at the top of the stairs, holding a mobile phone to her ear. She had long, damp hair and was wearing a green satin slip and nothing much else by the look of her.

'Who are *you*?' Lisa asked in shock.

'I might ask you the same,' the woman said. She didn't seem annoyed, put out or even embarrassed. 'Are you here for him? The agency didn't tell me. I haven't seen you before. I'm just ringing for a taxi.'

'Well, why are you ringing it here?' Lisa asked childishly.

Who could she be? You often heard of burglars coming into a house and just brazening it out with the householders. Maybe she was part of a gang?

Then she heard her father's voice.

'What is it, Bella? Who are you talking to?' And her father appeared at his bedroom door in a dressing gown. He looked shocked to see Lisa. 'I didn't know *you* were at home,' he said, nonplussed.

'Obviously,' Lisa said, her hand shaking as she reached for the front door.

'Who *is* she?' the girl in the green satin slip asked.

'It doesn't matter,' he said.

And Lisa realised that it didn't. It had never mattered to him who she was or Katie either.

'Well, who am I to say what you should do with your own money ...' The woman called Bella shrugged in her green satin underwear and went back into the bedroom.

Lisa and her father looked at each other for a long minute; then he followed Bella back into the bedroom as, unsteadily, Lisa left the house again.

Noel allowed himself to think that Stella would have been pleased with how he was coping with their daughter. He had been without an alcoholic drink for nearly two months. He attended an AA meeting at least five times a week and telephoned his friend Malachy on the days he couldn't make it.

He had brought Frankie back to Chestnut Court and was making a home for her. True, he was walking round like a zombie from tiredness, but he had kept her alive, and, what's more, the community nurses seemed to think she was doing well. She slept in a small cot beside him and when she cried he woke and walked around the room with her. He sterilised all the bottles and teats, made up her formula, winded her and changed her. He bathed her and burped her and rocked her to sleep.

He sang songs to her as he paced up and down the bedroom every night, every song he could think of even if some of them were mad and inappropriate.

'Sitting on the Dock of the Bay' ... 'I Don't Like Mondays' ... 'Let Me Entertain You' ... 'Fairytale of New York' ... Any snippet of any song he could remember.

One night he found himself singing the words to 'Frankie and Johnny' to her. The lyrics made him hesitate, but as soon as he stopped, she started crying again. Quickly, he started again. Why didn't he know the words to proper lullabies?

He had conducted three satisfactory meetings with Moira Tierney, the social worker, and five with Imelda, the community nurse.

His leave was over and he was about to go back to work at Hall's; he wasn't looking forward to it, but babies were expensive and he really needed the money. He would wait a while and then ask for a bit of a raise in salary. He was catching up with his lectures from the college – Lisa had been as good as her word – and was back on track again there.

He was tired all the time but then so was every young mother that he passed on the street or at the supermarket. He was certainly too tired to pause and wonder was he happy with it all himself. The little baby needed him and he would be there. That's all there was to it. And his life was certainly much better than it had been eight weeks ago.

He put his books away in the silent apartment. His cousin Emily was asleep in her room, little Frankie was sleeping in the cot beside his own bed. He looked out of his window in Chestnut Court. It was late, dark, drizzly and very quiet.

He saw a taxi draw up and a young woman get out. What strange lives people led. Then, two seconds later, he heard his doorbell ring. Whoever it was, was coming to see him – Noel Lynch – at this time of night!

'Lisa?' Noel was puzzled to see her on the entryphone screen at this hour.

'Can I come in for a moment, Noel? I want to ask you something.'

'Yes ... well ... I mean ... the baby's asleep ... but, sure, come in.'

He pressed the buzzer to release the door.

She looked very woebegone.

'I don't suppose you have a drink? No, sorry, of course you don't. I'm sorry. Forgive me.'

She had forgotten with that casual, uncaring, shruggy attitude of someone who was never addicted to drink.

Malachy had told Noel that it was this laid-back attitude that really got to him. His friends saying they could take it or leave it, bypassing the terrible urgency that the addicted felt all the time.

'I can offer tea or chocolate,' he said, forcing back his annoyance.

She didn't know. She would never know what it felt

like. He would not lose his temper, but what was she doing here?

'Tea would be lovely,' she said.

He put on the kettle and waited.

'I can't go home, Noel.'

'No?'

'No.'

'So what do you want to do, Lisa?'

'Can I sleep on your sofa here, please? *Please*, Noel. Just for tonight. Tomorrow I'll sort something out.'

'Did you have a row at home?'

'No.'

'And what about your friend Anton that you talk so much about?'

'I've been there. He doesn't want to see me.'

'And I'm your last hope, is that it?'

'That's it,' she said bleakly.

'All right,' he said.

'What?'

'I said all right. You can stay. I don't have any women's clothes to lend you. I can't give you my bed, Frankie's cot is in there and she's due a feed in a couple of hours. We'll all be up pretty early in the morning. It's no picnic being here.'

'I'd be very grateful, Noel.'

'Sure, then have your tea and go to bed. There's a folded rug over there and use one of the cushions as a pillow.'

'Do you not want to know what it was about?' she asked.

'No, Lisa, I don't. I haven't got the energy for it. Oh, and if you're up before I am, Emily, that's my cousin, will be getting Frankie ready to take her to the health centre.'

'Well, I'll sort of explain to her then.'

'No need.'

'What a wonderful way to be,' Lisa Kelly said in genuine admiration.

She didn't think she would sleep at all, but she did, stirring slightly a couple of times when she thought she heard a baby crying. Through a half-opened eye she saw Noel Lynch moving about with an infant in his arms. She didn't even have time to think about what kind of mind games Anton was playing with her or whether her father was even remotely embarrassed by the incident in their home. She was fast asleep again and didn't wake until she heard someone leave a mug of tea beside her.

Cousin Emily, of course. The wonder woman who had stepped in just when needed. She in turn didn't seem remotely surprised to see a woman in a black and red lace-trimmed dress waking up on the sofa.

'Do you have to be anywhere for work or anything?' the woman asked.

'No. No, I don't. I'll just wait until my parents have left home, then I'll go back and pick up my things and … find myself somewhere else to stay. I'm Lisa, by the way.'

Emily looked at her. 'I know, and I'm Emily. We met at Stella's funeral. What time will your parents be gone?' she asked.

'By nine – on a normal morning, anyway.'

'But this might not be a normal morning?' Emily guessed.

'No, it might not. You see—'

'Noel left half an hour ago. It's eight o'clock now. I have to go to the clinic with Frankie via the charity shop fairly soon … and I'm not quite sure what's the best thing to do.'

'I'm an old friend of Noel's, from college …' Lisa began.

'Oh, I know that.'

'So you wouldn't have to worry about leaving me here when you go out, but then you might not want to …'

Emily shook her head as if to get rid of any evidence of such deep thinking on her part.

'No, I was thinking of breakfast, actually. Noel made a banana sandwich for himself and then he'll have coffee on his way to work. I'm going to open up the thrift shop, when I've given Frankie her bottle; I'll have some fruit and cereal there. I thought you might like to come with me. Would that suit?'

'That would be great, Emily. I'll just go and give myself a quick wash.'

Lisa hopped up and ran to the bathroom. She looked quite terrible. All her make-up was smeared across her face. She looked like a tart down on her luck.

No wonder the woman didn't want to leave her in charge of the apartment. Nobody would let anyone who looked like Lisa did be in charge of anything at all. Maybe at the charity shop, Lisa might be able to buy something to take away the wild look of her. She cleaned her face and gave herself a splash wash, then put on over her dress a sweater Emily had given her.

Emily was ready to leave: she was dressed in a fitted green wool dress and she carried a huge tote bag. The baby in the pram was tiny – less than a month old – looking up trustfully at the two women who were realistically nothing to do with her.

Lisa felt a great wave of warmth towards the small, defenceless baby, relying on what were, after all, two strangers, Emily and Lisa, to get her through this day. She wondered if anyone had looked out for her like this when she was little. Possibly not, she thought bleakly.

It was the most unreal day Lisa had ever lived through. Emily Lynch asked nothing of Lisa's circumstances. Instead she talked admiringly of Noel and the great efforts he was making on every front. She told Lisa how she and Noel had known nothing about how to raise a child but between the internet and the health clinics they were doing fine.

Emily found a dark brown trouser suit in the thrift shop and asked Lisa to try it on. It fitted her well enough.

'I only have forty euros to see me through today,' Lisa said apologetically, 'and I may need a taxi to take my things out of my parents' home.'

'That's all right. You can pay for it by working, can't you?' Emily saw few problems.

'Working?' Lisa asked, bemused.

'Well, you could help in the shop until I take Frankie to the clinic, then we need to take her for a walk. Then you could come with me while I pop into the medical centre, and then we could walk down St Jarlath's Crescent where I look after the gardens, and you could push the pram around if Baby Frankie gets bored. That would be a good day's work and would well cover the cost of that trouser suit.'

'But I have to collect my things,' Lisa pleaded, 'and find somewhere to live.'

'We have all day to think about that,' Emily said calmly.

And the day began.

Lisa had never met so many people in one working day. She, who worked alone at her desk, tinkering with drawings and designs for Anton, had often spent hours without talking to another human being. Emily Lynch lived a different life.

They left the shop and moved to the clinic where Frankie was weighed and pronounced very satisfactory. There had been an appointment to see Moira the social worker, but when they arrived they heard that Moira had been called away on an emergency.

'That poor woman's life must be one long emergency.'

Emily was sympathetic instead of being annoyed that she had just made a totally unnecessary visit to the social worker's office. Then it was up to the health centre where Emily collected a sheaf of papers and spoke pleasantly to the doctors.

'This is Lisa. She's helping me today.'

They all nodded at her acceptingly. No other explanations. It was very restful indeed.

She was a pretty baby, Lisa thought. Hard work, of course, but babies were, weren't they? Or at least they were supposed to be. She didn't suppose she or Katie had ever had half the attention this one was getting.

Emily had left a parcel for Dr Hat, who was expected in shortly. He'd recently retired from full-time practice, but still did a day's locum work at the surgery each week. Emily had discovered that he couldn't cook and didn't seem anxious to learn, so she always left a portion of whatever she and Noel had cooked the night before. Today it was a smoked cod, egg and spinach pie, plus instructions on how to reheat it.

'It's the only meal that Hat eats in the week, apparently,' Emily said disapprovingly.

'Hat?'

'Yes, that's his name.'

'What's it short for?' Lisa was curious.

'Never asked. I think it's because he seems to wear a hat day and night,' Emily said.

'Night?' Lisa asked, with a sort of a laugh.

'Well, I have no way of knowing that.'

Emily looked at her with interest and Lisa realised that this was the first time today she had allowed herself to relax enough to smile, let alone laugh. She had been like a clenched fist, unable to think about the only family she had known and the only man she had ever loved.

'Right. Where to now?' Lisa was determined to keep cheerful.

'We could stop for lunch, go home, get something, give Frankie to her grandmother for a couple of hours, then I can make a start on this paperwork. I'll ask Dingo Duggan to drive you up to collect your things. He can use the thrift shop van.'

'Hey, wait a minute, Emily, not so fast. I haven't found anywhere to go yet.'

'Oh, you'll find somewhere.' Emily was very confident of this. 'You don't want to delay once you make a decision like this.'

'But you don't know how bad things are,' Lisa said.

'I do,' Emily said.

'How do you know? I didn't even tell Noel.'

'It must have been something very bad for you to

come to Chestnut Court in the middle of the night,' Emily said, and then seemed to lose interest in it. 'Why don't we see if they have any chicken livers down in the market. We could get some mushrooms and rice. Tonight's one of Noel's lectures. He'll need a good meal to see him through. Well, of course, you know that and you'll need all *your* papers and files and everything.'

'Oh no, I can't go to college tonight. The world is falling to bits on me. I have no time at all to go to classes!' Lisa cried.

'Always the very time we *must* go – when the world is falling to bits,' Emily said, as if it were totally obvious. 'Now, would you like a baked potato with cheese for lunch? I find it gives you lots of energy and you'll need that over the next couple of days.'

'Baked potato is just fine,' Lisa gasped.

'Good. Then off we go. And after the market we'll go on garden patrol. Could you have a paper and pencil ready and write down what we need for the various gardens in St Jarlath's Crescent?'

Lisa wondered what it would be like to have a life like this – where everyone sort of depended on you, but nobody actually loved you.

Dingo Duggan said that of course he'd drive Lisa to collect her things. Where would he bring them?

'We will be discussing that over lunch, Dingo,' Emily explained. 'We'll let you know when we see you.'

Lisa was almost dizzy with the speed with which it was all happening. This small, busy woman with the frizzy hair had involved her effortlessly in a series of activities and at no stage had suggested she explain the situation at home and why she had to flee from it.

Instead she had been to market and bargained at every stall. Emily seemed to know everyone. Then they had pushed the pram down St Jarlath's Crescent where Lisa had made lists of plants needed, weeds dug up, paint required for touch-ups. Some gardens were expertly kept, some were neglected, but Emily's regular patrol gave the street a comfortable, established air of being well cared for. Lisa had only begun to take it all in when they arrived at Noel's family home. Again, Lisa marvelled at Emily's speed.

The introductions to his parents were made briskly and briefly.

'Charles and Josie are very good people, Lisa. They do good works all day and are busy setting up a fund to have a statue erected to St Jarlath. We won't detain them from their good work for too long. This is Lisa. She's a good friend of Noel's from his college lectures and has been a great help today in looking after Frankie. And here is your beautiful granddaughter, Josie. She has been longing to see you.'

'Poor little thing.'

Josie took the baby in her arms and Charles beamed up from his unappetising-looking sandwich.

In Emily's room a bottle of wine was produced.

'Normally I don't have a drink anywhere around Noel, but today is special,' Emily explained. 'We'll wait until you've collected your things and then we'll have it with our lunch.'

'Yes, you must be worn out.' Lisa thought that Emily was referring to the hectic pace of the morning.

'Oh no, that's nothing.' Emily dismissed it. 'I meant that today is a day of decision for all of us. A glass of wine might be badly needed.'

At his restaurant, Anton was planning menus and talking about Lisa. 'I'd better call her,' he said gloomily.

'You'll know exactly what to say, Anton. You always do.' Teddy was admiring and diplomatic.

'Not as easy as it sounds,' said Anton, reaching for his phone.

Lisa's phone was switched off. He tried the number of the house where she lived with her parents. Her mother answered.

'No, we haven't seen her since yesterday.' The voice was distant, not at all concerned. 'She didn't come home last night. So ...'

'So ... what?' Anton was impatient with the woman.

'Well ... nothing, really ...' Her voice trailed away. 'Lisa is, as you must know, an adult. It would be fruitless, to say the least, to worry about her. Shall I give her a message for you?'

Lisa's mother had a voice that managed to be indifferent and courteous at the same time in a way that irritated him hugely.

'Don't bother!' he said and hung up.

Lisa's mother shrugged. She was about to go upstairs when her husband let himself in the front door.

'Has Lisa been talking to you?' he began.

'No, I haven't seen her. Why?'

'She will,' he said.

'Will what?'

'Will talk to you. There was an incident last night. I didn't realise she was at home and I had a young woman with me.'

'How lovely.' His wife's scorn was written all over her face.

'She seemed upset.'

'I can't imagine why.'

'She doesn't have your sense of detachment – that's why.'

'She hasn't gone for good. I see her door is open. She's left all her things here.'

Lisa's mother spoke as if she were talking about a casual acquaintance.

'Of course she hasn't gone for good. Where would she go?'

Lisa's mother shrugged her shoulders again. 'She'll end up doing what she wants to do. Like everyone …' she said and walked out the door that her husband had just come in.

'Where will we take your things?' Dingo asked Lisa.

'We're just going to leave them in the van, if that's all right?' Lisa said. She was feeling slightly dizzy from the many encounters that the morning had brought.

'Where are you going to live?' Dingo persisted.

'It hasn't been decided yet.'

Lisa knew that she sounded as if she was avoiding his questions, but she was actually telling the truth.

'So where do you plan to lay your head tonight, then?' Dingo was determined to get all the answers.

Lisa felt very weary indeed. 'Why do they call you Dingo?' she asked in despair.

'Because I spent seven weeks in Australia,' he said proudly.

'And why did you come back?'

She *must* keep the conversation going about him and avoid cosmic questions about herself.

'Because I got lonely,' Dingo said, as if this was the

most natural thing in the world. 'You will too, mark my words. When you're living with Josie and Charles and saying ten Rosaries a day, you'll look back on your own home and there'll be an ache in you.'

'Living with Charles and Josie Lynch? No, that was never on the cards,' Lisa said, horrified.

'Well, where am I to bring you back there when we've collected your things? Oh, look, here's your house.'

'I'll be ten minutes, Dingo.'

She got out of the van.

'Emily said I was to go in with you and carry out your things.'

'Does she think she runs the whole world?' Lisa grumbled.

'There's others who'd make a worse job of it,' Dingo said cheerfully.

It didn't take Dingo long to pack the van. He already had a dress rail installed in it, so he just hung up Lisa's clothes on that. He had cardboard boxes where he expertly packed her computer and files, and more boxes for her personal possessions. It wasn't much to show after a lifetime, Lisa thought.

The house was quiet, but she knew her father was at home. She had seen the curtains of his room move slightly. He made no move to come out and stop her. No attempt to explain what she had seen last night. In a way she was relieved, yet it did show how little he cared about whether she stayed or left.

As she and Dingo finished packing the van, she saw the curtains move again. However much of a failure her own life had been, it was nothing compared to his and her mother's.

She wrote a note and left it on the hall table.

*I am leaving the house key. You will realise now
that I have left permanently. I wish you both well
and certainly I wish you more happiness than you
have now. I have not discussed my plans with Katie. I
will wait until I am settled, then I will let you have a
forwarding address.*

Lisa

No love, no thanks, no explanation, no goodbyes.
She looked around the house as if she had never seen it
before. She realised it was the way her mother looked
at things.

Not long ago Katie had said Lisa was turning into
her parents and that she should leave home as soon
as possible. She longed to tell Katie that she had
finally taken her advice but she would wait until she
had found somewhere to stay. It would not be in St
Jarlath's Crescent with Charles and Josie, no matter
what Dingo thought, and no matter how Emily might
try to persuade her.

Back at the Lynches' house, Emily wanted to know how
it had all gone. She was relieved that there had been no
confrontation. She had feared that Lisa would say more
than she meant to.

'I'm never going to say anything to them again,' Lisa
said.

'Never is a long time. Now let's get these potatoes
into the microwave.'

Lisa sat down weakly and watched Emily moving
expertly around this little place that she had made completely her home, and suddenly it was easy to talk, to
explain the shock of seeing her father with a prostitute

last night, the realisation that Anton did not see her as the centre of his life, the fact that she had no money, nowhere to live, no career to speak of.

Lisa spoke on in measured tones. She did not allow herself to get upset. There was something about Emily that made confiding easy – she nodded and murmured agreement. She asked the right questions and none of the awkward ones. Lisa had never been able to talk like this before. Eventually she came to a full stop.

'I'm so sorry, Emily, I've been going on about myself all afternoon. You must have plans of your own.'

'I've telephoned Noel. He'll be here around five. I'll take Frankie back to Chestnut Court and Dingo can spring into action then.'

Lisa looked at her blankly.

'What action exactly, Emily? I'm a bit confused here. Are you suggesting that I live with Charles and Josie, because I honestly don't think—'

'No, no, no. I'm going to live there again for a little bit, and who knows what will happen then?'

Emily looked as if it should have been obvious to anyone that this was how things would be.

'Yes, well ... but, Emily, all my things are outside in Dingo's van. Where am I going to live?'

'I thought you could go to live with Noel in Chestnut Court,' Emily said. 'It would sort out everything ...'

CHAPTER SIX

Moira Tierney was good at her job. She had a reputation for following up the smallest detail. Her office was a model for young social workers with its faultless filing system. Nobody ever heard Moira moan and groan about her caseload or the lack of back-up services. It was a job and she did it.

Social work was never going to be nine to five; Moira expected to be called by problem families after working hours. In fact, this was often when she was most needed. She was never away from her cellphone, and her colleagues had become used to Moira having to get up and leave a meeting in the middle of everything because there was an emergency call. She was easy about it. It went with the territory.

Moira spent days and nights picking up the pieces for people where love had gone wrong: where marriages had broken down, where children were abandoned, where domestic violence was too regular. These were once people filled with romance and hope, but Moira had never known them in those days. They wouldn't have been in her casebook. It didn't make her deliberately cynical about love and marriage, it was more a matter of time and opportunity.

At the end of a day Moira had little energy left to go to a nightclub. Anyway, even if she had, she might well have had to take a call while on the dance floor – a call meaning that she would have to go to deal with somebody else's problems.

Yes, of course she would like to meet somebody. Who wouldn't?

She wasn't a beauty – a little squarish with curly brown hair – but she wasn't ugly either. Much plainer women than Moira had found boyfriends, lovers, husbands. There must be someone out there; someone relaxed and calm and undemanding. Someone much more peaceful than those she had left behind her at home.

Moira went back to Liscuan every few months. She took the Saturday train across the country and the bus to the end of their road. She came back the following day. She spent most of her time there cleaning up the house and trying to find out what benefits her father could claim.

Nothing ever changed, in all the years since she had left to study in Dublin things had been like this. Nothing altered.

People didn't much like coming to the house any more; and her father had taken to going to Mrs Kennedy's house, where she would give him a meal in return for cutting logs for her. Apparently Mr Kennedy had gone to England looking for a job. He might or might not have found one, but he had never come back to report.

Moira's brother Pat was left to his own devices. He worked around the place, milking the two cows and feeding the hens. He went for a couple of pints in Liscuan village on a Saturday night, so Moira had very little conversation with him. It made her sad to see him dress himself up in a clean shirt and put on hair oil for his weekly outing. Any more than in her own, there was no sign of love in Pat's life.

Pat said little about it all, just burned the bottom of one frying pan after another as he cooked bacon and eggs for supper every night. This cramped little farmhouse would never know the laughter of grandchildren.

It was lonely going home to Liscuan but Moira did it with a good grace. She could tell them nothing about her life in Dublin. They would be shocked if they knew she had dealt with an eleven-year-old girl constantly raped by her father and now pregnant, or a battered wife, or a drunken mother who locked her three children in a room while she went to the pub. Nothing like this happened in Liscuan, or so the Tierneys thought.

So Moira kept her thoughts to herself. This particular weekend she was glad of the time. She needed to think something through. Moira Tierney believed that you often had a nose for a situation that wasn't right, and this was your role in the whole thing. After all, it was what those years of training and further years on the job taught you, to recognise when something wasn't right.

And Moira was worried about Frankie Lynch.

It seemed entirely wrong that Noel Lynch should be given custody of the child. Moira had read the file carefully. He hadn't even lived with Stella, the baby's mother. It was only when she was approaching her death and the baby's birth that she had got in touch with Noel.

It was all highly unsatisfactory.

Admittedly, Noel had managed to build up a support

system that looked pretty good on paper. The place was clean and warm and adequately stocked with what was necessary for the baby. The sterilising for bottles was set up, the baby bath in position. Moira couldn't fault any of that.

His cousin, a middle-aged, settled person called Emily, had stayed with him for a time, and she still took the baby with her wherever she went. And sometimes the baby stayed with a nurse who had a new baby of her own and was married to a doctor. A very safe environment. And there was an older couple called Nora and Aidan who already looked after their own grandchild.

There were other people too. Noel's parents, who were religious maniacs and were busy drumming up a petition to erect a statue for some saint who died thousands of years ago; then there was a couple called Scarlet: Muttie and Lizzie, and their twin grandchildren, they were part of the team. And there was a retired doctor who seemed to be called Dr Hat, of all things, who was supposed to be particularly soothing to infants, apparently. All reliable people, but still …

It was all too bitty, Moira thought: a flimsy daisy chain of people, like the cast of a musical. If one link blew away, everything could crash to the ground. But could she get anyone to support her instinct? Nobody at all. Her immediate superior, who was head of the team, said that she was fussing about nothing – everything seemed to be in place.

She had tried to enlist the American cousin Emily on her side, but to no avail. Emily appeared to have a blind spot about Noel. She said he had made amazing strides in turning his life around so that he could look after his daughter. He was persevering at his job. He was even studying at night to improve his work chances. He had given up alcohol, which he found very hard to do, but he was resolute. It would be a poor reward for all this if the social workers were going to take his child away. He had promised the baby's mother that the child should not be raised in care.

'Care might be a lot better than what he can offer,' Moira had muttered.

'It might, but then again it might not.' Emily was not to be convinced.

Moira had to hold back. But she was watching with very sharp eyes for anything to go out of step.

And now it had.

Noel had brought a woman in to live in the flat.

He had done up the spare room for her to sleep in.

She was young, this woman – young and restless. One of those tall, rangy women with hair down to her waist. She knew nothing about babies and seemed defensive and resentful when asked about any parenting skills.

'I'm not here permanently,' she had said over and over. 'I'm in a relationship elsewhere. With Anton Moran. The chef. Noel is just giving me somewhere to stay and in return I'm helping him with Frankie.'

She shrugged as if it was simple and clear to the meanest intelligence.

Moira didn't like her at all. There were too many of these bimbos around the place, leggy, air-headed young women with nothing in their minds except clothes. You should *see* the dress that this Lisa had hanging on her wall! A red and blue designer outfit probably costing the earth.

Whatever doubts Moira had about Noel's judgment,

they were increased a hundredfold by the arrival of Lisa Kelly on the scene.

There were great plans afoot for a double christening. Frankie Lynch and Johnny Carroll, born the same day, minded by all the same people, were to be baptised together.

Moira was surprised to be invited. Noel had said that there would be a baptism in Father Flynn's church down by the Liffey, and a little reception in the hall afterwards. Moira was very welcome to join them.

She tried to put the right amount of gratitude on to her face. They didn't need to do this, but perhaps they were trying to underline the stability of their situation.

'What kind of christening gift would you like?' she said suddenly.

Noel looked at her in surprise.

'There's no question of that, Moira, everyone is giving a card to both Frankie and Johnny; we're going to put them in albums for them with the photographs so that they will know what this day was like.'

Moira felt very reproved and put down. 'Oh yes, of course, certainly,' she said.

Noel couldn't help being pleased to see her wrong-footed for once.

'I'm sure everyone will be delighted to see you there, Moira,' he said with no conviction whatsoever.

There was a much larger congregation than Moira had expected at Father Flynn's church. How did they know all these people? Most of them must be friends of Dr Carroll and his wife. Surely Noel Lynch wouldn't know half the church?

The two godmothers were there, Emily holding Frankie, and Fiona's friend Barbara, who was also a nurse in the heart clinic, carrying Johnny. The babies, both freshly fed and changed, were beautifully behaved and for the most part slept through the ceremony. Father Flynn kept it brief and to the point. The water was poured over their little foreheads – that of course woke them up, but they were quickly soothed and calmed; vows were made for them by the godparents and they were now part of God's Church and His family. He hoped that they would both find happiness and strength in this knowledge.

Nothing too pious, nothing that anyone could object to. The babies took it all in their stride. Then everyone moved to the hall next door, where there was a buffet and a huge cake with the names Frankie and Johnny iced on it.

Maud and Simon Mitchell were in charge of the catering: Moira remembered the names being listed among Noel's babysitters for Frankie. They seemed out of place in her vision of Frankie's life. But then, so did this whole christening party.

Moira stood on the outside, watching the people mingle and talk and come up to gurgle at the babies. It was a pleasant gathering, certainly, but she didn't feel involved. There was music in the background and Noel moved around easily, drinking orange juice and talking to everyone. Moira also noticed Lisa, who was looking very glamorous, her honey-coloured hair coiled up under a little red hat.

Maud noticed Moira standing alone and came over to her, offering her serving tray. 'Can I get you another piece of cake?'

'No, thank you. I'm Moira, Frankie's social worker,' she said.

'Yes, I know you are, I'm Maud Mitchell, one of Frankie's babysitters. She's doing very well, isn't she?'

Moira leaped on this. 'Didn't you expect her to do well?' she asked.

'Oh no, the reverse, Noel has to be both mother and father to her, and he's doing a really great job.'

More solidarity in the community, Moira thought. It was as if there was an army ranked against her. She could still see in her mind the newspaper headlines, *Social services to blame. There were many warnings. Everything was ignored ...*

'How exactly are you and your brother friends of Noel?' she asked.

'We live on the same street as he used to live, where his parents live now. But we're hoping to go to New Jersey soon, we have the offer of a job.' Her face lit up.

'No work here?'

'Not for freelance caterers, no, people have less money these days, they're not giving big parties like they used to.'

'And your parents, will they be sorry to see you go?'

'No, our parents sort of went ages ago, we live with Muttie and Lizzie Scarlet, and it will be hard saying goodbye to them. Honestly, it's too long a story, and I'm meant to be collecting plates. That's Muttie over there, the one in the middle telling stories.'

She pointed out a small man with a wheeze that didn't deter any of his tales.

Why had he brought up these two young people? It was a mystery and Moira hated a mystery.

*

At the weekly meeting, Moira's team leader asked for a report on any areas that were giving cause for alarm.

As she always did, she brought up the subject of Noel and his baby daughter. The team leader shuffled the papers in front of her.

'We have the nurse's report here. She says the child is fine.'

'She only sees what she wants to see.'

Moira knew that she sounded petty and mulish.

'Well, the weight gain is normal, the hygiene is fine – he hasn't fallen down on anything so far.'

'He's brought a flashy girl in to live there.'

'We are not nuns, Moira. This isn't the 1950s. It's no business of ours what he does in his private life as long as he looks after that child properly. His girlfriends are neither here nor there.'

'But she says she's *not* a girlfriend, and that's what he says too.'

'Really, Moira, it's impossible to please you. If she *is* a girlfriend you're annoyed and if she's not you're even *more* annoyed. Would anything please you?'

'For that child to be put into care,' Moira said.

'The mother was adamant and the father hasn't put a foot wrong. Next business.'

Moira felt a dull, red flush rise around her neck. They thought she was obsessing about this. Oh, let them wait until something happened. The social workers were always blamed and they would be again.

But not Moira. She would make very sure of this.

The next morning, Moira decided to go and examine this St Jarlath's Thrift Shop where the baby spent a couple of hours a day.

The place was clean and well ventilated. No complaints there. Emily and a neighbour, Molly Carroll, were busy hanging up dresses that had just come in.

'Ah, Moira,' Emily welcomed her. 'Do you want a nice knitted suit? It would look very well on you. It's fully lined, see, with satin. Some lady said she was tired of looking at it in her wardrobe and sent it over this morning. It's a lovely heather colour.'

It was a nice suit and ordinarily Moira might have been interested. But this was a work visit, not a social shopping outing.

'I really called to know whether you are satisfied with the situation in Chestnut Court, Ms Lynch.'

'The situation?' Emily looked startled.

'The new "tenant", for want of a better word.'

'Oh, Lisa! Yes, isn't it great? Noel would be quite lonely there on his own at night and now they go over their college notes together and she wheels Frankie down here in the mornings. It's a huge help.'

Moira was not convinced. 'But her own relationship. She says she's involved with someone else?'

'Oh yes, she's very keen on this young man who runs a restaurant.'

'And where is this "relationship" going?'

'Do you know, Moira, the French – who are very wise about love, cynical but wise – say, "There is always one who kisses and one who turns the cheek to be kissed." I think that's what we have here: Lisa kissing and Anton offering his cheek to be kissed.'

It silenced Moira completely. How had this middle-aged American woman understood everything so quickly and so well?

Moira wondered would she buy the heather knitted

suit. But she didn't want them to think that somehow she was in their debt. She might ask someone to go in and buy it later.

There was a notice on the corridor wall just outside Moira's office. The heart-failure clinic in St Brigid's wanted the services of a social worker for a couple of weeks.

Dr Clara Casey said they needed a report done, which she could show to the hospital management to prove that the part-time help of a social worker might contribute to the well-being of the patients who attended the clinic. The staff, though eager and helpful, were not aware of all the benefits and entitlements that existed, nor did they have the expertise to advise patients about how best to get on with their lives.

Moira looked at it vaguely. It wasn't of any interest to her. It was just politics. Office politics. This woman, Dr Casey, wanted to enlarge her empire, that's all. Moira couldn't have cared less.

She was surprised and very annoyed, therefore, when the team leader dropped in to see her. As usual, she admired Moira's streamlined office and sighed, wishing that all the social workers could be equally organised.

'You see, that job in St Brigid's, it's only for two weeks. I'd like you to do it, Moira.'

'It's not my kind of thing,' Moira began.

'Oh, but it is! No one would do it better or more thoroughly. Clara Casey will be delighted with you.'

'And my own caseload?'

'Will be divided between us all while you are away.'

Moira didn't have to ask, was it an order. She knew it was.

Moira had tidied up all the loose ends about Noel before her two weeks at St Brigid's. But she had one more stop to make. She called on Declan Carroll, who opened the door with his own son in his arms.

'Come on in,' he welcomed her. 'The place is like a tenement. Fiona is going back to work tomorrow.'

'And how will you cope?' Moira was interested.

'Oh, there's a baby mafia on this street, you know, we all keep an eye out for Frankie, well, they'll do the same for Johnny. My parents are dying to get their hands on him, turn him into a master butcher like my dad! Emily Lynch, Noel's parents, Muttie and Lizzie, the twins, Dr Hat, Nora and Aidan. They're all there for the children. The list is as long as my arm.'

'Your wife works in a heart-failure clinic?' Moira had checked her notes.

'Yes, up in St Brigid's.'

'I'm going there for two weeks tomorrow, as it happens,' Moira said glumly.

'Best place you'll ever work. There's a great atmosphere there,' Declan Carroll said effortlessly, shifting the baby around in his arms.

'Do you think Noel is fit to raise a child?' Moira asked suddenly.

If she had hoped to shock him into a direct answer, she had hoped in vain.

Declan looked at her, perplexed. 'I beg your pardon?' he said slowly.

Nervously, she repeated the question.

'I can't believe that you are asking me to give you a value judgment about a neighbour.'

'Well, you'd know the set-up. I thought I'd ask you.'

'I think it's best if I assume you didn't just say that.'

Moira felt the slow, red flush come up her neck again. Why did she think that she was good at working with people? It was obvious that she alienated everyone everywhere she went.

'That social worker is a real pain in the arse,' Declan said that evening.

'I suppose she's just doing her job,' Fiona said.

'Yeah, but we all do our jobs without getting people's backs up,' he grumbled.

'Mostly,' Fiona said.

'What did she expect me to say? That Noel was a screaming alcoholic and the child should be taken away? The poor fellow is killing himself trying to make a life for Frankie.'

'They're pretty black and white, social workers,' Fiona said.

'Then they should join the world and be grey like the rest of us,' Declan said.

'I love you, Declan Carroll!' Fiona said.

'And I you. I bet nobody loves Miss Prissy Moira, though.'

'Declan! That's so unlike you. Maybe she has a steaming sex life that we know nothing about.'

Moira had sent her colleague Dolores in to buy the knitted suit. Dolores was a foot shorter than Moira and two feet wider. Emily knew exactly what had happened.

'Wear it in happiness,' she said to Dolores.

'Oh … um … thank you,' said Dolores, who would never have got a job in the Secret Service.

*

Moira wore the heather-coloured suit for her first day at the heart-failure clinic. Clara Casey admired it at once.

'I love nice clothes. They are my little weakness. That's a great outfit.'

'I'm not very interested in clothes myself.' Moira wanted to establish her credentials as a worker at the coalface. 'I've seen too many people get distracted by them over the years.'

'Quite.'

Clara was crisp in response and yet again Moira felt that she had somehow let herself down. That she had turned away the warmth of this heart specialist by a glib, smart remark. She wished, as she wished so many times, that she had paused to think before she spoke.

Was it too late to rescue things?

'Dr Casey, I am anxious to do a good job here. Can you outline to me what you hope I will report to you?'

'Well, I am sure that you won't hand my own words back to me, Ms Tierney. You don't seem that sort of person.'

'Please call me Moira.'

'Later, maybe. At the moment Ms Tierney is fine. I have listed the areas where you can investigate. I do urge, however, some sensitivity when talking to both staff and patients. People are often tense when they present with heart failure. We are heavily into the re-assurance business and we emphasise the positive.'

Not since she was a student had Moira received such an obvious ticking-off. She would love to be able to rewind the day to the moment where she had come in; at the point when Clara had admired her outfit, she would thank her enthusiastically – even show her the satin lining. Some day she would learn, but would it be too late?

The head of the team had not said she must stay away from her caseload. Moira went home by way of Chestnut Court. She rang Noel's doorbell. He let her in immediately.

They looked like a normal family. Lisa was giving the baby a bottle and Noel was making a spaghetti bolognese.

'I thought you were going to work somewhere else for two weeks?' Lisa said.

'I never take my eye off the ball,' Moira said.

She looked at Lisa, who was now holding the infant closely and supporting the baby's head as she had been taught to do. She was rocking to and fro and the baby slept peacefully. The girl had obviously bonded with this child. Moira could find nothing to criticise; on the contrary, there was something very safe and solid about it all. Anyone looking in might think they were a stable family instead of what they were: unpredictable.

'Must be dull for you here, Lisa,' she said. 'And I thought *you* had a relationship.'

'He's away at the moment. Anton went to a trade fair,' Lisa said cheerfully.

'Bit lonely for you, I imagine.' Moira couldn't resist it.

'Not at all. It's a great chance for Noel and me to catch up on our studies. Do you want a bowl of spaghetti, by the way?'

'No, thank you. It's very nice of you, but I have to get on.'

'Plenty of it …' Lisa said.

'No … thanks again.'

And she left.

Moira was going back to her own flat. Why had she not sat down and eaten a bowl of spaghetti? It smelled very good. She had hardly any food at home: a little cheese, a couple of rolls. It wasn't compromising her whole stance to have stayed and eaten some of their supper.

But as she walked home, Moira was glad she hadn't stayed. This was all going to end in tears and when it did she didn't want to be anyone who had stayed and had dinner in their house.

Along the canal, Moira saw a small man surrounded by dogs walking towards her. It was Noel's father, Charles Lynch, marching along accompanied by dogs of different sizes and shapes: a spaniel, a poodle and a miniature schnauzer trit-trotting on their leads on one side and a huge Great Dane padding along on the other. Two elderly Labradors, unleashed, circled the group barking joyously. Charles Lynch should have looked ridiculous. Instead he looked blissfully happy.

In fact, Charles took his dog walking very seriously. Clients paid good money to have their pets exercised and he never short-changed them. He recognised the stony-faced social worker who had been dealing with his son and granddaughter.

'Miss Tierney,' he said respectfully.

'Good evening, Mr Lynch. Glad to see someone else apart from myself in this city is actually working.'

'But what easy work I have compared to yours, Miss Tierney. These dogs are a delight. I have been minding them all day – except Caesar, here, who lives with us now – and now I am taking them home to their owners.'

'There are two other dogs not on leads – whose are they?' Moira asked.

'Ah, those are just our local dogs, Hooves and Dimples, from St Jarlath's Crescent. They came along for the fun of it.'

And he nodded in the direction of the foolish old dogs that had just come along to share the excitement.

Moira wished that life was as simple for her. Charles Lynch didn't have to fear a series of articles in the newspapers, saying that yet again the dog walkers had been found wanting and that all the signs had been there ready for anyone to see.

Next day, Moira began to understand the nature of her job. She was helped in this by Hilary, the office manager, and a Polish girl, Ania, who had recently had a miscarriage and had only just returned to work. She seemed devoted to the place and totally loyal to Clara Casey.

There was, apparently, a bad man called Frank Ennis on the hospital board who tried to resist spending one cent on the heart clinic. He said there was absolutely no need for any social services whatsoever in the clinic.

'Why can't Clara Casey speak to him herself?' Moira asked.

'She can and does, but he's a very determined man.'

'Suppose she just took him out to lunch one day?'

Moira was anxious for this matter to be tied up so she could get back to her real work.

'Oh, she does much more than that,' Ania explained. 'She sleeps with him, but it's no use, he keeps his life in different compartments.'

Hilary tried to gloss over what had been said. 'Ania

is just giving you the background,' she said hastily to Moira.

'I'm sorry. I thought she was on our side.' Ania was repentant.

'And I am, indeed,' Moira said.

'Oh, that's all right then.' Ania was happy.

The whole atmosphere in the clinic was a combination of professionalism and reassurance. Moira noticed that the patients all understood the functions of the various medications they received and had little booklets with their weight and blood pressure recorded at every visit. They were all very adept at entering information and retrieving it from the computer.

'You wouldn't *believe* the trouble we had getting a training course organised. Frank Ennis managed to make it sound like devil worship. Clara practically had to go to the United Nations to get the instructors in,' Hilary told Moira.

'He sounds like a dinosaur, this man,' Moira said disapprovingly.

'That's what he is, all right,' Hilary agreed.

'But you say that Dr Casey sees him ... um ... socially?' Moira probed.

'No. Ania was saying that, not me – but indeed it is true. Clara has humanised him a lot but there's a long way to go still.'

'Does Frank Ennis know that *I'm* here?'

'I don't think so, Moira. No point in troubling him, really, or adding to his worries.'

'I like playing things by the book,' Moira said primly.

'There are books and *books*,' Hilary said enigmatically.

'If I am to write a report, I'll need to know his side of things as well.'

'Leave him until you've nearly finished,' Hilary advised.

And as she so often did these days, Moira felt she wasn't handling things as well as she might have. It was as if Hilary and the clinic were drawing away from her. She had meant to be there as their saviour, but somehow playing it by the book had meant that she had stepped outside her brief and that they were all withdrawing their support and enthusiasm.

It was the story of her life.

Moira worked on diligently.

She saw that there was a case for having a social worker attend one day a week. She looked through her notes. There was Kitty Reilly, possibly in the early stages of dementia, conducting long conversations with saints. There was Judy, who definitely needed a home help but had no idea where to turn to find one. There was Lar Kelly, who gave the appearance of being an extrovert, cheerful man but who was obviously as lonely as anything, which was why he kept dropping into the clinic 'just to be sure' as he put it.

A social worker would be able to point Kitty Reilly in the direction of day care a few days a week, find a carer for Judy, and arrange for Lar to go to a social centre for lunch and entertainment.

It was time to approach the great Frank Ennis.

She made an appointment to see him on her last day in the clinic. He was courteous and gracious – not at all the monster she had been told about.

'Ms Tierney!' he said, with every sign of pleasure at meeting her.

'Moira,' she corrected him.

'No, no, Clara says you are a "Ms" person for sure.'

'Really? And did she say anything else about me?' Moira was incensed that Clara had somehow got in ahead of her.

'Yes. She said you were probably extremely good at your job, that you were high in practicality and doing things by the book, and low in sentimentality. All the hallmarks of a good social worker, it would appear.'

It didn't sound that way to Moira. It sounded as if Clara had said she was a hard-faced workaholic. Still, on with the job.

'Why do you think they *shouldn't* have the part-time services of a social worker?' she asked.

'Because Clara thinks the hospital is made of money and that there are unlimited funds, which should be at her disposal.'

'I thought you and she were good friends ...' Moira said.

'I like to think we are indeed friends, and more, but we will never see eye-to-eye about this bottomless-pit business,' he said.

'You really do need someone part time, you know,' Moira said. 'It would round it all off perfectly, then St Brigid's can really be said to be looking after patients' welfare.'

'All the social workers and people in pastoral care are run off their feet in the hospital already. They don't want to be sent over to that clinic, coping with imaginary problems from perfectly well people.'

'Get someone new in for two or three days a week.' Moira was firm.

'One day a week.'

'One and a half,' she bargained.

'Clara is right, Ms Tierney, you have all the skills of a negotiator. A day and a half a week and not a minute more.'

'I feel sure that will be fine, Mr Ennis.'

'And will you do it yourself, Ms Tierney?'

Moira was horrified even at the thought of it.

'Oh no! No way, Mr Ennis, I am a senior social worker. I have a serious caseload. I couldn't make the time.'

'That's a pity. I thought you could be my friend in court: my eyes and ears, curb them from playing fast and loose with expenses and taxis.'

He seemed genuinely disappointed not to have her around the place, which was rare these days. Most people seemed to be veering away from her.

But of course it was totally impossible. She could barely keep up with her own work, let alone take on something new. And yet she would be sorry to leave the heart clinic.

Ania had brought in some shortbread for their afternoon tea to mark the fact that Moira was leaving. Clara joined them and made a little speech.

'We were lucky that they sent us Moira Tierney. She has done a superb report and has even braved the lion's den itself. Frank Ennis has just telephoned to say that the Board have agreed to us having the services of a social worker for one and a half days a week.'

'So you'll be coming back!' Ania seemed pleased.

'No, Ms Tierney made it clear that she has much more important work to do elsewhere. We are very grateful to her for putting it on hold for the two weeks that she was here.'

Frank Ennis had obviously briefed his girlfriend very adequately on the situation so far. Moira wished she had not stressed so heavily to Frank Ennis how important her own work was, compared to the work in the clinic. In some ways, it would be pleasant to come here on a regular basis. Apart from Clara Casey they were all welcoming and enthusiastic. And to be fair, Clara had been enthusiastic about the work Moira had done.

Hilary was always practical. 'Maybe Ms Tierney knows someone who might be suitable?' she said.

As if from miles away Moira heard her own voice saying, 'I can easily reorganise my schedule and if you all thought I would be all right, then I would be honoured to come here.'

They all looked at Clara, who was silent for a moment. Then she said, 'I feel that we would all love Moira to join us, but she will have to sign in under the Official Secrets Act. Frank will expect her to be his eyes and ears, but Moira will know that this can never happen.'

Moira smiled. 'I get the message, Clara,' she said.

And to her great surprise she got a round of applause.

The head of the social work team was not impressed.

'I asked you to write a report, not to get yourself yet another job, Moira. You work too hard already. You should lighten up a little.'

'I did there. I lightened up a lot. I know the set-up in

the clinic now. It makes sense that I do it rather than train someone new.'

'Right. You know what you *can* do and what you *can't*, and no more behaving like some kind of private eye.'

'I'm just watchful, that's all,' Moira said.

She went to Chestnut Court with her briefcase and clipboard. Noel was out, but Lisa was there. Moira went through the routine that had been agreed.

'Who bathed her today?' she asked.

'I did,' Lisa said proudly. 'It's quite hard on your own – they get so slippery, but she enjoyed it and she seemed to be trying to clap her hands a lot.'

The baby was clean and dry and powdered. Nothing to complain about there.

'When is her next feed?' Moira asked.

'In an hour's time. I have the formula there and the bottles are sterilised.'

Again, Moira could find no fault. She checked the number of nappies and whether the baby's clothes were aired.

'Would you like a coffee?' Lisa suggested.

Last time Moira had been rather swift and ungracious, so she decided she would say yes.

'Or, actually, I'm exhausted. You don't have a proper drink or anything? I could do with a glass of wine.'

Lisa looked at her with a very level glance.

'Oh no, Moira. We don't have any alcohol here. As you know, Noel has had a problem with it in the past so there's nothing at all. You *must* know that, you were always asking about it before, hunting for bottles stacked away and everything.'

Moira felt humbled. She had been so obvious. She was, indeed, like some kind of a private eye, except an inefficient one.

'I forgot,' she lied.

'No you didn't, but have a coffee anyway,' Lisa said, getting up from a table covered with papers and drawings to go to the kitchen.

'Did I interrupt you?'

'No, I was glad of the interruption. I was getting stale.'

'Where's Noel tonight?'

'I have no idea.'

'Didn't he say?'

'No. We're not married or anything. I think he went back to his parents' house.'

'And left you literally holding the baby?'

'He's given me a place to live. I'm very pleased to hold the baby for him. Very pleased indeed,' Lisa said.

'And why exactly did you leave home?' Moira fell easily into interrogation mode.

'We've been over this a lot, Moira. I told you then and I tell you now, it was for personal reasons. I am not a runaway teenager. I am a quarter of a century old. I don't ask you why you left home, do I?'

'This is different—' Moira began.

'It's not remotely different and honestly it's got nothing to do with the case. I know you have to look out for Frankie, and you do it very well, but I'm just the lodger helping out. My circumstances have nothing to do with anything.'

Lisa went into the kitchen and banged around for a while.

Moira sought subjects that wouldn't cause any further controversy. They were hard to find.

'I met Fiona Carroll. You know ... Johnny's mother.'

'Oh yes?' Lisa said.

'She said that you and Noel were doing a great job minding Frankie.'

'Yes ... well ... good.'

'Most impressed, she was.'

'And were you surprised?' Lisa asked suddenly.

'No, of course not.'

'Good, because I tell you I have *such* admiration for Noel. All this came out of a clear blue sky at him. He's been very strong. I wouldn't have anyone bad-mouthing him, not anyone at all.'

She looked like a tiger defending her cub.

Moira made a few bleating noises intended to suggest support and enthusiasm. She hoped she was giving the desired impression.

Her next visit was to a family where they were trying to make an elderly father a ward of court. To Moira, Gerald, the old man, was perfectly sane. Lonely and frail, certainly, but mad? No.

His daughter and her husband were very anxious to have him defined as being incapable and sign his house over to them, and then have him committed to a secure nursing-home facility.

Moira was having none of it. Gerald wanted to stay in his home and she was his champion. She picked up a stray remark from the son-in-law, something that made her think that the man had gambling debts. It would suit him nicely if his father-in-law were put away. They might even sell the house and buy a smaller place.

It wouldn't happen on Moira's watch. Her clipboard was filled with notes for letters she would send to the relevant people. The son-in-law collapsed like a house of cards.

The old man looked at Moira affectionately.

'You're better than having a bodyguard,' he said to her.

Moira was very proud of this. This was exactly what she saw herself as being. She patted the old man's hand.

'I'll get you a regular carer to come in and look after you. You can tell her if anyone steps out of line or anything. I'll liaise with your doctor also. Let me see … that's Dr Carroll, isn't it?'

'It used to be Dr Hat,' Gerald said. 'Dr Carroll is a very nice lad, certainly, but he could be my grandson, if you see what I mean. Dr Hat was nearer to my own generation.'

'And where is he?' Moira asked.

'He comes into their practice from time to time when they're short-staffed,' the old man said sadly. 'I always seem to miss him, though.'

'I'll find him for you,' Moira promised and went straight away to the doctors' group practice at the end of St Jarlath's Crescent.

Dr Carroll was there and happy to talk about the old man, Gerald.

'I think he's totally on the ball and playing with the full deck.'

'His family think otherwise.' Moira was terse.

'Well, they would, wouldn't they? That son-in-law would do anything to get his hands on the family chequebook.'

'That's my view, too,' Moira said. 'Can I ask you, does Dr Hat do house calls?'

'No, not really. He's retired, but he does the odd locum for us. Why do you ask?'

Moira chose her words carefully for once.

'Gerald thinks very highly of you, Doctor. He said that several times, but I think he finds Dr … er … Hat more in his age group.'

'Lord, he must be fifteen years older than Hat!'

'Yes, but he's fifty years older than you, Doctor.'

'Hat's a very decent man. He might well go round and see your Gerald as a social visit from time to time. I'll tell him.'

'Could I tell him, do you think?'

Moira had a history of people promising to do things that they fully intended to do but which never got done.

'Of course. I'll give you his address.'

For Declan Carroll it was just one less thing to do. She was efficient, this Moira Tierney, and dedicated to her job. Such a pity that she had taken so against poor Noel, who was breaking his back trying to keep the show on the road.

Dr Hat was indeed wearing headgear: a smart navy cap with a peak. He welcomed Moira in warmly and offered her a cup of hot chocolate.

'You don't know what I'm here about yet,' she said cautiously.

Maybe he might find this intrusive. She didn't want to accept a hot chocolate under false pretences.

'Yes I do. Declan called me so that I could be prepared.'

'That was courteous of him,' Moira said, though she would have preferred to handle this on her own.

'I like Gerald. I have no problem going to see him. In fact, we could play chess. I'd like that.'

Moira's shoulders relaxed. She would have the hot chocolate now. Sometimes things worked out well at work. Not always, but sometimes. Like now.

Just after she got back to her flat there was a phone call from home. Her brother Pat never called her usually: she was alarmed. She knew from experience that there was no point in hurrying him. He would take his time.

'It's Dad,' he said eventually, 'he's moved out. He's selling up.'

'Moved out where?'

'He's up with Mrs Kennedy. He's not coming back.'

'Well, can't you bring him back?'

'I did once and he wasn't best pleased,' Pat said. 'Couldn't you do something, Moira?'

'God Almighty, Pat, I'm two hundred miles away. You and Da have to sort this out between you. Go on up to Mrs Kennedy. Find out what he's up to. I'll come down next weekend and see what's going on.'

'But,' Pat asked, 'what am I to do? If he wants to sell up I'll have nowhere to go.'

'Why would he want to sell the farm?' Moira was impatient.

'You don't know the half of it,' said Pat.

Moira sat in her chair for a while, thinking about what to do. She knew how to run everyone else's lives but not her own. Eventually she pulled herself together and got on the phone. She had kept Mrs Kennedy's number in her huge address book in case she ever needed to contact her father when he was chopping wood up there. She asked could she speak to her father and, to use Pat's phrase, he certainly was not best pleased with the call.

'Why are you bothering me here?' he asked querulously.

'I'll be down next weekend. I need to see you, Dad, we need to talk about all this ...'

And she hung up before she could learn exactly how displeased her father was with this call.

Clara Casey turned out to be a friend rather than a foe. In fact, she even suggested that Moira come to lunch with her one day. This was not the norm at work. Her team leader would never have suggested a social lunch.

Moira was surprised, but very pleased. She was even more pleased when the restaurant turned out to be Quentins. Moira had thought they would go somewhere in the shopping precinct.

Clara was obviously known in the place. Moira had never been there before.

It was amazingly elegant and Brenda Brennan, the proprietor, recommended the monkfish: it was beautifully prepared in a saffron sauce.

'I don't suppose this restaurant is feeling any bad effects of the recession,' Clara said to Brenda.

'Don't you believe it. They're all drawing in their horns. Plus we have a rival now. Anton Moran is getting a lot of business for his place.'

'I read about it in the papers. Is he good?' Clara asked.

'Very. Huge flair and a great manner.'

'Do you know him?'

'Yes, he worked here once and came back to do the odd shift. A real heartbreaker – he has half the women in Dublin at his beck and call.'

Moira was thoughtful. Surely this was the name of the young man that Lisa Kelly had a relationship with? She had mentioned his name more than once. Moira smiled to herself. For once, it looked as if Lisa might not find the world going entirely her way.

Clara was easy company. She asked questions and was helpful about Moira's brother.

'You might want to stay there Monday morning and catch people at work,' Clara said. 'We can change your days around – no problem.'

Moira wished they didn't both have to go back to work. It would have been lovely to have had a bottle of wine and a real conversation where Clara could tell her about the other people who worked in the clinic and maybe even about this friendship she had with Frank Ennis, which seemed entirely improbable. But it was an ordinary working day. They each had one drink, a mixture of wine and mineral water, and they didn't linger over the meal.

Moira had learned little about Clara, except that she was long separated from her husband, she had two married daughters: one working on an ecology project in South America and the other running a big CD and DVD store. She had originally taken on the heart-failure clinic for one year, but it was now her baby and she would let nobody, particularly not anyone like Frank Ennis, take away one single vestige of its power or authority.

Clara was particularly sympathetic about Moira's mother having died. She said her own mother was straight out of hell, but she knew that this was not the case with everyone. Hilary, back at the clinic, had been heartbroken when her own mother had died.

Moira was to take the time she needed to sort out her family problems. It was as simple as that.

Of course it wasn't simple when she got back home to Liscuan. Moira had known that it wouldn't be. Pat had completely broken down. He hadn't milked the cows, he hadn't fed the hens, he babbled about his father's plan to sell the family home from under him and move in with Mrs Kennedy. This did indeed appear to be the case.

Moira asked her father straight out. 'Pat has probably got this all wrong, Da, but he thinks that you have plans to move in permanently with Mrs Kennedy and sell this place.'

'That's right,' her father said, 'I intend to go and live with Mrs Kennedy.'

'And what about Pat?'

'I'm selling up.' He shrugged, gazing around at the shabby kitchen. 'Look around you, Moira. I can't do it any more. I've dealt with this all my life while you were having a fine time up in Dublin. I deserve a bit of happiness now.'

With every single client in her caseload, Moira knew what to do. She had known how to set things in order for Kitty Reilly, Judy and Lar at the heart-failure clinic. Why was her own situation so totally impossible?

She spent the Monday helping Pat to look for accommodation. Then she wished her father well with Mrs Kennedy and took the train back to Dublin.

*

In Chestnut Court, Frankie was crying again. Noel was beginning to think that he would never know what the crying meant. Some nights she didn't sleep for more than ten minutes at a time. There was one level for food, but she'd just been fed and burped. Perhaps it was more wind. Carefully, he picked up his daughter and laid her against his shoulder, patting her back gently. She cried on. He sat down and laid her chest across his arm while he rubbed her little back to soothe her.

'Frankie, Frankie, please don't cry, little pet, hush now, hush now ...'

Nothing. Noel was aware that his voice was sounding increasingly anxious as Frankie cried on piteously. Perhaps for a nappy that needed changing? Could it be a changing job?

He was right. The nappy was indeed damp. Carefully he placed the baby on a towel spread over the table where they changed her. As soon as he removed her wet nappy, the crying stopped and he was rewarded with a sunny smile and a coo.

'You, Frankie,' he said, smiling back at her, 'are going to have to learn how to communicate. It's no good just wailing, I'm no good at understanding what you want.'

Frankie blew bubbles and reached up towards the paper birds flying from the mobile above her head. As Noel stretched out his hand to reach for the cleaning wipes, to his horror she twisted away from him and began to slip off the table.

Quick as he was, he was not in time.

It felt as though everything were happening in slow motion as the baby began to fall from the table. As Noel froze in horror, she hit the chair beside it, then fell to the floor. There was blood around her head as she started to scream.

'Frankie, *please, Frankie*.'

He wept incoherently as he picked her up and clutched her to him. He couldn't tell where she was hurt or how badly. Panic overwhelmed him.

'No, please, *dear God, no*, don't take her away from me, make her be all right. Frankie, little Frankie, please, please ...'

It was a few moments before he pulled himself together and called an ambulance.

Just as the train was pulling into Dublin, Moira got a text message on her cellphone.

There had been an accident. Frankie had cut her head. Noel had taken her to the A&E of St Brigid's Hospital, and he thought he should let Moira know.

She took the bus straight from the railway station to St Brigid's. She had *known* that this would happen, but she felt no satisfaction at being proved right. Just anger, a great anger that everyone else's bleeding-heart philosophy said that a drunk and a flighty young girl could be made responsible for raising a child.

It had been an accident waiting to happen.

She found a white-faced Noel at the hospital. He was almost babbling with relief.

'They say it's just a deep graze and she'll have a bruise. Thank God! There was so much blood, I couldn't imagine what it was.'

'How did it happen?' Moira's voice was like a knife cutting across his words.

'She rolled over when I was changing her and fell off the table,' he said.

'You let her fall from the table?' Moira managed to sound taken aback and full of blame at the same time.

'She hit the chair … it sort of broke her fall.' Noel was aware of how desperate this sounded.

'This is intolerable, Noel.'

'Don't I know that, Moira? I did the best I could. I called an ambulance straight away and brought her here.'

'Why didn't you get Dr Carroll? He was nearer.'

'I saw all the blood. I thought it was an emergency and that he'd probably have to send her here anyway.'

'And where was your partner while all this was going on?'

'Partner?'

'Lisa Kelly.'

'Oh, she had to go out. She wasn't there.'

'And why did you let the child fall?'

'I didn't *let* her fall. She twisted away from me. I told you …'

Noel looked frightened and almost faint from the stress of it all.

'God, Noel, we're talking about a defenceless baby here.'

'I know that. Why do you think I'm so worried?'

'So, what caused you to let her fall? That's what it was – *you* let her fall. Was your mind distracted?'

'No, no, it wasn't.'

'Did you have a little drink maybe?'

'*No*, I did *not* have a little drink or a big drink, though by God I could do with one now. It put the heart across me and of course I feel guilty but now I have you yapping at me as if I threw the child on the floor.'

'I'm *not* suggesting that. I realise that it was an accident. I am just trying to work out how it happened.'

'It won't happen again,' Noel said.

'How do we know this?' Moira spoke gently, as if she were talking to someone of low intelligence.

'We know because we are going to move the table up against the wall,' Noel said.

'And we didn't think of this sooner?'

'No, we didn't.'

'Can I have a word with Lisa when we get back to Chestnut Court? I'd like to go over some of the routines with her once more.'

'I told you, she's gone away.'

'But she'll be back, won't she?'

'Not for a couple of days. Anton has been asked to take part in a celebrity-chef thing in London and it's going to be televised. He's taking Lisa with him.'

'Is this Anton happy about his girlfriend living with you, do you think, Noel?'

'I never thought about it one way or the other. It suits her. He knows we aren't a couple in *that* sense. Why do you ask?'

'It's my business to make sure Frankie grows up in a stable household,' Moira said righteously.

'Yes, sure. Well, now that you're here, will you help me get her to the bus stop?'

'How do you mean?'

'You know, open doors for me and things. I didn't bring her pram, you see. I was afraid I wouldn't get it into the taxi coming home.'

Moira went ahead of him, opening doors and assisting him through the maze of corridors. He *did* seem concerned and worried about the child. Maybe this was the wake-up shock he needed. But she must be very firm with him. Moira had found over the years that firmness always paid off in the end.

Noel didn't want to let the baby out of his grasp. He lay back in his chair with Frankie clutched to his chest.

'You're going to be just fine, Frankie,' he said over and over as he rocked her in his arms.

If only he could have a drink to steady his nerves. He contemplated calling Malachy, but he was all right. The child was more important than the drink. He would manage.

'Here, Frankie, I'm going to stop talking to myself, I'm going to read you a story,' he said.

He put all the concentration in the world into reading her a story about a bird that had fallen out of its nest. It all ended very happily. It worked for Noel: it drove all thought of a large whiskey way out of his mind.

It worked for Frankie too, as she fell into a deep sleep.

Three days later Lisa Kelly phoned Moira.

'Oh, Moira, Noel asked me to call you. He said you wanted to go over some of Frankie's routines with me.'

'Did you have a good time in London?' Moira asked.

'So-so. What routines did you want to discuss?'

'The usual: bathtime, feeding, changing. You know she had an accident while you were away?'

'Yes. Poor Noel is like a hen on a hot griddle about it all. No harm done, I gather.'

'Not this time, but it's not good for a baby to fall on its head.'

'Well, I know that, but Declan has been round and he says she's fine.'

Moira was pleased she had obviously scared Noel enough to make him aware of the gravity of it all.

'And did your friend do well in the celebrity-chef thing?'

'No, not as well as he should have. But then I'm sure you read that in the papers.'

'I thought I saw something, yes.'

'It was all totally slanted the wrong way. You see, this woman April turned up out of the blue there, talking about column inches and potential. She knows nothing really except how to get her own name into the papers.'

'Yes, I saw she was mentioned. I was a little surprised. Noel told me that *you* had gone to assist him, but it made it seem as if she did all the work.'

'If drinking cocktails and handing people her business card is work, then she did a lot of that all right,' Lisa said. Then she pulled herself together. 'But about this routine you wanted?'

'I'll call round this evening,' Moira said.

Not for the first time, Lisa told Noel that Moira's social life must be the most empty and dull canvas in the whole world.

'Let's ask Emily to be here. She can take some of the heat away from us.'

'Good idea,' Lisa agreed. 'I was going to ask Katie to come to supper. The more lines of defence we can draw up, the easier it will be for us coping with Generalissimo Moira.'

Moira was surprised to see the little flat full of people. She wished that she had not been wearing the heather-coloured suit she had bought from St Jarlath's Thrift

Shop. Now they would know that she had sent Dolores to make the purchase!

Noel showed her the new positioning of the table. He stood obediently while she measured the formula out, even though he had been doing these bottles perfectly for months. Frankie went off to sleep obediently like a textbook baby.

'Please join us for some supper *this* time, Moira,' Lisa suggested. 'I put two extra drumsticks in for you.'

'No, really, thank you.'

'Oh do, for God's sake, Moira, otherwise we'll all fight over the extra bits,' Lisa's sister Katie said.

They sat down and Lisa produced a very tasty supper. Moira decided that for a brainless blonde she *did* have some skills. But then, of course, she was a chef's girlfriend.

Her sister Katie was practical and down to earth. She showed them pictures of her trip to Istanbul and talked affectionately of her husband Garry.

Neither she nor Lisa talked about their home life. But then, to be fair, Moira told herself, she didn't talk about her home life much either.

Instead they talked about Noel and Lisa's lectures. When Katie mentioned that Father Flynn was away visiting his mother in Rossmore, Noel mentioned that he'd first met the priest when he used to bring Stella cigarettes in hospital.

'Hardly a helpful thing to do under the circumstances.' Moira was very disapproving.

'Stella's view was that it was already way too late and she just wanted to enjoy the last bit,' Noel said.

'Why don't the clergy provide the priest with a place

to live? They do have these flats, I believe ...' Moira needed to know the answer to everything.

'He doesn't want that. Says it's like living in a religious community and he's more of a lone bird really.'

'And why didn't you go and stay in Katie's flat, Lisa, rather than here?' Moira asked.

Lisa looked at her impatiently. 'Are you *ever* off the job, Moira?' she asked, annoyed.

Emily stepped in to make peace. 'Moira has all the best qualities of a social worker, Lisa, she is very interested in people.' And then she turned to Moira. 'Father Flynn was installed before Lisa needed to move. That's right, isn't it?' She looked around her good-naturedly.

'That's it.' Lisa was brief.

'Exactly.' Katie was even briefer.

It would have been churlish to ask any more, like why Lisa had needed to move, so very reluctantly Moira decided to leave it there. Instead she said that the chicken was delicious.

'Just olives, garlic and tomatoes,' Lisa said, untensing. 'I learned it from Emily, actually.'

They *seemed* a normal enough group and there was no sign of alcohol anywhere during the meal. Moira sometimes wished she didn't have such a strong instinct for when things were going to go wrong. And she had felt this about Noel from the very beginning.

Anton's restaurant was advertising Saturday lunches. Moira decided to invite Dr Casey to return the hospitality at Quentins.

'There's no need, Moira,' Clara had said.

'No, of course not, but I'd enjoy it. Please say yes.'

It didn't suit Clara at all. Normally she had a relaxed

lunch with Frank Ennis on a Saturday and then they went to the cinema or a matinée at the theatre. Sometimes they went to an art exhibition. It had become an easy and undemanding routine. But what the hell, she could meet him later.

'That would be delightful, Moira,' she said.

Moira would book the table in person. She would like to have that effortless confidence that Clara had. She would like it if they knew her in Anton's and made a fuss of her as they had with Clara in Quentins. But that would never happen.

When she went to make the table reservation she was greeted by Anton himself. He was indeed very charming. Small and handsome in a boyish way, he pointed around the room.

'Where would you like to sit, Ms Tierney? I'd love to give you the nicest table in the room,' he said.

She pointed out a table.

'Excellent choice. You can see and be seen there. Are you inviting a friend?'

'Well, my boss actually. She's a doctor in a heart clinic.'

'Well, we'll make sure you both have a good time,' he said.

Moira left feeling ten years younger and much more attractive. No wonder this girl Lisa was so besotted with the boy. Anton was truly something special.

And he had not forgotten that they were to be well looked after. As soon as she entered the restaurant, the maître d' greeted her as though she were a regular and valued customer.

'Ah, Ms Tierney!' Teddy said, as she gave her name.

'Anton said to look out for you and to offer you and your guest a house cocktail.'

'Lord, I don't think so,' Clara said.

'Why not? It's free.' Moira giggled.

And they sipped a coloured glass of something that had fresh mint and ice and soda, some exotic liqueur and probably a triple serving of vodka.

'Thank God it's Saturday,' Clara said. 'Nobody could have gone back to work after one of these house cocktails.'

It was a very pleasant lunch. Clara talked about her daughter Linda, who was very anxious to have a child and had been having fertility treatment for eighteen months without success.

'Any babies coming up for adoption in your line of business?' Clara asked.

Moira gave the question serious attention. 'There might be,' she said, 'a little girl, a few months old now.'

'Well, I mean, is she available for adoption or not?' Clara was a cut-and-dried person.

'Not at the moment, but I don't think she's going to last long in the present set-up,' Moira explained.

'Why? Are they cruel to her?'

'No, not at all. They are just not able to manage properly.'

'But do they love her? I mean, they'll never give her up if they are mad about her.'

'They might have no choice in it,' Moira said.

'I won't tell Linda anything about it in case. No point in raising her hopes,' Clara said.

'No. If and when it does come up, I'll let you know immediately.'

Then they chatted about the various patients who

came to the heart clinic. Moira asked about Clara's friend Frank Ennis and learned that he was a very decent man in most ways, but had a blind spot about saving St Brigid's money.

Clara asked did Moira have anyone in her life and Moira said no because she had always been too busy. They touched briefly on Clara's ex-husband Alan, who was the lowest of the low, and on Moira's father, now happily settled in with Mrs Kennedy, who had asked only for one more crack at happiness and seemed to have found it.

Just as Moira was paying the bill, Anton arrived, accompanied by a very pretty girl who looked about twenty. He came over to their table.

'Ms Tierney, I hope everything was all right for you?' he said.

'Lovely,' Moira said. 'This is Dr Casey ... Clara, this is Anton Moran.'

'It was all delicious,' Clara said. 'I will certainly tell people about it.'

'That's what we need.' Anton had an easy charm.

Moira looked at the young woman expectantly.

Eventually Anton broke and introduced her. 'This is April Monaghan,' he said.

'Oh, I read about you in the papers. You were in London recently,' Moira said, gushing slightly.

'That's right,' April agreed.

'It's just that I know a great friend of yours. A *great* friend, Lisa Kelly, and she was there too at the same time.'

'Yeah, she was,' April agreed.

Anton's smile never faltered.

'How exactly do you know Lisa, Ms Tierney?'

'Through work. I'm a social worker,' Moira said, surprised at herself for answering so readily.

'I thought social workers didn't discuss their cases in public.' His smile was still there, but not in his eyes.

'No, no, Lisa isn't a client. I just know her sort of through something else ...'

Moira was flustered now. She could sense Clara's disapproval. Why had she brought up this matter anyway? It was in order to fill in the missing parts of the jigsaw in Chestnut Court. The unaccustomed house cocktail and the bottle of wine had loosened her tongue. Now she had somehow managed to spoil the whole day.

Everything settled into a routine at the heart clinic. Clara Casey seemed pleased by Moira's input into the heart-failure team, and could not fault her in terms of diligence and following up everything that needed to be checked. But the warmth had gone. Moira did not feel as included as she had thought herself to be.

The others were all welcoming, but Clara seemed to have lost respect for her and Moira had seen some forms on Hilary's desk, asking whether the part-time social worker was to be a permanent position.

Clara had attached a note: 'Tell them not yet. Position is still under review.'

So Clara Casey didn't really trust her, just because of a stupid, tactless slip in the restaurant. Moira redoubled her efforts on all fronts.

She got Gerald full-time care in his home to the great annoyance of his daughter and son-in-law. She had saved him from going to the old people's home, which he had dreaded, and he told everyone she was a knight in shining armour. She managed to get the children of a drug-addict mother fostered in a loving, happy home where they had warmth and toys and regular meals for the first time in their lives. She found a teenage runaway sleeping rough under a bridge by the river and invited her home for soup and a good talking-to. The girl slept for seventeen hours on Moira's sofa and then went back like an obedient lamb to her family home.

She managed to frighten a couple who were signing on for unemployment benefit at the same time as making a very reasonable living from a sandwich bar, and to terrify with threats of major publicity a factory owner who was paying much less than the minimum rate. She had even managed to get her brother Pat a flat and a job in a garage.

Her father had agreed to sell his house and divide the money between himself and his two children. Mrs Kennedy had apparently thought this was highly satisfactory and was busy planning a new kitchen. So there were *some* areas of Moira's life that were a great success.

But not all. Maybe she was just too ambitious about her strike rate.

Her father's house did not fetch a big price at the auction. It was a smallholding and this was the wrong time to sell. But it did mean that she had the deposit for a house. She must look around for somewhere to live.

'Make sure you get a place with a small garden,' Emily advised.

'Have somewhere near a tram or a bus,' Hilary, in the heart clinic, said.

'Buy a dilapidated sort of house and do it up,' said Johnny, who did the exercise routines at the heart clinic.

'Get a nice, modern place that isn't falling to bits,' said Gerald, who seemed to have a new lease of life now that she had rescued him from the prospect of being sent to a home, which he didn't want, and whose brain cells seemed to be working at full power.

She called at Noel's family home in St Jarlath's Crescent as she did from time to time. It was easier than bearding Noel and Lisa in Chestnut Court where they both seemed very resentful of her role in anything. At least Emily and Noel's parents could have a civilised conversation.

'This is exactly the kind of street I would like to live in,' Moira said. 'Do you know of any houses coming up for sale in the area?'

Emily knew that Noel wouldn't like Moira, who was regarded as 'the enemy', moving closer to him and being a neighbour of his parents.

'I've heard nothing of anyone moving,' Emily said and, as they did so often, Josie and Charles took their lead from her.

'It's nice to think that people would want to come and live here,' Josie said, heading off down memory lane. 'When Charles and I were young it was regarded as the last place on earth.'

'Maybe Declan might know of someone thinking about moving ...' Emily said.

She knew very well that Declan and Fiona had no great love for Moira, and thought her unnecessarily interfering in Noel's efforts to make a reliable home for himself and Frankie. Even if Declan knew that half the street was for sale, he wouldn't give the news to Moira.

Moira asked politely about the campaign for the statue to St Jarlath and Josie and Charles showed her some quotes they had from sculptors. Bronze was very expensive, but they hoped they might be able to afford it.

'Do you have a particular devotion to St Jarlath, by any chance?' Josie was always hopeful of recruiting others to the cause.

'Admiration, certainly,' Moira murmured, 'but devotion might be putting it a bit strongly.'

Emily hid her smile. When Moira was being diplomatic you could see she'd be good at her job. What a pity she couldn't see what huge strides Noel was making. Why did she have to behave like a policeman with him rather than an encourager and someone he could turn to if there were any problems?

As usual, Emily wrote it all to her friend Betsy back in New York. Somehow, typing it on her laptop made it seem clearer.

Honestly, Bets, you just have to get yourself over here. Maybe when you and Eric get married, as you will, sooner rather than later, I hope you will need a honeymoon. Find a good airfare and I'll find you somewhere to stay. But you have to meet this cast. Noel and his little girl. A changed man, he hasn't had a drink in months and he's working his butt off in this dreary company but he is keeping up with his lectures too.

He and a slightly kooky girl named Lisa live like an old married couple in their apartment, looking after the child and studying for their diploma. There's no sex because she is involved with some society guy – a celebrity chef, no less! They are being stalked by this social worker, Moira. She is doing her job, but she sort of hides in their garden and pounces on them, hoping to catch them at something.

And the campaign for the statue is going great guns. We are thinking of it being cast in bronze at this stage. And the whole business of the thrift shop has given Josie a new lease on life. She works away there happily with Molly Carroll and me. A lovely fedora came in last week and Josie took it to this man Dr Hat to add to his collection.

My uncle Charles has a very satisfactory dog-walking business now, even the hotel where he used to work has employed him to come and walk their customers' dogs.

He babysits for his granddaughter and takes care of her on the evenings when Noel and Lisa go to their lectures.

When I'm not helping out at the doctors' clinic, I'm busy doing gardens and window boxes – the whole Crescent looks just great. We might even win a prize in a competition for Most Attractive Street. In fact, I'm so busy that I haven't read a book or been to a play. And as for an art exhibition – it's been months!

Tell me about yourself and life back there. I have forgotten I ever lived in New York!

Love,
Emily

She got a reply in minutes:

Emily,
You must be psychic.
Eric asked me to marry him last night. I said I would if, and only if, you came back to New York

to be my maid of honor. Considering our great age, I thought a small wedding would be best, but nobody said anything about keeping the honeymoon low key.

Ireland, here we come!

Love,

Betsy

'I hear your aunt is going back to America for a vacation,' Moira said to Noel.

'She's actually my cousin, but you're right, she *is* going to New York. How did you know?' Noel asked, surprised.

'Someone mentioned it.'

Moira, who made it her business to know everything, was vague.

'Yes, she's going to her friend's wedding,' Noel said. 'But then she's coming back again. My parents are very relieved, I tell you. They'd be lost without Emily.'

'And you would too, Noel, wouldn't you?' Moira said.

'Well, I would miss her certainly, but as far as my mother is concerned the thrift shop would close down without Emily and my father thinks the world of her too.'

'But surely you are the one she has helped most, Noel?' Moira was persistent.

'How do you mean?'

'Well, didn't she pay your tuition fees at the college? Get you this apartment, arrange a babysitting roster for you and probably a lot more ...?'

There was a dull red flush on Noel's face and neck. He had never been so annoyed in his whole life. Had Emily blabbed to this awful woman? She had gone over to the enemy and told Moira all about things that were meant to be private between them. *Nobody* was ever going to know about the fees – that was their secret. He felt betrayed, as he had never felt before. There was no way he could know that Moira was only guessing.

She was looking at him politely, waiting for a reply, but he didn't trust himself to speak.

'You must have thought about who would take over her duties when she was away?'

'I thought maybe Dingo might help out,' Noel said eventually in a strangled voice.

'Dingo?' Moira said the name with distaste.

'You know, he does some deliveries to the thrift shop. Dingo Duggan.'

'I don't know him, no.'

'He only helps out the odd time when no one else is available.'

'And you never thought to tell me about this Dingo Duggan?' Moira asked, horrified.

'Listen to me, Moira, you give me a pain right in the arse,' Noel said suddenly.

'I beg your pardon?' She looked at him in disbelief.

'You heard me. I'm breaking my back to do this right. I'm nearly dead on my feet sometimes, but do you ever see any of this? Oh no, it's constantly moving the goalposts and complaining and behaving like the secret police.'

'Really, Noel. Control yourself.'

'No, I will *not* control myself. You come here investigating me as if I were some sort of criminal. Repeating poor Dingo's name as if he was a mass murderer instead of a decent poor eejit, which is what he is.'

'*A decent poor eejit.* I see.'

She started to write something down, but Noel pushed her clipboard away and it fell to the ground.

'And then you go and pry and question people. And try to get them to say bad things about me, pretending to look out for Frankie's good.'

Moira remained very still during this outburst. Eventually she said, 'I'll leave now, Noel, and come back tomorrow. You will hopefully have calmed down by then.'

And she turned and left the apartment.

Noel sat and stared ahead of him. That woman was bound to bring in some reinforcements and get Frankie taken away from him. His eyes filled with tears. He and Lisa had been planning her first Christmas, but now Noel wasn't certain that Frankie would still be with them by next week.

Noel picked up his phone and called Dingo.

'Mate, can you do me a great favour and come and hold the fort for a couple of hours?'

Dingo was always agreeable.

'Sure, Noel. Can I bring a DVD or is the child asleep?'

'She'll sleep through it if it's not too loud.'

Noel waited until Dingo was installed.

'I'm off now,' he said briefly.

Dingo looked at him. 'Are you okay, Noel? You look a bit, I don't know, a bit funny.'

'I'm fine,' Noel said.

'And will you have your phone on?'

'Maybe not, Dingo, but the emergency numbers are all in the kitchen, you know: Lisa, my parents, Emily, the hospital or anything. They're all there on the wall.'

And then he was gone. He took a bus to the other

side of Dublin and in the anonymity of a cavernous bar
Noel Lynch drank pints for the first time in months.

They felt great … bloody great …

CHAPTER SEVEN

It was Declan who had to pick up the pieces. Dingo phoned him a half an hour after midnight, sounding very upset.

'I'm sorry for waking you, Declan, but I didn't know what to do – she's roaring like a bull.'

'Who is roaring like a bull?' Declan was struggling to wake up.

'Frankie. Can't you hear her?'

'Is she all right? When did you last feed her? Does she need changing?' Declan suggested.

'I don't do changing and feeding. I was just holding the fort. That's what he asked me to do.'

'And where is he? Where's Noel?'

'Well, I don't know, do I? Fine bloody fort-holding it turned out to be. I've been here six hours now!'

'His phone?'

'Turned off. God, Declan, what am I to do? She's bright red in the face.'

'I'll be there in ten minutes,' Declan said, getting out of bed.

'*No*, Declan, you don't have to go out. You're not on call!' Fiona protested.

'Noel's gone off somewhere,' Declan told her. 'He left the baby with Dingo. I have to go over there.'

'God, Noel would never do that!' Fiona was shocked.

'I know, that's why I'm going over there.'

'And where's Lisa?'

'Not there, obviously. Go back to sleep, Fiona. No use the whole family being unable to go to work tomorrow.'

He was dressed and out of the house in minutes.

He was worried about Noel Lynch – very worried indeed.

'God bless you, Declan,' Dingo said with huge relief when Declan came into Chestnut Court.

He watched, mystified, as Declan expertly changed a nappy, washed and powdered the baby's bottom, made up the formula and heated the milk, all in seamless movements.

'I'd never be able to do that,' Dingo said admiringly.

'Of course you would. You will when you have one of your own.'

'I was going to leave it all to the woman, whoever she might be ...' Dingo admitted.

'I wouldn't rely on it, Dingo, me old mate. Not these days. It's shared everything, believe me. And quite right too.'

Frankie was perfectly peaceful. All they had to do now was to find her father.

'He didn't say where he was going, but I sort of thought it was for an hour or two. I thought he was going home to his parents for something.'

'Was he upset about anything before he went out?'

'I thought he was a bit distracted. He showed me all the numbers on the wall ...'

'As if he was planning to stay out, do you think?'

'God, I don't know, Declan. Maybe the poor lad was

hit by a bus and we're all misjudging him. He could be in an A&E somewhere with his phone broken.'

'He could.'

Declan didn't know why he felt so certain that Noel had gone back on the drink. The man had been heroic for months. *What* could have changed him? And, more important, how would they ever find him?

'Go home, Dingo.' Declan sighed. 'You've held the fort for long enough. I'll do it until Noel gets back.'

'Should we ring anyone on this list, do you think?' Dingo didn't want to abandon everything.

'It's one in the morning. No point in worrying everyone.'

'No, I suppose not.' Dingo was still reluctant.

'I'll call you, Dingo, when he's found and I'll tell him you didn't want to leave but I forced you to.'

He had hit the right note. Dingo hadn't wanted to leave his post without permission. Now he could go back home without guilt.

Declan looked down into Frankie's cot. The baby slept on as peacefully as his own son slept back at home. But little Johnny Carroll had a much more secure future ahead of him than poor Baby Frankie here. Declan sighed heavily as he settled himself into an armchair.

Where could Noel be until this hour?

Noel was asleep in a shed on the other side of Dublin.

He had no idea how he had got there. The last thing he could remember was some kind of argument in a bar and people refusing him further drink. He had left in annoyance and then found to his rage that he couldn't get back in again and there were no other public houses in the area. He had walked for what seemed a very long time and then it got cold, so he decided to have a rest before he went home.

Home?

He would have to be careful letting himself into 23 St Jarlath's Crescent – then he remembered with a shock that he didn't live there any more.

He lived in Chestnut Court with Frankie and Lisa.

He would have to be even more careful going back there. Lisa would be shocked at him and Frankie might even be frightened.

But Lisa was away. He remembered that now. His heart gave a sudden jump. What about the baby? He would never have left Frankie alone in the apartment, would he?

No, of course he hadn't. He remembered Dingo had come in.

Noel looked at his watch. That was hours ago. *Hours*. Was Dingo still there? He wouldn't have contacted Moira, would he? Oh, please, God, please, St Jarlath, please, anyone up there, let Dingo not have rung Moira.

He felt physically ill at the thought and realised that he was indeed going to be sick. As a courtesy to whoever owned this garden shed, Noel went out to the road. Then his legs felt weak and wouldn't support him. He went back into the shed and passed out.

In spite of the discomfort, Declan slept for several hours in the chair. When daybreak came he realised that Noel hadn't come home. He went to make himself a cup of tea and decide what to do.

He rang Fiona.

'Is today one of Moira's days up in your clinic?'

'Yes, she'll be there for the morning. Are you coming home?'

'Not immediately. Remember, don't say a word to her about any of this. We'll try and cover for him, but she can't know. Not until we've found him.'

'Where is he, Declan?' Fiona sounded frightened.

'Out on the tear somewhere, I imagine ...'

'Listen, Signora and Aidan will be here soon. They're collecting Johnny and will be going to pick up Frankie and then take them to their daughter's place ...'

'I'll wait until they're here. I'll have her ready for them.'

'You really are a saint, Declan,' Fiona said.

'What else can we do? And remember, Moira knows nothing.'

'Not a word to the Kamp Kommandant,' Fiona promised.

The clinic was in a state of fuss because Frank Ennis was paying one of his unexpected visits.

'You were out with him last night – did he not give you *any* idea he was coming in today?' Hilary asked Clara Casey.

'*Me?*' asked Clara in disbelief. 'I'm the very last person on earth that he'd tell. He's always hoping to catch me out in something. It's driving him mad that he hasn't been able to do it so far.'

'Look, he's talking to Moira very intently about something,' Hilary whispered.

'Well, we marked her card for her about Frank,' Clara said, 'and if Ms Tierney says a word out of order she's out of here.'

'I'll get nearer and see what they're talking about,' Hilary offered.

'Really, Hilary, I *am* surprised at you,' Clara said in mock horror.

'You go away and I'll hover,' said Hilary. 'I'm a great hoverer. That's why I know so much.'

As Clara made for her desk in the centre of the clinic, the phone rang. It was Declan.

'Don't say my name,' he said immediately.

'Sure, right. What can I do for you?'

'Is Moira near you?'

'Quite, yes.'

'Could you find out what she's doing after she leaves you today? I'll make myself clear. We share baby-minding arrangements with a friend and his baby. It's just that they're clients of Moira's and she's been a bit tough on him. He's gone off on a batter. I have to drag him back here and sort things out. We want to keep Moira out of the place until tomorrow, at any rate. If she discovers the set-up, then things will really hit the fan.'

'I see ...'

'So, if there was any other direction you could head her towards ...?'

'Leave it with me,' Clara said, 'and cheer up – maybe your worst scenario won't turn out to be right.'

'No, I'm afraid it's only too right. His AA buddy has just called in. He's getting him back here in about half an hour.'

Hilary came over to Clara with a report.

'He's pumping her for information. Like "does she see any areas of conspicuous waste", or "do the healthy cookery classes work or are they just a distraction?"

You know, the usual kind of thing he goes on about.'

'And what's she singing in response?'

'Nothing yet, but that may be because she's here under our eye. If he got her on her own, Lord knows what he'd get out of her.'

'Be more confident, Hilary. We're not doing anything wrong here. But you've given me an idea.'

Clara approached Frank Ennis and Moira.

'Seeing you two together reminded me that Moira hasn't seen the social work set-up in the main hospital. Frank, maybe you could introduce her to some of the team over there – today possibly?'

'Oh, I have a lot of calls to make on my caseload.'

Clara gave a tinkling laugh. 'Oh really, Moira, you're so much on top of everything, I imagine your caseload is run like clockwork.'

Moira seemed pleased with the praise.

'You know the way it is. You've got to be watchful,' she said.

'I agree,' Frank boomed unexpectedly. 'Everyone should be much more watchful than they are.'

'I *was* hoping, Moira, that you could link up with the whole system, but of course if you feel it's too much for you, then ...'

Clara had judged it exactly right.

Moira made an arrangement to meet Frank at lunch-time. Clara had managed to give Noel, Declan and the man from Alcoholics Anonymous a bit of a head start.

Aidan and Signora Dunne had arrived with little Johnny Carroll and taken Frankie with them. They would wheel the two baby buggies along the canal to Aidan's daughter's house. There Signora would look after all three children – their grandson Joseph Edward along with Frankie and Johnny – while Aidan gave private Latin lessons to students who hoped to go to university.

It was a peaceful and undemanding morning. If they had wondered what Dr Carroll was doing in Noel Lynch's place and why there was no sign of a normally devoted father, they had said nothing. They minded their own business, the Dunnes. Declan was glad of them many times, but never more so than today. The fewer people who knew about this, the better.

Malachy arrived, more or less supporting Noel in the doorway. Noel was shaking and shivering. His clothes were filthy and stained. He seemed totally disorientated.

'Is he still drunk?' Declan asked Malachy.

'Hard to say. Possibly.' Malachy was a man of few words.

'I'll turn on the shower. Can you get him into it?'

'Sure.'

Malachy was as good as his word. He propelled Noel into the water, letting it get cooler all the time until it was almost cold. Meanwhile Declan picked up all the dirty clothes and put them into the washing machine. He laid out clean clothes from Noel's room and made them all a pot of tea.

Noel's eyes were more focused now, but still he said nothing.

Malachy was not speaking either.

Declan poured another mug of tea and allowed the silence to become uncomfortable. He would *not* make things easy for Noel. The man would have to come up with something. Answers, or even questions.

Eventually Noel asked, 'Where's Frankie?'

'With Aidan and Signora.'

'And where's Dingo?'

'Gone to work,' Declan said tersely. Noel was going to have to speak again.

'And did he phone *you*?' He nodded towards Declan.

'Yes, that's why I'm here,' Declan said.

'And are you the only one he phoned?' Noel's voice was a whisper.

Declan shrugged. 'I've no idea,' he said.

Let Noel sweat a bit. Let him think that Moira was on the case.

'Oh my God ...' Noel said. His face had almost dissolved in grief.

Declan took pity on him. 'Well, no one else turned up, so I suppose I was the only one,' he said.

'I'm so sorry,' Noel began.

'Why?' Declan cut across him.

'I can't remember. I really can't. I felt a bit uptight and I thought one or two drinks might help and wouldn't matter. I didn't know it was going to end like this ...'

Declan said nothing and Malachy was silent too. Noel couldn't bear it.

'Malachy, why didn't you stop me?' he asked.

'Because I was at home doing a jigsaw with my ten-year-old son. I didn't hear from you that you were going out – that's why.'

Malachy hadn't spoken such a long sentence before.

'But, Malachy, I thought you were meant to—'

'I am *meant* to come when there's a danger that you might be about to go back to drinking. I am *not* meant to be inspired by the Holy Ghost as to when you decide on this kind of activity all on your own,' Malachy said.

'I didn't know it was going to turn out like this,' Noel said piteously.

'No, you thought it would be lovely and easy like the movies. And I bet you wondered what we were all doing at those meetings.'

Noel's face showed that this is exactly what he had wondered. Declan Carroll suddenly felt very tired.

'Where do we go from here?' he asked both men.

'It's up to Noel,' Malachy said.

'Why is it up to me?' Noel cried.

'If you want to try to kick it again, I'll try to help you. But it's going to be hell on earth.'

'Of course I want to,' Noel said.

'It's no use if you are just waiting for me to get out of your hair so that you can sneak off and stick your face into it again.'

'I won't do that,' Noel wailed. 'From tomorrow on it will be back just the same as it was up to now.'

'What do you mean *tomorrow*? What's wrong with *today*?' Malachy asked.

'Well, tomorrow, fresh start and everything.'

'Today, fresh start and everything,' Malachy said.

'But just a couple of vodkas to straighten me up and then we can start with a clean slate?' Noel was almost begging now.

'Grow up, Noel,' Malachy said.

Declan spoke. 'I can't let you look after our son any more, Noel. Johnny won't come here again unless we know you're off the sauce,' he said, slowly and deliberately.

'Ah, Declan, don't hit me when I'm down. I wouldn't hurt a hair of that child's head.' Noel had tears in his eyes.

'You left your own daughter with Dingo Duggan for

hour after hour. No, Noel, I wouldn't risk it. And even if I did, Fiona wouldn't.'

'Does she have to know?'

'I think so, yes.'

Declan hated doing it, but it was the truth. They couldn't trust Noel any more. And if he felt like that, what would Moira feel?

It didn't bear thinking about.

'We have to tell Aidan and Signora,' Declan said.

'Why?' Noel asked, worried. 'I'm over it now. I hate them knowing I'm so weak.'

'You're *not* weak, Noel, you're very strong. It's not easy for you doing what you do. I know. Believe me.'

'No, I don't believe you, Declan. You were always a social drinker; a pint in the evening and no more. That's balance and moderation – two things I was never any good at.'

'You took on more than most men would have done. I admire you a lot,' Declan said simply.

'I don't admire myself. I disgust myself,' Noel said.

'And what help will that be to Frankie as she grows up? Come on, Noel, it's her first Christmas coming up. The whole street is going to celebrate. You've got to get yourself into good form for it. No self-pity.'

'But Signora and Aidan?'

'They know *something* is wrong. We mustn't play games with them. They can cope with it, Noel. They've coped with a lot in their lives.'

'Anyone else I should tell?' Noel looked defensive and hurt by it all.

'Yes, Lisa, of course, and Emily.' Declan was very definite.

'No, please. Please, not Emily.'

'No need to tell your parents or my parents or anyone like that, but Emily and Lisa need to know.'

'I thought it was over,' Noel said sadly.

Declan forced himself to be cheerful. 'It will be over soon and meanwhile the more help you can get, the better.'

'Go back to the real world and heal the sick, Declan. Don't bother with me and my addictions. Get on with the real world.'

'What could be more real than the man whose daughter was born on the same day as our son? What would Stella be saying to you?'

'Thank God she doesn't know how it all turned out,' Noel said fervently.

'It turned out very well up until now and it will again. Anyway, according to people like your parents and mine, Stella *does* know and she understands it all perfectly.'

'You don't believe any of that claptrap, Declan, do you?'

'Not exactly, but you know ...' Declan ended vaguely.

'No, I don't know, I don't know at all. But if I have to tell Aidan and Signora, then I will. Is that okay?'

'Thanks, Noel.'

He had, of course, already told Fiona all about Noel. She was, as usual, practical and optimistic.

'He sounds shocked by what he did,' she said.

'Yes, but I wish I knew *why* he did it.' Declan sounded worried.

'You said yourself he was in bad form.'

'But he must have been in bad form a hundred times

during the last few months and he never went out on the town. He loves that child. You should see him with her. He's as good as any mother.'

'I know, I *have* seen him ... everyone has. That child has a dozen families round here who'll all do a bit more at the moment.'

'Noel's very sensitive about not letting people know, but he has to tell them. Until he does, don't say anything.'

'Quiet as the grave,' Fiona said.

Declan Carroll took his morning surgery. He had been two hours late, so Dr Hat had been called in to help.

'Muttie Scarlet rang a couple of times. He said you'd have some results for him today.'

'And I do,' Declan said glumly.

'I thought you might.' Dr Hat was sympathetic.

'Isn't it a shit life, Hat?' Declan said.

'It is indeed, but I'm usually the one who says that and you always say it's not so bad.'

'I'm not saying that today. I'm off out to Muttie's house. Can you stay a bit longer?'

'I'll stay as long as you like. They don't want me, though, they'll ask when the *real* doctor will be back,' Dr Hat said.

'I bet they do! They still ask me was I born when they got their first twinge of whatever they have and the answer is always that I wasn't.'

Muttie answered the door.

'Ah, Declan, any news yet?' He spoke in a low voice. He didn't want his wife Lizzie to hear the conversation.

'You know how they are,' Declan said. 'They're

so laid-back up there in the hospital they give a new urgency to the word *mañana* ...'

'So?' Muttie asked.

'So I was wondering, would we go and have a pint?' Declan said.

'I'll go and get Hooves,' Muttie suggested.

'No, let's go to Casey's instead of Dad's and your pub – too many Associates there ... we'd get nothing said.'

Declan saw from Muttie's face that he realised immediately that the news wasn't good.

Old Man Casey served them and, since there was no response to his conversation about the weather, the neighbourhood and the recession, he left them alone.

'Give it to me straight, Declan,' Muttie said.

'It's only early days yet, Muttie.'

'It's bad enough for a drink in the middle of the day, lad. Will you tell me or do I have to beat it out of you?'

'They saw a shadow on the X-ray; the scan showed a small tumour.'

'Tumour?'

'You know ... a lump. I've made an appointment for you with a specialist next month.'

'Next *month*?'

'The sooner we deal with it, the better, Muttie.'

'But how in the name of God did you get an appointment so soon? I thought there was a waiting list as long as your arm?'

'I went private,' Declan said.

'But I'm a working man, Declan, I can't afford these fancy fees ...'

'You won a fortune a few years back on some horse.

You've got money in the bank – you *told* me.'

'But that's for emergencies and rainy days ...'

'This is a rainy day, Muttie.'

Declan blew his nose very loudly. This was more than he could bear at the moment. He heard himself lying as he felt he had been lying all day.

'The thing is, Muttie, once this appointment is made, you can't cancel it. You have to pay for it anyway.'

'Isn't that disgraceful!' Muttie was outraged. 'Aren't they very greedy, these people?'

'It's the system,' Declan said wearily.

'It shouldn't be allowed.' Muttie shook his head in disapproval.

'But you'll go, won't you? Tell me you'll go?'

'I'll go because you can't get me out of it. But it's very high-handed of you, Declan. And if he suggests some mad, expensive treatment, he's not getting another cent out of me!' Muttie vowed.

'No, it's just to know the treatment that he would advise. One visit ...'

'All right then,' Muttie grumbled.

'You never asked me one single thing about the whole business,' Declan said. 'I mean, there are a lot of options: chemotherapy, radiotherapy, surgery ...'

Muttie looked at him with the air of a man who has seen it all and heard it all.

'Won't I hear all about it next month from the fellow whose Rolls-Royce *I'm* paying for? No point in thinking about it until I have to. Okay?'

'Okay,' agreed Declan, who was beginning to wonder would this day ever end.

*

By the time that Moira called at Chestnut Court, things had settled down a lot.

Noel had agreed not to drink today. Malachy had taken him to an AA meeting where nobody had blamed him but everyone had congratulated him on turning up.

Halfway through the meeting, Noel remembered that he had not let them know in Hall's that he wouldn't be in today.

'Declan did that ages ago,' Malachy said.

'What did he say?'

'That he was your doctor and you weren't able to go in. That he was telephoning from your flat.'

'I wonder how Mr Hall took that?' Noel was full of anxiety.

'Oh, Declan would have reassured him. You'd believe anything he said. Anyway, it was all true. You weren't able to go in and he *was* at your flat.'

'He looked very put out about everything,' Noel said. 'I hope he won't turn against me.'

'No, I think he was put out about something else.'

Malachy knew when there was a time to be very firm and a time to be more generous.

Moira viewed the presence of Malachy in the house with no great pleasure.

'Are you a babysitter?' she asked.

'No, Ms Tierney, I am from Alcoholics Anonymous. That's how I know Noel.'

'Oh really ...' Her eyes narrowed slightly. 'Any reason for the visit?'

'We were at a meeting together up the road and I came back for some tea with Noel. That's permitted, isn't it?'

'Of course – you mustn't make me into some kind of a monster. I'm merely here for Frankie's sake. It's just that we had a full and frank exchange of views yesterday and I suppose, well, when I saw you here, I thought that you might ... that Noel could possibly ... that all was not well.'

'And so now you are reassured?' Malachy asked silkily.

'Frankie will be coming back shortly. We want to get things ready for her ... unless there's anything else?' Noel spoke politely.

Moira left.

Malachy turned to Noel. 'One ball-breaker,' he said, and for the first time that day Noel smiled.

Everyone had been planning a Christmas party for Frankie and Johnny. Balloons and paper decorations had been discussed at length and in detail. It was going to be held in Chestnut Court: the apartment block had a big communal room, which could be rented for such occasions. Lisa and Noel had reserved it weeks back. Was it to go ahead or was Noel too frail to be part of it?

'We've got to go for it,' Lisa encouraged him. 'Otherwise when she looks back on her album she'll wonder why there was no celebration for her first Christmas.'

'She won't be looking back on any album with us,' Noel said grimly.

'What do you mean?'

'They'll take her from me, and rightly so. Who would leave a child with me?'

'Well, thank you very much from the rest of us who are doing our best to make a home for her,' Lisa said tartly. 'We are not going to give up so easily. Get her into the pram, Noel, and we'll head off and look at this room.'

Just then there was a ring on the bell.

'Noel, it's Declan, can we leave Johnny with you for an hour or so – it would be a great help.'

This was the first time since Noel's drinking incident that Johnny had been offered.

Noel knew it was a peace offering and an olive branch. But he also knew it was a vote of confidence. He stood a bit taller now.

'Sure, Declan, we'll take him off to see the room where he's having his first Christmas party,' he said.

And he felt that Declan was pleased too, glad to know the party was going ahead.

Having a party for the children three days before Christmas Day was a great opportunity for the families to get together. Most of them celebrated the day quietly, eating too much of their own turkeys and sitting in front of the television. But this was an excuse to get together and wear paper hats and pretend that it was all for the children.

Two small babies who would sleep through most of it.

Lisa was in charge of decorating the hall, and she did it in scarlet and silver. Emily helped her to drape huge red curtains borrowed from the church hall, Dingo Duggan had brought a van full of holly from what he described vaguely as the countryside, Aidan and Signora had decorated a tree that would be left in the big room over the Christmas season. They were going to bring their own grandson, Joseph Edward, to the party as a guest, and Thomas Muttance Feather, Muttie's grandson, was coming on the assurance that he wouldn't have to talk to babies or sit at a children's table.

Josie and Charles were wondering if a picture of St Jarlath would be appropriate in the decorations, and tactfully Lisa found a place for it. Somewhere it wouldn't look utterly ludicrous.

Simon and Maud had a job doing a house party, so they couldn't do the catering; but Emily had arranged a supper, where all the women would bring a chicken or vegetable dish of some sort, and all the men would bring wine and beer or soft drinks and a dessert. The desserts had of course turned out to be an immense number of chocolate ones bought in supermarkets. They were arranged artistically on paper plates on a separate table to be wheeled in after the main course was finished.

Noel showed Frankie all the Christmas decorations and smiled at her adoringly as she squealed with pleasure and sucked her fingers. Dressed in a little red Babygro and with a little red pixie hat keeping her little head warm, she was passed around from one doting adult to another, and featured in a hundred photographs along with Johnny. Even Thomas was persuaded to join in and posed for pictures with the three youngsters and a plate of mince pies.

Father Flynn had brought a Czech trio to play. They had been lonely in Dublin and missed their homeland, so he arranged a number of outings like this, which they enjoyed doing while they got a good meal and their bus money, and an audience cheering them on.

They sang Christmas songs and carols in Czech and in English. And when it came to

Away in a manger
No crib for a bed
The little Lord Jesus
Laid down his sweet head

a hush fell on everyone as they looked at the two sleep-ing babies. Then they all joined in the singing for the next bit:

The stars in the bright sky
Looked down where he lay
The little Lord Jesus
Asleep in the hay.

and everyone in the room, believers or non-believers, felt some sense of Christmas that they had not felt before.

'You're very good giving Muttie a lift,' Lizzie said when Declan called at the Scarlet house on a cold, grey January morning. 'He hates going to the bank, it makes him feel uneasy. He's dressed himself up like a dog's dinner, but he's been like a caged lion all morning.'

'Oh, don't worry, Lizzie, I'm going there anyway and I'd enjoy the company.'

Declan realised that Muttie had told Lizzie nothing whatsoever about his appointment with the specialist. He looked at Muttie, dressed in his best suit and tie, and couldn't help noticing how thin the older man had become. It was a wonder Lizzie hadn't realised it.

They drove in silence while Muttie drummed his fingers and Declan rehearsed what he was going to say when Mr Harris delivered the news that was staring at Declan from X-rays, scans and reports.

They called first at the bank, where Declan cashed a cheque just to prove that he had business there. Muttie withdrew five hundred euros from his savings.

'Even Scrooge Harris can't charge that much,' he said, nervously putting it in his wallet.

Muttie Scarlet wasn't happy about carrying huge sums of money like this, but he was even less happy still about handing it over to this greedy man.

As it turned out, Mr Harris was a kindly man. He was more than pleased to have Declan join them for the consultation.

'If I start talking medical jargon, Dr Carroll can turn it into ordinary English,' he said with a smile.

'Declan is the first person who grew up on our street who became a professional man,' Muttie said proudly.

'That so? I was the first in my family to get a degree, too. I bet they have a great graduation picture of you at home.' Mr Harris seemed genuinely interested.

'It replaces the Sacred Heart lamp.' Declan grinned.

'Right, Mr Scarlet, let's not waste your time here while we go down Memory Lane.' Mr Harris came back to the main point. 'You've been to St Brigid's and they've given me a very clear picture of your lungs. There are no grey areas, it's black and white. You have a large and growing tumour in your left lung and secondary tumours in your liver.'

Declan noted that there was a carafe of water on the desk and a glass. Mr Harris poured one for Muttie, who was uncharacteristically silent.

'So, now, Mr Scarlet, we have to see how best to manage this.'

Muttie was still wordless.

'Will an operation be an option?' Declan asked.

'No, not at this stage. It's a choice between radio-therapy and chemotherapy at the moment, and arranging palliative care at home or in a hospice.'

'What's palliative care?' Muttie spoke for the first time.

'It's nurses who are trained to deal with diseases like yours. They are marvellous, very understanding people who know all about it.'

'Have they got it themselves?' Muttie asked.

'No, but they have been well trained and they know a lot about it from nursing other people – what patients want and how to give you the best quality of life.'

Muttie thought about this for a moment.

'The quality of life I want is to live for a long, *long* time with Lizzie, to see all my children again, to see the twins well settled in a business or good jobs and to watch my grandson, Thomas Muttance Feather, grow up into a fine young man. I'd like to walk my dog Hooves for years to the pub where I meet my Associates and go to the races about three times a year. That would be a great quality of life.'

Declan saw Mr Harris remove his glasses for a moment and concentrate on cleaning them. When he trusted himself to speak again he said, 'And you *will* be able to do a good deal of that for a time. So let's look forward to that.'

'Not live for a long, long time, though?'

'Not for a long, long time, Mr Scarlet, no. So the important thing is how we use what time is left.'

'How long?'

'It's difficult to say exactly …'

'*How long?*'

'Months. Six months? Maybe longer, if we're lucky …'

'Well, thank you, Mr Harris. I must say you've been very clear. Not worth hundreds of euros, but you were straight and you were kind as well. How much exactly do I owe you?'

Muttie took his wallet from his pocket and laid it on the desk.

Mr Harris didn't even look at it.

'No, no, Mr Scarlet, you were brought here by Dr Carroll, a fellow doctor. There's a tradition that we never charge fellow doctors for a consultation.'

'But there's nothing wrong with Declan,' Muttie said, confused.

'You're his friend. He brought you here. He could have gone to other specialists. Please accept this for what it is, normal procedure, and put that away. I will write my report and recommendations to Dr Carroll, who will look after you very well.'

Mr Harris saw them to the lift. Declan noticed him shake his head at the receptionist as she was about to present the bill and Declan breathed a little more easily. Now all he had to do was to keep Noel on the wagon and, more immediately, go home with Muttie and help him tell Lizzie.

Thank God Hat was able to keep things going until he got back to his surgery.

Fiona knew there was something wrong the moment he came in the door.

'Declan, you're white as a sheet! What happened? Was it Noel?'

'I love you, Fiona, and I love Johnny,' he said, head in his hands.

'Ah, God, Declan, what *is* it?'

'It's Muttie.'

'What's happened to him? Declan, tell me in the name of God …'

'He has just a few months,' Declan said.

'Never!' She was so shocked she had to sit down.

'Yes. I was at the specialist this morning with him.'

'I thought you were taking him to the bank.'

'I did so that he could get the money for a specialist.'

'Muttie went private? God, he *must* have been worried,' Fiona said.

'I hijacked him into it, but the specialist waived the fee.'

'Why on earth did he do that?'

'Because Muttie is Muttie,' Declan said.

'He'll have to tell Lizzie,' Fiona said.

'It's done. I was there.' Declan looked stricken.

'And?'

'It was as bad as you'd think. Worse. Lizzie said she still had so many things to do with Muttie. She had been planning to take him to the Grand National in Liverpool. You know, Fiona, Muttie is never going to make it over to Aintree.'

And then he sobbed like a child.

Maud and Simon, who had grown up with Muttie and Lizzie and hardly remembered any former life, were heartbroken.

'It's not as if he was really old,' Maud said.

'Sixty is meant to be only middle-aged nowadays,' Simon agreed.

'Remember the cake we made for his birthday?'

'Sixty Glorious Years.'

'We'll have to put off going to America,' Maud said.

'We can't do that. They won't keep the job for us.' Simon was very anxious.

'There will be other jobs. Later, you know, afterwards.'

But Simon wasn't willing to let it go easily. 'It's such a chance, Maud. He'd want us to have it. We'll be earning a big salary. We could send him money.'

'When was Muttie ever interested in money?'

'I know … you're right. I was just trying to think of excuses, really,' Simon admitted.

'So let's try and get shifts in good Dublin restaurants.'

'They'd never take us on. We don't have enough experience.'

'Oh, come on, Simon, don't be such a defeatist. We have terrific recommendations and references from all the people we did catering for. I bet they'll take us on.'

'Where will we start?'

'I think we should invest a little money first, have dinner in somewhere like Quentins, Colm's or Anton's. You know, top places. And we'd regard it as research, keep our eyes open and *then* go back and ask for a job.'

'It seems a heartless sort of thing to be doing when poor Muttie is in such bad shape.'

'It's better than going to the other side of the earth,' Maud said.

They would start with Colm's up in Tara Road. They chose the cheapest items on the menu, but took notes on everything: the way the waiters served, how they offered the wine for tasting, the way the cheeses were brought to the table and how they were sliced according to the customers' wishes with some advice from the waiter.

'We had better learn our cheeses before trying here,' Maud whispered.

'That's the head guy there.' Simon pointed out Colm, the owner.

Colm came to their table.

'Nice to see a younger set coming in,' he said, welcoming them.

'We're in the catering business ourselves,' Maud said suddenly.

'Really?'

Simon was annoyed. They hadn't planned to blurt it out so quickly. Now they had exposed themselves as spies and not real diners.

'We have terrific recommendations and I was wondering if we could leave you our business card. Just in case you were short-staffed.'

'Thank you. Of course I'll keep it. Here, are you any relation of Cathy Mitchell of Scarlet Feather?'

'Yes, she trained us,' Maud said proudly.

'She was married to a cousin of ours, Neil Mitchell.' Simon saw no need to explain the situation any further.

'Well, well, if Cathy trained you, you must be great! But I won't have anything just for the moment. My partner's daughter Annie, that's her over there, she's just started here, so we're fairly well covered at the moment. Still, I'll put your names in the book.'

Then he retired to the kitchen.

'He was nice,' Maud whispered.

'Yeah, I hope he won't go checking up with Cathy on us just now. She's very upset about Muttie and it would look a bit heartless.'

*

They decided on chemotherapy for Muttie and by this stage everyone in St Jarlath's Crescent knew about him and had offered a variety of cures. Josie and Charles Lynch said that in recognition for Muttie's interest in the campaign for his statue, St Jarlath would put in a word for him. Dr Hat said that he would be happy to drive Muttie to the pub any evening he wanted to go. Hat wouldn't stay, but he'd come back and pick him up later. Emily Lynch managed to distract Muttie by planting shrubs for winter colour in his garden.

'But will I be still here to see them, Emily?' he asked one day.

'Oh, come on, Muttie. The great gardeners of history always knew that someone would see them. That's what it's all about.'

'That makes sense,' Muttie said, and put aside any thought of self-pity.

Declan's own parents saw that there was half a leg of lamb left over at the end of the day or four fillet steaks.

Cathy Scarlet called every day, often with something to eat.

'We made far too many of these little salmon tarts, Dad. Mam, you'd be helping me out if you were to take them.'

Often she brought her son Thomas with her. He was a lively lad and kept Muttie well entertained.

In fact, it was all going better than Declan could have hoped. He had thought that the normally cheerful Muttie would have fallen into a serious depression. But it was far from being the case. Declan's father said that Muttie was still the life and soul up at the pub and he had the same number of pints as ever on the grounds that there wasn't much damage they could do to him now.

Declan wrote to the specialist Mr Harris:

You were so kind and gracious when I brought Muttie Scarlet to a consultation. Your gesture about the fees was so appreciated that I thought you would like to know he is making very good progress, keeping his spirits up and generally living each day to the full.

You and your positive attitude have contributed greatly to this, and I thank you most sincerely.

Declan Carroll

Mr Harris responded by return.

Dr Carroll,

I was glad to hear from you. I have friends who run a general practice and they are looking for a new partner. They asked me, could I recommend anyone and I immediately thought of you. It's in a very attractive part of Dublin and would come with accommodation that would be available for purchase if required. I have attached some details for your interest.

These are very good, concerned people and just because their neighbourhood is affluent does not mean that their patients are rich people with hypochondria. They are sick and worried like people everywhere.

Let me know if it interests you and send me your CV and it can be arranged. Sooner rather than later, they tell me.

I will never forget your friend Muttie Scarlet. Only occasionally in life do you come across a genuinely good person like that. Someone with no disguises whatsoever.

I look forward to hearing from you.
Sincerely,
James Harris

Declan had to read the letter three times before it sank in. He was being offered a place in one of the most prestigious practices in the whole of Dublin. A house with a big garden and a posh school for Johnny. It was the kind of post he might have tried for in ten years' time. But *now*! Before he was thirty! It was too much to take on board.

Fiona had gone to work when the letter arrived so he couldn't share the news. Emily had come to pick up Johnny and wheel him up to Noel's to collect Frankie. Today the children were going to the thrift shop for the morning and back here to his parents in the afternoon. The system ran like clockwork and Noel seemed to be back on track also.

Declan's surgery began at ten so he would have time to call in to see Muttie and discuss the palliative care nurse who was arriving for the first time today. Declan knew the nurse. She was an experienced, gentle woman called Jessica, trained in making the abnormal seem reasonable and quick to anticipate anything that might be needed.

'He's his own man, Jessica,' Declan had warned her. 'He might tell you there's nothing wrong with him at all.'

'I know, Declan, relax. We'll get on fine together.'

And Declan knew that they would.

Moira was bustling down St Jarlath's Crescent when Declan went out. She seemed surgically attached to her clipboard of notes. Declan had never seen her without them. He waved and kept walking, but she stopped him. She clearly had something on her mind.

'Where are you heading?' he asked easily.

'I heard there was a house for sale in this street,' Moira said. 'I've always wanted a little garden. Do you know anything about it? It's number 22.'

Declan thought quickly; it belonged to an old lady who was going into an old people's home, but it was exactly next door to Noel's parents. Noel would not welcome that.

'Might be in poor condition,' Declan said. 'She was a bit of a recluse.'

'Well, that might make it cheaper,' Moira said cheerfully.

She looked nice when she smiled.

'Noel still okay?' she asked.

'Well, you actually see him more than I do, Moira,' Declan said.

'Yes, well, it's my job. But he can be a little touchy at times, don't you find?'

'Touchy? No, I never found that.'

'Just one day there recently, he pushed my notes out of my hands and shouted at me.'

'What was all that about?'

'About someone called Dingo Duggan who had been appointed as an extra babysitter. I asked about him and Noel shouted at me that he was a *decent, poor eejit* and used most abusive language. It was quite intolerable.'

Declan looked at her steadily. So *that* was what had tilted Noel that night. He hardly trusted himself to speak.

'Is anything wrong, Declan?' she asked. 'I get the feeling that I am not being told everything.'

Declan swallowed. Soon he would be far away from Moira and Noel and St Jarlath's Crescent. He reminded himself he must not explode and leave behind him a trail of confusion and bad feeling.

'I'm sure you were able to handle it very well, Moira,' he said insincerely. 'You must be used to the ups and downs of clients, as we are with patients.'

'It's good when you're told the full story,' Moira said. 'But at the moment I think something is being kept from me.'

'Well, when you discover what it is, you'll let me know, won't you?'

Declan managed to fix a smile on his face and moved on.

He called in at the thrift shop where his mother was working and kissed his son, who was sitting with his friend Frankie. The children were both like advertisements for Bonny Babies; they seemed to be endlessly fascinated with their hands.

'Who is his daddy's little boy, then?' Declan said.

His voice sounded different. Molly Carroll looked at her son, concerned.

'Did you come in for anything, Declan?' she asked.

'Just to say hello to my son and heir, and to thank my saintly mother and my friend Emily for making life so easy for us both.'

He smiled. A real smile this time.

'Well, isn't it the least I could do?' Molly was pleased. 'Haven't I got what every mother dreams of? Her son and now her grandson living at home! When I think of all the people who hardly ever see their grandchildren, I feel blessed every single day.'

Not for much longer, Declan thought to himself grimly. He went on to see Muttie and Lizzie. They were having a good-natured argument about how to welcome Jessica, who was going to arrive on her first call that day.

'I've made some scones, but Muttie thinks she'd like a good dinner. What do you think, Declan?'

'I think the scones would be fine and you can suggest lunch to her another time,' Declan said.

'Is she a married person or a single lady?' Muttie asked.

'She's a widow, as it happens. Her husband died about three years ago.'

'The Lord have mercy on him, it must be very hard on her,' said Lizzie, without any apparent acknowledgement that she, too, would soon be a widow.

'Yes, but Jessica has great heart. She puts everything into her family and her work.'

'That's very wise,' said Lizzie. 'And I hope she had a great doctor at the time like we do.' She looked at Declan fondly.

'You can say that again,' said Muttie.

'Stop that, Muttie, you're making my head swell!' he said.

'It deserves to swell. I've told everyone about that Mr Harris and how he wouldn't charge me because you were a professional colleague of his and I was your Associate.'

Declan felt a slight stinging behind his eyes. By the time that Muttie died, Declan and Fiona would be in a totally different part of Dublin. Not only would Muttie and Lizzie have lost their trusted doctor, but his own parents would have lost their son and grandson.

Before he got to work, he met Josie and Charles Lynch.

'I believe the house next door to you is up for sale?' he said.

'Yes, the notice is going up tomorrow. How do you know already?'

'Moira,' he said simply.

'Lord, that woman can hear the grass grow,' Josie said.

'She's been round to the house checking that there are no dog hairs. What kind of a world does she live in, thinking that dogs don't shed hairs?' Charles shook his head.

'She's thinking of buying the house,' Declan said.

'*Never!*' Josie was shocked. 'Lord, she'll be practically *living* in our house!'

Charles shook his head again. 'Noel won't like this … not one little bit.'

'Well, we always have Declan to stand up to her for us all.' Josie was good at looking on the bright side.

Not for long, Declan thought to himself.

In the surgery that morning all the patients seemed to need to tell him some story or recall some instance where he had helped them. If Declan were to believe a quarter of the praise he got that morning, he would have been a very vain man. He just wished they had not chosen today to tell him all this. Today, of all days, when he was just about to change his life and leave them all.

He booked a table at Anton's restaurant for dinner.

He wanted to tell Fiona in good surroundings, not in the house they shared with his parents where everything could be heard in some degree anyway.

'How did you hear of us, sir?' the maître d' asked.

Declan was about to say that Lisa Kelly talked of little else, but something made him keep this information to himself.

'We read about it in the papers,' he said vaguely.

'I hope we will live up to your expectations, sir,' said Teddy.

'Looking forward to it,' said Declan.

It seemed a long day until Dingo would come to pick them up at seven.

A couple of weeks before, Dingo had been to a party in a Greek restaurant and danced unwisely on some broken plates. Declan had tweezed the worst bits out of the soles of Dingo's feet. Money had not changed hands. It didn't, usually, in Dingo's case, but an offer of four trips in his van was agreed to be a fair exchange. This meant they could have a bottle of champagne when he told Fiona the great news.

Just before he left the surgery, Noel called in.

'Just three minutes of your time, Declan, please.'

'Sure, come on in.'

'You're always so good-natured, Declan. Is it real or is it an act?'

'Sometimes it's an act, but sometimes, like now, it's real.' Declan smiled, encouragingly.

'I'll come straight to the point then. I'm a bit worried about Lisa. I don't know what to do ...'

'What's wrong?' Declan was gentle.

'She's lost complete touch with reality when it comes to this Anton. I mean, she doesn't know what's real and what's not. Listen, I should know. I know what denial is. She's right in the centre of it.'

'Is she drinking or anything?'

Declan wondered whether Noel might have developed an alcoholic's sudden lack of tolerance for any kind of drinking.

'No, no, nothing like that, just an obsession. She's planning a future with him, but she's deluding herself all the time.'

'It's tough, all right.'

'She needs help, Declan. She's ruining her life. You're going to have to refer her to someone.'

'I'm not her doctor and she hasn't *asked* anyone to refer her anywhere.'

'Oh, you were never one to play it by the book, Declan. Get somebody ... some sort of psychiatrist to throw an eye over her.'

'I *can't*, Noel. It doesn't work that way. I can't go in off the side of the road and say: Lisa, Noel thinks you are heading in the wrong direction, so let's go and have a nice soothing visit to a shrink.'

'It *should* be the way things work, and anyway, you'd know how to say it,' Noel pleaded with him.

'But she hasn't done anything out of line. Your feelings about all this do you credit, but honestly there's no way that outside interference is going to help. Can't *you* get her to see sense? You live with her – you're flatmates.'

'Sure, who would listen to a word I say?' Noel asked. '*You* always did, to give you your due. You used to make me feel I was a normal sort of a person and not a madman.'

'And you *are*, Noel.'

Declan wondered, was there anyone left who hadn't told him how important he was to them?

Fiona was in great form. She said she had starved herself at lunchtime. Barbara had wanted them to go for lunch together for a long chat about the complexity of men, but Fiona had said that she was going to Anton's that evening, so Barbara said there was no point in talking about the complexity of men to her anyway, that she had got a jewel of a husband and there weren't enough of them to go round.

She was all dressed up in her new outfit: a pink dress with a black jacket. Declan looked at her proudly as they were settled in at the restaurant. She looked so beautiful. She had a style equal to any of the other guests. He took her face in his hands and kissed her for a long time.

'Declan, really! What will people think?' she asked.

'They'll think we are alive and that we are happy,' he said simply, and suddenly he made the second biggest decision of his life. The first had been to pursue Fiona to the end of the world. This one was different. It was about what he was not going to do.

He wouldn't tell her now about the letter from Mr Harris. In fact, he might never tell her. It suddenly seemed so clear to him.

'I was thinking ... I was wondering, should we buy number 22 in the Crescent? It would be a home of our own.'

CHAPTER EIGHT

'I have a bit of a problem,' Frank Ennis said to Clara Casey as he picked her up at the heart clinic.

'Let me guess,' she said, laughing. 'We used one can of air freshener too many in the cloakroom last month?'

'No, nothing like that,' he said impatiently, as he negotiated the traffic.

'No, don't tell me. I'll work it out. It's the brass plates on the door. We got a new tin of brass-cleaning stuff and I forgot to ask you? That's it, isn't it?'

'Truly, Clara, I don't know why you persist in painting me as this penny-pinching sort of clerk instead of the hospital manager. My worry has nothing to do with you and your extraordinary and lavish expenditure on your clinic.'

'On *our* clinic, Frank. It's part of St Brigid's.'

'It is in its foot. It's an independent republic – always was from day one.'

'How petty and childish of you,' she said disapprovingly.

'Clara, are you wedded to this concert tonight?' he asked suddenly.

'Is anything wrong?'

She looked at him sharply. Frank never cancelled arrangements.

'No, nothing is *wrong* exactly, but I do need to talk to you,' he said.

'Will you promise that it's not about boxes of tissues and packets of paper clips and huge areas of wastefulness that are bleeding your hospital dry?' Clara asked.

He actually smiled. 'No, nothing like that.'

'All right then. Sure we'll cancel the concert. Will we go out to a meal somewhere?'

'Come home with me.'

'We have to eat somewhere, Frank, and you don't cook.'

'I asked a caterer to leave in a dinner for us,' he said, embarrassed.

'You were so sure I'd say yes?'

'Well, in a lot of areas of life you are quite reasonable – normal even.' He was struggling to be fair.

'Caterers. I see …'

'Well, they're quite young. Semi-professional, I'd say. Haven't learned to charge fancy prices yet.'

'Slave labour? Ripe for exploitation, yes?' Clara wondered.

'Oh, Clara, will you give over just for one night?' Frank Ennis begged.

Maud and Simon were in Frank's apartment. They had set the table and brought their own paper napkins and a rose.

'Is that over the top?' Simon was worried.

'No, he's going to propose to her. I know he is,' Maud said.

'Did he tell you?'

'Of course he didn't, but why else is he making a meal for a woman in his flat?'

To Maud it was obvious.

They had laid out the smoked salmon with the avocado mousse and a little rosette carved from a Sicilian lemon. The chicken and mustard dish was in the oven. An apple tart and cream were on the sideboard.

'I hope to God she says yes,' Simon said. 'It's a heavy outlay for that man, all this food and the cost of us and everything.'

'She must be fairly old ...' Maud was thoughtful. 'I mean, Mr Ennis is as old as the hills. It's amazing that he still has the energy to propose, let's not even mention anything else!'

'No, let's not,' said Simon, with relief.

They let themselves out of the house and posted the keys back through the door.

Clara had always thought Frank's apartment rather bleak and soulless. Tonight, though, it looked different. There was subdued lighting and a lovely dinner table prepared.

And she noticed the red rose. This wasn't Frank's speed. She wondered whether the young caterers had dreamed it up. Suddenly she felt a great thud-like shock. He couldn't possibly be about to propose to her. Could he?

Surely not. Frank and she had been very clear about where they were going, which was a commitment-free relationship. They were both able to go out with other people. Sometimes when they went away for a weekend, and the time they had that holiday in the Scottish Highlands, they had stayed in the same room and had what Clara might have described as a limited, but pleasant, sex life. That was if she were to tell anyone about it. But she told nobody. Not her great friend Hilary in the clinic, nor her oldest friend Dervla.

Certainly not Clara's mother, who made occasional enquiries about her new escort. Not her daughters, who were inclined to think that their poor old mother was long past that sort of thing. Not her ex-husband Alan, who was always hovering in the background, waiting for her to come running back to him.

No, surely not. Frank could not have got his wires so hopelessly crossed. Definitely not!

He went into his study and came out with a sheaf of letters.

'This all looks very nice.' Clara admired the place.

'Well, good. Good. And thank you for agreeing to change your plans so readily.'

'Not at all. It must be important ...'

Clara wondered what she would say if he really *had* lost the run of himself and proposed. It would obviously be no, but how to put it without hurting him or making him look ridiculous? That was the problem.

Frank poured her a glass of wine and then passed the papers over to her.

'This is my problem, Clara. I've had a letter from a boy in Australia. He says he's my son.'

Simon and Maud had asked Muttie to test out for them that evening a recipe they had for koulibiac. In fact, they both knew the dish worked perfectly well. They just wanted to give themselves an excuse for going to the trouble for him and to give him a role to play. They showed Muttie carefully how they had folded the pastry leaves and prepared the cooked salmon, rice and hard-boiled eggs.

He watched with interest.

'When I was young, if we ever got a bit of salmon we'd be so delighted that we'd never wrap it up in rice and eggs and all manner of things!' He shook his head in wonder.

'Ah, well, nowadays, Muttie, they like things complicated,' Maud explained.

'Is that why you're always talking about making your own pasta instead of buying it in the shops like everyone else?'

'Not a bit,' Simon butted in with a laugh, 'she's interested in pasta because she's interested in Marco!'

'I hardly know him,' said Maud unconvincingly.

'But you'd like to know him more,' Simon responded definitely.

'Who's Marco anyway?' asked Muttie.

'His father is Ennio Romano, you know, Ennio's restaurant, the place we were telling you about,' explained Simon.

'We here hoping to get work there,' said Maud.

'Some of us were *praying* we'd get work there,' Simon added, laughing at his sister's blushes.

Maud tried to look businesslike. 'It's an Italian restaurant, it makes sense for us to know how to make our own pasta. And even if we don't get work there, it would be useful for our home catering. The clients would be very impressed.'

'And thinking they're knocking people's eyes out with envy,' Simon said.

'But what's the point of asking people to your house and then upsetting them?' For Muttie this was a real problem.

The twins sighed.

'I wonder, has he asked her yet?' Maud said.

'If he doesn't want his dinner burned to a crisp, I'd say he has.'

'Who's this?' Muttie asked with interest.

'A desperately old man called Frank Ennis is proposing to some very old woman.'

'Frank Ennis? Does he work up in St Brigid's?'

'Yes, he does. Do you know him, Muttie?'

'Not personally, but I know all about him from Fiona. Apparently, he is their natural enemy in the clinic where she works. Declan knows him too. He says your man is not a bad old skin, just obsessed with work.'

'That will all end if he marries the old lady,' Simon said thoughtfully.

'It will change for the old lady too, remember,' Maud reminded them.

'Has he paid you?' Muttie asked suddenly.

'Yes. He left an envelope for us,' Simon confirmed.

'Good. That's fine then. I hear from Fiona that he's a total Scrooge and won't pay his bills until the last moment.'

'He did mention thirty days' grace,' Simon said.

'You didn't tell me!' Maud said.

'I didn't need to. I said to him we operated a money-up-front, no-credit business. He totally understood.'

Simon was immensely proud of his negotiating skills and his command of the language of commerce.

Clara Casey was looking at the letter that Frank had handed to her.

'Are you sure you want me to read it?' she asked. 'He didn't write it to me ...'

'He didn't *know* about you,' Frank explained.

'But the question is, what does he know about *you*?' Clara asked gently.

'Read it, Clara.'

So she began to read a letter from a young man:

You will be surprised to hear from me. My name is Des Raven and I believe that I am actually your son. This will probably strike terror into your heart and you will expect someone searching for a fortune turning up on your doorstep. Let me say at once that this is not at all the case.

I live very happily here in New South Wales where I'm a teacher and – just to reassure you – where I will go on living!

If my presence in Dublin will cause embarrassment to you and your family, I will quite understand. I just hoped it might be possible for us to meet at least once when I am in Ireland. My mother, Rita Raven, died last year. She got a heavy pneumonia and didn't have it properly treated.

I have not lived at home for the past six years when I went to teachers' training college, but I always came home once a week and cooked her a meal. Sure, she put the washing through the machine for me, but she liked to do that. Truly she did.

Funny thing, I never asked her any questions about where I came from and what kind of a guy my father was. I didn't ask because she didn't seem very easy about the whole thing. She would say she had been very young and very foolish at the time and hadn't it all worked out so well? She said she never regretted one day of having me, which was good. And Australia had been good to her. She arrived here pregnant and

241

penniless when she had me and then she trained as a hotel receptionist.

She had a couple of romances: one fellow lasted six years. I didn't much like him but he made her happy … and then I think something marginally more interesting for him turned up. She had a lot of good friends and kept in touch with her married sister who lives in England. She was forty-two when she died, although she claimed to be thirty-nine, and I'd say, all in all, she had a good and happy life.

Of you, Frank Ennis, I know nothing except your name on my birth certificate. I found you on the internet and called the hospital from here and asked were you still working there and they said yes.

So here goes with the letter!

You have only my assurance that I will not make trouble for you and your present wife and family. I also know that you didn't know anything about where I lived. Mum was very adamant about that. She told me that every single birthday so that I wouldn't expect a gift.

I truly hope that we will meet.

Until then …

Des Raven

Clara put the letter down and looked over at Frank. His eyes were too bright and there was a tear on his face. She got up and went across to him with her arms out.

'Isn't this *wonderful*, Frank!' she cried. 'You've got a son! Isn't that the best news in the world?'

'Well, yes, but we've got to be cautious,' Frank began.

'What do we have to be cautious about? There was a woman called Rita Raven, wasn't there?'

'Yes, but—'

'And she disappeared off the scene?'

'She went to some cousins in the USA,' he said.

'Or to some non-cousins in Australia ...' Clara corrected him.

'But it will all have to be checked out ...' he began to bluster.

She deliberately mistook his meaning. 'Of course the airlines and everything, but let him do that, Frank, the young are much better at getting flights online than we are. The main thing is, what time is it in Australia? You can ring him straightaway.' She busied herself removing the clingfilm from the smoked salmon.

He hadn't moved. He couldn't bring himself to tell her he had had the letter for two weeks and hadn't been able to decide what to do.

'Come on, Frank, it's surely morning there and if you leave it any longer he'll have gone out to school. Call him now, will you?'

'But we'll have to talk about it?'

'Like what do we have to talk about?'

'But don't you mind?'

'*Mind*, Frank? I'm delighted. The only thing I mind is you, after all these years, having to talk to an answering machine.'

He looked at her, bewildered. There were so many things that he would never understand.

'How was Frank last night?' Hilary asked Clara the next day at the clinic. Only Hilary was ever given any information and she was the only one who dared to ask.

243

'Amazing,' Clara said and left it there.

'And did you enjoy the concert?' Hilary persisted.

'We didn't go. He arranged a catered meal in his apartment.'

'My God, this sounds serious!'

Hilary was delighted. She always said that they were made for each other. Something Clara continued to deny.

'Frank is as he always was and always will be: cautious and watchful, never spontaneous. Stop trying to matchmake, will you, Hilary?'

Frank had dithered so long last night that the telephone rang unanswered in Des Raven's home on the other side of the world. He had managed to miss talking to the son he hadn't known he had, just because he was anxious to talk it over and check it out. All this had led to nothing, but Clara told none of this to Hilary. It was still Frank's secret. She wasn't going to blurt it out.

'Where is Moira? Today's one of her days, isn't it?'

'She's just taken Kitty Reilly on a tour of residential homes. She has a checklist as long as her arm about what Kitty needs, you know, easy access to church, vegetarian food … that sort of thing.' Hilary sounded half impressed, half annoyed.

'She's very thorough, I'll say that for her,' Clara said, grudgingly.

'I know what you mean. If she smiled more, maybe?' Hilary wondered. 'Anyway, Linda rang you earlier,' Hilary said. 'You were with somebody, so I took the call.'

Hilary's son was married to Clara's daughter. The two women had schemed to introduce their children to each other and it had worked spectacularly well.

Apart from producing a grandchild. Despite a lot of intervention, there was no success. Both her son Nick and Clara's Linda were very despondent.

'She said no luck again.'

'If she's so het up, she will *never* conceive. She has a list of three dozen people she phones every month. You, me and about thirty more.'

'Clara!' Hilary was shocked. 'She's your daughter and she thinks you are as excited as she is at the thought of you becoming a granny, and of me becoming one at the same time!'

'You're right, I'd forgotten. Pass me the phone.'

Hilary watched as Clara soothed Linda and patted her down.

Linda was obviously crying at the other end. Hilary moved away. She would have loved Nick and Linda to have given them good news.

She could hear Clara saying, 'Of *course* you're normal, Linda. Please stop crying, sweetheart. You'll have horrible, piggy, red eyes. I *know* you don't care, but you will later on when you're getting dressed to go out ... Well, to Hilary's of course, that's where we're all going tonight. Don't even consider cancelling, Linda. Hilary has bought *the* most gorgeous dessert.'

'Oh, I have, have I?' Hilary said when Clara hung up.

'I had to say something. She was about to go home to a darkened room.'

'All right then. I had been going to serve cheese and grapes, but you've raised my game,' Hilary said. 'What did Frank Ennis serve last night as a dessert?'

'Apple tart,' Clara said.

'Are you *sure* he didn't ask you some question? Something you've forgotten to tell me ...'

'Oh, shut up, Hilary. Look, here comes Moira. Let's pretend to be doing *some* work here.'

Moira was triumphant. The fifth place they had looked at was perfect for Kitty Reilly – full of retired nuns and retired priests, and a vegetarian option at every meal. All you could ask for, in fact.

'Lord, I hope I'll ask for a lot more than that when the time comes,' Clara said piously.

'What would you like exactly?' Moira asked.

An innocent enough question, but Moira's tone seemed to suggest that for Clara the time probably had come already.

'I don't know: a library, a casino, a gym, oh, and a grandchild!' Clara said. 'What about you, Moira, when the time comes?'

'I'd like to be with friends. You know, people I had known for a long time so that we could do a lot of remembering together.'

'And will you do that, do you think? Get a group of friends and set up your own place?'

Clara was interested. She and her friend Dervla had often discussed doing just that.

'Probably not. I don't have many friends. I never had time to make friends along the way,' Moira said, unexpectedly.

Clara looked at her sharply. For a moment the veil had been lifted and she saw a very lonely woman indeed. Then the veil fell again and it was as before.

'Will you come round this evening and we'll call him? Earlier than we did last night ...' Frank called Clara full of plans.

'No, Frank, I can't tonight. Hilary's cooking dinner.'

'But you *have* to come!' He was outraged.

'I can't, Frank. I told you …'

'You're very doctrinaire,' he said, crossly.

'And so are you. If you had called immediately you would have caught him.'

'Please, Clara.'

'No. I'm not saying it again. Wait until the next night if you need me to be there and hold your hand for you.'

She hung up.

Frank sat listening to the empty line. What a fool he had been not to have telephoned the boy immediately! Clara was right. He *had* dithered and the only result of his delay was the boy would think he was having a door closed in his face. Of course he remembered Rita Raven. Who wouldn't have remembered her? His mother and father had been most disapproving.

Rita was from entirely the wrong kind of family. The Ennises hadn't worked hard and risen to this degree of respectability just to be dragged down by their son. Frank Ennis had parents who acted swiftly. Rita Raven had disappeared from everyone's life. Frank had thought of her from time to time slightly wistfully and now she had died. So young. He still saw her as the pretty seventeen-year-old she had been then. Imagine, she had gone all the way to Australia and had her child without ever letting him know. He had simply had no idea of this.

If he had known, what would he have done? He was uneasy thinking about it. Back then, on the edge of a career, back then, in a more disapproving climate, he might not have acted well. His parents had been so hostile about his relationship with Rita and so open in their relief that she had left the country. They couldn't possibly have known more than they said, could they? His stomach churned at the possibility of it. But they *couldn't*. Not paid a sum of money to buy her off. That was impossible. They were careful people with money. No, he mustn't go down that avenue of suspicion.

Damn Clara and her ladies' tea parties! He really needed to have her at his side.

Hilary served them an elegant meal. When she had gone to the gourmet shop to buy a deluxe dessert, she saw some unusual salads and bought those too.

The conversation was tense and stilted as it always was on the days after Linda had discovered that, yet again, she wasn't pregnant. Clara and Hilary looked at each other. Years ago it had been so different. There were orphanages full of children yearning for happy homes. Today, there were allowances and grants for single mothers.

Clara wondered if Moira had any further news about the child she said would shortly be going into care. The little girl was a few months old, exactly the same age as Declan and Fiona's baby. Lucky little girl if she got Linda and Nick as parents. No child would find a more welcoming home, not to mention two besotted grannies. She must ask Moira about it tomorrow.

Clara let her mind wander to Frank's apartment. She hoped he was being tactful and diplomatic with Des Raven. Had she stressed enough that he must *sound* delighted and welcoming? The first impression was crucial. This boy had waited for over a quarter of a century to talk to his father. Let Frank make it a good experience for him. *Please*.

*

Yet again the call went to voicemail.

Frank was unreasonably annoyed. Did this guy spend *any* time at home? It must be about six-thirty in the morning. Where *was* he?

Absently, during the evening he dialled again and to his surprise the phone was answered by a girl with what seemed a very strong Australian accent. Frank realised that Des Raven probably spoke like that too.

'I was looking for Des Raven …' he began.

'You missed him, mate,' she said cheerfully.

'And who am I talking to?' Frank asked.

'I'm Eva. I'm housesitting.'

'And when will he be back?'

'Three months. I'm walking his dog and looking after his garden.'

'Oh, and are you his girlfriend?'

'Who are *you*?' she asked with spirit.

'Sorry, I'm just a … friend … from Ireland.'

'Well, he's on his way to you, then.' Eva was pleased to have it all settled so easily. 'Probably there now. No, wait, he's going to England first because that's where he lands. It's near you, right?'

'Yes, under an hour's plane journey.'

Frank felt the entire conversation was very unreal.

'Right then, he knows where to find you.'

'He does?'

'Well, he left here with a briefcase full of papers and notes and letters. He showed a big batch to me. I think they were all from people he had written to who had written back.'

'Yes, yes, indeed …' Frank was miserable.

'So, can I say who called him? I'm keeping a list by the phone.'

'Have many people called?' he asked out of interest.

'Nope, you're the first. What shall I put down?'

'As you say, he'll be here in a day or two ...'

Frank Ennis had no wish to muddy these waters any further.

He contemplated telling Clara, but she was at this confounded tea party and might not value an interruption about his private life. It was *impossible* to know how women would react to anything. Look at Rita Raven, heading to the ends of the earth to have a child by herself! Look at how childishly pleased Clara had been to hear that Frank had fathered a child outside marriage!

He thought morosely about the women after Rita and before Clara. A line, not a long line, but they all had one thing in common: they were incredibly hard to understand.

The boy would have to get in touch through the hospital. He didn't know Frank's home address. He wasn't going to blurt out the whole story to whoever he met first. Frank had no fears on that score. The boy, Des, as he must learn to think of him, had written that he understood the moral climate might not have changed or moved on in Ireland as much as it had in Australia. He wished Des had sent a picture of himself, then he realised that the boy ... all right, Des ... didn't know what his father looked like either.

Quite possibly there was a picture of Frank many years ago. He hoped not. He hated being seen twenty-five years later, hair beginning to thin, stomach beginning to expand. What would Des Raven think of the father he had waited so long to meet?

The days seemed to be crawling by.

When it happened it was curiously flat.

Miss Gorman, who had been hired by Frank ten years previously because she was not flighty, came in to see him. The years had resulted in Miss Gorman becoming even less flighty, if this was possible. She had a disapproval rating about almost everything. A man with an Australian accent had been on the phone, wishing to talk to Mr Ennis on a personal matter. He stood condemned in her eyes because of his accent, his persistence and his refusal to define anything. Miss Gorman took it very personally. It was surprising, then, that Frank seemed to take it all so seriously.

'Where was he calling from?' he asked crisply.

'Somewhere in Dublin. He doesn't really know *where* he is, Mr Ennis.' Miss Gorman's sniff was unmerciful.

'When he calls again, make sure that you put him right through ...'

'Well, I am sorry if I did the wrong thing, Mr Ennis. It's just that you never, *ever* talk to anyone you don't know.'

'Miss Gorman, you didn't do the wrong thing. You are *incapable* of doing the wrong thing.'

'I hope that I have been able to make this clear over the years.'

She was mollified and withdrew to await the call.

'I'm putting him through, Mr Ennis,' she said eventually.

'Thank you, Miss Gorman.'

He waited until she was off the line, then in a shaky voice he asked, 'Des? Is that you?'

'So you *did* get my letter?' Very Australian but not very warm, not excited as his letter had been.

'Yes, I tried to call you but first it was the answering machine and then it was Eva. I talked to her and she told me that you had set out. I've been waiting for your call.'

'I nearly didn't ring ...'

'Why was that? Was it nerves?' Frank asked.

'No, I thought, why bother? You don't want to be involved with me. You've made that clear.'

'That's *so* wrong,' Frank cried out, stung by the unfairness of this. 'I do indeed want to be involved with you. Why else would I have called you in Australia and talked to Eva?' He could almost hear the shrug of shoulders at the other end of the phone. 'Why would I do that?'

Frank felt hollow. Somehow Clara had been right. He had paused when he should have gone enthusiastically forward. But that wasn't his nature. His nature was to examine everything minutely and when he was sure, and not a moment before, then he would pronounce.

'You probably thought I was coming to claim my inheritance,' Des said.

'It never crossed my mind. You said you wanted to get in touch. That's what I thought it was. I was as astonished as you. You know, I only just heard of your existence and now I'm delighted!'

'Delighted?' Des sounded unconvinced.

'Yes, sure, I was delighted.' Frank was stammering now. 'Des, what *is* all this? You got in touch with me, I called you back. Will you come and have lunch with me today?'

'Where do you suggest?' Des asked.

Frank breathed out in relief. Then he realised he had to think quickly. Where to take the boy?

'Depends what you'd like ... Quentins is very good and this new place, Anton's, is talked about a lot.'

'Are these jacket-and-tie jobs?'

Frank realised that it had been years since he had gone anywhere that a jacket and tie was *not* necessary. There would be a lot of adapting ahead.

'Sort of traditional but not stuffy.'

'I'll take that as a yes. Which place?'

'Anton's. I've never been there. Will we say one o'clock?'

'Why *don't* we say one o'clock?' Des sounded faintly mocking as if he was sending Frank up.

'I'll tell you how to get there—' Frank began.

'I'll find it,' Des said and hung up.

Frank buzzed through to Miss Gorman. Could she kindly find him the number for Anton's restaurant? No, he would make the reservation himself. Yes, he was quite sure. Perhaps she would cancel all appointments for the afternoon.

She called back with the number and then added that she had spoken to Dr Casey from the heart clinic who said that there was no way the 4 p.m. meeting could be cancelled. Too many people were setting too much store on the outcome. To have the meeting without Frank Ennis would be *Hamlet* without the prince. He would *have* to be back by four. What kind of a lunch would last three hours?

Chastened, Frank rang the restaurant.

'Can I speak to Anton Moran, please? Mr Moran? I have never begged before and I never will again, Mr Moran, but today I arranged to meet for the first time a son I never knew I had and I picked your restaurant. Now I am hoping you will be able to find me a table. I don't know where to contact the young man … my son … It will be such a messy start to our relationship if I have to tell him we couldn't get a booking.'

The man at the other end was courteous.

'This is far too important a matter to mess up,' he said gracefully. 'Of course you can have a table. Service today isn't full,' he added, 'but your story sounds so dramatic and so obviously true that I would have found a table for you even if I had to kneel down on all fours and pretend to be one.'

Frank smiled and suddenly he remembered Clara saying that he should be more immediate, more upfront with people. Nothing worked as well as the truth, she had advised him.

Another round to Clara. Was the woman going to be right about *everything*?

Frank was in the restaurant early. He looked around at the other diners, not a man without a collar, tie and smart jacket. *Why* had he chosen this place? But then again, if he had brought them to a burger place, it would hardly look festive. Or celebratory. It would look as if he was hiding this new member of his family. He watched the door and every time some man came in who might be about twenty-five his heart gave a lurch.

Then he saw him. He was so like Rita Raven that it almost hurt. Same little freckles on the nose, same thick fair hair and the same huge dark eyes.

Frank swallowed. The boy was talking to Teddy, the maître d', at the door and making signs around his neck. Seamlessly, Teddy produced a necktie and Des tied it quickly. Then Teddy was leading him over to the table.

'Your guest, Mr Ennis,' he said and slipped away.

Frank thought this man should have been an ambassador somewhere rather than working in what he realised was an outrageously expensive restaurant.

'Des!' he said and held out his hand.

The boy looked at him appraisingly.

'Well, well, well …' he said. He had ignored the hand that had been offered to him.

Frank wondered, should he attempt the kind of bearhug men did nowadays?

He was bound to get it wrong, of course, and knock half the things off the table. And maybe the boy, used to more rugged Australian ways, might pull away, revolted.

'You found the place,' Frank said foolishly.

Des shrugged and looked so dismissive.

'I didn't know where you were, you see. Where you would be starting out from …'

Frank's voice trailed away. This was going to be much harder than he had thought.

Near the kitchen door Teddy spoke to Anton.

'I've had Lisa on the phone.'

'Not again,' he sighed.

'She wants to come in for a meal sometime when we are not too busy.'

'Try and head her off, will you, Teddy?'

'Not easy …' Teddy said.

'Just buy me a week then. Tell her Wednesday of next week.'

'Lunch or dinner?'

'Oh God, lunch.'

'She has her eyes on dinner,' Teddy said.

'An early-bird dinner then.' Anton was resigned.

'She does work her butt off for this place. I don't think we ever pay her anything.'

'Nobody asked her to slave.'

Anton strained to hear what the newly united father and son were saying to each other. The conversation seemed to be limping along.

'Wouldn't families make you sick, Teddy?' Anton said unexpectedly.

Teddy paused before answering. Anton's family had not troubled him very much. Teddy didn't understand what was wrong with families from Anton's viewpoint, but he knew enough to agree with him.

'You're so right, Anton, but think of all the business we get out of the guilt that families create! Half the people here today are from some kind of family guilt. Anniversaries, birthdays, engagements, graduations. We'd be bankrupt without it.'

Teddy always saw the bright side.

'Good man, Teddy.'

Anton was slightly distracted. That man, Mr Ennis, was making heavy weather over his meeting with his son. Even from across the room you could cut the atmosphere with a knife.

Clara always said that when in doubt, you should speak your mind. Ask the question that is bothering you. Don't play games.

'What's wrong, Des? What has changed? In your letter you were eager to meet ... Why are you so different?'

'I didn't know the whole story. I didn't know what your family did.'

'What did they do?' Frank cried.

'As if you didn't know.'

'I don't know,' Frank protested.

'You don't fool me. I've got documents, receipts, signed forms – I know the whole story now.'

'You know more than I do,' Frank said. 'Who was writing these documents and filling in these forms?'

'My mother was a frightened girl of seventeen. Your father gave her a choice. She could leave Ireland for ever and she would get a thousand pounds. One thousand pounds! That's how much my life was worth. A miserable grand. And for this she was to sign an undertaking that she would never approach the Ennis family, claiming any responsibility for her pregnancy.'

'This can't be true!' Frank's voice was weak with shock.

'Why did you think she had gone away?'

'Her mother told me she had gone to America to stay with cousins,' Frank said.

'Yes, that's the story they all put out.'

'But why shouldn't I believe them?'

'Because you weren't a fool. If you played according to their rules you were in a win-win situation. Troublesome girl, irritatingly pregnant, out of your hair, out of the country. Everything sorted. You leaped at the chance.'

'No, I didn't. I didn't know there was anything *to* sort out. I never knew until I got your letter that I had a child.'

'Pull the other one, Frank.'

'Where did you hear all this about my parents asking Rita to sign documents?'

'From Nora. Her sister. My aunt Nora. I went to see her in London and she told me everything.'

'She told you wrong, Des. Nothing like that ever happened.'

'Give me credit for some brains. You're not going to admit it now if you didn't then.'

'There was nothing to admit. You don't understand. All this came to me out of a clear blue sky.'

'You never got in touch with her. You never wrote to her once.'

'I wrote to her for three months every day. I put proper stamps for America on them, but got no reply.'

'Didn't that ring any alarm bells?'

'No, it didn't. I asked her mother if she was forwarding the letters and she said she was.'

'And eventually you gave up?'

'Well, I was getting no response. And her mother said ...' He stopped as if remembering something.

'Yes?'

'She said I should leave Rita alone. That she had moved on in life. She said there was a lot of fuss made, but the Ravens had done everything according to the letter of the law.'

'And you didn't know what she meant?' Des was not convinced.

'I hadn't an idea what she meant, but now I see ... No, it couldn't be ...'

'What couldn't be?'

'My parents – if you had known them, Des! Sex was never mentioned in our house. They would be incapable of any discussion about paying Rita off.'

'Did they like her?'

'Not particularly. They didn't like anyone who was distracting me from my studies and exams.'

'And her folks, did they like you?'

'Not really, same sort of reasons. Rita was skipping her classes to be with me.'

'They thought you were a pig,' Des said.

'Surely not!' Frank was surprised at his calmness in the face of insult.

'That's what Nora says. She says you ruined everyone's life. You and your so-grand family. You broke them all up. Rita never came back from Australia because she had to swear not to. A perfectly decent family, minding its own business, ruined because of you and your snobbish family.'

Des looked very upset and very angry.

Frank knew he had to walk carefully. This boy had been so excited and enthusiastic about meeting him, now he was hostile and barely able to sit at the same table as the father he had crossed the world to meet.

'Rita's sister in London – Nora, is it? She must be very upset.'

'Which is more than you are,' Des said, mulishly.

'I *am* sorry. I tried to tell you that, but we got bogged down in a silly argument.'

'Silly argument is what you call it? A row that destroyed my mother's family!'

'I didn't know *any* of it, Des. Not until I heard from you.'

'Do you believe me?'

'I believe that's what Nora said to you, certainly.'

'So you think *she* was lying?'

'No, I think she believes what she was told. My parents are dead now. Your mother is dead. We have no one to ask.'

He knew that he sounded weak and defeated.

But oddly Des Raven seemed to recognise the honesty

in his tone. 'You're right,' he said, almost grudgingly. 'It's up to us now.'

Frank Ennis had seen the waiter hover near them and leave several times. Soon they must order.

'Would you like something to eat, Des? I ordered an Australian wine to make you feel at home.'

'I'm sorry, I like to know who I am eating and drinking with.' Des was taking no prisoners.

'Well, I don't know how well you'll get to know me … They say that I'm difficult and that I make a mess of things,' Frank said. 'That's what I'm told, anyway.'

'Who tells you that? Your wife?'

'No. I never married.'

Des was surprised. 'So no children, then?'

'Apart from you, no.'

'I must have been a shock.'

Frank paused. He must not say the wrong thing here. It was a time to be honest and speak from the heart. But how could he admit to this boy that his instincts and first reactions had been doubt and confusion and a wish to check it all out? He knew that if he were wholly truthful, he could alienate Des Raven for ever and lose the son he had only just met.

'It may sound odd and cold to you, Des, but my first reaction was shock. I couldn't believe that I had a child – my own flesh and blood – who had lived for a quarter of a century without my having an idea about it. I am a tidy, meticulous sort of person. This was like having my whole neat world turned upside down. I had to think about it. That's what I do, Des, I think about things slowly and carefully.'

'Really?' Des sounded slightly scornful.

'Yes, really. So when it had got clear in my mind, I called you.'

'And what had you to get clear exactly?'

'I had to get my head around the fact that I had fathered a son. And if you think that's something that can be accepted as natural and normal in two minutes, then you are an amazing person. It takes someone like me a bit of time to get used to a new concept and as soon as I did I called you and you had already gone.'

'But you must have been shocked? Afraid that people would find out?' Des was still taunting him.

'No, I wasn't afraid of that. Not at all.' He had to think what Clara might have said and it came to him. 'I was proud to have a son. I would want people to know.'

'I don't think so ... Big Catholic hospital manager having an illegitimate child. No, I can't see you wanting people to know.'

'There is no such word, no concept of an illegitimate child nowadays. The law has changed and society has changed too. People are proud of their children, born in wedlock or outside.' Frank spoke with spirit.

Des shook his head. 'All very fine, very noble, but you haven't told anyone about me yet.'

'You are *so* wrong, Des, I have indeed talked about you and said how excited I was to be going to meet you ...'

'*Who* did you tell? Not Miss Frosty in your office, that's for sure. Did you tell your mates at the golf club or the racetrack or wherever you go? Did you say, "I have a boy, too. I'm like you, a family man"? No way. You told nobody.'

Frank sat there, miserable. If he started to tell him about Clara, it made it all the more pitiable. There was only one person to whom he had told the secret. At that moment Anton Moran appeared at their side.

'Mr Ennis,' he said, as if Frank had been a regular customer since the place had opened.

'Ah, Mr Moran.'

Frank had the feeling of being rescued. It was as if this man was throwing him some sort of a lifeline.

'Mr Ennis, I was wondering, would you and your son like to try our lobster? It is this morning's catch, done very simply, with butter and a couple of sauces on the side.'

Anton looked from one to the other. A sudden silence had fallen between the two men. They were looking at each other dumbfounded.

'I'm sorry,' the younger man said.

'No, I'm sorry, Des,' said Frank. 'I'm sorry for all those years …'

Anton murmured that he would come back in a few moments to take their order. He would never know what was going on there, but they seemed to have turned a corner. At least they were talking and soon they were ordering food.

He looked over again and they were raising a glass of Hunter Valley Chardonnay to each other. That was a relief. As soon as he had mentioned the boy being the man's son, Anton had felt a twinge of anxiety.

Possibly he had been indiscreet? But no, it seemed to be working fine.

Anton breathed deeply and went back into the kitchen. Imagine – there were some people who believed that running a restaurant was all to do with serving food!

That was only a very small part of it, Anton thought.

CHAPTER NINE

Moira had an appointment with Frank Ennis. It was her quarterly report. She had to show the manager her case list and explain the work she had done, which was costing the hospital a day and a half's wages.

Miss Gorman, his fearsome secretary, asked Moira to take a seat and wait. Today she was, if possible, more fearsome still.

'Is Mr Ennis very busy?' Moira enquired politely.

'They never leave him alone, pulling him this way and that.'

Miss Gorman looked protective and angry. Maybe she fancied him and was annoyed that he had taken up with Dr Casey.

'He always seems so much in control,' Moira murmured.

'Oh no, he's at their beck and call all day. It's totally disrupting his schedule.'

'Who is doing this disrupting?'

Moira was interested. She liked stories of confrontation.

Miss Gorman was vague. 'Oh, people, you know. Fussing people saying it's a personal matter. It's so distracting for poor Mr Ennis.'

She *definitely* fancied him, Moira thought, and sighed over the way people wasted their lives over love.

Look at that Lisa Kelly who thought she was the girl-friend of Anton Moran despite all the women that he paraded around the place. Look at that silly girl in her own social-worker team who had refused promotion because her plodding boyfriend might have felt in-adequate.

Look at poor Miss Gorman, sitting here fuming because these people, whoever they were, were actually daring to ring Frank Ennis, saying that it was personal.

She sighed again and settled down to wait.

Frank Ennis was much more cheerful than on earlier visits. He checked Moira's figures and report carefully.

'You certainly seem to be taking a load off the main hospital ... the *real* hospital,' he said.

'I think you'll find that the heart clinic thinks of itself very much as the *real* hospital,' Moira corrected him.

'Which is why I wouldn't use such an expression in front of them. Credit me with *some* intelligence, Ms Tierney.'

'It's very well run, I must say.'

'Well, yes, they do deliver a service. I give them that much, but it's like a mothers' meeting in there – this one is having a baby, that one is getting engaged, the other one is getting married. It's like a gossip column in a cheap newspaper.'

'I couldn't agree with you less.' Moira was cold. 'These are professional women; they know their subject and they do their job well. They reassure the patients and teach them to manage their own condition. I don't see that as being in *any* way like a gossip column or a mothers' meeting.'

'But I thought I could talk to you about it. I thought you were my eyes and ears. My spy in there ...'

'You suggested that, certainly, but I never accepted the role.'

'That's true, you didn't. I suppose you've been sucked into it like everyone else.'

'I doubt it, Mr Ennis. I'm not easily sucked into things. Shall I leave this report with you?'

'Have I annoyed you in any way, Ms Tierney?' Frank Ennis asked.

'No, not at all, Mr Ennis. You have your job to do, I have mine. It's a matter of mutual respect. Why do you think you might have annoyed me?'

'Because apparently that's what I *do*, Ms Tierney, annoy people, *and* you look disapproving, as if you didn't like what you saw.'

Several people had said that to Moira, but usually in the heat of the moment when they were objecting to something she had to do in the line of work. Nobody had ever said it in a matter-of-fact way and an even tone like Frank Ennis.

'It must be the way my face is set, Mr Ennis. I assure you I'm not disapproving of anything you do.'

'Good, good.' He seemed satisfied. 'So you'll smile a bit from now on, will you?'

'I can't smile to order. It would only be a grimace,' Moira said. 'You know ... twisting my features into a smile ... it wouldn't be real or sincere.'

Frank Ennis looked at her for a moment.

'You're quite right, Ms Tierney, and I hope we will meet under some circumstances that do call for a real or sincere smile.'

'I hope so,' Moira said.

She thought that he was looking at her with some sympathy and concern. Imagine, this man pitied *her*! How ridiculous.

It was the weekend and everyone was going somewhere.

Noel and his parents were taking Baby Frankie to the country for two nights. They had booked a bed and breakfast place outside Rossmore. There was a statue of St Anne and a holy well there; Josie and Charles were very interested in it. Noel said he would probably give the holy well a miss, but he would take the baby for walks in the woods for the fresh air. He had shown Moira the case he had packed for the journey. Everything was there.

Lisa Kelly was going to London. Anton was going to look at a few restaurants there and she was going to take notes. It would be wonderful. Moira had sniffed, but said nothing.

Frank Ennis said that he was going to take a bus tour. It would take in some of Ireland's greatest tourist attractions. It seemed a very unusual thing for him to do. He had someone he wanted to show Ireland to and this seemed to be the best way. It was certainly going to be interesting, he told Moira.

Emily said that she was going to see the West of Ireland for the first time. Dingo Duggan was going to drive the van, taking Emily and Declan's parents, Molly and Paddy Carroll, too. They would have a great time.

Simon and Maud were going with friends to North Wales. They were bringing sleeping bags and a sort of makeshift tent. They would take the boat to Holyhead and then might find a hostel, but if not they could sleep anywhere with all their gear. There would be six of them altogether. It would be terrific fun.

Dr Declan Carroll and his wife Fiona from the heart clinic were taking their baby Johnny to a seaside hotel. Fiona said that she was going to sleep until lunchtime both days. They had babyminders there to look after young children. It would be magical.

Dr Hat was going to go fishing with three friends. It was an all-in weekend with no hidden extras. Dr Hat said he was a poor old pensioner now and had to be careful with his money – Moira never knew whether he was joking or not. It certainly wasn't the time to bring out one of those rare smiles.

Most of her colleagues were going away or else they were having parties or doing their gardens.

Moira suddenly felt very much out of it as if she were on the side of things looking on. Why wasn't she going somewhere, like sitting in Dingo's van heading west or going to see some statue in Rossmore or setting out for the lakes in the Midlands with Dr Hat and his mates?

The answer was only too clear.

She had no friends.

She had never needed them in life – the job was too absorbing – and to do it right you needed to be on duty all hours of the day. Friends would find it very tedious to go out to supper with someone who might well have to disappear in the middle of the main course.

But it was lonely and restless to see everyone else with plans for the long weekend.

Moira announced that she was going home to Liscuan. She talked so little about her private life, people assumed that there must be a big family waiting for her.

'That will be nice for you, to go home and meet everyone,' Ania said. 'You will have a great welcome, yes?'

'That's right,' Moira lied.

Ania lived in a world where everyone was good and happy. She was pregnant again and taking things very easily. The doctor had said that she needed bedrest and so she lay at home contemplating a great future with their child. This time it would happen and if lying around in bed would ensure it, then Ania was willing to do it.

Once a week, her husband Carl drove her into the heart clinic so that she could see everyone and keep up to date on what was happening. She was pleased that Moira was going to the country place for the weekend. It might cheer her up ...

Moira looked out of the train as she crossed Ireland towards her home. She had packed her little case and had no idea where she would stay. Perhaps her father and Mrs Kennedy might offer her a bed?

Mrs Kennedy was fairly frosty when Moira telephoned to speak to her father.

'He's having a lie-down. He always takes a siesta from five till six,' she said, as if Moira should somehow have known this.

'I'm in the area,' Moira said. 'I was wondering if I could call in and see him.'

'Would that be before or after supper?' Mrs Kennedy enquired.

Moira drew a deep breath.

'Or even *during* supper?' she suggested.

Mrs Kennedy was more practical than welcoming. 'We have only two lamb chops,' she said.

'Oh, don't mind about me. I'm happy with vegetables,' she said.

'Will you arrange that with your father when he wakes up? We don't know what he would want.'

'Yes, I'll call again at six,' Moira said through her teeth.

She had eased her father's passage to live openly with Mrs Kennedy and this was the thanks she got. Life was certainly unfair.

But then Moira knew that already from her work. Men laid off from work with no warning and poor compensation; women drawn into the drugs business because it was the only way to get a bit of ready money; girls running away from home and refusing to go back because what was there was somehow worse than sleeping under a bridge. Moira had seen babies born and go home from the hospital to totally unsatisfactory set-ups while hundreds of infertile couples ached to adopt them.

Moira sat alone in a café, waiting until her father woke from his siesta. Siesta! There would have been little of that in the old days. Father would come in tired from his work on the farm. Sometimes Mother had cooked a meal – most times not. Moira and Pat used to peel the potatoes so that that much was done anyway. Pat was not considered a reliable farmhand, so Dad would ensure that all the hens had been returned to their coop. He would call out until the sheepdog came home. Then he would pat the dog's head. 'Good man, Shep.' Every dog they had over the years was called Shep.

Only then would he have his supper. Often he had had to get the supper ready – a big pot of potatoes and a couple of slices of ham; the potatoes often eaten straight from the saucepan and the salt spooned from the packet.

Life had changed for the better in her father's case. She should be glad that he had that wordless Mrs Kennedy looking after him and cooking him a lamb chop of an evening.

Why was the woman so unwelcoming? She had no fear of Moira and she should know that. But then she was always stern and forbidding. She seldom smiled.

With a shock she realised that this is what people actually said about *her*. Even Mr Ennis had mentioned recently that Moira was very unsmiling and seemed highly disapproving of things.

When Moira rang back, her father sounded lively and happy. He said he spent a lot of time woodcarving nowadays. He had built on an extra room for his work. He had no news of Pat, but thought he seemed to have fallen on his feet and found a good job.

She took a bus out to Mrs Kennedy's and knocked on the door timidly.

'Oh, Moira.' Mrs Kennedy showed just enough recognition and acknowledgement that she had arrived, but no real pleasure.

'I'm not disturbing you or my father?'

'No, please come in. Your father is freshening himself up for supper.'

That was a personal first, Moira thought to herself. Her poor father used to sit down for whatever meal there might be with muddy boots and a sweaty shirt, ready to spoon out the potatoes to Pat and herself and to her mother, if she ever sat down. Things were very different now.

Moira saw a table set for three. There were folded table napkins and a small vase of flowers. There were gleaming salt cellars and shining glass. It was far from suppers like this that he had spent his former life.

'You have the house very nice.'

Moira looked around her as if she was a housing inspector looking for flaws or damp.

'Glad it passes the test,' Mrs Kennedy said.

Just then her father came out. Moira gasped – he looked ten years younger than the last time she had seen him. He wore a smart jacket and he had a collar and tie.

'You look the real part, Dad,' she said admiringly. 'Are you going out somewhere?'

'I'm having supper in my own home. Isn't that worth dressing up for?' he asked. Then, softening up a little, 'How are you, Moira? It's really good to see you.'

'I'm fine, Dad.'

'And where are you staying?'

So no bed here, Moira thought. She waved it away. 'I'll find somewhere ... don't worry about me.'

As if he worried! If he did, then he would ask his fancy woman to get a bed ready for her.

'That's grand then. Come and sit down.'

'Yes, indeed,' Mrs Kennedy said. 'Have a glass of sherry with your father. I'll serve the meal in about ten minutes.'

'Isn't she great?' Her father looked admiringly at the retreating Mrs Kennedy.

'Great, altogether,' Moira said unenthusiastically.

'Is there anything wrong, Moira?' He looked at her, concerned.

'No. Why? Should there be?'

'You look as if something's wrong.'

Moira exploded. 'God Almighty, Dad, I came across the country to see you. You never write … you never phone … and now you criticise the way I look!'

'I was just concerned for you, in case you'd lost your job or something,' he said.

Moira stared at him. He meant it. She must have looked sad or angry or disapproving – all these things that people said.

'No, it's just it's the long weekend. I came back to see my family. Is that so very unusual? The train was full of people doing just that.'

'I thought it was kind of sad for you: your home gone, sold to other people, Pat all tied up in his romance.'

'Pat has a romance?'

'You haven't seen him yet, then?'

'No, I came straight here. Who is it? What's she like?'

'Remember the O'Learys who run the garage?'

'Yes, but those girls are far too young. They'd only be fourteen or fifteen,' Moira said, shocked.

'It's the mother. It's Mrs O'Leary – Erin O'Leary.'

'And what happened to Mr O'Leary?' Moira couldn't take it in.

'Gone off somewhere, apparently.'

'Merciful hour!' Moira said. It was an expression of her mother's. She hadn't said it in years.

'Well, exactly. You never know what's around the next corner,' her father agreed.

He was in an awkward position, Moira realised. He couldn't really remonstrate with his son Pat for moving in with a married lady. Hadn't he done the very same thing himself?

Mrs Kennedy came in just then to ask, would Moira

like to freshen up before supper? Her father was nodding. Moira decided that she did want to freshen up. She took a clean blouse out of her suitcase and went to the bathroom.

It was an amazing room. The wallpaper had lots of blue mermaids and blue seahorses on it. There were blue and white china ornaments on the windowsill and a blue shell held the soap. A crinoline lady dressed in blue covered the next roll of lavatory paper in case people might know what it was and be affronted. There were blue gingham curtains on the window and a blue-patterned shower curtain.

Moira washed her face and shoulders and under her arms. She put on her clean blouse and returned to the table.

'Lovely bathroom,' she said to Mrs Kennedy.

'We do our best,' Mrs Kennedy said, serving melon slices with a little cherry on top of each.

Then she brought in the main course.

'Remember, vegetables are fine for me,' Moira said.

Her father waved her protest aside. 'I walked into town and got an extra lamb chop,' he said.

Mrs Kennedy looked as if Moira's father had given her a priceless jewel.

Moira showed huge gratitude.

She didn't feel that she could easily discuss Pat's new situation, so she ate her supper mainly in silence. Her father and Mrs Kennedy talked animatedly about this and that – his woodcarving of an owl; about a festival that was going to exhibit some local art. Mrs Kennedy said that of course he should offer some of his work to be put on show. This was also news to Moira.

They spoke about Mrs Kennedy's involvement in a

local women's group. They all felt that farming was finished and that there was no living to be made from the land. A lot of them were training to go into the bed and breakfast business. Mrs Kennedy was thinking she might join in. After all, they had three rooms more or less ready, all they'd need to buy was new beds. That would be six people and they would make a tidy living.

Moira realised that she didn't know Mrs Kennedy's first name.

If she had, she might say suddenly, 'Orla' or 'Janet' – or whatever she was called – 'can I sleep the night in one of those three rooms, please?' But she had never known her name and Dad referred to her as 'herself' and, when he was talking to her, as 'dear' or 'love'. No help there.

When she had finished the meal, Moira stood up and picked up her suitcase.

'Well, that was all lovely, but if I am to find a place to stay, I'd better go now. The bus still goes by at half past the hour, right?'

'Leave it to the next half-hour,' her father said. 'You'll easily get into the Stella Maris. They'll give you a grand room.'

'I was thinking of calling on Pat,' Moira said.

'He won't be there. He'll be up at the garage. Leave him till the morning, I'd say.'

'Right, I'll do that, but I'll go now as I'm standing. Thank you again for the nice meal.'

'You're very welcome,' Mrs Kennedy said.

'It's good to see you, Moira. Don't work too hard up there in Dublin.'

'Do you know what kind of work I do, Dad?'

'Don't you work for the government in an office?'

'That's it, more or less,' Moira said glumly and she set out on the road.

She wanted to go past her old home before the next bus came. She walked down the old familiar lane, a lane that her father must have walked many a time before he had officially left his home to live with Mrs Kennedy. And why would he *not* want to live with her? A bright, clean house where he got a welcome and a warm meal and maybe a bit of a cuddle as well. Wasn't it much better than what he had had at home?

She arrived at her old house. Straightaway she could see that the new owners had given it a coat of paint; they had planted a garden. The stables, byres and outhouses had all been changed, cleaned, modernised, and this was where they made their cheese. They had a successful business and it all centred around the house where Moira had grown up.

She went into the old farmyard and looked around her, bewildered. She must now see the house. If they came out, she would tell them that she had once lived here. She could see through the windows that there was a big fire in the grate and a table with a wine bottle and two glasses on it.

It made her very sad.

Why couldn't her parents have provided a home like this for Pat and herself? Why were there no social workers then who would have taken them away to be placed in better, happier homes?

Her mother and father had not functioned as parents over those years. Her mother, in deep need of help, and her father, struggling ineffectually to cope. Moira and Pat should have grown up in a household where they could have known the language of childhood. A family where, if Pat ran around pretending to be a horse, they would have laughed with him and encouraged him, and not cuffed him around the ears as would have happened in this house.

Moira had never had a doll of her own, not to mention a doll's house. There were no birthday celebrations that she could remember. She could never invite her school friends home and that was where she had learned to be aloof. She had feared friendship and closeness as a child because sooner or later that friend would have expected to be invited to Moira's home and then the chaos would be revealed.

There were tears in her eyes as she saw what the house could have been like when she was young. It could have been a home.

Moira caught the bus to town and booked two nights at the Stella Maris. The room was fine and the cost reasonable, but Moira burned with injustice. She had a father who had a home with spare bedrooms, yet she was forced to pay for bed and breakfast in her own home town.

She would go to see how Pat was faring the next morning. It was ludicrous to think of him with Mrs O'Leary, she was so much older. It was nonsense. Mr O'Leary couldn't have left because of Pat. Pat couldn't call her Erin.

She would find out tomorrow.

Next morning, she went to the garage. Pat was there on the forecourt, filling cars with petrol or diesel. He seemed genuinely pleased to see her.

'Have you got a car at long last, Moira?' he called.

'I have, but it's up in Dublin,' she said.

'Well, we can't fill it up for you from here then.' He laughed amiably.

He was totally suited to this work; easygoing and natural with the customers, good-tempered and cheerful in what some might have found a tedious and repetitive job.

'I came to see *you* actually, Pat. Do you have a break or anything coming up?'

'Sure, I can go any time. I'll just tell Erin.'

Moira followed him towards the pay desk and the new shop that had been built in a once falling-down garage.

'Erin, my sister Moira is here. Okay if I take a break and go and have a coffee with her?'

'Oh, Pat, of course it is. Don't you work all the hours God sends? Go for as long as you like. How are you, Moira? Long time no see.'

Moira looked at her. Erin O'Leary – about ten years older than Moira – a mother of three girls and the wife of Harry, who was a traveller and often travelled rather longer and further than his job required. He had now travelled right out of the country, it was said at the Stella Maris, where Moira had brought up the subject at breakfast.

Erin was wearing a smart yellow shop coat with a navy trim. Her loose, rather floppy hair was tied back neatly with a navy and yellow ribbon. She was slim and fit, and looked much younger than the forty-four or -five she must have been. She looked at Pat with undeniable affection.

'I hear you've been very good to my brother,' Moira said.

'It's mutual, I tell you. I couldn't do half the work I do without him.'

Pat had come back wearing his jacket and heard her say that. He was childishly pleased.

'I'm glad. He was a great brother,' Moira said, trying to put a lot of sincerity into her voice.

In fact, he had been a worry and had given her huge concern over the years – but no point in sharing that with Mrs O'Leary.

'I don't doubt it,' Erin O'Leary said, putting her arm affectionately around Pat's shoulder.

'And is all this a permanent sort of thing?' Moira asked, trying desperately to smile at the same time so that they would realise it was a good-natured, cheery kind of enquiry.

'I certainly hope so,' Erin said. 'I'd be lost without Pat and so would the girls.'

'I'm not going anywhere,' Pat said, proudly.

Would she have encouraged this set-up herself as a social worker? She might have examined Erin O'Leary's circumstances more carefully, checked that her husband would not return and evict Pat Tierney from his home and business. She would always have put the best needs of her client forward, but was there a possibility that, by challenging the living arrangements at Mrs O'Leary's, she might have deprived Pat of the loving home and workplace that he now seemed to have?

They went for coffee to a nearby place where everyone knew Pat. He was his own man with plenty to say.

People asked him about Erin and he told them how she had made a cake with his name on it for his birthday last week and they had all given him a present. And Erin must have told some of the regular customers too, because there wasn't room on the mantelpiece for all his cards.

With a heart like stone, Moira remembered that she had not sent him a card.

She had, she said, been to see their father.

'He seems happy with Mrs Kennedy,' she said, grudgingly.

'Well, why wouldn't he be? Isn't Maureen the best in the world?'

'Maureen?' Moira was at a loss.

'Maureen Kennedy,' he said, as if everyone knew her as that.

'And how did you find out her name?'

'I asked her,' Pat said simply, looking at his watch.

'Are you anxious to be back there?' Moira asked him.

'Well, she's on her own – there's only a young girl in the shop and she's a bit of an eejit with the till.'

Moira looked at him and bit her lip. She hoped that there weren't tears in her eyes. Pat reached over and took her hand.

'I know, Moira, it's hard for you having no one of your own and seeing Dad all settled with Maureen and me with Erin, but it will happen, I'm sure.'

She nodded wordlessly.

'Come back to the garage with me. Come in and talk to Erin.'

'I will.'

Moira paid for their coffee and walked like an automaton back to the garage.

Erin was pleased to see them. 'There was no hurry, Pat. You could have stayed longer.'

'I didn't want to leave you on your own too long.'

'Well there, Moira! Isn't that music to the ears?'

Pat had gone to put on his working gear again.

Moira looked at Erin. 'It's great that he's here with you. He has had so little warmth and affection. He was never in a loving family. You won't ... you wouldn't—'

Erin interrupted her. 'He's found a loving family now and here he will stay. Rest assured of that.'

'Thank you, I will,' Moira said.

'And come back and see us again and when you do, stay in our house, don't be paying fancy prices up in the Stella Maris.'

'How did you know I was there?'

'One of my friends works there. She rang and told me you were asking questions about me. Harry's long gone, Moira. He's not coming back. Pat is staying. He is exactly what we all need. He's cheerful and happy and reliable and always there. I didn't have that before and for me it's lovely too.'

Moira gave her an awkward hug and went back to the Stella Maris.

'I wonder if it will be an inconvenience if I cancel tonight's booking? I find I have to go back to Dublin on the afternoon train.'

'No problem, Ms Tierney, I'll just prepare your bill for one night. Will you be coming back to us again?'

Moira remembered that Erin had a friend here who reported things.

'Well, I may stay with Erin O'Leary next time. She very kindly invited me. I was so pleased.'

'Very nice,' the receptionist said. 'Always nice to stay in a family home ...'

*

Moira looked out the window at the rain-drenched countryside. Cows standing wet and bewildered, horses sheltering under trees, sheep oblivious to the weather, farmers in raingear going along narrow lanes.

Most people on the train were going to Dublin for some outing or activity. Or else they were going back to a family. Moira was going home to an empty flat halfway through the long weekend. She could not bear to stay in the place where her brother and her father had found such happiness and where she had found nothing but resentment and sadness.

It was still early enough to go somewhere. But where? She was hungry, but she didn't feel like going to a café or a restaurant on her own. She went into a shop to buy a bar of chocolate.

'Gorgeous day, isn't it? The rain's gone,' said a woman about her own age behind the counter.

'Yes, it is,' Moira said, surprised she hadn't noticed that the weather had improved.

'I've only another hour here and then I'm off,' the shop assistant confided. She had stringy hair and a big smile.

'And where will you go to?' Moira asked.

She wasn't being polite, she was interested. Possibly this woman, like everyone else in the universe, had a huge, loving family dying for her shift to finish.

'I'll go out to the sea by train,' she said. 'Don't know where yet, but maybe Blackrock, Dun Laoghaire, Dalkey or even Bray. Anywhere I can walk beside the sea, have a bag of chips and an ice cream. Maybe I'll have a swim, maybe I'll meet a fellow. But I wouldn't be standing indoors here all day with the sun shining outside and everyone else free as a bird.'

'And you'd do all this by yourself?' Moira was curious.

'Isn't that the best part? No one else to please, and all my options open.'

Moira walked out thoughtfully. She had never taken the train out to the seaside. Not in all her years in Dublin. If work had brought her that way, she would go. Not otherwise. She didn't know that people *did* that – just went out to the sea, like children in storybooks.

That's what she would do now. She would walk on beside the River Liffey until she caught the little train south. She would sit beside the sea, go for a paddle maybe. It would calm her, soothe her. Oh yes, there would certainly be crowds of people playing at Happy Families or being In Love with each other, but maybe Moira would be like the woman in the shop who was aching to have the sunshine on her shoulders and arms and watch the sea lapping gently towards the shore.

That's what she would do. She would spend some of the long weekend by the sea.

Of course it wasn't magic.

And it didn't really work.

Moira did not become calm and mellow. The sun did shine on her arms and shoulders but there was a breeze coming in from the sea at the same time and it felt too chilly. There were too many people who had decided their families must go to the seaside.

Moira studied them.

In her whole childhood she never remembered once being brought to the seaside and yet it seemed that every child in Dublin had a God-given right to go to the seashore as soon as the sun came out. Her sense of resentment was enormous and she frowned with concentration as she sat silently amid all the families who were calling out to each other on the beach.

To her surprise, a big man with a red face and an open-necked, red shirt stopped beside her.

'Moira Tierney as I live and breathe!'

She hadn't an idea who he was.

'Um, hello,' she said cautiously.

He sat down beside her.

'God, isn't this beautiful to be out in the open air? We're blessed to live in a capital city that's so near the sea,' he said.

She still looked at him confused.

'I'm Brian Flynn. We met when Stella was in hospital and then again at the funeral and the christening.'

'Oh, *Father* Flynn. Yes, of course I remember. I just didn't recognise you in the ... I mean without the ...'

'A Roman collar wouldn't be very suitable for this weather.'

Brian Flynn was cheerful and dismissive. He was a man who rarely wore clerical garb at all, except when officiating at a ceremony.

'Did your parents take you to the sea when you were a child?' Moira asked him, unexpectedly.

'My father died when we were young, but my mother brought us for a week to the seaside every summer. We stayed in a guest house called St Anthony's and we all had a bucket and spade. Yes, it was nice,' he said.

'You were lucky,' Moira said glumly.

'You didn't get to the sea when you were young?'

'No. We never got anywhere. We should never have been left in our home. We should have been placed somewhere ... anywhere, really.'

Brian Flynn saw where the conversation was leading. This woman seemed to have an obsession about taking children away from parents and into care. Or that's what Noel said, in any case. Noel was terrified of Moira and Katie said that Lisa felt just the same way.

'Well, I suppose things have changed a bit ... moved on,' Brian Flynn said vaguely.

He began to wish that he hadn't approached Moira but she had looked so lonely and out of place in her jacket and skirt, right in the middle of all the seaside people.

'Do you ever feel your work is hopeless, Father?'

'I wish you'd call me Brian. No, I don't feel it's hopeless. I think we get things wrong from time to time. I mean, the Church does. It doesn't adapt properly. And I get things wrong myself, quite apart from the Church. I keep battering away to get people a Catholic wedding and, just when I succeed, it turns out that they got tired of waiting and got the job done in a Register Office and I'm left like a fool. But, to answer your question, no, I don't think it's all hopeless. I think we do *something* to help and I certainly see a lot that inspires me. I expect you do too?'

He ended on a rising note, but if he was expecting some reciprocal statement of job satisfaction he was wrong.

'I don't think I do, Father Flynn, truly I don't. I have a caseload of unhappy people, most of them blaming their unhappiness on me.'

'I'm sure that's not true.'

Brian Flynn wished himself a million miles from here.

'It *is* true, Father. I got a woman into exactly the kind of facility she was looking for – a place with vegetarian cookery and, if you'll excuse the expression, with religion seeping from the walls. It's coming down with saintliness and she's still not happy.'

'I expect she's old and frightened,' Brian Flynn said.

'Yes, but she's only one of them. I have a very nice old man called Gerald. I kept him *out* of a home and stopped a lot of nonsense with his children, built up all the support systems for him, but now he says he's lonely all day. He'd like to go to a place where they play indoor bowls.'

'He's probably old and frightened too,' Brian Flynn suggested.

'But what about the ones who are *not* old? They don't want any help either. I have a thirteen-year-old girl who slept rough. I got her back to her family. There was a row over something – black lipstick and black nail polish, I think. Anyway, she's gone again. The Guards are looking for her. It needn't have got this far. All that talking, sitting under a bridge way into the night, and it meant nothing.'

'You never know—' Brian Flynn began again.

'Oh, but I *do* know. And I know how there's an army of people lined up against me over that unfortunate child who is being raised by an alcoholic …'

Brian Flynn's voice was a lot more steely now.

'Noel adds up to much more than being just an alcoholic, Moira. He has turned his life around to make a home for that child.'

'And that child will thank us all later for leaving her with a drunken, resentful father?'

'He loves his daughter very much. He's *not* a drunk. He's given it up.' Brian Flynn was fiercely loyal.

'Are you telling me, hand on heart, that Noel never

strayed, never went back on the drink since he got Frankie?'

Brian Flynn couldn't lie.

'It was only the once and it didn't last long,' he said.

Immediately he realised that Moira hadn't known. He saw that in her face. As usual he had managed to make things worse. In future he would walk about with a paper bag over his head and slits cut for his eyes. He would talk to nobody. Ever again.

'I hope you don't think I'm rude, Moira, but I have to ... um ... meet someone ... um ... further along here ...'

'No, of course.'

Moira realised that there was less warmth in his face now. But then that was often the case in her conversations.

Father Flynn had moved on. She felt conspicuous on this beach. It wasn't her place. Slowly Moira gathered her things together and headed towards the station where a little train would take her back into the city.

Most people liked the train journey. Moira didn't even see the view from the window. She thought instead of how she had been duped. They had even told that priest, who had nothing to do with the set-up. But they hadn't seen fit to tell the social worker assigned to the case.

Moira could not call to Chestnut Court armed with her new information since she knew that Noel and his parents had taken the baby off to some small town that she had never heard of – a place with a magic statue apparently. Or, to put it another way, Charles and Josie would be investigating the statue. Noel could well have the child in some pub by now.

She would deal with Emily when she came back from her sojourn in the West with Dingo Duggan, with Lisa when she and Anton came back from London, and eventually she would deal with Noel, who had lied to her. There were so many places where she could put Frankie Lynch, where the child would grow up safely with love all around her. Look at that couple – Clara Casey's daughter Linda and her husband Nick, who was the son of Hilary in the heart clinic – they were just aching for a baby girl. Think of the stability of a home like that: two grandmothers to idolise the child, a big, extended family and a comfortable home.

Moira sighed. If only there had been a magical social worker who could have placed Pat and herself in a home like that. A place where they would have been loved, where there would have been children's books on a shelf, maybe a story read to them at night, people who would be interested in a child's homework, who would take her to the seaside on a hot day with a bucket and spade to make sandcastles.

Coming fresh as she had from visiting the wreckage that was her own childhood, Moira was now determined that she would ease Frankie Lynch's path into a secure home.

It would be the only thing that might make any sense of Moira's own loss, if she could make it right for someone else. All she had to do was to get through this endless weekend until all the cast eventually came back from their travels and reassembled and she could get things going.

Lisa was actually back in Dublin even though Moira didn't know it. There had been some crossed wires in

London. Lisa had thought that it was a matter of visiting restaurants and talking to various patrons. April had thought it was a PR exercise and had arranged several interviews for Anton.

'They don't have a bank holiday in England this weekend, so it will be work as usual,' April had chirruped to them.

'Not much work at a weekend, though.' Lisa had tried hard to be casual.

'No, but Monday is an ordinary day in London and we can rehearse on Sunday.'

April's face was glowing with achievement and success. It would have been churlish and petty for Lisa not to enthuse. So she had appeared delighted with it all; she decided to get out with her pride intact.

She had loads to see to back in Dublin, she said casually, and saw, to her pleasure, that Anton seemed genuinely sorry to see her go. And now she was back in Dublin with nothing to do and nobody to meet.

As she let herself into Chestnut Court, she thought she saw Moira in the courtyard talking to some of the neighbours. But it couldn't be. Noel and the baby were off in this place Rossmore; Moira, herself, was meant to have gone to the country to see her family. Lisa decided she was imagining things.

But she looked over the wall on the corridor leading to their apartment and saw that it was indeed Moira. She couldn't hear the conversation, but she didn't like the look of it. Moira knew nobody in this apartment block except them. She was here to spy.

Lisa went out again and crossed the courtyard.

'Well, *hello*, Moira,' she said, showing great surprise. The two middle-aged women that Moira had been interrogating shuffled with embarrassment. Lisa knew them both by sight. She nodded at them briefly.

'Oh, Lisa … I thought you were away?'

'Well, yes, I was,' Lisa agreed, 'but I came back. And you? You were going away too?'

'I came back too,' Moira said. 'And did Noel and Frankie come back as well?'

'I don't think so. I haven't been into the apartment yet. Why don't you come in and see with me?'

The women neighbours were busy making their excuses and looking to escape.

'No, no, it wouldn't be appropriate,' Moira said. 'You've only just got back from London.'

'Moira is our social worker,' Lisa explained to the fast-retreating neighbours. 'She's absolutely great. She drops in at the least expected times in case Noel and I are battering Frankie to death or starving her in a cage or something. So far she hasn't caught us out in anything, but of course time will tell.'

'You completely misunderstand my role, Lisa. I am there for Frankie.'

'We're all bloody there for Frankie,' Lisa said, 'which is something you'd realise if you saw us walking her up and down at night when she can't sleep. If you saw us changing her nappy, or trying to spoon food into her when she keeps turning her head away.'

'Exactly,' Moira cried. 'It's too hard for you both. It's my role to see whether she would be better placed with a more conventional family … people with the maturity to look after a child.'

'But she's Noel's daughter!' Lisa said, unaware that the other women who had been about to leave were standing looking, open-mouthed. 'I thought you people were all meant to be keeping the family together and that sort of thing.'

'Yes, but you are not family, Lisa. You're just a roommate and Noel, as a father, is unreliable. We have to admit that.'

'I do *not* have to admit that!'

Lisa knew she looked like a fishwife with her hands on her hips, but really this was too much. She began to list all that Noel had done and was doing.

Moira cut across her like a knife.

'Can we move somewhere that we can have more privacy, please?'

She glared at the two neighbours she had been interrogating earlier, who were still hovering at the corner, and they vanished quickly.

'I don't want any more time with you,' Lisa said. She knew she sounded pettish but she didn't care.

Moira was calm but furious at the same time.

'In all this hymn of praise about Noel,' she said, 'you managed to forget that he went off the rails and was back on the drink. That was a situation where the baby was at risk and not one of you alerted me.'

'It was over before it began,' Lisa said. 'No point in alerting you and starting World War Three!'

Moira looked at her steadily for a moment. 'We are all on the same side,' she said eventually.

'No, we're not,' Lisa said. 'You want to take Frankie away. We want to keep her. How's that the same side?'

'We all want what is *best* for her.' Moira spoke as if to a slow learner.

'It's best for all of us if she stays with Noel, Moira.' Lisa sounded weary suddenly. 'She keeps him off the drink and keeps his head down at his studies so that he'll be a good, educated father for her when the time comes for her to know such things. And she keeps me sane too. I have a lot of worries and considerations in my life, but minding Frankie sort of grounds me. It gives it all some purpose, if you know what I mean.'

Moira sighed.

'I *do* know what you mean. You see, in a way, she does exactly the same for me. Minding Frankie is important to *me* too. I never had a chance as a child. I want her to have a start of some kind, not to get bogged down by a confused childhood like I did.'

Lisa was stunned. Moira had never admitted anything personal before.

'Don't talk to me about childhood! I bet mine could leave yours in the ha'penny place!' Lisa said in a chirpy voice.

'You don't feel like having supper tonight, do you? It's just that I'm a bit beaten. I was down in my old home and it was all a bit upsetting and there seems to be nobody in town ...'

Lisa ignored the gracelessness of the invitation. She didn't want to go back to the flat alone. There was nothing in – well, there might be a tin of something in the kitchen cupboard or a pack of pasta in sauce in the freezer. But it would be lonely. It might be better to hear what Moira had to say, but would it only be more of the same?

'Will we agree that Frankie is not on the agenda?' Lisa asked.

'Frankie who?' Moira said, with a strange kind of lopsided look on her face.

Lisa realised that it was meant to be a smile.

*

They chose to go to Ennio's trattoria. It was a family restaurant: Ennio himself cooked and greeted; his son waited on the table. Ennio had lived in Dublin for rather more than twenty years and was married to an Irish woman; he knew that to have an Italian accent added to the atmosphere.

Anton, on the other hand, had said to Lisa that Ennio was a fool of the first water and that he would never get anywhere. He never advertised, you never saw celebrities going in and out, he never got any reviews or press attention. It seemed like an act of independence to go there.

Moira had often passed the place and wondered who would pay seven euros for a spaghetti bolognese when you could make it at home for three or four euros. For her it was an act of defiance to choose Ennio's, defying her natural thrift and caution.

Ennio welcomed them with a delight that made it appear as if he had been waiting for their visit for weeks. He gave them huge red and white napkins, a drink on the house and the news that the cannelloni was like the food of angels – they would love it with an almighty love. When he opened his restaurant, his simple, fresh food had proved instantly popular. Ever since then, word of mouth had kept the place full to bursting almost every night.

Lisa thought to herself that Anton might be wrong about Ennio. The place was almost full already, everyone was happy. No client was attracted here by style or decor or lighting – nor, indeed, publicity interviews. Maybe Ennio was far from being a fool.

Moira was beginning to realise why people actually paid seven euros for a plate of pasta. They were paying for a bright, checked tablecloth, a warm welcome and the feeling of ease and relaxation. She could have put together a cannelloni dish, but it wouldn't be the same as this if eaten in her small, empty flat. It would not be the food of angels.

She started to unwind for the first time for a long time and raised her glass.

'Here's to us,' she said. 'We may have had a bad start but, boy, we're survivors!'

'Here's to surviving,' Lisa said. 'Can I begin?'

'Let's order his cannelloni first and then you can begin,' Moira agreed.

Moira was a good listener. Lisa had to hand her that. Moira listened well and remembered what you said and went back and asked relevant questions – like how old was Lisa when she realised that her parents disliked each other, and irrelevant questions – like did they ever take the girls to the seaside? She was sympathetic when she needed to be, shocked at the right times, curious about *why* Lisa's mother stayed in such a loveless home. She asked about Lisa's friends and seemed to understand exactly why she never had any.

How could anyone bring a friend home to a house like that?

And Lisa told her about working as a graphic designer for Kevin and how she met Anton and everything had changed. She had left the safe harbour of Kevin's office and set up on her own. No, she didn't really have any other clients, but Anton had needed her to give him that boost and he always said he would be lost without her. Even this time in London, this very morning, he had begged her not to leave, not to abandon him to April.

'Oh, April,' Moira said, breezily, recalling her first

lunch with Clara at Quentins. 'A very *vapid* sort of person.'

'*Vapid!*' Lisa seized on the word with delight. 'That's exactly what she is! Vapid!' She said it again with pleasure.

Moira gently moved the conversation away, towards Noel, in fact.

'And wasn't it great that you found somewhere to stay so easily?' she hinted.

'Oh yes, if it hadn't been for Noel, I don't know what I would have done that night, the night when I realised my father, my own father, in our own house ...'

She paused, upset at the memory.

'But Noel welcomed you?' Moira continued.

'Well, I suppose "welcomed" might be putting it a bit strongly ... but he gave me a place to stay, which, considering I hardly knew him, was very generous of him, and then we worked out with Emily that it might be best if I could stay, it would share the whole business of looking after Frankie and I could have a place to stay for free.'

'Free? You mean, Noel has to pay for you as well as all his other expenses?'

Moira's eyes were beginning to glint. More and more information was coming her way without her even having to ask for it.

Lisa seemed to recognise that she had spoken too freely.

'Well, not exactly *free*. I mean, we each contribute to the food. We have our own phones and we share the work with the baby.'

'But he could have let that room to a real tenant for real money.'

'I doubt it,' Lisa said, with spirit. 'You wouldn't get anyone paying real money to live in a house with a baby. Believe me, Moira, it's like "Macbeth shall sleep no more". It can be total bedlam at three in the morning with the two of us trying to soothe her down.'

Moira just nodded sympathetically. She was getting more and more ammunition by the second.

But, oddly, it did not delight her as much as she had once thought it would. In a twisted way, she would prefer if these two awkward, lonely people – Lisa and Noel – should find happiness to beat their demons through this child. If it were Hollywood, they would also find great happiness in each other.

Lisa knew nothing of her thoughts.

'Now you,' she said to Moira. 'Tell me what was so terrible.'

So Moira began. Every detail from the early days when she came home from school and there was nothing to eat, to her tired father coming in later and finding only a few potatoes peeled. She told it all without self-pity or complaint. Moira, who had kept her private life so very, very private for years, was able to speak to this girl because Lisa was even more damaged than she was.

She told the story right up to the present when she had left Liscuan and come back to Dublin because the sight of her father and brother having made something of the shambles of their lives was too much to bear.

Lisa listened and wished that someone – anyone – had ever said to Moira that there was a way of dealing with all this, that she should be glad for other people instead of appearing to triumph over their downfall. She might have to pretend at first, but soon it would become natural. Lisa had managed to make herself glad that Katie had a happy marriage and a successful career. She was pleased that Kevin's agency was doing well. Of course, when people were enemies, as her father was, and April was, then it would be superhuman to wish them well ...

As Lisa's mind began to drift, she realised that the woman at the next table was beginning to choke seriously. A piece of food had become lodged in her throat; the young waiter stared, goggle-eyed, as she changed from scarlet to white.

'What is it, Marco?' asked the young blonde waitress – was that Maud Mitchell? What was she doing working here, Lisa wondered – who then, taking in the situation at a glance, called over her shoulder, 'Simon, we need you here *now*!'

Immediately her brother arrived, and he too was dressed in a waiter's uniform.

'She's getting no air in—' Maud said.

'It's a Heimlich—' Simon agreed.

'Can you get her to cough once more?' asked Maud, in total control.

'She's trying to cough, something's stuck there ...' The woman's daughter was nearly hysterical at this point.

'Madam, I'm going to ask you to stand up now and then my brother is going to squeeze you very hard. Please stay calm, it's a perfectly normal manoeuvre,' said Maud in a voice both firm and reassuring.

'We've been trained to do this,' Simon confirmed.

Standing behind the woman and putting his arms around the diner's diaphragm, he pushed hard inwards and upwards. The first time there was no response but the second time he squeezed her abdomen, a small piece of biscuit shot out of her mouth.

Instantly she was breathing again. Tears of gratitude followed, then sips of water and a demand to know the names of the young people who had saved her life.

Lisa had been sitting mesmerised by the entire scene and suddenly realised she hadn't been listening to a word Moira had been saying for the last few minutes; though the entire episode had happened so quickly it looked as though few other people had noticed anything amiss. Really, those twins were something else. Out of the corner of her eye, she saw the waiter they'd called Marco shake Simon enthusiastically by the hand and then give Maud a hug that looked more than just grateful ...

Lisa and Moira divided the bill and began to leave, well pleased with their evening.

Ennio, in his carefully maintained broken English, wished them goodbye.

'Eet is always so good to meet the good friends who 'ave a happy dinner together,' he said cheerfully, as he escorted them to the door.

They were not good friends but he didn't know this. If they had been real friends, they would not have gone home with such unfinished business between them. Instead they had just touched on the levels of each other's loneliness but had made no effort each to find an escape route for the other or a bridge between them for the future. It was one night made less bleak by a series of circumstances and the warmth of Ennio's welcome, but it was no more than that.

It would have saddened him as he locked the doors after them: they had been the last to leave. Ennio was a cheerful man. He would have much preferred to think he had been serving a pair of very good friends.

CHAPTER TEN

Emily had a wonderful weekend in the West with Paddy and Molly Carroll. Dingo Duggan had been an enthusiastic, if somewhat adventurous, driver. He seemed entirely unable and unwilling to read a map and waved away Emily's attempts to find roads with numbers on them.

'Nobody could understand those numbers, Emily,' he had said firmly. 'They'd do your head in. The main thing is to point west and head for the ocean.'

And they did indeed see beautiful places like the Sky Road, and they drove through hills where big mountain goats came down and looked hopefully at the car and its occupants as if they were new playmates come to entertain them. They spent evenings in pubs singing songs and they all said it had been one of the best outings they had ever taken.

Emily had told them about her plans to go to America for Betsy's wedding. The Carrolls were ecstatic; a late marriage, a chance for Emily to dress up and be part of the ceremony, two kindred souls finding each other.

Dingo Duggan was less sure. 'At her age it might all be too much for her,' he said helpfully.

Emily steered the conversation into safer channels.

'How exactly did you get your name, Dingo?' she enquired.

'Oh, it was that time I went to Australia to earn my fortune,' Dingo said simply, as if it should have been evident to everyone and he wasn't asked by one and all.

Dingo's fortune, if represented by the very battered van he drove, did not seem to have been considerable, but Emily Lynch always saw the positive side of things.

'And was it a great experience?' she asked.

'It was really. It was ten years ago and I often look back on it and think about all I saw: kangaroos and emus and wombats and gorgeous birds. I mean, *real* birds with gorgeous feathers looking as if they had all escaped from a zoo, flying round the place picking at things. You never saw such a sight.'

He was settled happily, remembering it all with a beatific smile.

'How long did you stay there?'

Emily was curious about the life he must have led thousands of miles away.

'Seven weeks,' Dingo sighed with pleasure. 'Seven beautiful weeks and I talked a lot about it, you see, when I got back, so they gave me the nickname "Dingo". It's a kind of wild dog out there, you see ...'

'I see.' Emily was stunned at the briefness of his visit. 'And, er ... why did you come back?'

'Oh, I had spent all my money by then and couldn't get a job ... too many Irish illegals out there snapping them all up. So I thought, head for home.'

Emily had little time to speculate about Dingo's mindset and how he seriously thought he was an expert on all things Australian after a visit of less than two months, ten years ago. She had a lot of emailing to cope with to and from New York.

*

Betsy was having pre-wedding nerves. She hadn't liked Eric's mother, she was disappointed with the grey silk outfit she had bought, her shoes were too tight, her brother was being tight-fisted about the arrangements. She needed Emily badly.

Could Emily please come a few days earlier or there might well be no wedding for her to attend?

Emily soothed her by email, but also examined the possibility of getting an earlier flight. Noel helped her sort through the claims and offers of airlines and they found one.

'I don't know why I am helping you to go back to America,' Noel grumbled. 'We're all going to miss you like mad, Emily. Lisa and I have been working out a schedule for Frankie and it's looking like a nightmare.'

'You should involve Dr Hat more,' Emily said unexpectedly.

'I can't ask him.'

'Frankie likes Dr Hat. He's marvellous with her.'

'Do I tell Moira?' Noel was fearful.

'Most certainly.'

Emily was already busy emailing the good news to her friend Betsy; she would be there in three days' time, she would sort out the dull grey dress, the tight shoes, the cheese-paring brother, Eric's difficult mother. All would be well.

'Moira will be worse than ever when you're gone,' Noel said, full of foreboding.

'Just take Frankie in to Hat in the afternoons. He plays chess with a man in Boston – some student, I gather. Hat gets great fun out of it. He even asked me if I could go and visit him when I was in the States and give the lad a chess set, but I told him that I'd never have time to get all that way in such a short time.'

'Hat playing chess online! How did he ever learn how to use the computer?'

'I taught him,' Emily said, simply. 'He taught me chess in exchange.'

'I don't know the half of what's going on round here,' Noel said.

'Don't be afraid of Moira. She's not the enemy, you know.'

'She's so suspicious, Emily. When she comes into the flat she shakes a cushion suddenly in case she might find a bottle of whiskey hidden behind it and looks in the bread bin for no reason, just hoping to unearth a half-bottle of gin.'

'I'll be back, Noel, and Frankie will have grown, so she'll need a couple of new dresses from New York. Just you wait until she's old enough for me to teach her painting. We can start booking the galleries for twenty years ahead because she'll be exhibiting all over the world.'

'She might too.'

Noel's face lit up at the thought of his daughter being a famous artist. Maybe he'd take his art-supplies box out of the closet. He had made sure before he moved that there were no bottles hidden in it. He hadn't had time recently to draw but wouldn't it be a good influence on Frankie if he started again?

'If she wants it enough it will happen.'

Emily nodded as if this was a certainty.

'What about you? What did you want for yourself, Emily?'

'I wanted to teach art and I got that and then eventually, when they thought I wasn't modern enough for them, I wanted to travel and I've started that. I like it very much.'

'I hope you won't want to move on again from here,' Noel said.

'I'll wait until Frankie's raised and you've found yourself a nice wife.' She smiled at him.

'I'll hold you to that,' Noel said.

He was very pleased. Emily didn't make promises lightly, but if she had to wait for him to find a nice wife … Emily might well be here for ever if she were waiting for that!

They would all miss Emily. Down at the charity shop there was already confusion. Molly said that Emily would be able to judge someone's size and taste the moment that they walked in the door. Remember that beautiful heather suit that Moira had bought and pretended she hadn't? People whose window boxes she had planted and tended were beginning to panic that their flowers would wilt during Emily's three-week absence.

Charles Lynch was wondering how he could keep his dog-walking business in credit. Emily was always finding him new clients and remembering to segregate dogs of different sexes in case they might do something to annoy their owners greatly. Emily did his books for him so that nobody from the income tax could say that he was anything other than meticulous.

At the doctors' practice they would miss her too. Nobody seemed to know exactly where to find this document or that. Emily was a reassuring presence. Everyone who worked there had her mobile number, but they had been told that she couldn't be called for three weeks. As Declan Carroll said, it was unnerving, just like going out on a high diving board, facing all this time without Emily.

Who else would know all the things that Emily knew? The best bus route to the hospital, the address of the chiropodist that all the patients liked, the name of the pastoral-care adviser in St Brigid's?

'Perhaps you could get all this wedding business over within a week?' Declan suggested.

'Dream on, Declan. I don't want to "get it over with". I'm longing for it. I want it to go on for at least two months! My very best friend is getting married to a man who has adored her for years! I have to sort out shoes that turned out to be too tight, brothers, mothers-in-law, a dress that turned out to be dull. I can't be dealing with you, Declan, and where you put your dry-cleaning docket ...'

'I suppose we'll have to muddle through without you,' Declan grumbled. 'But don't stay away too long.'

Lisa was just the same. 'We can't phone you if Frankie starts to cough.'

'Well, you don't normally,' Emily said, mildly.

'No, but we *feel* that we could,' Lisa confessed. 'Listen, while I have you, Emily, I may have slightly ballsed things up with Moira. We had a meal together and I sort of said or let drop that it was fairly exhausting cleaning Frankie, feeding her, burping her and taking her from place to place. I meant it to be a compliment to Noel, you know, and how well we are managing things, but it came out sounding like a whine or a moan, and of course Moira picked up on it and wondered, were we capable of minding Frankie and all that, which was the *last* thing ...'

'Don't worry about it,' Emily advised. 'I'll have a talk with Moira.'

'I wish you'd stay and have a talk with her every day,' Lisa grumbled.

'You can always email me, but for the Lord's sake, don't tell everyone else.'

'Just about Frankie,' Lisa promised.

'That's a deal then – just about Frankie,' said Emily, knowing that no law was so strict that it couldn't be bent for an emergency.

Eventually Emily got away.

She could hardly imagine that it was just a matter of months since she had arrived here knowing nobody and now she seemed to be making seismic gaps in their lives by leaving for three weeks. It was amazing how much she had been absorbed into this small community.

She hoped she wasn't going to speak with an Irish brogue when she got back to the US. She hoped too that she wouldn't use any Irishisms like saying, 'Jaysus!' like they did in Dublin with no apparent blasphemy or disrespect. It had startled her at first, but then it had become second nature.

As she got nearer to New York she became excited at all that lay ahead. She tried to force the Irish cast of characters away from the main stage of her mind. She had to concentrate on Eric's mother and Betsy's brother, but images kept coming back to her.

Noel and Lisa in Chestnut Court soothing the baby as they did their preparation for a college degree that might or might not be any help to either of them.

Josie and Charles kneeling down saying the Rosary in their kitchen, remembering to add three Hail Marys for St Jarlath and a reminder that the statue campaign was going well.

Dr Hat playing chess with the boy in Boston who had something wrong with his foot and was off school for a week.

Molly in the thrift shop, wondering how much to charge for a pleated linen skirt that had never been worn.

Paddy Carroll bringing round big, wrapped parcels that contained juicy bones for the dogs that passed through.

Aidan and Signora singing Italian songs to three children: their own grandchild, as well as Frankie and little Johnny Carroll.

She thought about Muttie, wheezing happily to his dog Hooves or solving the world's problems with his Associates.

She thought about the decent priest, Father Brian Flynn, and how he tried to hide his true feelings about the statue of a sixth-century saint being erected in a Dublin working-class street.

There were so many images that Emily dropped off to sleep thinking about them all. And there she was in J.F.K. and, after collecting her luggage and clearing customs, Emily could see Eric and Betsy jumping up and down with excitement. They even had a banner. In uneven writing it said: 'Welcome Home Emily!'

How very odd that it didn't seem like home any more.

But home or not, it was wonderful.

Emily talked to Eric's mother in a woman-of-the-world manner. She managed to convey the impression that

Eric was very near his sell-by date and that he was very, *very* lucky that Betsy had been persuaded to consider him.

Betsy had, apparently, written over to Ireland that there were some 'obstacles' in the way of the marriage. Emily couldn't think what they might be. She looked Eric's mother in the eye and asked if *she* knew of any. Betsy's future mother-in-law, who was just a bit of a fusspot, started to babble a bit. Emily felt the point had been made. Betsy needed huge enthusiasm and support for her big day, otherwise she might pull out at the last moment and poor Eric would be left bereft.

Emily sorted the shoes simply by insisting Betsy bought a pair in the correct size; she sorted the dull dress problem by taking the very plain grey dress to an accessories store and asking everyone's advice. Together, they chose a rose-pink and cream-coloured stole, which transformed it.

She went to Betsy's brother and explained that since Betsy had waited this long to get married, it had better be a classy celebration; this way she managed to upgrade the menu considerably and arranged sparkling wine.

And, of course, the wedding was splendid. Emily was pleased to see her friend in comfortable shoes wearing a newly adorned dress. Betsy's brother had put on a very elegant spread and her mother-in-law had been like charm personified.

Betsy cried with happiness; Eric cried and said that this was the best day of his whole life; Emily cried because it was all so marvellous; and the best man cried because his own marriage was on the rocks and he envied people just starting out.

When all the relations had gone home and the best man had gone to make one more ineffectual stab at repairing his own marriage, the bride and groom set off with the maid of honour for Chinatown and had a feast. There would be no honeymoon yet, but a holiday in Ireland would certainly be on the cards before the end of the year.

Emily told them about some of the people they would meet. Eric and Betsy said they could hardly wait. It all sounded so intriguing. They wanted to go right out to Kennedy Airport and fly to Ireland at once.

To: *Emily*
From: *Lisa*

I know we agreed only to email about Frankie and there's no crisis – I just felt like talking to you. She is very well and sleeping much better.

Moira didn't seem to pick up on what I had said about Frankie being a lot of work, so with any luck that's all been forgotten.

Frankie seems to enjoy going to Dr Hat. He sings little sea shanties to her. He got her some jars of apple purée and spoons them into her all the time – she can't get enough of them!

Maud and Marco from Ennio's restaurant are a definite number, they've been seen at the cinema together. Nice for Maud because things are sad in that house, but I think Simon is feeling a bit left out.

Noel went out on a date last week. I set him up with a friend of Katie's called Sophie, but it just didn't take. When he told her about Frankie she asked, 'And when do you give her back to her mother?' Noel told her that Stella was dead and suddenly this girl Sophie wanted to be miles away. A man with a child! Beware! Beware!

Poor Muttie looks awful. Declan doesn't say anything, but I think it's not sounding too good.

Life is very good otherwise.

Everything going well. Anton's picture was in the paper today and April has blotted her copybook, I am delighted to say.

How was the wedding?

Love,

Lisa

Betsy and Eric asked a lot of questions and Emily explained people briefly. Moira was considered the enemy and April was considered a love rival of Lisa's; the twins were teenagers in the catering business, Muttie was their grandfather or uncle or guardian, no one quite knew. And Anton? The non-available object of Lisa's adoration ...

To: *Lisa*

From: *Emily*

Thanks for the news. The wedding was fabulous – will show you pictures.

What did April do? How did she blot her copybook?

Love,

Emily

To: *Emily*

From: *Lisa*

April told everyone that a group of food critics were coming to Anton's on Tuesday last and amazingly they never turned up: someone had told them it had been cancelled. Anton was so furious with her. He and I had a dinner together in the restaurant to cheer him up ...

Eric and Betsy, by now an established married couple, saw Emily off at the airport. They waved long after she had disappeared in the crush of people heading into Terminal 4. They would miss her, but they knew that soon she would be sitting on that Aer Lingus flight, resetting her mind and orienting herself towards Dublin again.

It sounded an insane place and it had certainly changed Emily. Normally so reserved and quiet, she seemed to have been entirely seduced by a cast of characters who sounded as if they should be on an off-Broadway variety show ...

Emily didn't sleep as so many of the other passengers did. She sat making comparisons between this journey and the one she had made across the Atlantic coming to Ireland for the very first visit.

That time she had been looking for roots, trying to work out what kind of life her father had lived back then in Dublin and how it had shaped him. She had learned next to nothing of this side of life but had become deeply involved in a series of dramas, ranging from helping to raise a motherless child who was living with a functioning alcoholic, to working in a thrift shop, trying to help her aunt raise money to build a statue to an unknown saint who, if he had ever existed, had died back in the sixth century, and organising a dog-walking roster for her uncle.

It seemed quite mad and yet she considered she was going home.

It was early morning in Dublin when the transatlantic flights came in and the crowds stood around the luggage carousels. Emily reached for her smart new suitcases – a gift from Eric to thank her for being maid of honour.

As they moved out through customs, she thought it would be nice if someone had come to meet her but then who would have been able to?

Josie and Charles didn't have a car. Neither did Noel and Lisa. Dingo Duggan, with his van, would have been nice, but was hardly likely. She would get the bus as before. Except this time she would know what she was going into.

Just as she came out into the open air, she saw a familiar figure; Dr Hat was standing there waving at her.

'I thought I'd come and meet you,' he said, taking one of her cases.

In the midst of all the crowds of people embracing each other, Emily was thrilled to see him.

'I'm in the short-stay car park,' he said proudly and led the way. He must have got up very early to be there in time.

'It's so good to see you, Hat,' she said as she settled into his small car.

'I brought you a flask of coffee and an egg sandwich. Is that as good as America?' he asked.

'Oh, Hat, how wonderful to be home!' Emily said.

'We were all afraid that you would stay out there and get married yourself.'

Hat seemed very relieved this was not the case.

'I wouldn't do that,' Emily said, flattered that they had wanted her back here. 'Now you can tell me all the news before I get back to St Jarlath's Crescent.'

'There's a lot of news,' Hat said.

'We've a lot of time.'

Emily settled back happily to listen.

It was mixed news.

The bad news was that Muttie had got a great deal worse. His prognosis, though not discussed or admitted in public, was no more than a couple of months. Lizzie seemed to find it difficult to take on board and was busy planning a trip to the sunshine. She was even urging the twins to speed up their plans to go to New Jersey – somewhere that she and Muttie could come and visit.

Simon and Maud realised that there would be no such journey; they were very down. Young Declan Carroll had been marvellous with them, giving them extra babysitting to keep their minds off things.

Hat's good news was that Baby Frankie was going from strength to strength. Emily didn't dare to ask, but Hat knew what she wanted to know.

'And Noel has been a brick. Lisa has been away a bit, but he manages fine.'

'Which means that you help him too.' Emily looked at him gratefully.

'I love the child. She's no trouble.'

Hat negotiated the traffic.

'Any more news?' Emily enquired.

'Well, Molly Carroll said you wouldn't believe how many garments she got from some mad woman.'

'Mad? Angry or crazy? I never know which you mean.'

'Oh, crazed is what she was. She discovered her husband had been buying clothes for another lady and she took them all and brought them to the thrift shop!' He seemed amused.

'But are we entitled to them? Were they the crazy lady's to give?'

'Apparently so. The husband was singing dumb over it all, saying that he had bought them for his wife, but they were entirely the wrong size and the wrong colour! Amazing things, I heard, like black and red corsets!'

'Heavens! I can't wait to get back,' Emily said.

'And you know the old lady who gave Charles the dog?'

'Mrs Monty, yes? Don't tell me she took Caesar away ...'

'No. The poor lady died – rest in peace – but didn't she leave all her money to Charles!'

'Did she have any money?'

'We think, amazingly, that she did.'

'Isn't that wonderful!' Emily cried.

'It is until you think how it's going to be spent ...' Dr Hat said, drawing a halo around his head with his finger.

Charles and Josie were waiting for her at number 23; they were fussing over Frankie, who had a bit of a cold and was very fretful, not her usual sunny self. Emily was delighted to see her and lifted her up to examine her. Immediately, the child stopped grizzling.

'She's definitely grown so much in three weeks. Isn't she wonderful?'

She gave the baby a hug and was rewarded with a very chatty babble. Emily realised how much she had missed her. This was the child none of them had expected or, to be honest, really wanted at the start – and look at her now! She was the centre of their world.

Dr Hat had been invited in for a cup of tea and was enjoying a game of picking up Frankie's teddy bear in order for her to drop it again; and Molly Carroll dropped in to welcome Emily back.

Noel rang from work to make sure she really *had* returned and hadn't decided to relocate to New York.

Frankie was fine, he said, a runny nose, but otherwise fine. The nurse had said she was thriving. Lisa was away again. She had missed three lectures now and it would be so hard for her to catch up. Oh yes, he had plenty of help. There was this woman called Faith at his lectures who had five younger brothers at home and had no time to study, so she had come to help Noel three evenings a week.

Faith was delighted with Frankie. She had a lot of experience bringing up younger brothers herself but had never been close to a little girl.

The evening slipped into an easy routine: bathtime, bottle, Frankie off to sleep, then revision papers and the internet notes to help them study. Faith sympathised deeply with Noel having to work in a place like Hall's: she was in a fairly dead-end office job but had great hopes that the diploma they were working for would make a difference. People in her office respected such things greatly.

She was a cheerful and optimistic woman of twenty-nine; she had dark curly hair, green eyes, a mobile face and a wide smile, and she loved walking. She showed Noel a great many places he had never known in his own city. She said she needed to walk a lot because it concentrated her mind. She had suffered a great blow: six years ago, her fiancé had been killed in a car accident just weeks before the wedding day. She had coped by walking alone and being very quiet; but recently she had felt the need to get involved with the world about her. That was one of the reasons she had joined the course at the college; and it was one of the reasons she had adapted so easily to Noel's demanding life.

She had bought a baby album for Frankie and put in little wisps of the child's hair, her first baby sock and dozens of photographs.

'Have you any pictures of Stella?' she asked Noel.

'No – none at all.'

Faith didn't enquire further.

'I could do a drawing of her, maybe,' he said after a while.

'That would be great. Frankie will love that when she gets older.'

Noel looked at her gratefully. She was very good company to have around the place. Perhaps later he might try to sketch her face too.

Lisa and Anton were at a Celtic food celebration in Scotland. They were looking into the possibility of twinning with some similar-type Scottish restaurant where they could do a deal whereby anyone who spent over a certain sum in Anton's could get a voucher for half this amount in the Scottish restaurant and vice versa. It would work because it was tapping into an entirely new market, mainly American.

It was Lisa's idea. She had special cards printed to show how it would work. The Scottish restaurant's name was a blank at the moment until the deal was done.

Several times Lisa felt rather than saw Anton's glance of approval, but she knew better now than to look at him for praise. Instead, she concentrated entirely on getting the work done. There would be time later over meals together.

At one of the hotels they had visited, the receptionist asked them if they'd like the honeymoon suite. Lisa deliberately said nothing. Anton asked, with apparent interest, if they looked like a honeymoon couple.

'Not really, but you *do* look happy,' the girl said.

Lisa decided to let Anton speak again.

'Well, we are, I hope. I mean, who wouldn't be happy in this lovely place and if there was a complimentary upgrade to the honeymoon suite, that would be the icing on the cake.'

He smiled his heartbreaking smile and Lisa noticed the receptionist join the long line of women who fancied Anton.

It was so cheering to be here with him and to know that April was out in the wilderness, not posturing and putting her small bottom in her skin-tight jeans on Anton's desk or the arm of his chair. April was miles and miles away ...

But then the trip was over and it was back to reality. Back to lectures in the college three nights a week, back to Frankie waking up all hours of the night, back to April, who was inching her way again into Anton's life.

Lisa noted that a lot of free events had been arranged at Anton's, occasions that would be written up in the papers, perhaps, but which did not put paying customers in seats, which was what they needed. She worried that too much was being spent on appearance rather than reality. The bottom line was the numbers of people you got in to pay for the meals and tell their friends who would also come in and hand over money. Not just another charity press conference with minor celebrities who would be photographed for gossip columns. This was April's world.

Lisa was not so sure it was right. But when she was alone with Anton, she kept quiet about her misgivings. Anton hated being nagged. To tell him he was high on publicity and low on paying punters could well have been considered nagging.

Lisa was not happy to be home.

Emily was walking towards Muttie and Lizzie's house when she saw Lisa and could judge Lisa's mood from a long way off. She wondered, was it going to be her only role in life from now on, cheering people up and stressing the positive?

'How are things, Lisa? Noel told me you've been on a great trip to Scotland,' Emily said.

'It was magic, Emily. Were you ever somewhere and wished that it would never end?'

Emily thought for a moment. 'Not really. I suppose there has been a day here and there that I never wanted to end. My friend Betsy's wedding day was one and driving round Connemara was another. I suppose there were good days when I was teaching art too.'

'I had days that were all like that in Scotland,' Lisa said, her face radiant at the thought of it all.

'Great – you'll have the memory of that to keep you going when you get back to your studies.' Emily knew she sounded brisk.

'Noel's been marvellous; he has had all his notes

photocopied for me, and he's arranged for Molly Carroll to take Frankie for a walk in the park, and he had to rearrange everything so that Bossy Boots knows all our plans. I'm just coming down here to make sure that Mrs Carroll has cover for the thrift shop.'

'You can't stand in the thrift shop all day – you have your studies to catch up on.'

'I have some of my notes here. It won't be that busy,' Lisa said.

'I'll look in after I've seen Muttie and Lizzie.'

'Not much good news there,' Lisa said, shaking her head. 'Muttie's chemo has stopped and Lizzie keeps making impossible plans for the future. Hey, you have enough to do, getting over jet lag and visiting Muttie. I'll survive in the thrift shop for a bit.'

'We'll see,' Emily said.

Muttie looked much frailer even after three weeks. His colour was poor and his face seemed to have hollows in it; his clothes hung off him. His good humour was clearly not affected, though.

'Well ... show us pictures of how the Americans do a wedding,' he said, putting on his spectacles.

'It's not very typical,' Emily explained. 'Fairly mature bride and maid of honour, for one thing.'

'The groom is no spring chicken either,' Muttie agreed.

'Look at the lovely clothes!' Lizzie was delighted with it all. 'And what are all these Chinese signs?'

'Oh, we went to Chinatown for dinner,' Emily said. 'Dozens of Chinese restaurants, Chinese shops and little pagodas and decorations everywhere.'

'That's where we'll go when we go to New York

later on in the year. Emily will mark our card.'

'That's if I can ever get myself on the plane.' Muttie shook his head. 'I seem to have run out of puff, Emily. Hooves here wants me to take him up to have a drink with my Associates, but I find the walk exhausts me.'

'Do you get to see them at all?'

Emily knew how much Muttie loved talking horses to the men in the bar while Hooves sat with his head on Muttie's knee and his eyes full of adoration.

'Oh, Dr Hat is very good. And sometimes young Declan Carroll gets a fierce thirst on him and he drives me up there for a few pints.'

Emily knew very well that Declan Carroll would often pretend 'a fierce thirst' and get himself a pint or two of lemonade shandy when he drove his elderly neighbour up to the pub.

'And how are all the family?' Emily enquired.

As she had expected, they all seemed to be making sudden visits to Ireland from Chicago, or from Sydney, Australia. Muttie was shaking his head at the coincidence of it all.

'I don't know where they get the money, Emily, I really don't. I mean, there's a recession out in those places as well as here.'

'And the twins? Busy as ever?'

'Oh, Maud and Simon are wonderful. There's less chat about their going to New Jersey, but then again Maud has an Italian boyfriend – a really polite, respectful, young man called Marco. They're all setting up this phone for us where you can see the person at the other end. It's called Skype and this weekend we'll be calling my daughter Marian in Chicago and we'll see her and all her family. It doesn't sound right to me.'

'Amazing thing, technology,' Emily agreed.

'Yes, but it's almost going too quickly. Fancy our children getting on planes and coming from the ends of the earth over here to see us and then this magic phone. I don't understand it at all …'

Emily went to the thrift shop and found the twins working there. Lisa was in a corner sighing over her notes. There were no customers.

'We don't all have to be here,' Emily said, taking off her coat.

'Maud and I were just wondering—'

'We don't want to put anyone out—'

'It's just there's this Italian cookery demonstration—'

'At Ennio's restaurant on the quays—'

'And Maud fancies the son of the house there rotten—'

Simon wanted everything to be clear.

'Not true. We've been out a few times—'

'But it's starting in half an hour, you see—'

'And if it was possible for us to work here some other time—'

Emily cut across this double act.

'Go now. This minute,' she said.

'If you're sure—'

'If it's not putting you out—'

'Is Ennio's the pasta house where I saw you working?' Lisa asked suddenly.

'You were there with Moira. Traitor!' Maud took no prisoners.

'You saw her socially.' Simon sounded disgusted.

'It was different. She was lonely.'

'I wonder why ...' Maud was unforgiving.

'Are you still here?' Emily asked, holding open the door of the thrift shop. As they left, she turned to Lisa. 'Go back to Chestnut Court and study properly, Lisa, and I'll do the pricing on the new clothes that have come in. Otherwise you and I will waste the morning and not a penny will be raised for St Jarlath.'

Lisa looked at her in surprise. 'But you don't believe any of this St Jarlath nonsense, do you, Emily?'

'I suppose we're just keeping our options open.' Emily was slightly apologetic.

'But think about it, Emily, if there were a God, then I would be engaged to Anton, Stella wouldn't have died in childbirth and Frankie would have a mother. Noel would be recognised for what he could do at Hall's, Muttie wouldn't be dying of cancer, you would be running the world or the Civil Service or something, with a nice, undemanding husband to cook you a meal when you got home every night.'

'What makes you think that's what I'd want a God to get for me?' Emily asked.

'What else would you want? Except to run things ...'

'I'd want something totally different: a home of my own, the chance to take up painting to see if I was any good at it, a small office from which I could run Emily's Window Boxes ... I don't want the undemanding husband or the great power of running the country. No way!'

'So you say.' Lisa knew it all.

'Is it going to be as hard to get rid of you as the twins?' Emily asked.

'Right. I'm going. Thanks, Emily. You're amazing. If I'd come back from America, I'd be on all fours rather than going straight in to work. I'm nearly a basket case and I was only in Scotland!'

'Ah well, you were probably much more active on your holiday than I was on mine,' Emily said.

Rather than work out what Emily might have in mind, Lisa left. As she walked up the road towards her bus stop she thought about Scotland. They had stayed in five different hotels and in every one of them Anton and she had made love. Twice in the place where they had the honeymoon suite. Why did Anton not miss this and want her to stay with him every night? He had kissed her goodbye when they got to Dublin Airport and said it had been great. Why did he use the past tense? It could all have continued when they were back home.

It was meant to continue.

He had said he loved her – four times he had said it – two of them were sort of jokey when she had got things right about various hotels and restaurants, but twice when they were making love. And so he must have meant it, because who would say something like that at such an intense time and not mean it?

In the thrift shop there was a beautiful green and black silk blouse. An 'unwanted gift', said the lady who had brought it in. It was still in its box with tissue paper. Emily hung it up on a clothes hanger and tried to price it.

When it was new it had probably cost a hundred euros, but nobody who came here would pay anything remotely like that. The lady who had donated it wouldn't be back to see how it was priced, but in any event Emily didn't want to price it too low. It was beautiful. If it were in her own size she would happily have paid fifty euros for it. She was still holding it when Moira came in.

'Just checking where Frankie is,' she said abruptly.

'Good morning, Moira,' Emily said, with pointed politeness. 'Frankie has gone to the park with Mrs Carroll. Declan's mother.'

'Oh, I know Mrs Carroll, yes. I was just making sure nobody had put Frankie in a "file and forget" folder.'

Moira smiled to take the harm out of her words. It was not entirely successful.

Emily had a touch of frost in her voice. 'That would never happen to Frankie Lynch.'

'You mean well, certainly, Emily, but she's not *your* responsibility.'

'She's family.' Emily's eyes glinted. 'She is the daughter of my first cousin. That makes her my first cousin once removed.'

'Imagine!' Moira wasn't impressed.

'Can I do anything else for you, Moira?'

Emily was still managing to hold on to her manners, but only just.

'Well, I'm going out to the heart clinic and the woman who runs it is like a clothes horse. She's interested in nothing but clothes.'

'I believe she's a good heart specialist also,' Emily said.

'Oh yes, well, I'm sure she is, but she's always commenting on what people wear ... I was just wondering if you had anything ... well, you know ...'

'This is your lucky day. I have a beautiful green and black blouse. It would look so well with your black skirt there. Do try it on.'

Moira looked very well in it.

'How much?' she asked, in her usual charmless way.

'Would be over a hundred in the shops. I was going to put fifty on it, but you're a good customer, so can we say forty-five?'

It was more than Moira had intended to spend, but they agreed forty-five and Moira headed off towards the heart clinic in her finery. The shabby grey blouse she had been wearing was wrapped up in the bottom of her briefcase.

As soon as she was gone, Emily telephoned Fiona at the clinic.

'I know this is a bit sneaky ...' she began.

'I *love* sneaky,' said Fiona.

'Moira Tierney is on her way to you wearing a smashing new blouse she bought here. She may start to regret her buy and grizzle about the price, so build her up to the skies.'

'Will do,' Fiona said enthusiastically.

There were already quite a lot of people at the clinic. Frank Ennis had come in for one of his unexpected and disliked visits. They were having tea when he arrived.

'Oh, nice biscuits,' he said, with a look of utter disapproval.

'Paid for by ourselves, Frank,' Clara said cheerfully. 'Every week someone gets to choose the biscuits and pay for them. Lord forbid that the whole of St Brigid's would have to come to a halt because the heart clinic charged the central fund for biscuits. Do have another while you're here ...'

Moira came in just then.

'You bring a touch of class to this place,' Frank Ennis said.

Ania, now visibly pregnant and looking tired, took offence.

'She doesn't have to wear a uniform,' she whispered to Fiona and Barbara, nodding her head at Moira.

To her bewilderment, Fiona didn't seem to agree.

'That's a beautiful blouse, Moira.' Fiona played her part perfectly.

Clara was looking at it too.

'You have a great eye for clothes, Moira. That's top-class silk.'

In a million years Moira would never tell them where she'd bought it. She murmured a bit, refused tea and biscuits and went straight to her small office.

She had three new patients to see today. The first man came in to see her. He was large, with a lined face and shaggy hair, and was fairly wordless. Moira flashed him one of her very brief smiles and took out a piece of paper.

'Well, now, Mr ... er ... Kennedy. Your address first, please.'

'St Patrick's Hostel.'

'Yes, I see you've been there since you left hospital. And before that ...?'

'In England.'

'Addresses?'

'Ah, well, I was here and there, you know ...'

Moira did know. Only too well. Irishmen who had lost years of their lives working on the buildings, using a different name every month, paying no tax, having no insurance, no record of years spent and their wages passed over in cash in a pub of a Friday evening.

'Before that then,' she said wearily. One way or another, she needed some kind of paperwork for this man.

'Oh, long ago I lived in Liscuan,' he said.

She looked up sharply. She had thought he looked somehow familiar.

It was Maureen Kennedy's long-gone husband. She was planning the future of the man whose wife now lived with her father.

Noel came back from Hall's tired.

He let himself into Chestnut Court and found Lisa asleep at the kitchen table with his college notes all around her. He had been hoping that she might have made supper and even gone down to the Carrolls' to collect Frankie.

But what the hell, she was probably worn out after her time in Scotland and was sorry to be home. He would go and collect Frankie. He might even bring home fish and chips. Thank God there were no lectures tonight. He might even drop in and see Muttie. Poor guy was looking desperate these days …

Muttie welcomed him with a big smile. It made his skull-like face look worse than ever.

'Lizzie, it's Noel. Have you a slice of cake for the lad?'

'No, thanks, Muttie. I'm collecting Frankie from Molly and Paddy. I only came to say hello. I have to get her home and put to bed.'

Maud and Simon were there, blond heads bent over a computer.

'We've put Skype on for Muttie,' Maud said proudly.

'So he can talk to people face to face,' added Simon, equally pleased.

'Well, when the two of you get settled in New Jersey, I can talk to you every week!' Muttie was bright and cheerful about it.

'Yeah, but we're not going to New Jersey,' Maud said.

'Too much to keep us here,' Simon added darkly.

'The cookery demonstration in Ennio's restaurant was brilliant today,' Maud said.

'He's a very nice lad, that Marco. You'd walk many a mile before you'd meet as nice a fellow,' Muttie said. 'Hurry up now, Simon, and find yourself a girl before it's too late for us all.'

They looked at him sharply, but he didn't mean anything sinister.

'It's too early to settle down,' Simon said carelessly.

'Who said anything about settling down?' Maud asked.

There was a knock on the door. It was a young man with black curly hair who came in carrying a huge saucepan of something bubbling in a tomato sauce.

'This is for the grandfather of lovely Maud,' he said.

'Well, thank you, Marco,' Muttie said, pleased. 'Lizzie, come in and see what's arrived.'

Lizzie came running in from the kitchen.

'Marco! Imagine, I was just about to get the supper.'

'So that was good timing, then?' Marco beamed around the little group.

'Well, I have to go.' Noel stood up. 'I'm Noel, by the way. I'd love to join you, but I have to pick up my daughter. *Buon appetito.*'

Noel wished he could stay. It was heartening to see such happiness in a house that was soon about to go through so much sadness.

In Chestnut Court, Lisa woke with a stiff neck. She saw Noel's coat hanging on the back of the door. He must have come in and left again. She should have made him some kind of supper or gone to pick Frankie up from Molly Carroll's. Too late now. He had scrawled a note saying he would come back with a fish supper. He was so kind. Wouldn't it have been so easy if only she could have loved Noel rather than Anton? But then life didn't work like that and maybe there would be even more obstacles in the way. She got up, stretched and set the table.

She would really love a glass of wine with the cod and fries, but that was something that would never be brought into this house. She thought back to the lovely wine they had drunk in Scotland. They had paid for the meals on alternate nights and so Lisa was seriously overdrawn now. But Anton never realised that. She hoped things would change; she would have to get a job if Anton didn't make a commitment.

Noel would be home soon and she mustn't be full of gloomy thoughts.

At number 23 St Jarlath's Crescent, Josie and Charles Lynch sat in stunned silence.

They had just closed the door behind a very serious lawyer in a pinstriped suit. He had come to tell them exactly how much they had inherited from the late Meriel Monty. When all the assets were liquidated, the estate would come, the lawyer said very slowly, to a total of approximately two hundred and eighty-nine thousand euros.

CHAPTER ELEVEN

It was good that Eddie Kennedy didn't recognise her, Moira thought. This way she could continue to be professional.

The hostel where he stayed was only a short-stay place, soon he would need something long term. If things had been different, she might have enquired more about the set-up in Liscuan, wondered whether he might even at this late stage be able to patch things up at home. After all, he didn't drink now. He might even be able to take up again with Maureen Kennedy, but the very thought of destroying the great content that her father had finally found late in a troubled life was a thought she could not bear to let into her mind.

Wherever Eddie Kennedy was to find his salvation, it must not be in Liscuan.

Moira sighed deeply and tried to remember what she would have done for this man if things had been different. If she hadn't known for certain that his long-abandoned wife was living with her own father. Wearily she continued with fruitless questions about any possible benefits that might be due to him after a lifetime of working in England. This man had never signed on anywhere or joined any system. It would be a progression of hostels from now on.

It would have been the same if he had come across

any other social worker, wouldn't it? Maybe one of them might have made enquiries back in Liscuan. And if enquiries *had* been made? Perhaps Mrs Kennedy and her father would have sung low, in which case there would have been nothing different to the way it was now …

Yet Moira felt guilty. This man shouldn't have his options restricted just because his social worker wanted her own father to continue undisturbed in what should have been his home. Moira wished, not for the first time, that she had a friend, a soulmate that she could discuss it with.

She remembered that meal with Lisa in Ennio's: it had been pleasant and it was surprisingly easy to talk to Lisa. But of course the girl would think she was quite insane if she were to suggest it again.

Worse – both insane and pathetic.

Muttie said to his wife Lizzie that something was worrying him.

'Tell me, Muttie.'

Lizzie had listened to Muttie for years. Listened to stories of horses that were going to win, backs that ached, beer that had been watered and, more recently, about some poor unfortunates he had met up at the hospital. Muttie had discovered there was a desperate lot of illness about – you just didn't come across it when you were in the whole of your health.

She wondered what she would hear now.

'I'm worried that the twins are putting off their trip to America because of my having to have these treatments.'

He said it defiantly as if waiting, hoping, for her to deny it.

If that was what he wanted, then that was what he got. Lizzie's face split in two with a great laugh.

'Well, if that's all that's bothering you, Muttie Scarlet, aren't you a lucky man? Have you eyes in your head at all? They didn't want to go because Maud is crazy about Marco. The *last* thing she wants to do is to go away and let some Dublin dolly get her claws into Marco. It has nothing to do with you whatsoever!'

He was vastly relieved.

'I suppose I was making myself the big man ...' he said.

Noel Lynch and Lisa Kelly were shopping for fruit and vegetables in a market where Emily had pointed them. Moira had complained that they did very little home cooking and that Frankie's diet might be lacking in all kinds of nutrients.

'She always moves the bloody goalposts,' Lisa said in fury.

'Why are home-made purées better than the ones we buy?' Noel said crossly. 'What *are* all these additives she talks about? And why do the makers put them in?'

'I bet they don't. It's just Moira making life more difficult. Right, show me the list Emily made. Apples, bananas. No honey, that can poison her. Vegetables, but no broccoli. We have stock, and it's low salt and organic, I checked.'

'Have we?' Noel was surprised. 'What does it look like?'

'Like a sort of toffee wrapped up. We have it, Noel. Come on, let's pay for this lot and we'll go home and purée it, and while it's cooking we'll go over the notes for that lecture we both missed. Thank God for Faith!'

'Yes, indeed.'

Lisa looked at him sharply. It was obvious to everyone except Noel that Faith fancied him. Lisa didn't feel at all drawn to Noel except as a housemate and friend, but she didn't want the situation complicated.

In some strange, odd way, Anton felt slightly more on his toes because Lisa lived with a man. It was more racy somehow. Once or twice Anton had asked if there was any frisson between the two of them. That was a very Anton type of word and he asked it casually as if he didn't care very much anyway.

But that was his way. He wouldn't have asked if he hadn't cared.

Lisa was comfortable in Chestnut Court. Noel made sure she went to her lectures when she wasn't running off with Anton at a moment's notice. And even though she wouldn't admit it to anyone, she had become amazingly fond of that little girl. Life without Frankie was going to be hard when it happened. As soon as Anton realised that commitment did not mean a life sentence, it meant the opening of doors.

Emily Lynch was also at the vegetable market; she had promised Dr Hat she would teach him how to make a vegetarian curry for his friend Michael who was coming to visit.

'Could you not just ... er ... make it for me?' Dr Hat begged.

'No way! I want you to be able to tell Michael how you made it.' She was very firm.

'Emily, *please*. Cooking is women's business.'

'Then why are the great chefs mainly male?' she asked mildly.

'Show-offs,' said Dr Hat mutinously. 'It won't work, Emily. I'll burn everything.'

'Don't be ridiculous – we'll have a great time chopping everything up – you'll be making this recipe every week.'

'I doubt it,' said Dr Hat. 'I seriously doubt it.'

The whole encounter with Eddie Kennedy had made Moira restless. Her own small apartment felt like a prison with the walls enclosing her more and more. Perhaps she was a kindred soul to him and would end up beached, with no friends, being looked after by some social worker who was still at school now.

It was her birthday on Friday. It was a sad person who had nobody to celebrate with. Nobody at all. Yet again her thoughts went back to that pleasant evening at Ennio's restaurant. She had felt normal for once.

What would Lisa say if Moira asked her to have a meal with her – except that she wasn't free? Nothing would be lost. She would go around to Chestnut Court now.

'God Almighty, it's Moira *again*!' Lisa said when she had put down the entryphone and buzzed her in.

'What can she want now?'

Noel looked around the flat nervously in case there was something that could be discovered, something that would be a black mark against them. Frankie's clothes were drying on the radiators – but that was good, wasn't it? They were making sure that the little garments were properly aired.

He continued spooning the purée into Frankie, who enjoyed it mainly as a face-painting activity and something to rub into her hair.

Moira arrived in a grey trouser suit and sensible shoes. She looked businesslike, but then she was always businesslike.

Noel looked at her properly for the first time. There was a sort of shield around her as if it were keeping people away. She had good, clear skin. Her hair was curly in a colour that suited her. It was just that it didn't add up to much.

'Will you have a cup of tea?' he asked her wearily.

Moira had taken in the domestic scene at a glance: the child was being well cared for. Anyone could see that. They had even listened to her about getting fresh vegetables and making purées.

She saw the books and note files out for their studies. These were her so-called hopeless clients; a family at risk, not fit to be minding Frankie, and yet they seemed to have got their act together much better than Moira had.

'I had a tiring day today,' she said unexpectedly.

If the roof had blown off the apartment block, Noel and Lisa could not have been more surprised. Even Frankie looked up startled with her food-stained face.

Moira never complained about her workload. She was tireless in her efforts to impose some kind of order on a mad world. This was the very first time she had even given a hint that she might be human.

'What kind of things were most tiring?' Lisa asked politely.

'Frustration mainly. I know this couple who are desperate for a baby. They would provide a great home, but can they get one? Oh no, they can't. People can ignore babies, harm them, take drugs all round them and that's perfectly fine as long as they are kept with the natural parent. We are meant to be proud of this because we have kept the family unit intact ...'

Noel found himself involuntarily holding Frankie closer to him.

'Not you, Noel,' Moira said wearily. 'You and Lisa are doing your best.'

This was astounding praise. Lisa and Noel looked at each other in shock.

'I mean, it's a hopeless situation, but at least you're keeping to the rules,' Moira admitted grudgingly.

Noel and Lisa smiled at each other in relief.

'But the rest of it's exhausting and I ask myself, is it getting anyone anywhere?'

Lisa wondered whether Moira might be having a nervous breakdown.

'It must be very stressful, your job. I suppose you have to try to compensate for it in your private life,' Lisa babbled, in an attempt to restore normality.

'Yes, indeed, if all I had to think about was Hall's, I'd be locked up by now,' Noel agreed. 'If I didn't have Frankie to come home to, I'd be a right mess.'

'I'm the same.' Lisa thought of Anton's. 'Honestly, the comings and goings, the highs and lows, the dramas. I'm glad I have another life outside it all.'

Moira listened to all this without much sign of agreement or pleasure. Then she delivered the final shock.

'It was actually about my social life that I called,' Moira said. 'I'm going to be thirty-five on Friday and I was hoping, Lisa, you might join me for supper at Ennio's ...'

'Me? Friday? Oh heavens. Well, thank you, Moira, thank you indeed. I'm free on Friday, aren't I, Noel?'

Was she looking at him beseechingly, begging him to

find some kind of excuse? Or was she eager to go? Noel couldn't work it out. Honesty seemed safest.

'Friday is my day on – you're free Friday evening,' he said.

Lisa's face showed nothing. 'Well, that's very kind of you, Moira. Will there be many people there?'

'In Ennio's? I don't know. I suppose there will be a fair number.'

'No, I mean to celebrate your birthday?'

'Oh, just the two of us,' Moira said and she gathered herself up and left.

Noel and Lisa didn't dare to speak until she had left the building.

'We should have said she didn't look thirty-five,' Lisa said.

'What does she look?' Noel asked.

'She could be a hundred. She could be any age. Why did she ask me to dinner?'

'Maybe she fancies you,' Noel said, and then, 'Sorry, sorry. I'm just making a joke.'

'Right, you can afford to make jokes. You're not the one having dinner with her on Friday.'

'She may be going mad,' Noel said thoughtfully.

Lisa had been thinking exactly the same thing.

'Why do you say that?'

'Well ...' Noel spoke slowly and deliberately, 'it's a very odd thing to do. No one normal would invite you to dinner. You of all people.'

She looked up at him and saw he was smiling.

'Yes, you're right, Noel. The woman's lonely and she has no friends. That's all.'

'I was wondering ...' Noel paused. 'I was thinking of inviting Faith to dinner. A proper dinner, not just a bowl of soup or something on toast. You know, to thank her for the notes and everything.'

'Oh yes?' Lisa said.

'I wonder would Friday be a good night? You'll probably be out late, hitting the clubs with Moira. I'd feel safer having a meal here. It's such a temptation to order a bottle of wine or have a cocktail in a restaurant.'

Noel rarely spoke of his alcoholism at home. He went to meetings and there was no drink in the flat. It was unusual for him to bring the subject up.

He must be interested in Faith after all.

Lisa's mind leaped ahead again. Suppose Faith really did move in with Noel? Where would that leave Lisa?

But she mustn't start to fuss. That was her least attractive quality. Anton had told her when they were in Scotland that she was an absolute angel when she didn't fuss. And Noel deserved some happiness in his life.

'That's a great idea. I'll do a salad for you before I go out and maybe you could cook that chicken in ginger you do sometimes. It's very impressive. And we'll make sure to iron the tablecloth and napkins.'

'It's only Faith. It's not a competition,' Noel protested.

'But you want her to realise you've gone to some trouble to entertain her, don't you?'

Noel realised with a shock that this was the first date he had ever planned in years.

'And in return you have to help me think of a present for Moira. Not too dear. I'm broke!'

'Ask Emily to look out something from the thrift shop for you. She finds great things – new things, even.'

'That's an idea.' Lisa brightened. 'Well, Frankie,

social life around here is getting very lively. You're going to be hard pushed to keep up with us ...'

Frankie stretched her arms out to Lisa.

'*Mama*,' she said.

'Nearly there, Frankie, but it's Lee-za, much posher.'

But from this child, 'Mama' was perfectly fine.

Faith was surprised and pleased to be invited.

'Will there be many people there?' she asked nervously.

'Just the two of us,' Noel said. 'Will that be all right?'

'Oh, fine!' Faith seemed very relieved. She smiled at him. 'Thanks, Noel, I'm looking forward to dinner.'

'Me too,' said Noel.

He wondered suddenly, was she expecting that they would go to bed together? He realised he had never made love in his life while sober. He had heard some terrible stories on this topic at AA. It was apparently fraught with difficulties and had disastrous effects of creating anxiety about performance. Many people had told his AA group that they had taken a quick shot of vodka just to see them right and were back on full-time drinking within a week.

But he would face that if and when it occurred. No point in destroying Wednesday by thinking about Friday. This one-day-at-a-time thing really worked.

Friday eventually came.

Emily had found a small mother-of-pearl brooch as a gift for Lisa to give Moira. She even produced a little box and some black velvet. Moira couldn't help but like that.

338

Anton had laughed when Lisa had said she was going to Ennio's with Moira.

'That should be a bundle of fun,' he had said dismissively.

'It will be fine,' she said, suddenly feeling defensive.

'If you want cheapo pasta, a bottle of plonk and a couple of Italians bunching up their fingers to kiss them and say *"bella signora"* ...'

'They're nice there.'

Why she was being protective towards this little trattoria, she didn't know.

'Yeah and we're nice in Anton's too, so why didn't you and the social worker choose us?'

'Be real, Anton. A Friday night! And anyway, it was her shout. She chose Ennio's.'

He looked like a small boy who had been crossed. 'I'd have given you early-bird rates all night.'

'I know that, she didn't. See you.'

'Are you coming round later? It's Teddy's birthday too and we're having a few drinks after closing time.'

'Oh no, we'll be hitting the clubs by then.'

She remembered Noel's expression. It was worth it to see the look of surprise and irritation on Anton's face.

Noel set the table at Chestnut Court. Lisa had left the salad in the fridge covered in clingfilm, and his chicken and ginger dish was under foil and ready to put in the oven for twenty-five minutes. The potatoes were in a saucepan.

Frankie had been delivered to Declan and Fiona's: she was going to have a sleepover.

'Dada,' she said as he waved her goodbye and his

heart turned over as it always did when she smiled at him.

Now he was back in the apartment, waiting for a woman to come to supper, just as someone normal would do.

Lisa had looked very well as she set out to the birthday celebration. It was so comforting to know that Anton was jealous, that he really thought she would go to a nightclub.

At Ennio's the host was waiting for them.

'*Che belle signore!*' he said, giving them a small bunch of violets each. Exactly as Anton had said he would. 'Marco, *vieni qui, una tavola per queste due bellissime signore.*'

The son of the house bustled towards them and dusted chairs. Moira and Lisa thanked him profusely.

Lisa spotted that Maud was working there that night and Marco saw Lisa recognise her.

'I think you know my friend and colleague Maud,' he said proudly.

'Yes, indeed I do, lovely girl,' Lisa said. 'And this is Moira Tierney who chose the restaurant for her birthday celebration.'

'Moira Tierney …' Marco repeated the words fearfully. 'Maud has mentioned your name to me.'

Written all over his face was the fact that the mention had perhaps not been the most cordial, but he struggled to remember his job of welcoming guests and handed them the menus.

They began choosing their food. If Moira said once that the mark-up on the food was enormous, she must have said it a dozen times.

'Imagine charging that for garlic bread!' she gasped, as if astonished.

'We don't have to have garlic bread,' Lisa said.

'No, no, we'll have everything we want. It's a celebration,' Moira said in a sepulchral voice.

'Indeed it is.'

Lisa was bright and positive. This looked like being a long night.

Emily went to Dr Hat's house to check that he had his curry ready for his friend Michael. She wanted to show him that he should have a dish of sliced bananas and a little bowl of coconut as well.

To her surprise the table was set for three.

'Will his wife be with him?' Emily asked, surprised. Only Michael had been mentioned up to now.

'No, Michael never married. Another crusty old bachelor,' Dr Hat said.

'So who is the third person?'

'I was rather hoping that *you* would join us,' he said hesitantly.

Paddy Carroll and his wife Molly were going to a butchers' dinner. It took place every year; the wives dressed up and it was held in a smart hotel. It was an occasion where Paddy Carroll had been known to over-imbibe, so Declan would drive them there and a taxi would be ordered to take them home.

Fiona waved them off as they left in a flurry, then she sat down with a big mug of tea to watch over the two little ones crawling around the floor before she had to settle them in their cots. They were both a bit restless this evening and she was going to have to separate them if they were going to go to sleep.

She was wondering if she might possibly be pregnant again. If she were it would be great and Declan would be so pleased, but it would mean that they would have to stir themselves and make sure the house was ready for them to move into before the baby was born. They couldn't put Paddy and Molly through all that business of a crying baby again.

Finally, along with the second bottle of wine, Moira broached the subject of Eddie Kennedy. Lisa thought she understood the situation, but she didn't really see the problem.

'Of course, you don't have to do anything for him,' she said. 'It was the luck of the draw that he got you as a social worker. You don't have to tell him about the cosy little homestead down there.'

'But he bought that house before he got addled with drink. He's entitled to live there.'

'Nonsense. He gave up all rights and entitlements when he went off to England. He chose to opt out of his old life. He can't expect you to turf your father out and get his wife to take him back. She probably wouldn't want him anyway …'

'But is he to die in a hostel because I don't want to disturb things?'

'He chose that route.' Lisa was firm.

'If it was your father—' Moira began.

'I hate my father. I wouldn't spit on him if he was on fire!'

'I feel guilty. I've always given my clients the best. I'm not doing this with Eddie Kennedy,' Moira said bleakly.

'Suppose you made it up to him in other ways? You know, went to see him in the hostel, took him out for the odd afternoon.'

Moira looked at her in disbelief. How could this be doing her duty? It would be crossing the thin line that divided professionalism from friendship. Entirely unsuitable.

Lisa shrugged. 'Well, that's what I'd do anyway.'

She caught Marco's eye and in thirty seconds a little cake with one candle came from the kitchen. The waiters sang 'Happy Birthday' and everyone in the restaurant clapped.

Moira was pink and flustered. She tried to cut the cake and all the filling oozed out of one side. Lisa took the knife from her.

'Happy birthday, Moira,' she said, putting as much warmth into it as she could. To her amazement she saw the tears falling down Moira's face.

Thirty-five and this was probably the only birthday party she had ever had.

Up in Chestnut Court the dinner was going very well.

'Aren't you a dark horse, being able to cook like this!' Faith said appreciatively. She was easy to talk to, not garrulous, but she chatted engagingly of her background.

She spoke briefly about the accident that had killed her fiancé, but she didn't dwell on it. Terrible things happened to a lot of people. They had to pick themselves up.

'Do you still love him?' Noel asked as he spooned out another helping of chicken.

'No. In fact I can barely remember him. And you, Noel, do you miss Frankie's mother a lot?' Faith asked.

'No, I'm a bit like you. I hardly remember Stella, but then that was in my drinking days. I don't remember anything much from those times.' He smiled nervously. 'But I love to have Frankie around the place.'

'Where is she now? I brought her a funny little book of animals. It's made of cotton, so it doesn't matter if she eats it!'

'Lisa dropped her in to Fiona and Declan's. Lisa's gone out to supper.'

'With Anton?'

'No, with Moira, actually.'

'A different kind of outing, certainly.' Faith knew the cast of characters.

'You could say that.' Noel beamed at her.

This was all going so well.

Fiona had just brought Declan a mug of coffee when she heard running feet outside the door.

Outside was Lizzie, dishevelled and distraught.

'Can Declan come quickly? I'm so sorry to interrupt you, but Muttie's been sick and it's all blood!'

Declan was already out of his chair and grabbing his doctor's bag.

'I'll come in a minute – I'll have to sort out the kids,' Fiona shouted.

'Fine.'

In seconds Declan was through the Scarlets' front door. Muttie was ashen-faced, and he had been vomiting into a bowl. Declan took in the scene at a glance.

'A thing of nothing, Muttie. They'll have you as right as rain in the hospital.'

'Couldn't you deal with it, Declan?'

'No, they're fierce for the back-up. They'd be suing me left and right.'

'But it will take for ever to get an ambulance,' Muttie objected.

'We're going in my car. Get in there right now,' Declan said firmly.

Lizzie wanted to go with them, but Declan persuaded her to wait for Fiona. He took her back inside the house and whispered that as the hospital might need to keep Muttie in overnight, the best thing was for her to go and pack a small bag for him. Fiona would bring Lizzie up to the hospital in a taxi when she was ready, and not to worry, he would make sure that Muttie was in safe hands. He knew that having something useful to do would calm her.

By now, Fiona had arrived, and they quickly realised that they had to find somewhere for Johnny and Frankie to spend the evening and do it fast, or there would be total confusion. Noel was having the first real date of his life; his parents were away. Lisa had gone out with Moira – which at least would keep the social worker out of their hair; Emily would be the one to call on.

Leaving Fiona to make the arrangements, Declan sped off with Muttie beside him looking pale and frightened.

Emily had insisted that Dr Hat served the meal himself. After all, he had made it.

Michael proved to be a quiet, thoughtful man. He asked her gentle questions about her past life. It was as if he were checking her out for his old friend Hat. She hoped that she was giving a good account of herself.

Hat was such a good and pleasant companion, she would hate to lose his friendship.

She was surprised when her phone rang in the pocket of her jacket as they were at the dining table. She wasn't expecting any calls.

'Emily, big crisis. Can you do baby patrol?' Fiona sounded frightened.

Emily didn't hesitate. 'Certainly. I'm on my way!'

She quickly excused herself and hastened down the road.

Outside the Carrolls' house all was confusion. Lizzie was there crying and clutching a small suitcase; Fiona was hovering between the Scarlets' front door and her own. Hooves was barking madly. Dimples was answering from the Carrolls' back garden. Declan had taken Muttie to hospital. The taxi was on its way for Fiona and Lizzie.

'I'm going up to the hospital with Lizzie to be with her while we wait for news of Muttie,' Fiona said as soon as Emily arrived.

'Can I move baby patrol up to Dr Hat's house? I'm sort of in the middle of a meal there.'

'Of course, Emily. I'm so sorry. I didn't mean to interrupt ...'

'No, it's fine, don't worry. Two crusty old bachelors and myself. This will lower the age level greatly. Good luck – and let us know ...'

'Right,' Fiona said, as the taxi pulled up outside the house. She grabbed Lizzie and the suitcase and bundled her into the back of the car. 'Emily, you are amazing. Key under the usual flowerpot.'

'Go now,' Emily ordered.

She ran to the Carrolls' house and picked Johnny up

out of his cot in the front room and fastened him into his buggy.

'We're going for a visit to Uncle Hat and Auntie Emily,' she said. She pushed the baby buggy out the door, locked it behind her and then put the key carefully under the flowerpot.

Dr Hat and Michael were suitably impressed with little Johnny. The little boy, exhausted from the journey, fell asleep on Dr Hat's sofa and was covered with a blanket. The meal continued seamlessly.

Hat admitted, when he produced dessert, that he had not made the meringues himself but had bought them in a local confectionery shop.

'I think he'd have got away with saying he made them himself, don't you, Michael?' said Emily.

Michael was flushed with wine and good humour. 'I'd have believed anything Hat were to tell me tonight,' he beamed at them. 'Never saw such a change in a person. If that's what retirement did for you, Hat, then lead on, I say. And I do admire the way you all look after these children. It was never like that in our day, people were stressed and fussed and never believed that anyone else could look after a child for more than two minutes.'

'Ah, they have it down to a fine art,' Dr Hat said proudly. 'Whenever Johnny and Frankie need a minder, they're all here on tap.'

'Frankie?' Michael asked.

Emily said, 'She's my cousin Noel's daughter. He's bringing her up as a single father and making a great job of it, too. Actually Noel has a date tonight. All of us chattering spinsters have great hopes of this girl Faith. He's entertaining her in his own apartment.'

'And so Faith is meeting the baby tonight?' Michael asked.

'No, she knows the child already, she goes in to study there, you see. But the baby is out for the night to give them a bit of space, I think.'

'So who's minding Frankie tonight?' Michael asked.

His question was innocent – he was fascinated by this Toy Town atmosphere with good Samaritans coming out of every house in the street.

Emily stopped to think.

'It can't be Lisa. She's going out with the dreaded Moira. The twins are out on the town. The Carrolls have gone to a butchers' dinner. Noel's parents, my uncle Charles and aunt Josie, are in the West ... Who *is* minding Frankie?'

Emily felt the first constriction of alarm in her chest.

If Noel had been going to bring in someone outside the circle, he would have told them. Moira had been behaving like a Rottweiler at the thought of any new face on the horizon.

'If you'll excuse me, I'll call Noel,' she said, 'just to set my mind at rest.'

'You'd interrupt the boy's first proper date with Faith?' Dr Hat shook his head. 'Think, Emily, she must be somewhere.'

'I have run out of options, Hat – let me call Noel.'

'I only want to say you'll be annoyed with yourself when it's all perfectly all right.'

'No. I'll be able to sleep easy,' she said.

'Noel, I'm so sorry,' she began.

'Is anything wrong, Emily?' He was alert to her tone immediately.

'No, nothing. I was just checking something. Where is Frankie tonight?'

'Lisa took her down to Fiona and Declan's earlier. I'm having a friend to dinner.'

'To the Carrolls' house?'

'Is everything all right, Emily?' he asked again.

'Everything's fine, Noel,' she said and hung up immediately. 'You two mind Johnny here. I must have left Frankie in the Carrolls' house. There was only one baby in the cot.'

She was out the door before they could ask any more.

Emily ran down St Jarlath's Crescent at a greater speed than she had known to be possible. What had Fiona said? She hadn't said 'babies'. She had said 'baby patrol'.

Her hand shook as she reached under the flowerpot for the key and opened the door.

'Frankie?' she called as she ran into the house.

There was no sound.

In the kitchen there was a second cot with some of Frankie's toys in it. Frankie's buggy was parked beside it. There was no sign of the child. The strength left Emily's legs and she sat down on a kitchen chair to support herself.

Someone had let themselves in and taken Frankie.

How could this have happened?

Then the thought struck her.

Of course! Fiona had come back home to check on things. Yes, that must be it.

She ran to Muttie and Lizzie's house. It was dark and closed. She knew before she started hammering on the door that there was no one in.

Now she was really frightened. Fingers starting

to shake, she dialled Fiona's mobile number. As the number connected, she heard a phone start to ring from inside the Scarlet house. It was Fiona's ring-tone, she recognised it. After a few seconds the ringing stopped and she heard the voicemail message start.

Declan. She had to call Declan.

'Emily?' He answered straightaway. 'Is everything all right? Is it the children?'

'Johnny's fine,' she said immediately. 'He's asleep on Dr Hat's sofa.'

'And Frankie?' Declan suddenly sounded alarmed. 'What about Frankie?'

But Emily had already started running.

CHAPTER TWELVE

They tried to be methodical about it but panic overwhelmed them; the list was checked over and over.

Signora and Aidan knew nothing about the child, but would join in any searches. No point in trying to contact Charles and Josie: they were miles away and couldn't do anything; they'd just get hysterical. It would be ages before Paddy and Molly would be home from the butchers' dance. Paddy would be fuelled with brandy and good cheer; Molly's shoes would be too tight.

Who could have come into the Carrolls' house and spirited Frankie away? She couldn't have got out herself and Emily had been back into the house and searched the place from top to bottom. Anywhere, any small space a child might be able to crawl into – she must be here somewhere.

She wasn't.

Could somebody have been watching the house? It seemed less than possible and there was no sign of a break-in. There must be a rational explanation. Should the police be called?

Having left Faith in the flat to answer any calls, and white-faced with anxiety, Noel ran in and out of all the houses in St Jarlath's Crescent. Had anyone seen anything? Anything at all?

He had sent Lisa a text and asked her to call him from the ladies', out of Moira's earshot. Lisa was shocked at how frightened she felt when she heard the news. For the time being, she was *not* to come home. It didn't matter where she went, as long as she kept Moira occupied. She felt sure that Moira must be able to tell something was wrong; nailing a smile on to her face, she went back to the table.

Up at the hospital, Lizzie wandered up and down the corridors, asking plaintively when she was going to be able to see how Muttie was getting on. Fiona persuaded her to come back into the waiting room and sit down. They would wait for Declan to come.

He arrived twenty minutes later.

'Well, he's stable now but they're going to keep him in for a while.' His voice was grim. 'They've made him comfortable and he's sleeping,' he said to Lizzie. 'You'll probably not be able to speak to him until tomorrow but he should feel better after a good night's rest. We should all go home.'

Lizzie was pleased with the news. 'I'm glad he's getting a good rest. I'll leave his suitcase in for him for tomorrow.'

'Do that, Lizzie,' Fiona said, realising that there was something Declan hadn't told her. Could this night get any worse?

It was a time of frantic comings and goings. Michael stayed with Johnny as Hat and Emily went through the whole thing over and over. At least a hundred times Emily must have said that she should never have gone along with the silly phrase 'baby patrol'. She should have asked what it meant and how many babies were involved.

Hat, in her defence, said that it was all Fiona's fault. Imagine having two babies in different rooms and not mentioning it! It was unheard of.

Noel was almost out of his mind with grief and worry and rage – what were those idiotic women doing, risking his daughter's safety like that? How could they be so stupid as to abandon her in that house, leaving her prey to – who knew what?

And as for him – it was all his own fault. Stella had trusted him with their daughter and he'd let her down, all because he'd wanted to spend some time with a woman. Now some monster, some pervert had taken his little girl and he might never see her again. He might never hold her in his arms and see her smile. He might never hear her voice calling him 'Dada'... If anyone had hurt her, if anyone had touched a hair of his Frankie's head ...

And in the middle of St Jarlath's Crescent, Noel kneeled down on the pavement and wept for his little girl.

Lisa managed to escape Moira on two occasions by going back to the ladies' room, but she couldn't go on doing this all night. She decided to persuade Moira to go to Teddy's birthday party at Anton's.

'But I won't know anyone,' Moira had wailed.

'Neither will I. Most of them will be strangers to me, friends of silly April, but come on, Moira, it's free drink and it's your birthday too. Why not?'

And as Moira agreed, Lisa dragged herself together. She wished that she was at home with Noel helping to co-ordinate the search. There *must* be an explanation. Lisa had heard very little except a trembling hysteria from Noel about what could have happened.

'Noel, don't hate me for saying this, but in the name of God, don't go back on the drink.'

'No, Lisa, I won't.' His voice was clipped.

'I know you're cross with me, but I *had* to say it.'

'Yes, I realise you did.'

'Go back to where we were before I said it. She's fine. There's been a misunderstanding. It will be sorted.'

'Sure it will, Lisa,' he said.

Sergeant Sean O'Meara had seen it all and done it all and, if he were honest, he would say that most of it was fairly depressing, but this occasion was just bizarre.

An extremely drunk man called Paddy Carroll had explained over and over that he had been at a butchers' dinner and someone had spiked his drinks. He had started to behave foolishly and so he agreed that his wife take him home in a taxi. The wife, a Mrs Molly Carroll, said that she was not a serious partaker of alcohol herself and had been delighted when her husband agreed to come home with her as her feet were killing her. But when they got home, they were bemused to find Frankie sitting on her own in the cot and their own family, son, daughter-in-law and grandson, nowhere to be found.

They had tried to contact several people, but hadn't been able to speak to anyone who might know what was going on. They'd tried to find the child's father but had arrived at his apartment block not knowing which flat he lived in. What sort of people don't put their names on doorbells, asked Paddy Carroll, looking around him accusingly. What sort of people don't want people to know where they live?

So what were they to do? The baby was crying; there was no answer from the doorbell they pressed; they couldn't find their son and his family; Emily wasn't in her house; Signora and Aidan had their phone on answer; there was no one at home in Muttie and Lizzie's; in fact, the whole street had gone into meltdown the moment the Carrolls had gone to the butchers' dinner.

'So, you want us to find this Noel Lynch. Is that it?' Sergeant O'Meara had asked. 'Had you ever thought of ringing him?' And he had handed a phone to Paddy Carroll, who had suddenly looked even more confused.

Faith had been pacing up and down at Chestnut Court. She had a sheet of paper by the phone and she perched nervously beside it, trying not to jump when it rang. Anyone who phoned in was asked for their telephone number; but she had little information to give out. Yes, Frankie was still missing. No, Noel wasn't there, he was out looking. No, they hadn't called the police yet, but the time was fast approaching when they would have to do so. They had agreed that if Frankie were not found within the hour, Faith would call the Guards. There wasn't long to go.

Noel had phoned her eight times already, knowing as he did that she would call him the moment there was any news.

She checked her watch again. It was time. She had to call the police. Hand shaking, she reached for the phone and as she did so, it rang. Her stomach lurched. Anxiously she answered.

At first, she thought it was a crank call. The man's voice on the other end of the phone sounded muffled, incoherent, angry she thought at first, but soon she realised he might be drunk.

No, Noel wasn't there, he was … No, he had been at home earlier in the evening but … No, his daughter was missing and the police were about to be called …

'But that's what I'm telling you,' the voice said. 'I've got his daughter here. She's with us now …'

And suddenly Faith heard the unmistakable sound of Frankie crying.

'She's *found*, Noel! Not a hair of her head touched,' she said. 'She's great. She's asking for her daddy.'

'Have you seen her? Is she there with you?'

'No. They brought her to the Garda Station. It was the Carrolls. It was Paddy and Molly Carroll. It was *all* a misunderstanding. They were looking for *you*.'

'What the hell did they mean by that? What do you mean, *looking for me*? We were in all night!' Noel was torn between overpowering relief and fury.

'No, it's all right, don't get angry. They got enough of a shock already.'

'They got a shock! What about the rest of us? What happened?'

'They came home early from their do and they found her in the cot alone in the house. They must have arrived just after Fiona and Lizzie set off for the hospital. They called on all the neighbours, but there was no one around – Declan and Fiona were at the hospital with the Scarlets, Emily was at Dr Hat's and, of course, Charles and Josie weren't there. They tried to call Fiona, but she'd left her phone at Lizzie's. Declan's phone was busy, so they came to Chestnut Court to see you. Only by the sound of it they'd got the wrong flat number and were pressing the wrong doorbell. By the time we knew Frankie was missing they were on their way to the Guards. They thought something was terribly wrong and quite rightly didn't want to put the child at further risk. But she's fine and we need to get over there to pick her up.'

But Noel was still distraught. 'Frankie's in a police station. What chance will I have of keeping her once bloody Moira gets to hear of this?'

'Don't worry – I'll call Lisa as soon as I put the phone down and let her know Frankie is found. Then I'll put together some things for Frankie – why don't you collect me here and we'll go up together? Let's get her home before Moira ever knows she was missing ...'

Sergeant O'Meara had no idea what they were all doing in a police station and he wished someone, anyone, would shut the screaming child up. Mrs Carroll kept bouncing the baby up and down, but the decibel level was getting higher. It was all starting to grate on him.

'Why *exactly* did you bring the child here? If you know who she is and all belonging to her?'

Paddy Carroll tried to explain. 'It seemed like the right thing to do at the time. Be on the safe side,' he said.

'The safe side of what?' Sergeant O'Meara asked, raising his voice above the din.

Paddy wished that his mind was less fuzzy and his speech more clear. 'Could I have a cup of tea?' he asked plaintively.

'It's a pity you didn't think of having tea earlier in the evening,' Molly Carroll said sharply.

Sergeant O'Meara organised tea, glad to get away from the screaming baby for a moment.

'So this Noel Lynch is on his way now?' he said wearily.

'There he is!' Paddy Carroll cried out, pointing at the glass door out into the front office. 'There he is! Noel! Noel! Come in here! We've got Frankie for you!'

And Sergeant O'Meara rescued Paddy Carroll's teacup just before it pitched on to the child as Noel threw himself at his baby girl.

'Frankie! Are you all right?' he cried, his voice muffled with emotion. 'Darling little Frankie. I'm so sorry, really I am. I'll never leave you again …'

Frantically, he checked that she was all right, uninjured in any way; then he wiped her face, her nose, and dried her eyes.

Behind him, meanwhile, stood a small, slim woman with green eyes and a big smile. She was carrying one of Frankie's coats and a woolly scarf; more important, she was carrying a bottle of baby food, which she handed to Noel straightaway.

As Noel fed his daughter, almost magically, the crying stopped, the baby calmed down and peace was restored.

Sergeant O'Meara was profoundly grateful that the situation seemed to be sorting itself out.

More and more people were arriving: a stressed-out, middle-aged woman with frizzy hair, and an older man wearing a hat like something from a black-and-white movie.

'Oh, Frankie! I'm so sorry …' The woman bent down to kiss the baby girl. 'I didn't know you were there. I'll never forgive myself. *Never*.'

The man in the hat introduced himself as Dr Hat; he looked like the only person with any degree of control.

'If ever there was a case of all's well that ends well ... it's here.' He beamed at everyone. 'And well done, Mr and Mrs Carroll. You did exactly the right thing in the circumstances. Noel, we'll all get out of here, don't you think, and leave Sergeant O'Meara to his business. No need to write a report at all – wouldn't you agree?'

The detective looked at Dr Hat gratefully. The writing of a report about this was going to be Gothic.

'If everyone's satisfied ...' he began.

'I'm so sorry about this,' Dr Hat said to him quietly. 'It's a terrible waste of your time, but I assure you that it was well meant. We're sorry to have disturbed you – but no harm done ...'

And as they all shuffled out of the police station, he heard them saying to each other in tones of relief that Moira need never know a thing about any of it. He wondered vaguely who Moira might be, but it was late and he could now go home to his wife Ita, who always had a hundred stories of her day's work on the wards in St Brigid's. He would tell her this one, if he had the energy to unpick who was who.

Muttie was asleep when Lizzie arrived at his bedside. They told her that he would need a scan in the morning but that he was comfortable now; far better for her to be at home and get a good night's sleep. She left the suitcase for him beside his bed.

'Can I leave him a note?' she asked, fearful of strange places and unfamiliar surroundings. A nurse brought her pen and paper.

Lizzie pinned a note to the suitcase.

Muttie, my darling, I've gone home but I'll be back tomorrow. You're going to be fine. The next time we use this suitcase will be when we go to New York and have dinner in Chinatown.

Love from,
Lizzie

She felt better, she told Declan, now that she had written a letter.

His relief at the safe return of Frankie was tempered by what he had just discovered: he had spoken to the medical team that had examined Muttie. The cancer had spread all over his body.

It would not be long now.

Lisa thought that the night would never end. Teddy's birthday party at Anton's was in full swing when they got there. They had just put on music and were beginning to dance. Straightaway she noticed April dancing around Anton.

'Hey, that's not dancing! That's lap dancing!' she called in a very loud voice. A few people laughed. Anton looked annoyed.

April went on weaving and squirming.

'Suit yourself,' she said to Lisa. 'You dance your way – I dance mine.'

Lisa, her rage fuelled by alcohol and jealousy, was about to engage in further conversation, but Moira interrupted quickly.

'I need a glass of water, Lisa. Can you come and get one with me?'

'You don't need water,' Lisa said.

'Oh, but I do,' Moira countered, pushing her towards

the ladies' room. There she took a glass of water and offered it to Lisa.

'You're not expecting me to drink this, are you?'

'I think you should, then we'll go home.'

Lisa was only just holding herself together. Moira must never know Frankie was missing.

'I'll think about it,' she said.

Moira spoke firmly. 'I think it would be wise. Yes, then I'll phone us a taxi.'

'No, we can't go home. Wherever we go, we can't go home!' Lisa said in fright.

Moira asked mildly, 'Well, where *do* you want to go, then?'

'I'll think,' Lisa promised.

Just then her own phone buzzed with a text message. Trembling, she read it.

All clear. Come home any time. F safe and sound.

'They *found* her!' Lisa cried.

'Who?' Moira paused in the middle of talking to the taxi firm.

Lisa stopped herself in time. 'My friend Mary! She was lost and now she's found!' she shouted, with a very unfocused look on her face.

'But you were talking to her earlier, weren't you?' Moira was perplexed.

'Yes and she got lost. And then found since then,' Lisa said foolishly.

Moira completed her call to the taxi and began to support Lisa towards the exit.

On the way, they passed Teddy, the birthday boy, who whispered in Moira's ear, 'Well done. Anton will owe you for this. We have an unexploded bomb here,' he said, nodding towards Lisa.

'Well, it's a pity he wasn't able to do something about it!' Moira retorted.

'Not his problem.' Teddy shrugged.

'Good enough to sleep with, but not important enough to be nice to, right?'

'I just said he'd be grateful to you. She was about to make a scene.'

Moira pushed past him, supporting Lisa into the taxi. Her dismal outlook on men seemed to have been confirmed tonight.

Lisa sang a little in the taxi. Sad songs about loss and infidelity, and then they were in Chestnut Court.

'Lisa's home, slightly the worse for wear,' Moira said into the entryphone.

'Can you help her inside, please, Moira?'

'Certainly.'

Noel put Frankie down for the first time since she had been found. He realised he had been clinging to her since they came back to the flat.

Faith had washed the dishes and tidied up the place.

Moira brought Lisa in the door and settled her in a chair.

'Partly my fault. We had a lot of wine at Ennio's and then we went to this party at Anton's.'

'Oh, I see,' Noel said.

'You'll be fine, Lisa,' Faith said, holding Lisa's trailing hand.

'Oh, Moira, I'm Faith, by the way. A friend of Noel and Lisa's from the college.'

'How do you do?'

Moira was gruff. She felt an unreasoning jealousy of Lisa. Nobody was blaming her for having become drunk. There was a household of people welcoming her. Even the child had stretched out her little arms towards Lisa as she lay slumped in her chair. If it had happened to Moira, she would have had to go home to an empty apartment. It seemed that almost everyone else in the world had sorted out their relationships while she, Moira, still was alone.

She left abruptly. Lisa let out a deep breath.

'I didn't tell her,' she said.

'I know you didn't,' Noel said.

'You did a great job,' Faith said, soothingly.

'Good. Glad it's sorted,' Lisa said, her voice slurring.

She began to slide off the chair, but they caught her before she reached the ground.

'When I think,' she said intensely, 'when I remember what I said to you, Noel, that it would be terrible if you were to fall into drink ... and then I went and did it myself ...'

'It doesn't matter, Lisa. You'll be fine tomorrow,' Noel said. 'And you did great work keeping Moira distracted. You did brilliantly.'

'Why don't we give Lisa a hand to get into bed?'

Faith made it all sound as if it had been a completely normal evening, what everyone did every night all over the place ...

When she got home, Lizzie was surprised to see so many people in her house. Her sister Geraldine was there; her daughter Cathy; and Cathy's husband, Tom Feather. The twins and Marco were there, and there were constant phone calls coming in from Chicago and Australia. Everyone seemed to be making tea and Marco had provided a tray of cakes.

'Won't Muttie be disappointed to have missed all

this,' Lizzie said and people looked away before she could see the pain in their faces.

Eventually they finally persuaded her to go to bed. The sitting room was still full of people. Cathy went upstairs with her mother and tried to reassure her.

'They're terrific in St Brigid's, Mam, don't be worrying about him. Geraldine's just been saying how good they are. All the best consultants and everything. They'll have Da right in no time.'

'I think he's very sick,' Lizzie said.

'But he's in the right place,' Cathy said, for the twentieth time.

'He'd prefer to be in his own home,' Lizzie said, for the thirtieth time.

'And he will be, Mam, so you're to get to sleep so that you'll be up and ready for him when he *does* come home. You're asleep on your feet.'

That worked. Lizzie made a slight movement towards the bed and Cathy had her nightdress ready. Her mother looked so small and frail; Cathy wondered would she be able to bear all that lay ahead.

Maud said that Marco had texted to say that he and Dingo Duggan would be available night and day with Dingo's van if anyone needed to be driven anywhere.

Marco had said, *I am so sorry about your grandfather. Please God, he will get better.*

'Please God, indeed,' Simon said, when Maud read him the text message.

'I think he just says that automatically.'

'Like Lizzie says "DV",' Simon agreed.

'Yes. I remember Mother used to say that too, except that she started to say "VD" instead,' Maud said. 'Dad would explain it over and over. DV meant *Deo volente*, God willing, but Mother always nodded and said VD.'

Simon and Maud talked very little about the parents who had abandoned them when they were young. This was their home. Muttie was the man they loved rather than the elegant father who had gone away on his travels. Lizzie was the mother they had never really had. Their own mother had always been frail with a light grip on reality. If they had heard that either of their biological parents had died, there would be a minor sense of regret. The news about Muttie was as if somebody had stuck a knife right into their bodies.

Nurse Ita O'Meara looked down at the man in the bed. He was in very poor shape. All she could do for him was to keep him under observation and make him comfortable.

'What's your name?' he asked her.

'I'm Ita, Mr Scarlet.'

'Then I'm Muttie,' he said.

'Well, Muttie, what can I do for you? A cup of tea?'

'Yes, I'd love some tea. Could you sit down and talk to me for a bit?'

'I could indeed, and would be glad to. We're not busy tonight.'

'Ita, you see, you don't know me from a hole in the ground.'

'That's true, but I'll get to know you,' she reassured him.

'No, that's not what I meant. I *want* someone that doesn't know me.'

'Oh yes?'

'It's easier to talk to a stranger. Will you tell me – am I for the chop?'

Ita had been asked this question before. It was never easy to answer.

'Well, you know your illness is serious and that we're at the stage where all we can do is make you comfortable. But you're not on the way out tonight.'

'Good. But some night soon, do you think?'

'It won't be long, Muttie, but I'd say you've time to sort things out.' Ita was reassuring. 'Is there anyone you want me to call for you?'

'How do you know I want to sort things out?' he asked.

'Everyone does at night, especially their first night in hospital. They want to make speeches and talk to lawyers and they want to talk to all kinds of people. Then, when they're leaving here, they've forgotten it all.'

Muttie's eyes beseeched her. 'And do you think I'll get out of here?'

Ita looked him in the eye. 'I tell you, as sure as I know my own name, you'll go home from here and then you'll forget all about us. You won't remember me and my cups of tea any more.'

'I will indeed remember you and how kind you are. I'll tell everyone about you. And you're right, I do want to make speeches and talk to lawyers and tell people things. I hope to do it all from home.'

'Good man, yourself, Muttie,' Ita said, as she took his empty teacup away.

She knew he didn't have long, but she'd do her best to make his mind easy. She sighed. He was such a warm little man. Why was he being taken when so many grumpy and sour-faced people were left for years with nobody involved in their lives? It was beyond understanding. She and Sean sometimes said it was very hard to believe in a kind, all-knowing God when you saw the random way fate worked. A decent man with a huge family and group of friends was about to die.

Sean would have similar stories from being a policeman. A kid who had joined a gang and had been caught on his first outing, faced with a criminal record; a mother who had no access to money of any kind, shoplifting to get food for her baby and ending up in court.

Life was many things, but it certainly wasn't fair.

It was clear that Muttie wanted to go home so they contacted the Palliative Care Team. Two nurses would visit him each day.

After three days, Ita handed him over to a small crowd of people, all of them delighted to see him coming home. Two of Muttie's children, Mike and Marian, together with Marian's husband Harry, had arrived from Chicago, which shocked him.

'You must be made of money that you fly all that way just to see me. Aren't I grand? I'm going home today and Ita's going to come and see me,' Muttie added.

'Oh, trust him to find someone else the moment I leave him out of my sight!' Lizzie said, with a laugh of pride in the notion of Muttie the Lothario.

Muttie's Associates from the pub were anxious to see him when he returned. Lizzie wanted to keep them at bay, but her daughter wasn't so sure.

'He relaxes when he's talking to them,' Cathy said.

'But is it sensible to have six big men in the sitting room when he's so tired all the time?'

Lizzie wasn't sure how much relaxation that would involve. Cathy knew that she was trying to restore order to the home; her brother and sister were, she knew, going to be staying for some time. They all realised their father had only a very short time to live.

Much as Lizzie and Cathy wanted to keep Muttie to themselves, with only the family around him, he did seem to blossom when friends, neighbours and Associates called. He had always been a man who loved talking with others. None of that side of him had disappeared. It was only his little, thin body that showed any sign of the disease that was killing him.

Hooves sat at his feet most of the day. He stopped eating and lay in his basket listlessly.

'Hooves and I,' said Muttie, 'we're not able to get up and about much at the moment. Maybe tomorrow ...'

Cathy and Lizzie provided endless cups of tea as a file of people passed through each day. The Associates all came together in a group and the women would hear bursts of laughter as they planned a great new world – a world without the present government, the previous governments, the banks and the law.

The Associates were mild men who talked big and Muttie had always been at their centre. They were jovial and blustering when they were with him, but Cathy could see their faces fall when they were out of his presence.

'It won't be long now, God save us all,' said one of the Associates, a man not usually known to respect the Almighty and ask for Divine help.

But mainly people came in one by one, monitored by Lizzie and Cathy.

They called to talk to him and were given fifteen minutes at the most. The kind nurse, Ita O'Meara, called. She spoke about everything except illness. They talked horses and greyhounds.

'Very sound woman,' he remarked approvingly when she left.

And they came in their droves, first asking Lizzie what would be a good time. She kept a notebook on the hall table.

Fiona and Declan came and brought little Johnny with them. They told their secret to Muttie: that they were expecting another baby. He said it would remain a secret right up to the end of his life.

Dr Hat came and brought some scones that he had made himself. Emily Lynch had been teaching him to cook and it wasn't bad at all if you put your mind to it. Muttie promised that when he got stronger he would think about it.

Josie and Charles came and talked about how a devotion to St Jarlath could help in almost any situation. Muttie thanked them and said he was as interested in St Jarlath as the next man, and that if ever he needed him he would certainly try to get in touch with the saint. However, fortunately, he was getting better now and would be back to full strength before long.

Like everyone else, Charles and Josie Lynch were mystified. They so wanted to talk to Muttie about their inheritance from Mrs Monty and how it should be spent or invested. Up to now they hadn't told anyone how much it was, not even Noel. But it seemed insensitive to talk about such things to a man who was so near death.

Could Muttie really not know that he was dying?

Molly and Paddy Carroll felt the same.

'He's talking of going to New York in a couple of months' time.' Molly was genuinely puzzled. 'Muttie won't go as far as the River Liffey, for heaven's sake – doesn't he know that?'

It was a mystery.

Noel came and brought Frankie. As Frankie sat on Muttie's knee and offered him her sippy cup, Noel talked more openly than he did to anyone. He told Muttie about the terrible fright when Frankie had been lost and how he had felt a pain in his chest as bad as if someone had put a great spade into him and lifted out his insides.

'You've made a grand job of this little girl,' Muttie said, approvingly.

'I sometimes dream that she's not my little girl at all and that someone comes to take her away,' Noel confessed, taking the child.

'That will never happen, Noel.'

'Wasn't I lucky that Stella contacted me. Suppose she hadn't, then Frankie would be growing up in a different place and she'd never know any of you.'

'And wasn't she lucky that she got you, even though you work too hard,' Muttie said.

'I have to work hard. I want to have some kind of a job that I'd be proud of by the time she's old enough to know what I'm doing.'

'And you gave up the gargle for her. That wasn't easy.'

'It's not too bad most of the time. I'm so busy, you see, but there are days when I could murder six pints. Those are bad days.'

'What do you do?' Muttie wanted to know.

'I ring my buddy in AA, and he comes over or meets me for coffee.'

'Marvellous bloody organisation. Never needed them myself, fortunately, but they do the job.' Muttie was full of approval.

'You're a great fellow, Muttie,' Noel said, unexpectedly.

'I'm not the worst,' Muttie agreed, 'but haven't I a great family around me. I'm luckier than anyone I ever heard of. There's nothing they wouldn't do for us, travelling like millionaires back from Chicago because I had a bit of a turn back there. And as for the twins ...! If I lived in a high-class hotel, I couldn't get better food served to me. They're always coming up with something new for me.'

Muttie's smile was broad at the thought of it all.

Noel held Frankie tight and she, with her interest in sharing the sippy cup now complete, returned her father's hug. Noel wondered why he dreamed that she would be taken away. She was his daughter. His flesh and blood.

Marco came to see Muttie. He was dressed in a collar and tie as if he were going somewhere very formal. Lizzie said that of course he must go in and see Muttie, but to go very gently. Hooves had died during the night and even though they had tried to keep it from Muttie, he had known there was something wrong. Eventually, they had had to tell him.

'Hooves was a great dog, we won't demean him by crying over him,' he said.

'Right,' Lizzie agreed. 'I'll tell the others.'

When Marco was ushered in, he came and stood beside the bed.

'I am so sorry about your dog, Mr Scarlet.'

'I never thought he'd go before me, Marco. But it's all for the best, he'd have been very lonely without me.'

'Mr Scarlet, I know you're not well and it's probably the wrong time to do this, but there is a question I would love to ask you.'

'And what would that be, Marco?'

Muttie smiled at the boy. The good suit, the anxious face, the sweaty palms. It was written all over him what question he was going to ask.

'I would like to ask you to give me the honour of your granddaughter's hand in marriage,' Marco said stiffly.

'You want to marry Maud? She's very young, Marco, she hasn't grown up properly and seen the world or anything.'

'But *I* would show her the world, Mr Scarlet, I would look after her so well, see that she wanted for nothing.'

'I know you would, lad, and have you asked her yourself?'

'Not yet – it's important I ask the father or grandfather first.'

'I'm not her grandfather, you know that.'

'She thinks of you as her grandfather, she loves you as if you were.'

Muttie blew his nose. 'Well, that's good, because that's the way Lizzie and I feel about her and Simon. But how can Maud marry you if she's going to New Jersey with Simon?'

'She's not going now, they've put that off,' Marco said.

'That's only because I have been sick. They'll go …
you know … afterwards.'

'You will be here for a long time, Mr Scarlet.'

'No, son, I won't, but I'm sure you and Maud have
it all worked out between you.'

'I couldn't tell her I want to marry her until I asked
you first …'

The boy's handsome face was beseeching Muttie to
give his blessing.

'And would she work with you in your father's restaurant?'

'Yes, for the moment, if she wanted to do that, then
we would both like to open a restaurant of our own.
It may be many years ahead but my father says he will
give me some money. You must have no fears about
her, she will be treasured by our family.'

Muttie looked at him. 'If Maud says she would like
to marry you, then I would be delighted.'

'Thank you, dear Mr Scarlet,' said Marco, hardly
daring to believe his good luck.

Lisa came to see Muttie also.

'I don't know you well, Mr Scarlet, but you're a great
character. I heard you'd been ill and I was wondering if
there was anything I could do for you?'

Muttie looked around to make sure there was no one
in the room with them.

'If I gave you fifty euros, could you put it on the nose
of Not the Villain for me?'

'Oh, Mr Scarlet, really …'

'It's my money, Lisa. Can't you do that for me? You
did say you wanted to help me.'

'Sure. I'll do it. What odds do you expect?'

'Ten to one. Don't take less.'

'But then you'd win five hundred,' she said, stunned.

'And you will get an enabler's fee,' Muttie said, laughing heartily as Lizzie bustled in to clear the teacups and arrange a little rest time before the next visitor.

Lisa didn't know where there were any local betting shops, but Dingo Duggan was able to come up with the name of a nearby place.

'I'll drive you there,' he said helpfully.

Dingo rather fancied Lisa and he liked to be seen with a good-looking girl sitting up front in his van.

'Got a good tip, then?' he asked.

'Someone asked me to put fifty euros on a horse at ten to one.'

'God, that must be a great horse,' Dingo said, wistfully. 'Wouldn't it be wonderful if you were to drop the name to me. I mean, it won't shorten the price or anything. I only have ten euros, but it would be great to have a hundred. Great altogether.'

Lisa told him the name of the horse but warned him, 'The source is not entirely reliable, Dingo. I'd hate to see you lose your money.'

'Don't worry,' Dingo reassured her. 'I have a very sharp mind.'

Lisa felt out of place in the betting shop and the presence of Dingo made it worse.

'Where are you off to now?' Dingo asked when the transaction was over.

'I'm going to see Anton,' Lisa said.

'I'll drive you there,' Dingo offered.

'No, thank you – I need a walk to clear my head and I've got to get my hair done, too.'

These were perfectly ordinary things to do, but Dingo noticed that Lisa announced them as if they were matters of huge importance. He shrugged.

Women were very hard to understand.

Katie sighed when Lisa came in. Yet another demand for a quick fix. The salon was already full. Had she ever heard of the appointment system?

'I need something, Katie,' Lisa said.

'It will be half an hour at least,' Katie said.

'I'll wait.' Lisa was unexpectedly calm and patient.

Katie glanced at her from time to time. Lisa had magazines in her lap, but she never looked at them. Her eyes and mind were far away.

Then Katie was ready. 'Big date?' she asked.

'No. Big conversation, actually.'

'With Anton?'

'Who else?'

'You'd want to be careful, Lisa.' Katie was concerned.

'I've been careful for years and where has it got me?'

Lisa sat looking, without pleasure, at her reflection in the mirror. Her pale face and wet hair showed up the dark circles under her eyes.

'We'll make you lovely,' said Katie, who seemed to have read her thoughts.

'It would help if I looked a bit lovelier all right.' Lisa smiled very weakly. 'Listen, I want you to cut it all off. I want very short hair, cropped short all over.'

'You're out of your mind, you've always had long hair. Don't do anything reckless.'

'I want it short, choppy, a really edgy style. Will you do it or do I have to go to a rival?'

'I'll do it, but you're going to wake up tomorrow and wish you hadn't done it.'

'Not if you give me a good cut, I won't.'

'But you said he liked you with long hair,' Katie persisted.

'Then he'll have to like me with short hair,' Lisa countered.

It was achieved in two hours: a full make-up, a manicure and a new hairdo. Lisa felt a lot better. She offered to pay, but Katie waved it away.

'Don't say anything to Anton in a temper. Say nothing that you don't want to stand over. Be very careful.'

'Why are you telling me this? You don't like Anton. You don't think he's right for me,' Lisa asked in confusion.

'I know. But you like him and I like you a lot, so I want you to be happy.'

Lisa kissed her sister. It was a rare thing to happen.

Katie felt it was unreal. Lisa, always so prickly and abstracted, had actually put her arms around her, hugged her and kissed her on the cheek.

What next?

Lisa walked purposefully towards Anton's. This was a good time to catch him. The afternoons were easier and less fussed. All she would have to do was get rid of Teddy and hunt April off the premises if she were there, then she would talk to Anton properly.

Teddy saw her coming in but didn't recognise her at first.

'Fasten your seat belts,' he hissed at Anton.

'Oh God, not today, not on top of everything else …' Anton groaned.

When Lisa came in, she looked well and she knew it. She walked confidently and had a big smile on her face. She knew they were looking at her, Anton and Teddy, registering shock at the difference in her. The short hair gave her confidence; it was much lighter than before, still golden and silky. She smiled from one to the other, turning her head so that they could get a good view of her and her changed look.

'Ah, coffee …' she said, apparently delighted. 'Teddy, will you forgive me, I have to talk to Anton about something for a short while?'

She spoke on a rising note as if she were asking a question to which there was only one answer.

Teddy looked at Anton, who shrugged. So then he left.

'Well, Lisa, what is it? You look terrific, by the way.'

'Thank you so much, Anton. How terrific do I look?'

'Well, you look very different, shiny, sort of. Your hair is gone!'

'I had it cut this morning.'

'So I see. Your beautiful long golden hair …' He sounded bemused.

'It just covered the floor of the salon. In the olden days they used to sell their hair for wigs, did you know that?'

'No, I didn't,' Anton said weakly.

'Oh, they did. Anyway, there we are.'

'I liked your hair, in fact I *loved* your long hair,' he said regretfully.

'Did you, Anton? You *loved* my long hair?'

'You look different now, changed somehow, still gorgeous but different somehow.'

'Good, so you like what you see?'

'This is silly, Lisa. Of course I like it. I like you.'

'That's it? You like me?'

'Is this Twenty Questions or what? Of course I like you. You're my friend.'

'Friend – not *love*?'

'Oh well, love. Whatever …' He was annoyed now.

'Good, because I love you. A lot,' she said, agreeably.

'Aw, come on, Lisa. Are you drunk again?' he asked.

'No, Anton. Stone cold sober and the one time I ever did get drunk, you weren't very kind to me. You more or less ordered Teddy to throw me out of here.'

'You were making a fool of yourself. You should thank me.'

'I don't see it that way.'

'Well, I was the one who was sober on that occasion – believe me, you were better out of here before even more people saw you.'

'What do you think of when you think of me? Do you love me a lot or only a little?'

'Lisa, these are only words. Will you stop this thirteen-year-old chat?'

'You say you love me when we make love.'

'Everyone says that,' Anton said defensively.

'I don't think so.'

'Well, I don't know. I haven't conducted a survey on it.' He was really irritated now.

'Calm down, Anton.'

'I'm totally calm …'

'It would make this discussion easier if you didn't fly

into a temper. Just tell me how important I am in your life.'

'I don't know … very important – you do all the designs; you have lots of good ideas; you're very glamorous and I fancy you a lot. Now will that do?'

'And do you see me as part of your future?' She was still unruffled.

There was a silence.

Lisa remembered Katie's advice not to be reckless, not to say anything she couldn't stand over. Maybe he would say no, that she wasn't part of the future for him. This would leave her like an empty, hollow shell but she didn't think he would say it.

Anton looked uncomfortable. 'Don't talk to me about the future. None of us knows where we will be in the great future.'

'We're old enough to know,' Lisa said.

'Do you know what Teddy and I were talking about when you came in and turfed him out?'

'No. What?'

'The future of this restaurant. The takings are appalling, we're losing money hand over fist. The suppliers are beginning to scream. The bank isn't being helpful. Some days we're almost empty for lunch. Today we only had three tables. We'd be better giving everyone who booked fifty euros and telling them to go away. Tonight we will only be half full. Punters notice these things. It needs some kind of a lift. It's going stale. You want to talk about the future – I don't think there is one.'

'Do you see *me* in your future?' Lisa asked again.

'Oh God Almighty, Lisa, I do if you could come up

with some ideas rather than bleating like a teenager. That is if we *have* a future here at all ...'

'Ideas – is that what you want?' Her voice was now, if anything, dangerously composed.

Anton looked at her nervously. 'You're a great ideas woman.'

'Okay. Light lunches – low-calorie healthy lunches in one part of the dining room where they can't see roast beef or tiramisu going past. And even that fool April could get you some publicity for this. Oh, and you could organise a weekly section on a radio show where people could send in their recipes for things that are under two hundred and fifty calories and you can judge them. Are those good ideas?'

'As usual you're right on the button. Will we call in the others to discuss this?'

'And what ideas do you have about me?' she asked.

'Are you still on this thing?'

'Just tell me. Tell me now – answer me and I'll stop asking you,' she promised.

'OK. I admire you a lot. I'm your friend ...'

'And lover ...' she added.

'Well, yes, from time to time. I thought you felt the same about it all.'

'Like what exactly?'

'That it was something nice we shared – but not the meaning of life or anything. Not a steady road to the altar.'

'So why did you continue to have me around?'

'As I've said, you're bright, very bright, you're lovely and you're fun. And also I think a little lonely.'

As she heard the words, something changed in Lisa's head. It was like a car moving into another gear. It was almost as if she were coming out of a dream. She could take his indifference, his infidelity, his careless ways.

She could not take his pity.

'And you might be a little lonely too, Anton, when this place fails. When Teddy has bailed out and gone to another trendy place, when little Miss April has flown off to something that's successful. There's nowhere in her little life for failure. When people say, "Anton? Isn't he the one who used to own some restaurant … popular for a while but it disappeared without trace." You might well be lonely then, too. So let's hope someone will take pity on you and you'll see how it feels.'

'Lisa, please …'

'Goodbye, Anton.'

'You'll come back when you're more yourself.'

'I think not.' She was still composed.

'Why are you so angry with me, Lisa?'

His head was on one side – his persuasive position.

But it didn't change her mind.

'I'm angry with myself, Anton. I had a perfectly good job and I left it because of you. I meant to get other clients, but there was always something to be done here. I'm broke to the world. I'm depending on a horse called Not the Villain to win a race today because if he does I get something called an enabling fee and I'll be able to buy my share of the groceries for the flat where I have a room.'

'*Not the Villain*,' Anton said slowly, 'that's how I see myself – I didn't think you were serious. I really am actually like that horse you've put money on. I'm not the villain here, you know.'

'I know. That's why I'm angry. I got it so wrong …'

*

381

Teddy heard the door bang closed and came in.

'Okay?' he asked.

'Teddy, if this place looked seriously like going under, would you go somewhere else?'

'Little bitch – she told you,' Teddy said.

'Told me what?'

'She must have seen me or heard somehow. I went to the new hotel on the river to know if there might be a vacancy and they said they'd see. This city is worse than a small village. Lisa must have heard it from them.'

'No, she didn't even know about it.'

Anton suddenly felt very tired. There had been something very final about the way Lisa had left the restaurant. But it was all nonsense, wasn't it? She hadn't been serious about any of it. Probably some of her girlfriends were settling down and getting pregnant and she felt broody. And that idea about the light lunches wasn't a bad one at all. They could get little cards designed with some kind of logo on them. Lisa would be great at that when she stopped all this other nonsense ...

Lisa walked out of the restaurant jauntily and as she moved through the crowded streets she was aware that people glanced at her with what she thought was admiration. She wouldn't think about what she had just said and done. She would compartmentalise things. Park this side of her life here and leave it until it was needed again. Concentrate on something else altogether. This was a city full of promise, potential friends and even possible loves. She would tidy Anton away and hold her head high.

*

Then, quite unexpectedly, she met Emily, who was wheeling Frankie in her buggy.

'I'm getting her used to shopping – she's going to spend years of her life doing it so she might as well know what it's all about.'

'Emily, you are funny. What have you bought today?'

'A bedspread, a teapot, a shower curtain. Really exciting things,' Emily said.

Frankie gurgled happily.

'She sounds happy now, but you should have heard her half an hour ago. I wonder if she's starting to teethe, poor thing. She was red-faced and howling and her gums look a little swollen. We're in for a bumpy ride if that's it,' Emily explained.

'Sure we are,' said Lisa. 'I think I'd better move out for the next few months!'

And, with a smile and a hug for Frankie, she was gone.

When Emily and Frankie got back to number 23 it was obvious that Josie had something important to say.

'Things aren't great down the road,' she said, her face grim.

That could have meant almost anything. That the takings were down at the thrift shop or that Dr Hat had put out some washing that had blown away in the wind or that Fiona and Declan were moving house. Then, with a lurch, she realised that Josie might be talking about Muttie.

'It's not …?'

'Yes. Things are much worse.'

Josie seemed unsure whether she should call on the household or not.

Emily thought not. They would only be in the way. Muttie and Lizzie would have lots of family already. Josie accepted this.

'I saw Father Brian going in there earlier,' she said.

Frankie chuckled, reaching out for Emily to be picked up.

'Good girl.'

Both women spoke slightly abstractedly, then each of them sighed.

Josie was wondering whether saying another Rosary would help. Emily was wondering what would be of most practical help. A big shepherd's pie, she thought, something they could keep warm in the oven for whenever anyone needed food. She would make one straightaway.

Muttie was annoyed that he felt so weak. Day and night seemed to merge and there was always someone in the room, usually telling him to rest. Hadn't he been resting since he came back from that hospital?

There were so many things still to sort out. The lawyer would drive you insane with the way he talked, but he did seem clear about one thing. The tiny amount of money the Mitchell family had paid towards the upkeep of the twins years ago, and which had stopped promptly on their seventeenth birthday, had all been kept in a deposit account and with it there was a percentage of Muttie's Great Win, the time he won a fortune and they all nearly went into heart failure.

The rest of the will was simple: everything to Lizzie and their children. But Muttie was very agitated in case the twins were not properly provided for.

'They will be well set up when they inherit all this,' the lawyer said.

'Well, so they should be. You see, when they came to us they gave up any chance of being in society. They were born to be with classier people than us, you see. They must be compensated properly.'

The lawyer turned away so that Muttie wouldn't see his face and watch him swallowing the lump in his throat.

Father Flynn came to see him.

'God, Muttie, and you grand and peaceful here compared to the world outside.'

'Tell me all about what's going on outside?' Muttie's curiosity was undimmed, despite his illness.

'Well, down at the centre where I work, there's all hell to pay over a Muslim wedding. This couple want one and I directed them towards the mosque. Anyway, some of the family don't want to go to it and some do. I said we would do the catering – your grandchildren could cook for anyone – and then there's a wing that says the centre is a Catholic place and run with money from the Church. I tell you, you'd be demented by it all, Muttie.'

'I wouldn't mind being out in it for a bit, though.' Muttie sounded wistful.

'Ah, you will, you will.' Brian Flynn hoped that he sounded convincing.

'But if I don't see it all again and I'm for the high jump, do you really think there's anything, you know ... up there?'

'I'm going to tell you the truth, Muttie. I don't know, but I think there is. That's the glue that has held me together for all these years. I will be one disappointed man if there isn't anything up there.'

Muttie was perfectly pleased with this as an answer. 'You couldn't say fairer than that,' he said, approvingly.

And as Brian Flynn left the house, he wondered, had any other priest of God delivered such a banal and bland description of the faith to a dying man?

Lisa Kelly came to call again. The family weren't sure he was up to seeing her.

'I have a secret I want to tell him,' she said.

'Go in then with your secret – but only ten minutes,' Lizzie said.

Lisa put on her biggest smile.

'I have five hundred euros for you, Muttie. Not the Villain won by three lengths.'

'Lower your voice, Lisa. I don't want any of them knowing I'm gambling,' he said.

'No, I told them I had a secret to discuss with you.'

'They'll think we were having an affair,' Muttie said, 'but Lizzie would prefer that than the gambling.'

'So where will I put the money, Muttie?'

'Back in your handbag. It was only the thrill of winning I wanted.'

'But, Muttie, I can't take five hundred euros. I was hoping for an enabler's fee of about fifty, that's all.'

'Spend it well, child,' Muttie said, and then his head drooped back on the pillow and Lisa tiptoed out of the room.

Immediately, Maud went in to see him.

Muttie opened his eyes. 'Do you love this Marco, Maud?' he asked.

'Very much. I know I haven't had a series of people to compare him to, like you should.'

'Says who?' Muttie asked.

'Says everyone, but I don't care. I'll never meet anyone better than Marco. They couldn't exist.'

He put out his hand and held hers.

'Then hold on to him, Maud, and find a nice girl for Simon too. Maybe at the wedding.'

Maud held the thin hand and sat with him as he fell asleep. Tears came to her eyes and trickled down, but she didn't raise a hand to brush them away. Sleep was good. Sleep was painless. Maud wanted Muttie to have as much of this as he could get.

Muttie's children knew it would be today or tomorrow. They kept their voices low as they moved around the house. They reminded each other of days in their childhood when Muttie and Lizzie had made a picnic with jam sandwiches and taken them on a train to the sea in Bray.

They remembered the time of a small win, which Muttie had spent on two roast chickens and plates full of chips. And how they had always been dressed up for first communion and confirmation like the other children, though this might have meant a lot of visiting the pawn shop. Muttie at weddings; their dog Hooves; Muttie carrying the shopping for Lizzie.

They had to share all these thoughts when they were out of Lizzie's hearing. Lizzie still thought he was getting better.

Ita, the nurse, came that day with a herbal pillow for Muttie. She looked at him and he didn't recognise her.

'He'll go into a coma shortly,' she said gently to

Maud. 'You might ask Dr Carroll to look in and the care nurses will do all that has to be done.'

For the first time it hit Maud really hard. She cried on Simon's shoulder. Soon there would be no more Muttie and her last conversation with him had been about Marco.

She remembered what Muttie had said when their beloved dog Hooves had died.

'We all have to be strong in honour of Hooves. He wasn't the kind of spirit that people go bawling and crying about. In his honour, be strong.'

And they were strong as they buried Hooves.

They would be strong for Muttie as well.

'It's going to be hardest knowing that he doesn't exist any more,' Simon said.

Brian Flynn was having a cup of tea with them. 'There is a thought that if we remember someone, then we keep them alive,' he said.

There was a silence. He wished he hadn't spoken.

But they were all nodding their heads.

If keeping people in your memory meant that they still lived, then Muttie would live for ever.

Lizzie said she was going to go in and sit with him.

'He's in a very deep sleep, Mam,' Cathy said.

'I know. It's a coma. The nurses said it would happen.'

'Mam, it's just—'

'Cathy, I know it's the end. I know it's tonight. I just want to be alone with him for a little bit.'

Cathy looked at her open-mouthed.

'I knew for ages, but I just didn't let myself believe it until today, so look at all the happy days I had when the rest of you were worrying yourselves sick …'

Cathy brought her mother into the room and the nurse left. She closed the door firmly.

Lizzie wanted to say goodbye.

'I don't know if you can hear me or not, Muttie,' Lizzie said. 'But I wanted to tell you that you were great fun. I've had a laugh or a dozen laughs every day since I met you and I've been cheerful and thought we were as good as anyone else. I used to think we were lower somehow. You made me think that even if we were poor, we were fine. I hope you have a great time until … well, until I'm there too. I know you're half a pagan, Muttie, but you'll find out that it's all there – waiting for you. Now won't that be a surprise? I love you, Muttie, and we'll manage somehow, I promise you.'

Then she kissed his forehead and called the family back in.

Twenty minutes later the palliative-care nurse came out and asked if Dr Declan Carroll was there.

Fiona phoned his mobile.

'I'll be there in fifteen minutes,' he said, and somehow they sat there for a quarter of an hour until Declan arrived and went into the bedroom.

He came out quickly.

'Muttie is at peace … at rest,' he confirmed.

They cried in disbelief, holding on to each other.

Marco had arrived and he was considered family for this. Some of Muttie's Associates, who seemed to fill the house with their presence, took out handkerchiefs and blew their noses very loudly.

And suddenly Lizzie, frail Lizzie who had until

today held on to the belief that she was going to go to Chinatown in New York with Muttie, took control.

'Simon, will you go and pull down all the blinds, please. The neighbours will know then. Maud, can you phone the undertaker. His number is beside the phone, and tell him that Muttie has gone. He'll know what to do. Marco, can you arrange some food for us. People will call and we must have something to give them. Geraldine, could you see how many cups, mugs and plates we have. And could you all stop crying. If Muttie knew you were crying he would deal with the lot of you.'

Somehow they managed a few watery smiles.

Muttie's funeral had begun.

The whole of St Jarlath's Crescent stood as a guard of honour when the coffin was carried down the road.

Lisa and Noel stood with Frankie in her buggy; and they were joined by Faith, who had heard so much about this man she felt part of it all. Emily stood beside her uncle and aunt with Dr Hat and Dingo Duggan. Declan and Fiona, with little Johnny in a sling, stood with Molly and Paddy. Friends and neighbours watched as Simon and Marco helped carry the coffin. They walked in measured steps.

The Associates stood in a little line, still stunned that Muttie wasn't there urging them all to have a pint and a look at the three-thirty at Wincanton.

Somewhere far away a church bell was ringing. It had nothing to do with them but it seemed as if it was ringing in sympathy. The curtains, blinds or shutters of every house in the street were closed. People placed flowers from their gardens on the coffin as it passed by.

Then there was a hearse and funeral cars waiting to take the funeral party to Father Brian Flynn's church in the immigrant centre.

Muttie had left very definite instructions.

If I die, which is definitely on the cards, I want my funeral service to be done by Father Brian Flynn in his centre, after a very brief sort of speech and one or two prayers. And then I'd like to give my bits to science in case they're any use to anyone and the rest cremated without fuss.

Signed in the whole of my wits,
Muttance Scarlet

Marco worked in Muttie and Lizzie's kitchen, producing platters of antipasti and bowls of fresh pasta. Lizzie had said he was not to hold back. He had brought forks and plates from his father's restaurant.

Before Muttie died, he had said he could ask Maud to marry him but he wouldn't – not until she had stopped crying for her grandfather. Then he would ask her. Properly. He wondered, would he and Maud be as happy as Muttie and Lizzie? Was he enough for her – she was so bright and quick.

There was a picture of Muttie on the wall. He was smiling as usual. Marco could almost hear him saying, 'Go on there, Marco Romano. You're as good as any of them and better than most.'

It was true what they had been saying: if people remember you, then you're not dead. It was very comforting.

At the church, Father Flynn kept the ceremony very short. One Our Father, one Hail Mary and one Glory

Be to the Father. A Moroccan boy played 'Amazing Grace' on a clarinet. And a girl from Poland played 'Hail, Queen of Heaven' on an accordion. Then it was over.

People stood around in the sunshine and talked about Muttie. Afterwards they made their way back to his home to say goodbye.

Properly.

CHAPTER THIRTEEN

Everyone in St Jarlath's Crescent was the poorer after Muttie's death and people tried to avoid looking at the lonely figure of Lizzie standing by her gate as she always had. It was as if she was still waiting for him. Of course everyone rallied round to make sure that she wasn't alone, but one by one her children went back home to Chicago and Australia; Cathy had to go back to her catering company, and the twins had to go back to work at Ennio's and decide on their future.

Everyone was slowly getting back to life but with the knowledge that Lizzie had no life to get on with.

One night she might be invited to Charles and Josie's, but her eyes were far away as they talked of the campaign for the statue. Sometimes she went to sit with Paddy and Molly Carroll of an evening, but there was a limit to what she could listen to about Molly's work at the thrift shop or Paddy's confrontations at the meat counter. She had no tales of her own to tell any more.

Emily Lynch was sympathetic company; she would ask questions about Lizzie's childhood and her early days working for Mrs Mitchell. She took Lizzie back to a time before Muttie, to places where Muttie had never walked. But then Lizzie couldn't expect Emily to be there all the time. She seemed to be very friendly with Dr Hat these days. Lizzie was glad for her but at the same time she mourned Muttie.

There were so many things she wanted to tell him. Every day she thought of something new: how Cathy's first husband Neil had come to the funeral and said that Muttie was a hero, how Father Flynn had blown his nose so much they thought he might have perforated an eardrum and how he had said the kindest things about Muttie and Lizzie's wonderful extended family.

Lizzie wanted to tell Muttie that Maud would be getting engaged to Marco and that Simon was happy about it and was still thinking about going to the US. She wanted to discuss with him whether she would stay on in the house or get a smaller place. Everyone advised her that she must make no decisions for at least a year. She wondered would Muttie think that was wise.

Lizzie sighed a lot these days but she tried to smile at the same time. People had always found good humour and smiles in this house and it must not change now. It was when she was left alone that the smiles faded and she grieved for Muttie. She often heard his voice coming from another room, just not quite loud enough to hear what he said. When she made tea in the morning, she automatically made a cup for him; she set a place for him at mealtimes and the sadness of it filled her with desolation.

Her bed felt huge and empty now, and when she slept, she did so with her arm around a pillow. She dreamed of him almost every night. Sometimes good dreams of happy days and joyful times; often they were terrible dreams of abandonment, loss and sorrow. She didn't know which was worse: every morning she woke afresh to the knowledge that he was gone and would never come back. It would never be all right again.

Dr Hat suggested to Emily that they go for a picnic as the summer had finally arrived and the days were long and warm. Emily suggested Michael come with them, though for some reason Dr Hat looked a bit odd when she raised it. She made sandwiches with the crusts neatly cut off and filled two flasks with tea. She brought chocolate biscuits in a tin and they drove in Dr Hat's car out to the Wicklow mountains.

'It's amazing to have all these hills so close to the city,' Emily said admiringly.

'Those aren't hills, they're mountains,' Dr Hat said reprovingly, 'it's very important to know that.'

'I'm sorry,' Emily laughed, 'but then what can you expect from a foreigner, an outsider.'

'You're not an outsider. Your heart is here,' Dr Hat said and he looked at her oddly again. 'Or I very much hope it is.'

Michael started to hum tunelessly to himself as he gazed out of the window. Dr Hat and Emily ignored him and raised their voices.

'Oh, Hat, you feel safe enough saying that to me in front of Michael as a sort of joke.'

'I was never as serious in my life. I *do* hope your heart is in Ireland. I'd hate it if you went away.'

'Why exactly?'

'Because you are very interesting and you get things done. I was beginning to drift and you halted that. I'm more of a man since I met you.'

Michael's humming got louder, as if he was trying to drown them out.

'You are?' shouted Emily. 'Well, I feel more of a woman since I met you, so that has to be good somehow.'

'I never married because I never met anyone that didn't bore me before. I'd like … I'd like you to …'

'To do what?' Emily asked.

Michael's humming was now almost deafening.

'Oh, stop it, Michael,' Emily begged. 'Hat is trying to say something, that's all.'

'He's said it,' Michael said. 'He's asked you to marry him. Now just say yes, will you?'

Emily looked at Hat for some clarity. Hat drew the car to a slow stop and got out. He went around to the passenger side, opened Emily's door and kneeled in the heather and gorse on the Wicklow mountains.

'Emily, will you do me the great honour of becoming my wife?' he asked.

'Why didn't you ask me before?' she wondered.

'I was so afraid you'd say no and that we'd lose the comfortable feeling of being friends. I was just afraid.'

'Don't be afraid any more.' She touched him gently on the side of his face. 'I'd love to marry you.'

'Thanks be to God,' said Michael. 'We can have the picnic now!'

Emily and Dr Hat decided that there was no reason for delay at their age; they would marry when Betsy and Eric were in Ireland. This way Betsy would get to be matron of honour and Michael would be best man. They could be married by Father Flynn in his church. The twins would do the catering and they could all go on honeymoon with Dingo driving them to the West.

Emily didn't want an engagement ring. She said she

would prefer a nice solid-looking wedding ring and just that. Dr Hat was almost skittish with good humour and for the first time in his life he agreed to go to a tailor and have a made-to-measure suit. He would get a new hat to match it and promised to take it off in the church for the ceremony as long as it could be restored for the photographs.

Betsy was almost squeaking with excitement in her emails.

And he proposed to you in the car in front of this other man, Michael? This is amazing, Emily, even for you. And you're going to be living around the corner from your cousins!

But can I ask, why is he called Hat? Is it short for Hathaway or was there an Irish St Hat?

Nothing would surprise me.

Love from your elderly matron-of-honour-to-be, Betsy

Emily still managed all her various jobs: she tended window boxes, she did her stints in the surgery, she stood behind the counter in the thrift shop – which was where she found her wedding outfit. It arrived in from a shop that was about to close down. There were a number of pieces that had been display items and the owner said she would get nothing for them and it was better they went to some charity.

Emily was hanging them up carefully on a rail when she saw it. A silk dress with a navy and pale blue flower pattern and a matching jacket in navy with a small trim of the dress material on the jacket collar. It was perfect: elegant and feminine and wedding-like.

Carefully, Emily put the sum of money she would have hoped to get for it into the till and brought it home straightaway.

Josie saw her coming through the house.

'The very woman,' Josie said. 'Will you have a cup of tea?'

'A quick one, then. I don't want to leave Molly too long on her own.'

Emily sat down.

'I'm a bit worried,' Josie began.

'Tell me,' Emily sighed.

'It's this money Mrs Monty left to Charles.'

'Yes, and you're giving it to the Statue Fund.'

Emily knew all this.

'It's just that we're worried about how much it is,' Josie said, looking around her in a frightened way. 'You see, it's not just thousands ... it's hundreds of thousands.'

Emily was stunned. 'That poor old lady had that kind of money! Who'd have thought it!' she said.

'Yes and that's the problem.'

'What's that, Josie?' Emily asked gently.

Josie was very perturbed.

'It's too much to give to a statue, Emily. It's sort of different from what we had thought. We wanted a small statue, a community thing with everyone contributing. If we give this huge sum we could have a huge statue up right away but it's not quite the same ...'

'I see ...' Emily held her breath.

'It's such a huge amount of money, you see, we wonder, have we a duty to our granddaughter, for example? Should we leave a sum for her education or to give her a start in life? Or should we give some to Noel so that he has something to fall back on if times got bad? Could I retire properly, and could Charles and I go to the Holy Land? All these things are possible, I know. Would St Jarlath like that better than a statue? It's impossible to know.'

Emily was thoughtful. What she said now was very important.

'Which feels right to you, Josie?'

'That's the trouble, they both seem to be the right way to go. You see, we were never rich people. Now that we are, thanks to Mrs Monty, could we possibly have changed and become greedy like they say rich people do?'

'Oh, you and Charles would never go that way!'

'We might, Emily. I mean, here am I thinking of an expensive tour to the Holy Land. You see, I tell myself that maybe St Jarlath would *prefer* us to spend the money doing good in other ways.'

'Yes, that is certainly a possibility,' Emily agreed.

'You see, if I could only get some kind of a sign as to what he wanted ...'

'What would God have wanted, I wonder?' Emily speculated. 'Our Lord wasn't into big show and splendour. He was more into helping the poor.'

'Of course, the poor can be helped by a statue reminding them of a great saint.'

'Yes ...'

'You're going off the idea of the statue, aren't you?' Josie said, tears not far from her eyes.

'No, I'm all in favour of the statue. You and Charles have been working on it for so long. It's a *great* idea, but I think it should be the smaller statue you originally thought of. Greatness isn't shown by size.'

Josie was weakening. 'We could give one big contribution to the fund and then invest the rest.'

'From what you know about St Jarlath, do you think he'd be happy with that?'

Emily knew that Josie must be utterly convinced in her heart before she abandoned the cracked notion of spending all this money on a statue.

'I think he would,' Josie said. 'He was all for the good of the people and if we were to put a playground at the end of the Crescent for the children, wouldn't that be in the spirit of it all?'

'And the statue?' Emily hardly dared to breathe.

'We could have it *in* the playground. Call it all "St Jarlath's Garden for Children".'

Emily smiled with relief. Her own view of God was of a vague benevolent force that sometimes shaped people's lives and other times stayed out of it and let things happen. She and Hat argued about this. He said it was a manifestation of people's wishes for an afterlife and to try to put more sense into the time we spent on earth.

But today Emily's God had intervened. He had ensured that Charles and Josie would help their son and their granddaughter. They would build a playground to keep the children safe. They would go to see Jerusalem and, most merciful of all, it would be a small statue and not a monstrosity that would make people mock them.

This would happen at a very good time for Noel. His exams were coming up soon and he had looked strained and overtired in the past few days.

'Once you and Charles have agreed, you should tell Noel,' Emily suggested.

'We'll talk it over tonight. Charles is out walking dogs in the park.'

'I have a lovely lamb stew for you,' Emily said.

She had actually cooked it for Hat and herself but this was more important. Josie must not be given *any* excuse to put off telling Charles about her decision. Josie was easily distracted by things like having to put a meal on the table.

Emily would make something else for herself and Hat.

They did their roster every Sunday night. A page was put up on the kitchen wall. You could easily read who was minding Frankie every hour of the day. Noel and Lisa each had a copy as well. Soon she would be old enough to go to Miss Keane's day nursery: that would be three hours accounted for each day. Only the name of who was to collect her would be needed for the mornings.

Lisa would take her to Miss Keane's and a variety of helpers would pick her up. Lisa wasn't free at lunchtime. She had a job making sandwiches in a rather classy place on the other side of the city. It wasn't a skilled job, but she brought to it all the skills she had. It paid her share of the groceries and little by little she told them her ideas.

A gorgonzola and date sandwich? The customers loved it, so she suggested little posters advertising the sandwich of the week and when they said it would be too expensive to do them, she drew them herself. She even designed a logo for the sandwich bar.

'You're much too good to be here,' said Hugh, the young owner.

'I'm too good for everywhere. Weren't you lucky to get me?'

'We were, actually. You're a mystery woman.'

He smiled at her. Hugh was rich and confident and good-looking. He fancied her, but Lisa realised that she had got out of the way of looking at men properly.

She had forgotten how to flirt.

She did other things to keep busy.

She joined Emily in the window-box patrol and learned a lot about plants as well as the lives of the people in St Jarlath's Crescent. She learned about feeding plants, and repotting. It was a different world, but she picked it up quickly. Emily said she was a natural. She could run her own plant nurseries.

'I used to be bright,' Lisa said thoughtfully. 'I was really good at school and then I got a great job in an agency ... but it all drifted away ...'

Emily knew when to leave a silence.

Lisa went on almost dreamily, 'It was like driving into a fog really, meeting Anton. I forgot the world outside.'

'And is the world coming back to you yet?' Emily asked gently.

'Sort of peering through the foggy curtains.'

'Are there things you meant to do before and didn't get to do them?'

'Yes, a lot of things and I'm going to do them. Starting with these exams.'

'It will concentrate the mind,' Emily agreed.

'Yes and keep me away from Anton's ...' Lisa said ruefully.

She knew very clearly that if she went back to the restaurant they would all greet her warmly. Her absence would not need to be explained. They would assume she had just had a hissy fit and had now come to her senses. Teddy would smile and hand her an espresso, April would look put out and Anton would look at her lazily and say she was lovely and the days had been lonely and colourless since she had gone. On the surface nothing would have changed. Deep down, though, it was all changed. He didn't love her. She had just been available, that was all.

But as she had said to Emily, there were still a lot of things that had to be done about other aspects of her life. One of these was arranging to meet her mother.

Since she had discovered that her father brought prostitutes home, Lisa's encounters with her mother had been sparse. They had coffee every now and then, and they'd had lunch before Christmas. A dutiful exchange of gifts was made and they both engaged in a polite fiction of a conversation.

Mother had asked about Lisa's design work for Anton's.

Lisa had asked about Mother's garden and whether she had decided on having a greenhouse or not. They had both talked a lot about Katie's salon and how well it was doing. Then, with relief, they had parted.

Nothing dangerous had been said, no forbidden roads had been opened up.

But this was no way to live, Lisa told herself. She must urge Mother to do what she had done herself and cut free from the old bonds.

She telephoned her mother immediately.

'Lunch? What's the occasion?' her mother asked.

'There's no law that says we can only meet on special occasions,' Lisa said. She could tell that her mother was confused.

'Let's go to Ennio's,' she suggested and before her mother could find a reason not to go it was all settled. 'Ennio's, tomorrow, one o'clock.'

Di Kelly looked well as she came into the restaurant. She wore a red belted coat with a white polo-necked sweater underneath. She must be fifty-three but she didn't look forty. Her hair showed that all that brushing had not been in vain and all that walking had ensured that she was trim and fit.

She did not, however, look at ease.

'This is nice,' Lisa said brightly. 'How have you been keeping?'

'Oh, fine. And you?'

'Fine also.'

'And have you any news for me?' her mother asked with an interested expression on her face.

'What kind of news exactly?'

'Well, I wondered if you were going to tell me that you and this Anton were getting married or anything. You've had him out on approval for long enough.'

She gave a tinkling laugh, showing she was nervous.

'Married? To Anton? Lord, no! I wouldn't dream of it.'

'Oh sorry, I thought that this was what this is about. You were going to ask me to the wedding but not your father.'

'No, nothing as dramatic as that,' Lisa said.

'So why did you invite me, then?'

'Does there have to be a reason? You're my mother and I'm your daughter. That's reason enough for most people.'

'But we aren't like most people,' her mother said simply.

'Why did you stay with him?' Lisa had not intended to ask this as baldly as it came out.

'We all have choices to make ...' Her mother was vague.

'But you couldn't *choose* to live with him, not after you knew what he was doing.' Lisa was full of disgust.

'Life's a compromise, Lisa. Sooner or later you'll understand that. I had options: leave him and be by myself in a flat, or stay and live in a house I liked.'

'But you can have no respect for him.'

'I was never very interested in sex. He was. That's all. I didn't enjoy it. You saw we had two separate beds ...'

'I also saw him bringing that woman into what was your bedroom,' Lisa said.

'It was only a couple of times. He was very ashamed that you saw. Did you tell Katie?'

'Why does that matter?' Lisa asked.

'I just wondered. She hardly ever calls. He thinks it's because you told her. I said she had stopped calling a long time ago.'

'And did it not upset you that both your daughters feel a million miles from you?'

'You are always very courteous, you've invited me to lunch to keep up the relationship.'

'What relationship? Do you think my asking you did the clematis grow over the garage, and your asking me whether Anton's is doing well is a relationship?'

Mother shrugged. 'It's as good as most.'

'No, it's not. It's totally unnatural. I live with a little baby girl. She's not yet one and she is loved by so many people you wouldn't believe it. She will never be left alone, bewildered, like Katie and I were. It's natural for people to love children. You were both so cold ... I just hoped you'd tell me why.'

Her mother was quite calm.

'I didn't like your father very much, even before we were married, but I hated my job more, and I had no money to spend on clothes, on going to the cinema, on anything. So now I have a part-time job, which I like, and I thought it was a fair exchange for marrying him. I didn't realise the sex thing was going to be so important, but, well, if I didn't want it, then it was only fair to let him go out and get it.'

'Or stay in and have it,' Lisa interrupted.

'I told you that was only two or three times.'

'How could you put up with it?'

'It was that or start out on my own again and unlike you I had no qualifications. I have a badly paid job in a dress shop. As it is, I have a nice house and food on the table.'

'So you'd prefer to share a man that you admit you don't like very much with prostitutes?'

'I don't think of it that way. I think of it as cooking and cleaning a fine house. I have a garden, which I love. I play bridge with friends and go to the cinema. It's a way of living.'

'You've obviously thought it through,' Lisa said, with some grudging acceptance.

'Yes I did. I didn't expect to tell you all this. Of course, I didn't expect you to ask.'

Her mother was self-possessed now and eating her veal Milanese with every appearance of enjoyment.

Maud was serving in the restaurant but realised that

this was a very intense conversation, so she steered away from personal chat. She moved gracefully around the room and Lisa saw Marco looking at her approvingly as he poured the wine for customers. That was what love and marriage was about – not this hopeless, downbeat bargain that her parents had made. For the first time ever, Lisa felt a wave of sympathy wash over her.

For both of them.

Faith stayed in the flat several nights a week now. She was able to look after Frankie and put her to bed on the evenings that all three of them studied. It was a curious little family grouping, but it worked. Faith said she found working like this so much easier than doing it alone. Between them they went over the latest lecture and talked it out. They made notes on what to ask the lecturer next week and they revised for their exams. They all felt that it had been worth doing and now that graduation was in sight they began to imagine how it would all work out for them when they had letters after their names.

Noel would immediately seek a better position at Hall's and if it wasn't forthcoming, then he would have the courage and qualifications to apply somewhere else. Faith would put herself forward as a manager in her office. She was doing that work in all but name and salary so they would have to promote her.

Lisa? Well, Lisa was at a loss to know what her qualifications would lead to.

At one time she had hoped to be a partner in Anton's. She had been going to invite Anton, Teddy and a few of the others to her graduation. She had even planned what to wear on the day.

But now? Well, she would have to return to the marketplace. It was humiliating, but she would have to contact Kevin, the boss she had left to go and work with Anton. That was last year when she had been reasonably sane and good at her job.

She picked up the phone with trepidation.

'Well, *hello*!'

Kevin was entitled to be surprised and a bit mocking. For months now Lisa had avoided him if ever they turned up at the same function; he had not been a customer in Anton's. It was very hard to call him and tell him that she had failed.

He made it fairly easy.

'You're on the market again, I gather,' he said.

'You can crow, Kevin. You were right. I should have listened. I should have thought it out.'

'But you were in love, of course,' Kevin said.

There was only a mildly sardonic tone to his voice. He was entitled to have a lot more I-told-you-so.

'That was true, yes.'

If he noticed the past tense he said nothing.

'So he didn't pay you in cash – I'm guessing. Did he repay you in love?'

'No, that's in pretty short supply these days.'

'So you're looking for a job?'

'I was wondering if you knew of anything? Anything at all?'

'But this may just be a lovers' tiff. In a week's time you could well be back with him.'

'That won't happen,' Lisa said.

'Right now I can only offer you a junior place. Somewhere to settle for a while. I can't give you a top job. It wouldn't be fair on the others.'

She was very humble now. 'I'd be more grateful than I could tell you, Kevin.'

'Not at all. Start Monday?'

'Can I make it the Monday after? I'm working in a sandwich bar and I'll have to give them notice … get someone else for them.'

'My, my, Lisa, you *have* changed,' Kevin said as he hung up.

Lisa went and told the young playboy Hugh immediately. 'I'll find you another sandwich maker in a week,' she promised.

'Hey, I want much more than that. I want a market adviser and a graphic designer as well,' he laughed.

'That may take longer, but anyway I wanted to tell you.'

'I'm sorry to lose you. I had ferocious designs on you actually. I was biding my time.'

'Always a mistake,' she said cheerfully. 'Now, Hugh, if you are to have any business at all, put your mind on sandwiches – what about a mild tandoori chicken wrap? They'd love that.'

'Let's go out in a blaze of glory for your last week.'

Lisa made the spicy chicken sandwiches and in between times texted Maud and Simon to look for a replacement. One of their friends would be able to do it without any problem. They had found somebody in a couple of hours.

'Send her up to me and I'll train her in,' Lisa suggested.

The girl was called Tracey. She was eager-looking but covered in tattoos.

Tactfully, Lisa offered her a shirt.

'We wear these here buttoned at the wrist,' she said. 'Hugh is very insistent about that.'

'Bit of an old fuddy-duddy, is he?' Tracey asked.

'Bit of a young fuddy-duddy; definitely a looker,' she said.

Tracey brightened. This job might have hidden benefits.

Lisa was amazed at how quickly she managed to adapt to a life that didn't centre around Anton's. Not that she didn't miss it; several times a day she wondered what they might all be doing and whether Anton would use any more of her ideas to beat the downturn in business. But there was plenty to occupy her and on most fronts it was going very well.

Lizzie found the days endless. The savage, raw pain of grief was now giving way to a gnawing ache and the void in her life was threatening to consume her.

'I'm thinking of getting a little job,' she confided to the twins.

'What work would you do, Lizzie?' Simon asked.

'Anything really. I used to clean houses.'

'You'd be too tired for that nowadays,' Simon said frankly.

'You could work at managing something, Lizzie,' Maud suggested.

'Oh, I don't think so. I'd be afraid of the responsibility.'

'Would you like to work in Marco's restaurant? Well, his father's restaurant. They're looking for someone to come in part time. I heard Ennio say they needed someone to supervise sending the laundry out and take in the cheese delivery and to sort yesterday's tips out from the credit-card receipts. You could do that, couldn't you?'

'Well, I might be able to, but Ennio would never give me a big responsible job like that,' Lizzie said anxiously.

'Of course he would,' Simon said loyally.

'You're family, Lizzie,' said Maud, looking down with pleasure at her engagement ring.

Ania's baby was due in a couple of months and there was great excitement in the heart clinic, mainly because Ania wouldn't begin her maternity leave.

'I feel much safer here,' she said piteously, so they let her stay even though everyone jumped when she took a deep breath or reached up to take a file out of a cabinet.

Clara Casey said that Ania had been so upset by her miscarriage that they must all be on hand to help her the moment there was the remotest sign of the baby. Ania's period of bedrest was over and she was back at work, but under constant supervision. Clara knew the girl was apprehensive – far from home, from her mother and sisters. Her husband Carl was, if possible, even more excited than Ania. He took to hanging around the clinic himself in case there should be any news.

Clara was very tolerant. 'Oh, work around him,' she told the others. 'The poor boy is distracted in case anything goes wrong this time.'

Clara herself was fairly distracted by matters on the home front: Frank Ennis and his son. The relationship had been prickly from the start, and hadn't improved much during the boy's visit. Des had gone back to Australia and they kept in touch from time to time. Not often enough for Frank, who put great effort into writing weekly emails to the boy.

'You'd think he'd do more than send a postcard of the Barrier Reef,' Frank grumbled.

'Look, be grateful for what you get. My Adi only sends a card too. I don't know where she is and what she's doing. It's just the way things are.'

Then came the word they had not expected.

I find myself thinking a lot about Ireland these days. I know I was rough on you and didn't really believe you when you said you didn't know what your family had done, but it took time to get my head around it all. Perhaps we should have another go. I was thinking of spending a year there, if that wouldn't put you out. I've been in negotiations about jobs and apparently my degree and diploma would be recognised in Ireland.

You must tell me if this is something you would be happy with and I would find myself an apartment, rather than crowd you out. Who knows, during my year there we might try the father–son thing and see how it goes. In any case, I'd like to meet Clara and even my nearly stepsisters.

They were both silent when they read the letter. It was the first time Des Raven had shown any sign of wanting a father–son relationship. And also the first time that he had any thought of meeting Clara …

The results of the examinations had been posted on the college notice board. Noel and Faith and Lisa had all done well and the diploma would be theirs. They celebrated with giant ice creams at the café beside the college and planned their outfits for graduation day.

They would be wearing black gowns with pale blue hoods.

'Hoods?' Noel asked, horrified.

'That's just what they call them – they're just the bits that go over our shoulders, to mark us out as different, not engineers or draughtsmen or anything.' Lisa knew it all.

'I'm going to wear a yellow dress I have already, you won't see much of it under the gown. I'll spend the money on good shoes,' Faith decided.

'I'm going to get a red dress and borrow Katie's new shoes.' Lisa had it sorted as well. 'Now, Noel, what about you?'

'Why this emphasis on shoes?' Noel asked.

'Because everyone sees them when you go up on the stage for your parchment.'

'If I polished up these ones?' He looked down dubiously at his feet.

The girls shook their heads. New shoes were called for.

'I'll get you a pale blue tie from one of my brothers,' Faith promised.

'And I'll iron your good shirt, any money there is, spend it on shoes,' Lisa commanded.

'It's a lot of fuss about nothing,' Noel grumbled.

'Nights of lectures, hours of study – and you call it nothing!' Lisa was outraged.

'And what about the photos to show Frankie?' Faith asked.

'I'll get the damn shoes!' Noel promised.

The day of the graduation was very bright and sunny. That was a relief: there would be no umbrellas or people squinting into the rain. Frankie was excited to see them all dressing up.

She crawled around the floor, getting under everyone's feet, and mumbled a lot to herself about it – words that didn't make much sense until they identified 'Frankie too'.

'Of *course* you're going too, darling.' Faith lifted her up in the air. '*And* I have a lovely little blue dress for you to wear. It will match your daddy's tie and you'll be the most beautiful little girl in the whole world!'

Noel looked very well. He was much admired by the women, who dusted flecks off his shoulders and examined his new shoes with cries of approval. Then Emily arrived to take Frankie in the buggy wearing her new dress and they all set out for the college.

Frankie behaved perfectly during the ceremony. Better by far than other babies, who cried or struggled at crucial times during the graduation. Noel gazed at her with pride. She was indeed the most beautiful little girl in the whole world! He had done all this for her – yes, for himself too, but all this work had been worth it for the chance to make a life for his little girl.

The new graduates filed on to the stage and the audience raked through the ranks until they found their own. The graduates also searched the audience. Noel saw Emily holding Frankie and he smiled with pleasure and pride.

Lisa saw her mother and sister both dressed up to honour the day; she saw Garry there and all their friends.

Then she saw Anton.

He looked lost; as if he didn't belong there. She remembered writing down this date in his diary months back.

It didn't mean anything to her that he was there and it had all been her own fault. Anton had never loved her. It had all been in her mind.

The President spoke warmly about the graduates.

'They had to give up a lot of social life to do this course. They missed television and cinemas and theatres. They want to thank you, their families and their friends, for supporting them on this undertaking. Each and every graduate here today has gone on a journey. They are different people to the people who started out with a leap of faith. They have much more than just mere letters after their names. They have the satisfaction of having set out to do something and seen it through.

'I salute them all on your behalf.'

There was tumultuous applause at this and the new graduates all beamed from the stage. Then the presentation began ...

They had planned a special lunch in Ennio's together with Noel, his family, Emily and Hat, Declan, Fiona, Johnny and the Carroll parents. Faith would bring her father and three of her five brothers. Lizzie was working there as a supervisor and she had reserved a big table for them and Ennio would give them a special price; the twins and Marco would be serving. Lizzie would even sit down and join them for the meal.

Lizzie had found the job a great help. For whole sections of the day she didn't stop and think of Muttie with that sad, empty look that broke her neighbours' hearts. Here it was too busy, too frenetic. There was too much shouting to leave any time to go over all she had lost. Ennio was always there with a coffee or a word of encouragement. She met new people; people who had never known Muttie. It wasn't really any easier, but it was less raw. Lizzie would admit that much and the twins were there for her every step of the way. She was a religious person. She thanked God every morning and every night for having arranged things so that Maud and Simon would come and live with them.

Ennio had said they should have a banner over the table – FELICITAZIONI – TANTI AUGURI – FAITH LISA NOEL – that would be in alphabetical order, so that nobody could be offended.

'What does it mean?' Faith asked.

'Congratulations, best wishes,' Marco said excitedly.

They were a mixed group including the two babies but they all got along very well and there was no pause in the conversation. More and more food and wine kept coming to the table. And finally a great cake arrived, iced in the shape of a mortar board and scroll.

People at other tables gathered round to see it.

'It was iced by Maud,' Marco said proudly.

'And everyone else.' Maud tried to shrug it off.

'But mainly by Maud,' Marco insisted.

And then there was sparkling wine for the toast and a glass of elderflower cordial for Noel. The health of the three successful scholars was drunk and they were cheered to the echo.

To everyone's surprise, Noel stood up.

'I think that, as the President said earlier, we owe a huge debt of gratitude to our families and friends and that we three should raise a toast to you also. Without you all, we wouldn't have been able to do all this and have this great graduation day and feast. To the families and friends,' he said.

Lisa and Faith stood up and all three repeated the toast.

'*To our families and friends.*'

CHAPTER FOURTEEN

Ania's baby was almost born in the heart clinic; not quite, but almost. It came too soon.

Her waters broke during one of the healthy-cookery demonstrations and they got her into the maternity wing of St Brigid's in the shortest possible time. Later that night the news went around: a baby boy, born prematurely and taken into the Special Care Baby Unit.

Everyone was concerned for Carl and Ania: it was going to be a traumatic time for both parents. They had been so anxious throughout the pregnancy and the worrying wasn't over yet. They were staying with the tiny baby by his incubator; Carl would come down to the clinic later and tell them what was happening.

Clara Casey called her ex-husband and asked him to drop by her house.

'Don't like the sound of this,' Alan said.

'Haven't I done everything you ever asked me: had two babies for you, left you free to follow your heart? I gave you a divorce when you wanted it. I never asked you for a penny.'

'You got my house,' Alan said.

'No. If you remember, the house was paid for by a deposit from my mother and every month by a mortgage that *I* earned. It was always my house, so we won't go down that road again.'

'What do you want to talk about if I come over?' He sounded sulky now.

'Various things … the future … the girls …'

'The girls!' Alan snorted. 'Adi's off in Peru doing God knows what …'

'Ecuador, as it happens.'

'Same difference. And as for Linda, she won't speak to me if I do get in touch.'

'That's because when she told you that she and Nick were going to adopt, you said you personally would never raise another man's son yourself. That was helpful …'

'You're hard to please, Clara. If I *am* honest, it's wrong; if I'm not honest, it's wrong.'

'See you tomorrow,' Clara said and hung up.

He looked older and shabbier than before. A succession of new ladies later he was temporarily without a partner. Alan, who always prided himself on having women iron his shirts, looked vaguely down at heel.

'You look wonderful,' he said, as he said to almost every woman almost all the time. Clara ignored him.

'Coffee?' she suggested.

'Or something stronger even?' he wondered.

'No, you can't handle drink like you used to. You start crawling over me when you've had a couple of glasses of wine and I certainly don't want that.'

'You liked it well enough once,' he muttered.

'Yes, that's true, but in those days I believed everything you said.'

'Don't nag, Clara.'

'No, of course not. I'm just showing you some courtesy here. Frank is going to be moving in here next week.'

'But you can't let him!' He was shocked.

'Well, I have every intention of doing so. I just thought you should hear it from me, that's all.'

'But, Clara, you're much too old for this,' he said.

'Imagine, you were once considered quite charming and dashing,' Clara said.

Emily had the spare room in Dr Hat's house beautifully decorated and she planned a series of outings to entertain Betsy and Eric. She had this ludicrous wish that they should love Ireland as she did. She hoped that it wouldn't rain, that the streets would be free of litter, that the cost of living would not be too high.

Emily and Hat were at the airport long before the plane arrived.

'It only seems the other day since you came out to meet *me* here,' Emily said, 'and you brought me a picnic in the car.'

'I had begun to fancy you seriously then, but I was terrified you'd say it was all nonsense.'

'I'd never have said that.' She looked at him very fondly.

'I hope your friend won't think I'm too old and dull for you,' he said anxiously.

'You're my Hat. My choice. The only person I ever even contemplated marrying,' she said firmly.

And that was that.

Betsy was bemused by the size of the airport and the frantic activity all around. She had thought the plane would land in a field of cows or sheep. This was a huge sprawling place like an airport back home. She couldn't believe the traffic, the motorways and the huge buildings.

'You never told me how developed it all is. I thought it was a succession of little cottages where you knew everyone that moves,' she said, laughing.

In minutes it was as if they had never been parted.

Eric and Dr Hat exchanged relieved glances. It was all going to be fine.

Emily was going to be given away by her uncle Charles.

Charles and Josie had finally come to the conclusion that a children's playground and a *small* statue of St Jarlath would fit the bill. They had been to see a lawyer and settled a sum for Noel and one for Frankie. Charles had even arranged for Emily to have a substantial sum as a wedding gift so that she wouldn't start her married life with no money of her own. It wasn't a dowry, of course, but Charles said that so often that Emily began to wonder.

Noel knew nothing about his inheritance. Charles and Josie had been waiting to talk to him on his own. There was always someone with him – Lisa or Faith or Declan Carroll. They could hardly remember the days before Frankie was born, when Noel was a man always by himself. Now the two of them were always the centre of a group of people.

Finally they found him alone.

'Will you sit down, Noel, we have something to tell you,' Charles said.

'I don't like the sound of this.'

Noel looked from one to the other anxiously.

'No, you are going to like what your father has to say,' Josie said with a rare smile.

Noel hoped they hadn't seen a vision or anything, that St Jarlath hadn't appeared in the kitchen asking them to build a cathedral. They had seemed so normal recently, it would be a pity if they had had a setback.

'It's about your future, Noel. You know that Mrs Monty, may God be good to her, has left us a sum of money. We want to share this with you.'

'Ah, no, Dad, thank you but that's for you and Mam. You did the dog minding, I wouldn't want to take any of it.'

'But you don't know how much she left,' Charles said.

'Is there enough to take you to Rome? Or even Jerusalem? That's wonderful news!'

'There's much more than that – you wouldn't believe it.'

'But it's yours, Dad.'

'We've made arrangements for an educational policy for Frankie, so that she'll never lack for a good school. And there'll be a lump sum for yourself, maybe the deposit on a house so you'd have your own place and not have to rent.'

'But this is ridiculous, Dad, it would cost a fortune.'

'She left us a fortune. And after a lot of thought we are spending it on a children's garden with a small statue, and on our own flesh and blood.'

Noel looked at them wordlessly. They had sorted out everything that was worrying him. He would be able to have a proper home for Frankie and maybe, if she'd have him, for Faith. Frankie would get a top-class education. Noel would have his rainy-day security.

All because his father had been kind to Caesar, a little King Charles spaniel with soppy brown eyes.

Wasn't life totally extraordinary?

On the morning of the wedding, before they set out for the church Charles made a little speech to Emily.

'By rights it should have been my brother doing this but I hope I'll do you credit.'

'Charles, if it were up to my father, he wouldn't have turned up or, if he had, he would have been drunk. I much prefer having you.'

Father Flynn married them. They could have filled the church five times over, but Emily and Hat only wanted a small gathering, so twenty people stood in the sunlight as they made their vows. Then they went with Eric and Betsy to Holly's Hotel in County Wicklow and back home to St Jarlath's Crescent where the honeymoon continued for the two couples and Dingo Duggan got new tyres to make sure that they got to the West and back.

They stayed in farmhouses and walked along shell-covered shores with purple-blue mountains as a backdrop. And if you were to ask anyone who they were and what they were doing, a hundred guesses would never have said that they were two middle-aged couples on honeymoon. They all seemed too settled and happy for that.

Two days after Emily's wedding, Father Flynn heard from the nursing home in Rossmore that his mother was dying. He got down there quickly and held her hand. His mother's mind was far from clear but he felt that by being there he might be of some comfort. When his mother spoke it was of people long dead, and of incidents in her childhood. Suddenly, however, she came back to the present day.

'Whatever happened to Brian?' she asked him.

'I'm right here.'

'I had a son called Brian,' she continued as though she hadn't heard him. 'I don't know what happened to him. I think he joined a circus, he left town and no one ever heard of him again ...'

When Mrs Flynn died almost the whole of Rossmore turned out for the funeral. At the nursing home, the staff had gathered together the old lady's belongings and gave them to the priest. They included some old diaries and a few pieces of jewellery no one had ever seen her wear.

Brian looked through them as he came back in the train. The jewellery had been given to her by her husband, the diary told, but they had not been given in love but out of guilt. Brian read with pain and embarrassment that his father had not been a faithful man and he had thought he could buy his wife's forgiveness with a necklace and various brooches. Brian decided to give the jewellery to his sister Judy with no mention of its history.

He looked up the date of his own ordination to the priesthood in the battered diary. His mother had written: *This is simply the best day of my life.*

It somehow made up for thinking he had joined a circus.

*

Ania's family were on their way from Poland to be with her as she and Carl watched over Baby Robert. He was so tiny, they could have held him in the palms of their hands; instead he was lying in an incubator attached to monitors and with tubes in and out of his little body.

Ania watched carefully as the monitor showed how Robert was having difficulty breathing on his own and how the machine was breathing for him. She was able to hold his tiny hand through the holes in the incubator. He looked so small, so vulnerable, so unprepared for the world.

Back at home, they had a nursery prepared, waiting for them to come home as a new family. The room was full of gifts given to them by friends and well-wishers. There were baby clothes and toys and all the equipment for a newborn child. Carl silently wondered if Baby Robert would ever get to use it.

On the third day, Ania was able to hold her baby in her arms. Unable to speak for the emotion, her face was wet with tears of hope and joy as she held him, so tiny, so fragile.

'*Mały Cud*,' she whispered to him. 'Little miracle.'

The honeymoon had been a resounding success. Emily and Betsy were like girls chattering and laughing. Hat and Eric found a great common interest in birdwatching and wrote notes each evening. Dingo met a Galway girl with black hair and blue eyes and was very smitten. The sun shone on the newly-weds and the nights were full of stars.

It was over too soon for everyone.

'I wonder if there's any news when we get back. I wonder how Ania's baby is getting on. I do hope he's going to be all right,' Emily said as they drew closer to Dublin.

'You're really part of the place now,' Betsy said.

'Yes, isn't it odd. I never had a real conversation in my life with my father about Ireland as well as about anything else, but I do feel that I have come home.'

Hat heard her say this and smiled to himself. It was even more than he had hoped.

When they did get back they heard the astounding news that elegant Clara Casey, who ran the heart clinic, was now living with Frank Ennis and, wait for it, he had a son. Frank Ennis had a son called Des Raven who lived in Australia and was coming to Ireland.

Fiona could talk of nothing else. It had completely wiped her own pregnancy off the list of topics. Clara *live with* Frank Ennis – didn't people do extraordinary things. And Frank had a *son* she hadn't met yet. Imagine.

Their first chance to celebrate properly as a family came when Adi returned from Ecuador with her boyfriend Gerry. Des had wanted to go back to Anton's.

'It will be like starting over,' he had said.

This time, there was no need to plead for a table, even though they were nine: Clara, Frank and Des; then Adi and Gerry; Linda came with Nick. Hilary and Clara's best friend Dervla made up the party.

The restaurant was half empty and there seemed to be an air of confusion about the place. The menu was more limited than before and Anton himself was working in and out of the kitchen. He said that his number one, Teddy, had gone as he needed new pastures. No, he had no idea where he had gone.

Des Raven was very courteous to his new

almost-stepsisters. He talked to Adi about teaching; he spoke to Linda about some friends of his who had adopted a Chinese baby; he talked easily of his life in Australia.

Clara asked Anton's advice about what they should eat.

'There's a very good steak and kidney pie,' he suggested.

'That's the men sorted, but what about the rest of us?' she asked.

She noticed he was tired and strained. It couldn't be easy running a restaurant that looked as though it might be on the way down.

'Small, elegant portions of steak and kidney pie?' he suggested with a winning smile.

Clara stopped feeling sorry for him. With a smile like that he would get by. He was a survivor.

Frank Ennis, in his new suit, was in charge of the table. He poured wine readily and urged people to have oysters as the optional extra.

'I talk about my son a lot,' he said proudly to Des.

'Good. Do you talk about Clara a lot?' Des asked.

'With respect and awe,' Frank said.

'Good,' intervened Clara, 'because she wants to tell you that her clinic needs some serious extra funding ...'

'Out of the question.'

'The blood tests take too long from the main hospital. We need our own lab.'

'I'll get your blood tests fast-tracked,' Frank Ennis promised.

'You have six weeks for us to see a real difference, otherwise the fight is on,' Clara said. 'He is amazingly generous in real life,' she whispered to Dervla. 'It's just in the hospital that his rotten-to-the-core meanness shows.'

'He's delighted with you,' Dervla said. 'He has said "My Clara" thirty times during this meal alone.'

'Well, I'm keeping my name, my job, my clinic and my house, so I'm doing very well out of it,' Clara said.

'Go on out of that, playing the tough bird, you're just as soppy as he is. You're delighted at this playing-house thing. I'm happy for you, Clara. I hope that you'll be very happy together.'

'We will.'

Clara had it all planned out. Minimal disturbance to their two lives. They were both people who were set in their ways.

Lisa was surprised when Kevin asked her out to lunch.

She was in a junior position in the studio. She didn't expect her boss to single her out. In Quentins she was even more surprised that he ordered a bottle of wine. Kevin was usually a one-vodka person.

This looked like being something serious. She hoped he wasn't going to sack her. But surely he wouldn't take her out to lunch to give her the push?

'Stop frowning, Lisa. We're going to have a long lunch,' Kevin said.

'What is it? Don't keep me in suspense.'

'Two things really. Did Anton pay you anything? Anything at all?'

'Oh, why are you dragging this up? I told you it was my fault. I went in there with my eyes open.'

'No, you didn't. Your eyes were closed in mad, passionate love and, fair play to you, you're not bitter, but I really need to know.'

'No, he paid me nothing, but I was part of the place, part of the dream. I was doing it for *us*, not for him. That's what I thought, anyway. Don't make me go on repeating all this. I *know* what I did for months ... it doesn't make it any easier having to do that.'

'It's just that he's going into receivership today and I wanted to make sure you got your claim in. You are a serious victim here. You worked for him without being paid, for God's sake. You are a major creditor.'

'I haven't a notion of asking him for anything. I'm sorry it didn't work for him. I'm not going to add to his worries.'

'It's just business, Lisa. He'll understand. People have got to be paid. It will be automatic. They'll sell his assets – I don't know what he owns and what is mortgaged or leased, but people have to be paid: you among them.'

'No, Kevin, thanks all the same.'

'You love clothes, Lisa. You should get yourself a stunning wardrobe.'

'I'm not smart enough for your office? Is that it?'

She was hurt, but she made it sound like a joke.

'No, you're too smart. Much too smart. I can't keep you. I have a friend in London. He's looking for someone bright. I told him about you. He'll pay your fare to London. Overnight in a fancy hotel and you don't want to know the salary he's offering!'

'You really *are* getting rid of me and you're pretending it's promotion,' she said bleakly.

'*Never* have I been so misjudged! I'd prefer you to stay and in a year or two I could promote you, but this job is too good to ignore and I thought that anyway it might be easier for you.'

'Easier?'

'Well, you know, there'll be a lot of talk about Anton's. Speculation, newspaper stuff.'

'Yes, I suppose there will. Poor Anton.'

'Oh God, don't tell me you're going back to him.'

'No, there's nothing to go back to. There never was.'

'Ah now, Lisa, I'm sure he *did* love you in his own way.'

She shook her head. 'But in ways you're right. I couldn't bear to be in Dublin while all the vultures were picking over the place.'

'You'll go for the interview?' He was pleased.

'I'll go,' Lisa promised.

Simon said it was time they talked about New Jersey. The amazing inheritance they had got from Muttie meant that Maud and Marco could put a deposit on their own restaurant and Simon could buy into the partnership of a stylish restaurant.

'I'll miss you,' Maud said.

'You won't notice I'm gone,' he assured her.

'Who'll finish my sentences?'

'You'll have Marco trained in no time.'

'You'll fall in love and live out there.'

'I doubt it, but I'll be home often to see Lizzie and you and Marco.'

Maud noticed he didn't include their father, mother or brother Walter. Walter was in gaol, Father was on his travels and Mother only had the vaguest idea of who they were.

As if he read her mind, Simon said, 'Weren't we so lucky that Muttie and Lizzie took us in? We could have ended up anywhere.'

Maud gave him a hug. 'Those American girls don't know what's coming their way,' she said.

It was a day of many changes.

Declan and Fiona and their son Johnny moved house. It was only next door but it was still a huge move. They arranged that Paddy and Molly Carroll should be part of it all so that they would realise how nothing had really changed. They would be next door, and when Johnny was old enough to walk he would know two homes as his own. And as for the new baby? That would be born into a two-house family.

The house had been painted in a cheery primrose colour, which brought sunshine into every room. They would think about proper colour schemes later but the most important thing was to make it bright and welcoming. Johnny's room was ready and waiting for his cot. Declan and Fiona would have room for their books and music.

They would have their own kitchen at last.

The time with Molly and Paddy Carroll had been happy but it couldn't go on for ever. They had both looked forward to and dreaded the day when they would have to move to somewhere with more space: this had been an ideal solution.

They walked the few steps between the houses carrying possessions and stopping for a pot of tea in one house or the other so that it underlined how much together they were still going to be. Dimples came in and padded around the new house and seemed to approve. Emily had brought window boxes already planted as a housewarming gift.

*

Dr Hat and Emily decided to open a garden store. There was plenty of room still beside the thrift shop. Now that so many residents of St Jarlath's Crescent had begun to take an interest in beautifying their gardens, there was no end of demand for bedding plants and ornamental shrubs.

They went up and measured it. It was now no longer a wish, it was a reality, they would do it together, it would be yet one more thing they could share.

In the disturbed world of Anton's restaurant the staff were making their plans. They would not open next week. Everyone knew this.

April sat around the place with her notebook, suggesting places for Anton to do interviews on the difficulties of running a business during a recession.

Anton felt unsettled. He wasn't listening. He wondered what Lisa would be saying.

It was the day that Linda and Nick decided to stop talking about adopting a baby and do something about it.

For Noel it was a good day also.

Mr Hall had said that there was a more senior position in the company that had been vacant for some time. He now wanted to offer it to Noel.

'I have been impressed by you, Noel, I don't mind saying that you did much better than I would have thought at one stage. I always hoped you'd have it in you to make something of yourself, though I confess I had my doubts about you for a while.'

'I had my doubts about myself,' Noel had said with a smile.

'There's always some turning point for a man. What do you think yours was?' Mr Hall seemed genuinely interested.

'Becoming a father,' Noel had said without having to stop and think for a second.

And now he was at home with Frankie, helping her take her first independent steps. There were just the two of them. She still liked the comfort of something to hold on to, and every now and then she suddenly sat down with a surprised look on her face. She had been making great efforts to tear up the cloth books that Faith had given her, but they were proving very resistant. She was frowning with concentration.

'I love you, Frankie,' Noel said to her.

'Dada,' she said.

'I really do love you. I was afraid I wouldn't be good enough for you but we're not making a bad fist of it, are we?'

'*Fst*,' Frankie said, delighted with the noise of the word.

'Say "love", Frankie, say "I love you, Dada".'

She looked up at him. '*Love Dada*,' she said, as clear as a bell.

And to his surprise he felt the tears on his face. He wished not for the first time that there really was a God and a heaven too because it would be really great if Stella could somehow see this and know that it was all working out as she had hoped.

CHAPTER FIFTEEN

Noel and Lisa planned a first birthday party for Frankie. There would be an ice-cream cake and paper hats; Mr Gallagher from number 37 could do magic tricks and said he'd come along and entertain the children.

Naturally, Moira got to hear of it.

'You're having all these people in this small flat?' she asked doubtfully.

'I know, won't it be wonderful?' Lisa deliberately misunderstood her.

'You should do more for yourself, Lisa. You're bright, sharp, you could have a career and a proper place to live.'

'This *is* a proper place to live.'

Noel was out at the washing machine so didn't hear.

'No, it's not. You should have your own apartment. You'll need one soon anyway, if Noel's romance continues,' Moira said, practical as always.

'But meanwhile I'm very happy here.'

'We have to stir ourselves from our comfort zones. What are you doing here with a man who is bringing up some child that may or may not be his own?'

'Of course Frankie's his own!' Lisa was shocked.

'Well, that's as may be. She was very unreliable, the mother, you know. I met her in hospital. A very wild sort of person. She could have named anyone as the father.'

'Well, really, Moira, I never heard anything so ridiculous,' Lisa said, blazing suddenly at the mean-spirited pettiness of Moira's attitude.

Wasn't life the luck of the draw? They could have got a very nice social worker like that woman Dolores who came to Katie to get her hair done at the salon. *She* would have been delighted with the way Frankie had turned out and would rejoice at such a successful outcome. But no, they were stuck with Moira.

Thank God Noel had been in the kitchen while stupid, negative Moira was talking. It was just a miracle that he hadn't heard.

Noel had, of course, heard every word and he was holding on by a thread.

What a sour, mean cow Moira was and he had just begun to see some good in her. Not now. Not ever again after such a statement.

He managed to shout out a cheerful goodbye as he heard the door. He wouldn't think about it. It was nonsense. He would think about the party instead. About Frankie, his little girl. That woman's remarks had no power to hurt him. He would rise above it.

First he must pretend to Lisa that he hadn't heard. That was important.

Moira walked briskly along the road away from Chestnut Court. She was sorry she had spoken to Lisa like that. It was unprofessional. It wasn't like her. And then, of course, she had her own worries about her father and Maureen Kennedy. Still and all, it was no reason to run off at the mouth about Noel. Mercifully, he was in the kitchen at the washing machine and didn't hear. Lisa was unlikely to bring the subject up.

Why did worries never come singly?

Moira's brother had written to say that their father and Mrs Kennedy were getting married. Mr Kennedy was now presumed dead after fifteen years' absence with no contact being made and his name not found on any British register. They would marry in a month's time and a few people were being invited back to the house. Everyone was very pleased, her brother wrote.

Moira was sure they were, but then they didn't have to cope with the fact that Mr Kennedy was alive and well, living in a hostel and on Moira's caseload.

'Father, it's Moira.'

He sounded as surprised as if the prime minister of Australia had telephoned him.

'Moira!' was all he could say.

'I hear that you're getting married again ...' Moira came straight to the point.

'Yes, we hope to. Are you pleased for us?'

'Very, and is everyone okay with you getting married, what with ...' She paused, delicately.

'He's presumed dead,' her father said in a sepulchral way. 'The state give a declaration of death after seven years and he's been gone years longer than that.'

'And ... um ... the Church?' Moira said.

'Oh, endless conversations with the parish priest, then they went to the archdiocese, but there's a thing called *presumptio mortis* and each case is argued on its merits, and since this boyo hasn't had an address or a record of any sort, there isn't any problem.'

'And were you going to invite me?'

436

It felt like probing a sore tooth. She hoped her father would say the wedding would be very small, and considering their age and circumstances they had restricted the numbers.

'Oh, indeed. I'd be delighted if you were there. We both would be delighted.'

'Thank you very much.'

'Not at all. I'm glad you'll be there.'

He hung up without giving her the date, a time or a place but, after all, she could get those from her brother.

Frankie's birthday party was a triumph.

Frankie had a crown and so did Johnny, since it was his birthday on the same day. Apart from the two birthday babies there were very few children coming to the party, but lots of grown-ups. Lizzie was helping with the jellies and Molly Carroll was in charge of the cocktail sausages.

Frankie and Johnny were much too young to appreciate Mr Gallagher's magic tricks but the grown-ups loved him and there were great sighs of amazement as he produced rabbits, coloured scarves and gold coins from the air. The children loved the rabbits and searched fruitlessly in the magician's top hat to know where they had gone. Josie suggested a rabbit hutch in the new garden, and the idea was received with great enthusiasm.

Noel was glad the party went well. There were no tantrums among the children, no one was overtired. He had even arranged for wine and beer to be served to the adults. It hadn't bothered him in the least. Faith and Lisa cleared up and quietly put the unfinished bottles in Faith's bag.

But Noel's heart was heavy. Two chance remarks

at the party had upset him more than he would have believed possible.

Dingo Duggan, who always said the wrong thing, commented that Frankie was far too good-looking to be a child of Noel's. Noel managed to smile and said that nature had a strange way in compensating for flaws.

Paddy Carroll said that Frankie was a beautiful child. She had very fine cheekbones and huge dark eyes.

'She's like her mother, then,' Noel said, but his mind was far away.

Stella had a vibrant, lively face, yes, but she didn't have fine cheekbones and huge dark eyes.

Neither did Noel.

Was it possible that Frankie was the child of someone else?

He sat very quietly when everyone had gone; eventually, Faith sat down beside him.

'Was it a strain having alcohol in the house, Noel?' Faith asked.

'No, I never thought about it. Why?'

'It's just you seem a bit down.'

She was sympathetic and so he told her. He repeated the words that Moira had said: that he was naive to believe he was Frankie's father.

Faith listened with tears in her eyes.

'I never heard anything so ridiculous. She's a sour, sad, bitter woman. You're never going to start giving any credence to anything she would say?'

'I don't know. It's possible.'

'No, it's not possible! Why would she have chosen *you* unless you were the father?' Faith was outraged on his behalf.

'Stella more or less said that at the time,' he remembered.

'Put it out of your head, Noel. You are the best father in the world and that Moira can't bring herself to accept this. That's all there is to it.'

Noel smiled wanly.

'Here, I'll make us a mug of tea and we'll eat the leftovers,' she said.

Moira went to visit Mr Kennedy in the hostel to make sure he was getting all his entitlements. He had settled in well.

'Did you ever think of going back home to where you were from originally?' she asked him diffidently.

'Never. That part of life is over for me. As far as they're all concerned I'm dead. I'd prefer it that way,' he said.

It made Moira feel a little bit, but not entirely, better. She was being unprofessional and when all was said and done she had nothing left but her profession. Had she fallen down on that?

She also regretted her outburst to Lisa when she questioned Noel's paternity of Frankie. It had been unforgivable. Fortunately he hadn't heard it or at any rate he was polite when she talked to him, which was the same thing.

Noel couldn't sleep so he got up and sat in the sitting room. He got a piece of paper and made a list of the reasons why he was obviously Frankie's father and another list of reasons why he might not be. As usual he came to no conclusion. He loved that child so much – she must be his daughter.

And yet he couldn't sleep. There was only one thing to do.

He would get a DNA test.

He would arrange it next day. He tore up the sheets of paper into tiny pieces.

That was all there was to it.

Noel didn't want to approach either Declan or Dr Hat about the DNA test. He had asked at the AA meeting if anyone knew how it was done. He made it seem like a casual enquiry for a friend. As always, the assembly was able to find an answer. You went to a doctor who took a swab of your cheek and sent it to a laboratory – couldn't be more simple.

Yes, that was all very well, but Noel didn't want Declan to know his doubts. He couldn't ask Hat either, since Hat was now family. So it would have to be someone totally new.

He wondered what advice his cousin Emily would give him. She would say, 'Be ruthlessly honest and do it quickly.' There was no arguing with that.

He looked up a doctor on the other side of the city. It was a woman doctor who was practical and to the point.

'It will cost you to have this test done. We have to pay the lab.'

'Sure, I know that,' Noel agreed.

'I mean, it's not just a whim or a silly row with your partner or anything?'

'It's nothing like that. I just need to know.'

'And if it turns out that you are *not* the child's father?'

'I will make up my mind what to do then.'

'You have to be prepared to hear something you don't want to hear,' she persisted.

'I can't settle until I know,' he said simply.

And after that it was straightforward. He brought Frankie in and swabs were taken. He would know for sure in three weeks.

Even though he had been told that it would take three weeks, Noel watched the post every day. The doctor had promised to let him have the results as soon as she got them. They had agreed that phones could be unreliable or too public.

Better to send it in a letter.

Noel examined every envelope that arrived, but there was nothing.

Lisa went to London for the interview and came back very excited. When she was offered the job, she accepted immediately; now she had to move pretty quickly and there weren't enough hours in the day.

But Noel had never felt time moving so slowly. The days in Hall's were endless. His need for a drink after each day was so acute that he went to an AA meeting almost every evening. Why could it take so long to match up bits of tissue or whatever DNA was?

He would look at Frankie sometimes and feel covered in shame that he was doing this to her – that he wanted so much to know.

Noel had a long history of being in denial. When he was drinking, he denied the possibility that anyone would ever discover this at work. When he stopped drinking, he banished all thoughts of comfortable bars from his head and memory. Mainly it worked for him but not always.

It was the same now. He banished the possibility that Frankie might *not* be his child. He just would not think what he would do then. The fact that Stella might have lied to him or been mistaken, and the heartbreaking possibility that Frankie might not be his little girl but somebody else's – it was too big to think about. It had to be left out of his conscious mind.

Once he knew one way or the other it would be easier. This was the worst bit.

The letter arrived at Chestnut Court.

Lisa left it on the table as she went out; in the silent flat Noel poured himself another cup of tea. His hand was too shaky to pick up the envelope. The teapot had rattled alarmingly against the teacup. He was too weak to open it now. He had to get through this day without shaking like this. Perhaps he should put the letter away and open it tomorrow. He put it into a drawer. Thank God he had shaved already, he could never do it like this.

He dressed very slowly. He was pale and his eyes looked tired, but really and truly he might pass for a normal person, not someone with the most important secret of his life tidied away unopened in a drawer. A person who would give every single possession he had for a pint of beer accompanied by a large Irish whiskey.

How amazing that he looked perfectly normal. Now, looking at him, you might think he was a perfectly ordinary man.

Lisa was startled to find him there when she arrived with Dingo Duggan and his van. She was going to take her possessions down to Katie and Garry's.

'Hey, I thought you'd be at work,' she said.

Noel shook his head. 'Day off,' he muttered.

'Lucky old you. Where's Frankie? I thought you'd want to celebrate a day off with her.'

'She went with Emily and Hat. No point in breaking the routine,' he said flatly.

'You okay, Noel?'

'Sure I am. What are you doing?'

'Moving my stuff, trying to give you two lovebirds more room.'

'You know, you're not in the way, there's plenty of room for all of us.'

'But I'll be going to London soon, I can't clutter your place up with all my boxes.'

'I don't know what I'd have done without you, Lisa, I really don't.'

'Wasn't it a great year!' Lisa agreed. 'A year when you found Frankie and when I ... well, when I let the scales fall from my eyes over so many things. Anton for one, my father for another ...'

'You never said why you came here that night,' Noel said.

'And you never asked, which made everything so restful. I'll miss Frankie, though, desperately. Faith is going to send me a photo of her every month so that I'll see her growing up.'

'You'll forget all about us.' He managed a smile.

'As if I would. This is the first proper home I ever had.'

She gave him a quick hug and went into her bedroom to check the boxes that were going to be driven over to her sister's.

'Give Katie my love,' Noel said mechanically.

'I will, she's dying to tell me something, I know by her voice.'

'It must be nice to have a sister,' he said.

'It is. Maybe you and Faith could arrange a little sister for Frankie one day,' she teased.

'Maybe.' He didn't sound very confident about it.

Lisa was relieved to hear Dingo arriving to carry the boxes. Noel was definitely not himself today.

Katie did indeed want to tell Lisa something. It was that she was pregnant. She and Garry were overjoyed and they hoped Lisa would be pleased for them too.

Lisa said she was delighted. She hadn't known that this was in the plan at all, but Katie said it had been long hoped for.

'Two career people? High flyers?' Lisa said, in mock wonder.

'Yes, but we wanted a baby to make it complete.'

'I'll be a terrific aunt. I don't know anything about having a baby but I sure as anything know how to look after one.'

'I wish you weren't going away,' Katie said.

'I'll be back often,' Lisa promised. 'And this baby will grow up in a family that wants a baby – not like the way you and I grew up, Katie.'

Emily and Hat were surrounded by seed catalogues, trying to decide from the huge amount on offer. Frankie sat with them and seemed to study the pictures of flowers as well.

'She's just no trouble,' Emily said fondly.

'Pity we didn't meet earlier – we could well have had a few of those ourselves,' Hat said wistfully.

'Oh no, Hat, I have much more the personality of

a grandmother than a mother. I like a baby that goes home in the evening,' she said.

'Is it dull for you here with me?' he asked suddenly.

'What do you mean?'

'Back in America you had a busy life, teaching, going to galleries, museums, thousands of people around the place.'

'Stop fishing for compliments, Hat, you know that I'm besotted with this place. And with you. And when we push this little pet back up to Chestnut Court I will make you the most wonderful cheese soufflé to prove it.'

'Lord above, life doesn't get much better than this,' Hat said with a sigh of pleasure.

The flat was very silent when Lisa and Dingo had departed with a chorus of goodbyes.

Noel opened the drawer and took out the letter. Perhaps he should eat something to keep his strength up. He had eaten no breakfast. He made himself a tomato sandwich, carefully adding chopped onion and cutting off the crusts. It tasted like sawdust.

He pulled the envelope towards him.

When he saw it all confirmed that he was Frankie's father, then everything would be all right. Wouldn't it? This hollow, empty feeling would go and he would be normal again.

But suppose that ... Noel would not allow himself to go down that road. Of course he was Frankie's father. And now that he had eaten his tasteless tomato sandwich, he was ready to open the envelope.

He took the letter from the drawer and slit it open with the knife he had used to make his sandwich. The letter was stilted and official, but it was clear and concise.

The DNA samples did not match.

A hot rage came over him. He could feel it burning around his neck and ears. There was a heavy lump in his stomach and a strange light-headedness around his eyes and forehead.

This could not be true.

Stella could not have told him a pack of lies and palmed off her child on him. Surely it was impossible that she had made all these arrangements and put his name on the birth certificate if she had not believed it was true.

Perhaps she had so many lovers, she had no idea who might be Frankie's father.

She could have picked him because he was humble and would make no fuss.

Or possibly Frankie's real father was so unreliable or unavailable that he could not be contacted.

Bile rose in his throat.

He knew exactly what would make him feel better. He picked up his jacket and went out.

Moira was having a busy morning at the heart clinic. Once the word had got around that she was an expert at finding people's entitlements, her caseload had increased. It was Moira's belief that if there were benefits, then people should avail themselves of them. She would fill in the paperwork, arrange the carers, the allowances or the support needed.

Today Mr Kennedy was coming to the clinic for his check-up; she would see him and make sure that he was being properly looked after. And unexpectedly Clara

Casey had asked if Moira could spare her ten minutes on a personal matter.

Moira wondered what on earth it could be. The gossip around the clinic had been that Dr Casey had moved Mr Ennis into her home, but surely Clara didn't want to discuss anything quite as personal as that.

Just after midday, when Moira's stint ended officially, Clara slipped into her office.

'This is not on the clinic's time, Moira, it's a personal favour on my time and yours.'

'Sure, go ahead,' Moira said.

A few months ago she might have said something sharper, something more official; but events had changed her.

'It's about my daughter Linda, she and her husband are very anxious to adopt a baby and they don't know how to set about it.'

'What have they done so far?' Moira asked.

'Nothing much, except talk about it, but now they want to move forward.'

'Fine, do you want me to talk to them sometime?'

'Linda is actually here today, she came to take me to lunch. Would that be too instant?'

'No, not at all, do you want to stay for the conversation?'

'No, no – but I do appreciate this, Moira. I've realised over the last months you are amazingly thorough and tenacious. If anyone can help Linda and Nick you can.'

Moira couldn't remember why she had thought of Dr Casey as aloof and superior. She watched as Clara ushered in her tall, handsome daughter.

'I'll leave you in good hands,' Clara said and mother and daughter hugged each other.

Moira felt an absurd flush of pleasure all over her face and neck.

At lunch in the shopping precinct Linda was bubbling over with enthusiasm.

'I can't think why you didn't like that woman, she was *marvellous*. It's all very straightforward. You go to the Health Board and they refer you to the adoption section and fill in a lot of details, and they come for home-assessment visits. She asked, did we mind what nationality the child would be and I said of course not. It really looks as if it might happen.'

'I'm so pleased, Linda.' Clara spoke gently.

'So you and Frank had better polish up your babysitting skills,' Linda said with unnaturally bright eyes.

Moira left the clinic in high good humour. For once it appeared her talents had been recognised. It was one of those rare occasions when people actually seemed pleased with the social worker.

She had warned them about delays and bureaucracy and said the most important thing was to be quietly persistent, keeping even-tempered no matter what the provocation. Linda had been delighted with her and, moreover, Linda's mother had given words of high praise.

This was a personal first.

Her steps took her past Chestnut Court and she looked from habit at Noel and Lisa's flat. Noel would be at work, but maybe Lisa was there packing her belongings. She was heading off to London soon. Anyway, no point in going in there and talking to Lisa and being accused of spying or policing the situation. She didn't want to lose the good feeling that had come from the clinic, so she passed by.

Emily got a phone call at lunchtime. It was Noel. His voice was unsteady. She thought he sounded drunk.

'Everything all right, Noel?' she asked anxiously, her heart lurching.

He should have been there to pick up Frankie. What could have happened?

'Yes. Everything's fine.' He spoke like a robot. 'I'm at the zoo actually.'

'The zoo?'

Emily was stunned. The zoo was miles away on the other side of the city. She didn't know whether to be relieved or horrified. If Noel was there, then he was safe; but then he was wandering around looking at lions and aviaries and elephants, rather than picking up his daughter.

'Yes. I haven't been here for ages. They've lots of new things.'

'Yes, Noel, I'm sure they do.'

'So I was wondering, could you possibly keep Frankie for a while longer?'

'Of course,' Emily agreed, worried.

Was he drunk? His voice sounded stressed. What could have brought all this on?

'And are you at the zoo on your own?'

'Yes, for the moment.'

Noel had been over and over it in his mind. For a year he had been living a lie. Frankie was not his daughter. God knew whose child she was.

He loved her like his own, of course he did. But he

449

had thought she was his own child and had no one else to look after her. His name was on the birth certificate, he had loved her and looked after her and fed her and changed her. He had protected her, given her a life surrounded by people who loved her; he had made her his. Did he regret all this?

She was a year old, her mother was dead – what sort of start in life would it be if he washed his hands of her now?

Could he bring up another man's child as his own? He didn't think so. She was someone else's child, someone else had fathered her and walked away, got away with it. Should he find out who it was? Would it be a wild-goose chase?

And what sort of man would he be if he ran away now? Could he abandon her when she needed him every bit as much as when she was that tiny helpless baby he had brought home from the hospital?

He pictured the flat that was their home: Frankie's toys on the floor, her clothes warming on the radiators, her photographs on the mantelpiece. The baby food in the kitchen, the baby lotions in the bathroom; he knew where she was every minute of the day.

He remembered the horror of the night she'd been missing. Everyone had been out looking for her, so many people had been concerned for her safety. She was with Emily and Hat now, and when they went to the thrift shop, they'd take her with them. His own parents knew her as their grandchild. She knew everyone in the neighbourhood, they were all part of her life as she was part of theirs. Was he going to end all that?

But could he bring up another man's child?

He needed a drink. Just the one, so he could see his way clearly.

When Moira called into St Jarlath's Thrift Shop and seemed surprised to see Frankie asleep there in her pram, Emily kept her worries to herself.

'What time is her father picking her up?' Moira asked.

She didn't really want to know, it was just a stance, she always liked them to know that she was in control.

'He will be along later,' Emily said with a confident smile. 'Can I interest you in anything in particular, Moira? You have such good taste. There's a very attractive bag here, it's almost a cross between a bag and a briefcase. I think it's Moroccan, it's got lovely designs on it.'

It was, as Emily said, very attractive, and would be perfect for Moira. She fingered it and wondered. But before she spent money on herself, she must think of a present for her father and Mrs Kennedy. Maybe Emily could help here too.

'I need a wedding present, something unopened, as it were. It's for a middle-aged couple in the country.'

'Do they have their own house?' Emily enquired.

'Yes, well, she has a house, and he's living there ... I mean, going to live there.'

'Is she a good cook?'

'Yes, she is actually.' Moira was surprised at the question.

'Then she won't need anything for the kitchen, she'll have all that under control. There's a very nice table-cloth, an unwanted gift apparently, we could open it to make sure it's perfect, then seal it up again.'

'Tablecloth?' Moira wasn't sure.

'Look at it, it's the best linen and has hand-painted flowers on it. I'd say she'd love it. Is she a close friend?'

'No,' Moira said. Then she realised that it sounded a little bit bald. 'I mean, she's going to marry my father,' she explained.

'Oh, I'm sure your new stepmother would love this cloth,' Emily said.

'Stepmother?' Moira tried the word for size.

'Well, that's what she'll be, surely?'

'Yes, of course.' Moira spoke hastily.

'I hope they'll be very happy,' Emily said.

'I think they will. It's complicated but they are well suited.'

'Well, that's what it's all about.'

'Yes, it is in a way, it's just that there's unfinished business, hard to explain, but that's what it is.'

'I suppose there always is,' Emily said soothingly.

She hadn't an idea what Moira was talking about.

Moira left with both the briefcase and the tablecloth; she was rapidly becoming one of the thrift shop's best customers.

There was something weighing heavily on her mind. Surely Mr Kennedy had a right to know that his house existed in Liscuan, that his wife was taking another man as her husband, and that this man was the social worker's father.

Moira knew that many would advise her to stay out of it. It would all have gone ahead without a problem if Moira hadn't come across Mr Kennedy and settled him into long-term hostel care. But there was no denying it. She had met Mr Kennedy and she could not let it go.

*

'Mr Kennedy, you're all right?'

They sat in the day room of the hostel.

'Miss Tierney. It's not your day today.'

'I was in the area.'

'I see.'

'I was wondering, Mr Kennedy, are you properly settled here?'

'You ask me that every week, Miss Tierney. It's okay, I've told you that.'

'But do you think of your time in Liscuan?'

'No. I'm gone years from there.'

'So you said, but would you like to be back there? Would you try again with your wife?'

'Isn't she a stranger to me now after all these years?' he asked.

'But suppose she got married again? Presumed you were dead?'

'More power to her if she did.'

'You wouldn't mind?'

'I made my choice in life, which was to go off, she's free to make hers.'

Moira looked at him. This was good – but she wasn't off the hook yet. She still knew what was going on. She had to tell him.

'Mr Kennedy. There's something I have to tell you,' she said.

'Don't worry about all that,' he said.

'No, please, you must listen. You see, things aren't as simple as you think. Actually, there's a bit of a situation I have to tell you about.'

'Miss Tierney, I know all that,' he said.

She thought for a wild moment that maybe he did,

but realised that he couldn't possibly know anything of life in Liscuan. He had been an exile for years.

'No, wait, you must listen to me—' she said.

'Don't I know it all, your father's moved into the house, and now he's going to marry Maureen. And why shouldn't they?'

'Because you are still her husband,' Moira stammered.

'They think I'm dead, and I am as far as they are concerned.'

'You've known all the time?' Moira was astounded.

'I knew you at once. I remember you well from back home, you haven't changed a bit. Tough, able to take things. You didn't have a great childhood.'

This man ending his days in a hostel pitied *her*. Moira felt weak at the way the earth had tilted.

'You're very good to tell me, but honestly, we should just leave things the way they are, that way there's the least damage.'

'But—'

'But nothing. Leave it, let them get married. Don't mention me.'

'How did you know?' Her voice was almost a whisper.

'I did have a friend I stayed in touch with, he kept me posted.'

'And is he there in Liscuan now, your friend?'

'No, he's dead, Moira. Only you and I know now.'

Secrets were a great equaliser, Moira thought. He wasn't calling her Miss Tierney now.

Linda told her mother that Moira was as good as her word. She had made appointments here and introductions there, and the process was now under way. Nick and Linda said they would have been lost in a fog without her. She seemed to find no obstacles in her way. A perfect quality in a social worker.

'I can't understand why none of you like her,' Linda said. 'I've never met anyone as helpful in my life.'

'She's fine at her work,' Clara agreed. 'But, God, I wouldn't like to go on a holiday with her. She manages to insult and upset everyone in some way.'

Frank agreed with her. 'She's a woman who never smiles,' he said disapprovingly. 'That's a character flaw in a person.'

'She had the strength of character to refuse to be your spy when she came to the clinic,' Clara said cheerfully. 'That's another point in her favour.'

'I think she must have misread the situation there ...'

Frank didn't want to bring disharmony into their home.

It was nine o'clock in the evening when Noel and Malachy turned up at Emily and Hat's house to collect Frankie.

Noel was pale but calm. Malachy looked very tired.

'I'm going to spend the night in Chestnut Court,' he said to Emily.

'That's great, Lisa's taken her things so it might be a bit lonely there otherwise,' Emily said neutrally.

Frankie, who had been fast asleep, woke up and was delighted to be the centre of attention.

'Dada!' she said to Noel.

'That's right,' he said mechanically.

'I've been explaining to Frankie that her granny and

455

granda are going to build a lovely safe garden where she and all her friends can play.'

'Great,' said Malachy.

'Yes,' said Noel.

'Your parents are going to have a sod-turning ceremony for the children's garden next week. The work is going to start then.'

'Sure,' Noel said.

Wearily Malachy got them on the road. Frankie was chattering away from her pram. Words that were recognisable but not making any sense.

Noel was silent. He was there in body but not in spirit; surely people were able to guess something was different. Frankie was just the same child she had been this morning but everything else had changed and he hadn't yet had time to get accustomed to the idea.

Malachy slept on the sofa. During the night he heard Frankie start to cry and Noel get up to soothe the little girl and comfort her. The moonlight fell on Noel's face as he sat and held the child; Malachy could see there were tears on his cheeks.

Moira took the train to Liscuan. She was met at the station by her brother Pat and Erin O'Leary.

'Who's minding the store?' she asked.

'Plenty of help, good neighbours, all delighted that we're going to your father's wedding.'

Erin was dressed to the nines with a rose and cream coloured outfit, a big pink rose in her hair. Moira felt dowdy in her best suit. She looked at Erin's dainty, girlish handbag and wished she had not brought her own serious-looking briefcase. Still, too late to change now. They would need to hurry to be in time for the ceremony.

There were about fifty people waiting at the church.

'You mean, all these people know that our father is getting married?' she asked Pat.

'Aren't they all so pleased for him?' Pat said. It was as simple as that.

And Moira prepared to sit through the whole ceremony, nuptial Mass and papal blessing, knowing that she was the only person present who knew the whole story. When it came to the part where the priest asked, was there any reason why these two persons should not marry, Moira sat dumb.

The presents were displayed in one of the reception rooms at the Stella Maris, and everyone seemed to think highly of the hand-painted tablecloth. Maureen Kennedy, now Maureen Tierney and her stepmother, drew Moira aside.

'That was really a most thoughtful gift, and I hope now that the situation has been regularised you will come sometime and stay under our roof, and maybe we will eat dinner with this lovely cloth on the table.'

'That would be lovely,' Moira breathed.

Faith had been away for three days and when she came back she rushed in to pick up Frankie.

'Have I brought you the cutest little boots?' she said to the baby as she hugged her.

'The child has far too many clothes,' Noel said.

'Ah, Noel, they're lovely little boots – look at them!'

'She'll have grown out of them in a month,' he said.

The light had gone out of Faith's face.

'Sorry, is something annoying you?'

'Just the way everyone piles clothes on her. That's all.'

'I'm not everyone and I'm not piling clothes on her. She needs shoes to go to the opening of the site for the new garden on Saturday.'

'Oh God – I'd forgotten that.'

'Better not let your parents know you did. It's the highlight of their year.'

'Will there be lots of people there?' he asked.

'Noel, are you all right? You look different somehow, as if something fell on you.'

'It did in a way,' Noel said.

'Are you going to tell me?'

'No, not at the moment. Is that all right? I'm sorry for being so rude, they're lovely shoes, Frankie will be the last word on Saturday.'

'Of course she will – now will I get us some supper?'

'You're a girl in a million, Faith.'

'Oh, much more than that – one in a billion, I'd say,' she said and went into the kitchen.

Noel forced himself into good humour, Frankie was unpacking the little pink boots from their box with huge concentration. Why couldn't she be his child?

He sat in the kitchen and watched Faith move deftly around, getting together a supper in minutes, something that would have taken him for ever.

'You love Frankie as much as if she was yours, don't you?' he said.

'Of course I do. Is this what's worrying you? She is mine in a way since I almost live with her and I help to look after her.'

'But the fact that she's not yours doesn't make any difference?'

'What are you on about, Noel? I love the child. I'm mad about her – don't you know that?'

'Yes, but you've always known she wasn't yours,' he said sadly.

'Oh, I know what this is all about, it's this ludicrous Moira who started this off in your head. It's like a wasp in your mind, Noel, buzzing at you. Chase it away. You're obviously her father, you're a great father.'

'Suppose I had a DNA test and found she wasn't – what then?'

'You'd insult that beautiful child by having a DNA test? Noel, you're unhinged. And what would it matter what the test said anyway?'

He could have told her there and then. Gone to the drawer and taken out the letter with the results. He could have said that he had done the test and the answer was that Frankie was not his. This was the only girl he had ever felt close enough to for him to even consider marrying: should he share this huge secret with her?

Instead, he shrugged.

'You're probably right, only a very suspicious, untrusting person would go for that test.'

'That's more like it, Noel,' Faith said happily.

Noel sat for a long time at the table when Faith left. He had three envelopes in front of him: one contained the result of the DNA test, one the letter that Stella had left for him before she died, and one held the letter she had addressed to Frankie.

Back in the frightening, early days when fighting to keep away from drink on an hourly basis, he had often been tempted to open the letter to Frankie. In those days he was anxious to look for some reason to keep going, something that might give him strength. Today he wanted to read it in case Stella had told her daughter who her real father was.

Something stopped him, though, perhaps some sense of playing fair. Although, of course, that was nonsense. Stella certainly hadn't played fair. Still, if he hadn't opened it back then, he would not do it now.

What had Stella got from it all anyway? A short restless life, a lot of pain and fear, no family, no friends. She never got to see her baby or know the little arms around her neck. Noel had got all this and more.

A year ago, what did Noel have going for him? Not much. A drunk in a dead-end job, without friends, without hope. It had all changed because of Frankie. How lonely and frightened Stella must have felt that last night.

He reached out and read the letter she had written to him in that ward.

Tell Frankie that I wasn't all bad ... she had said. *Tell her that if things had been different you and I would both have been there to look after her ...*

Noel straightened his shoulders.

He was Frankie's father in every way that mattered. Perhaps Stella had made a genuine mistake. Who knew what happened in other people's lives? And suppose somehow Stella was looking out for Frankie from somewhere, she deserved to know better than that the baby had been abandoned at the age of twelve months.

Noel had loved this child yesterday, he still loved her today. He would always love her. It was as simple as that.

He reached across the table and put the two letters from Stella into the drawer. The letter with the DNA results he tore into tiny pieces.

*

It was a fine day for the turning of the sod. Charles and Josie put their hands together on the shovel and dug into the ground of the small waste patch they had secured for the new garden. Everyone clapped and Father Flynn said his customary few words about the great results that came from a sense of community involvement and caring.

Some of Muttie's Associates had come to watch the ceremony and one of them was heard to say he would much prefer a statue of Muttie and Hooves to be raised instead of some long-dead saint whom nobody knew anything about.

Lizzie was there with her arm around Simon's shoulder. He was going to New Jersey next week but had promised to be back in three months to tell them all what it was like. Marco and Maud stood together; Marco had hopes of a spring wedding but Maud said she was in no hurry to marry.

'Your grandfather gave me his blessing to marry you,' Marco whispered.

'Yes, but he didn't say in the blessing *when* you were to marry me,' Maud said firmly.

Declan, Johnny and the now visibly pregnant Fiona were there, with Declan's parents and Dimples the big dog. Dimples had a love-hate relationship with Caesar, the tiny spaniel. It wasn't that he had anything against Caesar, it was just that he was too small to be a proper dog.

Emily and Hat were there, part of the scenery now. People hardly remembered a time when they were not together. Emily was noting everything to tell Betsy that night by email. She would even send her a picture of it all. Betsy too had fallen under the spell of this mixed community and was always asking for details of this and that. She and Eric had every intention of coming back again next year and catching up where they had left off.

Emily thought back to the first day that she herself had arrived in this street and heard her uncle and aunt's plans to build a huge statue. How amazing that it had all turned out so differently and so well.

Noel, Faith and Frankie were there, Frankie showing everyone her new pink boots. People pointed out to Noel that one of the houses in the Crescent would shortly be for sale, maybe he and Faith could buy it. Then Frankie would be near her garden. It was a very tempting idea, they said.

And as they wound their way back to Emily and Hat's house where tea and cakes were being served, Noel felt a weight lift from his shoulders. He passed the house where Paddy Carroll and his wife Molly had slaved to raise their son, a doctor, and then past Muttie and Lizzie's house where those twins had found a better home than they could have dreamed of. He blinked a couple of times as he began to realise that a lot of things didn't matter any more.

Frankie wanted to walk the length of the road even though she wasn't really able to; Faith followed with the buggy but Frankie struggled hard, holding Noel's hand and calling out 'Dada' a lot. Just as they got to Emily and Hat's place her little legs began to buckle and Noel swung her up into his arms.

'Good girl, Daddy's good little girl,' he said over and over.

His chest was much less tight, the awful feeling of

462

running down a long corridor had gone. Later tonight he would ring Malachy and then he would be ready for anything. He put his other arm around Faith's shoulder and ushered his little family into the house to have tea.

My dear, dear Frankie, my lovely daughter,

I will never see you or know you, but I do love you so very much. I fought hard to live for you but it didn't work. I started too late, you see. If only I had known that I would have a little girl to live for ... But it's all far too late for those kind of wishes now. Instead, I wish you the very best that life can give you. I wish you courage – I have plenty of that. Too much, some might say! I hope that you will not be as foolhardy and reckless as I was. Instead, may you have peace and the love of good people who will mind you and make you happy. Tonight I sit here in a ward where nobody can really sleep. It's my last night here, you see, and tomorrow is your first day here. I wish we had been able to meet.

But I know one thing. Noel will be a great father. He is very strong and he can't wait to meet you tomorrow. He has been preparing for weeks, getting things ready for you, learning how to hold you, to feed you, to change you. He will be a wonderful dad and I have this very clear feeling that you will be the light of his life.

So many people are waiting for you tomorrow. Don't be sad for me, you have managed to make sense of my life eventually!

Live well and happily, little Frankie. Laugh a lot and be full of trust, not suspicion.

Remember your mother loved you with all her heart.

Stella

ACKNOWLEDGEMENTS

I would like to thank my editor Carole Baron and my agent Chris Green, who have been hugely supportive and great friends to me during the writing of this book.

Read on for a special short
story by Maeve Binchy

CONTINENTAL
BREAKFAST

CONTINENTAL BREAKFAST

They had warned her about Frank. She couldn't say it had happened without a hundred warnings. He'll leave, they said, but it will look as if you were the one to throw him out.

But she had laughed. Kate would never throw Frank out, that was for sure. That was why she had lasted longer than any of his other girlfriends, she had allowed him the freedom to roam, she had given him a long rope. He always came back to her.

Kate knew that it wasn't the ideal way to love. That a lot of her friends shook their heads sadly over her. But let their heads shake. She had Frank, the man they would all have loved to claim. So it came as a big surprise to Kate when she found herself telling Frank it wouldn't work any more. They had gone as far as they could go. She would leave him, at the end of the week.

'Before our holiday?' Frank's dark eyes seemed disappointed. The holiday. She had forgotten it totally in the strange, empty, lonely realisation that he didn't love her any more. Perhaps ... No, it would be madness. It would be harder than ever.

'Well, it's your choice, angel,' he said. He called her angel always. He called a lot of girls angel, it was easier than remembering their names, safer than getting the names wrong. Kate realised, with a lump in her throat, that her friends had been right. He had managed to manoeuvre things to a state where she was doing the goodbye. He appeared like the reasonable man who didn't want to break anything up.

'You take the holiday anyway, angel,' he said.

It wasn't very generous of him to say that, she had paid for it. Frank didn't have the money for things like that. Too free a spirit for saving, and boring things like that. Time-consuming matters. Great on the flowers and the bottle of wine, not so good on the rent and the telephone bill.

Kate asked at the travel agency if she could get a refund. The girl had kind eyes, it was as if she could read Kate's soul. Perhaps she had heard about Frank or there were too many Franks in the lives of her clients.

'No,' she said, sadly. There would be no refund.

'My companion can't come with me,' Kate said.

'Find another companion maybe?'

In three weeks. It would be some challenge. Especially since Kate had given up men now. There would be no further romances upsetting her, hurting her and taking up her time.

'I'll go on my own,' she said.

'Great waste of a second bed and continental break-fasts,' the girl in the travel agency said.

Unexpectedly, Kate began to cry. She remembered the breakfasts she had eaten with Frank on balconies in Italy, and Spain, and France. This one would have been in Greece. Now she would sit alone and look out at the Mediterranean from yet another vantage point but with no handsome dark laughing face beside her. There would be no one to plan the day with, no laughing man

4

to say that really they didn't have the money to hire a car, but who would sit proudly and happily at the wheel when Kate paid with her credit card.

She sat weeping with the loss of it all.

Other people buying their holidays looked away embarrassed. They didn't want to be reminded of reality and sadness when they were booking a dream.

Kate accepted the tissues, and blew her nose.

'It doesn't have to be a man, you know.' The girl at the counter was helpful.

She was right of course, it didn't have to be a man. There were two beds in the room, Kate could invite her mother. Her mother? Who had said she was making herself cheap over this man, and was also endangering her immortal soul? Or her sister Helen, who said that she would suffer for it later, and that Frank would leave her as he had left a string of others? Or her best friend Jane, who would say nothing at all, who would offer no criticism, not a word of I told you so? But between them would hang the memory of a hundred conversations, a million warnings, none of them heeded.

She said nothing at work. But she knew they knew. And anyway, her secretary knew since there were no loving phone calls any more, the kind that made Kate kick the door of her office shut. There were no flowers coming at odd times.

There was no Frank standing handsome and relaxed, open-neck shirt and perfect smile, as confident as any of the buttoned-up suits that manned the big company Kate worked for. He looked and felt their equal in every way, and indeed he was. Didn't he have all the success and comforts and admiration that they did without having to work a punishing day to achieve it?

Oddly, Kate missed the flowers more than anything. The single rose. Or the bunch of freesias. Sometimes once a week. Maybe three days running if they had been particularly loving.

After a week she phoned the florist, and ordered for herself a dozen dark red roses with some fern. She cleared a space for them on her desk as she spoke.

'Same name for the giver as for the receiver?' The florist was anxious that he had got it right.

'There isn't a law against that, is there?' she snapped at him, and felt sorry the moment she had put down the phone. The man was only doing his job making sure that he hadn't misunderstood. After all, there can't be that many people who phone in to send themselves flowers.

A large pale-faced boy arrived with the roses.

'Someone loves you,' he said as he handed them over.

'I love myself,' Kate said. 'I sent them to myself.'

'Right. I'd do that if I could too. I'd send myself a big, big bunch of those tiger lilies,' he said.

'You work there, you don't have to.'

'No, I don't. I got fired today. This is my last job, delivering your roses.'

'I'm sorry. What did you do to get fired?'

'I was the last one in, so I'm the first one out. It's a bad crime to be the last in these days.'

'Have they paid you off?'

'Yes. What little there was. They were sorry, they said so. They might have meant it too.'

'Would you like to go for lunch?' Kate asked him.

He looked at her, startled. Kate, thirtyish, dark, good-looking, dressed in a power jacket and very high heels, her own office, her own assistant sitting at a desk outside the door. Kate, who had bought for herself the most expensive roses by credit card, was asking him to lunch.

Written over his large pasty features was disbelief. He even looked over his shoulder in case someone worthy of lunch had come into the room without his noticing.

There was no one else.

'Me?' he said, as Kate knew he would say.

'Yes, why not? At least it would make the day less bad.'

'You needn't … I mean, you mustn't feel you have to …'

'I don't feel I have to. Will we go?'

'We have to put the flowers in water first,' he said.

'My secretary will do that.'

'No, they're lovely flowers. You wanted them, you must enjoy them.'

Kate looked at him in amazement, a big pale boy, fired from an unskilled job delivering flowers in a van. And he put off the chance of going to lunch in order to get water for the bloody roses. She sat there leaning on her desk watching as he got the vase, found the water and arranged the flowers.

It took him about seven minutes. He stood back, pleased with his work.

'Now we go to the canteen,' he said.

'I haven't eaten in a canteen for nearly a decade,' Kate told him. 'I have no intention of starting again.' When she told him the name of the restaurant he started to back away.

'You're making fun of me,' he said.

'I'm not. I want lunch there, I'll book a table.' He

watched while she leaned across and called the restaurant. She asked for her usual table, and asked them to have a jacket and tie. 'It's *their* silly rules, so they can damn well sort that out themselves,' she said.

Kate's secretary watched amazed as she left, arm in arm with the delivery boy.

'I'll be late. Don't fix for me to talk to anyone this afternoon,' she said.

And as they got into the lift at least half a dozen people standing there must have heard Kate asking, 'What *is* your name by the way? I never asked you, did I? I'm Kate, but then you know that already.'

His name was Tommy, he was twenty-six. He lived with his married sister, his parents lived in the country. He went home once a month to see them. They would be disappointed about the job. He had been there for five months and he had liked it. It was good to work with flowers, even though he wasn't allowed to touch them much, only deliver them.

He had been slow at school, not stupid but just slow. He didn't do well in exams, he had never trained for any job. He just liked being where there was a good atmosphere. He minded his sister's children, and then he did odd jobs there to pay for his keep. He saved his wages. One day he was going to go on a great trip and see some of the world.

He showed Kate his deposit book from the building society. He thought he saw tears in her eyes. Perhaps he was boring her.

'Should I not be telling you things like this?' he asked. She said nothing. She seemed to be biting her lip.

'Am I talking too much for a place like this?' He looked around wonderingly at the smart restaurant, the discreet service, the thick heavy tablecloths and the shining crystal glass.

'No, it's very interesting.' Her voice was soft.

Tommy looked at her, pleased. He couldn't understand why she seemed to like him talking, after all he had been burbling on. When he did this at home his sister would tell him to stop, or his mother. Even in the flower shop they had asked him not to tell such long rambling tales. But this woman, this beautiful Kate who had taken him to lunch in a place that he wouldn't have dared enter, seemed to think it was perfectly fine. She was easy to talk to. He looked at her and smiled.

Kate had chosen for him because the menu was in French. He had told her he liked chicken to give her a guideline.

'Have you a passport, Tommy?' she asked.

'Well, not yet. You see, I thought I'd wait until I was sure of going on a trip before I went to the trouble and expense of getting a passport.' He was eager to show her that he had it all worked out.

'Would you like to come to Greece with me?' Kate said. She spoke slowly and deliberately.

'I don't think I'd have enough,' Tommy said, looking at his savings book. Kate looked at the book with him. His savings would not cover a holiday to Greece. 'I suppose it would depend, though.' Tommy's brow was furrowed. 'It might cover a holiday that wasn't full board. What do you think?' He looked at Kate hopefully.

She, who could read menus in French and arrange for the restaurant to lend him a jacket and tie, who was powerful enough to send herself the most expensive dark roses in the shop, would know whether his savings would do.

'Just get a passport, that's all. I'll look after everything else. You see, my friend wasn't able to come on the holiday and so I have the friend's ticket here in my bag. It wouldn't cost you anything.'

Tommy sighed with pleasure. Things were so much better than he had thought a couple of hours ago.

They used to say that Kate was mad to love Frank. But Kate thought to herself they ain't seen nothing yet. As soon as any of them hear what I'm up to now, then they really will have the place booked in the funny farm for me. But she didn't care. Any more than she had cared about Frank being a philanderer. She had loved him with all his faults, she had closed her mind to his other women, his easy lies and the way he took, took, took, giving so little except his loving and his easy smile.

And she wouldn't care when they all told her she was mad to travel with Tommy, a half-simple boy she'd only just met. They would say that it wasn't fair to him, to build up his dreams, to get him used to a lifestyle that he would have to leave.

Perhaps he would say no, maybe he would think it was all too much. That might be for the best. Less explanations, less justifications, to herself as well as to everyone else. It would all be debated and argued as the business with Frank had been.

Tommy knew none of her thoughts. 'How do I get a passport?' he asked.

She told him. 'What will they say?' she asked.

'Who?' Tommy seemed surprised.

'Your sister, your parents, the people you know?'

'They won't say anything. I won't tell them until I come back.'

'But you have to say where you're going … don't you?'

'I'll say I'm going to Greece. I'm grown up, Kate. I'm twenty-six. I don't have to tell them every step of the way, do I? I always get told off for telling too much as it is. They tell me people aren't really all that interested in my doings.'

She listened. Nothing she had heard at any management course, nothing she had read in any motivational book, had been so useful. High-flying, extrovert Kate, Kate who got things done, Kate who was always out there at the front punching, she had felt it necessary to tell them all about her personal life as well as her business plans. Part of her style.

What did she know about her sister Helen's marriage for example? Nothing at all, only what she was told, which was very little. Any conversations with Helen over the last months, even years, had been about Frank. And Jane, good kind Jane, told her little of life with the quiet Robert. Maybe it was too quiet, maybe Robert was rarely around. Kate felt a pang of guilt that she hadn't known, or thought to ask. As always, it had been Frank they talked about. Frank was the shining star in all their lives. He was so bright there was no room for other people's loves or lives at all.

'What will I need to take with me?' Tommy asked.

She thought about what Frank would have taken. Six of the shirts she had bought him, the smart pants that he said he had bought for himself as a treat, but Kate knew they had been a present from some other woman, a woman foolish like herself, a woman who believed that if you bought a gift for Frank you bought his time and attention.

Frank would have brought no suntan lotion to Greece, no mosquito repellent. He would look better than any other man on the island, and yet the local Greek men would have liked him and invited him to drink with them, taught him to dance maybe, brought him into their circle. While Kate would sit white-knuckled and tense, hoping that the showy redhead at one table or the tiny blonde at another wouldn't catch Frank's eye.

She forced her mind back to the big, anxious, white face beside her. She told him about heavy-duty sun-block bars, about anti-insect spray, and suggested shirts that would cover up shoulders she knew would burn.

They agreed to meet at the airport in two weeks' time. He seemed pleased, but not over-excited.

'How do you know I mean it?' she asked.

'Because you meant it about having lunch here.' He looked around again, as if to imprint every bit of the smart restaurant on his memory.

'And why do you think I'm doing it?' she asked. She was probing it like a sore tooth. She wanted the boy to say something crass, ungrateful, something to call the whole deal off.

'Because you are very kind,' he said simply.

She threw herself into work for the two weeks.

When they asked how was Frank, where was Frank, as they always did ... she realised that this was because Frank questions were the only ones to get a light in her eye. Now she just answered that Frank was around. If they wagged their fingers and shook their heads she didn't know. She didn't try to catch them unaware, try to read her future in their uncertainties as she used to.

*

Two days before the holiday Frank came into the office. He stood leaning against her office door like he always had, his head on one side, his smile lopsided, heart-breaking.

He knocked lightly even though he knew she had seen him.

'Just to wish you *bon voyage*,' he said. He had brought a rose.

'That's lovely of you.' She took it and put it in with the dark roses she had bought for herself. His rose looked a little unimportant somehow. In other times she would have got a separate vase.

'You have another admirer, then?' He jerked his head towards the roses.

'No, I sent those to myself.' She smiled easily. She didn't care if he believed her or not.

'That'll be the day,' but he looked put out. She said no to lunch and no to a farewell drink.

'You found another travelling companion?' He seemed to care. All those months when she wanted to hear that note in his voice.

'The delivery boy from the florist's,' she said. She didn't smile, shrug or apologise.

He didn't know what to make of her. It was like those early heady days at the start of their affair, when he hung on everything she said and tried to work out what she meant. But he knew enough to know he was getting nowhere.

'Love Greece then,' he said and moved out, giving one of his very special smiles to Kate's secretary.

Tommy was at the airport early. He had a carnation for her, all done up with silver paper as if for a lapel at a wedding. She thanked him and, even though it looked ludicrous on her light linen travelling suit, she pinned it on.

Tommy had never been on a plane before. He tried to pay for the lunch.

'It's complimentary,' said the stewardess.

'I'm not a very experienced traveller,' he said with a smile.

Kate and the stewardess exchanged smiles too. Usually she hated them when they smiled at Frank. This was different.

The little van took them to their hotel, all painted white with little flower-filled balconies looking out over a deep blue sea.

'This must be very expensive for you,' Tommy said anxiously. 'I hope I have enough to buy all the lunches and the dinners.' He fumbled anxiously with his money belt, a present from his sister.

Frank had offered to pay for so little. 'That's fine, Tommy, we'll sort it out,' she said.

The hotel had little balconies, all of them with a sea view.

'We can wave at each other when we're having our continental breakfasts,' he said happily.

Kate took a deep breath. 'It's going to be the same balcony,' she said, trying to be light and casual about it.

'We're going to share a room?' He looked startled.

'It will have two beds.' She spoke too quickly, as if apologising. But then she *was* apologising. For having brought him here under false pretences.

'I see.' He looked cast down, sad, and even sympathetic, as if he were sorry for her.

Kate flashed with anger. 'It's all right. I won't have my wicked way with you.' She knew her voice sounded cutting and sarcastic. Of course, it had been a ridiculous idea, patronising even. But she hadn't thought that he would baulk so much at the thought of sharing a room with her. Tears came into her eyes. She, Kate, whom so many of the men at the office had tried to take to bed, being rejected by this ... this ... stupid boy.

They were standing, waiting to check in. She had been about to present her voucher at the desk. Now it was all ruined. Over before it had begun.

'I'm sorry,' she said to him, as tears ran freely down her face.

He put his arm awkwardly around her shoulder. 'I didn't know it was a love that let you down, I thought it was just a friend,' he said.

She couldn't bear the sympathy and concern in his voice. 'Yes, well, you know now.' She tried to wipe her eyes but the tears wouldn't brush away on her hand.

He took out a big tissue and dabbed her face. He took the voucher from her hand and gave it to the smiling Greek woman who was allotting the rooms. 'I hope we have a lovely view,' Tommy said. 'It's our first time in Greece, you see.'

The woman smiled as she would have at Frank, but it was a different smile, warmer, less challenging. They said no words to each other until they were in the white bedroom with the wooden beds, each covered with a long white bedspread. They looked around at the pictures on the wall, fishing scenes, harbour paintings. There were pottery bowls and vases scattered here and there, and a bright rug on the floor. Local work, things they could buy in the souvenir shops.

Tommy opened the door to their little bathroom. 'Imagine,' he said. 'Six towels.'

Her heart was heavy as she sat on one of the beds. Kate said nothing.

'Why don't you take the one nearer the window?' he suggested. 'It's got a nicer view.'

'I'm sorry, Tommy,' Kate said.

'And I'm very sorry too. It must be very sad for you.'

There was something very genuine about him. He was sorry that a kind woman like Kate, who had taken him on a holiday, should have had this blow in her life. It wasn't that he was afraid to sleep in the same room with her.

'Thank you. I know you are.' It sounded curiously formal to her, but Tommy seemed to think it acceptable.

He nodded. 'I hope it will be a help to you having me here, not a hindrance,' he said.

'Of course it will,' she laughed. 'We'll show them all.'

'Who are they all?' he asked innocently.

And for a second time she realised there was nobody to show. Her life and Frank's part in it were not centre stage for anyone except herself. Maybe this time it would stick. Maybe she would believe it in her heart as well as in her head.

'There's no all,' she said, sad in a way to lose the imaginary audience, but relieved at the same time.

'Will we go for a swim?' He was eager, eager as the child he still was in many ways.

'Yes, but only if you put on lots of sun cream.'

'You sound like my mother,' he laughed.

Frank used to say, 'You're making noises like a wife.'

Kate used to protest at that. Protest too much, so that Frank would never know just how much she wanted to be his wife, so that he wouldn't be frightened away. But it was an act. Like almost everything else she had done.

There was no more acting. 'I'll be worse than a mother to you,' she threatened him. 'I see it as my mission to get you back home from here in one piece and without sunstroke.'

He laughed, delighted with her.

She could see by his open, honest face that he was glad that whatever storms there were seemed to have passed. That it was going to be a great holiday after all. And she laughed back … without wondering how it would sound. She wasn't free yet, but she would be.

Maybe even at the end of the holiday.

P.D. Viner is an award winning film-maker and creator of the highly successful SmartPass audio guides. He's married to an American Doctor of Linguistics and, along with their five-year-old daughter, he is her test-subject. He has lived abroad for ten years, working and studying in the USA, New Zealand and Russia, and has been a pretty bad stand-up comedian, produced mime shows for Japanese TV and written theatre for the Shakespeare festival, produced in London and Verona.

This is his first murder.

THE
LAST WINTER
OF DANI LANCING

P.D. VINER

EBURY
PRESS

1 3 5 7 9 10 8 6 4 2

First published in 2013 by Ebury Press, an imprint of Ebury Publishing
A Random House Group Company
This edition published in 2014

Copyright © P. D. Viner 2013

P. D. Viner has asserted his right to be identified as the author of this Work in
accordance with the Copyright, Designs and Patents Act 1988

This novel is a work of fiction. Names and characters are the product
of the author's imagination and any resemblance to actual persons,
living or dead, is entirely coincidental

The Random House Group Limited Reg. No. 954009

Addresses for companies within the Random House Group can be
found at: www.randomhouse.co.uk

A CIP catalogue record for this book is
available from the British Library

The Random House Group Limited supports The Forest Stewardship
Council® (FSC®), the leading international forest-certification organisation.
Our books carrying the FSC label are printed on FSC®-certified paper.
FSC is the only forest-certification scheme supported by the
leading environmental organisations, including Greenpeace.
Our paper procurement policy can be found at:
www.randomhouse.co.uk/environment

Printed and bound by CPI Group (UK) Ltd, Croydon, CR0 4YY

ISBN   9780091953348

For Lynne
My A-muse

PART ONE

PART ONE

ONE

Saturday 18 December 2010

'There's no such thing as monsters,' he tells her.

The girl screws up her nose. 'Look anyway. Please.'

'Okay.'

She hugs Hoppy Bunny tight as her dad slides sideways off the bed and onto the floor, pulling the duvet to one side and peering into the shadows.

'Nothing there.'

'Are you sure?'

Even at five years old she knows that grown-ups can't be trusted with this stuff. They aren't clear about what is and isn't in the dark.

'I am absolutely, totally sure there's nothing under your bed.'

'Check the wardrobe.'

With an exaggerated sigh, he moves across the room and pulls the doors open quickly. Dresses and coats sway violently, like zombie hordes.

'Dad!'

'It's okay.' He grabs the clothes. 'Nothing to worry about.' He pushes them aside and peers into the back of the wardrobe. 'Just clothes, no lions or witches.'

Her eyes widen. 'Did you think there would be?'

'No. No... I was just being silly.' He sits back on the edge of her bed. 'There's nothing there, darling.'

'Nothing now! What if a monster slides under the door when I'm asleep?'

'Once I kiss you goodnight the room is sealed, nothing can come into your bedroom in the night.'

She frowns. 'What about the tooth fairy?'

'Well...'

'Santa?'

'I meant...' He frowns too. 'Nothing bad can come in, and Hoppy Bunny's here to keep you safe.'

'How?' She looks dubiously at the small stuffed rabbit.

'Hoppy was specially trained, he only lets in good fairies or Santa.'

'Hmmm.'

'Don't worry, Dani. Mummy and I are downstairs. Nothing bad is going to happen. I promise.' He kisses her forehead...

... and the memory starts to fade.

Dani watches her younger self melt into the shadows of the night. Frozen in time, for a moment longer, is her father. The sight of him, so young and handsome, makes her smile – a sad smile. Slowly, the black hair, smooth face, elegant clothes slip away. Left behind, lying in the bed, is the older version. His hair is salt and pepper now, his face craggy and lined. He sleeps, but it's not the sleep of the just. His nights are pained by visions. More than twenty years of night terrors – and she is the cause.

She sits in the chair by the door and watches him sleep just like she does every night, watching for the shadows to take his dreams. When they come, she will sing to him. Sometimes, when he whimpers or calls out, she aches to lean forward and kiss his forehead – but she can't. Nearly forty years have passed since he banished

4

the monsters from her room. Now it's her job – to keep him safe in the night.

She curls her arms around herself. The room is cold, though she doesn't notice, she just likes to feel arms around her. She wishes she could call the child back, see herself again from all those years ago. How old – five? So serious and confident, when had it all disappeared? But of course she knows the answer to that. 'Dani...' he calls out in his sleep.

'Shh, sleep safe. I'm here.' And softly she sings a lullaby she remembers from all those years ago.

'Care you not and go to sleep, Over you a watch I'll keep...'

'Not her!' He calls out in pain from the thickness of his nightmare.

'Shh, Dad.' She slides off the chair to kneel by his bed.

'Dani...' he calls softly.

'It's okay.'

'I can't find you.'

He's sweating. His face is pinched and his legs begin to jerk like he's running.

'Dani!' he yells, his hands flail, jaws grind.

'I'm here, Dad,' she tells him, hoping her voice might worm its way down into his dream.

He twists sharply and cries in pain. 'Are you safe?'

She hesitates. 'Yes, Dad, I'm safe.'

He shakes, whimpering like a child. 'Dani. Where are you?'

'Dad, I'm here,' she whispers. 'I came back.'

His face contorts and he moans loudly.

'I can't see through the snow. Dani, I can't—' his body is suddenly rigid. His jaw grinds and darkness knits his brow. His back arcs – like he is having a seizure.

'Sleep, Daddy. I'm here.'

He makes a low moan and, like a sudden storm, the danger passes as tension slips away from his body and he slides deep into the undertow of sleep. She watches him, listens as his breath softens until it's barely audible. He's still. He's safe. The monsters have left him alone – for tonight. He should sleep until morning.

She stretches in the chair. Her back aches and the pain in her hip cuts through her. She can't sit any longer, so lies on the floor beside him. She rocks from side to side, trying to get comfortable. It was such a long time ago, surely it shouldn't still feel like this. Phantom pains. On the ceiling, the faintest movements of shadow – greys and blacks – skirmish above her head. Slowly, the pain recedes and she sinks into the floor. She lies still, missing her night-light, wants something to eat the darkness away. She longs for dawn, for her dad to wake. She wants to talk, go for a walk, maybe see a movie? What time is it now – 2 a.m.? Tiredness sweeps across her. He'll sleep – she wishes she could.

She lies still for a long time, listening to his breath rise and fall. Finally she rolls over onto all fours – stretches like a cat – and leaves. Outside his door, she pauses for a few moments, continuing to listen to his breath. One day it will end. Will she be there at that moment? Hear the body draw its final inhalation, the lungs expand and then just stop so that the air seeps away and there is nothing. Nothing. The thought scares her. The loneliness terrifies her.

She turns to her own room. Inside is her single child's bed, the same bed her father knelt under to check for monsters all those years ago. She feels a tiny shudder run through her.

'Someone walked over your grave.' That's what her gran would have said.

The room is too dark, only a little moonlight spills in from the hallway. She isn't sure she can stay there. The shadows are alive sometimes.

'Be brave, Dani,' she tells herself. But the old fears are strong. What would Dad do?

She bends down and looks underneath the bed. Cobwebs. No monsters – unless you're a fly. She smiles a fake smile, even though there's nobody there to see it, and she feels braver.

'Go on, Dan,' she whispers, and stretches out her fingers to the wardrobe door. It swings open with a little haunted-house creak. The dresses and coats are long gone. It is totally empty. Of course it is. Real monsters don't hide in wardrobes.

TWO

Saturday 18 December 2010

She cuts him.

His body twists. She tightens her grip on his hand as the pain draws him back from the oblivion of sedation. Eyes flicker. For a second they open: confusion, pain, fear. His palm pools with blood.

'Shh,' she whispers, as if to calm a baby, squeezing his fingers tight.

He struggles one final time, but the tape she's wrapped around his body holds him securely. He drops back into the darkness.

With an unsteady hand she fumbles in her pocket for the sterile swab.

'Damn,' she spits, frustrated by the delicate touch needed. With a bloodied finger she pokes her glasses, holding them in place so she can peer through the oval at the bottom. His blurred hand sharpens into focus.

She dips the bud into his palm; the cotton bloats, gorges itself. She lets his hand drop – it arcs to the floor and swings, splattering red like a child's painting, and then comes to rest, weeping onto the carpet. She's cut far deeper than was needed; bone shows through the deep trench of flesh. She doesn't care, just runs the swab across the slide, leaving a bloody smear. Done. She feels giddy. Finally she's done it. Patricia Lancing has her man. She leans forward, her mouth brushing his ear to whisper, 'You are a monster.'

'He needs a plaster,' A small voice says.

Patty looks across at Dani, who with a shy smile holds up the toy she's squirted with ketchup.

'Hoppy Bunny needs a plaster. He's poorly.'

'Oh dear, let's get him one. Maybe Doctor Duck should take a look.'

'Oh yes, Mum. I'll go get him.' Her daughter pads away, the memory fading.

'Danielle,' Patty calls to her five-year-old daughter, but she is gone. Long gone.

She looks back to the man tied to the chair. 'Why Danielle?'

The question hangs in the air between them as it has done for over twenty years, poisonous and all consuming.

'Why my daughter?'

There is no sound from him. She looks at her watch. 3.42 a.m.

She takes the slide with his blossom of blood, puts it back in its box and seals it. With reverence she walks it over to the cooler and places it inside. All is done. She hears her husband's voice slide back to her through the years: 'Now what, Patty? Now what will you do?' Jim asks, but she doesn't know what to say to him, her mind too full of shadows.

She turns back to the man she has abducted. With a finger, she reaches out and tips his head. His skin is waxy, lips flecked with the drool of insensibility. She takes his eyelid and peels it back; there is nothing but a poached-egg smear. He sickens her. She raises the knife and presses it into his soft throat. It would be easy... so... she closes her eyes.

She opens them. The hotel room has gone. She coughs and the shop assistant looks up from what he's reading.

'Yeah?' He looks fourteen, all spots and surly resentment.

She points behind his head, to the serious hunting knives in the locked cabinet. He grunts, then takes a stubby key from his pocket and slides the glass away. He points to one and she nods. It's vicious, designed to slice through flesh and muscle, hack through bone. One edge a razor, the other a saw. She's come all the way across London to this little shop in Wimbledon, somewhere nobody knows her, to buy a specialist hunting knife. She carries no ID, just cash – a cover story all worked out: her husband will be hunting for the first time, big promotion up for grabs and he needs to impress. So she will have to gut, slice and cook whatever he manages to shoot. She's pleased with her invention and has topped it off with a disguise: waxed jacket and riding boots she bought from Oxfam yesterday. She's also wearing lots of make-up. Mutton dressed as mutton. She spent all morning in front of a mirror perfecting her cut-glass home-counties accent, reborn as Hilary Clifton-Hastings. Nobody can refuse to sell a hunting knife to a Clifton-Hastings.

'That will do nicely' she says and hands it back. The shop assistant peels the price sticker from the back with a fingernail that is almost pure soil.

'Thirty-five fifty.'

Hilary Clifton-Hastings slides the cash across the counter; he scoops it up and scatters it in the till. No questions, barely a glance from him. She does not need her alter ego. He sizes her up in a microsecond; small, thin, grey woman in her sixties: harmless.

Harmless!

That was two days ago.

She opens her eyes. She's cold. That afternoon's snow falls on her once again. The watery sun's dipped below the horizon and the light has died. She stands, a statue, alone in the long-stay car park alongside the metal carcasses that poke from the growing carpet of snow. If anyone were watching her, they'd think she was a crazy woman. But nobody is watching, not even on CCTV. Broken yesterday and not repaired, tut tut.

She hasn't dressed for the weather. The ferocity of the cold has surprised her: Siberia in south-east England. She knows she should go and sit in her car but everything looks so beautiful in its white coat. All around the ground is pure, unmarked, as if no living thing exists to disturb the peace. It would be terrible if she destroyed it. So she stands still and waits.

She sticks out her tongue and counts... one elephant, two elephants... a swirling snowflake lands and dissolves, wet and slightly metallic. Others fall on her eyelids and trickle away as mock tears, some alight on her skin and nuzzle into her silver hair. Each flake is perfect – an intricate and exquisite ice world – unique. Some see the hand of God in this. Not her.

Fewer and fewer planes have been landing over the last few hours as the snow has got heavier. If she had her phone she could check the weather report, check the plane schedule, but she doesn't have it. She carries nothing that could identify her if... if things don't go to plan.

'Shall I just stand here and wait?' she thinks. 'But for how long? He's already hours late, may not come at all.' Does she wait until she freezes?

She watches the snow and listens for the first mutterings of an engine. She feels as if she's been placed in a magician's cabinet, waiting to be sawn in half.

Then, in the darkness some way off, she hears the chug of a motor. She shakes a little, though not her sickness shakes. She doesn't need her medication – this is first-night nerves.

All is dark. Jim flicks the light on. He stands in the doorway, holding a tea towel where the door should be. 'Ladies and gentleman. I now present for your delectation and delight a master of the art of prestidigitation…'

'Dad!' Dani shouts from the hallway. 'I'm doing magic.'

'Sorry. Ladies and gentlemen, I give you the Magic of Madame Danielle Lancing.'

The tea towel is pulled away with a flourish and a six-year-old Dani enters, wearing a black top hat made from an old porridge container and a paper plate. She sports a black cape that was once a towel and waves a cardboard wand that came free in a Rice Krispies packet and has been sat on quite a few times.

'I am Mystical Dani and you will be amazed,' she says in as low a voice as a six-year-old can manage.

She whips the wand into the air.

'Abracadabra!' She pulls off her hat and Hoppy Bunny is on her head, dressed in a tutu.

Jim claps wildly. Dani grins, showing her missing front teeth. She waves her dad over, and once again they whisper.

Patty watches them with pleasure, and perhaps a twinge of jealousy. They're thick as thieves those two. Always have been, always…

'Now my beautiful assistant will help me,' Dani shouts as if she were in a real theatre, and Jim bows and blows kisses to the crowd, 'with the Many Knives of Doom illuj-ion.' She waves a plastic knife in the air.

Patty feels the weight of the hunting knife in her own hand, its edge bloody. Her husband and daughter dissolve – smoke and mirrors. They were not real, a thirty-five-year-old memory that rose to the surface; the heft of the blade in her hand is real though. What she must do with it is real. She grips it tight.

Headlights arrive, arresting the freezing flakes in mid-air. It's too big to be a car, it must be the shuttle. The excitement thaws her toes and fingers; she moves slowly towards the line of cars that will hide her from view. Finally the shuttle reaches the entrance to the car park and turns in. She feels her heart slow as the bus crawls towards her.

'Let him be on it,' she speaks aloud, though the wind rips her words to shreds the moment they emerge from her mouth. The bus skids a little as the driver applies the brakes. Inside it's dark. There is no movement. She ages and dies many times before the door finally cracks open and the interior is illuminated. The driver hops down the stairs quickly, keen to get this done and get back to the warmth of the terminal. He opens one of the luggage stores under the bus and pulls out a set of golf clubs.

'How funny,' she thinks as she watches him struggle with them. Shivering, the driver holds them out, as a single passenger alights. The metal whale then pulls away with a little slide of the wheels, heading back to civilisation.

She watches the passenger wrestle with the golf clubs and a little pull-along suitcase. She cannot see clearly; he's too far away and in the shadows. She holds her breath while he inches towards her. From somewhere she hears:

'Mum.' A voice from the dark.

'I'm nearly there, Dani. So close.'

'Patty.' Jim's deep voice rattles in her ribcage.

'Please don't ask me to stop, Jim.'

Patty digs her gnawed fingernails into the skin of her arm – as hard and deep as she can – and the passenger stumbles closer. Face still hidden, snow billowing around him. There is a yellow pool of light and he is almost there... he steps into it, like an actor moving into a spotlight: Duncan Cobhurn.

He's not tall but he's stocky. He looks like a rugby player who's stopped exercising but still enjoys his food and beer. Mostly bald, just a clipped halo above his ears, black flecked with grey. His face is fleshy and pink – a mix of blood pressure and sun. He has a few days' growth of beard, which is mostly white. He's dressed in linen, a stylish white suit that might have looked great in Lisbon but is going to get ruined in the snow. He looks frozen already.

'Good,' she thinks. 'That will make my job easier.'

The clubs are on his shoulder and swing heavily as he walks. He has to stop every few feet to clear away the little snowmen his case keeps building. As he approaches she slowly draws back into the shadows and slides towards her car.

She opens her eyes. She's back in the hotel room with Duncan Cobhurn – a sedated and bleeding Duncan Cobhurn. The room is stifling. She misses the clean sterile cold of the afternoon. No snowflakes fall here; instead motes of dust dance. She remembers how Dani, when she was about five, believed they were sugarplum fairies dancing in the moonlight. The imagination of a child... It's just dirt and decay. This room is filthy. The walls are beige but speckled with greasy spots and chocolate-coloured scabs. The ceiling was probably white once, but is now nicotine beige, and the floor... Christ knows what bodily secretions have seeped into it. There's a stain, just by the foot of the bed, that she thinks is the spitting image of Gandhi. Now, what would he have done? Forgiven Duncan Cobhurn? She is not Gandhi. She cuts him.

THREE

'Wha—?' Jim Lancing wakes with a start. No idea where, frozen – panic.

'Dad.' Dani is beside him in an instant.

'I'm okay darling. Go back to your room, I'm fine. It was just a nightmare, just another nightmare.'

'I should stay.'

'No, no really. Please Dani. I'm okay.'

'Are you sure?'

'Please.'

She nods, a little reluctantly, and leaves him.

He lies back down and concentrates on slowing his heart, pulling himself back from wherever his dream had taken him. He pictures a lake in his mind, mountains surrounding it – a calm place. Slowly the fear recedes and he is himself again. He rubs his hand, it hurts. He looks across at his bedside table. Glowing numbers read 3.42.

'Damn.'

He really needs more sleep than this, but he knows that won't happen. He lies there in the dark. On his tongue there's the faintest taste, and in the air there seems to be something, tangible and smoky, but he can sense it rather than smell it. He feels sweaty from his nightmare and already the prickles of sweat are turning cold; he realises what the taste in his mouth is: blood.

16

He rolls over onto his side and then out of bed and onto the floor. The first few steps are little more than a hobble until his creaking joints and muscles warm up. He walks down the hall-way to the loo. This is the biggest show of how age has crept up on him: that he can't go through the night without the need to pee. And then, once he's there, he stands longer than ever before. Sometimes he even sits, like a girl. Tonight he sits immediately, knowing he will be in there a long time. After a couple of minutes he takes a newspaper that's folded under the sink. He looks at the Sudoku.

'I haven't got a pen,' he calls out.

'Isn't there one in the medicine cabinet?'

He looks and finds a stubby pencil in with his razor.

'Got it. Thanks,' he shouts to his daughter.

'Okay,' she calls back. 'I'll be downstairs. Waiting for you.'

He finishes the Sudoku and Killer Sudoku while he's there, then cleans his teeth, trying to remove the taste of blood. He looks at himself in the mirror and isn't unhappy with the reflection. He's got pretty terrible bed-head and his eyes look saggier than usual, but generally he's not too bad for a man of sixty-four, especially at this time of night. Not gone to seed, like many others he could name – he's pretty lean. He can bend over and touch his toes without too much huffing and puffing. He would be the first to admit that his stomach isn't flat like it once was; there's a slight paunch but it's not bad, just a little loss of muscle tone to show how gravity hates the old. He rinses his mouth and then runs his wet fingers through his hair. It's still a pretty good crop, even if it has gone stone grey at the temples and the rest, once raven black, is now dusted with grey. He has always thought his features a little too pronounced, his nose too big and his mouth too wide, but he seems to have grown into them over the years.

He shivers, the chill of the morning creeping into his bones. He runs a shower, nice and hot, and steps into it. The pressure is strong – it pounds and buffets him, releasing knots.

'Jim,' a voice breathes from inside the cascade of water.

'Patty?' He strains to hear – can her voice be in the water?

'Help.'

He feels something deep in his heart – a tug that says something's wrong with her, his wife. A wife he has barely seen in twelve years. In the churn of the water his nightmare comes back to him.

'Are you coming down yet?' she calls up the stairs.

'Just coming,' he replies, feeling guilty for not going down before now. He knows how much she longs to talk after a sleepless night, how lonely she gets during the long stretch of darkness. But right now he's too rattled by the images in his head to talk to her. He tries to push them back inside the box and paste a smile on his face.

'You need to get down here,' Dani shouts.

The smile wastes away on his face. He heads downstairs. 'Where are you?'

'Hide and seek,' is her reply.

He finds her curled up in the big leather armchair in the room they laughingly call his den. When she was a child it had been the family dining room. But he couldn't remember the last time the house had any actual dining in it. Instead the room had become a sort of den-slash-library-slash-watching-the-world-slide-by room. It's pretty Spartan: two chairs, a small table and an old fish tank. Once, a long time ago, the tank had been home to Dani's tropical friends but now has some very creepy-looking cacti in among multi-coloured stones. It's the only room in the house that's allowed to be a little untidy. Newspapers are on the floor; he only buys the Saturday *Guardian* and Sunday *Observer* each week but they certainly mount up. Books and correspondence are piled on a small coffee table. Every couple of months he forces himself to sit down and catch up with the world; he should probably do that pretty soon, he thinks.

She turns in the big chair to look up at him. Her long dark hair curling over her shoulder, pale skin flawless and her large brown eyes glittering with excitement. It shocks him a little – probably the aftermath of his nightmare – that she still looks so young. He forgets that sometimes... after all that has happened to her.

'You okay?' she asks with a half smile.

He nods a yes.

'Then sit down and buckle up – you are in for a treat.'

She swings back in the chair to face the doors that lead to the garden. Jim sits in the other, less comfortable chair and angles it to match Dani's view. Outside it's black but he can just see someth— a light snaps on in the garden next door, bleeding across their lawn, revealing an amazing vista. Huge flakes of snow drift on the wind, buffeted and brawling like bumper cars at the fair.

'Oh my God.' He's amazed by the sight.

The two of them sit watching the snow until the sensor light turns off.

'It'll go back on soon.'

They sit in the dark, waiting. Jim suddenly thinks of the animals out there: Willow, Scruffy, George and others – guinea pigs, hamsters, cats and two dogs buried over the years in solemn services. He has never seen their ghosts, which he's glad about. If Scruffy came back to be stroked, like some zombie Disney cartoon, that would scare the life out of him. But he wonders where they are now. Is there an animal afterlife? Do they have souls like he does, like Dani does?

The light flips back on – catching a squirrel in mid-scurry – and Jim is once more in awe of the scene before him. The snow swirls like the Milky Way, so close he could reach out and touch it.

'Are you out there, Patty?' he thinks. 'Somewhere in the snow?'

FOUR

Saturday 18 December 2010

Tom stops to get his bearings. Peering into the dark, he can see the mouth of the bridge stretching over the Thames but by halfway across, it fades to nothing. A wall of blackness with snow rippled through it. The streets are empty but for a second he thinks he sees someone walking towards him across the bridge. It looks like... but then there's no one. Just snow whipped up by the wind. Who? Something scratches at his thoughts, tugging at strands of memories that just refuse to come. For a second, he knows... but it just fades from his mind.

He looks at his watch, it's 3.42 a.m. Everybody's asleep, except him.

He turns back to the path and kicks at the snow. For days he's been dragging a heavy heart along in a sack but now there's snow. How can anyone feel depressed when faced with this? He feels like a kid who's bunked off school to see the circus come to town, 'oohing' and 'ahhing' as the tufts of candyfloss parachute towards him.

'I love snow,' he tells the world.

He looks over the sluggish water to the park; it could be anywhere, anywhen. The snow is already quite thick, deadening all sound, building banks and drifts. The moon's fat, nearly full, but half-hidden behind skyscrapers of cloud. He stands for a long time, a solitary figure in a snow globe, then finally turns towards the ark of glass that juts out over the river and trudges towards home.

He's left his car outside her house. He's already thinking he'll send a constable to collect it in a day or two, in case she's watching out her window.

'What a mistake,' he tells the snow.

He'd known she was divorced, had two children – and that could have been fine, he's good with kids. The problem was that he'd not seen how needy she was. They'd had dinner a week ago – she'd drunk a little too much and been a little loud by the end of the evening, but he thought that was nerves. She was at least ten years younger than him, thirty, with long, deep brown hair and tall, long-limbed. That was what had attracted him to her profile. And in her picture she smiled quite beautifully – genuine, unconcerned. Just like *her* smile had been.

'And?' he asks himself. 'The truth?'

Truth? He thinks. It has nothing to do with truth, or admitting anything. He knows why he'd been drawn to this woman. He knows why some women draw his eye and not others. Why he'd turned down at least two women who could have made him happy, who could have loved him. The truth was because he was in love. Still in love after all these years.

And that photo on the website had been so like her. So like Dani. He had made the date, wanting to see her smile again. Except in real life he didn't see Dani's smile. Instead there was a thin half-smile, darting across her lips like an apology, and she dipped her head to hide how tall she was. Her voice had grated on him from the start too – rough sloppy diction – *you know*, *you know like*. But dinner had been fine. At the end they had walked to the Tube and she'd leant into him and kissed him. He felt her small breasts push into his chest and a flick of her tongue brush his lips. She called him the next day and they had agreed to meet again. She invited him to dinner at her place. Stupid. Her place – it was obvious where that was heading. Stupid to go to bed with her. Out of her clothes she was so unlike Dani. She had tattoos, which he hated. From the start she apologised for everything. Sorry for her M&S knickers, the sheets, the children down the hall, her inexperience, how cold her hands were. 'Next time it will be perfect,' she whispered in his ear as he pushed himself into her.

Afterwards she went to the toilet. He imagined her in there, crying for her lost life and the desperate compromises she'd been forced to make. He had to get out of the house. When she returned with minty breath, he told her he had to leave, still had a test to prepare for Year Four. He saw her flinch as he lied to her – clearly she was a woman who'd heard a lot of lies and had good radar for them – but he couldn't bear to snuggle up with her and talk about the future. It actually made it worse that she looked like Dani. Only skin deep though. He smiles at the thought of Dani and his cheeks tighten and ache. His eyes have little frozen lakes in the corners.

It wasn't his first lie to this woman either. His profile on the dating site says he's a teacher of history at an under-performing comprehensive. He never tells anyone he's a policeman. Even those few people close enough to him to know he works for the police don't know exactly what he does. Only a few other high-rank-ing officers know he heads a special unit, and that he looks into the eyes of dead girls and promises them he will try to find the men responsible. And he tries. He tries. Detective Superintendent Thomas Bevans. The Sad Man.

He walks, feeling the snow give way under his feet.

'I should've put a bet on a white Christmas – the odds will be useless now,' he tells the trees.

He loves the silence. Of course, at almost 4 a.m. on a Saturday morning, it is going to be pretty quiet – but the deadening effect of the snow and the low cloud has removed all trace of the world. No music of the spheres. He stops and closes his eyes. He's a boy again, remembering the first time the silence descended, a truly white Christmas. 1976.

He was eight and pretty sure he'd never seen snow before – not real snow that settles on the ground. But he remembers the rush of excitement that morning, like man had landed on Mars or something. The road outside their flat was amazing. Nothing had driven through it, not even a bike. Pure. Virgin. White. He ran out. His mum was still asleep and he ran and ran through the snow, then turned to see his tracks – the only human being on earth. Until he got to the park. And there she was. He remembers thinking 'What the bloody hell is she wearing?' She was in a white nightdress, flimsy and sheer. He could see the curves of her body beneath it – but is that just wishful remembering? No, she was fully clothed underneath, with a big sailor's jumper. She wore the nightdress over the top. She was lying in the snow waving her arms. He saw her and hid in some bushes, watching. She lay there for a while and then got up and walked away – her dark hair streaked with snow. He waited until she was out of sight and walked over to where she'd lain. There was an angel in the snow.

Christ, even at eight years old, she had done something to him. Danielle Lancing, the girl he loved. Loves.

As memories of her flit through his mind he feels a shiver run through him as if somebody is dancing on his grave. But it's just the vibration of his mobile on silent. He pulls it out and reads the short message, a missing person report. Normally he wouldn't be notified unless it was a high-profile victim. This isn't, just a Durham businessman who'd been reported missing by his wife. But the name is one that he'd recently added to a high-security alert list: Duncan Cobhurn. And the memory slots into place – the woman he thought he saw in the swirling snow on the bridge, Patricia Lancing. Dani's mother. He feels lost.

'Christ.'

He turns to head back the way he's come. He begins to run.

FIVE

Patty sits in the dark. She had to turn the lights out so she could no longer see him – she wants to cut his throat. She needs to get calm so she can go and check the blood, to make—

Light snaps on outside the room, headlights from a car skidding into the car park behind the hotel. The glare spills around the edges of the curtains. The blood pooled at his feet glows. Her heart somersaults. Panic. She hadn't considered the curtains; they're a cheap fabric and don't fit very well. There must be no chance someone can see inside. She grabs the gaffer tape and begins to run it across the gaps, sealing the two of them in a cube. It takes a few minutes to remove all vestiges of light seeping in from the outside world and plunge the room into pitch black.

Dani is standing on a chair; she's eight and looking intently at the problem before her. Jim has sunk a little so that she can reach around his neck. He's wearing a rented tuxedo that's a little snug in places. Dani has the two ends of a bowtie in her hands and a slip of paper with instructions on how to tie it.

'I think…' Jim starts.

'Shh!' Dani holds her finger to her lips and then frowns back at the paper.

'If you...' he tries.

'Shh. If you want this tied properly you need to keep quiet.' She reads, 'Fold the left over the right...' She proceeds to follow the directions carefully, concentrating on the diagrams.

'Eureka!' She jumps up and down doing her happy dance. It's a little loose, but a recognisable bowtie. Dani beams broadly, proud of herself. From the door there is a wolf-whistle. Jim turns to see Patty. He gives her a twirl.

'I could rent you out as a gigolo,' she says huskily.

'Sorry, I'm a one-woman man. You look fantastic.'

She rolls her eyes; compliments are not something she likes to hear.

'Cab will be here in five minutes.'

'Will Jenny be here soon?' asks Dani.

'Any minute. She'll give you some supper, then into jammies, stories and bed. Got that?'

'Yes,' says the eight-year-old with a little roll of her own eyes, as if to say: *I'm eight. I can understand simple instructions and I don't really need a babysitter any more anyway.*

'If you win will you wake me up and show me your prize when you get home?' she asks.

'No.' 'Yes.' Patty and Jim answer simultaneously.

'I won't win – it's just stupid,' Patty shakes her head.

'Daddy says you fight for truth and justice.'

'Oh does he? I just write stories in a newspaper.'

'I'm going to be a superhero when I grow up,' says Dani as she jumps off the chair and lands with a slam at her parents' feet.

'And what superpowers will you have?' Patty asks her. Dani thinks for a moment.

'To make people be nice.'

Patty snaps the light back on in the room. She checks the tape again. His mouth's totally covered, but just to make sure, she pulls his head back to rest on the chair and wraps layer after layer of tape around and around. He can't possibly move now. There is no dignity. He's wet himself; it drips down the chair and onto the floor, joining his blood. The smell is rank. It looks as if he's melting, like the Wicked Witch of the West.

When she's finished with the tape, she turns her attention to the room. A double bed dominates. She has lain on it; it's lumpy. She didn't pull back the sheets, sure they wouldn't be clean and not wishing to leave any evidence. She wears gloves, has done each time she's entered the room. She also wears a shower cap and plastic pinafore, as if she works in a meat-pie factory. There's a bedside table with alarm and telephone, a chair by the window, a wardrobe that contains a mini-safe and an ironing board. She looks down. The blood will be difficult to get out of the carpet.

'Maybe when I'm finally done with this room I'll leave a pile of money for the poor cleaner who finds all of this... If all goes well,' she thinks.

According to the plan, she should return in less than eight hours to find nothing disturbed and her prisoner still unconscious. If not... then she must leave no trace. She checks all the drawers, they're empty; not even the Gideons see any point in coming here.

She moves to the bathroom: cracked white tile and a faint smell of bleach over damp and mustiness. The shower curtain has mildew along the bottom. She brought no toiletries with her, has not touched the two small plastic beakers, nor the two small bottles of shampoo and body wash. There's a hand towel. She wonders if she used it and decides to take it with her just in case. She stuffs it into her bag.

'Better safe than prison,' she thinks.

She turns to leave and catches sight of herself in the mirror. Blood is smeared on her glasses and arcs over her cheek, sweeping across her right eye. She draws back from her reflection, horrified for a second and then... exhilarated. Fiery eyes blaze through a red cowl of his blood. She smiles at her bloody twin. She likes it, would like to keep it for ever, a red badge of courage. Nemesis – the Red Revenger. But she's no superhero. She wipes the blood away with a wet-wipe she pockets after. In the mirror is a crone once more. She gives the bathroom one final look and heads back to the bedroom. Everything is clean. She looks at her watch: 5.30 a.m. Time to go. She checks she has the room key and then switches the light off and plunges the room once more into darkness.

From somewhere far-off she hears Jim ask her: 'Patty, what would your superpower be?'

She whispers into the dark. 'To bring back the dead.'

SIX

Saturday 18 December 2010

Tom sits at his desk. He should get moving – he doesn't have much time – but he can't move. For the last ten minutes he has read from a small purple book. The same page over and over. On the cover, written in bold black letters: 'Private – do not open.' He takes the diary and slides it back into the safe in his desk. Inside there are two other diaries and a small photo album, full of pictures of Dani. He locks the safe and slides the desk drawer closed, then locks that too. No one knows he has a small safe in his desk; he fitted it himself one weekend.

Tom goes through his checklist one last time. He'd signed in twenty minutes ago, chatting to old Charlie on the desk for a while, asking about his daughter just as he always did. Then he took the lift up to his office on the third floor. He'd unlocked it and turned his computer on, logging in at 5.22 a.m. and started an email. Now it is 5.36 a.m. Time to go. He heads into the corridor and takes the stairs down to the first floor, the main ops room for Operation Ares.

It's a large room with floor-to-ceiling glass composing one wall. Almost every other inch of wall space is taken up with whiteboards covered with lists of names, photos of victims, schedules of surveillance, reports and statements. Seen from eye level it's a mess, a Rorschach test in three dimensions. Yet from above

30

it resembles a hive city with maze-like avenues created from dozens and dozens of dividers forming little rooms or corridors where desks can congregate. Everywhere, everywhere is paper. Great, towering skyscrapers of paper. In some places they are still intact, in others smashed down or mashed into other towers as if Godzilla has rampaged through central Tokyo. Some of the paper skyscrapers spill onto the floor like a river that's burst its banks. In other spots, reams and reams are scrunched into balls and lie under desks or scattered around empty bins. A sorry testament to the lack of basketball skills in Britain.

At this time of the morning, before natural light begins to spill through the glass, it feels oppressive. A city of paper, dark and shadowy. Except for one desk that blazes in the very centre of the web. This is where the graveyard shift works, or more likely dozes, while they wait for information on breaking crime. Mostly they file reports for later attention by the day shift, but sometimes they need some poor bugger woken up and dispatched to some draughty wasteland to look at a body. Tonight they had just passed on a run-of-the-mill missing person's report... but that had made Tom head directly there, not passing go and not collecting £200.

Tom looks at his watch: 5.38. In under an hour the graveyard shift will be over and the morning staff will start to arrive – he has to move. He can feel his stomach spasm; he's the boss, he should be beyond reproach. What he's about to do is misconduct at best. He vowed to himself, twenty years ago, that he would be straight, that his conduct would be whiter than white, that he would never do anything that he knew was wrong. Not again. Not since... That was why he was the youngest special-operations superintendent in the Metropolitan Police; that was why he had the loyalty of his team. And will he jeopardise that now – for her? For Dani? Of course he will.

He takes a deep breath and swings the door open, making straight for the only officer – Eddie Matthews. Fat Eddie. As he walks towards Eddie, Tom can see from the way he slumps sideways that he's asleep. He comes level without disturbing him, then slaps him hard on the shoulder. The big man jumps like he's been electrocuted.

'What the fu— Guv? What are you doin' 'ere?'

'No peace for the wicked, Eddie.' With a Cheshire cat smile, Tom sits on the desk and looks the big man up and down. 'Honestly, Eddie, have you got a shirt that isn't covered in Pot Noodle and tomato sauce? You look like you're bloody homeless.'

'Sorry guv, I'll—' Eddie looks like he might cry for a second and then hauls himself out of his chair and shambles off towards the gents.

Tom watches him go and feels a pang of guilt. It was a cruel thing to say. The reason Matthews had been given the graveyard shift was because his wife had kicked him out and he actually was homeless. A WPC had found him sleeping rough one night and called Tom rather than move him on or arrest him. Now Matthews had a rollaway bed under his desk, a corner of the gents had his suitcase in it and a mug with a razor and toothbrush. As long as no one had to see him with his shirt off and he didn't smell, everyone was pretty pleased to have an officer permanently on nights.

Tom watches the big frame amble into the gents and then quickly pulls out Eddie's chair and sits at the desk. Any tracing request needs to come from Matthews's computer; that would make everything look normal. If Tom did anything from his own computer or accessed any of the Serious Crime Squad's PCs there would be trouble. Of course, he's the boss and he knows Matthews's username, Fat Eddie. But he doesn't have his password. It takes just one guess. Rachel. Eddie's wife's name, poor bastard.

It takes a few seconds to open up all the information on Duncan Cobhurn, then he copies it into the management pensions file on another server – a report so boring nobody has accessed it in six months – closes down the file and logs out.

He slides the chair back and swings himself onto the desk. Then he waits for the gents door to open. It takes about a minute, then, as Eddie appears, Tom opens his desk and takes out a Picnic bar.

'Guv!' Eddie wails.

Tom smiles broadly and takes a big bite.

'That's me last one.'

'I'm saving you from yourself, Eddie.'

'I don't need saving.' Eddie approaches his desk, sullenly reaches into another drawer and pulls out a Snickers.

'Last one?'

'Last bloody Picnic, I love those. I've still got Snickers, Mars and a couple of Lion bars.'

Tom shakes his head. 'See ya, Eddie.'

Tom starts to walk off but Eddie asks, 'Didn't ya want something, guv?'

He calls back over his shoulder, 'Just some sugar Eddie. Cheers.'

Back in his own office Tom opens the pension file and cuts the missing person report from it. He excises any trace of it and saves it in his personal documents on his desktop. Then he opens it and reads quickly but carefully.

Missing person: Duncan Cobhurn.

Date of report: Friday 17 December 2010, 11.45 p.m.

Reported by: Audrey Cobhurn. Wife.

Called wife at 4.20 p.m. to say he had arrived and would see her in three hours.

Landed at Heathrow from Lisbon. Flight BA147

Arrival confirmed by BA at 4 p.m.

Additional notes:

Cobhurn car found in long-term car park. Tyres slashed. Snow has obliterated any signs of potential struggle. Bags missing.

House keys discovered in glovebox of car.

Status of investigation:

Potential abduction enquiry.

'Christ!' Tom's face drains of all colour as he reads the report. Something was happening after all this time. He needs to see them again, Jim and Patty. They will have to talk about what happened twenty years ago.

Tom opens his drawer, then the safe, and fishes the diary out once again. He reads, though he probably could recite the page from memory.

3 October 1985

Tom said today he is applying for Cambridge too. Probably King's to read literature. I'm sure we'll both get the results we need, but is he going there because of me? I don't know. I love him, of course I do – he's brilliant. My best friend and he's been so amazing the last year. There is no way I would have held it together without him but… what if he suggests we get a flat together? In one sense it would be great but in another, I don't know. He wants more. What do I want? I wish I could ask Dad about it but really I think his head would explode if I talk love and sex. I'll ask Izzy, but she has a bit of a blind spot when it comes to Tom. I know he's the best friend in the world, but...

SEVEN

Saturday 18 December 2010

It's 6 a.m. Still a couple of hours before the sun will be up and even then it will probably be pathetic, wishy-washy grey light like dishwater. They have been watching snow swirl for a while and playing games. I Spy fizzled out quickly, but naming films and books with heavy snow scenes lasted quite some time.

'I need a coffee,' Jim finally tells his daughter.

She starts to lift herself out of the chair.

'No, stay here and watch the snow.' He turns away before he can see her face. He just feels like he needs some time on his own.

Three measured spoons into the grinder, top on, a triple tap on the side to make sure all the beans are in the centre and then he presses the button and counts to thirty before the beans are ground. It's all a little OCD. He tips the coffee into the pot, the roasted scent swirling around the room. He pours the almost boiling water on (starting the little timer on the fridge) and watches the black mass fizz and bubble as a creamy skin forms on top. He slowly stirs the pot with a chopstick. Why is Patty back in his thoughts? From somewhere deep down in his body he feels a sense of dread start to build again, to... The beep of the timer pulls him back to earth and he plunges the coffee. He pours and sips. The black tar catches in his throat, acrid and syrupy, and sits uneasily on his empty stomach. Maybe a piece of toast would make him feel better. He slices himself a thick piece and puts it under the grill. The echo of her voice plays through his head. Urgent, desperate and needy. His heart begins to race and his chest tightens.

'Dad,' Dani is next to him. 'Just breathe.'

He immediately starts to calm. Dani has always been able to cheer him and calm him. That's why he needs her. Why they need each other.

'Dad. Dad, the toast's on fire.'

'Oh hell.' He pulls the grill pan out and dumps the blazing slice into the sink. Dani doubles up laughing.

'It's not funny.'

'It is, it so is.'

He turns the taps on full and the blackened bread disintegrates and washes down the plughole.

'Bit of luck the smoke alarms don't work any more.'

The kitchen smells bitter and smoky. It reminds Jim of a Bonfire Night from many years ago. He closes his eyes and can see Dani – she must be about six or seven. That night he nailed Catherine wheels all along the outside wall and made a big production out of lighting the first one, which spun and shot vicious sparks everywhere. He'd made a mistake; the fireworks were much too close, the sparks from the first hit the next and the next. Suddenly they were all alight. Spinning, squealing and roaring until one of them shot off the wall and landed in the bin, setting it ablaze. The next-door neighbours called the fire brigade, thinking it might spread. Of course, by the time the firemen arrived it was out and they were pretty annoyed at being called to something so minor on the busiest night of the year. He was really embarrassed but Dani sat there in silence, her face illuminated first by the sparks and flames, then by the flashing blue lights of the fire engine, all the time smiling so broadly. When it had all finished and the grumbling firemen had left, she said 'Do it again, Daddy.'

'Do you ever talk to your mother?' he asks. It suddenly seems such an obvious question but he's never asked it before.

Dani scowls. For a second he's scared she doesn't know who he's talking about – has she forgotten her mother? Then she shakes her head. 'No,' she answers sadly. 'You miss her?'

Jim can only nod. Miss is such a plain little word to describe how he feels. And after his nightmare he can't shake the sense that something awful has happened.

EIGHT

Saturday 18 December 2010

As soundlessly as possible, Patty opens the door and cranes her head out, first left and then right. Empty. She steps out into the hallway, pulls the door closed and slips the DO NOT DISTURB sign onto the handle. She peels off the gloves and slips them inside her bag, then the shower cap. She hopes she looks normal once again. She draws a deep breath into her lungs and holds it there. She will succeed. She releases the breath and walks to the service lift. She almost uses her bare finger to call the lift, but stops herself just in time.

'Think, Patty. Think.'

She pulls a rolled-up glove from the bag and pokes the button through it. The lift arrives quickly and she takes it down to the lower depths.

The door opens and she strides out, trying to look as confident and non-kidnapperry as possible. The effect is immediately ruined as she jumps out of her skin at the explosion of sound her heels make on the concrete.

'Christ.' She stands shaking for a full minute before she can pull herself together again.

She's lucky. There is no one to hear or see her. The car park has no CCTV; this was one of the factors that made her choose this particular hotel. She slips off her shoes and walks to her car. She opens the driver's door and slides in. Then she locks herself inside. It's not something she would normally do, but this morning it makes her feel safer. She turns the engine over, wincing a little at how loud it seems, and then she slowly drives up the ramp and out into the street.

Slide.

'Fuck.'

She loses control. The top of the ramp is sheet ice, the wheels slew to the left and the brake does nothing. The nose of the car hits the wall and she hears the crack of glass. She turns the wheel slowly and bites down on the accelerator. The wheels spin but don't catch.

'Fuck.' She floors the accelerator, the car pitches forward, she brakes hard and the car slides into the street completely out of control and veers sideways into a parked car. She closes her eyes tight as metal crunches into metal.

She sits for a few seconds while her racing heart slows a little. She tries the clutch again, slowly, until it bites and the car creeps forwards. Okay. She slowly pulls into the middle of the road and... there's a snowman. Where the hell did it come from? It has a carrot for a nose and lumps of coal for eyes. Where did someone get coal?

Past Frosty, illuminated in small pools of yellow streetlight, she can see bank after bank of snow – it looks like Narnia. There's no moon, just oppressive cloud covering the sky. This was never part of the plan. She slowly lets the clutch bite and pushes forward, nudging the snowman in the tummy and then collapsing him. The head lands with a bump on the bonnet of the car and looks at her sadly, before it rolls off as the car swings... steer, steer... the wheels won't do what she wants and again she lurches into the kerb. Crunch.

From somewhere she can hear the clatter of grit being shot at high speed, pinging off metal and concrete. She feels panic building.

'Shit shit shit shit oh shit. Patricia, breathe.'

She has driven this route three times over the last six weeks, each time obeying the speed limit, and it has taken her forty minutes. But today?

'Do not have a panic attack, Patricia. Do not. You have time, you have hours.'

She has no idea if the streets are passable. All she can hear echoing in her head is Dustin Hoffman whining 'I'm an excellent driver.'

She pulls out into the street once more, and immediately feels the car slipping as the wheels slur away from her.

'Steer into the spin, not away.' She remembers that from some TV show or something. 'I am an excellent driver, dammit,' she says through gritted teeth.

She gains some control and pulls away again, creeping forwards at about two miles an hour. 'I have planned this meticulously. I have driven this route; I know it like the back of my hand,' her voice is level but intense. 'I have change for the parking meter in a Ziploc bag and I have his blood. I am not letting this fucking weather stop me.'

* * *

She winds slowly through the streets. Everywhere there are cars skidded, crashed and abandoned. Some have run into other cars, some into brick walls. She thinks once or twice that she sees heads slumped against windows as drivers sleep in their cars. There will be many, many war stories for people to tell their loved ones when day breaks. In the distance sirens and car alarms wail like babies. Instead of forty minutes it takes two hours to drive the distance to the lab. While she drives the snow falls around her.

She remembers the first time her parents took her into Central London – maybe she was six – to see the Christmas lights shining all the way down Oxford Street. Someone famous turned them on, a singer. She can't remember his name all these years later, but she does recall how magical it all was.

'I declare these lights…' Flick – from nothing to great beauty, all in a split second. After that, her parents took her for dinner somewhere swanky, or at least to her it felt like a palace. They ordered her spaghetti – it was the first time she'd ever had pasta and it seemed so exotic. Then the biggest treat – the London Palladium to see *Peter Pan*. When the pirates were on she remembers squirming in her mother's arms and watching through her fingers, ready to close them tight when it all got too scary. But more than anything she remembers Tinker Bell. She can still feel the tears of her six-year-old self as they run down her cheeks when the fairy drinks poison.

'Save her, Peter!' six-year-old Patricia screams, along with about two thousand other girls.

'We can all save her,' Peter Pan shouts, 'if you believe in fairies.'

'I believe, I believe!' Patricia screams, everyone screams and the air is full of fairies, dancing, flying… just like the snowflakes.

Patty brakes, softly at first until she feels the wheels skid and glide. Then she pumps her foot hard. The wheels bite, the car slows and slides until the kerb stops it with a little jerk. She looks at her watch. It's 7.38 a.m. She's parked directly opposite the main entrance to the testing labs. On previous trips at this time, even before the doors were opened, there were lights on inside, preparation for the day ahead. Now, however, inside it's black – no glimmer of light. Snow still falls, a fresh blanket to cover the ground. She doubts the

Tube will run, maybe some buses. But will any of the lab staff make it to work?

'I need to breathe,' she thinks and slips out of the car into the icy air. On one of her reconnaissance trips she had gone to an all-night cafe for a mug of tea. It was very close by, so she turns to head for it. As she walks away from the car she feels a slight tug – his blood seems to call her.

NINE

Jim stands by the phone, which sits on the arm of a chair in the living room. He looks at his watch. Almost 9 a.m. He was brought up never to phone anyone before 9 a.m. or after 8 p.m. – that was just how it was.

'What about a movie?' Dani calls from another room.

Jim looks out through the windows as the snow still swirls in the grey light – banked up against the garden fence and the door.

'I can't see any cinemas being open today. Maybe tonight,' he calls back.

'What about a soup kitchen?'

'To help the homeless?'

'No, I thought you might need some soup, old man,' she says with a smile as she walks in. 'I know how hard those dang-fangled ring pulls are to open.'

'You cheeky—'

The phone rings. Jim grabs at it.

'Patty?' He turns his back on Dani.

There is only the sound of someone breathing.

'Patty?' Jim's desperation oozes into his voice. 'Patty?'

'No. No it isn't Patty, Jim. It's Tom. Tom Bevans.'

'Tom?'

'Tom,' Dani echoes his name, though Jim cannot hear her any more.

'Long time, Jim.' His voice seems to come from far away.

'Has something happened to Patty?'

'Dad.' Dani tries to get his attention, but her voice is suddenly so small. She feels giddy – unreal, like she weighs nothing, is nothing. She starts to feel a little scared.

'No, no, that isn't why I'm calling.'

'Then why? I don't underst—'

'We need to talk about Dani. About what happened.'

'I—' Jim's head pounds.

'Did Patty tell you I saw her?' Tom asks.

'You've seen Patty, when?'

'She told me she'd tell you.'

'Tell me what?'

Tom pauses, annoyed – unsure how to proceed. 'Dani's case is being looked at again, potential new evidence but—'

'What are you talking about?'

'That can wait, something else has happened and I need to see y—'

'Dad.' Her voice is so tiny, but Jim hears the fear in it. He turns.

'Oh my God.' He drops the phone.

'Help me, Dad,' she pleads.

His twenty-one-year-old daughter looks as if she has aged a thousand years in seconds.

'I need a hug.' She stretches out her arms.

'You know I can't.'

'I need you to hold me, Dad.'

'I want to but—'

'I'm begging, Dad.'

'Dani.'

She moves to him, but he pulls away.

'Dad,' she says, with such hurt, and turns her back on him.

'Jim… Jim…' the phone is calling from the floor. Tom desperate to know what has happened. Jim puts the phone back on its cradle and then pulls the little clip out of the socket so the phone is dead. He looks for his daughter – she is gone.

'Dani?'

No reply.

He finds her standing in the garden, her head down. He walks out to join her, bracing himself against the intensity of the wind.

'Come back inside darling.'

She looks up at him. Her face pale and beautiful again.

'I need someone to hold me – to feel something.' She lifts her arms for snowflakes to fall on them; she longs to feel the bite of cold as the crystals strike and melt.

'I want to feel life again.'

'I'm sorry,' is all a father can say to his daughter.

The snowflakes drift through her to strike the ground. They cannot touch her.

'Dani—'

'What is wrong with me Dad?'

'Nothing Dani. There's nothing wrong with you.' He tells his dead daughter.

She looks at the ground, sees his footprints alone in the snow.

INTERMISSION ONE

Tuesday 14 February 1989

Jim hears them enter the street and walks outside to meet them. He watches the horse-drawn carriage arrive. Black and sleek, the horses shake their heads and flick their tails. The youngest of the funeral directors has a pocket of carrots and Polo mints to keep them in line.

'Say goodbye in style,' the funeral arranger had said, as if there was something to celebrate. So Jim had booked horses. As a girl Dani had loved them; they'd gone to Devon when she was six and she'd ridden a big brown carthorse. She squealed with delight the whole time. So why not get horses? Because he hadn't thought about the size of them, the smell of them, the rank deposit one of them would make outside the house while they wait. There is no 'style' in saying goodbye to Dani.

The funeral director's mouth moves, but Jim hears nothing. He feels sick, but there's nothing in there to come out. For the last few days, all he's taken into his body has been a little water, a few cups of tea and a bottle and a half of cheap Scotch. At six that morning it was just dry heaves.

His back hurts. He spent last night in Dani's bed. He'd never realised how soft the mattress was. It had seemed a good idea that evening, even though Jacks had warned him. He thought it would be time to say goodbye. Instead he had lain awake all night, hearing her voice, sensing her every time sleep seemed about to claim him. He misses her. He misses his daughter so very much.

The funeral director repeats his words. 'It's time, Mr Lancing,' he says, waving his plump hands.

Jim goes back into the house. Patricia's still on the sofa, slumped even further against Tom. She's so heavily sedated she doesn't know up from down. Maybe that made it a little easier now, but what would they pay for all this in the end?

In the kitchen Jacks and Ed, their oldest friends, finish the washing up. They'd been there last night. Jacks had slept next to Patty and Ed was on the couch. Thank Christ for friends.

For a second, just for a second, he wishes his mum was there, that she could hold his head in her arms and coo to him like she did when he was a boy. But there's no one to coo. She's dead and gone as well. His life has always been about women, his women: Dani, Patty, his mum and long ago his gran – Nanny Lily. He'd always been a mother's boy; Patty had often taunted him with that but... he liked it. And she did too, really. Patty wasn't interested in machismo. But as much as he misses his mum, he knows that she's lucky to be gone. His mum had been mad about Dani and she had adored her gran. If he believed... but he didn't. He could fantasise about his daughter being greeted into paradise by his mum but that was all it was, fantasy.

'Just get through today. Just today,' he thinks.

He feels Ed's hand on his shoulder and a whisper in his ear. 'Time to go, Jim-boy.'

He nods, thankful for the darkness to be blown away, even for a few moments. Glad to have his best friend there, though anxious about what will happen once Ed and Jacks have gone. Jim and Patty have so few people in their lives. Their parents have gone. No brothers or sisters to lean on, no nieces and nephews to get caught up with. Jim and Patty are only children who had an only child. Why had that happened?

They could all have fitted in one car, but the funeral directors sent two. So Ed and Jacks travel in one long black car and Jim, Patty and Tom in the other. The trinity of the pained. Jim likes the speed the horses move at, slower than slow. He sees drivers fume all around, dying to honk and swerve round the cortège – but unable to cross that Rubicon of disrespect.

The three of them sit in their snail of a car, watching the horses draw the casket forwards. All is silent, except for raspy breaths from Patty, a side effect of the sedatives. Jim sneaks a sidelong look at his wife. Her eyes are glassy, her mind trapped somewhere in an amber of Valium and God-knows-what. This fact makes his stomach lurch and anger fizz deep in his empty belly. She was meant to have been off the strongest drugs for today, the doctors had promised him that she would be awake. But this morning there had been 'an episode'. That was what the nurse had called it. She'd shot Patty up with something 'to calm her'. Zombify her, more like.

'She will hate me for this,' he thinks. He already hates himself. But he doesn't have the strength to tell everyone to go home. He needs today to break the pressure of the storm that's built over them. He needs to see others who loved her, Dani's friends. So many of them have called, written and even knocked on the door. That has moved him so much. And, most importantly, Jim needs to remember the girl he raised and loved above all others, to remember her how she was. Not as the lifeless, defiled body he saw in the morgue.

When they arrive Reverend Chapman is waiting for them. He has the whitest teeth Jim ever remembers seeing. Jim dislikes him intensely. Reverend Chapman never knew Dani, feels no real sympathy but there aren't many places where you can bury someone and seat two hundred mourners.

'Hypocrite fuck,' Jim whispers to himself.

He knows Patty would never have let God anywhere near their Dani. But she's out of it and he had to make the decision. Alone.

Jim gets out of the car. Tom holds Patty until Jim's ready, then between the two of them, they manhandle her out. Jim shakes the vicar's hand.

'This is my wife Patricia.'

'I am so sorry for your loss.' He holds her arm for a second, squeezing – then he lets her go.

'This is Police Constable Thomas Bevans.' Jim pauses for a second. 'He was Dani's boyfriend.'

It's a kind lie. Tom feels his gut clench and his eyes turn gritty. He takes the clergyman's hand.

'I am so sorry.' The white teeth gleam.

They walk through the vestry. The walls are covered in photos, snapshots of Dani. Notes pinned to them, flowers and jewellery scattered all over.

'Your daughter was loved.'

Jim nods. Love. He thinks of his mother.

On an easel outside the chapel Jim sees his mother's photograph, and underneath it reads: Grace Lancing, 1901–1976. Eight-year-old Dani stands in front of it frowning and asks 'Who's that lady?'

'That's Gran,' Jim answers.

She looks at him crossly and shakes her head. 'That isn't Gran, we're at the wrong funeral. That's some other lady. She isn't old enough to die.'

Jim looks closely at the photo. It had been taken before he was born – his mother as a young woman, between the wars. She'd been picking hops in the country with her sister. Even in black and white he could see how healthy and fit she looked. Happy.

'It is Gran, just a long time ago, when she was young.'

'Oh. Olden times.' Dani nods sagely. 'How old is she there?'

'Nineteen or twenty, I think.'

'Oh yes. That's much too young to be dead.'

Reverend Chapman leads them out of the vestry and into the church. He nods across to the organist who strikes up 'Nearer my God to Thee'. Jim looks across at him angrily; he'd said no hymns, no church music. Chapman does not meet his gaze, instead he leads them into the centre aisle and the four of them process towards the front pew.

They walk slowly, like the horses, and Jim looks out at the sea of faces. Students from Dani's university have come by coach from Durham, organised by the students' union. They sit together in a group. Already tears stream down faces and pretty blonde girls lean against each other, clutching hands and promising to stay in touch their whole lives, no matter what. Jim smiles at them even though he recognises only two or three. In another group, closer to the front he recognises most of the sixth form from Dani's school and in another pew is the entire running team. He's so deeply proud that Dani had been so popular. He can see them, there in the pews, sharing anecdotes and memories, tears and even some laughter. Halfway down, Jim suddenly realises he will never lead his daughter down the aisle to be married. He stops dead.

Chapman sees Jim freeze, the colour drain from his face and his legs start to shake. He immediately steps back and kindly but firmly takes his arm and leads the three of them down to the front. He deposits them there, in the place of honour, then walks to centre stage. He lets his eyes move across the congregation as the final lines of the hymn fall away. Then he walks across and lightly touches the casket, directly above where the head lies. It's a small ritual of his – a final blessing for those he is about to deliver from this earth. It's subtle but the families always like it: a little bit of theatre that gives them permission to go up and touch the casket later, to say goodbye to the girl they loved. He knows how important that is, to release the grief and to stop any thought of the body inside – of the tests, the prodding and indignities that come with violent death. With rape and murder.

He looks down the aisles and sees the row after row of pretty young women whose thoughts must be so conflicted this morning. Anger, fear, grief and some guilt. Some part of them all must think – it wasn't me, thank God it wasn't me. But it was their friend. Towards the back there are men in uniform. Policemen of all rank from low to high. Some are there to support their colleague who has lost his young love. Others are there to be seen, a public act of contrition for their failure to find those responsible. Chapman finds it distasteful – the motives of these men are tainted. They are there for the press not the family. Then behind the uniformed men are the press. Again, a few are there to support a colleague and the mother of the murdered girl, yet most of the others are beasts full of the scent of blood. A photogenic, middle-class 'good' girl missing for three weeks and found raped and murdered. Tabloid gold. He hopes they will behave – in church, at least. He looks back to the schoolfriends, and then slowly onto the family.

It will be an emotional service and Chapman's prepared. Large boxes of tissues have been placed at the end of every aisle and there are four professional grief counsellors on hand for free advice after the funeral – he's pulled out all the stops to make this one work. After all, the press are here and so is the archbishop.

This is bigger than the jockey and the serial bigamist combined. Showtime.

Reverend Chapman waves to someone at the back, and the sound of Siouxsie and the Banshees sweeps out from the speakers above the pulpit.

In the front pew Jim bows his head and pulls Patty close to him. Beside them, Tom Bevans's heart breaks.

At the back of the church, someone slips in and stands behind a stone pillar, unseen by other mourners. Tears slide down his face. He knows he should not be there but can't help himself – the pull is too strong.

'I am so sorry, Dani. I never meant...' His words are swept up in the howl of the Banshees.

TEN

Jim makes hot chocolate, piping-hot milk with heaps of dark cocoa. He pours two mugs and sets one on the table in front of her. The curling steam circles her face and seems to shift the lines, smudging her cheeks, turning her features to air.

'I think I can smell it.' She turns her face up to him, a huge smile.

'That's great.' Jim beams back, though he knows it can't be true. Maybe she's remembering the scent – drawing on happy childhood winters or perhaps it's just wishful thinking. He sips his own, it's bitter with too much chocolate. He watches her – lost in thought somewhere.

Finally she snaps back. 'How's yours?' she asks.

'Oh it's good. Really good. Especially on a day like today.'

She nods.

'How about we go for a walk in the park?'

She seems not to hear him at first, then responds slowly. 'I'd like that.'

'Great.'

They sit together in silence, until his mug is empty and hers is stone cold.

'I'll run up and get something warmer.' He tells her, and heads upstairs.

He doesn't exactly remember when he first saw Dani – Dani like she is now. For a while, after her death, she seemed to be always there in the corner of his eye, but when he turned to find her she was gone, melted away or morphed into another face. But that flash of her was enough to keep him going somehow.

But there came a point, maybe a year after her death, when it wasn't just a glimpse. One day, soon after he'd resigned his job, he saw her straight on. She was on a train he'd just left. For some reason he turned back as it was about to leave the station, and there she was. She winked at him. A week or so later she waved from a taxi. She looked as she had that last time he saw her alive: dark brown shoulder-length hair held off her face by a clip, freckles dotting her nose and upper cheeks like they did even in winter. She wore no make-up and looked healthy. Looked happy. He never told Patty he saw her. He knew what she'd say: 'You are cracking up, my friend, you need to see someone.'

That was pretty much what she said to him most days back then. He hated it when she called him '*my friend*' and of course she knew it made him crazy. And, in part, it was why she said it. She knew long before she left him that she would, and a part of her wanted to make him hate her, make him glad she was gone instead of just feeling abandoned. Of course that plan was futile. Without Dani, Jim held on to Patty harder than ever. He knew deep down it stifled her, pushed her away, but he couldn't help himself. The fear of being alone was too deep, but that very fear made it inevitable. The man who loved women but who was left by them all.

It took Patty eight years to leave him. Eight years after Dani died to feed the resentment and build the courage to leave the man she loved. When she did, Jim fell apart. He called for her, howled for her, and for Dani. Then when Jim hit rock bottom, about a week after Patty left, Dani came back to him. He'd been in the living room and he thought he heard the front door. He rushed out, like a dog desperate to see its owner.

'Patty?' he shouted.

The hallway was empty. He just stood there, staring at the front door, his brief moment of optimism deflated like a ruptured balloon. The sun was going down and the glass of the door was flaring with the last few rays. It was actually quite beautiful, reminded him for a moment of Notre Dame at dusk. Then, within the shimmering orange-gold light, a shape seemed to coalesce. The sun slipped away and Dani stood there. She was wearing a red duffel coat and held a beaten-up suitcase.

'I thought you might want some company,' she said with a smile. 'Can I come in?'

He nodded and she walked past him into the living room. Not floating, not see-through. She left the suitcase in the hall. Later he noticed it was gone. That night he asked her to take her old room and she did. He asked where she had been, what she remembered. She said there was nothing. He accepted it, though he liked to imagine she'd been travelling – seen the world like she'd always planned. Once she'd graduated. Had she lived.

'It's so quiet.'

Jim nods.

Father and daughter walk together towards Greenwich Park. Jim steers them on a slightly longer route than normal; yesterday he saw a poster on a tree: missing cat. He knows to avoid it. The streets are empty. It's not even 10 a.m. but the greyness feels like dusk. Snowflakes still fall but not so thickly; the wind has died so they gracefully drift towards the earth, turning slowly.

As they approach the park, they begin to hear the first sounds of the day – whooping and yelling. They enter the park at the top of the hill leading down to the Thames and the sprawling vista of London. Today the skyscrapers stand like grey mountains in among the clouds. The two of them stop to view the scene. Jim feels the cold in his chest, watches his breath billow like a dragon's smoke. But when he turns to Dani there's nothing.

'What's going on in your head?' he asks her softly.

She turns her back on him and walks away. He watches her for a moment and then follows.

'Dani!' he calls to her and she turns.

She is just twenty-one, frozen in that state for ever and... her face is shattered, a snowball punches through it.

'Be more bloody careful,' Jim screams at the kid.

'It weren't anywhere near you,' the kid shouts back.

'You hit my daught—' He stops. Looks at Dani, her face is back to normal – and she bursts into laughter.

'Sorry, kid,' he calls back and starts to laugh himself.

'Your face.' She points, still laughing.

'Your face.'

And they walk to the observatory – like they've done a hundred times over the years.

❄

'Do you remember anything?' he asks.

The day she came back to him he asked the same question, and he kept asking for months but she always shook her head. He could see the pain, so he stopped. But after his nightmare, and the call from Tom – he feels like something is coming.

'I... Dad, I don't know.'

'It's okay.'

'Is it?'

Her face pinches, mouth becomes hard.

'You said you came back for me.'

'I did. You called me.'

'Where were you?'

'I don't know.'

They're both silent. They sit on the wall of the closed observatory and watch children sledge down the hill.

'In my day we used a *Rupert* annual,' Jim says, pointing at the sleek blue sled that a small flame-haired boy is dragging up the hill. The snow has started to fall a little heavier again. Jim watches it settle on the wall beside him. The spot where he can see Dani sitting. Suddenly he jumps up and runs towards the flame-haired kid who has finally got the sled to the top of the hill.

Dani watches him pull something from his pocket and gesture wildly to the boy. Then he turns and with the broadest smile, waves at Dani and motions her to come. He hands something to the child and takes the sled. He sits on it and waits for Dani to scramble onto the back. Then kicks off.

'Whhhheheehehhheheheheeeeeeeeeeeee...'

The sled shoots off down the hill. Dani screams. Jim puts his arms in the air – the wind biting his face, his hair billowing out – and wipes out. The snow shoots up his shirt, down his neck, in his mouth and down his pants. The cold hits him like an electric shock, and he rolls and rolls until the hill runs out.

He lies there, wet and cold but most of all scared. Dani stands over him. She is twenty-one years old, beautiful. He is petrified he is going to lose her again. That was his nightmare – that is always his nightmare – being alone.

'Are you okay?' she asks.

He can't answer, doesn't trust his voice. He feels the weight of twenty years bear down on him.

We need to talk about Dani. About what happened. Tom's words echo through his mind.

⁂

At the top of the hill, directly above Jim, stands DS Tom Bevans. He had planned to talk to Jim, had walked a long way through the snow, but seeing him like this – having fun like a child – he can't. Instead he turns his back on the older man and trudges back the way he came. In his pocket the diary feels heavy. He should have returned it to Jim and Patty years ago – but it's too late. Everything feels too late.

⁂

Saturday 27 September 1986

This will be my last entry in this diary. Tomorrow I'm packing everything up and on Monday I will be gone. This feels a little like the journal of a child. Time to grow up. I hope when I come back to read this in years' and years' time – maybe when I've got a child of my own going off to university – that I'm not too embarrassed by my immaturity. Anyway, this is the end of an era, the end of a life. I won't be like Mum, though. When she went to uni she never went home again. I know she never saw Gramps after she left and Nanny had to get the coach to us if she wanted to visit even when she was dying – I won't be like that, couldn't cut Dad out of my life. But... I do have to push Tom back a little. I shouldn't have said he could come up on Monday – I don't know how to let him down easy. I hope he'll find some pretty policewoman soon. I need to start the page again, reinvent myself. A new Dani Lancing.

Finis

PART TWO

ELEVEN

Sunday 31 December 1989

S-E-B M-E-R-C-H-A-N-T

She writes his name in her tiny, precise hand on a yellow Post-it note. In a zip-like motion she sticks it to the wall below the word *boyfriend*? Above *TORTURE*. Her eyes flick across the wall – layers of photos, press clippings, witness statements, police reports – hundreds of documents pinned and stapled, all covered in questions on yellow notes. Always questions – why, how, who – almost a year of questions. She has stood before this board for months, adding nothing but dead ends, theories – nothing concrete. Ahab, standing at the wheel, scouring the infinity of the ocean for a sign. But today the whale has been sighted: Seb Merchant is found. She steps back, knocking a pile of frames that are on the floor. She kicks them further into the corner, hearing glass splinter. They used to hang in front of her – two diplomas and three awards for journalism. They had once been her proudest achievements, now they have no place on the walls.

She feels the broil in her stomach; this will end soon. She's a little light-headed – she should probably eat something, can't remember the last time she had, and she will need her strength for later. From downstairs she hears a clatter. They're still here, she'll wait for them to go before venturing out.

She falls into her old office chair, it tips back like an astronaut waiting for the kick of G-force. The wall fills her vision, making her feel... she looks down. With a bent paper clip she digs into the quick of her fingernail. She watches the little bead of blood she's teased from her finger, imagines it swimming with life, and then brings it up to her mouth and sucks it away. The taste makes her want to heave. Downstairs she hears another thud and crash – Christ, he is so obvious, she knows what he wants and she feels so tired of disappointing him, so tired of seeing his pain. He has no idea what she needs, what they need.

'Help. Professional help,' he had said with his big sad cow eyes, adding the killer blow: 'Dani would have wanted this.'

She agreed and they went to see Alice Bell, for thirty-four minutes.

'Bereavement counsellor. Fucking joke. Fucking joke, Jim,' Patty snapped at him afterwards. 'BACP, UKRCP. They aren't real qualifications, might as well include the fifty metres backstroke.'

She remembers the pain in his face as she spat out her poison. It shames her now, remembering the vitriol. It was almost six months ago but the memory feels fresh. His pain feels so fresh.

'Fucking joke. And did you see that photograph?' she snorted.

He had seen it, the only personal item on her desk. It showed Alice Bell, maybe ten years younger, though you can clearly see it was her, with arms around a child in a wheelchair – they both beam with happiness.

'What the fuck does she think she's saying with that? "I know pain too, I know what you are going through, but it isn't all bad"? Bitch.' She spits out the final 'bitch'. She sees Jim cringe at the coarseness of her language; he's never heard his wife speak like this before. Jim didn't sit on the news desk and watch her trade crude insults night after night with leery old men who hated working with her but wanted to fuck her anyway. She used to keep work and family life separate: Jim and Dani were like oxygen for her – she needed them to live – but her career was food, the nutrients for a healthy Patricia. Now she had neither. Her editor himself had said she lacked focus, had lost her journalistic balance. He smiled, of course, offered a leave of absence. She told him to stuff it. She knew her 'balance' wasn't coming back. Not until she had revenge. That was what kept her going now.

She knew Jim had liked this Alice Bell, had found her calm voice and kind eyes comforting. Patricia had only seen danger in those eyes, the kind that could lull you into trust. Trust could kill them. She knew Alice Bell's kind of help was not what she needed.

'To come to terms with Dani's death—'

'Dani's multiple rape and murder,' Patty interrupts her, bearing witness to the truth of it, the horror of it. She sees the blood drain from Jim's face, a sadness creep across the professional Ms Bell.

'Your loss is terrible...'

Patty hears the first few words and then drifts away – it's all blah blah blah. She isn't looking to come to terms with Dani's death. She's looking for vengeance and justice. Only then might there be peace.

Jim treads carefully up the stairs, virtually silent. As he reaches the top stair he can see Patty through the slats, sitting at her desk and staring at the wall. He hates that wall. He knows it's totally irrational, how can you hate a wall? But he hates it. Hates the curled and flapping paper covered in questions, hates the lists, the accusations, the anger spewed over every surface. But worst of all are the photos – the room she was found in and two taken of her after. When there was no more Dani, just a husk that looked like his daughter but had none of her life. They make him die inside.

He needs to ask Patty one last time if she'll come with them. He already knows the answer, knows she'll say no just as she has done at least half a dozen times over the last twenty-four hours, but he'll give it one last try. He'd be so happy if she would go with them.

'Patty,' he calls. Then waits. 'Tom and I are going. Please come with us.'

She tilts her head, the tiniest movement, so she can look at him and then, without answering, kicks the door so it swings closed.

'Okay,' he says to no one in particular and walks back down to Tom, who is waiting in the kitchen.

'No?'

Jim shakes his head sadly. Tom nods to show he understands, then picks up his overcoat and they head out into the bitter cold.

It's only ten in the morning but the sky is gunmetal grey. They drive to the crematorium. It's the same route they took for the funeral but now they move faster. The heater's on full blast to keep the windscreen from icing over. Nothing is said.

At the crematorium they park and get out. Tom slams the door, which echoes through the cemetery like a gunshot. The trees stand skeletal, waving fingers in the sky. Everywhere you look an angel stands sentinel over a fallen loved one. Tom pulls his overcoat closer to his throat, breath streams from his mouth. Jim carries a bouquet of yellow roses. Tom can't imagine where he got them on a day like this. Tom carries nothing but inside his breast pocket he has a slim volume of poetry – Keats. He will read one and then leave the book for her.

They walk in silence, both knowing where they are going, neither knowing that the other has made this walk twenty or thirty times already – alone. In the garden of remembrance there is a small plaque, chosen together in those first few days.

DANI, LOVED DEARLY AND MISSED DEEPLY

They stand close to it, her men, Dani's men. Slowly Jim moves forward and places the flowers on a ledge just below the plaque. He whispers something to the air and then steps back while Tom draws out the slim volume and reads.

'Bright star, would I were steadfast as thou art.'

As the front door closes Patty gives an involuntary shudder. It's time. She's excited but there are other emotions too. Darker ones, that she holds just below the skin, willing them down until the time is right. She opens her bag one final time and checks the contents. Tickets, notebook, keys, whistle and pepper spray just in case. She feels the weight of the small canister in her palm and wonders if she will use it today. A big part of her hopes she will.

She's not told Jim her plans. Not told him she's going to Durham or that she's done something the police couldn't do: track down the elusive Seb Merchant, Dani's ex-boyfriend. Secret ex-boyfriend that her parents never met, never heard her mention once. Patty only knows about their relationship from fellow students. His name has come up time and time again. Most of them say he's trouble.

He was missed by the police in the initial trawl for statements, as he wasn't a student with Dani – he'd been a student five years before but had dropped out halfway through his second year. He stayed in Durham, and each year he made noises as if he'd start his degree again but he never returned to college. No one knew how he made his money; a few suggested he was independently wealthy.

The police had finally put him on the list of people to talk to but they couldn't find him. Patty has.

She feels something tingle, deep down. This is the breakthrough – she knows it. He has something, something to tell her that will reveal the truth at last. And. And. There is a possibility he is Dani's killer. And... and...

'What would you do?' asks Alice Bell near the end of that thirty -four minutes.

'I don't understand,' Patty says coldly.

'You say you are investigating Dani's death.'

'Murder.'

'Dani's murder. You are looking for her killer, yes?'

'Yes.'

'So what would you do if you found him?'

Patty is impassive. She watches the woman before her, the soft kind eyes and mouth that twitches a little – sharing the pain. Patty will not answer her, instead they will let the final minutes drain away into nothingness. But she knows her reply.

I will find him. I will kill him by cutting his heart out. I swear.

❄

'Should be a bloody florist,' the young man says, cocking his head towards the pile of bedraggled bouquets swept into a corner of the garden. Jim looks at his own yellow roses lying by her plaque. He will leave them here and they will rot and turn to mush. Who decided flowers were a suitable tribute for the dead?

'Instead of a copper?' Jim asks.

Tom kicks at the gravel, sending a shower pinging against the fountain in the centre of the garden.

'More public respect, more useful, better hours.'

'Really,' Jim shakes his head. 'No florist is going to find who killed Dani.'

Tom feels himself flush with shame. 'No. Not likely.'

The two men stand in silence. Tom knows what Jim wants – some assurance that Dani's killer will be found. He wishes he were anything but a policeman right now. Both men stand and think of Dani. At some point tears come for them both. They lose all feeling in their feet from the cold, yet neither wants to be the one to suggest leaving. Any connection with the girl they love is better than none.

Finally it's Jim who makes the move.

'A drink, maybe a bite to eat?' Tom asks, hoping to keep the link alive.

'Maybe another day. I think I should get back to Patty.'

'Course. Yeah,' Tom nods and starts to wiggle the toes he knows are in his shoes somewhere. He wonders if this is the last time he'll see Jim. Then together they walk to the car, hobbling slightly on their frozen feet.

'Patty,' Jim calls as he walks through the front door. He's bought an extra large portion of chips from the Sung Lee and two giant pickles. He imagines them sousing them in malt vinegar, sprinkle of salt and then Heinz poured all over. Maybe they could eat on the sofa, in front of the TV – see the New Year in together. A new start, maybe. They could hold each other. Make love in their bed. Wake up in the morning and talk about Dani and love each other again.

'Patty?'

But there's no reply. He finds a note on the kitchen table.

Gone. Back later. P.

No little x of a kiss. Jim wonders for the thousandth time if his wife can bear to be with him any longer.

'Will you stop staring at me, I feel like I'm on fucking suicide watch,' she'd said just yesterday.

He makes himself a coffee, and sits at the kitchen table, staring deeply into the patina of the wood until it swims before his eyes. He loves this table. He and Patty found it in a junk shop in Chichester soon after they were married. It was a beautiful shape but scuffed and scratched, a piece hacked out of the middle. They bought it for next to nothing and restored it, the two of them, a shared project. They found a piece of wood that was as close as close, its twin, and joined them together. Jim traces his fingertips across the top, following the grain with his hand. Even though he knows where to look for the piece they grafted in, he can barely see it. The scar has healed and the wood bonded.

He remembers how happy they'd been working together, sanding and planing. It's a beautiful memory and he allows it to wander through his head and warm his thoughts. Then it passes and the cold invades his mind once more.

There is a light knock on the door.

'Are you okay?' a woman calls out.

Patty can't answer. She sits on the toilet and sobs as the train sways beneath her. In the bowl her bile and small flecks of the little she ate this afternoon swill about and will not flush away. Tears flow freely, splattering down into her lap as she leans forward. It had taken her all this time to find him, months. Sending letters, pestering his family, putting posters around, all to find this Seb

Merchant and… and it was such a fucking waste of time and now there is no lead, there is no suspect, there is no hope.

She sits there, on the foul-smelling toilet, and lets the grief and frustration bubble up and die. She's lost. She's used up every last favour and dried up the last reserves of goodwill. She knew it was coming, has seen how old colleagues shy away from her or run the other way when they see her. How the Durham students take a step back from her when she tries to question them, thinking they've told her every last thing they knew about Dani. She knows how she's pestered them, but she thought something would give, someone would crack, and allow her a glint of hope. But what happens now?

'Are you okay? I'll get the guard,' the voice calls through the door once more. Concern mixed with more than a little annoyance.

'I'm…' Patricia begins. 'I don't need the guard.'

She hears the woman grumble and walk off, possibly searching for another toilet. Patricia tries to stand but the nausea sweeps across her once more and she drops back feeling everything unravel. She is so scared, scared that nothing of Dani will remain, even her face is fading in her thoughts. In her bag she keeps a photo. She stares at it every day but she knows that more and more it is the photograph she remembers and not Dani. She can do nothing for her now, all those years of feeding, washing, dressing, encouraging and loving – loving, always loving. But at the end it was all shit, all such shit, all arguments and disappointments and all fucked up. With no goodbye, no time to prepare. That Christmas. Oh God, the Christmas – last Christmas.

'I forced her away.' Patty cramps at the memory. Dani was meant to stay for a week and it was just two days. They argued so bitterly.

'That was what I left her with. She hated me.' The tears will not stop.

'It will get better, time heals all wounds,' Jim had said. Fucking liar. The only thing that will ease the pain is to find the man who did this and…

'How do I do that?' she shouts. 'How do I find him?'

The train rattles on.

Finally the river runs dry and she can clean herself up and leave the small cubicle. She sits in the first empty seat she finds where she can be alone. Then she closes down.

It's dark when Jim looks about him. He must have fallen asleep, curled up in his chair. Again.

'Christ… arrgh.' His leg's asleep. Pins and needles dance along the sole of his foot and march up his leg. He feels scrunched up, a tall man forced into a box and— the phone. It's ringing and that's what's woken him. He launches himself out of the chair and limps into the hall.

'Hello?' he tries to keep the urgency out of his voice.

'Have you been watching it all? Dancing on the Berlin wall, the crumbling ripped-down bloody Berlin wall, who would have thought it? We won. We're giving peace a chance.' It isn't Patty but Ed, sounding a little boozy.

'It's good to hear from you,' Jim replies. It really is good to hear from his oldest friend. Ed and Jacks have done so much over the last year.

'Well, I watched the moon landing with you, I think this is the next big thing. And it was pretty obvious you'd be at home while the rest of the world celebrates the end of nuclear war. Greenham Pat must be wetting herself.'

Despite himself, Jim smiles at his wife's old nickname.

'She isn't here.' He thinks for a second. 'I have no idea where she is. What's the time?'

'It's ten o'clock. If you're on your own, get the fuck over here and get drunk with us and forget, just for one night, about this fucking awful year.'

New Year's Eve, he'd forgotten. He cradles the phone between chin and ear and pulls his sleeve away from his watch. He squints in the near dark. It's ten past ten. On the table the unopened chip packet has gone cold and soggy. There will be no new start with Patty tonight.

'So come. Jacks wants you to.' In the background there is a snort. 'And there's twenty or so people here that don't know you're the most miserable fuck in the world and—'

'I can't. Patty might be back in time.'

'In time to do what? Give you a kiss to ring in 1990, say "It'll all be fine next year"? I love…' Ed pauses, thinking he might have gone too far. 'Oh, Jim. I'll come over and get you.'

Jim hears Jacks in the background saying that Ed's too drunk to drive.

'Thanks, Ed, but I can't,' Jim cuts in.

'Leave her a note and drive over. You can make it by midnight. Don't be by yourself. Not tonight.'

'Thanks, Ed. Love to Jacks.'

'You fuc—'

Jim misses the rest as he puts the phone down. The silence in the room seems so profound all of a sudden. He appreciates Ed's try at getting him over, but he can't betray Patty. Betrayal? What a strange idea. He just needs to be there for when she needs him, that's all. Isn't that love?

He closes his eyes tight and indulges himself in a happy memory: the first time he saw Patricia.

She was looking down reading a story as he walked into the university newspaper offices. He was going there to see Connie Tunstall. She had kept telling him he ought to contribute and he always said he was too busy. But that night he and Connie had arranged to meet to go and see a film and he was half an hour early, so he decided to pick her up at the newspaper office.

So, he walked in. The editor's office was at the back, overlooking everything, but at that exact moment Patricia was standing at a desk by the door looking over some boy's shoulder, reading his text. As Jim walked in she looked up for a second and caught him full blast with these eyes. Kapow! 'Come to bed eyes' is how he described them to Ed the next day. Hazel with flecks of gold, languid like they couldn't be bothered to look at you, sexy as hell. And then there was her mouth. Full, soft – perfect. He fell in love with that mouth there and then. He may even have drooled a little. He was immediately drawn into her orbit like a love-struck moon. She was the editor, in her second year reading politics, and by all accounts had turned an unloved, barely read monthly into a must-read weekly and was advising other universities on what to do with their crumbling old titles. As he watched her advising and guiding the cub reporter through his story, he was immediately struck by how she took charge with such a deft touch, getting the best out of him not by domineering but by persuading and suggesting. Jim had already fallen a little in love with her that first night, before he even got to her desk and offered his services as cartoonist.

He flicks on the overhead light, which seems too bright somehow. He hears some thumping music from somewhere close, maybe two doors down. The sounds of the party make him feel even more alone. He wishes he could have a drink but there's no alcohol in the house. He indulged a little too much in the months after Dani's death and cut himself off. Maybe for New Year's Eve... but he doesn't want to go out in case Patty calls. So the best he can do for a treat is a squashed Quality Street from the back of the sofa.

He turns on the TV but keeps the sound off. The cameras keep flipping between countries where fresh-faced young people smile and dance and look so hopeful. 1990 really is going to be a new world for them all to live in. But how will he live in a world without Dani?

At five minutes to 1990 he switches on the sound and watches while the world calls in to show what an amazing decade the nineties will be. It can't be worse than the eighties, surely.

Finally it's time to countdown from Trafalgar Square as Big Ben winds up for the momentous dongs.

The crowd begins its chant.

Ten

The phone rings. Jim grabs it.

'Patty?'

Nine

'Jim,' she sobs.

Eight

'Where are you?'

Seven

'I thought I had him, Jim. Thought I'd found him.'

Six

'Who, Patty?'

Five

'The killer, Dani's killer.'

Four

'But it wasn't him?'

Three

'I can't find him, Jim. I can't find him.'

Two

'Let's just let... I love you, Patty.'

One

The crowd roars. Otherwise there is only silence.

INTERMISSION TWO

Monday 14 June 1982

He cannot take his eyes off her, this lovesick, pale boy. For about another minute that will be fine, watching her is acceptable while she runs. But soon she'll finish the race, and then he'll have to stop, peel his eyes off her skin and look elsewhere. She's coming into the final stretch, miles ahead of the competition, she runs fluidly, seemingly with little effort.

He's watched her for a long time – years – since they started school together at five years old. His first real recollection of her was as Mary, mother of our Lord. She was chosen to lead the nativity and for a glorious day and a half he was to be her husband Joseph. Mr Chinns explained the story to them, and Tom tried to imagine what living with Dani and their child would be like. On the run on a donkey: romance, tragedy and adventure. This was the first time his creative imagination had swung into gear and it flipped a switch in him. They were bonded, and it was strong; a desire to protect and love Danielle Lancing was etched on Thomas Bevans's young heart.

It was only a day and a half of married bliss. There wasn't even a rehearsal, so they never got to stand next to each other as man and wife. Instead, he began to itch, and broke out in red welts that were diagnosed as chicken pox. He missed three weeks of school, had a pretty miserable Christmas, and it was all over. He was lucky – there wasn't a single scar from the pox. At least, none on the outside. Inside, it felt like there was a tiny little arrow embedded that cut every time he thought about or saw Danielle Lancing.

Despite the dig of pain, he watched her whenever he could. In the eight years following their doomed nativity they barely spoke, even though they continued to be in the same class all the way through primary and into secondary school. Tom was too shy, Dani too popular.

Then at the start of this school year, when they were both assessed and found to be in the top twenty per cent of the population in terms of intelligence, they were placed in English Literature One. Together, at the same desk, they were forced to talk about love. John Keats.

She breaks the tape, no one anywhere near her. He claps, watching her swing around the extra bend as she slows, her limbs powering down. He must stop gazing now… now… now! He pulls his head away with some effort, and looks across the stand. Her father's there; he's still watching her and clapping hard. He seems not to know the decorum of school sports day. A few other parents look at him with some distaste. They believe he's gloating, although Tom thinks he's merely a man visibly filled with pride. For a second he wonders what it would be like to have such a father. Then the man, still clapping, looks sideways and sees the boy staring at him. For a second their eyes lock and then the boy holds up both of his thumbs signalling he too is in the Dani Lancing fan club. The man smiles, then turns back to admire his daughter once more. The boy can feel himself turn red. Even at fourteen he knows the double thumbs is juvenile (for a short while Arthur Fonzarelli had made it fashionable, but anybody actually cool knew that time had long gone).

He picks up the briefcase his mother insists he uses, even though he is mocked for it, and walks down the line of seats towards the exit. He'll not look back at her. He knows that by now she will be surrounded by handsome athletes. He walks away. There's a kiosk nearby that sells ice cream, cake and drinks. He doesn't feel like going home just yet, so he heads over and buys a Zoom. He sits on a bench overlooking the bowling green and bites into the cold. He replays the race in his head, watching Dani stretch and—

'Excuse me,' a voice calls out from a little way off.

The boy does not look up, assuming someone else is being called.

'Excuse me... Mr Briefcase.'

Tom looks up and sees it's Dani Lancing's father calling him. The man half-waves, then walks across the bowling green towards him.

'I'm sorry, sorry to shout. I don't know your name so, Briefcase. Nice case by the way. My grandfather had one just like it.' The older man reaches the younger one and stops. 'Jim. Jim Lancing. I'm Danielle's father.'

'Tom,' the boy says, not standing. Jim holds out his hand and awkwardly they shake.

Though it is still a pretty warm afternoon, Tom can't help but feel a chill run down his back. Is it obvious, can this man see how Tom feels about his daughter?

'How can I help?' Tom asks.

'You seemed to know Dani.'

'A little. We're in English Lit together.'

'Well, have you any idea where she might have gone? I was meant to be taking her home, at least I thought I was but...'

There was a party for the sporty and attractive kids, something Tom would never be invited to. He was about to tell her father the address but some alarm bell went off in his head.

'No. No sorry I don't know where she is,' he lied.

'Okay.' They both just stand there. Tom feels his Zoom begin to drip. Finally the older man says, 'Well, thanks.'

Jim Lancing walks off, a little unsure about where to go and what to do. Tom watches until he disappears. Then he picks up his case and heads towards Islington and the party. Obviously he wasn't invited, but now he bears a message. That is his ticket to get in and get close to her. It's slight, he knows that, but maybe it's just enough to allow him entrance to the inner sanctum.

TWELVE

Saturday 18 December 2010

Patty walks to the cafe, all the while feeling the pull of his blood. There is only one customer, a cab driver, sitting alone in the far corner. Patty looks him over. People-watching is still one of her favourite ways to pass the time and she can't resist trying to unpick his life story. They make eye contact for a moment. He has a haunted look, like a man who is pushed or pushes himself very hard. Does he need the money to fund some addiction? Or does he just need to keep moving, keep awake like a shark, desperate just to keep going, no time to think? And what might he see in her – does she stink of desperation? Can he tell that she has lived and breathed revenge – has stayed alive for one purpose: to catch the man who took Dani's life and pitched them all into this everlasting, ferocious winter of grief and loss?

From behind the counter a figure emerges. A bleary-eyed young man, dark and handsome.

'Tea, please.'

'Ereogo?'

'I don't understand.'

He mimes, pointing at the seats or out the door.

'Oh, yes of course. I…'

She would like to sit there and drink the hot tea, cradle the ceramic bowl in her hands and let the heat seep through into her icy fingers. But the blood is in the car and what if someone tries to steal it?

'Take-away, please.'

He takes a Styrofoam cup and fills it from the urn, then splashes a little milk into it before sealing it with a white plastic cap. Patty takes it from him with a mumble of thanks and drops two coins onto the counter. She turns on her heel and walks back to the door, immediately sorry for her decision to opt for take-away as the heat is dampened by the foam of the cup and her fingers stay cold. Outside, on the street, she pours some of the tea directly onto her skin and it turns a bright and angry red, but she can't feel it.

Patty perches in the doorway of the lab, waiting for the staff to struggle in, the blood cradled in her arms. Her anxiety is building but she tries to keep it in check.

'Just wait,' she tells herself. And she can wait. She is the queen of waiting. It seems like all she has done for the longest time. Finally, her patience pays off. The first staff member arrives. He looks at her nervously.

'Can you stand back?' he asks.

'Oh, of course. Yes.'

Patty steps away from the stairs and the keypad. The staff member taps in his code and then edges in, keeping his eyes glued to Patty. It's only once he's inside that Patty realises he thought she might try and force her way in to get drugs or start begging for something. When the next staff member arrives, Patty moves away and immediately launches into her best Hilary Clifton-Hastings, non-threatening cheery voice.

'Hello. Just waiting to have someone run some tests. That's all.'

They look at her like she's crazy. That may be better than fearing she's an axe-wielding junkie.

Finally the door is open to the public and she can walk inside. Roberta is there, the woman she'd met with the week before. At that meeting, she had given Patty the slide and refrigerated box as well as instructions on how to take the sample. There were two options, she had said. The easiest was with a swab inside the cheeks, Invasive but did not hurt in any way. The other option was a blood sample – a prick was all that was needed. Patty had decided on blood, but a little more than just a prick. Patty hands her the box with the slide of blood. Roberta checks it is sealed correctly.

'Please take a seat.' She motions to two chairs in the corner and then she punches digits into a keypad and disappears into the main part of the lab. Patty can't sit. She stands. After about twenty minutes Roberta returns.

'The sample is well collected and seems clean. It can be matched with the sample you brought in before. We will have the result tomorrow.'

'I'm sorry,' Patty tries to keep the scream out of her voice. 'We had agreed a four-hour test time.'

'I know. Normally that is possible but we are understaffed today, the sn—'

'I understand there may need to be an extra fee for expediting the result. Needless to say I will be happy to pay it,' Patty smiles.

'I see,' Roberta nods. 'Four hours. And the expedited rate is an extra fifty per cent.' She smiles a snake-like smile.

'I'll come back for the result.'

She begins to retrace her steps to the cafe, following the breadcrumbs of memory, but finds a modern coffee shop open on the way. It's a corpo-chain shop but all the better for anonymity. Plus it offers bagel and baguette breakfasts, as well as superskinnysoy-moccacinolattes. Patty orders and pays. The staff do not make eye contact, they have no interest in her life story, why she is there, what she wants. Perfect. She sits and closes her eyes. Immediately tiredness sweeps over her. She's exhausted but must not sleep. Soon she will be able to. Then she can catch up on more than twenty years of sleep. She sips her coffee and feels her mind slip back twenty years – that last Christmas won't stay out of her thoughts.

'Dad.' Dani hugs him tight. Father and daughter seem to become a single being for a few seconds, and then release.

'I'll take your bag in.' He lifts the backpack over a shoulder and walks it inside.

'Mum.' Dani embraces Patty, but it doesn't have the same warmth or urgency. Patty can't help but feel that old jealousy. They break their embrace, or is it that Dani tries to break free but Patty holds on? She looks her daughter in the face. Dani looks tired around the eyes and her face is fuller. Patty can tell her daughter has completely given up on training, less lean than she has been for years, even a little tummy forming. Student diet is a killer.

'I am so looking forward to bread sauce,' Dani says with a huge grin. She firmly twists from her mother's grip and heads inside.

'Do you remember this?' Dani holds up the treasure she has unearthed.

'Do I?' says Patty, laughing. 'That's Hoppy Bunny. I bought her for you when I was pregnant. I'd only just found out. We were living in Clapham and I went to Arding and Hobbs. Three shillings she was.' Patty smiles, thinking she's finally connecting with her daughter, that whatever is going on with Dani will come out. Instead, she watches a cloud sweep across her daughter's face as she closes off once more. Patty watches her go through the old boxes for a while longer and then leaves her to get on with it. In the kitchen she makes coffee and wonders for the millionth time what is up with her. She'd been home two days and was so morose. Even Tom and Izzy coming over hadn't cheered her up. Patty lights a cigarette, opens a window a crack and blows the smoke out.

She remembers the absolute joy she had felt when she bought Hoppy, her first real acknowledgement that a life was growing inside her. And she can remember so clearly how Dani's eyes had lit up the first time she saw it and how she squirmed as Patty bounced the bunny on her tummy.

'Hoppy loves Dani, hop, hop, hop.'

As a child Dani had loved her mother best of all but the older she got the closer she and Jim became, until one day Patty felt an outsider in her own family. Maybe it was puberty; the teen years were tough. She finishes the cigarette and flicks the butt out of the open window, staring out into...

'Mum.'

'Christ,' Patty jumps at her daughter's voice. 'I didn't hear you come in.'

'I'm not going back to uni. A year—'

'Don't be stupid.'

And the row strikes like a tsunami.

'It's Christmas Eve,' Jim pleads with them, but he knows it's futile. They're both too stubborn to back down now.

'I'm going.' Dani is adamant.

'Stay till after Christmas day at least,' he asks.

'Let her go. She can think about how stupid she's being,' Patty almost spits.

'Don't worry, I'm not staying here.'

'Dani, please sweethe—'

'I'm sorry, Dad. Bye.'

There was no goodbye for Patty.

That was the last time they saw her.

Alive.

INTERMISSION THREE

Tuesday 14 February 1984

Dani and Tom sit back-to-back, leaning against each other. He has the cigarette, takes an amateur pull on it, does not inhale, and passes it back to her. She takes it from him like a precious relic and in a gracious sweep brings it to her mouth. She drags the smoke deep into her lungs, holds it there and then, with a practised pucker, releases a perfect smoke ring. It sails away, slowly breaking down until it dissolves. She wonders if she could blow a smoke ring over an erect penis. She takes another deep draw on the cigarette and aims at an imaginary erection.

'Good smoke ring,' Tom says looking round. She doesn't tell him what she was aiming at.

He casually drops his eyes to his watch. 'I think we need to get back, Dani.' He stands, making sure she doesn't tip backwards.

She looks down at the cigarette, knowing he's right but feeling resentful. Geography and chemistry will never be as useful to her, in real-life situations, as being able to smoke with style. She imagines she's Julie Christie as she takes the cigarette up to her mouth and draws softly but intensely on the tip, the end glowing powerfully red. She rolls the smoke around her mouth like she's seen her dad do with wine, then pushes the smoke out through her nose, a perfect dragon drag. Satisfied, she flicks the butt into the corner. It bounces underneath the spare pommel horse.

Inside their corrugated metal smokehouse it was dry, but outside the air is damp – as close to rain as you can get without it actually raining. Both feel their hair start to curl slightly at the ends and their school uniforms dampen. They walk back to the main building in an uneasy silence. He's dying for her to mention the card – the one he delivered to her house at five o'clock that morning. He hadn't signed it, of course, but desperately wanted to hear about it from her. Was she excited? Who could her mysterious admirer be? How did she feel about what was inside the card – a ticket for Siouxsie and the Banshees at the Apollo the following week. E4, upper circle.

Dani was thinking about the card. Of course she knew it was from Tom, just like she knew he had the ticket next to hers. If he'd said, 'Let's go see the Banshees', she would have gone, probably would have let him buy her ticket. But this romantic bullshit made her feel uneasy. She should never have kissed him. He'd caught her a little upset, more than a little drunk, on the rebound and easy prey. It had been stupid. She didn't want to lose him, he was her best friend but she'd let him imagine something he couldn't have. He wasn't someone she could have fun with – at least, not just fun. With the athletes and sporty-boys it was easier; they didn't ask any searching questions and had no real feelings to hurt. She could talk to Tom; they both had issues with their mothers and had dreams of the future. Tom was cool... but not cool enough. Not for a boyfriend. And he wasn't sexy, and Dani was starting to appreciate sexy.

'Are you training later?' he asks. She doesn't respond right away. The answer's 'no', but that didn't mean she was free to hang out. Instead, she was going to take the Tube into town and mooch around the pub opposite Goldsmiths in the hope that she'd see *him* again. She knew very little about him; they called him Bix and he did something with Lego and dog shit. He was tall and arrogantly, jaw-droppingly handsome. He was a friend of Toni's brother and they had all met up on the Saturday. Bix hadn't talked to Dani directly, but she'd watched him as he dominated the group, talking with passion about art and sculpture as he drank cider and smoked his short, stubby roll-ups, which he made look fucking sexy. In part, this was why she was smoking at lunchtime – to get good enough to smoke with him. The other part was that she wanted to get stoned very soon, and knew you had to be a smoker or it didn't work.

'Yes, I'm training. My sprinting needs some work,' she says into the air, not catching his eye. She hates lying to Tom. If it had been anything else she'd have told him. In the last year he'd become her closest friend, even listening as she droned on about her mum and bloody Greenham Common. Not even her Dad was so attentive, but she knows Tom wants boyfriend/girlfriend. No matter how selfish her mum says she is, she will not screw Tom over and make him listen to her moaning about love stuff.

'We could get together after training.'

'No. No idea how long I'll be.' She keeps her eyes ahead, trying not to blush at the lie.

He nods like he agrees, but feels disappointed. He had wanted this to be their first Valentine's together. They carry on, walking in silence, until the school gates come into view.

'The careers fair is on Friday ha—'

She groans. 'God Tom, I have no idea what I want to be when I'm a grown-up. Not dead and not a journalist, that's about it.'

'Okay,' he says, trying to sound upbeat.

They reach the school gates and push inside. This is where they part. He knows she's off to geography. He has her timetable memorised.

'Tomorrow, seven thirty at the bus stop?' she asks.

He nods. She squeezes his arm and walks off. He watches her cross the playground. His stomach tightens when she finally disappears. He knows something is happening, changing. Over the last six months he's seen how she's slipped out of her training regime, started to wear make-up and think about what she's wearing, but he doesn't know what it means. In his pocket the Siouxsie and the Banshees ticket burns a hole. They often spend their evenings together, sometimes studying but mostly just talking, but there is nothing about these evenings that could be called 'romantic' and he wants a real date. He can still felt the adrenalin of their kiss, even after more than two weeks. It's like some super battery, revving him up. He wants more, wants everything. He wants Dani. From inside the closest building he can hear the bell ring. He runs to class.

THIRTEEN

Saturday 18 December 2010

'Maybe we should go to her house,' Dani suggests.

Jim shakes his head. 'If she was there she'd answer the phone.'

'Unless…' Dani realises her mistake and stops. Jim switches the radio on and they listen, but can only bear it for a few minutes. Everything is closed, cut-off, trapped, lost, buried, worst since records began. The end is nigh. He's called Patty five times over the last few hours, and of course he's imagined her lying on the floor unconscious but… deep down he knows his fear isn't really about Patty being hurt.

'I need to get in touch. Tom might…' But he's afraid to call Tom. For some reason he needs to talk to Patty first. And…

'The Lost Soul.' He suddenly realises there is someone who might know where Patty is, or at least have a mobile phone number for her. Jim runs upstairs.

'Dad?' Dani calls after him.

'I'll be down in a minute.'

He stands before her door. He hasn't been in there since the day she left. He puts his hand to the door and… push. A rush of stagnant air, the slight sweetness of damp hits him. The room is empty. The wall is gone. The pictures and endless reports, the questions – all gone. The desk is empty but he hopes he'll find a leaflet in the drawer. Yes.

'But it's miles Dad.'

'I can do it. I know the short cuts.'

'But she might not even be there.'

'I know, but I have to do something.' Jim smiles at Dani and heads out. He knows she's right, it's a long way and the news says there's no trains or buses – but it's the only thing he can think to do. He's tried calling but just gets an answering machine. He has to try and see Karan Noble. As he walks, he tries to remember Karan's story.

Karan Noble had twin girls, Emma and Tamsin. At the age of eleven they disappeared. It was 1976, the hottest summer for decades, and the girls had been playing in the garden in an inflatable paddling pool they'd been given for their birthday. Karan had called them in for dinner at about six o'clock and there was no reply. No girls. Nobody was sure when they could remember seeing them last. There was lots of media interest initially, pretty girl twins, photo-genic and newspaper-selling. But that died away as the reporters came up against a brick wall with the family. Karan shut herself away from the world and left it all to the husband who was a cold fish. With little media attention, the police found the trail quickly became cold. With no prodding from the family, it just all dropped. It was a mystery for seven years. Then, an accident in their street led the gas board to dig up most of the road and some gardens behind the houses. The twins' bodies were found in the garden of Karan's next-door neighbours, Ken and Sarah. For Karan, who had almost got her life back together, it was like losing them all over again. Maybe worse – now she knew there was no hope. And she had trusted Ken. He had been the first person she had called when she found the girls missing. He had led the search around the neighbourhood.

'We won't give up, we'll find them, Karan. Have faith,' he had said to her on the third day and she had wept in his arms. That memory, after her children's bodies had been discovered, had made her physically sick.

He was arrested and pleaded guilty. He said he had invited them in for a cold drink and put on a film, a film of men having sex with teenage girls. When they tried to leave he stopped them. The police searched the house and discovered an entire cupboard filled with films and photographs of children being abused. There were photographs of Emma and Tamsin. He was convicted of their murders. Karan's marriage had lasted just a few months after the girls went missing. By the time their bodies were found, their father was remarried, living in France with a four-year-old son. About a year after the neighbour was convicted, Karan Noble set up the charity Lost Souls. Its agenda was the campaign for stiffer penalties for endangering, harming and killing children, no matter the circumstance. As a secondary goal, it tried to fight for state funding to provide counselling for grieving parents, their extended family and friends.

Karan had passion for her cause, but no real knowledge of how that message could be put across to politicians and the press. Then she met Patty about six months after Dani was killed. In many ways they were made for each other. Patty was both a journalist and activist. She knew how to get stories in the papers and who to harangue. Oh, she could harangue. Karan was someone who could organise and structure. Patty was never someone who was going to build a charity from the ground up, but she could help to shape someone else's cause. So Karan took on Patty as a kind of manager, to shape policy. Under Patty, Lost Souls became a lobbying group, a powerful mouthpiece for anyone who had lost a loved one to violent crime. And of course it was Patty who became the public face of Lost Souls. When children went missing or were murdered, she was one of the first to be called by the press or TV for comment. Jim had hated that; he hadn't liked the friendship that had developed between Patty and Karan. To him it didn't seem based in support for each other but in a shared spite and pain. It hadn't surprised him at all when Patty had confided in him, about a year after joining the charity, that Karan regularly paid money to see that the man who killed her children was beaten and abused in prison.

Jim walks without pausing until he reaches the South Bank, directly opposite St Paul's cathedral, snow scattered over its dome like icing sugar. There he stops and leans on the railings. The beauty of it makes his heart soar.

'It's lovely.'

He turns to see his daughter. He smiles, pleased to see her.

'Do you rem—' he starts.

'I remember you boring me witless talking about Wren and the dome and the flying buttresses.'

He laughs.

'Happy days.' She grins.

Silently the two of them stand by the river and watch London, a thousand years reflected in the shimmer of water.

'Shall we go?' Jim says as the cold sneaks into his fingers.

They push on, cold breath billowing from his mouth like steam. They walk past the National Theatre, towards Big Ben and Parliament. Then over the Thames, as the snow begins to fall once more; hard and heavy as the afternoon light dies.

They stand before the slate-grey building on the edge of Dryden Street and look up at its darkened windows. There might be a faint glow coming from the very top floor, it's hard to tell. He looks at the run of intercom buttons down the right side of the door; the top two are for Lost Souls. He pushes them both, one after the other. There is a long wait before a weirdly crackling and rather irritated voice asks, 'The office is closed. Who is it?'

'It's Jim Lancing. You might remem—'

The intercom buzzes and the door pops open slightly. He pushes it forwards, holding it wide as he turns back to Dani.

'I think it best if you stay down here.'

'Good, I'll window shop.' She sounds quite excited.

'Okay. I don't suppose I'll be that long – an hour at most.'

'Rendezvous back here at seventeen hundred hours?' she asks.

'Fine.'

Dani smiles and turns away to walk towards the heart of Covent Garden.

He climbs three flights of a very steep circular staircase to get to the Lost Souls office. Theatre posters adorn the walls of the first two flights. The second floor seems to be home to theatrical agents, though judging by the posters they seem only to represent second-rate ventriloquists, mesmerists, the runner-up in some ancient talent show and a fizzy blonde dance troupe that have had ten years airbrushed off them.

The top floor opens out onto an area which resembles a private dentist's waiting room. There's no one there, but there is a sign, propped on a small table. It reads: PLEASE TAKE A SEAT.

There's an old leather sofa and three less comfortable-looking chairs. At the far end is a small receptionist's desk. He chooses the sofa and sinks comfortably into it. There's a coffee table, but all it contains are the glossy flyers and annual reports of Lost Souls. He doesn't pick one up. He's seen them many times before and knows that on page four there is a picture of a stricken Patty holding up a photograph of Dani. He'd argued against its inclusion but Patty insisted. 'Jim, the charity needs a public face. You need to poke people and show them the reality: loss and grief. Loss and grief sells.'

'Charities aren't selling anything.'

'What century are you in?' she laughed. 'Charities need to sell harder than anyone.'

Of course, deep down, Jim knew Patty was right. But he deeply resented their grief being used like that.

It takes Karan Noble about ten minutes, but finally she appears from a small door Jim hadn't noticed. She's a tall, slim woman, somewhere in her late sixties. Her hair is up, which gives her a sense of elegance. This is further enhanced by her plain silver jewellery, which highlights the silver in her hair. Jim has met her twice before. Both times he had felt she didn't like him, didn't trust him. Her eyes told him that he was judged. Now he sees something new in her eyes. She's wary and looks a little afraid. He wonders what's changed. She walks to the desk and stands behind it, as if it affords some protection to her.

'Mr Lancing.'

'Mrs Noble. I was hoping you might—'

'I really can't help you. I don't have any information I could share with you. Even if I had, I wouldn't.'

Jim looks surprised. 'I… it's Patty.'

'Patty has made her own choice. She needed to act and she has done so.'

'What, hang on what choice?' Jim stands and Karan Noble steps back. 'I just want to know about Patty. I've tried to call and can't reach her. I thought you might know something.'

She pauses. Karan Noble knows, she knows everything. She had watched Patty lose hope over the years, watched her anger die. She had even thought it a blessing; no one could live with that much rage. Then suddenly the fire burnt again. Patty said nothing but Karan knew only one thing could make the anger return: the chance to catch him. The chance to kill him. She would never betray her friend.

'I don't. I know nothing, Mr Lancing.'

'A mobile number, an email she might check.'

She pulls her arms tight around her defensively. 'Nothing.'

'Please. Somewhere she might be?'

'I can't. I would like you to leave.'

'I'm worried about Patty. I'm sure—'

Karan's face clouds over. 'My understanding is that Patty hasn't seen you for years. That doesn't sound like a man who cares.'

'That's not right. I mean it is years, but... I just...' he feels a headache begin. 'This will sound crazy. Out of the blue I suddenly started thinking about her and I've been worrying about her ever since. I can't get her out of my mind.'

Karan snorts a little and starts to shake her head.

Jim continues. 'Something is happening and... and I think you know what it might be.'

She raises her eyebrow and then a wry smile creeps across her face. 'My husband, ex-husband, had a heart attack two months ago. Not fatal, but serious.'

'I'm sorry.'

'Don't be, it's more than thirty years since he meant anything to me. I mention it because there was a time when I thought that if anything happened to him – anything at all – that I would know, some intuition or something. But...'

'But everything changes when a partner moves on,' says Jim softly and Karan meets his gaze properly for the first time. She nods.

'I can't help you, Mr Lancing.'

'Can't or won't?'

She smiles. 'Can't, won't – they're the same thing. Now, please leave.'

Jim feels the blood pound at his temples. He opens his mouth to argue with her but at that second there is the slam of metal and brick from somewhere close by. A car alarm immediately sounds and various voices begin to shout. Jim and Karan both move to the window, three or four figures can be seen scurrying around the corner, heading to something. Jim looks down. Dani is in the middle of the road waving manically. From that distance he can't really see her expression, it's more like a smudge, but he knows something is very wrong.

He turns to Karan Noble 'I have—' he doesn't finish, but rushes out of the room.

'What the hell?' Karan Noble shouts after him but he's gone.

He takes the stairs two at a time, bouncing off the walls of the narrow staircase until he hits the bottom. He tumbles out into the cold evening air. Dani runs to him, so panicked she runs through a parked car.

'Dad!' She looks scared, so pale – even for a ghost.

'What? What's happened?'

'Dad, this way...'

She turns and runs into the road; Jim follows.

'Watch it!' the driver screams, as Jim swerves at the last moment to avoid being hit by the only car on the street. Dani runs around the corner. As he gets into Drury Lane, Jim sees a group gathered around a man lying in the middle of the road. A car has crashed into a wall to the left of them – the driver has got out of the car and is swaying slightly – he looks both dazed and angry. Jim slows and comes to a halt next to Dani, who watches the group.

'I should help.'

'No need, he's dead,' she tells him in a small voice.

'How…?'

'I saw it.' She turns to Jim. 'He collapsed right in front of me, but…'

'What?'

'He… his body fell but another part of him stayed up, standing there. Like his flesh just fell away and his spirit was still upright. He looked right at me – could see me. He looked shocked, confused… he looked down and saw his body and then…'

She screws her face up, the memory cutting into her.

'Then he just seemed to freeze. The spirit part of him that was standing opened its mouth. I think he was going to say something to me. Ask what had happened, but he just suddenly seemed to shake – like a huge current was running through him and he lit up like the sun – and then…' she struggles to express it. 'He turned to steam, or something like smoke, and was gone.'

She closes her eyes, replaying what she'd seen in her mind.

'I don't understand, Dani,' Jim tells her.

'He was gone, Dad. Gone.'

'What?'

'Not like I can – he was gone. Nowhere. His spirit just went.'

'Dani…'

'Then the car came – the driver saw the body in the road at the last second and steered away, hit the wall. Lucky he was moving so slowly.'

'Oh,' is all Jim can say.

They stand silent while the wail of the ambulance builds around them. It trundles through the still treacherous streets. As soon as it arrives two paramedics jump out. Dani finally lifts up her face to meet her father's gaze. Her eyes seem to dance with a firelight Jim has never seen before.

'I don't remember it, Dad. I don't remember my death. I don't know why I'm here. Why didn't I go like he just did? What...?' She can't complete the sentence. Instead she turns and starts to walk away.

'Dani,' Jim calls to her. 'Please don't go.' But she fades from sight.

He waits for a while, hoping she will come back, but after half an hour his fingers and feet are frozen. Full of questions he trudges back to the Lost Souls building. Now it looks totally dark. He knows Karan Noble would never let him back in. But she had confirmed something was going on – 'Patty has made her own choice. She needed to act and she has done so' – that was what she'd said, but what did it mean?

He sighs heavily. He's no closer to finding Patty, and is even more worried than he was that morning. With a heavy heart, Jim heads slowly up Dryden Street towards home.

※

Patty suddenly sits up like a marionette, her strings jerked – ready to perform. She has no idea where she is for a second, the sound and images so alien – then it all rushes back: the knife, the blood, the drive through the snow, handing the sample over, the end to her long, long wait.

On the table the superskinnysoymoccacinolatte is cold, a film formed over the top. Her hand reaches up to her lip and she feels drool. She reaches into her bag and pulls out a packet of tissues to mop her lips. She looks at her watch – 11.30. The four hours are almost up. It's time to go back to the lab.

She feels like she's moving through mud; the air is sodden with the weight of loss: lost laughter, lost moments, lost... She moves slowly through the streets, almost like a bride moving down the aisle, she feels like she is about to shed her old life and become someone new.

She climbs the stairs to the lab. She asks for Roberta, again trying to smile and affect the cheery Home Counties voice.

Roberta enters. She is all frowns, but as she sees Patty she smiles.

'It is good news I think.'

Patty imagines the blade in her hand, sees herself slide it into him, spit in his face. She cries her tears that splash down upon him as his life slimes away. The blood and tears mingle, blood red pain and crystal joy. Both will free her.

Roberta, still smiling, tells her the result. Her lips move but the sound is distorted. Patty starts to sway; she looks down at her hand covered in his gore. Blood spews onto the floor like broken waters as a baby squirms in the dirt, fighting for breath. She tumbles forward. All is black for Patricia Lancing.

INTERMISSION FOUR

Monday 8 February 1999

She stands on the threshold. The train station behind her, looking down the path that winds into the middle of town. She's made this walk so often – dozens of times over the last ten years – but today her legs feel like jelly. She has come to despise this city and its occupants, maybe not all but certainly the young ones, with their long limbs, super white teeth and clear skin. They strut around like they own the place – she hates it – the arrogance of the young and privileged. Even the student selling the *Socialist Worker* sounds like a refugee from the House of Lords.

She pushes herself forward and starts to trundle down the path. It's five months since she was last here, then it was the start of the new university year. She had quizzed the staff for the thousandth time – nothing. Very few remain from Dani's day, a couple of secretaries, two senior masters and no students; they have masters and PhDs now and are scattered all over the planet. The police gave up on Dani long ago, even Tom has moved on. And Jim... Patty suddenly stops and grabs hold of the metal rail. Behind her a Japanese student with a large trundling suitcase has to make an emergency stop.

'Excuse me.'

Patty takes no notice. The path ahead swims, she sits down – feeling damp from the ground seep into her jeans. The diminutive Japanese student swears under her breath as she manhandles the enormous suitcase around the madwoman sitting in everyone's way. There is no way forwards – that is the only thought in Patty's head. Ten years. There are no leads, no evidence, no chance. She feels sick. Tired and sick. She hates Durham. Before Dani came here Patty knew nothing about the city. No, that isn't quite true – she had known one girl from Durham, a prostitute who worked out of a slum in King's Cross. Tina. Tina? When Patty first met her she was still pretty, only twenty, slight but not addict thin. She'd arrived from Durham a few weeks before – running from someone or something. Running to the big smoke where the streets were paved with gold. Stupid girl. She had a son who was in care – she swore she'd get him back. She begged Patty to help. What a fucking joke, he was better off without her. Fucking Durham.

Patty sits on the step and lets the day slide away from her. At some point her stomach grumbles so loudly that she gets up and walks down the path to find something to eat. In a greasy spoon she orders a cheese sandwich and glass of milk. There's a phone box outside and she considers calling Karan. She wants someone who might understand. Might appreciate what ten years of death feels like… but she doesn't ring her. Truth is there is no one who can know what she has gone through, feel the frustration of her failure to find Dani's killer, know the guilt she feels about those first few days when she was drugged up to the eyeballs and no help. She feels the shame nuzzle her heart even now, gnaw at her:

'You fell apart when you were most needed. Ninety per cent of all crimes are solved in the first twenty-four hours and you were no use – you might as well have killed her.' That is what her head tells her. The milk seems to curdle in her mouth. She takes one bite from the sandwich but can't force it down. She spits it into a napkin. Why did she come here? She envies Karan Noble. She lost her daughters but at least she knows who to blame, who to hate. She has the pleasure of knowing his life is being made a hell in prison – that she pays for him to be beaten and worse every week. That is something. Something.

'Really. Would that make you happy, Patty? To have a man raped and beaten for your pleasure?' Jim-in-her-head asks.

'Yes.'

'Are you so lost?'

'You have no idea who I am these days.'

'I am so sorry for you.'

Patty gets up and pays the bill. Outside it is quite dark. The day is lost. She stands there stuck. She could go to a hotel and start early in the morning. Maybe the local paper has… but instead she turns towards the path back to the station. The chance to avenge Dani has gone. There is no revenge for her. This has been a long way to come for a bite of cheese sandwich.

'Sorry,' the man says as he hits her shoulder, walking the other way.

'Watch where you're going,' she calls back to him.

❄

He goes a few steps more and looks back. He recognises her immediately from the church. Ten years – but it's her mother. His chest tightens as he watches her walk up the hill. He feels a force, like a rubber band stretched between them. He follows her, keeping his distance as she heads up the hill.

In the station she turns to the platform heading south, and he walks to the opposite platform and sits, watching her across the tracks. She has a thin jacket on; she looks frozen but seems oblivious to the cold. She's lost a lot of weight since he last saw her; she looks lean now, like a runner. She looks more like Dani – how Dani might have looked when… if… he feels a tear breach his defences and roll down his cheek.

Patty looks across the train tracks and sees a man crying. He reminds her of Jim for a second – so close to tears all the time. She wonders why he's crying... and then the London train rattles into the station wiping the image from her sight. Was the man real – or just Jim-in-her-head? She will not admit to missing him. Not allow the loneliness to flood back in. She had to leave him; the closeness was killing them both.

She rises slowly and walks to the train. She will not make this journey again. There are people she can help through Lost Souls, there are men she can punish, laws to change and young women like Dani to protect. Maybe she could even write again... maybe...

He walks to the edge of the track and tries to catch a glimpse of her on the train. A part of him wants to run through the tunnel to the steps and get on the London train. Maybe he could sit opposite her and... what? Say sorry. Say sorry for the pain, sorry for his part in Dani's— from nowhere a hand grabs his arm and pulls him back as a train rushes past his nose.

'You need to be careful,' a voice tells him.

'Yes. Yes thank you. Thank you.'

From the air, a disembodied voice announces the London train is about to depart. The man stands there and watches as it pulls out of the station. Then he heads back to the twisting path that leads to his wife and daughter.

PART THREE

PART THREE

FOURTEEN

Monday 4 October 2010

Tom stands on the doorstep, frozen. His arm raised, finger pointing towards the doorbell, yet he cannot move. It's a cool autumn day, but his hairline is beaded with sweat. His eyes are wet with tears that threaten to stream. He lowers his arm and pulls at his jacket, which is a little too snug along his back. The insignia on his chest and shoulders pronounces him Detective Superintendent in the Metropolitan Police; inside the uniform he feels like a child, knocking on the door to ask if his friend can come out to play. He breathes and steadies himself once more. This should be easy, it isn't like he's calling to tell someone their loved one has been killed. Not this time.

Inside the house, a body lies on the floor. She looks dead, but not at peace, her brow puckered, her mouth pinched. The doorbell rings, the body doesn't move. The doorbell sounds a second time and the face creases with annoyance. Patty opens her eyes, they swim, unfocused for a second and then fix on the world. She had been lost inside her head somewhere in a fog. Her stomach growls, she has no idea when she last ate. The doorbell rings again.

'Go away!' she shouts. She doesn't open the door these days. She doesn't answer the phone either. It's never anybody real any more.

The doorbell sounds three times in quick succession.

'Christ,' she mutters and rolls over onto all fours, then pulls herself upright and walks to the door. She doesn't know why; it was just that the three quick rings reminded her of something.

On the doorstep, Tom braces himself.

'What the hell is it?' Patty glares at him angrily for a moment and then softens as she recognises…

'Pup,' she whispers. She takes a step forwards and her hand reaches out to trace the lines around his eyes.

'Hello, Patty,' he manages to squeeze the words past the lump in his throat. Her fingertip is suddenly wet and she pulls her hand away, embarrassed.

'Tom. It's good – a surprise – but good to see you. Come in.' She steps back and he follows her in.

She takes him into the lounge. It's quite Spartan – there are two chairs and a small table covered with leaflets. She says something but he can't quite sync her mouth with the sound. It looks like Dani's mouth, which is odd because it never used to. It had been very full, soft and inviting. He remembered Jim telling him one day – one drunken night really – how it had been Patty's mouth he had fallen for that first night, the greatest mouth he had ever seen. Now it was thinner and tighter. Tom wondered if it ever laughed any more.

'I am so sorry. I have no tea or coffee or anything really.' Her stomach growls again and she hopes he can't hear it. 'Water?'

'No, I'm fine.'

She stares at him, not knowing what to do – it's years since she had to entertain. He stands awkwardly, waiting for her to offer him a seat, until he realises she never will.

'Can I sit down?'

'Yes, yes of course. Where are my manners? I don't have any tea…' she trails off knowing she's said that already. She flushes with embarrassment.

'You look good.'

'Liar.' She sits opposite him and studies his face – so hard to see the boy in there now. She remembers how he had aged suddenly after Dani... after Dani. But now he doesn't just look merely old but craggy, weathered – it suits him. Suits his position, he has authority about him. She likes it, and yet, feels a stab of pain.

'It is good to see you,' she says, and means it.

'I was sorry about you and Jim.'

She waves her hand as if she were swatting a fly – wiping away the past.

'It's twelve years. Too long to care about.' She wonders for a moment if they still see each other – Tom and Jim. They used to go for drinks, after they'd been to the garden of remembrance. Remember what? The good old times.

'You've done well for yourself. I've seen your name in the news over the years.'

He ducks his head. 'Luck.'

'Don't be silly. Intelligence and a good heart – that will get you high in the police. So few of them have it.'

'Well,' he starts, but doesn't know what to say. He remembers Dani yelling at him. 'Don't join the police, for God's sake! Mum, Mum tell him.' And Patty shot him a look that was so full of disappointment he almost gave in.

'Where are you at the moment?' Patty asks. 'You were family liaison weren't you?'

'Yes, I was always the one called in to tell the bad news.'

She nods. She knows what they used to call him: the Sad Man.

'Now I head up a special operations unit, small but...' he trails off again.

'What does the unit do?'

He looks at her. He can feel his face crumble a little. 'We investigate sexually aggravated murders, usually multiple victims.'

She nods. The irony is not lost on her.

'Children?'

'No, the Child Protection Unit deals with under eighteens.'

'No, sorry... I meant: do you have any? Are you married?'

His face is blank for a second. 'No.'

From nowhere, a thought hits her that takes her breath away: 'Why is Tom here, in uniform?' Numbness spreads across Patty's chest, her stomach starts to churn. Tom is the harbinger of death – it's Jim... A tremor begins, a bad one.

'I'm sorry I... I... could you...' Patty stammers, hands already shaking. She stands and makes her way over to the mantelpiece with intense effort. There is a bottle of pills there. Tom strides over and tries to help, but she brushes him away. She takes two of the small pills and swallows them down without water.

'Patty?' Tom asks with obvious concern.

'I'm fine.' Patty can hear how sick her voice sounds; it embarrasses her. She sounds like an old woman. She pulls herself together.

'Tom, is it Jim? Is he...?'

'Oh no, sorry no. Patty no, no. This isn't a bad news visit. Christ I'm sorry.'

He takes her hand and leads her back to the chair.

'Could you get me a glass of water?' She points towards the kitchen and he rushes off.

He returns with a full glass and hands it to her. She drinks greedily; it triggers more growls from her stomach.

'Good. Thank you,' Patty closes her eyes. She breathes into the tremor – feeling it lessen and finally ripple away.

Tom stands waiting until she finishes the water. He takes the empty glass and sits back down, a little shocked.

'Why?' she asks breathlessly. 'Why are you here?'

What does he say? He feels lost.

'Is it an official visit?'

No nods, he tries to speak but his voice seems a long way off. It's stupid, he has done this a thousand times.

'There is a chance…' he stops and starts again. 'Patty, there have been breakthroughs, scientific breakthroughs in forensic technology, DNA matching and profiling over the last few years. Pretty amazing steps forward – you probably know this already.'

'I haven't kept up with the technology lately, I…' she trails off.

'Okay, well there's been a revolution in forensic analysis, and it's meant that cold cases all over the country are being reviewed. There's a series of teams looking at every unsolved murder case. Families are being contacted and…'

The penny floats in the air and then drops like a hand grenade. 'Dani? Will they review Dani's case?'

He pauses, a little scared by the small flame he has seen ignite in her eye.

'Yes. Dani's case is on the list. They would have sent an officer round from family liaison but…'

'You volunteered.'

He nods. He could add: 'I wanted to see your face when you got the news, I wanted to manage your expectations – not to get your hopes up.' But he doesn't. He can't.

They sit silently together for quite some time. Patty's mind is whirring. She used to keep up with the changes in procedure and testing; it had been part of her job. She remembers sitting in the British Library reading the *Journal of Forensic Science*, but when did she do that last? She was at a conference in Berne on DNA profiling. When was that? 2000? 2001? Ten years ago? When did she stop looking? When did she give up on Dani? She shakes her head, trying to clear the brain fog, feeling the cogs start to engage once again.

'What do you mean by forensic analysis?' she asks.

'It's an evidence-based review. They'll go through the file and look at whether any of the recent technical advances can be used to develop DNA matches, looking at samples taken at the time to consider if they can be tested.'

'Samples?'

She remembers the cold and damp of the room. Spider webs that not only have spread into the corners but seem to creep over the ceiling, and down onto the metal struts of the shelves, knitting the darkness together. She can't imagine this room ever having been cleaned, the must of decaying paper and mould making her sneeze again and again.

She waits while the man who manages the evidence store tracks down the files she needs. He moves slowly, far more slowly than she has patience for.

'Really, I could find it myself.'

'No. No sorry to say I couldn't allow that, my dear – authorised personnel only.' His voice has a sibilant hiss; his skin looks mottled with mildew. Maybe all the years down there have turned him into a half-man. Certainly looks like it.

Finally he emerges with a green file. She knows that means an open case. Open but cold.

'Now, miss, you understand I am doing this as a favour to PC Bevans, up there in Greenwich.'

Patty nods.

'Officially, you are not here.'

'I understand.'

He nods over at a desk and chair. 'You can sit over there.'

'Can I make any copies?'

'No. You can make notes and sketches. No photographs and you can't leave this room with any of the papers. Want a cuppa?'

She nods and accepts this kindness from a stranger. He walks off and she prepares herself. She slips her hand down her leg and into her boot, removing the tiny Leica camera. She quickly photographs each page. She can only hope she has got the exposure right; the head photographer on the paper had given her lessons, though she hadn't told him what she planned.

She hears Tom's warning echo through her head. 'Careful Patty. Take care of yourself.'

She knew what the warning meant. It wasn't merely 'Don't get caught'; it was 'Don't be disappointed'. He had told her many times that the file had nothing – no leads. But the file held photographs.

'From after she was found... in that room,' Tom told her with a shaking voice.

'I understand.' And of course she had understood; she'd seen crime-scene photos and autopsy photos many times. She could handle it. She had to see everything. Tom had nodded, looking defeated and a little worried.

'I'll arrange it.'

She photographs each page methodically and quickly with the little spy camera, but does not read anything, barely glances at the content. Not until she has finished and stowed away the camera does she begin to read the file.

Patty shakes those memories away; she needs to concentrate on Tom now, not twenty years ago.

'What forensic testing... of what evidence, Tom? I saw the files back then and there were no DNA samples taken.' She tries to remember the exact wording. She's sure it said: 'Samples collected for storage: none.'

'I haven't seen the original report. Perhaps they weren't classified as samples because by the standards of twenty years ago they weren't.' Tom tries to make it sound like he isn't guessing.

'But today? Today these tests...'

'Minute traces can be tested today whereas twenty years ago you needed so much more. And samples can be taken from so many more surfaces and materials.'

'And does the file have—'

'Patty, I don't know. Maybe, but...'

He feels out of control. Normally he wouldn't give the family any technical detail, just be calm and reassuring without getting anyone's hopes up. But this is Patty.

Tom continues. 'They sent me a scan of the log sheet – it's a one-page summary on the front of the file. It says there were fluid samples taken and clothing samples retained.'

Patty feels tears break through the levee and begin to run down her cheeks. She thought she'd cried every tear her body was capable of years ago; she'd become desiccated through so much sobbing, but they still come. Tom stands and moves forward slowly, like a trainer with a wild animal. He puts his arms around her shoulder, and... Flashback to twenty years ago and he is breaking the news to her and she begins to scream and scream, he holds her tight. The same woman twenty years later... He can feel a fury build in his own chest but he holds it down.

Later, when he is alone, he will scream Dani's name until his lungs feel like they will burst. Then he will cry for her and her mother. He will cry for them all. Now, he and his love's mother are wrapped together before the last sob wracks Patty and she pulls herself away from him. She gets up and goes in search of some tissues. All she can find is a roll of toilet paper.

'Patty, you have to know that the chances are slim. Really slim that anything is even usable, let alone could provide evidence.'

'But possible?'

He should say 'no'. He can see her hopes rise. He should say 'no' to save her more torment, but he can't. 'Yes, it's possible.'

Possible. The word seems to burrow into her, letting the fog out. Her heaviness falls away, like one of Salome's veils dropping to the floor revealing the shape of something indistinct, a tease, but something is there. Patty feels alert, for the first time in years.

'Do you have any idea about the timescale? When will Dani's murder be reviewed?'

Tom hesitates. 'Forty-eight months,' he tells her, deeply embarrassed. 'Probably about forty-eight months. I'm very, very sorry.'

'Oh Tom,' is all she can say.

They sit together for a while longer, though there is not much more to be said. Tom gives her a web address and tells her that a letter will arrive soon restating pretty much what he has just told her.

'Jim will be informed too,' Tom tells her.

'I can tell him,' Patty offers.

'Or I can.'

'It would be better if I told him.'

'Fine,' Tom nods.

In her heart, Patty knows she won't tell him and thinks it better if he doesn't know. Not for a while at least. Finally Tom makes moves to leave and Patty shows him to the door.

'Oh. Wait,' and she runs off.

Tom stands at the door awkwardly as time ticks by. She is gone for at least five minutes, before she finally returns.

'There is this. I thought you might... I don't know why I have it. I have almost nothing else but...' She hands him a small metal cup on a fake marble plinth. On the front is a gold-coloured plaque that reads:

14 JUNE 1982
800M CHAMPION
DANIELLE LANCING

He smiles as he runs his finger along the rim of the trophy. He remembers the day as if it were yesterday, not almost thirty years ago. She broke the school record that day, and that night was the first he talked to her, talked to her properly, just the two of them.

'Tom. Isn't there something you can do to bump her up the list? Surely there must be.'

He looks at her as the memories crash around him. Patty was good. She had ambushed him at his most vulnerable.

'There is nothing I can do,' he manages in a small voice.

'That can't be tr—'

'Cold cases are looked at by another unit. I can't ask for preferential treatment, and they wouldn't give it. Besides, I think the chance any review will uncover something is so small. Really, Patty, I don't want you to have false hope.'

He holds out his hand to her, but she pulls away. He can see her harden before his very eyes. He hears it in her voice too. The ice queen.

'Don't worry about me,' she tells him and opens the door. 'Bye, Tom.'

'Patty.'

He walks away from the house. Darkness has fallen while he was inside and the night air is chill. He hopes he made the right decision, to see her himself rather than have a junior FLO deliver the news. He doesn't know what four years of waiting will mean to her. He remembers all too vividly those first few months, that first year or two. She was like a hunting dog, pulling apart everything. He didn't know how Jim could stand it back then, watching the obsession grind her down and waste her away. He desperately hopes this will not rekindle that madness. There is no chance that the samples will provide the evidence to find the killer – this isn't TV. There is never going to be an answer to who killed Dani.

Patty watches him walk down the road, away from the house. As he retreats, she feels the tremor begin. She rides the crest, surfing the crashing wave out... out... out... It takes a long time for her to come back to her body. She has found over the years that the tremors are like ripples made by a stone thrown into a lake. A small splash and there's just a gentle undulation that carries you outwards until calm returns. A big stone and it's a roller coaster. And this? Well, this was no small stone, this was Atlantis, sliding under the churning ocean creating waves that could last for all time.

FIFTEEN

Tuesday 5 October 2010

The dead leaves crunch underfoot as Patty runs. She knows it's some kind of addiction – she craves the endorphins her body ekes out like some crack-dealing Scrooge. She runs every day, has done for the last six or seven years. Sometimes only a few miles but often fifteen or more. Always alone. It depends on how much thinking she has to do, or how desperate she feels. On desperate days she runs the furthest and fastest.

It's cold. Autumn is really biting, but the sky is clear and there's some watery sun that shines through the brown papyrus of the leaves. She can see her breath.

Still less than a day since Tom's visit. It feels like she's been struck by lightning. 'She's alive, she's alive!' She imagines some mad scientist howls at the moon in glee that Patty Lancing is reanimated.

'When did I die?' she asks herself.

'When you gave up hope,' he echoes through her head.

'Oh, are you back in my head, Jim?'

'I never left, just waited for you.'

Patty speeds up, trying to outpace the truth. Because, of course, she had given up. She had looked under every rock, tried to dig out every secret surrounding her daughter's death, but there was nothing. She hit brick wall after brick wall as if someone were blocking her at every stage. But she still went around the maze time and time again. Month after month and then year after year. And then – she can't pinpoint the time or the place, but she started to slow down. Then she fell to her knees and crawled and finally she lay down and died. That was probably when she started to run. Her body still worked, but inside there was nobody home. When was the last time she shed a tear, the last time before yesterday? Years. Years and years. Silent and cold, dead but running. Until now. Bolt from the blue and... her case will be reviewed. Something to live for. But four years? She runs faster.

Her lungs burn, and finally force her to stop. She has lost all sense of time; it's dark and she has no idea where she is. The temperature's dropped, suddenly it's freezing. She looks up to the moon and to the side sees the Pole Star. She could wish on it. The thought makes her smile.

'Star light, star bright, first star I see tonight. I wish I may, I wish I might...'

But what does she wish for? She closes her eyes and a face she had almost forgotten fills her mind.

SIXTEEN

Friday 8 October 2010

The *bizness 4 U* building had been launched, with great fanfare, by a government minister five years before – all slick and shiny. Two hundred subsidised luxury offices to boost London's entrepreneurial spirit. Today, half are empty, the other half full of massage therapists, women baking organic flapjacks and media start-ups. Patty arrives on level four and peers out from the lift. It looks exactly the same as levels two and three, both of which she has walked around for the last twenty minutes. The carpet is luxuriant, but hideously turquoise. Large plants in pots have been placed every ten feet, real plants, but the lack of light has caused them to brown at the edges and curl like old toast. At least half of the light bulbs are blown and a large pink penis has been drawn in the lift. This is the last floor she will look at, she decides, and heads out. Nothing, nothing, nothing… But then the final door reads MARCUS KEYSON INVESTIGATIONS. She feels a little sick.

She has spent the last four days, since Tom's visit, in the British Library reading the *Journal of Forensic Science*. She realises now just what an explosion there's been in criminal investigations in the last four or five years. The uses of DNA matching and profiling have boomed over this time and she had sleepwalked through it. For four days she has read voraciously, yet after all that, she has no greater insight into Dani's case. She does not know if her killer can be found. What she does know, however, is that she needs to find out what samples the police gathered in 1989. Then she can discover what can be done with that evidence and see where it might lead.

She knocks. The door is opened by a stunning young woman, petite with auburn hair cut into a bob and, refreshingly, no make-up. She smiles. 'Mrs Lancing?'

Patty nods. Doesn't correct her, not trusting her own voice.

'Please take a seat. Dr Keyson will be with you soon.'

She indicates a row of four chairs with a wave, then turns to walk back to her desk. Her hip drops, as if she has been hit, then rights itself and she drags her foot forward. It is the worst limp Patty has ever seen – she immediately feels sympathy for her – then catches herself. 'Stupid,' she thinks. 'She doesn't need sympathy from the likes of me.'

Patty walks to the seat furthest from the receptionist and scans the room. It is nothing like she'd expected; it looks more like a high-end psychiatrist's office. Two pieces of large expressionist art dominate the room as well as four smaller contemporary sculptures. In front of the chairs is a low-slung coffee table, which, thankfully, does not have nine-month-old gossip magazines resting on it. Instead there are gallery catalogues, most in English, but some in Spanish and French. In the corner is a crate full of children's toys. Patty wonders who brings a child to an appointment like this. Apart from the entrance, there are two other doors. On the walls there are a few small, delicate drawings and a series of framed diplomas, which mostly hang above the pretty girl's desk, highlighting that Marcus Keyson is indeed an accomplished doctor of forensic sciences. She wonders why he is here, in this run-down building. She has seen his name mentioned in two or three of the articles in the journals she has been devouring. In each one he was lashing out at the police, saying that they missed too much evidence, that they did not have the proper training needed to keep a crime scene clean. She had googled him. It was obvious that he had been a shining star in the firmament of forensic investigation, but something had happened and, like Icarus, he had tumbled down to earth. She couldn't find what but did discover that he acted as an independent investigator on forensic assessment of evidence and DNA. His website said he had strong links to the Metropolitan Police and that total privacy was assured. Free initial consultation. So she had called.

'Can I get you a tea? Or coffee?' the receptionist asks.

'No. No, thanks... actually yes, yes I would like a tea. Black, black please.'

'Of course.'

The girl leaves her desk and limps towards one of the mystery doors. It must be a kitchen, or at least a room with a kettle. Patty doesn't really want the tea, but she needs something to do with her hands, to quell the tremor that is beginning to build. In her pocket she feels the weight of her medication. She could take two small white pills, which would control the shaking but it would dull her too. And that is not acceptable; she needs to be sharp.

After a few minutes the girl returns with a tray. On it are three mugs, a small dish of sugar sachets and a plate of biscuits, fancy ones coated in Belgian chocolate. Two of the mugs are stylish Pantone designs, the third is a beaten-up old thing, its surface pitted by a thousand buffets in a dishwasher. But you can still see the faded legend: WORLD'S FAVOURITE DAD. The girl puts the tray down and takes one biscuit and the DAD mug and walks to the third door and knocks. There is a muffled response and she enters. Patty takes the mug of black tea into her hands and holds it. It's been made from real tea and not a bag; a few specks of leaf swirl in the depths as the undertow forces them to the top, only to drag them down once more. Her shakes are almost under control. She closes her eyes and visualises them fading. 'I am not solid; I am not rigid. I am liquid; I am air. I am—'

The door opens and the receptionist limps out. 'Dr Keyson can see you now.'

'—I am blood.'

Patty rises from the chair and walks slowly, keeping herself steady. The pretty receptionist smiles and touches her arm, just for a second.

Marcus Keyson is sitting on the edge of his desk, his coffee mug wrapped in a bear paw of a hand. He smiles and stands to greet Patty. He's tall, about six foot five. Late thirties, early forties, which Patty finds amazing, given the diplomas liberally covering the walls in the outer office. He has strawberry-blond hair, very expensively styled, with eyebrows that seem almost white. His skin is tanned and slightly ruddy. He wears white linen suit trousers and a long shirt with a granddad collar. No tie. No jacket. No shoes. He has bare feet. He has bare feet. Patty stops dead, thinking she's come to the wrong place – this is some new-age therapist who's gonna yin her yang.

'I think there might be some mistake,' Patty starts.

'Marcus Keyson. Forensic investigations. This is the right place, Mrs Lancing.' He stretches out a hand to her and with it, guides her, like they're dancing, to a chair. Then he sits back on the corner of his desk and looks questioningly at her. He says nothing.

'Dr Keyson—'

'Marcus.' He smiles, then nods for her to continue.

'Dr Keyson, your website details a specialism in forensic assessment.'

'That's right. How's your tea?' he asks with an open smile and sympathetic eyes.

'Erm. Okay.'

There is silence. Patty can feel a cold invade her chest. She needs to get out and starts to rise. But he's quicker. He puts his hand gently on her shoulder and presses her down firmly.

'Would you like to tell me about your…?'

'Dr Keyson.' She closes her eyes. She has stood and looked into the chasm so often… she leaps.

'My daughter was kidnapped, raped and murdered.' Just facts, headlines, nothing of Dani. He remains silent. 'Good,' she thinks, 'there's no *poor you.*' She has been hollowed out by *poor you.* He stays silent, his eyes coolly assessing her.

'When did this happen?'

'She was found in February 1989. She had been missing for three weeks. There were no leads and no one was ever arrested.'

'I'm sorry, there is nothing I can do for you. 1989.' He says the date like it is the dark ages.

'I fully understand the—'

'1989.' He stands, dismissing her. She does not catch his eye; instead she begins her story.

'I was visited by the police a few days ago. My daughter's case falls into some criteria for re-opening her file.'

He flicks his eyes to the clock behind her head, makes some internal calculation, and nods slowly. 'Yes, cold cases are being reviewed systematically,' he stops and looks like he's choosing his words carefully. 'It's purely evidence-based, so that would indicate that there was some kind of sample taken at the time.'

'Exactly.' She fishes in her pocket, pulls out a notebook and reads from it: 'Fluid samples taken and clothing samples retained.'

She closes the book again. 'That's what he said, but it made no sense. I saw the notes, back then, and I was sure there were no—'

'A police officer told you all this?'

She nods.

'I'm surprised they were so… candid.'

'I was insistent.'

He looks at her, and his brow furrows. 'Not a good sign,' Patty thinks.

'I still don't think I can be of any help, Mrs Lancing.'

Patty can feel the shake. A vibration runs through her and down the chair to the floor. She clenches her hands and feels the nails cut into her palm, but they are too bitten-down to draw blood.

'Could I have a glass of water, please?'

He looks as if he is about to say no, then nods and leaves the room. Her head swims as though she might pass out. She takes one of the pills from her bag and places it on her tongue. He returns with a glass of water. It has ice and a slice of lemon; she almost laughs. She manages a polite 'Thank you'. He looks concerned. Patty knows she must have turned white, like a ghost.

'Are you?'

'Fine. I'm fine. Please.'

'To be honest, Mrs Lancing, the samples taken in the eighties will be no good now for any kind of analysis. Procedure back then was…' he whistles through his teeth, 'neanderthal.'

'But there have been successes, with Low Copy Number analysis. Some of those samples date as far back as 1981.'

'You?'

'I did some research.'

She doesn't tell him she has barely slept in four days, reading and rereading a hundred case studies.

'Hmm.' He nods, drumming his fingers on the desk. 'That's true but...' He pauses. 'In 1989 you really needed to have had a forward-thinking officer at the crime scene for any samples to be viable today. Twenty years...'

'But it's possible?' She is strong, not needy or desperate.

'It isn't beyond the realms of possibility,' he says carefully. 'It's not inconceivable that a DNA profile could be produced from the sample.' He frowns. 'If – and I cannot stress strongly enough – *if* it were cleanly taken and well stored.'

'Then it could be matched on the police DNA database?'

'Potentially, *potentially* it could be matched with DNA previously taken.' He shakes his head. 'But there are big *ifs* in the mix.'

'I see.'

She closes her eyes. 'I must not get my hopes up,' she thinks.

'But hope is the only thing keeping you alive.' Jim-in-the-head says.

Keyson pulls a small notebook from a desk drawer and takes a pen from his pocket. 'Were you given any kind of timeline on the review?'

Patty nods slowly. 'He said it could be four years.'

Keyson stabs the pen into the notebook. 'Okay, so it's a grade two case.'

'Grade two?'

'Grade two or priority two cases. Firstly, there's no one being held in custody for a crime, so there's no potential miscarriage of justice to address. Secondly, there's no indication of a link to another murder or serious crime – those cases are priority one. Otherwise, where there's the potential to solve a cold case, those are graded priority two.'

He smiles and knocks back the last mouthful of his tea.

'So my daughter's killer could be identified?'

'Without access to the case notes I couldn't comment.'

'But a sample exists, a sample of DNA that could identify her murderer?'

'Patricia, can I call you Patricia?' He doesn't wait for her reply. 'I cannot, in all my experience, hold out any hope that a sample taken from your daughter would shed any light upon the identity of her killer. In 1989 no police investigation could analyse a forensic sample and cross-match it with a DNA database. Now they can. It's an enormous advance. And yet...' He sees the hope in her. 'Perhaps, in another four years...'

'Dr Keyson, I don't have four years. I'm dying. I have cancer.' She had not rehearsed the lie. She hadn't even consciously decided she would lie. But she realises she will do anything. 'I can't wait for the police. I have waited over twenty years already and cannot continue. I will not be here in four years.'

'I'm...'

'DS Bevans made it seem—'

'Tom Bevans?'

'Yes. You know him?'

'He's a senior officer. The head of Operation Ares.'

'Yes.'

'He personally gave you this information?'

'Yes. He has been involved from the start – with Dani's murder.'

'Dani?'

'My daughter. Danielle.'

'Your daughter is Dani – and she was murdered in London.'

'No. No she was killed in Durham. She was a student there.'

'Durham.' Patty can see the cogs churn in his head. Then he swings himself off the desk and walks behind it. Something in him has changed, his eyes no longer sympathetic, instead they burn with intelligence.

'Let's start from the beginning.'

INTERMISSION FIVE

Monday 20 February 1984

Downstairs is a heaving mass of bodies, writhing like worms in mud. Dry-ice, cigarette smoke and sweat curl up and fill the air. Upstairs, the seating makes it more organised but still bodies bounce and jerk to the pounding rhythm. All is dark except for dim green exit signs and the strobe lights on stage, which catch the band in frozen image after image. Tom feels car sick. Nic Fiend wails into the darkness.

The sea of sound is overpowering. Tom feels it in his body, working him like a marionette, pulling him this way and that as the band crash, guitar and drums pitched at incredible decibels. To compete, the singer has to screech ever higher and louder. They don't play like a team but like competitors racing to the finish. Exhilarating – but his head hurts.

Tom would rather be outside away from the smoke but he has to be in his seat: E5. It's the only place he knows for sure she'll be. The Banshees won't be on for ages. Alien Sex Fiend have just started and there are another two support bands he's never heard of. To be honest, he doesn't know much about Siouxsie Sioux – just that Dani loves her. And he loves Dani.

He would have preferred to have taken her to a movie. *Footloose* or *Police Academy* – they both sounded good. In a cinema they could hold hands and share popcorn while they watch. And after he could lean over and kiss her.

Yeah, right! Like that was going to appeal to Dani Lancing. No, Dani will love seeing the Banshees, and he will bask in that.

A final screech of guitar and vocal cord end their biggest number and the crowd scream and clap. He joins in, though his applause is a little lacklustre. As the band launch into another song, Tom turns round to scan the doors once more. She probably won't come until the first chord Robert Smith plays, but he can't help himself. He knows he should feign nonchalance, get caught up in the music. He should watch the bands. Even after she arrives and sits next to him, he should pretend not to know she's there until a song ends and he calmly notices her.

'Oh hi, Dani. This is cool.'

Except, even he knows that saying anything's *cool* would be romantic suicide. Maybe he should keep quiet. And not dance. Christ, it's really difficult – especially when his heart's flailing like Keith Moon on a bender.

Under the chair he has a hip flask for them, well, mostly for her, filled with vodka he's nicked from his mum's stash under the bed. When she arrives he should say nothing, just hand her the flask and go back to the music. That is wha—

Someone moves in next to him, into Dani's seat.

'No, that's ta—'

'Hi, Tom,' the girl shouts, smiling broadly.

'Tash?'

She leans across and pecks him on the cheek, then smiles a little flirtatiously. She's a girl from their class, not someone he knows well. She's pretty with a very sharp nose. He's only ever seen her in glasses before, but she must be wearing contact lenses. Her hair seems glittery too. She has a lot of lipstick on; he thinks he must have a little kiss tattoo from her peck on his cheek.

'Good to see you, Tash. Someone else will be here in a minute though, that's her seat.'

'No. It's mine.' She waves the ticket stub at him. 'I bought it this afternoon off Dani Lancing.'

'Oh!'

'She said you'd be here. Said you'd look after me.' She smiles broadly. He pulls the hip flask from under his chair and passes it to her. She takes a chug from the flask, cut short as she coughs and splutters from the bite of the alcohol in her throat.

She laughs. 'Shit, Tom.'

Later he walks her home. His eardrums still throb and hum. Tash had loved the night. She'd danced, screamed and drunk the whole hip flask. Her face is deeply flushed and she walks with a pronounced sway. She hadn't been bad company, but Tom was deeply disappointed by the evening. He would have liked to have gone straight home to bed, pulled the covers up over his head and escaped into sleep. Not an option. He couldn't leave Tash to get home alone, could he? But he was a bit worried about her parents chasing him down the road, screaming that he'd got their darling daughter drunk.

They barely speak on the walk home. Tash doesn't mind; in fact it helps to build the mystique of this pale thin boy. She has just had one of the best nights of her life and is thinking this edgy young man has earned himself a reward. Just before they get to her road, she stops by a house with a large hedge. The house is dark and the closest streetlight is broken. It's almost black in that little part of London. She takes Tom's hand and pulls him towards her. She leans over and plants her mouth on his, her tongue pushing forward through his closed lips and into his mouth.

He kisses her back, eyes closed, imagining it's Dani. She tastes like vodka. Tash takes his hand and brings it up to her shirt. He cups her breast.

'Nice,' she says and kisses harder, her teeth nipping his lip. The little dab of pain breaks the spell – it isn't Dani. Tom takes his hand away from her breast and gently ends the kiss.

'We need to get you home,' he says and draws her out of the shadows, the way you might lead a toddler, and walks her home.

In a small grubby flat above a kebab shop on Streatham High Street, Dani lies on a sofa. There isn't much light in the flat. What there is shows the walls are covered in drawings, like some primitive cave. The smells of greasy roasting flesh fill the room, mingling cloyingly with a sweet incense of vanilla and sandalwood, both scents fighting against the heavy fug of dope smoke.

Dani tries to get up, off the sofa, but her body doesn't respond like it normally does. It's as if she's floating in treacle. Everything is disjointed. She tries to speak, but slurs, she understands nothing she hears. She feels the joint back at her lips, but she no longer has the ability to suck the smoke into her lungs. There is music from somewhere, plaintive and soulful, but she can't make out the lyrics.

Her beautiful art student takes a final draw on the joint and holds it there, looking down at the young woman almost comatose on his sofa. Then he leans forward, opens her mouth with thumb and finger, and blows the smoke in, watching it billow around her lips and then up into the air.

She feels the tug but is not sure what it is. Her jeans are pulled down and taken off. Then her knickers. She falls asleep.

SEVENTEEN

Monday 18 October 2010

A cheeseburger waddles past, waving a handful of flyers.

'Happy Meal?' it asks.

Patty looks blankly at it.

'Okay, have a good day,' it shrugs and ambles away to accost a large group of tourists. Patty turns to the restaurant and peers through the glass; she can see very little evidence of anyone inside feeling any joy. She pushes the door and goes in. The traffic sounds die behind her, to be replaced by the hubbub of twenty different languages fighting to be heard over the noise of deep-fat frying.

She spots Keyson immediately. He sits in the corner. Somehow he's folded his large frame into a garishly coloured booth that seems designed for toddlers. He looks like a giant in a fairy tale, made all the more surreal as he's surrounded by a group of yelping Japanese exchange students who crowd the tables around him. Patty takes a deep breath, as if about to dive underwater, then she steps forwards.

There is ketchup in the corner of his mouth, making him look a little like a vampire – eyes glazed over, sated by his gorging. Then he sees her and a genuine smile creases his face. She crosses the room, avoiding the mustard and BBQ landmines. He pulls his coat from the seat opposite and she slides into it.

'No trouble finding the place?' he asks.

'I used to work close by.'

'I'm giving evidence at the Old Bailey later, so it was a good option to meet here.' He slurps the last of his shake and dabs at his large mouth with a tiny serviette.

Then something shifts and a cloud crosses his face as he slips awkwardly into professional mode. He starts to say something but it's obliterated by a sudden cackle of Japanese. 'Where the hell is Godzilla when you need him?' Patty thinks.

'I missed that, can you repeat what you said?' she asks with annoyance and leans towards him close enough to smell the tang of gherkin and special sauce.

'There was a prime suspect in your daughter's case, did you know that?'

The world becomes silent. Around her, mouths from across the globe chew the cud of news from home: latest fashions, crazes, diets or plain who-fancies-who and what they did or didn't do. The world goes on around her, but nothing touches her consciousness. Nothing but Keyson's words.

'Prime suspect... no.'

Keyson nods sagely as if confirming some ground-breaking theory. 'The detective at the time seemed to feel there was a strong case. I'm reading between the lines, of course, but there was a partial print from your daughter's left hand on the boot of this man's car.'

He punches her hard, the lip is ripped by the teeth, blood vessels burst bleeding into soft tissue, the bruise blossoms like poppies on her cheek. The blow spins her, balance shifts and she falls sideways – her hand strikes the car just before her hip does. Slam! She is lifted off her feet for a fraction of a second as her head snaps back. Even six years of ballet can't keep her on her feet as she begins to fall. Her arms start to wave, trying to regain balance but it is too late, she is past the point of no return as she falls. In a second he is on her, punching her chest, face, shoulder, forehead – until all goes black.

'Patricia?' Keyson waves his hand in front of her face, bringing her back.

'Yes, yes, I'm… please, tell me the rest.'

He hesitates, seeming to be unsure of what to say next. 'There is also a sample of…' he stops and looks down to his notes.

'Tell me,' she holds her breath.

He coughs and, in a monotone, continues. 'Semen was recovered post-mortem. It may be adequate for testing.'

Patty gulps in air. 'That's wonderf—'

'But…' he cuts her dead, '… there is no sample from any suspect.'

'I don't fully understand what—'

'It means that when the police get around to your daughter's case they can profile the DNA and check it against the national database.'

'And that's over five million people.'

'Exactly. And you might be lucky and find that the killer is in there.'

'But…'

'The *but* is that your prime suspect may not be in the database – won't be, unless he's had a DNA sample taken for another reason.'

Patty nods. She feels the hopelessness spreading around her like ink in water.

'And…' he shakes his head, 'I spoke to someone at the DNA database. Your man was right – it will be at least four years before your daughter's case is opened. I even told them you might be dead before then. They didn't care.'

Patty wants to roll into a ball. Tom was right: she shouldn't have got her hopes up. 'Is there anything we can do?'

'Well...' he leans in closer to her. 'I have a contact.' He stops and chews his lip.

The penny drops; now she understands why they've met here and not at Keyson's office. She's seen men act like this many times, when they had information to sell to the newsroom. This is about a bribe.

His voice drops as low as it can possibly go. 'I can get your daughter's case file. That would include all samples.'

'But...'

'You're right, there is a big but. Two big buts. The first is that I would need a pretty hefty amount of money to secure this.'

'How much?'

'Ten thousand pounds. That's for my contact, you understand.'

She nods. 'The second but?'

'Do this – get the evidence illegally – and it will destroy any case against the killer.'

'But if the sample matches?'

'Doesn't matter. If the evidence is out of police control, even for a second, it's useless.'

'But with the DNA match I could prove it was him, show the results to the news.'

'You could. But he'd still have to give a DNA sample voluntarily. And the publicity would mean he could never be charged. Any legal case would be impossible. You'd never get justice through the courts.'

'Justice...' She wants to laugh at such an outmoded concept. Funny guy. 'I'll get you the money, Dr Keyson. Thank you.'

She stands and holds out her hand, like shaking on the promise of a new job or the price of a house.

'I'll be in touch,' he tells her.

'Soon,' she says. 'Soon I hope.' She turns and leaves.

He watches her walk to the door. She is swallowed up by the maelstrom of London life. Then he smiles.

INTERMISSION SIX

Friday 4 May 1984

Dani holds Tom's hand tight, almost crushing it. He doesn't mind. They don't speak, there's nothing to say. It was all said last night when she lay on his bed and told him the story.

'I can't tell them, I can't, Tom. They'll be so disappointed in me – I am so fucking stupid.'

'Dan—'

'Don't, Tom. I'm an idiot, a comedy stereotype: teenage and pregnant. A fucking joke... a joke.' She finishes with a tiny voice, then lies her head back on his pillow and sobs.

The injustice burns in Tom's stomach like poison. He's never felt anger like this, sulphuric in his veins. He wants to run out into the night and kill him, to beat him to a pulp. Except he needs to stay here, with her, to hold her and tell her it will be okay. Tell her that he loves her. But he does neither. Instead, he sits and watches as the girl he loves falls apart on his bed.

Even as Dani lies there crying, she knows it's unfair on poor Tom; she feels so ashamed of how she has treated him. She can't tell him that it happened on the night she should have been with him at the concert. Of course, had she have been there, she would never have been in this state. She feels so lost, alone and stupid. She loves her parents, but could never tell them what she has done. They would help her, of course. They would love her, of course, but they would always look at her with such disappointment. Her mum would hold it over her – in some weird way Dani thought Patty might be pleased. It would prove for ever that her daughter doesn't have the strength, the moral purpose, the drive that she had. And her dad... oh, her dad. He adores her and she could not bear to watch the disappointment, even pity, spread across his face for the first time in her life. She could not, would not, be less than the perfect daughter for them.

'So will you come with me tomorrow?' she asks Tom.

'Of course. I'll always be there when you need me.'

'Thank you,' she says as she takes his hand and squeezes it.

The appointment was made through rape crisis to make sure her parents would not find out the truth.

When they first arrive at the clinic they are led into a private room. The nurse asks Dani to come in alone but she refuses, wanting Tom to be allowed in. The nurse eyes him with distrust. She obviously wants to make sure this is not coerced; she assumes Tom is the father... father? Hardly a father. Inseminator, perhaps?

Tom blushes under her gaze. He is not the man who has done this – but inside, to his shame, he can't help but think that he would give anything to have been the one who had begun a life inside Danielle Lancing. And he hopes that one day he will, when they are married.

After Dani gives her details she's examined. This time Tom stays the other side of the curtain. Then they are both asked to wait.

They sit with four other pregnant teens – two of them are obviously with their mothers, all tearful. One teen sits alone, her back rigid, her head held high. The last has fourteen-month-old twins, who play with Lego on the floor. She looks like the devil is at her heels.

They wait for two hours until Dani is called. She smiles weakly at Tom when finally it's her turn.

'I'll be here when you come round,' he says.

'I know you will. You're my Galahad,' and she kisses him on the cheek. There is no passion, but for Tom it's the best kiss of his life: there will never be another to beat it. Then she turns and follows the nurse.

An hour later he's called to see her in the recovery room. She sits up in bed wearing one of those awful gowns that no one can be glamorous in. Dani sits drinking tea that is so sweet it makes her grimace with every sip. She looks incredibly pale. Tom thinks her more beautiful than anything he has ever seen.

'I can go any time. I just need to get my clothes on.'

He nods. 'I'll go and call a cab.'

'I can get the bus.'

He shakes his head, taking charge, possibly for the first time in his life.

'No. You get dressed and I'll get a cab.'

She holds onto his arm as they walk down the front steps. The cab sits there, the diesel engine chugging, ticking the clock round. Tom had raided his room – the large Roses chocolate jar and his Star Wars pencil case had been full of change. Now about thirty pounds in coins weighs down his backpack. He hopes the cabby won't make a scene about being paid in shrapnel.

They get inside and Tom reels off Dani's address but she corrects him and instead gives Tom's. She looks at him, her eyes pleading. He nods. Then the cab wheels away.

They sit on the back seat and Dani slides sideways and lays her head on his lap. Tom watches the cabby tilt his mirror down so he can see if any funny business is going on in the back. Tom strokes her hair and tries not to get an erection.

At the end of the journey he pays the fare. He gives a decent tip to stop any complaint.

Then Dani laces her arms around him and he helps her up to his room. He puts her into his bed, fully clothed, and she falls asleep. He sits in a chair and watches her.

At about 9 p.m. she wakes and asks for water. Then she gets up and uses the phone, calling home to tell them she's staying the night with a friend. Her dad answers, he wants more details, but she tells him all is fine, that she's tired and is going straight to bed. He isn't pleased but says 'okay'. Then she goes back to Tom's room, strips to her underwear, gets into his bed and sleeps for another eighteen hours.

When she finally awakes she finds him sitting in an armchair by the bed, watching over her. She holds her hand out to him and pulls him onto the bed with her. They spoon together though she is under the sheets and he on top of them.

'Thank you,' she says softly to the back of his head. He tries to turn but she stops him. She likes him to be close but doesn't want him to see her.

'I want to say something… not to you, exactly, maybe like a New Year's resolution. I think I just have to say it to get it out there.'

'Okay.'

'I won't ever do that again.'

He stays silent, waiting to hear if there's more.

'I don't know how I feel about kids, I… I'm not sure my mum's the best role model for balancing a career and motherhood. But I

142

didn't take care of myself and... and look at the mess I got myself in. I need to look out, think – not just jump at things for the challenge, to see what happens.'

Tom nods but doesn't really understand. His own desire is so focused on Dani that it skews his natural inquisitiveness. He notices other women, especially their breasts and bums, but always in comparison with Dani. For him there is no one else.

'I need to get my shit together,' she says, forcing a smile that's more like a grimace.

They lie there for a while and then Dani sighs, gives him a last squeeze and gets up to face the world again.

EIGHTEEN

Thursday 21 October 2010

The next few days Patty spends in some kind of limbo. Waiting. Waiting for news from Keyson. Waiting for the name of her daughter's murderer and, of course, considering how she might end another human being's life. Planning a killing. Really anticipating, imagining, and relishing the taking of his final breath. Both in her waking life and in sleep, she is consumed by a bloodlust that has lain coiled around her heart for twenty years and is now ready to strike.

She has become an early riser. Not because she goes to bed early – she doesn't – but because she's weaned herself from the need for sleep. Four hours is all she's needed for many years. Even that seems a luxury now, as she rises at five o'clock after just three hours of sleep. But she wakes refreshed, buzzing with adrenalin. She's moved the telephone next to her bed and during the day walks around the house with it in her pocket, desperate not to miss the call from Keyson. She still leaves the house to run but she's gone for only an hour and takes her mobile. When she returns, she checks the answering machine and calls the talking clock to make sure the phone has no fault. She waits.

She waits for four days and three hours. Then the phone rings. They speak for a few seconds. That afternoon, she goes to her bank and withdraws the money. She is surprised at how small ten thousand pounds is, just a paper bag about the size of a sandwich.

Friday 22 October 2010

Patty drives into the NCP car park and all the way to the top level. That high, it's almost totally empty. She parks in the outer rows looking out over the Thames. It's a crisp autumn day with barely a cloud in the sky. The sun is bright, but not warm. She stands on the edge of the parapet and looks out. If she leans forward and cranes her neck out, she can see down the river to St Paul's. The majesty of it takes her breath away and for a moment makes her forget why she's there – what she will soon do – but just for a second.

She watches boats motor along the Thames, mostly tourists boarding in the shadow of Parliament and going downriver. So many years since she has done anything like that – enjoyed the city she had once loved so much. She and Jim used... oh what good will that do? The past is buried, burned black, and should not be dug up. Instead, she thinks once again about how his filth can be examined on a cellular level. How each cell bears his signature; his blood and piss and seed all spell his name and will prove his guilt. Then, once it is proven beyond doubt, she will kill him.

She wades in her daydreams for about ten minutes before another car drives up the ramp. Keyson is at the wheel. He's alone. She feels inside her coat once again to make sure the money's still there. She realises she's enjoying the cloak-and-dagger aspect. Keyson parks his car and gets out; he wears a World-War-Two-style trench coat, slightly turned up at the neck. In his hands is a metal box.

'Mrs Lancing,' he nods in greeting, then tips his head to indicate the box. 'This is the sample.' He holds it gingerly. He hands it to her as if it might explode. She takes it with her fingertips. He hands her a wad of paper.

'These are the instructions on how to store the sample. You need to get it home and in your freezer quickly. Did you prepare it like I said?'

She nods. 'I did everything like you said.'

She had stripped all the food out and taken it to a soup kitchen rather than throw it away. Then she'd bleached the interior and lowered the temperature to minus eight degrees.

'Good. That's good.' He puts an envelope on top of the sample box in her hands, then reaches into his inside coat pocket and pulls out a file folded in half. 'These are the case notes.'

He places those on the box too. Then he grins at her. 'It's a beautiful day and hopefully we'll have a really nice week. Anything planned for the weekend?'

She ignores the question. Instead she walks to her car and carefully places the box on the passenger seat. From her pocket she takes the brown paper bag and hands it to him.

'Thank you. I hope you find what you're looking for,' he says, offering his enormous hand for her to shake. She reaches up to him and lets him squeeze her fingers once. She watches him drive away and then she collapses.

❄

She wakes some time later, freezing. She can feel foam fleck her lips. She has rolled herself half under her car, probably had a small seizure. She slowly rolls onto her side and then gets up, her joints straining and her teeth beginning to chatter. Her vision swims slightly, her focus shifting, not too much but enough to worry her. She has barely eaten in three days.

'Get your bloody act together, Patricia,' she hisses to herself. She gets into the car and starts it up. No heat yet.

In her kitchen she stands by the sink and eats a packet of biscuits from her almost bare cupboard. She finishes them and forces herself to drink a large glass of water. Then she turns to the box. She tears the security tape from around it and takes out one small, squat jar. There is a label on the outside; the ink is faded and the paper dried-out from twenty years in a fridge. The faded and stained label around the jar reads: 'Case HTR234y678d: Danielle Lancing. Multiple rape and Murder. 7 February 1989. Sample: semen from vagina recovered post-mortem'.

She places the jar in the freezer and closes the door.

Patty switches on the lights and settles into an armchair, unfolds the document wallet and, as if curling up to read a good book, she begins. After half an hour she stops. Her heart is beating triple time. He had been right, Dr Keyson. The officer in charge had felt there was a very strong case against this man, this prime suspect. He had been a client at the health club Dani had temped at in the summer after her first year at university. He'd been linked to her during a routine questioning of her colleagues. One of them had said that he'd given Dani a lift home once. He'd denied this, but his car was checked and hair, which seemed to match hers, was found on a jacket on the backseat and a partial print was found on the boot. That had been enough to question him but no further link could be made. He'd argued that she could have just been walking through the car park and touched his car, and her hair was similar to his own daughter's and it was probably hers. No charge could be brought. He was top of the suspect list for months and eventually the investigation petered out.

She reads the report again and again, at first becoming angry that the investigation had failed to make the final link: they let the bastard go. But soon the anger seeps away and is replaced by a steely calm as she settles into the knowledge of what will happen now. His name is here in black and white: Duncan Cobhurn.

When Patty finally looks at her watch, it is 3 a.m. She should sleep, but sleep's for the dead. Now it's time to plan.

Saturday 23 October 2010

Patty finds him online. She ignores an actor Duncan Cobhurn, who's a Winston Churchill look-a-like, and there's a guy who values property for some huge investment bank but he's too young. She also disregards the evangelical preacher from Arkansas who believes God will produce a fireball that will purge the Earth of all homosexuals in 2020. But there's a story from 2008 in the *Durham Chronicle*: 'Local businessman runs for mayor'.

She clicks on it. Sixty-three-year-old Duncan Cobhurn, owner of the successful Porto Pronto chain of Mediterranean furniture design shops, is running for office. Blah blah blah... it's him. Must be. A later story shows he lost the election; some kind of smear campaign was blamed. Another story about him has a picture; she clicks on it. The grain makes it hard to see details, but that is her Duncan Cobhurn. He's shaking some teenager's hand and handing over a cheque, blood money probably. He reminds Patty a little of Bob Hoskins and... Jim. A short, squat Jim.

She finds another photo from election night. He's with his wife Audrey and their daughter Lorraine. Patty examines the daughter – she doesn't look a bit like Dani, but they must be about the same age. If Dani had been allowed to live, they would be about the same age. Patty can feel the blood around her heart boil. She googles Porto Pronto and finds the website. They open at nine. She calls at 8.50 a.m. and lets the phone ring a long time before a slightly distracted receptionist answers.

'Por—'

'Is Duncan there?' she asks in as friendly and girly a voice as she can manage.

'Sorry no, we don't actually open till—'

'Do you have the authority to book me an appointment with him?'

'I—'

'We're old friends. I'm just in from Seville. My time is pretty limited. I'm about to jump on a train, I only have a minute or so.'

'Okay. Erm, let me see. Could you see him…? This week is pretty bad, he's in Lisbon…'

'Oh, is he already there?' Patty asks as nonchalantly as she can.

'No, he's in London today. He flies out from Heathrow Monday morning. So you could see him next Monday, maybe?'

'I'm gone then. Oh dear… I really wanted to see him, it's been absolutely ages… well, it will have to be next time. Or maybe… Lisbon, does he fly there often? I have a holiday home there, you see.'

'Well…' the receptionist hesitates.

'Maybe I'll call Audrey instead and try to see her.' Patty tries to make it casual, but planting the wife's name works a treat.

'Well, he flies to Lisbon every month, mostly the last Monday so…'

'Oh you have been so helpful. Tell me, sweetheart, what's your name, I must tell Duncan how wonderful you've been.'

'Greta, it's Greta.'

*

She calls back at 12.20, recognises Greta's voice immediately and hangs up. At 1.10, however, there's another receptionist.

'Greta, please.' Patty tries to sound her most authoritative.

'Greta's on lunch. Can I help?'

'Oh hell. Well, I bloody hope you can help. It's Monarch travel. Our computer's gone mental and I know your boss is flying Monday morning out of Heathrow.'

'That's right. Lisbon.'

'Well, we've got no records available so I've no idea if he needs a cab...'

'No he's driving himself. He leaves it in the long-term there.'

She rolls the dice. 'And it's the 9.20 a.m. BA flight?'

'That's the one, and back on Friday morning.'

Patty quickly scans the BA printout of flights to Lisbon. 'The 11.40 coming back.'

'That's it.'

'Lovely, my darling. All right, let's hope the IT department can get their fingers out of their arses long enough to get us back online.'

'Good luck,' she says, which makes Patty smile.

*

Monday 25 October 2010

Patty gets up at 4 a.m. and grabs a bucket of mud from the garden. She smears it all over the car, making sure to obscure the number plate. Then she gets dressed in clothes from the back of her wardrobe that she hasn't worn in years. They come from an era when she had curves and filled them – perfectly, according to Jim. Now they hang like tents. She should have given them to charity but they have a sentimental pull. The old life.

She completes the ensemble with a scarf, hat and sunglasses. In the mirror she cannot recognise herself. Then she drives to Heathrow.

She arrives at 6.30 a.m. and parks in the long-stay car park. She reasons that if he uses it often he must know exactly where the shuttle picks up passengers, so parks close to that. The spot is directly below a CCTV camera, which she hopes will make it harder to view her. It's all automated so there is no actual person in the car park to notice that she's just waiting. Only cameras, like so much of England now.

She gets out of the car and goes into a dumbshow, looking angrily at the car and then opening the bonnet. She swears, stamps her foot and then calls someone on her phone. If a security guard shows up she'll tell them she's broken down and is waiting for the RAC.

Then she gets back inside and settles down to wait for Duncan Cobhurn.

She has almost given up hope when, finally, at 7.45 he arrives. He speeds into a spot and leaps out looking flustered. He grabs a pull-along suitcase from the back seat and runs to the shuttle stop. Her heart is pounding. She hasn't thought about what to do now. She can see the shuttle come through the gate and make its way slowly to the stop. Should she get on the shuttle too? She's paralysed. She watches him jump on the little bus, which then trundles away to the terminal. Once it's out of sight, she opens her car door, swings her head out and vomits violently.

Thursday 16–Friday 17 December 2010

She takes a train out to a town she's never been to before. She only carries cash with her; no cards, no ID. She doesn't use her Oyster card. In charity shops she buys two outfits. She also gets a pair of large sunglasses, a hat and a wig. In a pharmacy she buys a bright lipstick, a shade she would not normally be seen dead in. At a hardware store she adds two rolls of gaffer tape and a small rubber ball.

She finds a park that has a public toilet that's reasonably clean and has no attendant. Inside she changes into one of the suits and, in the cracked mirror, applies the lipstick. The sunglasses and hat complete her transformation. She rides a bus out to an address she'd found the previous day in *Loot*. There, from a very friendly but highly suspect man called Dave, she buys a car for cash. No log book – no questions. She drives the car home and parks it in her garage. Her own car is parked on the street. She does the trick with the mud again until it is impossible to see even the make of car. Then she showers and dresses in the second outfit. She takes the Tube out to Amersham, reasonably close to the airport but not right there. She walks to the hotel she's chosen. She has stayed there three times already, each time checking in as Joyce Adams and paying the bill with cash. She pays for three nights, telling the bored clerk she's on business and is eight time zones out – she does not want anyone disturbing her so she can sleep. No room service, no cleaning. She needs nothing.

In the room she sits and watches TV for two hours. After that she turns off the TV and leaves the room as quietly as possible. She places the DO NOT DISTURB sign on the door and takes the lift down to the parking area. She saunters through as if her car is just at the end of the row... but walks all the way out to the street. She sees no one. From there she walks back to the Tube station and retraces her steps home. She gets back at midnight as Friday slides into being. Today is the day. She does not sleep.

At 8 a.m. it is time for her to get ready. She dresses in the second outfit she bought yesterday. She puts on the wig and threads the sunglasses into it, then applies the unnaturally bright lipstick and looks in the mirror. A stranger stares out. She logs onto the Heathrow site to see the flight arriving from Lisbon at 11.40 a.m. It's in the air but the weather report is poor and deteriorating. She opens her bag and checks the contents: money in Ziploc bag, the hypodermic and drug vial, the tape, the ball, a long knife. In the hall is a folded wheelchair to put in the car. It is time to go.

It cost £500 to have the CCTV put out of action in the long-term car park. That had been Patty's main concern right from that first morning she watched Cobhurn get on the shuttle. She had known then that, with luck, the long-term parking was where she would kidnap him from. She had to put herself in the mind of the police. Once Cobhurn was reported missing they would retrace his steps. They would find that he landed and took the shuttle, and they were bound to look at CCTV footage from the car park. She called someone on a London paper; she'd known him years before when he was just a cub reporter. Now he runs the crime desk. She asked him for a snitch, pretended to be working on a book of true crime. He gave her a name and that name gave her another. After five degrees of separation Patty had some kid who had twelve ASBOs ranging from tagging his school gym to exploding garden gnomes in the local shopping mall. She left his money and instructions in a Hello Kitty bag on a park swing, a few days before she planned to kidnap Cobhurn. At 10 p.m. on Thursday 16 December he shot the head off every camera in the car park. Money well spent.

She arrives at 10.30 a.m. and as she waits the first snow begins. She watches the flakes – their beauty mesmerises her and yet she curses them. As the storm thickens she realises that very few planes are landing. She had not factored in God.

After two hours of sitting she cannot stay in the car any longer and gets out, feeling the snow crunch beneath her feet.

'There is something very Zen about watching snowflakes tumble through space as you turn to ice yourself,' she thinks, slowly accepting the idea that he will not be arriving – that his plane had been grounded somewhere or redirected to another airport.

'If I have to wait I will.' She knows she must get him. And something keeps her there, in that cold parking lot, until the sounds of the shuttle break the dead silence.

She sees him alight and struggle forward with his golf clubs and little pull-along case. She steals back to her car; it must be timed perfectly. He waddles forwards, dragging his case and bouncing the club bag. Finally he gets to his car and throws his bags down in anger as he realises what has happened. She must time this just right. She knows that. She eases out of her parking space and slowly moves towards him just pulling alongside as he gets out his phone. She winds her window down and shouts:

'Are you okay?'

He looks over at her; she can see he's shaking with cold and anger. 'Some fuckers have slashed my tyres.'

'Bastards. Kids today see something they want – a beautiful car – and they just have to wreck it,' she nods sadly.

'If I could get my hands on 'em, I'd wring their fucking necks.'

Patty smiles. 'Do you want a lift back to the terminal? You could get security to call a repair truck or something.'

He starts to shake his head but stops. Wind whisks freezing flakes into his face and he looks down at what he's wearing.

'Yeah.' He nods. 'Thank you. Yeah.'

Patty gives him her most dazzling smile, then flips open the boot. He walks around to it and throws his bag and clubs in.

'Be careful of the wheelchair,' she shouts back to him.

He closes the boot and gets in beside her.

'I really do ap—'

'Seatbelt, please,' she interrupts.

And as he reaches over to find it, she slides the hypodermic into his neck and pushes the plunger home. He jerks away, but not far enough and she manages to push the plunger all the way home. He looks at her, incredulous, his lips try to form a word, an expletive – *fuckers* – but the syllables crumble, soundless, and then he does too.

She shoves him back in the seat and clips the belt home. Done.

Her first stop is a skip she'd noticed on the drive there. She puts gloves on and then pulls out his case and clubs and throws them inside. She slides him out of his jacket and throws that in too, including his wallet and ID. Then she drives directly to the hotel, parking in the deepest recess of the underground car park. There is nobody else about. She walks to the back of the car and takes out the wheelchair. She unfolds it, and then, with every ounce of her strength, manages to manoeuvre his body into it and strap him in. She wheels him to the service lift and they go up to level two. Her room is close to the lift. She has the key ready. Luck is with her; there is no one around. She opens the door and wheels him in.

She looks around at the room. It is exactly as she left it the night before. No one has been in. She turns on the TV and then turns to the man in the wheelchair. The man she has abducted.

From her bag she pulls one of the thick rolls of gaffer tape. She pulls at it and it makes a sound like fabric ripping – she loves that sound. Then she begins to wind the tape around him, like a snake coiling its prey.

She knows what she is about to do. She will restrain him so that there is no chance he can escape or call out. Then she will take a sample of his blood. She has already delivered the semen sample from the killer to a private lab in the city. Once she has his blood sample they will compare the two and when they match them – proving his guilt – she will return to this hotel room and then will cause him pain before she takes his life. After that there is probably nothing. Finally, after more than twenty years of waiting, Patricia Lancing takes a knife and cuts his flesh.

INTERMISSION SEVEN

Friday 9 January 1981

Patty looks at her watch: 5 a.m. Christ, she's bored. She sits alone in her battered green Cortina with just her nan's old Thermos, Trebor mints, a Zippo and two packs of B&H for company. She tries to stretch, but it's a little car. She'd like to get out and walk around but she's on surveillance and it's really not good to get spotted by a nosy neighbour. Instead she lights a cigarette and smokes it like her granddad showed her – wrapped inside his hand like he did in the trenches. She can't open the window and so the small car fills with smoke, nice.

She wonders, for the thousandth time, if this is all a waste. An anonymous tip-off to the crime desk and she beats five boozy hacks, who all think the story should be theirs, and scuttles up to Leeds. This isn't how it should happen. This is not investigative journalism – it's a fucking feeding frenzy. Journalists calling in favours, throwing out back-handers, threatening ponces, pressuring whores – anything and everything to get an angle on him – and Patty is raking through shit with the best of them. She is the best of them, she knows she is. It just pisses her off that she has to work so hard to get those bastards to see it, and that she has to keep proving it. But this one would set it in stone – that she was the equal of any man. The Holy Grail of blood and murder, Sonia Sutcliffe. The police had taken her into protective custody at first, but they let her go, to 'be with relatives' a couple of days later and – gone. No statement, nothing. Nobody knows where she is or who she is, this woman who married a monster, who might be a monster. That's why Patty's sitting, desperate for a pee, in a cramped smoky car all night. The thought of interviewing a female killer – multiple killer of women, a modern day Bonnie Parker – well, it makes her heart soar. This was what she went into crime reporting for: to cut open the belly and see the filth and shit. To shine a spotlight into the corners and watch the spiders and cockroaches run. That is the only way she can see it getting better.

'This is such a mind-numbing waste of time,' she thinks, just as the front door shoots open. Three men come out, walking quickly – they're huge. A fourth figure emerges, much smaller – a woman. The men form a rugby scrum around her. From somewhere, behind Patty, there's the sound of an engine turning over.

'Fuck.' She's out of her car in a second, running to the house. She'd parked across the street but they must have known she was there.

The three goons walk quickly and are at the gate just seconds after Patty – the front two stretch out enormous hands. The third, comically, is trying to throw a blanket over the woman in the centre, who shoves it back at him.

'I have no camera,' Patty shouts, holding her hands up in the air like it's a robbery.

The blanket is thrown to the ground as the front two men separate, revealing Sonia Sutcliffe.

'Sonia,' Patty calls. 'I'm on my own. I just want to talk; hear your side.'

Sonia steps out onto the pavement and Patty moves to bar her way. The front two men hesitate, unsure how to treat a woman reporter with no camera.

'Your words, Sonia, not some hatchet job. That's all, I promise. My name's Patricia Lancing.' Patty holds out her hand.

Sonia looks down at the outstretched fingers – then up into her face. For a moment she thinks she sees Sonia's eyes soften – but there is no trust. Patty sees a woman who has heard too many promises that turned out to be lies. Sonia breaks the contact, turns and moves forwards. A car screeches into the kerb. Patty tries to follow but a giant hand holds her shoulder.

'There's big money in it, for your story,' Patty shouts after her – desperate to keep her there. Sonia doesn't look back. The car door opens and she gets in, followed by the three men.

'Sonia, please tell me. How could you not know? Sonia, how do you live with a monster? How do you live with yourself?'

The car speeds off. It had all taken no more than a minute.

'Bollocks.'

She stands there, feeling the cold creep into her bones. Finally she gets back into her Cortina to finish the Thermos of lukewarm coffee and have a cigarette. She sits in the driver's seat and goes over the encounter again and again. There was no interview, no story – but there was something. Sonia could have gone out the back way and avoided any confrontation, but she didn't. She wanted to walk tall, not skulk away. That said a lot about her, but was that a story? It certainly wasn't news. Patty finishes the cigarette and then has two more while she thinks. She should drive home. She could be there for the afternoon – but that makes the trip a waste and she wants a story.

She drives to the hotel she'd booked. The room's basic – it smells of stale smoke and dust. The overhead light doesn't work; she has to turn on the bathroom light and use a shoe to hold the door open. The only window is painted shut. The saving grace is that the water is scalding hot. She runs a deep steamy bath and lies there for over an hour, smoking the rest of the pack and turning into a giant prune. The towel looks disgusting, so she drips dry on the carpet. She pulls back the sheets – they look okay. She falls into the bed naked and grabs a few hours' sleep.

It's 11 a.m. when she wakes. She has to be out of the room in an hour so she dresses quickly and goes down to the breakfast room. There's no food but she does manage to get a black coffee out of a young Italian girl. Deep in her notebook she finds a phone number she jotted down some months before. A Bradford number. It's the home phone of the mother of one of the victims. No reply for quite some time but Patty is patient. She lets it ring and ring. Finally a woman answers dozily and agrees to meet.

'Hello. Hello. We spoke on the telephone earlier,' Patty shouts through the letterbox. There is no reply. Patty waits a minute before trying again.

'You said I should come. Patricia, my name's Patricia Lancing.'

She can't see anything inside the flat but she can wait. She stands back from the door and turns to look out over the balcony. She's on the third floor of a block of flats where four identical squat blocks face each other with a courtyard below. To one side there is an area of grass and some rotating clothes dryers but they're naked, much too cold and wet for clothes to dry. The sky is grey, one of those English days where it won't ever get properly light, merely go from dark to grey to dark again. Kids are running about in the courtyard.

It takes two cigarettes and another round of pounding on the door before a bolt snaps back, a chain scrapes and the door opens. The woman doesn't step out onto the balcony, merely beckons Patty inside with a wave of the hand. As she walks in, Patty can feel eyes on her from all directions. Patty follows the hand into the living room and it points to the sofa.

'Tea?' the woman asks over her shoulder as she walks into the kitchen.

'I'd love some,' Patty replies, even though she hates the industrial-strength tea they always serve in the north.

While the woman makes a pot, Patty looks around the room. It's pretty bare. On the walls she can see the tell-tale signs of pictures having been removed. Every family picture has been taken down. Destroyed, or stored away for a time when seeing them won't cause such pain?

The woman enters with a small tray – two mugs of tea and a little plate of biscuits. She pulls out a table from a nest and puts Patty's tea and the biscuits next to her, before sitting in an armchair across the room, cradling her tea in her hands. Patty's notes say this woman is forty-seven but she looks sixty-five. Her hair has fallen out in clumps all over her head. Her fingertips are speckled with dried blood where the nails have been shredded.

'Thank you for agreeing to see me.' Patty smiles.

The mother says nothing but their eyes meet. All Patty can see in them is helplessness. The air swims with pine air freshener and Patty feels a little light-headed.

'I'm not here to drag up awful memories.'

'Me memories ain't bad. They're all I've got now,' the mother says in a voice that seems both raw and soft at the same time.

'Tell me something wonderful, a great memory of the two of you.'

The woman closes her eyes for a second, her forehead wrinkles.

'She weren't a bad girl. I know some a me neighbours'll say different, but I had owt trouble. She were only seventeen.' Her eyes glisten.

'Her father?'

The woman frowns, as if she doesn't understand the question at first.

'Gone. Long gone. They're all gone.' She gazes into her tea. 'Tap.' She says suddenly.

Patty shakes her head, not understanding.

'She loved tap. Gene Kelly and Fred Astaire. Whenever there were one o' them films on we'd watch it. She 'ad the shoes. I got 'em for 'er – sixth birthday, I think. She 'ad tap every Saturday morning. I loved to watch 'er... that were a special time.'

Patty nods. She keeps nodding as the woman talks about her daughter, unfolds her box of memories. The mother talks for an hour.

'I 'ave to go to church now. I go every day. Will youse come too?'

They leave the council flat and walk down the stairs and across the courtyard, both silent. In the air are the sounds of a baby crying, and from somewhere far-off, a dog howling. The estate is only about twenty years old, but it already looks shabby and unloved. They walk through the courtyard and into a small alleyway, which Patty knows she would not walk down alone after dark. The alleyway leads into an identical courtyard, which leads to another scary alleyway. Through that they come to a small modern church, built as part of the estate.

Inside, the church is Spartan. There are pews that look more like the kind of stackable chairs you'd find in a school. No stained glass; in fact, there are only three small windows – mounted quite high so very little light can enter. The only decorations are tapestries that look machine woven, depicting the twelve stages of the cross. One is particularly harrowing – Jesus being stabbed by a centurion. It's in front of that image the two women stop. Patty stands, uncomfortable, while the grieving mother bows and crosses herself. Then she kneels and prays for her seventeen-year-old Lamb of God, slaughtered by Peter William Sutcliffe. Patty sits next to her, feeling like a fraud in the house of prayer.

They sit in silence for twenty minutes and then it's time to leave. Patty follows the mother out. While they were inside the light died; it's turned dark and bitterly cold.

'Thank you,' the mother says, throwing her arms around Patty, pulling her close, making Patty feel very claustrophobic. She lays her head on Patty's shoulder and a great sob convulses her.

'I am sorry for your—' Patty pauses. 'For your daughter. I'm sorry.'

The mother smiles a watery half smile before wearily heading back towards her flat. Patty stands outside the church for a while. She lights a cigarette, smokes it greedily all the way to the butt, and then heads back to her car for the long drive.

It's after midnight when she finally arrives home. Soon, after she left Bradford, she had felt a great pull, a real need to get back to Jim and Dani. Especially Dani. She realises with shame that she never did call her today, she really had meant to, but...

The house is quiet and dark. Once inside, she goes directly to Dani's room and pushes the door open. There her daughter lies, asleep on her side. Not dead, not lost, but at home with them. As soon as she sees her, Patty realises she has been nervous all the way home – scared she would not be there when she got back. She watches Dani sleep for a long time before she can tear herself away.

In the dark of their bedroom she puts her pyjamas on. Jim lies on her side of the bed but as she pulls back the covers he rolls over into the cold half, leaving her to snuggle into the warmth he'd just left.

'Did you speak to her?' he asks, his voice a little slurry from sleep.

'No, just a glimpse. She had three thugs. Spoke to the mother of one of the girls, though. Poor fucking woman. Heartbreaking.'

'I'm sure.' He rolls over to face her, blinking some of the sleepiness away.

'What about here, how'd it go?' Patty asks.

'I cooked a big lunch.'

'Love-struck pup come?'

'Of course Tom came. Good too, he does the dishes.'

'You don't think he seems a bit too interested?' She pauses. 'You know what I mean.'

'They're just friends.'

'He's here an awful lot.'

'I don't think he likes to go home. He likes Dani.'

'That's the problem.'

'Why's that a problem?'

Patty doesn't answer, not sure she can explain what she means. She worries that Dani has no sense of proportion. She's got a dad who puts her on a pedestal, and some love-struck kid who would do anything for her.

'Just that she might be a bit big-headed.'

'Well, you keep her grounded,' he says, and Patty can't tell if that's barbed or not.

'So did she like it?' Patty asks.

'Oh yes, she was really happy with it. After school we took it over to the lane and tried it out.'

'Did you have cake?'

'She said she was too old for cake. We had fish and chips and a semi-frozen cheesecake from over the road. I put a candle on her cod. Thirteen wouldn't fit.'

'Rubbish portions over there. Was it just you two?'

'And Izzy. We missed you.'

'Yeah, well. Now she's a teen she's meant to hate me.'

'Do something nice for her in the morning.'

She shakes her head. 'I need to be in the office at the crack of dawn if I'm gonna get anywhere with the story.'

'Okay,' he says without a hint of reproach. He kisses her softly on the forehead. He means it as a loving gesture but Patty finds it annoying. Within seconds he is asleep. Patty lies there wide awake. She can't smoke in bed any more, not since setting fire to the duvet, but she feels desperate for some nicotine goodness. For a long time her mind whirrs, thinking about Sonia and the grieving mother, about how both their lives have just been turned upside down. Then her thoughts drift back thirteen years, to when she is in hospital cradling her newborn daughter. At the time, the world seemed to offer everything, nothing scared her. Dani could grow up to be anything she wanted – and she would be safe and protected. Patty would never let any harm come to her – she would keep men like her own father from hurting Dani. And she would have the kind of relationship with her own daughter that had been impossible with her mother. Where had that gone wrong? How were they drifting apart as Dani got older?

'Where do we go from here?' Patty asks the night.

PART FOUR

NINETEEN

Sunday 19 December 2010

Patty tries to open her eyes but they're glued together. Panic starts to rise. She can hear something, some snatches of speech, but none of it makes sense. She's cold, naked from the waist down. Panic spikes, out of control.

'Christ, w w w where…'

Her throat is so dry, she tries to claw at it. She pulls at her arm but it doesn't respond. Panic surges. She pulls and twists. There's something holding her. Her arm hurts, a scratch and tug as she struggles.

'Oh Christ, he's got me.' A scream builds in her chest, billows up her body. She doesn't want to die. She doesn't want to die now.

Hands hit her shoulders, push her back.

'No! Help!' She can feel his hands slide around her throat. 'Jim, help me!'

'Quiet, sweetheart.' A lilting voice, insistent but not threatening envelops her. The hands are firm. They push her back down. 'Careful now, darling, that there tube's for your own good. You need that for water and nutrients. I'll get someone to put it back.'

The hands push Patty back down onto the bed, her head sinking into the pillow. Then the sound of soft footsteps. Patty shakes, every muscle in her body burns. Her eyes feel stitched shut. She forces them apart – they crack and tear. Light flickers in, like flame scorching. A faint shape. She can't focus, all just a charcoal smudge.

More footsteps, different this time, heavier. Someone is moving her arm, pinching her really hard and there's a burning.

'You gave us quite a scare you know. There we go...'

The burning stops. The voice is a woman's, older than the first.

'I'm going to call a doctor. Tell them you're awake.'

She leaves, heels clicking on the hard floor. Patty feels her stomach tighten. A doctor? Where the hell is she? She tries to sit up but everything swims and black bleeds in.

❄

'Hello there. I'm Dr Frobisher.'

There is a light, white hot. Just for a second, but it burns itself into Patty's sight and floats there like a storm cloud. Water pours from her eyes. There is some spray, a cloth.

'Your eyes have been weeping and are swollen shut. This should make you feel better and the swelling should calm. Try to open them very slowly.' With the cloth he wipes under her eyes and around her mouth. She can feel her lips are cracked. She tries to suck on the cloth. With a 'tut' he pulls it away.

'You have an intravenous drip in your right arm. Do you understand what I mean by that?'

She nods. She'd like to tell him that she isn't a bloody idiot, but her throat won't cooperate.

'I had Sister tape down the tubes so they stayed in while you were unconscious. But I've moved them so you can sit up... can you try for me? We do have a lift we can use at the back.'

Patty slowly sits up and an arm snakes behind her to help. Under normal circumstances she would recoil from the forced intimacy of the touch. Under normal circumstances, but she's too weak and so she allows the unseen arm to sit her upright. She can see down her body. She's dressed in a hospital gown, hence the lack of underwear and basic dignity. The doctor continues to prod and poke her like a cow being valued for a quick sale.

'You're a bit of a mystery, you know,' he says as he lifts first one foot then the other and pinches her toes. 'We don't even know your name. Could you tell us your name?'

Patty looks blankly at him.

'You had no form of identification on you, no bag, no purse, nothing. Were you robbed?'

Blank.

'Not sure? You had a fall, there's a bang to your head – nothing serious. We were more worried by how dehydrated and undernourished you were. So we sedated you and we've been feeding you by drip and line. Do you understand?'

Blank.

'Now you're awake, we would like you to start eating. We need to build your strength up.'

'How lon—'

'I can't hear you,' he tells her gruffly. She motions to a water jug and glass on the cabinet. He pours a little water for her and hands it over. She rolls the water around her mouth. It feels better but she can't swallow and has to spit back into the cup. Dr Frobisher grimaces.

'How long was I sedated?'

'Twenty-four hours – just over, maybe.'

'Twen—' Her throat fills with the bile of a scream. Weight bears down on her chest. A day lost. They'll have found him and…

'No. Naaaaaa…' she remembers Roberta's words. Her wail fills the ward.

'Now, I—' Doctor Frobisher starts to panic in the face of raw emotion. 'I'll get…' he runs off to find help. The inhuman sound gets even louder. Two women in their nineties begin to cry, both believing a bombing raid is about to start. One whimpers with fear; the other sobs for the man she loved and lost so long ago.

The ward sister rushes over. 'What the hell is going on?' The sister grabs hold of Patty and shakes her. 'What? What's the matter.'

'It wasn't him.'

'Who?'

'It...' Patty's eyes are wild, snapping back and forth. 'The killer, he was...' she feels the ward sister draw away...

'Killer?'

...and that snaps Patty back. 'Can't get caught now – the killer is still out there. I kidnapped the wrong man,' she thinks.

'It, it was a bad dream. I had a bad... please excuse me.'

'I don't understand.' The sister eyes her patient with some suspicion. 'You're okay? Are you in pain?'

'No. No pain.'

'Okay, then please lie down, I'll go and prise our Dr Frobisher out of the toilets and we can see about getting you something to stabilise you. Maybe get some meat on the bones, eh?' She smiles. 'Okay?'

Patty nods. The sister leaves and Patty lies back, feeling her heart pulse – reliving Roberta's words– the mouth moving and the air suddenly becoming hot and toxic 'Not a match.' Not. It wasn't him. Duncan Cobhurn didn't kill Dani.

'Oh Christ.' She allows the dam to break and the tears to flow free. She sobs for ten minutes and then, with an absolute force of will, pushes the wall of self-pity away and starts to drag herself up from the pit.

When she is almost herself, she begins to look around and plan her next step. To her side there is a locker. She leans awkwardly over and pulls the door open. No clothes – but her glasses are there – she puts them on and the world becomes slightly less blurred. She can see a ward of maybe eight beds. Old people. Bloody old people. It's the ward her mother-in-law died in.

'I am not old,' she croaks, but nobody acknowledges her. She pulls off the covers; she needs to get away. She tries to swing her leg out, but the tubing pulls and pain burrows deep. She has a catheter.

At some point a woman, possibly the first voice she heard, approaches with a mug of tea and places it on the tray next to her. Patty takes it. It's sweet but very refreshing. She closes her eyes again and listens to the staff as they patrol the ward. She begins to distinguish the voices, gets an understanding of who's in control. What they do there. Twenty-four hours. 'So it's Sunday – morning or night?' she thinks to herself. She looks at her wrist and then in the locker, no watch – she wore no jewellery. Even the bifocals were an off-the-peg pair from the chemist's. No prescription, nothing that could be used to trace her. Except her, of course. Except for the fact that she's lying down like a fucking dog waiting to be found. Obviously Duncan Cobhurn will be free – when? He would have woken up at some point on Saturday afternoon. If she was lucky he would have slept until the evening, but as soon as he'd woken he would have started making a lot of noise. Enough to wake the dead. So he'd have been found at some point last night – the best she could hope for would be this morning. Then what? She tries to rifle through the filing cabinets of her mind for all the cases she's reported on over the years. How long does it take to take a statement? Make a photofit? He only saw her for a minute and she was in disguise – what would the police have? Nothing more than a general description: woman in her mid-sixties, tall and thin. But they're not idiots. At some point they will work out what the cut in his hand was for. Maybe it was good that she cut so deep – it isn't obvious that it was for a blood sample. But they will realise it quickly, and then they'll check all testing facilities. The lab will be discreet, but an ambulance was called from there for a tall, thin woman in her sixties who had collapsed. Christ, the trail leads directly to her. It is only a matter of time.

'Nur…' Patty croaks and looks up, and sees not just a nurse walking at the end of the ward but a man too. A policeman. Patty feels a tremor start to build.

'Oh fuck. Calm. Calm Patty.' She lies back and closes her eyes, trying to keep the shakes away.

'I understand she's awake,' a male voice says.

'She was, but now she's resting.'

'Well, I'm happy to wait.'

Patty opens her eye a crack to see him.

'Ah, there she is.'

'Ahh!' Patty screams and rolls her head, kicks her legs, looks terrified.

'Officer, move back.' The sister dives in, shoving the policeman back and grabbing Patty's hand. She writhes and screams – not sure herself what part is real and what an act.

'It's okay, he's leaving. Don't worry,' the sister says, trying to reassure her.

'I'm sorry, love, didn't mean to frighten you.' But he doesn't back off.

'Ahh!' Patty screams again and thrashes harder.

'That's it. Out.' The sister shoves him back.

He holds his ground. 'Just a few words.'

'Now.' The nurse uses her body and literally bumps him back. He looks angrily at her but can tell she won't budge. 'Out, officer.

Come back tomorrow morning,' she says with an edge of threat to her voice.

He nods and walks away slowly from the ward.

Patty starts to calm as he retreats. What does he know? Will she be arrested in the morning or does she have time? Time, what the hell is the time…? So Cobhurn wasn't the killer?

The ward sister returns and sits on Patty's bed. 'Well, you're quite the enigma aren't you?'

'What's the time?' Patty asks softly.

'Six twenty.'

'Sunday… morning?'

'Night. It's pitch black out. Do you need to know the month too?'

'I know the month, and I know who's prime minister.'

'Then you know more than most people here. But do you know your name? Your address? Do you remember anything about what happened?'

Patty shakes her head.

'Are you on any regular medication? If you are then you should be taking it. Warfarin, maybe?'

'I…' She almost tells her that she takes 9mg of Ropinirole, but can't let even a crack of her real self open. 'Nothing. I'm tired,' Patty tells her, noticing her own voice for the first time. It sounds empty and hollow, like her grandmother's before she died.

'Okay.' The sister leans over her and pulls the bedclothes up and tucks them in tight. Patty notices her breath is Tic-Tac sweet. She must be covering something. Smoking perhaps, or booze.

'I'm going home soon. But I'll ask the night-shift to look after you, and I'll see you in the morning before the police get here.' She pauses. 'If you have anything you need to tell, to anyone, I urge you to speak soon. The police are quite unsympathetic when they have to do all the work.' And with that, she walks away. Patty listens to the click of her heels as she walks as far as the nurses' station and then talks to one of the newly arrived night staff. Patty strains her ears to try and hear.

'Bed three... malnourished... quite possible she's had a mini-stroke... what caused her to collapse... seems not to have directly affected her speech... recall has been degraded... possibly. She may be faking that, or at least making it appear worse than it seems. Not sure why, but she seems afraid. We need to keep a close eye on her.' Then the ward sister leaves.

Patty lies there for some time as the staff change over and medicines and cups of tea are brought round. All the time, she's thinking she needs to get out before morning. The fact that they sent a constable means they don't know exactly who she is or what she did. The ward sister wouldn't be around for the night; she has her suspicions that something is wrong, but didn't convey that directly to the night staff. They just think she needs extra care. Maybe Patty can work that to her advantage. She looks around the ward and quickly sees what she needs. A mobile phone sits on the short wardrobe between one of the sobbing old women and a skeletal woman who has not moved. She can make this work; she knows she can. In fact, she feels more confident, stronger than she has done in a long time. Maybe she needed a day in hospital. But no more.

At 10 p.m. they turn down the lights. Patricia has no intention of sleeping, which she thinks is lucky because the last place that encourages sleep is a hospital. She continues to watch the nurses buzz around, waking the poor old dears every damn hour to stick something in them or make them swallow this and that or just fiddle. Because they can. But she learns quickly about the routines on the ward and which nurses will bend the rules if you annoy them enough.

She waits until midnight, when things start to slow. She props herself up in the bed and looks around. Everyone seems to be asleep in the ward. Her bed is halfway down the room, too far from the light switches. Above her bed is a large, extending lamp. She can't reach up to it, but there is a cane hanging from the handle of the chest of drawers to her right. She reaches over to it and loops the leather cord at the end around her wrist. Then she takes aim and swings the cane violently at the light. She means to turn it on. Instead the cane swings like an executioner's axe and lops the head of the lamp off, flinging it out into the centre of the ward where it crashes to the ground with an explosion of metal and glass.

'Nurse! Nurse!' someone screams. Lights flare on and nurses run. There is pandemonium. It is time for Patty to go to work. She has her target in her sights. Nurse Lucy, who has texted her boyfriend forty-seven times in the last two hours and given at least two old women the wrong medicine. As Nurse Lucy rushes past Patty grabs at her.

'Nurse!' she barks.

'I can't...'

'I need to go to the toilet.'

'You don't need it; you got a thingy. You don't need to get up.'

'My dear girl, I am Hilary Clifton-Hastings and I have been taking myself to the toilet for sixty years. Please remove this catheter.'

'I can't.'

'I would appreciate being left with my dignity.' She almost shouts the word dignity and can feel all the other old dears in the ward nodding their agreement.

'Really I—'

'Please. Dignity.' Patty knew that would push the nurse's buttons. It's all about dignity these days – can't keep old dears on their backs, drugged up, peeing and pooping with nothing to do until MRSA and bedsores get them.

'Honestly, it's dead busy…'

'Then who is the senior consultant on call? I might well know them from the Rotary club?'

She sees Lucy stiffen. She hates to bully the girl but she has to get out of there.

'Okay.' Nurse Lucy pulls the bedclothes back and with a snap of surgical tape and a tug – she removes the catheter. 'You'll need a walking frame. Your legs'll be a bit wobbly. Wait here.'

Patty watches Nurse Lucy grab a Zimmer frame from by the door. She wants to yell out, 'I'm not old! I don't need that', but she thinks better of it. Better to play along and act like some frail old fool.

'Here ya go. Hold onto the bar and hoist your—'

Patty grabs the bar with disdain and pulls. Her legs give way, they're jelly. She collapses back onto the bed.

'Marta!' Lucy calls out to a colleague.

'Christ,' thinks Patty. 'I am an old fool. Jelly on a plate, jelly on a plate, wibble-wobble, wibble-wobble, old crone in a state.'

Patty needs both nurses to hold her up while she does the latest St Vitus dance craze.

'Back to bed,' says Marta. 'You need the catheter still.'

'No. I will use the toilet myself – like a normal person.' And Patty takes a step. She doesn't tumble, the momentum takes all three women forwards. She has to keep them going. Together the nurses and Patty weave drunkenly to the toilet, propelled by the sheer force of Patty's will.

The nurses want to take her inside, but she refuses.

'My legs are fine now. Please let me do my business in privacy, I am not an animal.'

'Okay,' says Lucy and Marta walks off. 'I'll wait right here, and you must leave the door open in case I need to come in and help.'

'Of course, my dear,' Patty agrees through tight lips.

As soon as she is inside the lavatory, Patty curses the situation. She's got herself free of the catheter but that won't help if her damn legs won't work or if the nurse hangs around all the time. She punches at her legs.

When she can't punch any more she leans over the sink and runs a basin of cold water to dunk her face in. The water feels good. She looks at herself in the mirror.

'Look at you – old, old woman. What a bloody mess,' she tells herself. 'Christ. Did a mouse die in my mouth?' she thinks, running her tongue around her dry mouth. She hobbles back to the door and looks out. The younger nurse is still there, hovering, waiting for her.

'Clean teeth, I must clean my teeth!' And she exhales in the young woman's face.

The nurse recoils. 'Okay. Wait here. I'll be back in a sec.' She trots off to find a toothbrush and toothpaste. Patty eyes the journey back to the bed and beyond, to the bed by the window and the mobile phone.

'I can do it.'

She pushes off with the frame and begins to walk, tottering and swaying like a marionette with half her strings cut. Jelly legs flying everywhere. Her eyes start to stream; she bites at her lip. She is falling to one side.

'Come on, you silly old cow.' She pulls up on the frame. The distance is narrowing; she is almost there. She makes it to her bed and stops to rest. She listens hard: is someone coming?

No. Geronimo! She is off again. Step after step, her legs almost useless, her arms trembling with the exertion. The phone, she can see the phone.

'Think about prison,' she hisses to herself as she crosses the final yards to the phone. She grabs at it and nearly tips over. The old woman next to her whimpers and turns over. The skeleton merely lies there. Patty flips the phone open, praying to a non-existent God for some battery power.

'Yes!' The time flickers at her. 12.57 a.m. She dials a number she has not called in many, many years, but will never forget. It rings.

'Come on come on come on come on come on come on come...'

'Hello?' His voice is sleepy.

The years stretch into eternity.

'Hello? Is somebody there?'

Patty finds she's mute. She had no idea what a profound shock it would be to hear his voice again, really hear him, not just the constant echo of him in her head.

'Hello?' he repeats. 'I'm going to hang up now.'

'Jim,' she says in a voice that sounds a thousand years old.

There is silence, just his breath. Patty thinks she would have been happy to have listened to that breath for a year and a day, but her toothpaste will be here any moment.

'I'm in trouble. I need your help. Please go to my house; there is a spare key taped inside the blue recycling bin in the alley, to the left of the front door. I need you to go in and get me a change of clothes, including underwear and shoes. Bring them, in a bag, to the Royal. I'll meet you by the toilets next to X-ray; remember where they took your mum when she broke her hip. Meet me there at exactly 3 a.m. Don't park in the car park, park in a side street. Then take me home. I'll explain it all, I have to go now.'

She flips the phone closed and sets it back down on the cabinet. No one seems to have heard her. There is no alarm, no pointing finger, no searchlight. She spins the Zimmer round and heads off back to the toilets, faster than before. Her legs are hers again. As she gets to her own bed, the nurse returns.

'Oh. I thought you were going to wait for me in the loo,' she says, a little peeved.

Patty snatches the brush and paste from her and charges for the toilet, this time slamming the door and locking it. The nurse is shocked for a second and then runs to the toilet and bangs on the door.

'Let me in. Right this second, or I'll call security to take the door off.'

'I will be out in one minute but I want some privacy,' Patty screams through the door. She angrily brushes her teeth until her gums bleed. Then she sits on the toilet seat and weeps.

TWENTY

Jim slides the key into the lock as if he owns the place and pushes the door open – he quickly steps inside. Behind him, Dani hesitates.

'Come in quick,' he hisses.

'Do you think it's okay – can I come in?'

'You're not a vampire. Get in quickly, we don't want a nosy neighbour calling the police.'

'But…'

'Sorry.' He closes the door on her. He pulls a torch from his pocket – he flicks it on and the beam falls on a small mountain of pizza flyers and minicab cards, as well as three days' worth of newspapers. Jim scoops them up as Dani walks through the door.

'That was rude,' she says, waving the torch away from her face.

'We looked suspicious and a bit crazy, plus we don't have much time. We need to get your mum in less than an hour.'

'It was still rude to slam the door in my face.'

'I didn't slam it. I closed it.'

'Thanks for the apology.' She walks off to explore downstairs.

Jim takes the pile of junk mail and newspapers into the lounge where he drops them on a small table. He shines the torch around the room, trying to keep the beam away from the windows. The room is almost bare. One chair and the small table.

'Nunnery chic,' Dani says walking in.

'She seems quite minimalist,' Jim agrees. 'Not much to show for a lifetime,' he thinks.

'I'm going upstairs to find some of her clothes.'

'I can be fashion consultant.'

'No, you wait here – I'll be quick.'

He walks upstairs, holding the light down to the floor. He has no idea where her bedroom is, so pushes randomly at a closed door and it slides open. He raises the torch and the light hits…

'God.' The air is knocked out of him. His hand shakes. The torchlight skitters across the wall. *The wall* – in all its glory, recreated just as it had been in their house all those years ago. Though now it's even bigger, with more Post-it notes and more pictures. The day Dani arrived at Durham – so happy. Home at Christmas, her birthday… then those other pictures of her, his child defiled. Dead. So pale and yet beautiful. The same as she is now – the same as she is downstairs. Full of life. He feels sick, doubles over.

'Dad?' she calls.

'Dani, don't come up here,' he shouts back, his stomach cramping. 'Don't come…'

'What are you going to do? Slam the door in my face again?' She floats through the door. 'I can go anywhere. I'm the Ghost of—' She sees the photos, sees herself: her hands tied, her body bare, the bruises covering her arms and legs. Post-it notes scream 'torture', 'multiple rape', 'faeces and urine'. Around her the air seems to turn tar black.

'Dani…' Jim reaches out to her, he tries to scoop her into his arms – if only he could hug her –but she dissolves. The torch blinks out, there is only black – the shadows seem to suck all life from the air.

'Dani, Dani, please come back.' But there is nothing. The torch flickers once again – the beam catches her image one last time. Dead.

Jim takes a final look at the hateful wall. 'Oh Christ, Patty.' He walks backwards out of the door, closing it gingerly, as if there's an unexploded bomb inside. He pauses for a moment, unsure of what to do. Then slowly he moves to the next room, her bedroom.

Inside there is just an unmade bed, a tatty old wardrobe and a few boxes. The bed makes him feel sad. Sad and old. It all feels intrusive and voyeuristic, especially going through her clothes to put together a bag for her, but he does as she asked. He is also saddened by the fact that he recognises every item of clothing. Hasn't she shopped in twelve years? With the bag ready, he closes the door and goes back down.

Dani sits in the living room. He would have missed her but for the slightest sigh as he passed the doorway. He strains into the darkness and makes out her faint shape.

'I'm sorry, darling.'

'Not your fault. You did warn me.' She pauses. 'Why don't I remember?'

'Did seeing the pictures…?'

'No. Maybe. I can see flashes.'

'Faces?'

'I… yes.'

'Do you recognise them?'

She opens her mouth to speak, but it all seems too unclear. She closes it again.

'Can you describe them?'

'No. No, it's all deformed, hazy – like I'm seeing everything underwater.'

'Maybe… maybe that's best.'

She shakes her head slowly. 'All I remember clearly is hearing your voice far-off, and then opening my eyes and I was me, but not myself any more, not whole. I felt scared and so alone.'

'Never alone.'

'Really?' She shakes her head sadly. She feels alone so often.

'Let's go and get your mum,' he says softly.

'Okay.'

He drives to the hospital. He remembers not to park in the hospital car park but doesn't trust the side streets. Instead he pulls over on the main road close to a bus stop. There won't be any buses tonight. The drive had been more than a little scary for him; Dani had loved it. From the moment she'd yelled 'shotgun' to the final skid into the kerb, it had been like a roller-coaster ride. He would not have gone out in those conditions for anyone else.

'I'll go in alone.'

'Dad!'

'Wait at the car, please.' He turns on the radio for her and gets out into the icy wind. He walks towards the hospital slowly, a little like a penguin as the snow shifts under his feet. He feels guilty about asking Dani to stay in the car, but he doesn't want her with him while he confronts Patty. He's starting to get worried about why she's in the hospital – in his mind he visualises *the wall* once again. Is Patty still obsessed by finding Dani's killer after more than twenty years? What might she have done? The snow begins to fall once more. He can't move.

'Are you okay?' Dani calls from the car. Jim turns and waves to her, though he doesn't trust his voice. 'Shout if you need me,' his daughter calls out.

His mouth feels like black pepper has been ground into it as he walks slowly inside. Right inside the door is a desk that, during the day, is manned by volunteers. Of course, at this time of the morning it's empty. Lying on the top is a pile of maps with a handwritten sign saying: PLEASE TAKE. On the board behind the desk is a list of the departments and the buildings they occupy. Jim looks for the department of psychiatry. He's relieved to see there's no unit or secure ward listed. He remembers waking from the nightmare – how scared he was for her. Have faith, he thinks, and heads towards the X-ray department. He knows the way – he has been to this hospital many times over the years. His mother died here, he had his prostate poked here. Now what?

X-ray reception is closed when he arrives. The air seems to fizz with the smell of bleach and the ageing institutional lino floors seem tacky as he walks on them. He sits in the central bank of chairs, probably the only time he's ever managed to get a seat here. Normally patients stand three or four deep waiting for their close-ups. To complete the zombie-movie aesthetic, the strip light above him flickers. He checks his watch: 3.02.

'Maybe it's a joke,' he thinks with no conviction. Then he hears footsteps from behind and turns. He doesn't recognise her for a second. She's thin – marathon runner thin. It shocks him a little.

'The clothes, Jim, for Christ's sake, we don't have much time. Is that it?' She snatches up the bag and heads for the women's toilet in the next corridor.

Jim watches her go. Only a few seconds – but he knows she isn't mad. She's Patty – she looks older, leaner but… 'Christ.' The intelligence flares in her eyes. She's illuminated from within. He realises that, after all this time, he desperately wants to hold her.

Patty storms out of the toilets after a minute. She throws the bag, Jim isn't sure if it's to him or at him. She looks angry.

'What the hell were you thinking?' She indicates her body.

Jim looks down at her and blushes. The clothes he picked out make her look like a clown.

'You...' He wants to say: 'You used to be taller, fuller, more...' but he dries up. She is thin and bird-like, angular and pointy... and amazing. And angry.

She walks towards him and her head leans as if to kiss, but instead hisses 'Go out the Warren Street exit and I will meet you on the corner by Wimpy.'

'Patty...' he starts but she's already heading away. Jim watches her stride purposefully away towards the main exit. She walks quickly but erratically, correcting herself as she veers slightly from one side to the next. Then she turns the corner and is gone. Jim feels like he's in a dream. He looks at the sign above him; the Warren Street exit is on the other side of the hospital. He needs to head into the belly of the beast – Accident and Emergency. He gets up and goes forward. Corridors wind and turn like in a maze, then suddenly the corridor opens out onto a full room of men clutching arms and heads, girlfriends with hands covered in gore and children asleep on laps. Except for the red flash of blood, all is pallid and miserable under the glare of strip lights. Everywhere, people seem to huddle and wait for help. That's what hospital emergency departments are at night: a sodium-lit purgatory.

As he walks through, hollow eyes look up, pleading with Jim to diagnose, advise, and administer drugs so they can get home to bed. Everyone looks so desperate. But all Jim can do is shrug apologetically and try to avoid stepping in the fresh drops of blood. They look like scattered breadcrumbs leading the lost back home. Jim looks around – why is there no one with a mop at this time of the night?

Close to the exit Jim sees a man with green skin, eyes that are a huge black void, hair matted with blood, kicking a vending machine.

'Where is my fucking Coke?' the man repeats over and over. Each time the searching question is underlined by a thump to the Perspex cover. 'The hospital is a place for philosophers,' Jim thinks. 'Where indeed are our fucking Cokes?' Jim stops and gently hits A11 on the machine. The mechanical arm moves, trundles across and delicately plucks a red-and-white can from the shelf and drops it into the chute. Jim nods. He can't heal anyone but he can at least deliver some succour. The automatic door slides open and he walks out into the night. The door slides back and he can just hear the man.

'I wanted Diet Coke.'

The street is empty and cold, still snow-spewed as it continues to fall. The car is on the other side of the hospital – Jim hopes Dani is okay, he wishes she were with him now. He crosses the treacherous street and can see the restaurant. He approaches the Wimpy with caution. He can't remember the last time he saw one; he thought they'd gone out of business years ago. They seem to be something from a bygone age – before the Whoppers and Big Macs came and swept them away. He assumes Patty will be in the doorway, but as he gets level, it's empty. No one inside; just enormous close-ups of meat. It reminds him of the hospital. The mixed grill looks like pictures he's seen of men eviscerated in war and they make him feel a little queasy. Where is she?

Then he sees her pushed into the doorway of an off-licence. She's rocking slightly on her heels, back and forth, looking tightly wound. He opens his mouth to shout but stops. Instead he moves slowly, his hands outstretched, showing he has nothing in them, as if he's approaching a dangerous animal. Patty catches sight of the movement and instinctively pulls into the shadows.

'It's okay, it's me.'

She relaxes a little and steps forwards.

'What's up?'

'It's good to see you, Jim.' Her voice is husky with intense tiredness. She smiles and he feels like he's twenty again. 'What took you so long?' The years melt away. She'd said those exact words the first time he kissed her. He'd been gathering his courage for weeks. Finally the dam had burst and he had launched himself at her in the clumsiest way. Instead of a clean kiss they had bumped chins and clattered teeth.

'If we're going to do it, then let's do it properly,' she had said and grabbed his jacket, pulling him to her and... fireworks.

'Patty...'

'Can we get to the car? I'm cold and you didn't exactly bring me winter clothes.' She sounds exhausted but her prickliness has melted away.

'I'm parked a little way away. Have my coat.' Jim peels off the jacket and holds it open so she can slide inside. He feels her move against him – brittle, bird-like. A memory hits him hard – that first night – the curves and full breasts, the weight of her as she lowered herself onto him with her hands on his chest – taking his breath away. He can't help himself as he puts the jacket around her – he pulls her into him and closes his arms around her like he did all those years ago. Then, she melted into him like syrup – tonight she pulls away and her face is a mix of rage and fear.

'I... Sorry. I was just...'

She doesn't make any reply, just shudders a little from the cold. Jim motions with his hand towards where the car is parked and she moves off. Nothing is said as they walk. Clouds roll by, mostly unseen in the dark night until the moon is revealed just for a few seconds. Jim slides back through the years: he is walking with Dani, right on the spot where he is now. They are crossing this same tarmac strip. How old is she? Eight? They have just visited her gran, who is dying. They walk in silence. Her small, warm hand in his. She's deeply thoughtful, then she looks up to him and asks: 'Where do we go after we die, Daddy?'

'The next right,' he shouts to Patty, who is ahead of him. His hand seems a little warm, clammy as if it has held a small, sticky little mitt. The moon disappears once more as the clouds roll by. Ahead, Patricia strides forward.

'Just there, on the left. Red Saab.'

The moon skids back and Jim can see Dani sitting on the bonnet of the car. She smiles broadly and waves, happy to see him. He waves back to her, not thinking. Patty turns and sees him; she jumps.

'I've got this bad shoulder. I was just stretching it.' It's a terrible lie. On the car Dani laughs.

'I'll open it.' He pulls out the little leather fob and for a second it feels like a small hand rests in his.

Where do we go after we die, Daddy? The air seems to carry the echo through the decades.

Dani slides off the bonnet and walks over to her mother, looks directly into her face, but Patty sees nothing and climbs into the passenger seat. The clouds scud past once more and the moon is so bright, it feels like daytime for a second, then it fades to black as the clouds roll past again.

Jim climbs into the driver's seat. He can see Dani in the rear-view mirror, leaning forward on the back seat, her face blank. Jim wonders what she's thinking, the three of them together after all these years. In the back seat Dani sighs and then yawns. Patty silently stares out of the window. Jim pulls away from the kerb, the wheels skid but he slowly moves forwards, heading to Patty's house. The roads are clear of traffic and the main roads are pretty well gritted. After ten minutes he allows himself a sideways look at his wife. She's closed her eyes, might be asleep.

'Do you remember Monty?' Dani asks from the back seat.

'Of course,' he says softly. Monty had been Dani's dog. One day, it must have been her last term or so of A levels, Dani came home with him. Patty was fine about it and Jim loved dogs, so Monty stayed. Of course, when Dani went off to university she couldn't take him, so he stayed with them. Jim had thought that he would end up being the main carer for the big lump, but when it came to it, Patty had been the one to replace Dani in terms of walking and feeding. Jim hadn't minded; he thought it was good for her and gave Patty and Dani something to talk about. In some ways it was a little bit of a bribe for Dani: don't just come back to see us but to see Monty too. He'd been a great dog, adored Dani, so happy to see her when she came home. Until she didn't, of course.

Patty withdrew her love then. It was almost as if Dani's death burned all affection out of her. She didn't show anybody or anything any love. Maybe a cat could have survived the loss of love, but not Monty. He would literally howl into the wilderness that was Patty's face, trying to get her to see him, to respond to him, but there was nothing. Jim thinks it broke the poor dog's heart. They gave him to some friends about three months after Dani's death. Within a year he had developed cancer and was put down. Jim never told Patty. By that time, he thought, the capacity for grief had left her.

'I remember Monty.' Jim flicks his eyes to the rear-view mirror but cannot see Dani's face in the murk of the back seat.

Where do we go after we die, Daddy?

Jim tries to recall his exact words to his poor little girl who was losing her beloved gran.

'Mrs Henson said heaven was where Gran would go. Will she go to heaven, Daddy?' She asked him.

Jim feels shame. He could have planted the seed of hope in his daughter. Let her believe that, no matter what terrible things happen to us in life, that death honoured the just, good and blameless lives of ordinary people. But he didn't.

'Dani, I really don't know. I think that Gran will have no pain any more, which will be really good, but probably there is just nothing when you die, darling. Nothing.'

Nothing? Had he really believed that? The man who lives with his daughter's ghost? 'I am such a bloody hypocrite,' he thinks.

The moon slides behind the clouds once more and is finally gone. He sneaks another peek across at his wife. The closeness of her makes his chest burn a little. He has been so lonely. The worse loneliness had been in those between years – when Patty supposedly was still with him and yet she was so distant. Then he had no one. During that time he left his work – he even volunteered for the Red Cross. For a year he drove trucks of medicine and aid, usually flying to the nearest safe haven and then driving truckload after truckload of life and hope and aid to desolated areas. He delivered food and medicine to Sri Lanka, Turkey and Haiti. He saw so much destruction – but it hardly affected him. Whenever his truck had rolled into town, a group of children would follow. He always kept his pockets stuffed with energy bars so that when they caught up with him, he could hand them out. There were never enough. In those moments he didn't feel powerful, no Santa or Jesus – not even some low-rent Robin Hood. Instead he felt needy, desperate to buy some love, to show himself he could do good in this shitty world. Just for a moment to see pain turn to a smile. That was what he failed to do in the years with Patty, after Dani died. To turn off the darkness inside his wife, just for a second. Even with those poor kids, he could do nothing. After a year of volunteering he stopped. Instead he drove a minicab in London. He liked to keep moving – he thought he might die if he stopped. Then Patty left him and... but tonight, when she needed someone, she called him. If it weren't nearly four in the morning, and he hadn't just broken someone out of hospital, he'd feel heartened by it. Maybe tomorrow he would. Right now tiredness was starting to sweep through him and make him feel nauseous. His introspection is broken by the sound of snoring. He glances across at Patty and allows himself a chuckle.

Jim finally pulls up outside Patty's house at 4 a.m. and cuts the engine. Next to him Patty breathes softly, lost deep inside some inner world. He opens his door and slides out of the car, his back crunchy from sitting. He slams the car door; it does the trick and wakes Patty. She drifts for a second in some calm waters and then, as memories flood back in, she tenses once more.

Jim opens her door and bends down. 'You're home.'

'Do you have the spare key?' she asks, her speech thick with tiredness.

'Of course.' He hands it to her and watches as she walks into the house. She wobbles slightly as she walks, as if she's on too-high heels. At the door she fumbles with the key, pushing and scratching, until finally the metal slides into its sheath and she goes inside. She leaves the front door open.

'Dad,' Dani calls from the car.

'Yes, darling.'

'She's left the front door open.'

He nods.

'You need to go and close it.'

'True.'

'I'll wait. Don't worry about me.'

He nods to her and walks over to the house. He holds the door, feeling the heft of the wood in his hand. He could shut it and leave; deep down he thinks this would be best. But instead he follows Patty inside and shuts the door behind him.

The house is dark. Jim tries to remember the layout from his brief visit earlier. Suddenly there is a cry, a scream of pain. Primal, animal, intense pain. In the darkness Jim is enveloped by the scream, the pain. It tears into him; he knows what it is. He rushes forwards, unsure where to go. He sees a bar of light under a door and hits the wood. The scream rises in force, hitting him in the chest and ripping the years away from him. Patty is on the floor in the lounge. In her hand is one of the newspapers and she waves it around, then claws at the front page. She screams again, then rolls into a ball. She is having a fit – some kind of seizure – just like when she'd heard Dani was dead. A scream of pure pain. The intensity of loss, the hunger of despair – it cuts right through him.

'Patty. Patty. Look at me, calm down.'

He tries to put his arms around her and hold her, calm her, but she lashes out – forcing him back. Her body arches; she looks as if she could snap in two. He lunges again, trying to grab her arms, but she beats at him. The scream rises even higher.

'Patty, Patty, calm down.'

She writhes and twists. Jim holds on for dear life like a cowboy at a rodeo. She butts him in the face – so much pain. His lip is cut and there's blood.

'Mine or hers?' he thinks, frightened and not knowing whether to call the hospital or the police or to try and ride the roller-coaster to the end. He grabs her shoulders and pulls her closer, tighter.

'Patty, we love you,' he moans into her hair. Then he starts to rock her, tiny movements he has not made since Dani was a baby.

And he sings, barely audible, but he sings for her soul. Finally she starts to slow. Her screams collapse into shakes as her entire body vibrates. Slowly the muscles start to unwind, and she softens and curls into his arms from choice. She wraps her arms around his neck pulling herself into him, almost crushing his chest. Her sobs start to calm and she fades to black.

They are still for half an hour. She lies curled in his arms while he breathes in the perfume of her hair and her skin. Then suddenly, as if a momentous decision had finally been reached, Jim lifts her, supporting her head as he would a child, and carries her upstairs. He lies her down on her bed. She rolls onto her side and curls. She is so thin, so small. He searches, first under the bed and then in the wardrobe. He discovers a large duvet and spreads it over her. He feels like forty-five years of his life have melted away – it is that first night once again. She is so beautiful. Her skin is aglow and her hair ripples down her back in cascading waves. She is once again his pre-Raphaelite queen on a bower. He cannot help himself, but leans forwards and kisses her head, then strokes her hair. Then he lies down on the bed. He does not plan to sleep, just to lie there in case she wakes, just a few inches between them. He closes his eyes.

Patty wakes, and for one blissful moment, floats above the world like a newborn, innocent. Aware of the press of another body against her, she feels the warmth of contact and is drawn into that gravity, yearning for embrace, her arms folding around the other figure. Then the memories flood back, swamping her, stealing her breath as they have done every morning for more than twenty years, grinding her under their heel. She begins to shake.

Jim feels the tremor beside him. Through the sticky curtain of sleep he holds out his hand and she grabs at it; they grip hard, harder. Just like they had done with her morning sickness. 'Squeeze. Tighter, Jim, squeeze tighter.'

He did, with all his might. And if it didn't work, then he held the hair away from her face while she retched... then wiped her vomity mouth for her.

'Oh, that's disgusting, Jim. You don't have to do that,' she'd say.

'I don't care.' He didn't.

He wakes. The pressure on his hand and the allure of the past draw him from sleep. For one terrible moment he is lost, buried, at the bottom of a hole as it fills with sand and he is running, scrambling, trying to climb out. Then the hand holding his own calms him. He remembers where he is. Their hands squeeze together, they roll face to face. Scared, needy, hungry and as old as the earth. Patty reaches out to his face and strokes it, feels the stubble, the grey stalks of hair forcing their way through his toughened skin. She could never have described it to another person, could not even have formed the words to tell herself about his face, his cheek. Yet she knows every contour of his face and body. A lifetime melts away, she does not see him now, not the sixty-four-year-old Jim, but he's a boy in her bed. So fine, so fine.

He opens his arms and she rolls into them, they hug so tightly. She feels so different in his arms, there is no curve and heft – now she is air and breath. Her once alabaster skin ravaged by loss, grief and despair. And yet.

'You are so beautiful,' he whispers.

'You bloody idiot.'

He looks into her face. Her smile dazzles him like the sun and her lips caress his. He can taste the salt of tears.

'I love you, Patty. I love you,' he breathes into her, overwhelmed by the rush of emotion and desire that he finds in his heart and mind and body.

She leans into him, snuggles her mouth into his hair and whispers.

'Jim. I killed a man.'

REPORT OF SURVEILLANCE

Sunday 19 December–Monday 20 December 2010

3.58 a.m.: Car arrives outside residence. Red Saab. Licence plate: SD54 GRD

3.59 a.m.: James Lancing (positive identification from photos) exits car and opens passenger seat. Helps woman out of car, she is incapacitated, appears drunk. (Positive identification of Patricia Lancing.)

Img007/008/009 Three photos taken of couple.

4.02 a.m.: Sounds of commotion, screams etc. from suspect's house. Next-door neighbour's lights on for a few minutes. Lasted duration of 2–3 mins.

Log end.

Parked almost directly opposite Patty's house is a white van with tinted windows. Inside, invisible to anyone in the street, is Grant Ronson. He sits in the driver's seat writing up his log.

It is now almost 4.30 a.m. and there has been nothing since the screaming. The house is quiet and dark. The young man is bored again. He had thought this job afforded some glamour, even danger, but it is mostly bloody boring. On the seat next to him he has yesterday's *News of the World*, an iPod and a well-thumbed copy of *Escort*.

There is a rubber tube coiled off the seat and onto the floor, which snakes back behind him into a large jug that is almost completely full of his urine. It's starting to smell. He has another two hours until his shift is over and the dayshift arrives. He yawns. He picks up the paper again and scans the front page.

The headline reads: MURDERED MAN IDENTIFIED.

He reads the article:

The body discovered on Sunday at the Thursdowne Hotel close to Heathrow has been identified as Duncan Cobhurn, a businessman from Durham, owner of the Mediterranean furniture company Porto Pronto. He had been missing since Friday when he was due to return home via Heathrow from a business trip to Lisbon. Police have speculated that this was a kidnapping that had gone disastrously wrong. Police insiders have said they think that the perpetrators used too great a dose of narcotic and bound Mr Cobhurn too heavily, resulting in death from asphyxiation before ransom demands could be made. There is, however, evidence of torture which has also prompted comparison with the Soviet spy Alexander Litvinenko who was poisoned in London in 2006...

Ronson throws the paper down, bored. He yawns. If nothing happens soon he's going to have to masturbate again. At least that will kill some time. Janet from Edinburgh deserves more attention. He sits for a few minutes and then unzips his trousers.

PART FIVE

TWENTY-ONE

Tuesday 13 February 2007

'Two dog walkers found the body on the allotment,' DI Thorsen explains to Tom as they half slide, half drag themselves through the glossy mud. 'They called it in at about 6.20 a.m. A local response officer was here in about ten minu— careful!' Thorsen grabs his arm as he slips sideways down an oozing incline. She steadies him. She's got Wellington boots on. He wears black Oxford brogues. They both know which of them is the more stylish – and who's ruined their shoes.

'Luckily the kid was bright enough to radio it in as Operation Ares.'

Tom nods. He walks with knees bent and feet splayed. They reach the bottom of the treacherous hill. Tom looks across the mud – rain falling a little heavier now. He sees a shoe lying alone, an evidence marker pushed into the mud alongside it. It's the size of a child's shoe – but the heel shows it was made for a woman. A shoe to dance in, have fun in. Not die in. It seems so alone, sitting there in the rain.

Around them, officers buzz like flies, taping off areas, erecting tables – making an island of hi-tech in the mud. Over the body is a makeshift tent, not much better than the kind Tom had made as a kid, though then he'd used blankets and dining chairs and now it was plastic sheets and metal struts. Over to one side three officers stand, puzzling over a laminated manual, trying to build a tent wide enough to cover the body and surrounding area. Tom watches them slowly turn the manual 180 degrees, scratch their heads and slowly turn it back the other way. Christ, they're idiots.

'Could you?' he asks his efficient DI and points to the three stooges. She shrugs and trudges over to them, already barking orders. Tom knows she'll get it built.

He closes his eyes for a second and the world around him slows and disjoints, moves out of focus. Then he moves to the covered body – there is only the victim. He pulls aside the plastic sheet… a dead young woman. The latest in a litany of lifeless young women into whose eyes he has gazed. Another young woman he will silently promise to avenge. He looks at her face – her eyes are open – staring. Grey-blue eyes and the palest skin. In life she may have been ruddy, healthy but now her life-blood was a part of the mud that lapped at her face.

'Guv,' Thorsen calls to him and he looks up to see the full tent ready to slide over the body. He nods and steps back, thinking it doesn't matter much anyway – this rain has almost certainly washed away any really helpful DNA evidence. He sighs, watching his breath spiral up. It will be another long day. The SOCO team will start to gather evidence. Take photos, bag the clothes, take samples from the victim – trim her nails, swab her mouth, vagina, anus – nothing is private. Not today. And at the end of all this, Tom doesn't expect there to be much more learned than he saw from a casual glance.

The body is Sarah Penn's. She's been missing for three days. He recognised her from photos. Her mum and dad brought the snap-shots in the day she was reported missing. Holiday photos from Ibiza last year, though death has wiped away her smile, and the rain has uncurled the bounce of her hair and left it smeared across the ground.

She's naked – her clothes thrown all around. She has been beaten and sexually assaulted. She is without most of the skull above her left eye. Claw hammer is Tom's opinion, based on twenty years of seeing death and on having seen the same injuries twice before – Heather Spall and Tracy Mason. Sarah Penn is victim number three.

'Guv?' DI Thorsen calls to him, miming a drink. He nods and she grabs a Thermos. He turns back to the body.

'I'm sorry, Sarah.'

He remembers thinking when he saw her photos, 'what a pretty girl'. A tear runs down his cheek for all the pretty dead girls. It melts into the rain. Within an hour or two, he'll be standing at the front door of her parents' house about to tell them the news they've dreaded for the last three days, if not the last sixteen years. He knows there'll be tears, maybe screams, denial, blame. All the while he will be there to share their pain. To show them that the police care about their loss, the country cares. That is what he does. He tells families they have lost someone they loved. He is the Sad Man.

Thorsen holds out the metal cup. He takes it from her with a nod.

'Same MO as Spall and Mason?'

He nods.

'I'll send a FLO.'

'No. I'll go.'

He doesn't think of himself as much of a policeman; there are no *little grey cells*, no deductions and last-minute reveals. But what he is good at – what he is best at – is winning trust. Opening a dialogue with witnesses, family, their friends, and teasing out information. People look at him and trust him, especially the damaged and needy. They see a kindred spirit in Tom. They see someone else in pain and they open their hearts to him. No family liaison officer has ever opened up partners, kids, parents or friends like he does. That's why he's the Sad Man and why he runs Operation Ares. He named the unit himself – Ares the destroyer, the god of fruitless violence, a coward who kills for the sake of killing.

Suddenly the tempo of the rain changes: more aggressive, faster and harder. Hailstones. The seventh plague of Egypt. Big chunks of ice slam into the plastic sheets. The officers buzz around more quickly. More plastic is stretched, arced over skeletons of metal. DI Thorsen yells, points – then men run for cover. Tom looks around the allotment. Any early buds are going to be smashed and splintered. Luckily there are no fruits yet, no tomatoes to crush, no strawberries to mash. Tom should get under cover too but he can't leave Sarah. Something more than hailstones rained down on her. She deserves more than this, so much more than this. Little girl lost. Found in body, but for ever lost. Tom waits out the storm, feels the ice bounce off his cap and splash mud over him, but he stands sentry over Sarah until the hail thins and is gone. Now it's just rain.

'Bevans,' a loud voice booms out.

Tom looks up to see an idiot juggling a trowel, a watering can and a packet of seeds. It's impressive juggling but it all makes Tom feel so tired. Were it one of his team he would scream at them to have some respect. Instead he waves a tired hand at his friend and pulls his shoe up out of the mud. It squelches satisfyingly, like a movie sound effect.

'You're meant to set an example,' Tom hisses to the tall pathologist when he gets over to him.

'I am. This is work–life balance. See?' He throws the items even higher, catching the can and seeds, but the trowel spins out of control and shoots into the ground. It sticks in the mud, pointing straight up like an arrow, sending a billow of muddy water up Tom's leg.

'Whoops,' the pathologist laughs.

'Grow up, Dr Keyson.'

Tom walks away, frustrated by the man who, he believes, doesn't comprehend the concept of the chain of command. He seems to have no respect for authority. Tom wonders for a thousandth time if his new friend is autistic to some degree; brilliant people often are. And there's no denying that Marcus Keyson is special; highly intelligent and charming, he's the youngest pathologist working with the Met by ten years, but there is something a little odd about him, something cold and calculating, something that disconnects him from everyone else.

'Or is that just paranoia?' Tom asks himself. Or maybe even a little jealousy? Or is it just remorse? After being closed off for so many years, Tom had finally opened up a little to someone, and now he wished he hadn't. It was stupid. Drunk stupid. Lonely stupid. Tom knows he shouldn't drink, but his loneliness had got the better of him. He should have bought a hamster, not tried to have a friend. He'd gone so many years without one – why had he tried now? But of course that was the point, wasn't it? It had been 6 February – the anniversary.

'Why?' Keyson asked.

'No one is meant to drink alcohol on police premises.'

'They all do.'

'I don't care about that. I'm the boss and I need to be beyond reproach, or at least look like I'm following the rules'.

With a shrug, the tall man pops the top off the bottle and takes a swig.

'Christ, Marcus.'

The pathologist pops another bottle and hands it to Tom, who takes it furtively and then sits at his desk and pulls out two mugs from the bottom drawer. He hands one to Keyson that reads KEEP 'EM PEELED. The second he keeps for himself. They pour their bottles into the mugs, then Tom puts the empty bottles into his drawer.

'World's Greatest Dad?' Keyson points at Tom's mug.

'I. It… My…' Tom stammers.

'Nobody expects the Freudian Inquisition?' jokes Keyson.

Against his better judgement, Tom laughs. 'Okay, Siggy. I bought it for my dad, when he was still with us. I was about twelve. Big fucking joke.'

'You kept it. Waste not, want not?'

Tom nods but it isn't the case. He kept it to act more like a warning, something he would see every day. Be careful who you raise to the level of a god.

Tom sits at his desk, Keyson opposite him in the bollock chair, so named as you only sat in it if you were getting a bollocking. The two men raise their mugs and drink in silence. As they drink, a tear runs down Tom's cheek.

'Is this why they call you the Sad Man?' Keyson asks, pointing to the tear.

'Jesus.' Tom pulls a box of tissues out of his desk. He takes one and wipes his face.

'Sorry,' Marcus Keyson manages to make an apology sound more like an accusation.

'I have no control of my eyes. I just tear up…' Tom doesn't finish the thought – 'I tear up when I think of anything sad.' Tom knows full well what everyone calls him; he even thinks of himself as the Sad Man, but no one says it to his face. That's the problem with Marcus Keyson – no off switch, no self-censor. Tom picks up the beer and drinks the whole mug down in one go. The genie is out of the bottle.

'How old do you think I am?' Tom asks.

Keyson knows the answer, but remembers how surprised he'd been when he discovered it. He mimes supreme concentration. 'Forty-eight?'

Tom smiles. 'I'm thirty-nine.'

Tom knows that forty-eight is a kind guess. Most people say early fifties. And that's now – even when he was thirty, people guessed he was fifty. The first three times he tried online dating he was accused of lying about his age on the form. Once it led to a stand-up row in a Pizza Express. After that he started putting down forty-eight. He didn't change the age he wanted, twenty-five to thirty-five, and was amazed that he got more responses when women thought he was nearing his fifties.

Beer number seven slides down. Now, both men are lying on the floor, heads almost touching. The time is uncertain; all they know is that the building is mostly dark and out of the seventh-floor window there is nothing to see. No stars and no moon, all hid by brooding clouds. Tomorrow it will rain. And the next day.

'Don't look that way. The wind'll change and you'll get stuck like that.'

Tom laughs, more a schoolboy snigger, really. The beer has taken twenty years off him. 'My mum would always tell me that. I thought it was just more of her crap – but it turned out to be true. Dani died, I cried, and all the fun was over. I got stuck like this.' He laughs a touch hysterically, but truthfully. It feels good to tell someone.

'When?' Keyson asks.

'1989. She was twenty-one.'

'You loved her?'

The tears run sideways and pool in his ears. He can only nod.

'And that's what made you join the police? You wanted to win justice for her?'

'No.' He feels the guilt rise in him. 'I'd already joined.' He can hear them: his mum, teachers, Dani asking him, 'Why, why?'

'Why?' She wasn't angry; she just didn't understand it. Dani could not comprehend why he wasn't going to take the place at Cambridge.

'Explain it to me,' she asked. But he couldn't.

'I left school and joined. It was for her, though – it was for justice. For Dani. Somebody had hurt her and—'

Tom holds the pint glass. It feels awkward in his hand. The alley smells of urine. It's dark and he can't see much except for the pub over the road, which throws rectangles of light into the black street. He's in the perfect position to see the front door, see when it swings open and *he* leaves. Tom knows the man is in there; he checked it out. Bix was there. Lego-and-dogshit Bix.

Tom had walked into the pub, bought himself a pint, taken a few sips, then left with the glass and crossed over to the alley. He'd tipped the beer down a drain and settled down to wait. At 10.50 he heard the last-orders bell clang. Soon. He stretched his stiff legs. A few minutes later a group of lanky men came out, five of them all looking the same as each other. Floppy hair, black T-shirts and jeans, leather jackets, canvas bags slung over a shoulder. Individuality – three cheers for that. They slapped backs, arms or palms before each one peeled off, heading in a different direction. Tom nearly set out to follow the wrong man, but at the last minute one of them shouted.

'Tomorrow, Bix!'

'Right,' Bix replied, and Tom saw his mistake; he should be following the other lanky, arty bastard. He switched to following him. He slammed the glass against the wall and it sheared in half leaving a jagged edge, a nasty-looking weapon. In ten minutes it would cut through the young man's face. Ending his pretty boy looks for ever.

The room is swimming a little. Tom thinks Marcus might have fallen asleep. He knows he should get up soon; his bladder feels distended, but it all seems like such an effort. The glass slices into skin, flesh – then grinds on bone. There is blood and a scream.

'I did something awful,' Tom's voice slurs a little, part alcohol and part melancholy. 'I did it for her, Dani. For her. To defend her. She'd been hurt and I knew he'd do it again, hurt more women. I stopped that.'

That is what he has told himself for years. In front of Marcus Keyson, however, it sounds a little thin.

'I thought about it a lot afterwards. I did my A levels – even applied to university with Dani. But I couldn't stop thinking about what I'd done. I joined the police.' He says in little more than a whisper.

He would like to tell Keyson what he did, that he *glassed* a man. But he cannot. It still shocks him today. And he avoids the obvious question: would he do it again? He hears the scream. The warmth of the blood. The bile rising in his throat. He knows the answer is yes.

'So, the love of your life was murdered?' Keyson's voice sounds warm and surprisingly sober.

Tom is pulled from the nauseating memory. 'Yes. Her last year at university. When she graduated we would have been married, but...' The air above him feels heavy as he lies alongside his confidant, looking up at the ceiling.

'Durham. She was reading classics. I hate Durham.'

'Really?' Keyson sounds a little wistful, enough that Tom rolls his head slightly to look at his friend. 'I love it.'

'All surface. It looks beautiful but underneath... there are maggots.'

The two men are quiet for a few minutes, each lost in their own memories. Tom hears his new friend sigh and looks across to see tears running down his cheeks towards the floor.

'Are you...?'

'I was at boarding school,' Keyson begins. 'I'd gone from the age of five. I was the sad child with big eyes who waves goodbye to all his friends at holiday time and spends a boring break with the sadistic form master and kindly matron.'

'Your parents?'

'Gone.'

That single word is all he says on the subject of his parents. There is a minute of silence as the two men reflect on this new level of intimacy between them.

'One year, maybe I was nine, I was invited home for Christmas by one of the other boys. We weren't even that close and I thought it was a cruel joke at first, but at the end of term a car came and collected both of us and our trunks and we went to his home for the holiday.'

'Durham?'

'Yes. The boy's father had spoken to the headmaster. It had begun a little selfishly, really. The boy had lost his mother and his father was concerned for him. He thought that if he had a friend to play with, that Christmas would be... tolerable.' He pauses and lets that word fill the air around them. Tom knows how keeping busy makes life tolerable.

'Anyway, it was the best two weeks of my whole life. Sad?'

'No... no.'

'I went home with Paul every holiday after that. His father bought us bunk beds and, well, they were my family. My father and brother.'

'You still see them?'

The pause tells Tom everything he needed to know. 'I'm really sorry.'

'I loved them both. Gerald, Paul's father, inspired me – he was the coroner there, the most dedicated man I ever met.'

'In Durham?' Tom feels ice shift in his chest.

'I followed him into the work, something to prove, I suppose. Oh...' Both men suddenly feel a weight push down on them. 'Christ, Tom, your girl died in Durham.'

Simultaneously both men imagine Gerald's scalpel cutting deep into a young woman's chest. Marcus Keyson reaches out and puts his hand on Tom Bevans's arm. Such a little gesture but Tom could not remember the last time anyone showed him such kindness. Tom feels his own hand begin to stretch and, with the lightest of touches, he rests his hand on the other man's arm. Together, swimming in the memories of those they once loved, they lie and stare at the ceiling.

TWENTY-TWO

Tuesday 7 February 1989

There is a strange crackling from the body on the bench. It happens three times before the figure moves, rolling slightly to free a hand from the black cocoon. It pulls out a squat brick with an antenna, and holds it close to what must be a mouth.

'PC Bevans,' is all it says, in a voice syrupy with tiredness.

There's a long pause. Tom pushes himself up on his park-bench bed, keeping the sleeping bag pulled up to his neck. His shoulders are killing him and his lower back feels compressed, as if he'd been carrying a rock uphill for the longest time. He waits for the voice in the machine to tell him the news.

'They... found 'er.' The voice just peeks through the static. 'Call just came in from Durham CID.'

Tom knows the news is not good. He shakes his head free of the last cobwebs of fatigue.

'She's dead?'

The silence says it all.

'Mate, I am so sorry,' Sarge finally manages.

'How can they be sure?' Tom asks, deadpan – dead.

'An anonymous tip-off just before midnight. A male. He said they'd find Dani Lancing at a private address in Durham. A car went straight there and found the body, the first officer on the scene called it in.'

Tom's stomach pitches.

'But are they sure it's her?'

'The first OS had taken the file – all the missing-persons photos. He said he was sure it was her but they called the flatmate over anyway. She made the positive at about one this morning.'

From somewhere an owl hoots. Tom's mouth feels rank. He spits into the grass.

'How had...? What's the cause of death?'

'Don't know. There'll be an autopsy later.'

Silence. Chill.

'Had she been...?' Tom tries to ask.

'Oh, mate. I don't know.' Sarge sounds like he might cry; he hates breaking bad news. It was part of the reason he'd taken the desk job in the first place – so he didn't have to deliver the worst news to people and watch as they disintegrated before his eyes. But he owes something to this young policeman. He grits his teeth.

'She was tied up when they found her... Tom, I'm sorry. That's all I know, the full report will be in later. Sorry.'

'What about her mum and dad?' Tom's voice barely registers.

Sarge twists the volume dial and asks him to repeat.

'Her mum and dad, who's going to tell them?'

'Durham CID are sending someone down. They wanted one of their own to see her parents and talk to the papers – you know, with everything that's gone on.'

'Oh yeah. The reporters.'

They had been like flies on shit the last couple of weeks, plastering Dani's picture all over the front page. Hounding them, wanting anything, everything. And that bastard from the *News of the Screws* – he'd been the worst – disgusting. Well, at least he wouldn't be bothering them again.

'When will the Durham team be here?'

'Hour, maybe two. They're going to meet the DS at some cafe on the way. Get a quick briefing, then the pair of them will drive in together. I think the plan is to get there at about six. I think they're gonna ask the parents to do a secondary ID of the... of Dani. But they're dealing with it as a known victim.'

'Thanks, Sarge. Over.'

Tom feels frozen. He puts the radio down on the bench and swings his legs off. He puts them tentatively on the ground – pins and needles run up and down like electric charges. He feels like a zombie, dragging around a dead body because he's too stupid or too cowardly to lie down. The radio squawks once more.

'I'm re-jigging the rota. Don't come in till Thursday night,' Sarge says through the static.

Three days to recover from the loss of your one true love.

'I need to bring the radio back.'

'Thursday's fine. Go home, Tom.'

'Sarge.'

Tom takes his thumb off the radio and lets the silence engulf him.

He sits for about forty-five minutes, not really thinking, not really doing anything. It's still dark. Last night the moon had been so bright, but it's gone now and Greenwich Park is purple and navy. Tom can just about make out shapes. He hobbles over to a bush and pees into it. He hopes none of it is splashing onto his boots, but really, what does that matter? Once again he's slept in the park like a tramp. He had the idea after Dani had been missing for six days, to keep a walkie-talkie with him at all times. He talked to Sarge about it and he agreed that whoever was on duty would let Tom know any news that came in. The first few nights he'd been at home but he couldn't sleep, worrying that if a call had come in he couldn't get there quickly enough. He wanted to be at the Lancings' the second there was news. So he started to take a sleeping bag onto the heath, only a five-minute walk from their house. It was cold, but nothing that the four-season Everest sleeping bag couldn't deal with.

He used his uniform as a pillow, wrapped up in a soft waterproof, and he always remembered to take a change of underwear and a sponge bag. If he was on duty, he'd wash at the station house; if not, then there were public loos that opened at 7 a.m. on the other side of the bridleway. Normally that was fine, but this morning it isn't good enough. His teeth need a good clean and his chin's scratchy with a lot more than Mickey Rourke stubble. In the dark he can't see that the hairs poking through his skin are pure white, like those spreading out from his temples.

Maybe three weeks ago. Maybe then, he would still have been described as a boy: the pale, skinny boy. Of course, nobody who knew him would say it to his face, but he heard it. Old ladies would see the uniform, stop him in the street and then argue with him, insisting he was a tall child dressing up. One even threatened to call the *real* police. He'd tried to grow a beard, but it had been a disaster. He had been thinking about ordering a pair of glasses with clear glass to see if they made him look older... That was three weeks ago. This morning, no person on earth would mistake him for a boy.

He looks towards the old, old tree, where the woods seem to curve down to the horizon. There, that's where the sky will start to glow soon. In all seasons and all different daybreaks, he always knows when it's about to start – when that first barely perceptible change will come. It's no innate skill in him; it's the birds. No matter what month it is, the birds will begin their chorus two minutes before he sees the first ray. He doesn't know if they sense the change or if their eyes are just that much more sophisticated than his, but something alerts them and they sing the new day into being.

For the past nine days, except for two shifts of night duty, he has lain on this bench and slept at least part of the night here before waking for the miracle of dawn. He'd never slept here before Dani went missing, but he had sat in this spot and watched the dawn arrive. He'd done it some two dozen times over the last five years, and always the same thought had been in his head and heart: is this the day I can persuade Dani Lancing to love me?

The first time it had been Valentine's Day 1984. He'd delivered a card to her house – anonymous of course, and then had run out to the park, amazed by his daring and full of excitement and expectation. He'd not planned to watch the dawn break; in fact it had surprised him. It was an accident – he'd been looking directly at the spot where the sun rose and... He was amazed by the beauty of it. A golden-orange light exploded in the grass and rose to form a miasma around the trees, for a short while making them look like angels; at least they did to a romantic teenager, who had just delivered his first declaration of love.

'Is this an omen of good luck?' he thought. Of course it was not the day Dani Lancing fell for him... in fact, it had been a bit of a disaster, but a love of watching the daybreak from this spot had been born in him. Today, once again, he will watch the dawn from this bench.

The birds begin the overture and there... ta-da. Raspberry ripple smudged into the dusky grey of the sky. It's morning: 7 February 1989. The worst day of his life. The weather forecast predicted a dry warmish day. Not the weather for this news. It should be raining. Storming. Torrential rain to batter and destroy – thunder and lightning. Drama.

She's dead.

He doesn't actively think 'I'll break my orders' but he looks at his watch at 5.30 a.m. and is aware that he should be telling Patty and Jim that Dani is gone. He pulls the walkie-talkie out of his pocket and slides the button down. He croaks into it.

'Sarge?'

'Bevans?'

'I'm heading over to the Lancings'.'

'Oh fuck, Tom, don't do that. The brass'll be there in half an hour or so. Let them deal with it.'

'Sorry, Sarge. I'm not in uniform, I'm off-duty and a family friend. I won't say anything about hearing the news from you. Sarge… Jack, I am very grateful.' Tom drops his finger off the call button.

'Bevans. Bevans… Fuck.'

Tom turns the volume down low and puts it in the bag with his uniform. He knows his sarge is right, but this is his duty. The DS from Durham can deal with the shit from the press. Tom can't think about that, all he knows is that two people are in pain. And, it strikes him only now, that it's two people he loves. Sort of, certainly two people he has become close with, cares about. Is that love? He stands and swings his bag onto his shoulder. Then he heads out.

'What the hell are you doing? Do you know what they call you? "The pup". Stupid love-struck pup. She says you follow me around drooling like some lost dog.' He hears Dani's voice in his head.

It had been his third visit to her in Durham, the third term of her first year. He'd gone for the weekend and right from the start she'd been eager to pick a fight. He'd said something about Patricia – something nice – and Dani had blown up. Tom hadn't risen to the bait; he could see what was going on. A lot of their friendship had been born out of each of them moaning about their mothers. Dani liked to riff on her absent, career-obsessed mother and Tom would tell stories of his mother's drinking, offensive boyfriends and the beatings. Then his mum died.

It was the middle of Dani's second term, that first year. Dani hadn't come to the funeral. He had hoped she would, had asked her to, but she was busy and had tests. It was a dismal turnout. An aunt he barely knew. A woman who said she knew her from bingo and three drinking mates who sat in the back row and raised cans of Special Brew to their lips as a parting toast.

Tom sat alone, in the front row. He wore his uniform. He wasn't sure why but it helped keep him strong – it was unseemly for a copper to blub in public. He sat there waiting for the vicar, wishing for the day just to be over. Then someone slipped in beside him and a hand gripped his. He looked over and it was Patricia. She didn't say anything, just winked at him.

After the funeral they walked together, around the cemetery. There was no wake. No sandwiches starting to curl in the back room of a pub somewhere. Instead, the young policeman and the mother of his love walked and talked. Well, she smoked and he talked. He talked of his mother – but it wasn't the complaints and horror stories he might have told Dani. Instead it was tales of laughs, fun and shared happiness: the time when this happened, that broke, they got lost going there, she used salt instead of sugar... good times. And under the outstretched wings of a stone angel, in a field of the fallen, Patricia folded Tom into her arms and stroked his head while he cried.

'Poor pup,' she had said, comfortingly.

Of course, the minute he'd heard that Dani was missing, he had gone to them. 'What can I do? What do you need?' Patricia and Jim appreciated it. They weren't being taken seriously in Durham, they said. They wanted him to check out the progress from inside the force. That was his mission – if he chose to accept it. He did.

After Dani had been missing for seven days, Tom was at the Lancings' every evening for an update. On his days off he went to Durham and talked to the police there. He went alone, even though he knew Patricia was going too – sometimes with Jim, but other times alone. He liked spending time with Jim, but often Patricia scared him. He had no idea what drugs the doctors had prescribed for her, but he thought no human being should be that tightly wound. Her grief scared him. It felt like a violent cloud that hung over anyone that came close to her. In her presence he felt frustrated – like a child furious at the injustice of the world and yet unable to do anything to change it. At least with Jim he could put a hand on his shoulder, connect at some level. With Patricia, she was inside some private bubble, waiting and waiting and waiting for her daughter to come home.

'Oh, Jesus.' A sob convulses him. She isn't coming home. Not for them and not for him.

'Dani!' he howls, filling the park with pain.

For a second he's outside his body looking in, watching some old, old man weep for his lost love. The pain screws his face until it shatters like fine porcelain in a fire. Then the wind changes and he's stuck like it. The Sad Man is born.

Jim stands in Dani's bedroom and looks out at the encroaching day. He likes to be in there; it still smells of her: coconut shampoo and menthol cigarettes. She'd been home for just two disastrous days at Christmas. They had rowed and… they hadn't had enough time. They hadn't even spoken to her on her birthday. The first time… but he mustn't think like that. She'd be back soon and the room –

her room, was ready. He'd changed the bedding only a few days before and bought a new toothbrush and the toothpaste she likes. When she's found, she'll need to be looked after, be in comfort and safety. That's their job, their only… Through the window he sees Tom enter their road, walk a little way and stop on the corner. Jim feels his stomach churn. He can see the young man batting at his face, like a wasp is buzzing around. Then he realises Tom is crying.

Jim's throat closes up; he finds it hard to breathe.

'Patty.' He thinks of his wife next door, asleep for the first time in days – even if it is purely due to sedation. Tom will be here, will knock in about a minute. Why is he crying?

Jim is out of the front door as quietly as he can. He's in the street before he realises he's still in his pyjamas. He looks down the road – Tom's still where Jim last saw him – was that good news? He walks towards Tom, each step becomes a wish, a prayer. 'Let her be alive. Found alive. Found alive.' Hope.

Tom sees him approach and tries to pull himself together. He remembers the first time they ever spoke, after they both watched Dani run. He even remembers the stupid thumbs up he gave him that day. The pain spasms the policeman. Jim sees the pain and slows. There is no good news. There is no hope. Their eyes lock like two gunslingers facing off at dawn. Tom shakes his head and the tears stream. With a cry, like he's been shot, the pyjama-clad man falls to the ground.

TWENTY-THREE

Friday 8 October 2010

Marcus Keyson sees the way her hand shakes. After a while he discounts nervous energy and decides she has Parkinson's, probably early stages, and isn't fully managing her medication yet. While she talks he watches her. She looks like a runner, very thin but muscular, powerful. She could have been a looker when she was young; she has the bone structure for it. Her eyes are the real point of attraction, they actually seem to burn as she talks about her daughter. Though, truth be told, he's pretty much zoned out of her story, just the odd nod here and there. Something she said early on sent his mind spinning.

Finally she stops talking and looks at him expectantly, like a puppy. He nods slowly; that always seems to put people at their ease.

'Mrs Lancing, I will need to look into this further. I have ex-colleagues I can talk to, I have a relationship with the Durham coroner's office. But just to recap, you mentioned Detective Inspector Tom Bevans – he's an old friend – was he involved with the original investigation?'

'No, not really, just by... he... he was Dani's friend.'

'Friend?'

'He... does it matter?'

'I don't know. Maybe.'

'He was... he loved her.'

'She loved him?'

She pauses. 'No, not in that way.'

Bingo.

After she leaves, he googles her. Award-winning crime journalist, first with the *Northern Echo* and then the *Independent*. There are dozens of articles she'd written over the years. Two books, one titled *Wives of the Killers*, which seems to be a series of interviews, and *The Ugly Man*. Both have great reviews and the second won two prestigious awards. There are also press releases and news stories linking her to Lost Souls, a charity campaigning for victims' rights. Next he googles images of her and there are many: one of her accepting an *Evening Standard* prize, a National Journalism Award for an interview with Sonia Sutcliffe, another of her on a demo and a few at Greenham Common. The best is one of her haranguing Margaret Thatcher. He was right: she had been quite a looker back then. He feels excited, his whole body tingles. The long-dead girl and Tom Bevans. And... something else is pulling at threads in the back of his mind. A long-ago tragedy. He struggles to remember – a note he had seen twenty years before. A suicide note. It spoke of shame, corruption and... lance. Was that it? Lancing? He shakes his head – the thread will not unravel. Instead he turns back to the job in hand and flicks the intercom.

'Can you come in here please, Lauren?' he asks.

A few seconds later his assistant limps in.

'I need you to find me an investigator in Durham. They're to find out names and addresses for anyone involved in the investigation of a murder. Danielle Lancing, February 1989.'

Lauren starts to make notes.

'I want to know the name and current address of every copper on the murder team back then. I also want to know who was writing up the notes, and where any samples and evidence are kept. Okay?'

She smiles. Everything is okay as far as she's concerned.

'And...' He pauses. 'Gerald Spurling. I think you'll find he was the coroner on the case. I'd like to see his reports from the public record.'

'Okay,' she nods.

'And can you check on the state of forensic review with Durham CID, make it sound general but I need to know about this girl, Dani Lancing. Why is her case coming up now, is it just luck or did someone request a review?'

'Will do,' she smiles.

'And call Ronson and ask him to come and see me ASAP. Oh, and I want all the murder team members cross-referenced with a London officer – DS Tom Bevans. He was a PC back then.'

Lauren stops making notes.

'He's the one who—'

'Yes. Yes he is, so do a thorough job. Okay?'

She smiles and moves to walk around to the back of his chair; she stretches her fingers as she walks and reaches out for the back of his neck.

'Not now.'

She blushes at the rebuff. 'Of course,' and she leaves.

Marcus Keyson sits back in his chair and dares to dream – of revenge. A chance to get back at the man who made all this happen – who destroyed his career, tarnished his reputation and betrayed him. His Judas. Maybe all this could be turned to some financial advantage as well. Tom Bevans should pay. Maybe Patricia Lancing should pay too; he could do with clearing some of the debts – even get away from this awful place.

'This is so good. So good.'

TWENTY-FOUR

Monday 11 October 2010

Keyson pushes the heavy doors open and stands on the threshold of bedlam. He whistles 'The lunatics have taken over the asylum' as he steps inside the special ops room for Operation Ares. As he does so, he slips the ID card from around his neck and drops it into his pocket. It's a fake, of course, and impersonating a police officer is a serious offence. He smiles.

For all the chaos, it's the sound that really makes an impact. Officers howl into their phones, each having to project over the din of colleagues and the incessant squawking of dozens of unanswered phones demanding attention. Added to that are the slams of filing cabinets, the squeals of felt-tip markers and the pacing of a lot of nicotine-deprived, overweight men.

The air is sticky with testosterone and cheap aftershave, knock-off Calvin Klein from Petticoat Lane market. Keyson had forgotten its pungency. He takes a deep breath and heads for the centre of the web. This had never been his office but he'd spent so much time here it had almost been home – once. For three years, unless he was actually scrutinising a cadaver, he had been here, among the living. He'd believed he'd made friends. For a while, he thought Detective Inspector Jane Thorsen might be the one. Not a long while, though. He reaches the heart of the operations room, unnoticed, and stands there waiting.

He watches his ex-colleagues and imagines them all dead. Violent, blood-splattered deaths, and he's the man brought in to solve their murders. It cheers him enormously. Finally he's noticed. A nod, a shake of the head, a whistle, someone pointing and then the wall of sound deadens and flat-lines. Close by there is a chorus of 'I'll call you back'. Phones are replaced on their receivers. The room is quiet.

'What the fuck do you want, Keyson?'

He turns. Of course, it's Clark. Clark, who used to call him 'Marcus'. Who had invited him to both his stag night and his wedding. Clark, who had once vomited on his shoes – suede shoes – and told him he'd never loved his mother and now she was dying of cancer and what could he do? Clark, who had practically offered him his own sister once, but who had spat in his face after the tribunal. The two men square up. Keyson would be only too glad to fight Clark.

'Clark,' Thorsen barks through a megaphone. The sound echoes off the walls filling the room. 'If you lay a hand on a civilian, you'll be on a fucking charge so fast.'

'But—'

'Get back to work. Stay where you are, Keyson.'

Grumbling, the crowd dissipates back to desks and phones. The noise level builds again and all is back as it had been. Thorsen waits to make sure everyone has obeyed, then walks over to Keyson. As she approaches him, she notes the small changes. He is still well groomed, always spent freely on his hair and skin, but his clothes are a little shabbier than before. The coat is the same he had three years ago and his shoes are worn. There is a shine to the knees of his suit – not worn-out, but the old Marcus Keyson replaced his wardrobe every year. Interesting – life in the independent sector not quite so sparkling for God's gift to forensic science.

He is still bloody handsome, though, she thinks as she stops in front of him.

'Why the hell are you here, Marcus?'

'Good to see you too, Jane,' Keyson says, with what he believes is a winning smile.

Thorsen crosses her arms and glares at him. Keyson notes how she hides her chest, breast reduction in her late teens due to backache. In bed he had kissed the tracery of fine scars. He never told anyone, not even after she'd maced him. That should have earned him something, shouldn't it? He'd even met her mother.

From behind DI Thorsen, a small, bespectacled man emerges, looking a little mole-like: DI Jenkins.

'I think, unless you need something, that you should turn around and get out, Dr Keyson.' Jenkins – the voice of reason. The only one who didn't turn against him after the tribunal. How he hates Jenkins.

'I'm here to see the Sad Man,' Keyson says to Jane, ignoring Jenkins altogether.

'I'm sure the guvnor has no desire to see you again,' she says, her voice level but full of fury at the disrespectful use of Tom's nickname.

Keyson nods, then takes a pad and pen off an adjacent desk and quickly scrawls a note. He folds it in half and hands it to Thorsen.

'Please give him this. Tell him I'll be over the road in Munchies. I'll get him a tea. Four sugars, if I remember correctly.'

He turns on his heel and walks back towards the door. He feels the daggers in his back from all quarters, but he's pleased with how it went. If he can avoid food poisoning in Munchies, this will be a good day.

DI Thorsen stops for a second outside Tom's office; she's shaking a little. She feels so angry at the ex-pathologist that she needs to pause. Marcus Keyson betrayed them both, but in a funny way it's Tom who has been more deeply affected. She was the one who'd slept with him, had even taken him to meet her super-judgemental mother – and annoyingly her mum had been thoroughly charmed by him – but she has other friends, real friends. She's been on a lot of dates since, slept with a number of men, and it's water under the bridge as far as she's concerned. But Tom doesn't make friends, at least none that she knows of, certainly none in the force. That was why it had seemed so strange that he and Keyson had become close. She knows better than anyone how seductive Marcus Keyson can be – clever, funny and a great listener. She remembers that Tom and Marcus had even talked about holiday plans, a long weekend in Copenhagen for some conference. Didn't happen in the end. Instead, Professional Standards took Keyson into custody one afternoon and closed the unit down for three days while they investigated accusations of gross professional misconduct. They had all been questioned. The entire department had fallen under suspicion, especially Detective Inspector Jane Thorsen, the idiot who had been dumb enough to sleep with him, and Detective Superintendent Tom Bevans – his friend. Detectives from DPS had been through both of their files and their personal lives with fine-tooth combs. It took months, but eventually the only person reprimanded was Keyson, though there remained a stain on the reputation of the whole Serious Crimes Unit and Operation Ares in particular.

It was hushed up, of course. No press got wind of it. They discharged Keyson with no pension, but there were no criminal charges. She still doesn't know how the slimy bastard managed it. That had been three years ago. Since then she had barely thought of Marcus Keyson. He had no lasting power over her life, though she feels that Tom is still hurt by the loss of his friend. So, how would he react now? There is only one way to find out. She knocks.

'Come in,' he calls.

Tom Bevans stands by the window looking out onto the street outside. The grey December light makes him look even paler than normal; his silver-white hair shines a little. He turns towards her, his face seeming to contain both a little boy and an old man simultaneously. Though he is her superior officer, she wants to hug him to her and make him eat some soup.

She holds up the note. 'Marcus Keyson just slimed in.'

'Keyson. Why?'

'He asked me to give you this.' She waves the note. 'And to tell you he'd be in Munchies and would get you a tea.'

He walks over and takes the note.

'Cheeky bastard, well he can go—' He unfolds the paper and dries up.

'Guv? Guv, are you okay?' She thinks he's seen a ghost.

'You said he's there, now?'

'He came in, gave me the note and left.'

'Well, how the fuck did he get in here? He doesn't have clearance.'

'I don't know, sir.' He had never shouted at her before; she feels herself contract a little, like when her father had come home.

'Okay.' He sees her flinch from him and immediately feels guilty. 'I'm sorry, Jane. Thanks, thanks for bringing this up to me. You go back to work, I'll… you go back.'

She nods and walks towards the door, feeling the tension in the air. She can see he wants her gone. She'd like to offer help, but she leaves instead.

Tom waits until Thorsen has gone and then calls down to security for them check the log. There's no Dr Marcus Keyson entered.

'Well, he was just here,' Tom tells them angrily. 'Read me the names of everyone admitted into this building in the last half hour – I don't care how fucking busy you are.'

The sixteenth name strikes a bell: Lewis Mason. There'd been a detective about ten years ago with that name but he'd transferred to Cardiff and then left the force. He'd become a hypno-therapist, specialising in helping the gullible and weak give up smoking and lose weight.

'Check Mason right now,' he ordered. Security checked – Lewis Mason's level one clearance was still operative; it had never been rescinded.

'Well bloody do it now!' barked Tom. 'Then, start going through all existing access and check that the officers are alive and still work here... I don't care how long it'll take. We just had someone break into the Ares op room; he could have been a suicide bomber.'

Tom slams the handset down. In all likelihood this was probably worse than a suicide bomber. Damn Keyson. The scrap of paper Jane had handed him was still lying on his desk. He picks it up and opens it again. Two words, but they make the pit of his stomach lurch.

Danielle Lancing.

TWENTY-FIVE

Monday 11 October 2010

From somewhere a trumpet plays 'Joy to the World', but plaintively, as if performed by a heartbroken elf.

'It's only mid-October,' Tom grumbles under his breath as he stands under a grocer's awning and scans the road. The rain is falling harder now and the street ahead's a wind tunnel, threatening to slice anyone salami-thin if they venture into it. Tom's hand slides through his white hair. He should have brought an umbrella. From where he stands he can get to Munchies in about two minutes – but he will arrive looking like a drowned rat. Normally he wouldn't mind – he's not a vain man – but Marcus Keyson brings out the worst in him.

'Come on, calm down for a couple of minutes,' he tells the rain. Of course, it gets harder instead. 'Typical.'

He can't delay this much longer. It's already forty-five minutes since Thorsen gave him the note. After checking security, he quickly scanned the last six weeks of crime digest – an online summary of crime. He filtered it using as many keywords as he could think of: Keyson, Lancing, Durham University, Durham gang, Merchant and Cobhurn – nothing came up.

Then he washed in the gents – used Fat Eddy's deodorant and razor – and put on the spare shirt and tie he kept for snap inspections. Waste of time. The new shirt is now completely soaked and he already smells a bit.

'Over the top,' he sighs, and makes a dash for it. He hits a paving stone and it rears up, shooting mucky brown water up his leg and into his crotch. He remembers his old religious education teacher, Vicar Tim, standing in front of them intoning in his deep sombre voice: 'With pestilence and with blood, I will rain down upon him.'

'What shit has Dr Marcus Keyson come to rain down on this sinner's head?' Tom wonders. Then he catches himself and realises he's in full-on apocalypse mode. 'Really, Tom. Really – Bible quotations now? You need to get out more. And you need to stop thinking about yourself in the third person.'

He walks on, waddling like a duck as the muddy water soaks through his crotch.

Finally he reaches the cafe, but stops short of the door. Rain runs off him in little waterfalls, his socks are wet and his underpants squelch. He wants to shake like a dog but where's the dignity in that? Instead he squeegees his hair with his hand and composes himself. At least there are unlikely to be any of his colleagues inside the cafe. *Real* coppers went to Fred's – a large greasy spoon just around the corner. Fred's is cheap, decidedly cheerful, and gives you the kind of home comfort that most coppers don't get at home. Unpredictable hours, and the fact that most of the women they know work long hours too, means most male coppers defrost and microwave their own suppers in front of the telly or computer. Or they eat at Fred's and flirt with his two plump daughters. The women coppers are similar; they either go home and heat up ready-meals for their husbands and kids – who are jealous of the time they spend on the job – or they eat a super-food salad from M&S on their own, knock back three or four vodkas and fall asleep in their clothes. This is modern policing.

While the worst of the storm drips off him, Tom reads the specials board through the window: sunblush tomato and feta quiche, balsamic roasted parsnip soup, halloumi and couscous salad. Was this a date?

Below the board, sitting in the far corner, he sees Keyson, whose table is littered with empty cups and a teapot. Stone cold, thinks Tom. As if he knows he's being watched, Keyson slowly turns and looks straight at Tom. He waves.

Tom pushes the door open and steps inside. A very pretty waitress waves him towards a table by the door, but he shakes his head and indicates Keyson's table.

'He's my plus-one – finally,' Keyson calls to her. Both he and the waitress laugh. Tom grimaces. He takes off his coat and hangs it by the door, on a rack that is supposed to look like deer antlers. Keyson stands as Tom approaches and holds out his hand. Tom ignores the gesture and pulls out the other chair at the table – but as he does so he looks down. Scattered across the table are papers and photographs: Dani, Patricia, Jim and a face he barely recognises – but it's circled in red ink. Ben Bradman.

Tom reels. 'I… I'll be just a second.'

'Gents is over there.' Keyson points with a smile.

Tom heads off.

TWENTY-SIX

Monday 30 January 1989

'Peace, man.' The reporter flashes a two-finger salute as he opens the door and sees a uniformed police constable standing there.

'Mr Bradman?' asks PC Tom Bevans, controlling a desire to punch him.

'That's me, Mr Policeman.' He smiles.

'I wonder if I could come in and ask you a few questions, Mr Bradman?' Tom asks in a level and friendly voice.

'Well now, I am not at all sure about that. I would have to make clear I was in no way waiving my rights and not agreeing to my premises being searched or—'

'This is not about you directly, Mr Bradman. Let me assure you I am not interested in what might be in your flat. I just want to ask you a few questions concerning the disappearance of Danielle Lancing. In your article this weekend you seem to hint at information you may have obtained—'

'Whoa, whoa there, officer. A reporter's source is sacrosanct. When he talks to me, that is like a priest hearing confession.'

Tom has trouble seeing Ben Bradman as any kind of priest, but he tries to keep the incredulity out of his face and voice. 'Mr Bradman, I have no desire to shatter the integrity of your relationship with your source. But I would like to ask about the information itself, and I do not think your hallway is the place to do this.'

Bradman thinks for a second. 'Okay, but wait here.'

He closes the door behind him and goes into his flat. Tom stands stock still. He assumes Bradman's hiding his dope stash. Even through the door he can smell the oppressive fug of cannabis. He waits about two minutes and Bradman reappears. He nods and Tom follows him in, closing the front door. As he walks over the threshold, Tom slips his hand into his pocket and fingers a brass knuckleduster taken from the evidence room. He slips it on his hand. He follows Bradman into the living room. The curtains are closed.

'Anyone else here?' he asks.

'In a flat this size? You're jo—'

Tom swings hard and fast; he feels a snap and hears the crack of cheekbone and his own knuckle pop out of its socket.

'Fuck' both men shout together. Bradman drops to the floor, his hand to his face – blood showing through his fingers. It reminds Tom of how a torch glows red through your hand when you cup it. Tom pulls off the knuckleduster and pops his finger back into its socket.

'Jesus shit. Shit.' Bradman keeps repeating.

'Stay down or I will hit you again,' Tom says, in his best hard-man voice. He really hopes Bradman does stay down. His hand hurts so much he doesn't think he could hit him again.

'Franco will get his fucking money. I just need another day or two,' Bradman is almost hysterical.

'I'm not from Franco.'

'What?'

'I'm not from Franco.'

'Then…' His brain reels: who is this guy if he's not from Franco? 'So, what do you want?' he asks, starting to get angry.

'I told you. I want to talk about the story you wrote on Dani Lancing.'

'You are shitting me.' He starts to get up.

Tom kicks at his knee, smacking him back down to the floor. Bradman grunts and grabs at the knee, smearing blood all over his jeans, which are filthy already. Tom unfolds a sheet of newsprint from his pocket.

'Dani Lancing has been painted as a promising student, sports star and much loved daughter – a good girl. However the truth may be very different. There is evidence to suggest Dani was involved with drugs in her first year at Durham University and was selling them to finance her lavish lifestyle—'

'Freedom of spee—' Bradman interrupts.

'You fucking liar!' Tom shouts, kicking wildly at Bradman's leg.

'I reported fairly,' Bradman whines.

Tom kicks at his leg again, this time just hitting into the thigh. '*Fair*, you don't know the meaning of the word. You smeared a poor sweet—'

'Oh please. I read all that shit in the *Independent* and *Echo*. I heard stuff about Snow White.'

'What?' Tom drops to the floor, making Bradman squeal a little. 'What did you hear?'

'She... she used to be the bitch of the campus pusher: king of the uni smackheads.'

Tom feels his stomach freeze. 'You liar.' His voice is a little uncertain.

Bradman seizes on that; he continues, more brazen now. 'She got turned. Happens to students all the time. She's probably drying out somewhere – or stuffed to the tits on junk.'

Tom punches hard, into the floor by Bradman's head. He hears his knuckle pop again but doesn't feel it – his body is awash with adrenalin.

'I love her!' Tom screams into his face.

All colour drains from Bradman's face, finally understanding what has happened. 'I... I'm sorry.'

'Sorry? Sorry?' Tom barks.

'You're right, right of course. It's not true. I embroidered, embellished. You gotta understand, there's a pressure...'

'Pressure?' asks Tom, in a small voice.

'I can see what I've done now.' He laughs a nervous, edgy laugh. 'I've tried to shoehorn two stories together: student druggies and your missing girlfriend. I'm sorry. We can do a big story – get the public looking under every rock and stone. Telling them how brave she is, about how amazing her parents are...'

'What did you hear?' Tom almost whispers into the reporter's ear.

'Look. We can—'

'What did you hear?' Just a breath.

'Probably nothing, I—'

Tom swings again – the knuckleduster connects with chin – blood in the mouth.

'Fuck, fuck... I heard rumours. Okay, just rumours.'

'Who from?'

'I can't—'

'Give me a name.' Tom takes the knuckleduster and drives it into the reporter's hand, crushing it into the floor. He screams.

'A jazz guy, trumpet player in Durham. Diamond earring in his right ear, shaved head. I don't know his name. Honest.'

Tom pulls the brass knuckleduster off his hand. Bradman pulls his fingers into his chest and rolls from side to side, tears rolling down his face.

'Thank you for your help, Mr Bradman.' Tom stands up – it's over.

Bradman lies there and watches the policeman rise. He suddenly realises it's done, just a hurt hand and knee – that's all this is. He laughs. Then he opens his arms as if to embrace humanity, his face sad – what can you do? Life.

It was the gesture Tom hated: supplicant and weak – a victim. It reminded him of all the ponces he'd arrested, the women he'd seen battered, his own fucking father after he'd beaten his own son and he opened his arms as if to say 'It was your fault after all, but I forgive you.' Tom sees red. He grabs the knuckleduster and punches – once hard. There is a crack – metal on bone, a pistol shot. Bradman lies unmoving.

Was it premeditated? That's what Tom has asked himself so many times over the years. Ben Bradman and Bix Lego-dogshit.

He looks down at the body in front of him. Feels for a pulse – weak, but there. He isn't dead. Tom runs into the bathroom and throws up. When he's finished he cleans the bowl and bleaches it thoroughly. Whether Tom had planned to knock him out or not, he hadn't planned what to do next, but it came to him in a rush. He started to search the flat; he knew Bradman had hidden something. He found it quickly but it was very disappointing, a small bag of dope – not enough.

'Think, Tom,' he tells himself. He needs Bradman out of the picture for a while. He can't have him investigating Tom and Dani again.

Bradman's keys are in the back of the front door; he'd used them to open up when Tom arrived. He checks Bradman's pulse again. He'll be out for a while.

'Okay.' He grabs the keys and leaves the flat, locking the door behind him. He runs down the three flights of stairs to the street and out into the night. It's almost ten o'clock but where he's going, that's like morning. Bradman had given him the answer to the problem himself. Franco.

It isn't far. He's only been there once before, as extra support if a riot occurred. Franco ran drug distribution for almost the whole of East London. Pretty amazing, considering he is eighteen years old. Tom runs the whole way there. The base of Franco's empire is a four-storey block of ex-council flats sold off by Thatcher in the mid-eighties. Now it is equipped with armed guards on the roof, a helipad and the most sophisticated set-up of surveillance cameras in London – including those around MI5. As soon as Tom gets to the forecourt of the block, he can feel eyes on him. He knows at least one rifle will be trained on his head. He stops at the entranceway. It's dark, but he knows how misleading that is. Blackout curtains mask the fact that most of the flats are being used to manufacture crack, PCP, amphetamines and a wide variety of mood enhancers and brain-cell killers. Tom doesn't care.

He stands on the threshold of the enemy kingdom and looks up. He's wearing his uniform, which was great for getting into Bradman's flat, but makes him a terrible target now.

'Into the valley of death rides the idiot. Cannon to left of him...' Tom holds his hands up, showing his palms.

'I want to see Franco,' he shouts.

There is nothing for a while and then a booming voice calls out, 'Strip.' And from all around there are the deep, throaty laughs of bored men.

In ultra-slow motion Tom slides out of his jacket, then unbuttons his shirt and removes it. Then he undoes his belt and trousers – they fall to the floor. He slides his hands into the waistband of his...

'Leave the underpants on. We don't wanna see your skanky white cock,' a voice calls out.

'I need to see Franco,' Tom shouts back to the unseen voice.

'We's thought you were auditioning for the Chippendales.' A whole gang of voices laugh and there are the slaps of high-fives.

'I have a proposition for Franco.'

'Some naked white guy gonna propose to Franco!' another voice shouts and a peal of laughter echoes around the block.

'Come on up, Officer Dribble!' shouts the first voice and Tom walks out of his trousers and heads up into the jaws of Franco's headquarters.

The stairs smell of piss and weed. He takes them two at a time, starting to feel pretty cold.

Once he gets to the top floor, there is a group of armed men waiting for him. Even though he is near-enough naked they still frisk him for weapons. One of them cups his balls and grips his penis.

'This is no time to get an erection,' he tells himself. Thankfully it's cold and the frisk only lasts a few seconds.

'You can see I don't have anything. No weapon, no wire, nothing. I'm not here as a copper but as a regular citizen. I need a favour from Franco,' Tom tells the assorted men, none of whom seem to be in charge. A nod seems to run around the group and one of them disappears inside.

'Nice night,' Tom says, trying to be friendly.

The gunmen laugh and then melt into the shadows leaving him seemingly alone. He stands shivering for ten minutes before the door opens again and he is motioned inside. Once over the threshold he is frisked again by a giant of a man before being led into a large room.

'Wait here,' he's told, and the giant leaves.

The room is empty, except for a huge sofa. On one end is a beautiful young woman, maybe eighteen, with flawless cinnamon-coloured skin. She wears a silk sarong that looks like the sun, it's so bright. She is as high as a kite. Her eyes are rolled back in her head and she sways to music only she can hear. Occasionally she giggles. Tom sits at the other end of the sofa, as far from the girl as he can be.

'I really need to see Franco quickly,' Tom says to the air, assuming a hidden camera somewhere. Bradman will wake up within an hour or two and time is short. 'Ben Bradman owes Franco a lot of money. I am here to buy that debt from him... as well as something else.'

Tom hears a click from somewhere.

A minute later the giant reappears and ushers Tom from the room and into another. This room is even larger. Tom wonders how it's possible – the entire storey of the block must have been knocked through into one flat. In this room there's a full-size snooker table. Franco is playing a long red. He pots it expertly and straightens up. He's a tall and imposing figure; the story Tom had heard was that his bloodline was ancient African royalty, and the young man holds himself ramrod straight. Franco turns towards Tom and for a second seems so young, a gawky teen with a slightly cheeky smile and swagger. Tom feels a smile start to break, then recalls a body he saw a month or two ago. A mutilated corpse, punished by Franco, and his smile fades. The story goes that Franco inherited this empire from his uncle, who had built it up over twenty years using a mixture of loyalty, brutality, fear and clever pricing models. The uncle had been known to be cruel and heartless. Franco was said to be worse. Tom looks to the other player. He recognises him off the telly – an up-and-coming snooker star.

'Police Constable Bevans, do you play?' Franco asks as he eyes up another long pot.

'There's a table in the station house. I've played a few times,' Tom replies, trying to keep his voice level. Of course his uniform is downstairs with his warrant number on it, someone must have linked the number to the name. Still, it was quick work to get a name.

Franco nods and folds himself back over the cue. He wears sunglasses, which he pushes down his nose so that he can look over the top. He pulls the cue back and shoots the white ball down the table. It clatters into the black, which dances in the jaws of the pocket before spilling back onto the table.

'Bad luck there, Franco. Do you want another try?' says the professional. Tom can hear the fear in his voice.

'No,' Franco says, sounding a bit brittle. 'I'm done.' The professional looks like he wants to cry. 'Fuck off, pool boy.'

The giant reappears and leads the snooker player out.

Franco walks off, through another door. Tom looks around and then follows him. The new room is even larger. Pinball machines line one wall and a large office table sits in the middle. Covering one wall is a huge noticeboard, breaking up East London into the areas led by its chief distributor. Shit, this is gold dust for the anti-drugs unit, Tom thinks, but he looks away. He isn't here as a policeman. A rolled-up dressing gown hits him in the face.

'Please put that on, PC Bevans.'

Tom does as he's asked. It is a flaming red and yellow kimono – a dragon.

'Looks good on you. Very Hendrix. Keep it as a gift.'

'Thank you.'

Franco sits down at his desk, feet up on it. He pushes the sunglasses back on his head. Even though he's tall, the desk dwarfs him – Tom cannot help but think he looks like a child playing businessman. Tom is left to stand.

'So what do you want, Mr Policeman?'

'Ben Bradman, reporter with the *News of the World*.'

'A filthy rag. A friend?'

'He is no friend.'

'I am pleased to hear it. The man is scum.'

'He owes you money. I will buy that debt from you.'

Franco raises an eyebrow. 'Why would you do that, Mr Policeman?'

'That's my business, Mr Franco.'

Franco smiles. 'He owes me four thousand pounds. I will sell that debt to you for eight thousand.'

'Agreed.' Tom doesn't stop to think where he could possibly find the money. 'Of course you can see I do not have the money on me.'

'When we shake on the deal, you will have two days to deliver the money.'

'Fine.' Tom pauses. 'There is something else I would like to ask of you. Something... more unusual.'

'More unusual than buying this debt?' asks Franco, intrigued.

'I think you will find it so.' He pauses to concentrate his courage. 'Heroin, Mr Franco. I want a large amount of heroin. Enough so that when it's found by the police, it will result in the person in possession being sent to prison for a long time. But I do not want to buy the heroin, I want to borrow it and return it. Probably in three months' time.'

For a few seconds there is nothing, then Franco's throat erupts into a deep laugh. 'You are right, Mr Policeman, that is indeed most unusual.' He laughs again. 'You are a strange man PC Bevans.'

'Call me Tom.'

Franco reacts like he's been slapped. He is up and across the room in an instant. In one fluid motion he grabs Tom by the throat, kicks his legs out from under him; he falls with a crack to his knees. Franco jabs a small blunt-nosed gun into Tom's neck.

'Tell me, friend, Tom, why do you do this?'

Tom feels the cold metal press harder into his throat. 'You wouldn't understand.'

'Try.'

A pause.

'My… a woman is missing. She is my best friend and Ben Bradman told the dirtiest lies about her.'

Franco lets him go, almost like Tom burns him, and turns away.

'I am sorry.' He pauses. 'Tom.'

Tom stands, the gun is gone. Franco returns to his desk, though this time he does not put his feet up on it.

'Okay, I will give you half a kilo of dirty heroin. It's cut with bathroom cleaner; it is likely that any conviction for supplying contaminated H would result in the judge throwing away the key. Would that suit your purposes?'

'Yes.' Tom feels shame for a second, then remembers Bradman's words and his story in the newspaper.

'I do not require the heroin back. I do not sell dangerous product. It was cut by a business associate. An ex-business associate.'

Tom remembers the mutilated body – was that his crime? 'Thank you. I will also need some… other evidence.'

Franco nods. 'I can supply that also. I suggest you will need to administer at least one dose of genuine product to Mr Bradman to complete the frame. You may also have that free and gratis. I do not like this man, you understand.'

Tom nods.

'Do you know how to administer such an injection?'

Tom creases his brow. 'I saw a police training film at Hendon.'

Franco grimaces. 'I know that film – it is useless. Come with me.'

Franco walks Tom back through the snooker room and into the sofa room. The beautiful woman is asleep.

'Wait here.' Franco leaves for a minute or so and returns with a carrier bag, which he hands to Tom. Then he leans forward and pulls open the woman's sarong.

'Lovely, yes?'

Tom doesn't reply, but he cannot help but think she is exquisite, flawless, except for her shoulder where there is a sore red welt. It is a brand that has been burnt upon her, a single F. She is the property of Franco.

Then Franco pulls her legs apart and Tom sees she has a line of tracks spreading along her inner thigh. Some are pinpricks, others little scabs, and two are little open mouths. They spread from her like a butterfly emblazoned on her body.

'Here.' Franco takes a syringe out of the bag and pushes the lever up. A drop of liquid is pushed out of the needle. 'You will have seen this on TV – there must be no air in the syringe. Use it to create a number of pinpricks on Mr Bradman's arm, then do the final one into a vein. Tie this around his arm. We do not need to protect Mr Bradman's pretty arms.'

He shows Tom how to tie a rubber tube around the girl's arm, then he flicks her forearm to show the vein.

'You see?'

Tom nods. She stays asleep through all this. Somehow it makes it worse. From somewhere the giant reappears with a bag marked Homepride Flour.

'Here is all you need.'

'Thank you.'

Franco holds out his hand. Tom looks at it nervously for a second and then extends his own. Franco's grip is like a vice. He hold's Tom's hand and does not let go.

'Tom, do you know how I happen to run this business?' asks Franco.

'I understand that you inherited the business from your uncle.'

'True. And do you know what happened to him?'

'I do not.'

'I slit his throat and drank his blood. That is, by tradition, how we transfer power in my tribe. When the old ruler became too weak he would choose a successor. That man would then drink his life and his strength. Her name?'

'Danielle.'

'And for her?'

'I would drink a man's blood.'

He nods. 'Two days, Mr Policeman,' and releases his hand. 'This act of faith, of trust from me, will be repaid. You understand?'

Tom nods.

'One day, friend Tom, one day I will ask something of you.'

Downstairs Tom puts his clothes back on. They are cold and wet – he doesn't like to think about what the wet could be. He returns to Bradman's flat. It had all taken a little more than an hour. The reporter is still unconscious. Tom thinks of the beautiful human pincushion back at Franco's. He feels sick, but rolls up the reporter's sleeve, takes the needle and presses it into his arm.

Later, Franco tells his men that he will be alone with the cinnamon-coloured beauty. There are sniggers and winks – each man knows why he wants to be alone with her. He tells them not to disturb him under any circumstance, and closes the doors to her room. She lies on the sofa in a drug-induced sleep. He sits beside her and draws her towards him, her head down to rest on his lap. He smoothes her hair and strokes her face. She means nothing to him. He would not kill for her, would not lift a finger for her. There is no one in the world he would risk himself for, no one for him to care if they live or die. With that thought in his head, he sheds a tear. The first since he was four years old.

TWENTY-SEVEN

Monday 11 October 2010

Tom walks back into the cafe – at least he's dry now, after nearly twenty minutes of wringing out his clothes and keeping the air dryer going. He walks over to Keyson's table and sits down. The table is still strewn with photos and newspaper cuttings dating back to Dani's disappearance. He's seen all of the photos of Dani except one: her at some swanky party. She looks all dressed up. It's folded; he reaches out to open it.

'No – no.' Keyson puts his finger on it and slaps Tom's hand away. 'Tea's cold, Tom. I'll get you another.' He waves at the waitress who quickly comes over.

'Another tea for my friend and I'll have a black Americano. Candy – what biscuits do you have?'

'Rich tea, Bourbons, custard creams, Garibaldi…'

'That's it. Garibaldi – a plate of those please.'

The waitress skips off, eager to please.

As soon as she is out of earshot, Tom growls, 'What's this about?'

'Oh, Tom, can't two old friends get together and chat?'

'We are not old friends. If that's all this is, then I'm off.' He kicks his chair back with a squeal like fingernails on blackboard.

'Please sit down, Detective Superintendent Bevans, and you will learn something very much to your advantage.'

He remains standing. 'Just spit it out, Ke—' He dries up as Candy skips back with the plate of biscuits.

'Thank you, Candy.' Keyson says with his night-time DJ voice. Candy oohs a bit, then leaves.

'I did not come here to watch you flirt with waitresses.'

'No, but you did come.' He smiles, knowing he has all the aces. 'I have been retained by Patricia Lancing. You do know Patricia Lancing, don't you, Tom?'

Tom feels the skin tighten on his scalp. He sits back down.

'Her daughter was murdered and... well, you know all that, don't you?'

Tom remembers the two of them lying on the floor next to each other, heads almost touching. He remembers how good it felt to finally tell someone about Dani.

'You told me the story of your one true love – do you remember?'

Tom is silent. He looks coldly into the other man's eyes.

'The night, I believed, we became real friends.' His eyes flash a deep anger. 'If I recall correctly – she studied at Durham. Classics, wasn't it?'

'You know it was.'

'You never told me her surname but... fancy her mother coming to me to look into her death. To help solve the twenty-year-old mystery.'

'Marcus...'

'Of course, it could have been a coincidence, there may be many murdered Danis – but I told her I'd look into the case and I did. I went to Durham.'

Tom's eyes widen. 'You were there as a child. The coroner...'

'Yes. I shared that with you didn't I? My mentor, my second father.'

Tom breaks eye contact.

'I hadn't been back since his death. More than ten years but I still had contacts – he had been much respected. It wasn't difficult to get to see the case notes.'

'Those are sealed – active officers only.'

'Your name appears all over her case notes.' He pulls a folder from the pile, Tom snatches it and leafs through. He recognises his handwriting on most pages.

'I could charge you for having these.'

'Possibly. You're probably right. I shouldn't have them.'

'Here we are at last. These'll warm you up.' Candy reappears with the drinks and places them down on the table. She seems not to notice the bubbling tension between the two men. She has unbuttoned her blouse a little.

'You are a treasure, Candy.' Keyson winks.

She blushes and walks off.

'Excellent.' Keyson picks up a biscuit and dunks it into his coffee. 'Named after Giuseppe Garibaldi, you know.'

'The man who unified Italy in the nineteenth century – I know.'

'Tom—'

'Detective Superintendent Bevans, if you don't mind.'

'Okay. Fine. Detective Superintendent. I have been retained by Patricia Lancing to help expose the killer of her daughter Danielle Lancing in February 1989. I have ascertained this is the same Dani you claimed to have loved—'

'Damn you, Marcus.'

'Claimed would have married you – which was news to her mother.'

Tom just catches himself in time – his fist balls and he wants, so much, to send it into this man's face. This… Calm, he must stay calm.

'Patricia Lancing has entrusted me with photos, newspaper clippings and authorised me to access her daughter's case notes. I also have the coroner's report...', he pauses theatrically, relishing the flames of unease that lick across Tom Bevans's face, '... and his examination notes. His personal examination notes.'

'Where the hell did you get those?' Tom asks, angry to be so wrong-footed by Keyson.

'Oh Tom, and you're one of the bright ones. I don't think that's actually important – what is crucial in finding the man responsible for your Dani's murder is discovering why the final report and the initial notes vary so much.' He dunks another biscuit. 'Because the funny thing – and it genuinely is a funny thing – is that these notes are full of inconsistencies, inaccuracies and blatant mistruths.'

Tom sits there feeling himself shrink, little by little. He wants to say something but his mouth is parched and no words form.

'I have been able to piece together some of the story, the true story. I spoke to a retired sergeant, Ray Stone. You knew him a little, I believe. He ran the Durham evidence store back in 1989. Fascinating man; he has throat cancer and talks out of his neck with a stick. He said to say "hello".'

'Don't remember him.'

'Tom!' Keyson wags a finger as if at a naughty schoolboy. 'You have got to work on your poker face. How did you get where you are today?' He grins.

Tom gulps, he thinks the same sometimes.

'So you don't remember Sergeant Stone? Well, he remembers you.'

'That's nice. If you have his address I'll add him to my Christmas card list.'

'Oh good idea – then you'll need more stamps – I have another name to add. Journalist. Ben Bradman. Ring a bell?'

'Bradman,' Tom whispers.

With a single finger Keyson slides one of the newspaper clippings around to face Tom. He recognises it immediately as Bradman's *News of the World* story. Out of Tom's left eye slides a single tear.

'We talked for quite a while, he and I. He had a lot to say about you, Detective Superintendent Bevans, none of it complimentary. You know he didn't do well in prison, don't you?'

Tom says nothing. He knows that Bradman was sentenced to seven years and spent four years and eight months in prison before he was paroled. He knows, from reading the governor's reports, that he'd been beaten and sexually abused there. Tom lowers his eyes, not wanting Keyson to see the shame burning in them.

'I know nothing about him. I only met him the once.'

'Quite a meeting, though. I should think every one of his nightmares ever since features you. I wouldn't have thought you had it in you, Tom. You devil.'

Tom feels bile rise in his throat. 'You know nothing about me, Keyson.'

'But we were such good friends,' he says with a frosty smile.

Tom wants to deny it and yet... and yet. 'You betrayed that friendship.'

'Me?' Keyson's face turns scarlet. 'I betrayed you? Liar – you destroyed me. You dragged me through the mud and had me fired.'

Tom stands quickly, pushes himself away from the table, scared.

'You threw away your career, Marcus, you did it to yourself.'

With a squeal, Keyson pushes the table away so nothing stands between the two men – he reaches out to grab him by the throat.

'Is everything okay?' Candy is by Keyson's shoulder looking concerned. 'Do you need...?' She places her long fingers on his arm. Keyson pulls his arm away like it's been burnt and turns – snarling at the interruption.

'Get the fuck back to—' he pulls his arm up to swat her away.

Candy screams and shrinks back afraid.

'I'm sorry. So sorry. I—' he is immediately a civilised man again, but too late – she scampers back to the kitchen. A second later the chef emerges, a cleaver in his hand in case of trouble.

'Misunderstanding, nothing more. Sorry about that. We'll leave immediately. Maybe the bill?' He smiles his most winning smile. The chef grunts and walks back into the kitchen. Keyson swings back to Tom.

'No more time for niceties. Patricia Lancing, the mother of your one true love, came to me to help find her daughter's killer.'

Tom nods. 'Changes in DNA profiling. The potential for matching samples with—'

'Oh drop it, Tom. DNA technology – don't make me laugh. I don't need a fucking microscope to solve this mystery. I just need to look past the cover-up.'

'What do you—'

'I've done it, Tom. I've found the killer of Danielle Lancing.'

The blood drains from Tom Bevans's face.

Marcus Keyson smiles. 'You killed her, Tom.'

PART SIX

PART SIX

TWENTY-EIGHT

Monday 20 December 2010

She watches them sleep. Her parents. It probably crosses a line, to sneak into the bedroom and watch them – Dani isn't sure her moral compass is so accurate these days. She sighs. They're both fully clothed. Her mother is wrapped in a blanket. She's drawn her legs up into her stomach, like a baby in the womb. Her father lies on the outer edge, almost falling off the bed, but his legs curl against Patty's and they hold hands.

'Did you know that otters sleep holding hands?' Dani remembers telling her parents that fact one day when she was five or six. For a long time afterwards, at bedtime, she was an otter and her dad would hold her hand while she fell asleep.

She reaches out to their entwined hands – maybe she could. She holds her hand just above theirs – it looks as if the three hands are joined – but they aren't. She cannot grasp them and her hand slips through… she pulls it back. She can't feel, can't touch. Just watch. She knows she should be happy – if her parents could be together again, it would make her dad so happy. But what would it mean for her? Would he need her? He is her only link to the world – would she fade for him? Might she be completely alone? The thought fills her with dread. It's hard enough at night, being alone while he sleeps and having nothing to do but watch over him and blow the cobwebs of fear from him when the nightmares come. If he turns his back on her she will have nothing. Will she even exist with no anchor to life?

She looks out of the window. Snowflakes turn in the air once more. It will be dawn again soon – a new day. She closes her eyes and stretches out her hand to the glass; it slides through. She rises on her toes and leans – leans – leans forwards and... she is through the glass and outside, in the air, falling? No, floating. Slowly she turns in the air like the snowflakes, twisting down, gravity has no effect on her, nor does the icy wind. She floats softly in the sky. A shooting star. There is a flash in her head – an explosion. She feels arms on her, holding her down – feels immense weight on her hips – something snaps. She hears a scream of pain – it must be her own voice. Hands squirm all over her, sharp pain in her arms – her wrists – smells of sweat, beer, sick. Her flesh is twisted, mouths bite her, suckle from her – a tongue forces into her mouth. White-hot, searing pain. She is violated. She falls through the air. The snow catches her. Her limbs and joints scream out – she burns. She opens her eyes. A face, a form.

'Tom?'

But he isn't there. Just a memory.

*

'Jim. I killed a man.'

Patty's words ricochet around his head. Alongside him she sleeps. It took a while to fall under after her confession. She wept, she curled in his arms and wept. He feels guilty but it made him happy. To hold her again.

He has no idea what the time is, but can see a dim light seep through the crack of the curtains. His body would appreciate more sleep but his mind is doing star-jumps. Patty killed a man.

He heads downstairs. In the kitchen he opens cupboard after cupboard – desperate for coffee. It's a kitchen with a lot of storage, but it's mostly empty. There isn't even any salt or pepper.

'Oh thank you, Saint Java,' he exclaims when he finally strikes gold. In a scrunched up carrier bag, stuck down the back of the sink, he finds an old, half-empty jar of Nescafé. It's nestled in the bag alongside a pile of individually wrapped plastic cutlery, a mound of sugar sachets and about twenty little ketchup pots and a mayonnaise dip with a sell-by date that passed three years ago. He pulls out the coffee jar and, with some effort, unscrews the lid. Inside the granules are congealed into a solid lump. He tries to hack some out with a plastic knife but it just snaps. So he boils some water – in a saucepan – and pours it into the jar. The granules start to dissolve and he pours them into a cup. He sips at the coffee – it's disgusting, but he still drinks it.

'Jim. I killed a man.'

'Slow down, Patty. Tell me slowly.'

'Tom came to see me.'

'Tom... Tom Bevans?'

'He told me that Dani's case would be reviewed – that there was a new way of analysing evidence samples.'

'Hang on, Tom told you. Was he talking as a policeman, was it an official visit?'

'Yes, it was official. He said he wanted to do it himself rather than send some family officer.'

'So...' Jim's head reels. 'What did he say?'

'That a team, a dead case team, in Durham will investigate.'

'That's wond—'

'Jim, he said it could be years. Another four years.'

'It's already been twenty.'

'I can't do another four years. I won't.'

'So... what did...?'

'I hired someone. An ex-police pathologist named Keyson. He knew who to talk to and who to bribe.'

There is silence while the last piece of information sinks in.

'And?' Jim asks – suspecting that he doesn't want to know the answer.

'He found a suspect, a prime suspect, someone the police had thought could be the murderer. They had been almost sure but there wasn't enough evidence. But they had samples from Dani. Samples that were useless back then, but now – now could prove his guilt. They could catch him. I could... I could...' Silent tears flow.

'Patty.' He reaches out to her but she pulls away.

'It wasn't him.'

'We can look ag—'

'You don't understand. His photo – it's on the cover of every Sunday paper.'

'Why?'

'He's dead. Jim, I killed him.'

Jim feels cold in his bones as he cradles the coffee. He isn't going to drink any more, he just wants the warmth. He stands in the kitchen unravelling last night's conversation. She'd kidnapped a man and killed him. That was what triggered her seizure. He feels scared all of a sudden. He heads to the living room, he needs to see the man who threatens to take his wife away again.

The floor is strewn with shredded newspaper. He bends down and pulls out yesterday's *Sunday Times*. Only the headline is legible: HEATHROW TORTURE MAN IDENTIFIED.

'Christ, Patty.'

Under that is the *Observer*. The front page is also obliterated, but on page three there's a photograph. A man in his early sixties, close-cropped hair, bullet-shaped head. His name is Duncan Cobhurn.

'Oh my God.' Jim recognises the face, knows the man. He wants to be sick; he needs air. He pulls open the curtains and – there's a body lying in the snow outside.

'Dani!' Jim runs to the front door and out, around the side of the house and into the garden.

'Dani.' He stands over her. Her lips are blue, eyes closed – skin pale. She looks like she did in the morgue. That awful day when he—

'Dad,' she opens her eyes, they brim with fear. 'I saw them. They hurt me, they hurt me so much.'

'Dani.' He desperately wants to hold her.

'They laughed, Dad, they held me and wouldn't stop and… Tom. I saw him too.'

'What? When?'

But Dani's eyes are taken by the scrunched-up paper Jim still holds. She sees the photo and her eyes widen.

'Dad, why – why is there a picture of Duncan in the—'

Jim pulls it away but she's seen the caption.

'Murdered? Duncan murdered?'

'She—' Jim clams up.

'She? Christ! What happened, Dad?'

TWENTY-NINE

Friday 30 September 1988

Jim has a key; the landlord sent it after he called. The van he's borrowed is parked downstairs. Inside there's a ladder, dustsheets, two tool kits, filler and plaster, primer and paint – lots of paint. He loads himself up with as much as he can possibly carry and takes them up – clanking all the way like the Tin Man. He only wants a heart. He manages to juggle it all at the front door, and he slides the key home and pushes the door open.

He only gets a few steps inside when the bedroom door flies open and a blur rushes out; a man, naked except for a towel that he's still tucking round himself.

'Who the fuck are you?' he shouts at Jim.

'I… I'm sorry, this was meant to be—' he starts to explain when another figure appears from the bedroom, wrapping a sheet around her. It's Dani. Jim sees red.

'Dad, don't!' Dani screams.

'Dad?' the man says, as Jim drops the paint and pulls back a fist.

The naked man responds by holding his hands up in surrender – his towel falls off. He stands there naked and smiling. Jim hits him in the face – a knock-down.

'Dad!' Dani shouts and drops down next to the naked man. 'I'm sorry, darling,' she says to the naked man, using the corner of the sheet to wipe a stripe of blood from his lip.

'Dani. What th—' starts Jim.

'Dad, just go.'

'But—'

'Now.'

Jim doesn't move. He looks down at the man he's punched. He's at least forty years old. He's shorter than Jim, squatter but more toned with muscular legs, like a rugby player. His hair is short, greying and there's the beginning of a bald patch at the back.

'Bloody cavemen,' Dani tells them both, talking to them like naughty children. She helps the fallen man to his feet. He wraps the towel back around himself and holds it securely.

'This is my father, Jim Lancing. Dad, this is Duncan. Duncan Cobhurn.'

Duncan holds out his free hand to shake – Jim keeps his hands by his side.

'Okay, so we're going to play that game,' Dani bites at her lip. 'Dad, please go over the road. There's a cafe there – the Grange. It's okay, nice eggs. We'll be over in twenty minutes.'

'Just you, not… him. I'd like to talk to you.'

She pauses.

'That sounds like a good idea.' The naked man squeezes her hand. She gives him a small nod, then turns back to Jim.

'Just me. I'll be over soon.'

Jim grunts something and leaves.

※

In the kitchen of the Grange Cafe is a tall, skinny man. Serving out front is a bubbly young woman who gives Jim a big smile when he walks in. He sits at a table; in the middle is a laminated hand-written menu propped up between two globes, red ketchup and brown sauce. He picks up the menu but can't read it; his brains are scrambled. The waitress gives him a minute before coming over, notepad in hand.

'What can I get for you?'

'Coffee.'

'No food?' She looks very disappointed.

'I'm waiting for my daughter.'

She trots off, leaving Jim to stew.

Twenty minutes later Dani arrives. Jim's pleased to see she's alone. She sits down opposite him. He looks over to the waitress and for a second can see a strange look flick across her face. Confusion? Had she seen his daughter in here with an older man before? Had she thought they were father and daughter? The look is replaced, almost instantaneously, by a smile. They both order a cheese and onion omelette with chips.

'The omelettes are good here,' Dani tells him once the waitress has retreated.

'Good.'

'You came to decorate. A surprise for me. That was really nice of you.'

He shrugs. 'I thought you were in the Isle of Wight.'

'My plans changed. I should have let you know.'

'You... no. No you weren't to know. That's why they call them surprises.'

'And the surprise was on you,' she tries to joke. It falls flat.

They sit in silence. The waitress brings Dani a herbal tea.

'You look... you look well,' Jim finally tells her. And she does. He can see that her hair has been cut recently, her fingernails aren't bitten down like they have been the last few times he'd seen her. She's even put on weight – she actually looks a little cuddly rather than being lanky and gazelle-like. He likes it – makes her look more like Patty. All her life people have said Dani looks like Jim, and she does, but he can see Patty there too. He likes this new look.

She smiles. 'I'm happy, Dad.'

'Dani, I really don't mean to pry or anything, but—'

'Shut up, Dad.' She doesn't say it with any malice or anger. 'Please let me say some things.'

Jim zips his lips, like he used to when she was a girl. It makes her smile.

'You think I'm being stupid, don't you?'

'Dan—'

'Listen, Dad. Look, I know how awful all that shit with Seb was – I will never forget what you did for me then. You saved me, but that's over. I've grown up so much in the las—'

The waitress walks over with the omelettes. Dani stops talking while she waits for her to leave.

'I know he's older than me – he's forty-four.'

'He's my bloody age.'

'Dad. His name's Duncan. He imports furniture, rugs and tapestries from the Mediterranean. He's really successful. Don't look like that, Dad.'

'Forty-four?'

'Don't you trust me?'

Jim sucks air in through his teeth. Reluctantly he nods.

'He loves me, Dad. I love him. He's proposed.'

'Oh, Dani.' Jim throws his cutlery down. The clatter echoes through the cafe, causing the waitress and cook to look over.

'Butterfingers,' he says loudly, waving the digits. The waitress smiles and she and the cook go back to reading magazines.

'Don't you want me to be happy?' she asks in little more than a whisper.

'That isn't fair, darling.'

'It is. It's all about trust, Dad. This isn't like with Seb.'

'I should bloody hope not – you swore to me that would never happen again.'

'And it won't, Dad. I am not the same person I was then. You helped me so much when I needed you. But Duncan has too. He knows all about it, all about how awful it was and he's kept me sane and... I love him, Dad. He loves me.'

'And he said he wants to marry you.'

She nods and then drops her eyes again.

'What? Dani, what?'

She doesn't reply. Instead she holds up her left hand and wiggles the ring finger.

'You are joking? Oh Dani.'

Father and daughter eat their omelettes in silence.

***

'The chips were good,' Jim says finally, when both plates are licked clean.

'Tony's the cook and owner,' she points at the tall, skinny man. 'He double cooks them for crispiness. His lasagne's great too.'

'With chips?'

'Of course – what else do you eat with lasagne?' she smiles.

'I told your mum I'd be gone till Friday. The plan was to do repairs today, then paint tomorrow and touch up any last-minute things Friday morning before going home.'

'Duncan's gone. I told him I'd call tomorrow... maybe we could...'

'Decorate together?'

She nods and smiles.

He remembers the fun they had. There was no more talk of Duncan and there was no more talk of Seb Merchant. They listened to the radio and worked. Mostly Radio 1, but they switched to local stations to avoid Dave Lee Travis. When they were tired, they went out for food and beers, and in the evening they listened to John Peel. It was the last of the good times. After that, there was only that awful Christmas and then...

THIRTY

Monday 20 December 2010

'Dani. Please let's go inside. I'm freezing.'

'Not until you tell me what happened to Duncan.'

'He…' Jim shakes his head. 'Could he have been responsible for your death?'

'No.' Her eyes flash. Jim has not seen her angry once in the last twelve years – but she is now. The paleness of her skin is burnt away as the anger rises.

'He wanted to marry me, Dad. You know that.'

Jim feels sick to his stomach. So many secrets, so much unsaid. 'I never told your mum about him. I hoped it would end, that you'd realise he was too old for you.'

'I loved him.'

'He…' Jim feels shame creep in on top of the cold. 'He was the prime suspect in your murder.'

'He wouldn't…'

'The police didn't realise you were… lovers.'

The snow starts again, falling into Jim's hair – the flakes drift through Dani.

'Samples were taken – when you died.'

'From me?'

'Yes. The man left… anyway, they couldn't test the samples then. They can now.'

270

'The man who...'

'... could be found. Yes. That's what your mum was trying to do. She bribed a man to get the samples and then...' Jim stops. He is shaking. 'She needed to test them against the prime suspect.'

'Duncan?'

'She tied him up...' He doesn't need to finish – Dani can see where he's headed.

'Oh my God!'

'Dani.'

'Mum killed him.'

'She was doing it for you.'

'Mum killed him.'

'She didn't know...'

'She didn't know he wanted to marry me,' Dani says in the smallest voice. She looks at her father, so full of sadness. Then she fades.

'Dani,' he calls, 'Dani don't go. Please come back. Dani!' But he knows it's futile. 'Dani.'

She looks at herself in the mirror, remembering the excitement she felt seeing his blood smeared over her face – like a mask, a super-hero's mask. The Red Revenger – when was that, two days ago? Now there is none of that hope, none of that energy. She flew too close to the sun and fell. She has failed.

In the bedroom she stands and watches him sleep. Jim, the white knight who came to save her. What mess has she gotten him into now? What further misery will she pile on his head? She'd like to lie back down, snuggle into him, let him protect her, just for a day. Or two. But no. He looks so innocent lying there. He looks like Dani. She has failed them both. She slides down the wall, her legs suddenly jelly-like. It should all be over now. Roberta was supposed to confirm his guilt and then – armed with that proof – she was to take her revenge. End his life as he ended Dani's. And then... then Patty was to leave his stinking corpse, go home, finish the letter on her computer – the story of his crime and punishment. Then... then... then... she can't even say it to herself. But now? Oh Christ – it breaks on her like a tsunami – she has killed an innocent man. She is as bad as Dani's killer. She knows there is only one thing she can do, but... Dani will never be revenged. Never.

'Jim. Jim.' A hand shakes his shoulder. 'It's five in the afternoon. I thought I'd better wake you.'

He rolls over, opens his eyes – it's all a bit blurry and dark.

'Five?' He can't believe what she said. Something's wrong – and then he realises the problem: he slept well. No nightmare.

'When did you fall asleep?' she asks.

'I... I don't know. I went downstairs to look for coffee.'

'Did you find any?'

'None that was fit for human consumption.'

'Oh well, if you're going to be picky...' she leaves the room.

He remembers the morning: finding the newspaper, seeing Duncan Cobhurn's picture. Dani's pain. He rolls over and walks downstairs.

He finds her in the lounge – she is staring out the window. 'Is this the man you killed?' he holds the newspaper – the same photograph Dani saw.

Patty nods. 'An innocent man.' Her eyes hollow out with the memory of his death – bound and gagged, blood oozing from his hand.

Jim shakes his head. 'Maybe he wasn't so innocent.'

'I had his DNA matched with the killer's – not the same.' She crosses her arms across her chest. 'Last night you were great, when I needed you...' She stops. He can see how hard she's trying to keep herself together.

'Patty, we can—'

'I'm a murderer. I need to call the police and confess.'

'Patty?'

'Jim. He has a wife. Can you imagine how our lives would be different if the police had found the man who killed Dani? If we hadn't had all that worry – not knowing why. All that time I searched...'

'Dani's death wasn't an accident – this was.'

'Was it?' Patty asks, looking frightened. 'I almost slit his throat there in the chair. I tied him, cut him and left him with no water or food – pumped up to the gills with horse tranquilliser. How does that sound like an accident?'

'I...' The brutality of Patty's words stops him short. 'I don't know. I don't care. I just don't want to lose you again.'

'Jim.' Her eyes flare. She wants to tell him he lost her twenty years ago. Last night was just an echo of something long dead.

'Patty, don't decide now. Just spend the day with me.'

She can't say no, it's what she wants more than anything in the world.

❄

Jim showers first, then Patty. She stays in that stream until the hot water is exhausted. How can a person feel so happy and so sad, all in the same moment? She loves Jim, she has throughout the last forty years, and she can have him back. But at what cost?

When she gets downstairs, Jim is in the kitchen and the room is filled with mouth-watering smells. He's run out to the shops, bought a pile of newspapers, fresh coffee and a coffee maker, eggs, bread and cheese. There are these tiny little tomatoes and olives with a box of salad leaves, plus little pre-cooked potatoes with basil. It all looks very year-in-Provence-y. He has the plates warming in the oven like Patty's mum always did when entertaining guests. Posh.

'Can I do something?'

He shakes his head. 'Just sit down.'

'Where? I don't have a dining table.'

She goes to her bookcase and pulls out two large coffee-table books, *A Pictorial Journey Around the Galapagos Islands* and *The Bloody Monks*.

'We can use these as trays.'

Patty watches as he efficiently pulls plates from the oven, flips an omelette and slices it in two. Molten cheese oozes from the wound. He scatters some leaves on the plate and spoons quartered tomatoes, olives and pesto-covered potatoes on the leaves.

'That looks like a painting,' she says, a little awed. 'My stomach is growling.'

He shrugs, 'Let's hope it tastes okay.'

As soon as the plate is in Patty's hands, she tears into the food. She eats ravenously.

Jim watches, amazed. 'There's no more, but I could knock some up quickly.'

'Toast. I really want some toast. Is there any butter?'

He nods and starts to rise.

'No, eat yours. I can make toast.' But even as she says it, she wonders if she actually can. She hasn't made it in more than twenty years, but surely it's something you don't forget.

She walks into the kitchen and stops dead. She has no idea if she has a toaster. She assumes she doesn't but looks around, just in case. There's a sliced loaf on the side, another of Jim's purchases, and she pulls out two slices and puts them under the grill. The oven came with the house and she has barely used it – just the hob. For years she has literally lived on tea and sandwiches or soup bought from Marks and Spencer. She can't remember the last time she was hungry – really hungry – craving sustenance. Jim walks into the kitchen to see her finish her fourth round of toast and popping two more under the grill.

'I can't stop,' she laughs, as tears run down her cheeks. 'I can taste it too,' she says with astonishment. 'It tastes good. Better than good. It tastes, I don't remember the last time I actually tasted something.'

He says nothing, but pours himself more coffee and returns to the living room. She eats four more rounds of toast before leaving the kitchen to find him. He sits there, sipping coffee and scouring the newspapers for news of Duncan Cobhurn's murder.

Patty pulls the paper from his hands and slips onto his lap. She takes his head in her hands – there is a symmetry between this and Duncan Cobhurn – she held his head like this, but then his glassy eyes didn't look back. Now Jim's eyes brim with hope and love and sadness and... and... she kisses him.

❋

'Jim, the funeral is next Tuesday. I need to go.'

'No. Please, it's crazy.'

'A whole week away. I'll see her, see his friends and family and... decide.'

Decide whether to confess. It means she loses all this. Loses Jim, and any chance of justice for Dani.

'Patty...'

'Jim, let's have Christmas. We can have a week without any mention of Duncan Cobhurn or his family or – anything. Just us. Then we can talk about this and plan what will happen on Tuesday. But let's just have Christmas. You can love me like it's 1979.'

THIRTY-ONE

Saturday 25 December 2010

They walk hand-in-hand through Greenwich Park at dawn. There's still snow under the trees and frozen leaves crack underfoot. They have had five days together. They went to the zoo, up in the London Eye at twilight and walked the length and breadth of the National Gallery, Tate Modern and St Paul's. They've eaten Vietnamese and Thai food and, after so many years apart, they made love. They have not spoken once about Duncan Cobhurn – in fact, they have not talked about the last twenty years at all. They have talked about their friends at university, especially Ed and Jacks. They've laughed, sung, and people-watched. They agreed not to buy presents for each other, though both have a little something tucked away at home for after breakfast. The last two nights they've spent back at the family home, the home they bought together some thirty-five years before. Now they walk. There is nothing to say – they both just bask in the other's presence.

At the crest of the hill they stop and look out over the sweep of London. They have always loved this spot, this view over the park into the heart of the city. He feels her hand slip from his, but he is lost in thought. He is thinking about Duncan Cobhurn – about him and Dani. Jim still has not told Patty about those days decorating with Dani. He wishes now that he had told her the truth all those years ago, but then it was Dani's secret. Just like the trouble with Seb Merchant had been their shared secret. He had not wanted Patty to worry, either time. But knowledge of both worry him. He needs to tell…

'Aaaaah!' His face is wet and freezing. Patty scoops up another handful of snow and shoves it right in his face.

'Patty!'

'No. You were being maudlin. It's Christmas.'

'You sound like Noddy Holder.'

'Do not take his name in vain.'

They both laugh. Patty scoops up another handful and cups it – pressing the snow into a ball.

'You dare!'

It hits him in the chest. 'Oh, you asked for it.' He starts to gather his own snowball. It's war.

An hour later they reach home. Both are frozen, covered in snow, and happy.

'Go get changed,' he tells her. 'I'll make hot chocolate.'

Patty goes upstairs and Jim walks into the kitchen. He stands there, quietly, listening. He whispers to the air: 'Dani? Where are you?'

He has not seen his daughter since he told her of Duncan Cobhurn's death. He misses her. Cannot bear the memory of the sadness on her face. It reminds him of one other time, soon after she came to live with him.

'Can you tell me?' he had asked.

She thought for a second, her nose crinkling with concentration.

'I don't know what to say, Dad. I don't remember what it felt like. It just all changed, slipped away and… I think I just winked out from one way of being and then there was something else. I just wasn't alive any more.'

He had nodded at her words, but doesn't really understand them.

'I used to see you, just catch a glimpse of you in a crowd.'

'I kept my eye on you.'

'Why?'

'I was worried. You seemed so sad.'

'Did you watch your mum?'

'Not really. She was stronger.'

'It was her that fell apart when you died.'

'Yes. That surprised me, really.'

'Then you came back properly. After your mum and I...' he paused, the pain of that time shifting in his chest once more. 'Why did you come back to me?'

'You called me.'

'Did I?'

She nodded.

'I needed you,' he sighed then looked sadly at his daughter. 'Was there pain?'

'Oh Dad, you keep asking that. If there was I don't remember, and it doesn't make any difference now.'

'And the man who...'

'Dad!' she dropped her head. They had agreed he would not ask that again. 'I told you I don't know. I can't remember.' She kept her head down for a while then raised it and smiled at him – that beautiful open smile.

The memory of her fades and Jim is alone in the kitchen once more. 'Where are you, Dani? Have you remembered more?' he asks the air. There is no answer.

It's 11 p.m., Christmas night. One hour left of their holiday from life and responsibility. Tomorrow reality will wash back in. Today they have made love, watched twenty minutes of *The Great Escape* on TV and made a roast dinner. Now, they are back in the park, where the day started. The sky is black, yet the scene is ablaze with lights and the occasional firework that arcs into the darkness above the cityscape. Jim and Patty came prepared for the cold. They have a Thermos of hot coffee and several blankets. Jim puts a bin-bag on the bench and then a blanket. They sit and pile the other blankets on top of themselves.

'Tomorrow...' Patty starts.

'Shh. No tomorrow, just tonight.'

They snuggle together and watch the city lights wink at them until the cold finally sneaks into their bones. Then Jim pulls a bag from under the bench.

'I was wondering what you had in there.'

'I hope it still works.'

Jim pulls out a black case, which he flips open to reveal a little portable record player.

'Oh my God. The Dansette Transit. You kept it?'

'I kept everything. Here.' He pulls out a cloth bag and places it alongside the record player, then pulls out a small, shiny vinyl disc.

'You haven't—'

'1963, "Heatwave" by Martha and the Vandellas.'

'You romantic bastard.'

'Birmingham University dance hall. You were all Peter, Paul and Mary.'

She laughs. 'And you were all Johnny Cash, man in black.'

'But we danced to Martha and the Vandellas. Our first dance.'

She shakes her head. 'You're crazy.'

'And Elvis, the Beatles.'

'Even Cliff Richard.' She makes a gagging face.

He puts the needle on the record, and through the hiss and crackle, the song starts.

'Dance with me?' he asks and holds out his hand. Patty nods and takes his hand, melting into him. In the cold of the wee small hours, they dance.

When the song ends, Patty lifts the needle and starts it again. They dance six times to the same song, before Jim suddenly stops and pulls out his phone.

'Who are you calling?'

Jim holds his hand up to quieten her as he listens to the phone ring for ages before it's answered.

'Hello. Who's that?' a sleepy voice asks.

'Listen to this.' Jim puts the needle back on and places the phone close to the little speaker.

'Is that you, Martha?' the voice on the other end croaks.

'What's going on?' a second voice, more distant, and very sleepy, comes from the phone.

'Do you remember, Ed, November 1963, Birmingham University?'

'I remember an old friend from those days who must be fucking dead because he hasn't called me in years.'

'Merry Christmas, Ed. Love to Jacks.'

'I think you owe us at least eight birthdays and Christmases.'

'It's almost midnight,' Jacks says, with sleepy annoyance, in the background.

'Is there a point to this call, Jim?' says Ed. 'We could have a pint next week or have you got some horrible terminal disease and you're running down memory lane before you snuff it tomorrow?'

'I'm in Greenwich Park, dancing in the dark with my wife.'

'Remarried – good for you. I hope she's a looker.' He whispers to Jacks, 'New wife.'

'Congratulations. Now let us get back to sleep!' shouts Jacks.

Patty grabs the phone. 'No, still the same old wife.'

At home in Dorset, Ed and Jacks jump up in bed like they've been electrocuted.

'Patty?'

'I think the object of this call is to ask you to dance with us again,' she says.

'It's almost bloody midnight. I'm sixty-five,' Ed says in disbelief.

'We all are,' says Patty. 'Isn't it great?'

She puts the phone back down by the Dansette and lifts the needle again. She drops it on the first groove and takes her husband in her arms to dance.

In a bedroom 134 miles away, a couple who have not danced together in a long, long time, get out of bed. They put on the speaker-phone and dance with their oldest friends.

When the song ends, both couples kiss and Ed takes the phone.

'We love you. Let's get together soon. I think we have both really missed you. But now bugger off so we can get some sleep.'

'We love you too,' Jim tells them before he ends the call. He stands there for a while, silent, thinking about his oldest friend.

'What else do you have?' Patty asks.

Jim opens the bag and looks through. 'Carole King, Four Tops, Diana Ross, Donovan...'

'Anything. You decide. I need to pee.' Patty runs off behind a bush. Jim continues to fish through the bag until he finds something that makes his heart skip a beat. He pulls it out and looks at it in the moonlight.

'I remember that from my first party.'

Jim turns to see his daughter standing there.

'Good to see you,' he tells her.

'Do you remember? I danced to it with...'

'Gary, Gary Rohr. Buck teeth.'

'My first kiss.' She smiles, remembering such an innocent time. Behind her there is a flare of firework from somewhere behind Canary Wharf.

'Come up and see me...' he starts.

'... make me smile,' she finishes.

He puts it on. Steve Harley's unmistakable voice cuts through the air. Jim holds his hand out and the ghost drifts over. Without touching the two of them move and spin together.

They dance until Patty returns and steps through her daughter's image, making it shatter into a million fragments, to take her husband's hands and dance with him.

'This was...' she starts.

'...Dani's favourite,' he finishes her sentence.

THIRTY-TWO

Sunday 26 December 2010

They danced in the park and watched the stars until four that morning before they went home. Now, at 2 p.m., they sit surrounded by newspapers and with a laptop open. They are back in the rushing of time that is real life. Patty sits at the table, head down over her laptop, searching, intently scrolling and noting down things in a small Moleskine notebook. Jim stands to the side, alternating his gaze from the road outside to the side of his wife's head, his mind in an absolute turmoil.

'What are you looking for?' he asks. 'What are you hoping to find?'

'I don't know,' she tells him, though she knows full well what she's searching for. She wants to see photographs of the wife... widow. Ideally two photos: before and after; happy and sad – the eternal opposites.

The first would be the couple, together and happy. The second would be of her alone, after his death. Patty wants to see her grief.

'Bloody hell, that sounds sick,' she thinks. 'Why do I need to see that?' But she knows the answer: because she wants to judge her sorrow.

In her own wallet she has two photographs of herself. She never leaves home without them, though she hasn't looked at them for a very long time. She just needs to know they're there. The first shows her happy... no, not happy, that is far too bland a word. She is absolutely ecstatic – caught in a moment of rapture with her husband and her child. She is whooping, whooping with delight. Her perfect child has just won the English prize at school and Patty dreams she will follow her into writing, noble writing for great causes, something to make her so very proud. Patty can close her eyes and see that photo in every detail. It is taken in the grand hall of her school. Dani is about twelve and is standing on the stage holding a cup aloft – her prize. Slightly behind her are Jim and Patty. Jim stoops slightly to make sure his head is in the picture. His hair is still a brilliant black, he's dressed like a cut-price Steve McQueen – he looks great. Patty has long hair – probably the longest she ever wore it. It suits her, spilling over her shoulders. She wears a clingy dress – a floral pattern that shows off her fuller figure; hourglass many people called it. Patty knows it's her and yet she barely recognises herself.

It's the woman in the second photograph, the *after* image, taken maybe three years ago and thirty years after the first, who she recognises in the mirror today. Sat alongside the first photo, it reminds her of some champion slimmer standing next to the cardboard cut-out of their former giant self. The contrast between the two Pattys, especially in the face, scares her a little – showing how the acid of loss strips away the flesh, etches the lines of pain and rage into the body. This is how she judges pain and loss. And that is why she must see Audrey Cobhurn. To weigh up her loss like a butcher judging a cut of meat. But the search yields nothing. There is only a half-turned shot of her from her husband's failed election bid. It tells Patty nothing.

'I've got to go to the funeral,' she says.

'You won't do anything stupid though, will you?' he asks nervously. 'You won't confess without talking to me first?'

'No,' she lies.

In the middle of the night Patty wakes. Jim is curled into her, as if they are one body. His body heat keeping her warm.

'I must remember this, all this. If nothing else, I must never let this memory go,' she tells herself.

She can see what it means to him – he sees it as the continuation of a forty-year love affair. He's the romantic one. For Patty it's new and exciting, a final fling before everything rusts away or falls off; something that can live away from the burden of their previous life together. Could she ever be that Patricia again?

She slips out of the bed, as quietly as she can. As her flesh pulls away from his, she feels the separation – the pop of the skin disengaging. It makes her heart dip.

She walks downstairs as quietly as she can and makes her way to the den. The curtains are not drawn here, and moonlight illuminates the room. What she sees most in the room – in the whole house – are the missing things. Once upon a time this room had been filled with photographs, certificates, diplomas and trophies. Dani had been a winner. If she ever sees this room again she will replace those pictures. The time for grieving is long gone. They should remember their beautiful girl and sing her praises to the heavens – not hide her away like they're ashamed of her.

She walks over to the fish tank – well, ex-fish tank. Dani used to keep her beautiful little friends in here. Jet-propelled flashes of neon that would fascinate her for hours and hours. That was before running became her big passion. At some point, when she was about twelve, they stopped replacing the ones that died. After about a year they were all gone and the tank was drained. No one wanted to get rid of it and so the bottom was spread with soil and brightly coloured stones. Then exotic cacti were planted – the kinds that would be all right after you left them for months with no care.

Patty pushes her long, slim fingers down inside the tank. Through the stones and into the soil, the dry soil. She moves her fingers like worms through the crumbling bed until she finds the buried treasure. She had placed it there many years before. The memory of that day shames her.

She had been sitting at the kitchen table. It was early; she had barely slept – again. She was smoking – again. She had promised Jim she wouldn't smoke in the house but... but what? She had thought: 'Fuck him and his stupid rules.'

He had come down and seen her sitting there, wreathed in smoke. He hadn't said a word, just looked at her, a pained expression on his face like a fucking martyr. She took the cigarette and ground it out in her own hand. It hurt. She had wanted a reaction, wanted him to scream at her: 'You idiot, you stupid self-obsessed cow, you weak, feeble woman. If you want to harm yourself then do it properly, kill yourself and do the world a favour.'

He hadn't screamed. He had said nothing like that. Instead he cleaned the wound, slathered it in antiseptic cream and bound it in a bandage. All the while looking at Patty with love and compassion. It was then that she knew she had to leave him. When he left the house that morning she packed a small bag, wrote a note and, lastly, walked over to the cacti tank.

She blows on the treasure, removing the little bits of soil attached to it. It's still a little grubby but seems fine. She slips it back onto the second finger of her left hand. Perhaps she could try to be that Patty again.

THIRTY-THREE

Tuesday 28 December 2010

She drives to Durham. She leaves plenty of time and so arrives early at the churchyard. She stands outside and waits. She's well insulated against the cold, but still finds herself hopping from foot to foot and clapping to keep the blood circulating. She sucks in the chill air and feels it burn her throat a little.

The church itself is impressive, flint and cobble hewn from the earth and tamed into a house of worship. The churchyard looks ancient; the headstones are a little like medieval teeth and tree roots have burrowed beneath them forcing them to stick out at odd angles. It is a dramatic place to be laid to rest; a dramatic place to be unmasked as a murderer too.

Patty has a story all worked out if anybody asks who she is, or why she's there. She'll be Carol, Carol Plimpton, née Hawkins. She worked with Duncan a long time ago, before he set up on his own. She carries no identification and, once again, all her clothes are from a charity shop, except the underwear.

It's a long time since she's walked inside a church, years, and much longer since an event of joy beckoned her in. In her twenties and thirties it was weddings, then christenings; now it's funerals. She's stopped attending obsequies though, now she sends condolences, in a few instances a tasteful floral tribute, but she can't attend in person. There were two or three funerals of contemporaries from university; she went but found she had to fake compassion, pretend some sadness; it made her face ache and stomach churn. Of course, there was another reason: she was avoiding Jim. The last funeral she attended was seven or eight years ago. Poor Connie Tunstall, the woman who was responsible for Patty and Jim meeting, though of course Patty knew Connie kicked herself for that. Connie had always had a thing for Jim. And of course Jim had been there too and... she had hated seeing him then. Why? She smiles. These last few days things have begun to get clearer – clearer than they've been for twenty years. She did not want to see him for fear he would cheer her up. How idiotic, to be so married to grief.

'Christ, am I going to be cursed with epiphanies now that I'm a murderer?' she laughs to herself. Then she remembers Audrey Cobhurn and feels ashamed by her flippancy. Her head swims a little and she walks further into the churchyard, all the way to the wall that separates the church from the farm. She looks out and sees beauty all around. She sniffs the air; it's tinged with that scorched leaf smell she remembers from childhood and knows that somewhere there must be a bonfire. She remembers that there used to be a man at the end of the street who roasted chestnuts on a brazier. The smell drove the kids wild, but Patty remembers that when she finally tried some they were disappointing. The hot, sweet nuts were not as tasty as the smell they gave off. In her mind that man was always there, in the street, ringing his bell and yelling through all seasons, but it can only have been December and maybe January too. In summertime it was Tonibell ice cream.

Duncan Cobhurn is being interred in the earth. Patty finds that surprising. She thought everyone was burnt nowadays, that there was no room left for the brittle dust of mortal remains. But she does understand it. The thing about burial is that there's somewhere to visit, a plot to tend and make beautiful. She would have liked to have had Dani buried so there was somewhere to go... but she was *unavailable* for the funeral planning. Jim made the decisions. Now, each year on Dani's birthday, Patty goes to a park, always alone. She knows that Jim goes to a garden of remembrance where Dani's ashes were scattered but Patty doesn't want to go with him. Especially not to somewhere that celebrates her death. Instead, Patty goes to a park, the closest point she can get to where Dani was born. The hospital itself was pulled down years ago and is now a supermarket. She went in there once. Worked out that Dani was born in the deli section. It could have been worse; feminine hygiene and incontinence were close by. Patty bought some cold cuts, salami, breaded ham and a baguette. She thought about eating them there and then, but it seemed a little crass. Instead she walked outside and wandered around the area, until she found a little park.

She sat in there, that first time, and ate and thought of Dani. She went back a week later – this time she had a sapling with her, in a plastic bag. The man at the garden centre said it was really sturdy and would grow quickly. She also bought a little spade plus that stuff like chicken wire you see around baby trees. She dug a hole, popped the tree in, then pushed the soil back and put the coil of wire around it. There's no plaque or anything, but Patty knows it's hers. It has thrived over the years and now gives enough shade in the summer to allow her to picnic underneath.

Cars begin to arrive, a fleet of them sweeping in formation like geese headed for home. Black. Traditional. The first setting the speed, slow and dignified. One by one they sweep in and park. Only when all the cars stop, does a tall, silver-haired man with military bearing walk forwards and open a door. Patty can see why he became a funeral director. She immediately trusts him; maybe she should tell him she's the murderer and get it all over and done with.

'Christ, Patty, that's not funny,' Jim's voice-in-her-head tells her.

From the phalanx of cars there is now a steady pouring of black suits into the courtyard around the church. Some walk straight in, others take the opportunity for one last cigarette before they receive the reminder of their mortality. Patty insinuates herself into a clump of middle-aged mourners and they file in.

'Just look at her if you have to, but please, please do not try and speak to her. Please,' Jim had asked her that morning.

'Okay, fine,' she had said without meaning it.

The church interior is just as impressive as the outside, with delicate stained glass and tapestries that shimmer across the walls. The pews are ornate and each one has a series of hand-embroidered cushions on them depicting a Bible scene.

'Hope I get Sodom and Gomorrah,' Patty thinks.

The most impressive part of the church, however, is the carved Jesus which towers over the congregation, his face a bloody mask of pain, his blood congealed to gore in puckered orbits on hands and feet. Arms outstretched to... to what? Absolve, condemn? He is a wooden man, spindly, grotesque, a mahogany Pinocchio with no strings to hold him down. He dominates the room, his eyes following Patty around, seeming to say: murderer. She takes a seat towards the back, away from the altar and the towering Jesus, but on the aisle close to the exit.

Funereal black is a lifesaver. She is bulked up: three jumpers, jacket and then a black suit. Huge and baggy without the padding, but with it... grieving fat woman. The ensemble is topped off with a black hat and veil from Cat Rescue. Patty had hoped the body would be on show – she had wanted to see his face one last time but this is no open-casket freak show.

Slowly, a trickle of people arrive and the chairs start to fill. She holds firm to the aisle seat and moves aside so people can squeeze past her intimidating bulk. The room is full by the time the vicar enters, and even then, as the organ strikes up 'Nearer my God to thee', there is another wave of mourners who have to stand along the walls and at the back. There are at least two hundred people in the room before the service begins.

Finally, two women enter, arm-in-arm; both tall and slim – widow and daughter. The older woman walks fully erect, her chin hyper-extended to show she is bowed by nothing. The younger is slightly curved and leans a little into her mother. Both are dressed in elegant black dresses. The two women process down the aisle and take their places centre stage, below the all-encompassing Jesus.

'What is a man...' the priest begins and Patty shifts her attention to the other mourners. She has never been a fan of organised religion, always thought it destroyed the questioning mind. Her eyes scan the room and her blood turns cold. There is the policeman who tried to question her in the hospital, but he isn't in uniform. He is looking straight at her: their eyes latch, she holds her breath. Finally, his gaze moves on. He seems to be scanning the congregation, is he searching for a killer there? Patty feels herself shake, though it's not her illness, merely the shudder of blood unfreezing and starting to pump again. She has no idea if her disguise held up to scrutiny. He certainly didn't seem to register any recognition and yet policeman are also actors, trained to morph into friend and confidant of the criminal, to blur the distinction between good, bad and ugly.

For a second she wishes Jim were there with her – then feels guilty for that thought. It was bad enough that she got him into trouble this far; she cannot endanger him any more. 'Shit.' She suddenly realises everybody is standing except for her. She blushes and, with some difficulty, pulls herself up for a hymn.

God sent His Son, they called Him Jesus; He came to love, heal, and forgive.

Patty moves her mouth a little, to look as if she's singing. She cranes forward, trying to see the widow, is she singing? She can't tell. The hymn finally ends and everyone sits again. Now the vicar begins to recount a litany of charity work done by Duncan Cobhurn. A long list of young people's charities, homeless and drug-addicted teens mostly. Around Patty, men and women nod their heads, many shed tears and some hold hands; some of these mourners are the drug-addicted teens, now grown up and made good: Duncan Cobhurn helped save them. Patty feels her stomach lurch. He sounds like a saint.

'Here you go,' a whisper comes from beside her. A hand is flapping a tissue, she realises she's crying.

'Thanks.' Patty dabs away her Judas tears.

Lorraine, his daughter, rises to read from his favourite book. She makes it through ten lines of *Watership Down* before tears make it impossible for her to continue. Patty gets it though: poor bunnies, life sucks. Then a favourite song: 'Lola' by the Kinks. The congregation is told it was playing on the radio when Duncan met Audrey, his wife of more than forty years. At this the widow's head sags and she leans into her daughter, both heads touch and seem to merge into one conjoined grief.

Patty's throat is dry and mouth sour like that little taste of reflux sick. She cannot see the widow's face or look into her eyes and yet knows what is written there. She sees that her need for revenge has sliced love from this poor woman's heart, destroyed her life as callously and as starkly as Dani's murder ruined Patty's. She should stand and announce her guilt, let Audrey Cobhurn have the satisfaction of seeing her ripped to shreds like an exhausted fox set upon by hounds. She should… but is too afraid. Patty is disgusted with her own cowardice. Two more songs, then a last reading and it's the final hymn.

The vibrato of the organ hangs in the air as the final words die away and the funeral is over. The widow and her daughter walk hand-in-hand up the aisle. The older woman is still bent into her daughter, deflated like a burst balloon. As they pass she reaches out and touches Audrey's arm, then widow and daughter are gone. Patty can't breathe. She needs to get out. She makes for the door: one step, two, three, four… Hand outstretched… and is through. She staggers over to the teeth of headstones, leans on one… the world is smeary with snotty tears and her chest heaves, she has to breathe or will blac—

'Where – why am I face down in grass?' Patty asks herself, not sure where she is or… the funeral. It leaps back at her. 'Crap,' her knee hurts, she puts the slightest pressure on it and it burns – maybe twisted, definitely swollen. Her chin is wet, maybe with blood. She fishes around in her pocket and finds a tissue; she wipes at her chin and it comes away with only tears and mucus. She has no idea how long she's been down here – seconds or minutes or hours? She gets up, slowly, supporting her knee, holding onto a headstone. Died 1824 – they won't mind then. Her hat is crushed, she leaves it where it is. Most cars have gone but a couple remain – she prays the policeman isn't still here. But why pray when she plans to confess?

She can see her little car and slowly walks towards it. She is almost there when somebody comes out of the church. Patty turns – force of habit – and looks directly into the eyes of Audrey Cobhurn. A sign. It's time to confess. She walks over to her.

'You don't know me, Mrs Cobhurn...'

'I bloody do,' the widow's face turns quickly from puzzlement through recognition to fury. She pulls her arm free from her daughter.

'She knows me, my God she knows who I am and what I have done,' thinks Patty, incredulous – but then all thought is stripped away as Audrey Cobhurn slaps Patty, who staggers back under the onslaught.

Patty is dazed by the ferocity – her ears ring and cheeks flare. Audrey's hands strike Patty's chest, sinking into the woollen blubber of the disguise – she looks at Patty with wonder. Then lashes out again.

'I buried my fucking husband here today. You have no right, no right.'

The punches start to lessen and then die away as the demon departs her. Her daughter manages to grab her arms as she falls forwards, clutching at Patty, oozing into the padding as her rage is replaced by the utter desolation of loss. She falls to her knees, still grabbing Patty's body – sliding down her. She looks up as she drops, her face a mass of streaming colours and all she can do is mouth...

'You shouldn't have come here. I did what I had to do for...' and there is nothing except streaming tears. Patty kneels down and takes the widow in her arms, they hold each other and together they sob. Patty sobs for Dani and Jim. Audrey wails for her Duncan.

Lorraine gently grasps her mother's shoulders and pulls her away from Patty. Her own face is a flood, all has been washed away. She turns her mother around and slowly walks her towards their car. Patty stays on her knees, watching the two women walk towards their car. Suddenly she is bombarded by questions: 'How did Audrey Cobhurn know who I was? Why did she have such an angry reaction? Does she know I killed her husband? If she does – then why not call the police? What just happened?'

She sees Lorraine put her mother in the car, say a few words, then she turns once more and walks towards Patty. When she reaches her, Lorraine does not meet Patty's eyes.

'I didn't come here to cause you pain. Not you or your mother.'

Lorraine nods.

'I don't know why I came really... I just...' Patty trails off – she has no idea how to end that sentence.

'We can't cope with you too,' Lorraine says almost inaudibly, still looking down at the ground between them.

In the distance a new group of black cars drives through the gate and down to the church – black suits emerge. Next funeral... death goes on. Lorraine watches them arrive and forces herself to continue: 'What we did to you, what Mum did – all that time ago. It's never left us. I think it cursed us. Dad has tried to pay it back; he tried to make good. I... am... sorry! I know we all need to bury our dead.'

Patty can't breathe.

'Please don't hate us.' She pulls her bag open and fishes in it, finding a card and a pen. She scribbles something and then hands it to Patty. It's a business card, 'Lorraine Summers designs', and then a mobile number scrawled on the back. She hands the pen and a blank card to Patty who, with numb fingers, writes her own mobile number on it.

'I can't talk now, Mum needs me. Please call tomorrow and we can meet.'

She smiles at Patty, a conciliatory smile.

'Maybe it has been a good thing that you came today. Maybe you can forgive us after all these years, Mrs Lancing,' and she turns and walks back to her mother.

Patty cannot move: she has looked into the heart of Sodom, like Lot's wife, and been turned into a pillar of salt. The cold suddenly blows up and she is dissipated into the air.

THIRTY-FOUR

Jim feels anxious. He's been pacing around the house ever since he kissed Patty goodbye that morning. He looks at his watch again – the funeral was supposed to have started ten minutes ago. Christ, what will she do? She had held his hand and kissed him so tenderly, like a permanent farewell. He had asked to go with her, but she had held firm.

'I have to go alone.'

'I don't understand why you have to go at all.'

'I'll be back this evening.'

'Promise?'

'Scout's honour.'

He knew she was telling him what he wanted to hear. It was more likely that she would see the weeping widow and then find the nearest policeman to confess to. In many ways he admired that, admired her. But what consolation was that? Admiration – he'd had twenty years of admiration and it didn't fill his empty heart. He feels so alone. Where was Dani? Was he going to lose them both?

Suddenly the phone rings, he snatches it up.

'Patty?'

There is no answer, just a faraway sound of breath.

'Who is this?'

'James Lancing?' it's a voice Jim doesn't know.

'Who is this?' Jim asks.

'A friend, Mr Lancing. I have some information for you. For you and your wife. Could you meet me?'

'I have not seen my wife in—'

'Please don't bother lying to me, Mr Lancing. You have been with her for the last few days.'

Jim feels sick. He lets the information sit there for a few seconds before he can speak again.

'When do you want to meet?'

'Now. Now would be good.'

'My wife isn't here, we can't both meet you.'

'You alone will be fine, Mr Lancing.'

Jim is silent for a few moments. 'Where?'

'The birthplace of time?'

'When?'

'How about twenty minutes?'

There is a click and the call is ended. It takes Jim just a few minutes to get ready. He stands in the hall looking at the door. His stomach is full of moths. He's scared. He heads out into the cold.

'There he goes,' Grant Ronson pulls the binoculars from his eyes and slips them into his pocket. He bloody loves this. He grabs the bag and makes for the door, shouting back as he heads out. 'You were brilliant – bloody Blofeld. We have information, Meester Bond – classic.'

'Remember what we are looking for, Mr Ronson.'

'Mr Ronson – classic.'

'A small leather book – not a regular published book, the spine will almost certainly be blank.'

'Got it, Ernst Stavro.' And he is out of the door and gone.

Marcus Keyson watches him go. An idiot. But loyal and good in a scrap – that was Keyson's assessment of his employee. But it was the 'idiot' bit that worried him at the moment. The last time he had asked Ronson to break into a house to recover something, he had taken far longer than he should, as he'd been raiding the wife's lingerie drawer and leaving her a 'present'. They had an hour maximum. They had to be quick.

Jim was only at the end of the road when he realised he didn't have his phone. Patty might need him. He turned and rushed back to the house. He knew exactly where it was. He would grab it and still be at the Royal Observatory in time to meet the mystery voice.

As soon as he opened the front door he knew something was wrong. It wasn't any kind of sixth sense. Someone was upstairs, opening drawers, moving furniture and whistling *The Dam Busters* theme very loudly. What should he do? Not confront the man – he should back out and call the police – but his phone was just inside the kitchen. He could get it in a few steps, then get out and call the police. The intruder upstairs was making too much noise to hear him. He couldn't see a second man. Jim moved as slowly as possible. It was twenty paces to the kitchen. He got the phone in his hand, flipped it open – dialled 99…

Jim crumples from the blow to the top of his head. The phone spills onto the floor. Keyson retrieves it and turns it off. He looks down at the unconscious man.

'I am very sorry, Mr Lancing. This shouldn't have occurred,' he steps over the body. 'Ronson you idiot,' he screams up the stairs.

He feels his head move – not that he did it himself. No, someone is holding it and... 'Shit. Shit. Shit.' A finger pokes into his skull and everything explodes. Sticky and wet. Jim feels sticky and wet.

'Jim. Jim.'

There is a voice from somewhere. Jim tries to open his eyes but...

'Too hard.'

'Jim. Here.'

Something pressed to his lips. Water. At least he thinks its water. He manages a sip.

'Need sleep.' Jim starts to slip away again.

'Jim!'

Water hits his face.

'Try and talk,' the voice says again. Jim attempts to open his eyes to see who's talking. He thinks it may be God or an angel.

'Jim.' God says with a slap to his face.

'You are an angry god,' Jim croaks.

'Jim, you've been cracked on the head. There's a lot of blood but I don't think it's serious.'

You don't expect that sort of talk from God.

'Jim. Can you understand me?'

'Who are you?' Jim asks, beginning to think it isn't God.

'Jim, it's Tom. Tom Bevans. We need to talk.'

Jim forces his eyes to focus. 'Tom. It's good to see you. I might pass out again.'

'No you don't. Come on, walk around – have you got any painkillers?'

'Kitchen.' Tom helps him to his feet and walks him into the kitchen. Jim sits at the table – pointing to the drawer with pain-killers. Tom finds them and gets a glass of water.

'Thanks.' Jim takes the ibuprofen and swallows them down. 'What time is it?'

Tom looks at his watch. 'Eight o'clock. When were you hit?'

'Erm... one-ish. I think.' It all seems very hazy. Jim opens his eyes to see he is in the living room but the room has been demolished.

'Patty.' Jim suddenly starts to panic. 'Where's Patty?'

'You've got a few texts.' Tom hands over Jim's phone. 'I hope you don't mind – I read them. Patty's fine but she isn't coming home tonight. She says she's got a hotel room – there are things she needs to think about. But...' Tom pauses, 'she isn't going to confess, she says. What do you think she means, Jim?'

Jim looks into Tom's face. He has not seen the younger man for a few years. He tries to keep his expression neutral. 'I have no idea, Tom.'

Tom sighs. 'Oh Jim. I know all about Duncan Cobhurn.'

Jim looks Tom in the eye – but he doesn't feel scared.

Tom sighs and holds his hands palms up. 'Patty is safe from me. I'm not here as a policeman, but I don't know how safe she actually is. She's in trouble, Jim.'

'Why?'

'She's got involved with a nasty piece of work. Do you know who hit you?'

'Didn't see him. Someone was upstairs, pulling things apart and whistling *The Dam Busters*.'

'That'll be the charming Grant Ronson.'

'Who?'

'He's listed as a private detective, but really he's an errand boy used for your more unpleasant jobs. He's been most recently in the employ of Dr Marcus Keyson.'

'Hang on,' Jim fights the swirling broken thoughts in his head and tries to piece his memory back together. 'Patty saw him – he's a pathologist.'

'He's a psychopath.'

'She hired him – he was helping her.'

'Helping himself, more likely. Look, he and I have some history and, take it from me: he is not a good guy.'

'And that's who could be trouble for Patty?'

'He's trouble for all of us.'

'So why was he ransacking the place here?'

'I think he wanted something you had.'

'Had?'

'I assume he found it.'

'What?'

Tom hesitates; his eyes fall away from Jim's gaze. 'Dani's diary.'

'There are lots of diaries, she always kept a…' Jim trails off. 'You mean her university diary?'

Tom nods.

'But, how did he know about it? You told me you'd wiped all trace of it from the files.' Jim starts to panic.

'I did. The investigating officers never saw it but… I missed something. I never changed the evidence sheet from the crime scene. I mean nobody ever goes back and looks at those.'

'But this Keyson obviously did.'

'He has the entire file. I don't know how he got it, but he has. He's got the original log. All you have to do is compare the two and see the diary was logged in at the crime scene but never made it to the evidence list.'

Jim closes his eyes and desperately thinks back. That day at the morgue, Tom had disappeared to do some paperwork with a hatchet-faced officer. Afterwards, they'd waved something in his face to sign. Later Tom gave him a small bag.

'Here. Don't look now, just take it home. We can't leave it here for the investigation.'

Jim hadn't realised what he had at the time. It was only when they were back in London that he looked. There, in the bag, were two small diaries. He'd been excited at first, hoped it might tell him something – even have clues as to who had killed Dani. But of course there was nothing. The diaries only reached the end of that first miserable year. Nothing to do with her death but told of that dreadful time with…

'So he knows all about Seb Merchant?'

Tom nods.

'Has he told Patty?' Jim asks, worried.

'I have no idea.'

'Hell,' Jim feels a sharp pain cycle round his head. He tries hard to concentrate again. 'So who is this Keyson? What does he want?'

Tom looks across at the older man; he's worried about his head wound.

'First, let's give that head some attention. We can talk while I clean it. Do you have iodine?'

'Bathroom – under the sink.'

Tom nods and walks away. He returns shaking his head. 'This stuff is five years past its sell-by-date.'

'Wouldn't worry.'

Tom takes a small cloth and tips the iodine into it and then dabs at Jim's bloody head. Jim winces but says nothing.

'Marcus Keyson – he worked with us – he was the pathologist allocated to Operation Ares.'

'I don't know what that means.'

'Sorry, Jim. I forget you aren't a copper. Operation Ares is a special taskforce, a unit within the Serious Crime Division. I head it up – we investigate sexual murder where we think there are multiple victims or there's some unusual element to the case.'

Jim nods slowly. It was a bigger memorial to Dani than he could imagine.

'You save lives? Punish the wicked?' Jim asks.

'We try.' Tom sees Sarah Penn's face. The photo from Ibiza and her dead face morph together. Three years dead. She's waiting for him in the dark somewhere with the others, needing his attention and help. 'I try.'

'So he worked with you?' Jim tries to get Tom back on track.

'Yeah... Keyson was our pathologist – a brilliant man. Quite honestly there are two murderers – at least – who we would not have caught without him.'

'So why did he hit me over the head if he's a good guy?'

'Oh, I don't think Marcus Keyson's a good guy. But I didn't think he was a bad guy either.' Tom stops to concentrate as he cleans into the deepest part of the wound. 'He was kicked off the force. Dishonourable discharge, no pension, no consultancy, no references – nothing. He was lucky he wasn't arrested; they just kicked everything under the carpet.'

'What did he do?' Jim asks.

'He took bribes to tamper with evidence. Not on any of our cases, but others he worked on. There were two cases in particular. In the first he was caught changing drug results on a hit-and-run drink-drive. They found Keyson was sleeping with the wife and daughter in payment to get the father acquitted. There was another big case: a woman was driving over the limit – she ploughed into three children on the pavement. Two dead, one in a wheelchair for life. He purposefully contaminated the evidence against the driver – at trial it all fell apart and she walked away scot-free.'

'But I don't understand what this has to do with us.'

'I...' Tom looks ashamed. 'I'm the reason he was investigated. He was my friend. I was at his house one night after work. I

305

dropped by with a bottle, out of the blue. The wife of the defendant was there and I recognised her. I called the DPS. I sold him out and got him kicked off the force.'

'So he hates you.'

'Pretty much. He certainly blames me for everything that's gone wrong for him.'

'But why was he at my house?'

Tom hesitates.

'I told him about Dani – years back, when we were still friends. Told him she was murdered and I loved her. Then, a couple of months ago, Patty went to see him to ask him to investigate Dani's death. It was a freak coincidence that she found him. She mentioned me and he saw it as a way to get his revenge, to hurt me.'

'How, how could he hurt you?'

Tom's eyes flash for a second. 'He knows I... he knows I withheld evidence from the reports on Dani.'

'I see. He got kicked off the force for tampering with evidence and he wants you to get the same treatment.'

Tom nods. 'But... there's something else.'

'Something to do with Dani's death.'

'Something I did that I'm ashamed of. If he makes it public it will ruin me, my work, the team will be disbanded. Those girls... they need to be remembered.'

Jim nods. 'I need to get to Patty,' he tries to take a step but is still woozy. He staggers and Tom catches hold of him.

'I'll drive,' Tom tells him. 'It's a while since I've been to Durham.' He almost smiles.

The front door slams into place as they leave. As Jim walks away from the house he thinks he sees a slight shape inside. He holds his hand up and waves awkwardly. Dani waves back; his chest flares, he is so happy to see her again. He puts his lips to his mouth and blows her a kiss. He needs her to know she is loved.

'Jim?' Tom is at the car. He turns, unsure of what Jim is doing.

'Coming, Tom.'

From inside, Dani watches the two men get into the car and drive off. Tears trickle down her cheeks. She didn't know a ghost could cry before this. She does now.

She is scared for them. And for herself. Slowly her pale face fades from the room until she is gone.

THIRTY-FIVE

Tuesday 28 December 2010

The widow is alone. After the morning's funeral Lorraine brought her home. She would not go to bed and so her daughter made a day-bed for her in the sitting room. On the table there is a sandwich, untouched. Cold tea sits there too, a scum formed on the top. Audrey had tried to lie down but she felt nauseous and sat up. For a long time she has just stared out of the window, but she feels a need for... Lorraine has gone through the room removing anything and everything she thought might trigger her mother's grief. Normally the room is awash with family photographs – but now they are all packed away somewhere. Audrey feels a deep desire to see his face again.

She opens the door slowly, quietly. From the kitchen she can hear sounds of life – Lorraine is washing up. Audrey walks carefully through the downstairs and into the room at the back. Duncan's home office. There on the corner of a filing cabinet is a silver-framed photo. Her Duncan grins out from it looking relaxed and happy. He wears black tie. He still has hair and is thinner than he has been over the last few years; it must be at least fifteen years ago. She takes the photograph back to the lounge and sits on the sofa with her Duncan one more time. Earlier in the day, seeing the photo might have tipped her back into the overwhelming grief that had gripped her after the funeral, but since returning home she has self-medicated for the pain; V&V – vodka and Valium. Everything is hazy and colours seem muted. She cannot tell when her eyes are open or closed as pictures still play across her vision. There seems to be no way of telling the past from the present, except he can't be here in the present, can he? But she sees him open the door... young, he is amazingly young. That first day.

He opens the door; she catches a glimpse of him in her peripheral vision, a breeze of colour. All is in slow motion as she turns and... The spotlight of that smile is turned on her, dazzling her senses. The smile blots out everything else. Then slowly she sees how his eyes twinkle... oh boy, is he trouble.

He opens the cafe door where Audrey Hall works as a waitress. She is seventeen and has worked there for two years after leaving school with no qualifications.

She turns as he enters; he smiles and her heart slows – like now with the pills. She starts to drool... He sits down at one of my tables. She can barely catch her breath then... or now. She wants it to stop, she cannot see him like that, young and beautiful.

She has the pill bottle. The doctor said if she needed a quicker relief she should chew so she grinds each pill to powder with her teeth and knocks them back with vodka. It's not part of the prescription but the pain is too much to bear alone.

He smiles. 'Egg and chips please love, and a big mug of tea.'

The cafe is gone and she is dressed in white, in a church. Today it was black now it is white. He kisses her.

'I love you,' he says.

'And you loved her too. Didn't you?'

Duncan Cobhurn smiles at his wife and shrugs his shoulders. 'All too long ago, darling. All too long ago.'

From somewhere far-off there is the sound of a bell. Audrey Cobhurn half registers it, and then hears raised voices from the hallway. She pulls herself up off the sofa... immediately her knees begin to buckle but she steadies herself. The room shifts like at a funfair, lines seem to curve in a way that physics should not allow. But she manages to get to the door and open it. A man stands there, seeming to argue with her daughter. When he sees Audrey he pushes himself into the hall, muscling Lorraine to one side so he can talk directly to her mother.

'I am so sorry for your loss, Mrs Cobhurn.' He holds out a wallet. She doesn't understand.

'Detective Superintendent Tom Bevans. I really need to ask you a couple of questions.'

'Mum, he can come back tomorrow,' Lorraine says, trying to lever him out the door, but he won't budge.

The widow smiles, not really sure what is being asked of her, the pills and vodka swimming in her stomach and her brain, but she likes the look of him. Tall and young, with sandy-blond hair and eyebrows so blond they are almost white.

'Please, you can see the state she's in. Come back tomorrow,' Lorraine asks.

But the man doesn't reply. Instead he pulls out a photograph – carefully, almost like a conjuror drawing you into his sleight of hand. The widow looks at it bemused. How odd, she thinks. It's the same photo from his office, the one she has been staring at for so long. Why does this policeman hav—

Then the man takes the photo and opens it. His copy was folded in half. He opens it to reveal... drum roll: Dani Lancing. Dani Lancing in a gorgeous silver dress, and she is holding onto Duncan's arm.

Audrey Cobhurn is unconscious before she hits the floor.

PART SEVEN

PART SEVEN

THE DIARY OF DANIELLE LANCING

PRIVATE

Monday 29 September 1986

So let's start as I mean to go on – with a lie. It's actually Tuesday, technically, as it's three in the morning. I've just got home and I promised I would start this diary thing again so... University: day one, Monday 29 September 1986.

God, Mum has such a stick up her arse. Dad was his usual quiet, great self. Tom... oh what about Tom? Tom needs to meet someone – he should have gone to uni, and I don't understand why he didn't. He's so clever but so stupid. And then there's Seb. Wow!

He's not a student – well, he was but he left the course he was on. The philosophy of economics – something weird like that. He came out of nowhere after Mum and Dad left and we started talking and we just talked and talked. We walked over to the cathedral and sat on the grass outside by some graves. It was cool. He rolled a joint – it was mild but I got a bit spacey. We kissed, but he was a real gentleman. He walked me home. I'm meeting him tomorrow. Goodnight, diary.

PS: Just found box from Mum in bed – a bloody letter. She saw me all day, and hardly said a word. She goes on about not saying what she means so she writes – crap. Communication is communication.

Tuesday 30 September 1986

Met Seb for a drink in C1 bar. After he came back to the dorm and I gave him a shoulder rub and a little bit more. Nikki came back early, so we couldn't do too much, but I am really looking forward to seeing him again.

Monday 6 October 1986

What an amazing weekend. Went with Seb to a party on Saturday, at a student house in Walltown. Philosophy and ex-philosophy students talking death, the afterlife and Hitchhiker's Guide to the Galaxy. Then a whole crowd of drama students started acting out Monty Python sketches as if they were performed by Neil and Vivien from The Young Ones. I wet myself. It was pretty druggy too, not just joints. There was a room where someone was cooking up heroin. Seb said we should watch – like we were anthropologists studying a tribe recently discovered in the Amazon. I couldn't look when they actually injected themselves. For a few minutes after they talked just like before, then they got all smiley and floppy – they looked like they were having the biggest orgasms and sagged down onto the floor. Three of them, out cold, but looking like they didn't have a care in the world. Seb said a lot of crap gets talked about drugs because the authorities are too frightened of how it liberates young people. So many of our greatest poets and thinkers took drugs to free their imaginations – but governments don't want you knowing that.

Wednesday 22 October 1986

Should have been at a lecture this morning but too hung-over. Went to Seb's last night and stayed over. He had some new weed and rolled a joint that was almost hallucinogenic. An old friend of his was over – a girl I hadn't seen before, Lucy; she had some really big tattoos, the best was a rose with a dagger through it that said Mum. We played truth or dare – Seb dared me to snog Lucy. I did. I quite liked it. Maybe I'll be bi.

Tuesday 4 November 1986

Not written for over a week, not sure what to say. Seb and I went to a party on Saturday – before last. It was at the same place we'd gone once before, in Walltown. It was pretty fun – I had a joint and then Seb took me upstairs. Some of his friends were shooting heroin. We watched them once before but this time Seb said he wanted to join in. It was safe and we shouldn't be cowed by all the stupid taboos society laid on us. I wasn't sure – but for him I said yes. It was amazing. Everyone should try it. You don't realise how small the world is until you do. And then when you come down off it – it's really disappointing. It's like going on an amazing holiday to the sun – where all the colours are really amazing and the weather is just the best and you come back to dingy England. We did it again this Saturday and last night. Was fantastic again – even better. This time Lucy was there and we got off with each other while we took the stuff. Incredible.

Friday 14 November 1986

Money is such a mind-fuck. Seb seems to be rolling in it – I don't know where he gets it from. Last night we were gonna shoot some stuff but he said I needed to pay for it this time. I wasn't thinking about money – he always took care of it – but he said he needed £500. I mean that's a lot of money. He said I should call my dad. I said it was okay I just won't have any.

Monday 17 November 1986

Fucking Seb. I didn't see him all weekend. I really miss him. I hurt. Why has he done this? I called Dad and told him I need some money. Afterwards I went to the cathedral and sat for a while. It was calming and quiet. I prayed – Mum would have a fit, but it felt pretty good.

Friday 21 November 1986

Finally. Finally he comes over. I am like sweating, even though it's so cold out. I give him the money and we go out for a curry but I can't eat. I keep telling him I need the stuff. After the starters he takes me into the toilets and gets me to suck him off before he gives me a tiny little bit of smack. I am so fucking grateful. I think I need some help. I went back to the cathedral and sat in my pew. Stupid – I think of it as mine. There were lots of tourists, and they can be a pain but I sat through a service and even sang a hymn. I kneeled down on a cushion that had been made for the Coronation – crazy. I took a pen and wrote my name right at the bottom. Maybe in another thousand years someone will wonder who I was.

Sunday 23 November 1986

Seb is just the sweetest boyfriend. He turned up with flowers yester-day and took me out for lunch at this really nice place. Then later we went back to his place and shot the best stuff I have ever had. Today he is taking me out again – he said he'd be here by noon. Should be here soon.

Monday 24 November 1986

He never fucking came. I waited and waited. He called at seven. Said he was caught up – I could hear music and laughing in the background. He wouldn't tell me where he was – I told him I needed him. That junk on Saturday had been perfect – we should do that again. That shit didn't come cheap, he said – told me I needed to find one thousand pounds. What am I going to do? I sat in my pew again and I must have a looked a right wreck because someone came over, a priest or something, and asked if I was all right. I wanted to tell him. But I ran.

Thursday 27 November 1986

The money from Nan has gone. I've even sold my coat. What do I do? I'm missing too many lectures and they're starting to ask questions. I can't let them know – I can't let anyone know.

Friday 28 November 1986

I saw Lucy this morning. I thought Seb might be there – I had been looking everywhere for him. She told me all about his lies. The prison stretch, how the uni had expelled him for drug dealing. No wonder he's got money. Oh shit.

Thursday 4 December 1986

I called Dad an hour ago. He's coming to get me. He's taking me somewhere for a week or two before I go home – can't do this with Mum looking at me with those judgemental eyes. Oh Christ, I am so fucking dumb. I am going to stop writing this after today but – future Dani: don't do this any more. Remember yesterday and the shame.

In the weekend, Seb had come round with some shit on Saturday morning and we had got high. Then went to some friends in the evening, four of them. His friends, he said, but they didn't look like his kind at all. Merchant bankers, Midas-rich and mean with it. We went somewhere expensive – Seb had asked me to dress up all fancy. There was champagne with dinner but I didn't drink any. Afterwards we all went back to a hotel room – a suite. Seb and two of them went off into the toilet. I was left with the other two – they looked at me like I was meat. I knew Seb was selling them drugs in the loo and I was a sweetener – he was giving them me as well. When the drooling pair went into the toilet too, I ran. I was not going to be his whore. Seb caught up with me when I was almost home. He kicked me. Called me... called me something I would never even write down.

On Sunday he brought flowers round. I wouldn't let him in. He called Monday and Tuesday. I didn't want to let him in but... I needed the stuff. Being without it burned. I let him in yesterday. He started out all sweet then got mean. Told me if I wanted him to keep me in the manner to which I had become accustomed then I needed to be nicer to him and nicer to his friends. Then he dragged me out of the halls and up to the cathedral. He remembered that I loved to sit in the cathedral library. It is the most amazing room I have ever been in – spiritual but you can feel the centuries of learning, of truth seekers searching through the books. It's tangible, right in the fabric of the building. Whenever I sit there I am filled with awe. The ancient wood that holds the room together is steeped in knowledge – the carvings and ornate stone hold so much pure love of learning. In one room is humanity's striving to learn and grow – a thousand years of human endeavour. And I can never go back. He defiled the place for me, defiled me in there. He pulled me to the back of the study room, behind a bookcase and made me kneel down and suck him, there in the library. At one point a nun walked by and he groaned so that she would see us – see me. I saw her shock and pity. He laughed. I am so dirty. I don't know how I will ever be clean again.

It is the final entry. Marcus Keyson closes the book.

THIRTY-SIX

Thursday 9 February 1989

Heavy doors swing open. Jim stares into a room and feels his stomach clench. It is the final stop after a maze of corridors that have led down and down and down – into the bowels of the hospital. The morgue. Steel, steel, porcelain and more steel – all scrubbed down and smelling faintly of bleach. In the centre of the room is a table. A blue sheet covers it, though it's not flat. Of course it's not, there's a body under it. Alongside Jim is a middle-aged woman with a kind face. She is his guide into the underworld to find Persephone.

'Do you need a minute?' she asks.

He looks at her blankly, not understanding the question. 'To do what?' He asks. She smiles and waits. 'Oh. I see.' She means a minute to brace himself. 'No. No, I'm fine.'

He's been told he doesn't need to do this. Tom had tried to get him to stay in London, near to Patty. Dani's flatmate was called out and has positively identified the body, so there is no need for Jim to make an identification – not legally, anyway.

'Don't go, Jim', Tom's voice is soft and kind.

'I need to see her.' Tom stares off into space for a moment and then nods. Of course Jim needs to go – they both know why. Jim opened his heart to the young man on that dreadful day he brought the news that Dani was dead. He had held it inside for so long he thought he might explode if he didn't share it, so he had told Tom all about Seb Merchant. The drugs and the lies, the shame and that terrible call he got from her begging him to help. How he'd rushed to Durham and took her away from there, from that awful situation. How he found her a clinic and took her there. How he'd hidden it all from Patty and how he had been scared for his daughter ever since.

Tom heard his confession without a word and at the end he said he would accompany Jim to the morgue in Durham.

'Such a kindness,' thought Jim.

Jim's guide moves over to the body and pulls the sheet back to reveal a dead face.

'Oh, sweetheart,' he whispers, then hides for a moment in a memory.

❄

'This is stupid.' Dani calls out. Jim walks into the living room to find her scowling at the radio. She's about nine years old.

'What's stupid?'

'This song.'

Jim listens. It's Donovan.

'First there is a mountain, then there is no mountain, then there is – that's stupid. Mountains are big, they don't walk away to have their tea some place.'

'You're right.'

'So what is he saying?'

'It's very complicated...' Jim begins.

Dani scowls at her father.

'It's Zen, I think. One can get over-analytical in this world...'

'What?' she asks, getting annoyed.

'Okay,' he sits down next to her. 'You can look at stuff so hard – like a jigsaw puzzle – trying to work out what it is, what it does – that you forget it's just a simple piece of cardboard. It's a song about just accepting the world as it is and not looking for anything deeper.'

'You have no idea, do you?' she frowns in concentration. 'Is it about aliens taking mountains away?'

'Maybe.' He shrugs. 'Maybe there never was a mountain.'

She nods. 'That's probably the answer.'

'That's my daughter,' Jim tells the kind guide.

She takes a notebook from her pocket and writes down the time of his formal identification.

'Could I have a moment alone with her?'

She shakes her head. 'I'm sorry.'

'PC Bevans will be here. I won't touch her.' Tom looked into the rules and told Jim that would be allowable, though not encouraged. If she knew Tom and Dani's history she would definitely say no. But…

'Of course.' She nods slowly and carefully. 'I'll be in the waiting room, take as long as you like and come out when you're ready.' She smiles and holds out her hand – one human being to another. Jim takes it and feels a little squeeze. A mother to a father.

'Thank you.'

She goes to the door and beckons Tom inside. She whispers something to him and then leaves.

'Jim,' Tom hisses.

'Please stay by the door, Tom – this will just take a second.'

Jim moves until he stands over her, his face cranes down to just above hers; it's pale, and the tiny traceries of veins can be clearly seen through the papery skin. Not at all like her glowing skin in life. He knows she is not merely asleep and yet… he slides his arm under the sheet and holds her hand. It's cold.

'Warm me up, Daddy,' she says from far-off. He squeezes her hand but nothing can warm it now.

'Goodbye, pumpkin.' He gives her the gentlest of kisses on her pale lips.

'And I am so sorry to do this.' He pulls back the sheet. She has been shaved for the autopsy and he's shocked by the nakedness between her legs.

'Please forgive this intrusion, Dani,' he asks her.

She is covered in bruises, all over her breasts, thighs and where they have shaved her. Her right hip looks terribly swollen. Her ankles and wrists are sliced where she was tied. Tom had told him that the blood settles, making the skin look worse, the marks more livid – but… but this is his girl. With all the strength he can muster, he takes her arm and holds it up. He's looking for something, something he prays he will not find. Tom has walked over to his side and together they see that all over the inner arm there are puncture wounds, track marks.

'My darling, darling girl,' Jim whispers to her.

He places her arm back down and takes the sheet, pulling it up over her body, leaving just her head exposed. He leans forward and kisses her one final time.

The kind-faced guide is there as he exits. She has been talking to another police officer, a hatchet-faced man with a pencil moustache who disappears once Jim walks over.

'A tea perhaps?' she asks Jim.

'A coffee would be really…' tears come and he can't fight them. He goes and sits, his head down. After a minute or two someone brings him a coffee. All sounds seem to come from underwater. Her arms…

The coffee is almost cold when Jim is finally able to lift his head. In the corner Tom is making the arrangements for the body to be sent to London once the coroner releases it. Jim watches him – he is so thankful to the young man. He is so grateful to him for helping. But now what? How did she lose her way again? Did the drugs make her a target? Is that why she was killed?

'Jim.'

Jim doesn't hear Tom, he's so lost.

'Jim.' Tom shakes him by the shoulder – softly.

'Miles away. Sorry.'

All Jim wants is to get home and get into bed with Patty. She's still sedated, a nurse is with her. She has been drugged to the eyeballs for almost two days now and Jim is terrified that Patty may be lost to him too.

'We should go. All the arrangements are made but you need to sign something. Come here and meet one of the senior officers.'

Tom leads him over to the hatchet-faced DI. The three men talk, there's a document signed. Then Tom guides Jim out of the underworld and back up to the land of the living.

They walk – heading to the station but in a meandering way.

'Do I smell?' Jim asks. He hasn't washed or shaved in two days, can't remember cleaning his teeth either.

'No,' Tom answers too quickly. 'A little… you could brush your teeth.'

They stop at a pharmacy and buy a toothbrush, toothpaste and mouthwash. At the station, Jim goes into the toilets and cleans his teeth. He also washes his face and, as no one else is there, takes off his shirt and cleans under his arms.

On the platform, Tom is in the waiting room. There are twenty minutes until the London train.

'Thank you, Tom,' Jim says, handing him a bar of Fruit and Nut he just bought from a machine.

Tom nods his head – his own greying head. He hasn't shaved today either and the whiskers are starting to poke through the skin; each one is white.

'She should be in London in a couple of days,' Tom says chewing a cube of slightly stale chocolate.

Jim doesn't know who he means for a second – then realises he means Dani. Dani's body. The two of them sit quietly for a few minutes, then Tom breaks the silence.

'There will be an inquest, maybe next week...' he pauses. 'Certain things will be excluded from the coroner's report and missing from the inquest.'

'What do you mean?'

'The drug use – it isn't relevant to the case.'

'Surely the police need...'

'Nothing will damage the police investigation. I just think there are certain things we don't need made public. Patty needn't know.'

'Is that possible?'

Tom nods solemnly. 'Dani was a wonderful girl, a model student who met a tragic end.'

'That newspaper story?'

'Jim, don't worry. Ben Bradman retracted that piece of filth and won't repeat the allegation. Don't worry. Trust me. And here.' Tom gives Jim a small bag. Jim looks inside – Dani's diaries.

Jim nods, immensely grateful. Then he slides back into the mire of his thoughts while they wait for the train.

THIRTY-SEVEN

Wednesday 29 December 2010

Audrey Cobhurn is sober now. She was pretty sober before she took the silver photo-frame from Duncan's office, undid the small black metal clasps and slid out the photo and mount. The mount had been glued and when she pulled it away, it took small scabs of the photograph with it. Below the mount she could see that the picture had been cut – but she could still see that resting on his arm was a hand, with long fingers that said: 'He's mine.' It was Dani Lancing's hand.

It's a little after midnight. All good children should be in their beds. She walks slowly through the dark house. It had been a family home just a fortnight ago, everyone looking forward to Christmas. Now it's a mausoleum. She reaches the front door and turns to the coat rack. Lorraine's jacket is there. Audrey pats it until she finds a lumpy pocket. Inside is her daughter's phone and a small card; she slips both into her own pocket. Taking extra care to be silent, she opens the front door and takes a step outside. It's a chill night; she wasn't thinking. She grabs a big duffel coat from beside the door and puts it on. It's too big – was Duncan's – still smells of him. She breathes deeply.

'Careful…' a voice from a long way off – was that him?

She wraps her arms tightly around herself – she's about to pull the door shut but remembers something. She goes back inside and pats at another of Lorraine's pockets. Inside is a packet of cigarettes. She takes them and then shuts the door.

She hurries off, not wanting Lorraine to follow if the door woke her. When she's turned a left and a right she slows down to a normal pace. She pulls out the packet of cigarettes and looks inside. Three left, plus a slim lighter. She takes one and lights it. She sucks the smoke deep down. It's the first one she's had in more than ten years. She'd given up for Duncan.

'Those things'll kill ya,' he'd said.

He gave them up one day, just like that. He didn't preach at her, but you could see he didn't like her smoking. She'd carried on about nine months after him and then stopped. But her stopping required patches, gum and a mink coat from Harrods. Even then she fell off the wagon a few times. But now, what's the point? Who wants to live for ever?

She smokes it right down to the butt, maybe even a little beyond. Then she takes the little card and taps the number into Lorraine's phone. She dials. It takes at least twenty rings but finally it's answered.

'Patricia Lancing,' a sleepy voice answers.

'It's Audrey Cobhurn. I realise this is late, but I hoped we could meet.'

* * *

Patty rushes, the little heels of her black shoes typewriter-clacking on the paving stones as she heads through the empty market-place, up to the cathedral and Audrey Cobhurn. Patty steals a glance at a clock on a small church – it's just before 1 a.m. She puts on a further burst of speed. The path is steep and twists; she has to be careful. She wishes she'd brought her running shoes with her – anything other than funeral clothes. To her left are the gates to

Dani's college. If she goes up to them she could probably see Dani's dorm room where they delivered her all those years ago. All... she stops as her stomach twists and sends pain up her back and down her legs. She's eaten nothing since she left Jim that morning – yesterday morning now. Nothing, except about a dozen assorted pills. She remembers that day so clearly. Freshers' week 1986. Patty had never been to Durham before Dani applied. She immediately saw how beautiful it was – Dani's school at the top of the city, nestled in the bosom of the cathedral like Mount Olympus. But she remembers feeling unease – were these children the new gods? They seemed to think they were with ramrod straight backs, ultra white teeth and confidence oozing from every pore of their perfect skin. It was the kind of privilege she had so often complained about... and there was Dani inside it all.

'I'm not just some young version of you, Mum. Your values make me sick. Physically fucking sick.' The words echo through Patty's head all this time later.

Patty runs on, turns a corner and suddenly it's there. The claustrophobic feel of the twisting streets breaks into the magnificence of the Cathedral Square dominated by the grandeur of the building itself. It takes Patty's breath away. Directly in front of the edifice is a rectangular lawn. To the side is an ancient burial ground, stones toppled like steed fallen in battle. Surrounding the lawn, the ground is cobbled, undulated like strafed soil. It's freezing. Patty can see the breath roll from her mouth and float upwards, disappearing into the night. Patty doesn't trust the cobbles, and walks onto the grass – heading straight to the maw of the cathedral.

'I'm not just some young version of you, Mum. Your values make me sick. Physically fucking sick.' The same words again. Patty remembers them so clearly: she said them to her mother on the day she left for university. And she never went home again. Did she deserve them – her poor mother? Patty doesn't really remember. But what is a mother for – to keep you safe and protect you – isn't that what a mother should do? Her own couldn't. So Patty never went home again. And Dani?

'Here.' A voice calls out from the shadows.

Patty can just make her out – standing before huge oak doors, almost close enough to touch sanctuary. Yesterday she reminded Patty of a swan – elegant and long but bowed. Grief piled on her head and shoulders and yet she carried it with a great dignity. But in this moonless half-light, Patty's impression is of a hawk. Her head is hooded yet her eyes sparkle from the shadows, her talons ready to strike. This does not seem the same woman.

Patty walks to her, like a fly approaching a spider. Audrey stands there, in the shadow of the cathedral. Patty can't see her face, but can see that her arms shake.

'You asked me to come,' Patty calls out.

'Did you kill my husband?' Audrey Cobhurn steps forwards, out of the gloom. She is completely altered – her face twitches, writhes as if worms tunnel beneath a mask. She looks as if she is consumed by the hunger to know the truth. Patty knows that look, has seen it on a hundred women at Lost Souls, and on her own face for so many years. She feels sick. This is it: she cannot run, would not want to.

Patty feels herself slice into the hand of Duncan Cobhurn.

'I... cut him.'

All she needed was a few drops of blood. Instead, she cut a river into his hand, through muscle and tendons – down to bone. She caused pain, damage, took revenge; tortured an innocent man. Tears stream down her face. All over, all gone. She thinks of Jim. All she wants now is to hold Jim's hand, to walk with him down to the river, kiss him and tell him that she loves him. She wants to live again. But it's too late.

'Please,' Audrey Cobhurn says in a small voice. 'Tell me the truth.'

Patty breathes. So many images flash through her mind. Dani's face on the missing poster, Jim's tears when he thought he couldn't be seen, Tom's face cracking open with grief, and her own face palsied by loss. The faces of all those students – children really – hundreds of them, saying how they loved and missed Dani. Each one thanking God it wasn't them. Patty feels the shame and guilt of the countless hours she had wished each and every one of them had been raped and murdered, so long as it hadn't happened to Dani. Blame and shame and guilt. Blame and shame and guilt. She wouldn't wish that on anyone – not if she could save them.

'Yes. I killed your husband.'

'I so wish you hadn't said that,' says Jim-in-her-head.

She sighs, knowing she has lost him now, lost all the love she had known those last wonderful few days.

'I had to, Jim,' she tells the man in her head. 'She needs peace. I can't let her suffer like we have, not knowing. I couldn't do that to another human being. And the truth is that I killed him.'

'You killed him accidentally.'

'No I didn't. I took revenge... I killed him. Please, Jim, let me go. I need to take my medicine.'

Patty closes her eyes, expecting the world to end. Either Audrey will pull out a phone and call 999 – come and arrest a murderer — or she will take a carving knife from her pocket and run Patty through. She waits, prepared for either. For what seems like an eternity there is nothing – Audrey Cobhurn merely watching her husband's killer – but she does not move or make a sound. Then she pulls something from her pocket.

'Here it comes... here it comes... Be brave,' thinks Patty.

'Look,' Audrey says, her voice cracking with emotion. She holds something. Patty stays bowed.

'Look, damn you!' she screams, crossing the distance between them until they are almost nose to nose. Patty opens her eyes, and sees that Audrey holds a photo.

'Dani?'

Audrey drops the photo, it spins to earth – Patty instinctively moves to catch it, like a leaf spilling from a tree in autumn. It lands face up in her hands and she cups it.

'I've never seen this picture...' she whispers, more to herself. She does not remember Dani ever being so glamorous, ever looking so grown up and happy.

'Where did you get this?' Patty asks the widow.

With a cruel smile, Audrey produces another picture... no, the same picture, the other half of the same picture. She holds it just by the corner – as if it might burst into flame.

'My husband,' she says, like an introduction at a party.

Twenty years younger, but him. Patty recognises the man she killed. Audrey hands the two pieces to Patty who puts them together. They fit perfectly.

'I don't understand.'

'Forgive me,' the widow says.

'What? Why?' Patty's head is spinning.

'I didn't mean it to happen, I just couldn't lose him – I loved him so much, he was my world. I told Lorraine – but she already knew – knew her from university. Knew your daughter, had seen them together.'

'What do you mean, together?' Patty asks but Audrey Cobhurn doesn't hear the question. She sees the young beautiful woman again. Sees Dani Lancing, who has listened to all Audrey has to say – all she has to offer and then…

'I don't want your money – you can't buy me. I'm not a whore.' Dani's voice cuts through her – then she laughs, deep and throaty – it makes Audrey Cobhurn spasm.

'I had begged Lorraine to tell me where to find her so I could talk to her. I had to make her see what she was doing to me, to us – to his family. I went to see her – offered her money, anything to leave him alone.'

Patty can't feel her arms or legs – totally numb.

'I couldn't believe he'd want her – she was a kid, the same age as our Lorraine. I gave him everything you know. He owed me – we were a team. Then this snot of a girl came in and threatened to ruin it, destroy it. I knew it wouldn't last, he'd have realised he loved me, but then she tricked him. Dug her claws into him with the oldest trick in the book…'

Patty feels bile rise in her throat.

'She got pregnant.'

Patty's hand drops to her stomach unbidden, some physical memory hardwired into her. In a rush she is back at Christmas with Dani. That final Christmas, with Dani so moody, so fractious. So plump. So pregnant.

'Oh Christ.' How had she not seen it?

Audrey Cobhurn reaches out with her hand, lays it on Patty's arm and grips her hard.

'I was at the end of my rope. I didn't want her hurt…' Audrey Cobhurn breaks down, tears stream down her face. 'My brother knew some men. I asked for them to frighten her, scare her off so we could get back to how it was, the three of us.'

'Oh my god…' Patty tries to pull away from her, but Audrey holds on – Patty twists her body – but Audrey won't let go.

She needs Patty to listen; she needs her to know – to hear her confession.

'They went to see her, those men my brother got me, and they told her to leave us alone – leave Duncan alone. She wouldn't listen, threatened to call the police and so they grabbed her. Things got out of hand.'

THIRTY-EIGHT

Monday 9 January 1989

He checks the notes and signs the box to start his rounds. It is 2 p.m. He walks onto the ward and goes to the young woman's bed. She has been there for two days. She has barely spoken in all that time, first name but no address. She has one question, which everyone has avoided answering.

The doctor dreads sitting down with her. Her bruises are healing well. She has three cracked ribs but they'll soon knit and begin to mend. She has lost two teeth, but not at the front; so long as she doesn't smile she looks fine. Smiles are probably not on the agenda for a while anyway. On the ward everyone else is at least fifty and most are sixty plus – that is the normal age for women to have hysterectomies. Of course he has, sometimes, dealt with younger women, those with ovarian cancer generally, never someone who has been kicked repeatedly and savagely in the stomach. It had been a matter of life and death when she'd been brought in, and while she may know that – understand the truth of it…

'Will I be able to have a child in the future?' she asks him the question.

He cannot say the words to her. All he can do is shake his head. He avoids her eyes and their hope for another answer.

'The pain…'

'Of course.'

He writes a note for extra medication. He can see how tight her jaw is, how she grits her teeth when it gets bad. He leaves quickly, writes that a counsellor should see her tomorrow or the next day, then continues his rounds.

A nurse sits on her bed a short while later and washes her, helping her to move as the pain tramps around her, making her woozy and weak.

'Is there no one to come see ya, pet?'

'No. No one,' she wants Duncan, but she can't tell him what has happened. It is all such a mess. She grits her teeth, more at the thought of telling him, than the pain flecking her abdomen.

'I'll get ya some morphine love.' And the angel rises and leaves.

Later, as evening draws in around her, she remembers how she felt when she had her abortion. How stupid she had been to let it happen, and with that bloody art student who was such a shit. How could she ever have been interested in him? Back then she had told herself that she wasn't killing anything, she was just postponing the moment when she met her child and held it. That was what she told herself then. Now, she will never hold a child from her own womb. Life plays such awful tricks.

'Happy birthday to me. Happy birthday to me. Happy...' She is twenty-one. In Greenwich she knows her Mum and Dad will be worried – they have never missed seeing her on her birthday. Birth-day...

When the nurse returns she will call Duncan. She needs him.

Duncan sits in the dark. Waiting for Audrey. A bag lies by his feet, packed.

Finally, there is a scratch at the lock and the front door opens.

'Lorraine, why are you here, pet?' Audrey calls out as she arrives – knowing someone is in the house. 'You'll not guess where I've been,' she calls out excitedly, glad to have someone to share the gossip with. She'd been to a salon – exclusive. Had her hair done, her nails as well – feet and hands – plus a wax. Downstairs. It feels really odd. All part of her plan to get him excited in her again.

'Aud.'

She almost jumps out of her skin. She flicks on the light and sees him at the table. She knows it's awful news. His skin is chalk, his eyes bloodshot and his cheeks are streaked with tears. But it is the bag that tells the story.

'I love you, Audrey but… she needs me.'

There was no need to reveal her name. Duncan knows his affair is an open secret.

'No!' she moans.

'Don't make this harder than it has to be. I owed it to you to tell you face to face. But I'm going.'

'You can't, Dunc. We're your family.'

'You will always have everything you need.'

'Lorraine…'

'She's grown, Aud – she doesn't need me and neither do you.'

'We do!' she is on his lap in a second, wrapping her arms around his neck. Trying to kiss him.

'Don't, Audrey. Have some dignity.'

He pushes her off his lap and she lands on the floor.

'Do you want me to beg? Look, I'll beg.' She is on her knees, shuffling forward, arms outstretched. 'Please, Duncan. Don't do this to me, to us.'

'I'm sorry, Audrey. Christ, I shouldn't have come home.' He goes to walk around her but she grabs his leg.

'No, No. No!' she screams.

He tries to shake her off but she won't budge. 'Audrey, don't. Christ, sweetheart, don't make this worse.'

'It can't be worse. You can't leave.'

'She needs me.'

'I need you!' Audrey screams.

'She lost a baby. She lost my baby.' He is all tears now, they stream out of him, snot too. 'Someone beat her to a pulp – almost killed her. They killed my baby.'

Audrey lets go, and slides to the floor. He walks around her.

THIRTY-NINE

'He left,' Audrey Cobhurn continues as Patty tries to reel her mind back into her body.

'I lay there on the kitchen floor, shocked. I'd called my brother. He said it all went fine and she wouldn't be troubling me again. He said nothing about the violence – I found that out later. They'd beaten her badly. She'd been lippy and they were the type of men who liked hitting woman and… I hadn't told them she was pregnant.'

The cold bites at the two women.

'I lay there all night, praying, cursing… then, at dawn, the front door opened. He was back. He didn't say a word. Just came in and unpacked his bag. Showered and went to bed. I didn't know what to think, didn't know what happened – but he stopped with us. I thought they must have had a fight, him and your daughter. Or he realised it were just the baby that had brought them together. We never talked about it and then a few weeks later we saw her photo in the papers. She was missing.'

Patty remembers how she and Jim had finally driven up to Durham. She had been so angry with Dani. Starting with that stupid Christmas visit – how the hell could she give up on her education when she was so close to finishing? Then keeping quiet on her birthday, her twenty-first. She had seen how all this had hurt Jim. He kept asking Patty to get in touch with Dani, but she refused. Then they had a letter from the university, asking if Dani was deferring her final year or had dropped out. They had to speak to her. They called and called, but no reply. They decided to drive there.

When they arrived there was no one there. They let themselves in, they had a key, and waited. After a few hours the flatmate came back, very surprised to see them. She hadn't seen Dani since before Christmas.

'I knew she'd gone home to tell you she didn't want to do her final terms. I think she was going to defer them but… I thought she was with you. There's a pile of post…'

Jim went through the stack of mail for any clue to where she might be. Nothing. Patty sat on the sofa. She already felt something awful had happened. That evening they went to the police and reported her missing.

Audrey continued. 'Duncan was beside himself. He was out every night – I think he was searching for her. He didn't talk to me, or Lorraine. Didn't go to work – left his assistant to run the business. Almost ran it into the ground. Duncan was in the same house with me but wasn't my husband any more. I know that if he'd have found her, he would have left me. Just know it. I prayed she'd stay gone – for ever. And then… then she was dead.'

Patty sees Tom's mouth move but she doesn't understand. The drugs have slowed everything, disengaged her eyes from her ears.

The words make no sense. Then she looks to Jim and she knows what Tom was saying. Jim's face says it all.

Patty closes her eyes and her heart.

'I never said anything to Duncan about what I'd done. But in those early days I saw what it did to him. He thought he'd let her die and it was killing him. That's when the charity work started: young offenders, drug addicts. I helped him with it and we slowly became a team again.'

For a few seconds Audrey Cobhurn is lost in her thoughts, memories of the two of them fighting the system, the dynamic duo. Then she is back in the cold reality.

'I thought he'd forgotten her. That it was all over. Then he dies, my poor lovely man. And you show up at his funeral. I hadn't even put him in the ground and you were there. Of course I recognised you right away – knew you were her mum. Then the policeman comes and shows me the photo – this photo.' She holds up the picture of Dani and Duncan.

'Now I don't think he ever got over her. I think he loved her for twenty years.'

She looks lost, caught in a maelstrom of memories – reaching out to touch them and judge if they're real. Remembering each kiss and thinking – did he mean that for me or for her? Suddenly her face changes – pain streaks it.

'The policeman told me you killed Duncan.' Her eyes flash naked hatred for a second, directly at Patty.

Patty closes her eyes. 'I thought your husband killed Dani, all those years ago. I kidnapped him to force him to tell me and… I killed him. I didn't mean to. I didn't—' but her words sound empty. Patty knows she wanted him dead.

The widow sighs and folds into the earth, whispering softly, 'I might as well have killed them both.'

The two women are quiet, both locked into their own grief. Until something in Patty's brain switches on. She suddenly feels a chill in her chest, realising the importance of something Audrey had said.

'What policeman?'

Audrey Cobhurn says nothing, lost, dancing somewhere far away with her Duncan.

Patty grabs at her coat and pulls her up. 'What policeman?' she feels something under her hand. She pulls at the coat and jumper; there's a box tucked into Audrey's waistband – a wire runs out of it to a microphone taped to her chest.

Patty panics, she pushes Audrey away from her, and she staggers but doesn't fall.

'That policeman.' Audrey points to a figure on the other side of the Cathedral Square, walking towards them.

'He told me you did it, killed Duncan, but he was wrong... it was me. I killed him – all those years ago. Killed the baby, killed our love and then killed him.'

Patty is superglued to the spot – watching the figure get closer and closer – until...

'He isn't a policeman,' she calls out to Audrey. She knows him. This is all wrong. She backs away, her eyes searching for an escape.

'Don't run, Mrs Lancing,' Marcus Keyson calls out as he walks closer. He waves a box in his hand. 'I have you on tape, confessing to the murder of Duncan Cobhurn. Stay right there.'

He is almost on her. She can't run anyway, not in these stupid shoes. She pulls her leg back...

Keyson calls. 'There's nowhere to—'

Patty lashes her leg out with all the speed and agility she has. The shoe flies off her foot, streaking like a bullet and slams into Marcus Keyson's face.

'Hell.' He staggers and drops to his knees. Patty kicks the second shoe off and runs as fast as she can. She can see, by the side of the graveyard, there's a path that leads back down into town. She goes hell-for-leather towards it.

Marcus Keyson feels his nose. It's tender but not broken. There's a dull ache and he will have quite a bruise there tomorrow, but he doesn't care. He watches Patty run to the side of the graveyard and drop out of view. He could probably catch her, she's in her sixties and he's twenty-five years younger, but it doesn't seem worth it. He's got what he needs. The thought makes him all warm inside. He walks over to the other woman, kneeling on the cobbles.

'Hello, Audrey, thanks for finding Patricia for me. I have her confession on tape, well not tape, of course, all digital now – but you get my point. You should be happy.'

He smiles. Audrey curls into herself a little more, wanting him to go away.

'I do have a teensy confession to make though. Patricia was right: I'm not an actual policeman. Sorry. I really wanted her confession – and as a bonus, I got you too, ouch nasty. Having a young woman almost beaten to death and her pregnant. Not good, really. Not something we want in the papers, is it – and they would love it, I'm telling you.' He laughs. 'It's been a bad Christmas for you, hasn't it?'

Patty runs as fast as she can, on cobbles that threaten to tip her over and break an ankle at every step. She almost falls as she reaches the Market Square. If she can only...

'I see her,' a shout comes from somewhere to her left. She veers away from the voice, towards the little church at the end of the square. To the left, in the shadows, is the entrance to the indoor market.

'Where is she, Ronson?' Keyson calls out from somewhere behind.

She slams into the wooden door – it's chained and padlocked. The wall curves into a black corner – a dead-end, she can't go that way.

'No!' She slams the heel of her hand into the gate. A slat gives ever so slightly. She pushes at it, and a tiny gap appears; barely wide enough for a child to crawl through. Patty scrapes through it, and tumbles into the dark of the market hall.

She lies where she's fallen; her hands are scraped but there's nothing more serious. Her eyes strain into the dark, trying to see something, anything, of her surroundings. She can see nothing. The only sound she can hear is the pounding of her own heart. Suddenly she is hit again by the awful knowledge that Dani was pregnant – it folds her into a ball, clawing her stomach. She wants to scream, howl, but she can't. She needs to get away first, that is the priority. Any thought of confessing to the police for the murder of Duncan Cobhurn has evaporated, this is survival now. She wants to live and she wants to be free. She wants Jim.

With a supreme effort of will, she pushes herself onto her hands and knees. Grief can wait. The drumming of her heart begins to lessen and she listens. To her right she hears footsteps – they're so close, but they're on the other side of the fence. Slowly her eyes adjust to the darkness and she can see she's in some sort of walkway between stalls. She can just about see a large pile of second-hand books and a tray of CDs and DVDs. It will be difficult to get past them without making any noise – and she will need to be totally silent as the men chasing her are so close. From behind her she hears the slam of boots on the gate into the market, testing it to find a way in, just like she had done.

'Where the hell is she?' a voice she doesn't recognise calls out.

'She can't have gone far – keep looking,' Keyson yells back.

She can't stay in there, they'll find the way in soon and then she'll be trapped. She crawls on, through a mass of dropped clothes hangers and past a stall smelling of fish. Up ahead she can see a light, spilling through from somewhere. It may be a street light. She can…

Her phone rings. 'Oh shit.' She rolls onto her side and scrambles in her pocket, desperate to extinguish the sound as quickly as possible.

'I hear something, boss,' the unknown man shouts. 'She's in the market. How the hell did she get in there?' He starts thumping on the fence, hard and loud.

The phone screen shows Lorraine Cobhurn's number.

Patty answers in a whisper. 'What?'

'I asked you to forgive me,' Audrey Cobhurn's voice sounds far-off, barely audible above the wind and sounds of traffic.

'I heard you,' Patty answers in as low a voice as possible. 'I can't forgive you.'

'I didn't really expect you to. I wouldn't if I were in your shoes. And I don't forgive you either – for Duncan. I just don't blame you. I can't imagine twenty years of feeling like this.'

Patty could say it gets better. But it doesn't, time heals nothing.

'I… I am sorry. For your loss, I—' Patty falters.

'Don't, you cannot have the right to apologise. There is only one thing you could do to make it up to me.'

'What?'

'Kill yourself. That would do it. I think you should kill yourself, really I do, and I think it would make you happier.'

'You're crazy,' deep down Patty knows it's her grief talking and she understands the urge to make the pain stop.

'Maybe I am crazy, honestly I could be,' Audrey tells her. 'But it seems very clear to me that I cannot live like this and I'm pretty sure you can't either. How you have coped for twenty years I can't imagine. So I think we should die together. A pact.'

'Audrey, don't be an idiot.'

'I think it's the best way for both of us, but if you won't then you have to live with what you've done – to Duncan and Lorraine and me. If you can live with it, then great. I know I can't live without Duncan, not now I know that I'm to blame.'

'Audrey – what are you saying?' Patty hisses. Scared to be too loud.

'Will you do something for me?' the widow asks.

'Audrey, think straight – Lorraine—'

'Say goodbye to her. Tell her I love her.'

'Audrey!' Patty shouts, forgetting the two men hunting for her.

'Goodbye.'

Suddenly the noise of the wind screeches in the phone, then a blare of an airhorn as a truck bellows into the night – a scream of brakes and a sickening thud as the truck strikes Audrey Cobhurn's body. There is an explosion of sound and the phone goes dead.

Simultaneously, from outside the market, somewhere on the ring road behind the cathedral, Patty can hear an enormous crushing sound of metal on concrete; almost immediately followed by a cacophony of car horns and car alarms. Patty's hands start to shake.

'She's right here, I heard her,' shouts the unknown man. Then there is the crash as a part of the fence gives way under the crunch of his boot.

'I'm in,' he yells.

'Oh my God. Oh my God.' Patty starts to crawl again towards the light. Fighting to put thoughts of Audrey's death out of her head and concentrate on getting away. The floor is gritty and she feels pieces of glass cut into her left palm, her knees feel shredded. She will have to stand but then she'll lose the cover.

'Come out, my little piggy.' The unknown man laughs and then starts to hit the plastic tubs.

Patty almost screams. She feels the blood soak into her trousers as her knees are cut. She needs to get up and... there's a doorway up ahead. She can make out a blob of light that spears through it. It looks like it leads to an outside area and maybe to freedom. If she can only... there is a crash to her left, as she sends a tray of CDs spinning to the floor.

'There you are,' the unknown man screams and heads towards the sound – crashing into a stall himself and sending it flying. Suddenly a line of light shoots out – he's got a torch. He catches her in the arc of light and her eyes widen in fear.

'Got you.' He whoops in delight and lunges forward, grabbing at her arm... but the stalls are in the way and she is just out of his reach. He grunts in frustration, bats aside a pile of clothes and forces his way into the aisle directly behind Patty. She had been frozen for a second but now the spell is broken and she runs forwards at full pelt.

There are stairs to her left. She bolts up them, trying to stay out of the beam of light that tries to track her like a searchlight. She has to keep moving. Below her, on the other side, there is another crash as part of the fence falls into the market and Keyson steps inside.

'Ronson!' Keyson yells. 'Where is she?'

'Up the stairs, she's gone up to the second level.'

'Go up after her. I'll look for another staircase.'

Patty hears Ronson start to head up the stairs. It's too dark up here for her to blindly stagger about, but she knows that as soon as he gets up with the torch, she'll be a sitting duck. There is only one thing to do. She rolls to the top of the stairs and flattens herself as low as she can get. Then as Ronson's head gets level with her foot, she lashes out, kicking him in the side of the head.

'Christ...' he flails, trying to grab at her leg as he starts to topple backwards. He touches her heel, tries desperately to get a hold on her as he falls back, but he can't keep his footing and he crashes backwards down the stairs, head over heels into a crumpled heap at the bottom. Patty is up and after him, running down and jumping over his body.

She hopes he's unconscious but with a roar of anger he is up and on his feet in seconds. She runs as fast as she can, hoping the path ahead is clear. She can see a rectangle of light further on; it must be a door – but where to? She prays it leads outside. She reaches it and – yes, she can see through the gloom to the end of a storage area and there's a fence she could scale that leads to the open world. She could escape. She takes a breath to ready herself for a sprint and jump, her adrenalin spiking. She can do this. She leaps forward, accelerating as quickly as possible – sees the gap with the fence beyond – seconds away, she speeds up and—

'Got you.' From nowhere an arm shoots out and grabs her. She tries to spin sideways but it grips on tight, pulling her into a bear hug.

'You've been a bit naughty, ain't ya,' Grant Ronson laughs. His other arm pulls her around and his hand clamps a cloth over her face. She twists and kicks like a mule, tries to pull her face away, breathe clean air, but his hand stays firmly around her nose and mouth. Slowly her energy begins to wane as the chloroform starts to take effect.

'Time to sleep,' he says as she turns to deadweight. He swings her onto his shoulder like a sack of potatoes. She drops her phone but he bends down and retrieves it. Then, whistling the theme to *The Dam Busters*, he carries her outside.

❄

It's colder out in the open. Wisps of mist have started to trail through the Market Square. Keyson stands under a streetlamp, a sodium-orange pallor making the bruise above his nose look quite nasty. He stamps his feet, partly due to the cold, partly in annoyance.

'Here we go, guv.' Ronson gives his boss a broad smile.

'Phone?'

He hands Patty's phone to Keyson, who nods and scrolls through the address book. He finds the name he wants and hits dial. It only rings once.

'Patty. Thank God, I was so worried about you,' Jim's voice blasts from the phone. Keyson pulls it back from his ear a little.

'You will never guess what just happened – a woman jumped off a bridge and landed just in front of us, we had to swerve but a truck hit her. Christ, it was awful. Patty? Patty?'

Keyson smiles. 'Hello, Jim, hope your head's feeling better.'

In the car, Jim digs his fingernails into the seat, digging small ovals into the leather. He looks across to Tom and whispers, 'It's Keyson.'

'Oh hell.' Tom feels a little sick. He looks out of the windscreen at the anarchy in front of him. Two cars have crashed into the middle barrier. One is crushed into the tunnel support, closing the entrance. A trail of blood is smeared from the tunnel at least twenty yards to where the truck dragged the body; the body itself lies like a battered rag doll, its stuffing pulled from it and smeared all around.

'Where's my wife?' Jim asks coldly.

'Wife? Haven't you been separated for years?'

'She is still my wife. Where is she, Keyson?'

'Okay, let's not split hairs, Mr Lancing. Your wife is safe. No one is getting hurt, I am not that kind of man.'

'Oh, I've heard exactly what kind of man you are, Dr Keyson.'

'From who?'

'Detective Superintendent Tom Bevans.'

'Oh, Jim. Honestly, I would take anything he tells you with a pinch of salt. He's not your friend.'

'And you are?'

'Me? No, "friend" is too strong a word – but I am going to tell you some truths, including a particularly juicy one. I am going to tell you who killed your daughter.'

From somewhere the sound of sirens begins to wail, getting closer. He turns to see the flashing lights – red and white, rotating – making the blood on the road shine like a trail of bright red breadcrumbs leading to hell. In the mirror, just for a split second, Jim thinks he sees Dani frozen in the red stroboscopic light from an ambulance. She waves solemnly, then she is gone.

Jim strains into the darkness, hoping to catch another glimpse of her but...

Whack! The truck driver slams into the car.

'Jesus!' Jim jumps.

The driver is in complete shock, staggering around in a circle. Jim sees a medic jump out of an ambulance and run towards him.

'Are you still there, Jim?' Keyson's voice calls from the phone.

'Yes. Yes, I'm here. Patty was in Durham, are you still there?' Jim asks Keyson.

'Yes, old Durham town,' Keyson replies. 'Don't tell me you're here too.'

'Yes.'

'How wonderful. Let's meet and have a lovely chat about abduction and murder.'

'Where?' Jim asks coldly, not wanting to get drawn into anger by Keyson's levity.

'How about the cathedral. Lovely spot. Begun in 1093 and is in the Norman style with some beautiful Gothic flourishes. I've got a pile of guidebooks if you'd like one?'

Jim looks out of the side window and up to the heavens. He can see the cathedral above them, dominating the skyline of the town.

'I can be there in fifteen minutes,' Jim tells him.

'Alone?'

'I may have DS Bevans with me.'

'Oh, Jim. That would be perfect. Please bring him.'

But Jim's no longer listening. He unclips his seatbelt and opens the door.

'Jim, Jim, where are you going?' Tom asks, but gets no reply. Instead he watches his friend dart across the blocked carriageway and start to climb the hill that leads up to the cathedral.

'Shit!'

Tom slides out of the car and slams the door, pocketing the keys as he does so. He looks around wildly for a second. All is pandemonium as more and more emergency vehicles arrive, each one adding another flashing light and wailing siren. He should help out, move the car to the side, but Jim is getting away from him and he can't let him meet Keyson alone. He looks around. The truck driver is being helped and it is going to take a lot of time to remove the dead woman from the roadway. There is nothing he can do.

'Damn.' He runs after Jim.

FORTY

Above them, at the top of the city, Keyson holds Patty, still unconscious, in his arms and watches Ronson work on opening the
cathedral door. It is huge, solid oak reinforced by thick slats and
possibly metal rods. Keyson doubts it can be breached but he's seen
Ronson perform some remarkable feats and Ronson has told him
he will get them inside. Keyson presses himself against the door,
deep into the shadows and waits. There is a sudden snap and the
door shudders on its hinges and arcs forward.

Ronson catches it as it moves. 'There you go,' Ronson says with
pride as it swings, wobbling on a shattered hinge. 'No alarms, and
I can't see any CCTV neither.' Ronson grins and holds the door for
his boss to walk through.

Keyson enters the enormous structure, looking up, as he does
so, to see a parade of saints glowering down at him. Each is suffused
with moonlight and looking furious at this intrusion.

'Gentlemen,' Keyson waves cheerily to them. He walks to the
baptismal font and places Patty's limp body on the cold stone.
Then, switching on a torch, he begins to explore. There is something he desperately wants to find. He locates the rose window,
an enormous wall of stained glass in the shape of a flower. It
orients him to the correct set of pews and he kneels down in the
central isle and shines his torch into the rows – examining each

pew until he finds what he wants. In the faintest of writing he sees her name.

DANIELLE LANCING. 1986.

He sits in the pew trying to imagine her there. It is uncomfortable and draughty sitting, so he kneels and uses a cushion embroidered in 1952 for the Coronation.

'The lord is my Shepherd I shall not...' he begins to intone... but there is nothing. Nothing of her to feel. Nothing of anyone to reach out to, in the draughty ancient room. He gets up and walks further into the belly of the cathedral. Now he can give the place his attention. It is magnificent, vaulted ceilings with fingers of wood that worm through stone to hold up the sky. The great rose of stained glass dominating the centre of the cathedral. During the day it blazes with light but in the darkness it seems somewhat sinister, a shadow-play of pain and anguish. Keyson likes it.

Jim walks up the final slope towards the cathedral, his legs like pistons – his eyes ahead. In his chest the feeling of panic is slowly being replaced by the fizzing of anger. Behind him Tom follows, not knowing what to do. His professional wisdom says: stop and call for back-up – but this is not professional, it's personal. He pulls out his phone, sees the time is 3 a.m. He punches in a number and listens to it ring. An answer phone picks up – his own voice.

'You've reached Tom Bevans. Sorry I'm not here at the moment but please leave a message and I'll get back to you. Thanks.' Tom smarts a little at the message. Plain Tom Bevans, no DS – in case a woman he lied to is calling.

'I need to get a life once this is over,' he tells himself.

The phone beeps once.

'It's 3 a.m. Wednesday 29 December 2010. I am approaching Durham Cathedral in pursuit of Dr Marcus Keyson and Grant Ronson, who I believe have abducted Patricia Lancing for the purpose of extortion. I am following her husband James Lancing to the ransom drop-off point. If for some reason I...' He stops for a second. 'Jane, just get the bastard.'

He flicks the phone closed and hurries off after Jim. Tom catches up with him just as he is crossing the central lawn that leads directly to the main cathedral door, which stands massive and black in the night. Hung in its centre is the sanctuary knocker – a blazing metal sun behind a face with soulless dark eyes. By royal decree those who use it to call for the door to be opened can ask for sanctuary. It was granted even to the guiltiest of souls. Tom reaches his fingers out to touch it.

'Oh please, sanctuary – for you?' Keyson appears from the shadows.

'It isn't even the real thing, it's a fake.' Tom says a little sadly.

'Nowhere is safe for a murderer nowadays. Isn't that right, Tom?' Keyson asks with a smile.

'Hello, Marcus.' Tom attempts to smile back, but in his tired face it looks forced.

'Please.' Keyson motions for them to enter as he pushes the door open.

'Into the cathedral?' Jim asks.

'Pretty please.'

They enter and Keyson closes the door behind them.

Inside it's mostly dark except for rectangles of moonlight that spill across the floor. The light from the stained glass seems alive, dancing across the flagstones – deep purple, blood red and under-sea blue. Jim looks up and sees the parade of saints who smile down on him.

'Your daughter loved it in this cathedral, she came often. I think it fitting that this is where we all finally meet to unravel this mystery.' Keyson smiles but both Jim and Tom feel goose bumps spread over their flesh.

Keyson takes a slim book from his pocket and offers it to Jim. 'I do apologise for the way I borrowed this.'

Jim snatches Dani's diary back. 'Where is my wife?'

'Towards the back, she's perfectly safe – Mr Ronson is with her.'

Jim gives Keyson a filthy look and leaves the two men. He walks quickly, almost running, though he has to take care; the flagstones are smooth like ice, and he can't see where they dip and bow from a thousand years of wear. His head is full of the rushing of his blood as he fights the panic that threatens to overwhelm him. Ahead of him the room stretches for ever – the size of a football pitch at least. Jim's footsteps echo throughout, filling the air like a million insects scuttling through the house of God. As he rushes forwards, towards the enormous rose of stained glass that beckons him on, for a second he sees Dani sitting in a pew, her hands linked together in prayer. She turns to look at him; her face is so pained, and then she is gone. Ahead he sees an area fully lit, a room off the main throughway – a chapel. He heads to it.

He steps inside, amazed to see it isn't electric light that illuminates the room but more than a hundred small votive candles, which have been lit around a massive sculpture carved from drift-wood. It is of a woman who seems to be cut more from pure pain than wood. Her face is long, her lips pursed and her eyes weep. The wood itself seems weathered by a thousand years of sun and sea and salt; the form appears to bear the scars of humanity. At the woman's feet lies a man, twisted, half on his side; he looks emaciated – stripped of hope and life. Mary, the mother, and Jesus, her murdered child. Jim does not appreciate the theatricality of all this. He walks up to the figures until he stands by Jesus' head and the mother towers over him, almost double his height. Then he sees her. With her hands tied and mouth taped, sitting directly before the mother and child, is Patty. Grant Ronson stands beside her like some cut-price nightclub bouncer, his hands cupped in front of him. Jim moves to untie her, but Ronson pushes him back.

'It's fine, Mr Ronson. Let him untie her,' Keyson calls out as he and Tom step inside the chapel.

Ronson steps aside and Jim scrambles forward. He quickly gets the rope undone and pulls the tape off her mouth.

'Patty. Oh Christ, Patty, I am so glad to see you. I was so worried.' He hugs her and she holds on to him tightly.

'Jim, I am so sorry to drag you into all this mess.'

'I don't care. Just as long as you're safe and we're together.'

She pulls him into her so tight they become a single entity for a moment.

She buries her head in his neck. 'I'm not confessing – I'm not giving in, I want to be with you.'

'You will be,' he tells her.

'I told his wife – she needed to know and I had to tell her.'

'Of course you did.'

'Keyson taped it… me admitting to killing Duncan Cobhurn.'

Jim feels all the blood drain from his face.

'And she told me – oh Christ, she told me something, Jim. She told me something awful and then. Oh God, she killed herself.'

'His wife?' Jim asks.

'She jumped in front of traffic or something – I could hear the truck.'

Both Jim and Patty heard the death of Audrey Cobhurn and Jim saw her body fall. The sight will haunt him for the rest of his life.

'They were lovers – Dani and Duncan Cobhurn. And she was pregnant, Jim. Dani was going to have a baby. That Christmas she was pregnant and I screamed at her, told her she was wasting her life, but I didn't know. Jim, I didn't know she was carrying our grandchild.' Patty has tears streaming down her face.

Jim grips her tight, his throat closing up as he thinks of Dani that last time he saw her – the rounded tummy he thought was too many chips.

'Audrey found out and confronted Dani, telling her to leave him alone, and when she wouldn't... when she wouldn't...' Patty dissolves in tears.

Keyson kneels down next to Jim. 'Audrey Cobhurn had your daughter beaten until she miscarried. I wouldn't waste a tear on Mrs Cobhurn if I were you.' Keyson then removes the final pieces of rope from Patty and helps her and Jim up, before dropping a hand onto his shoulder.

'There we go. I am sorry for the inconvenience. Don't worry that you missed Audrey's revelation, Mr Lancing, there are many more to come.'

Keyson walks across to Ronson and whispers in his ear. Keyson gives him the recording machine from his pocket and Ronson walks off.

'Mrs Lancing, I apologise. You are my employer after all and I really have acted badly – but I think ultimately you will thank me.'

'I can't see that happening, Dr Keyson,' Patty says, trying to keep her voice level.

'We shall see, because I am about to tell you who killed your daughter.'

Despite herself, Patty feels her heart stop for a second.

Tom steps forward with his arm outstretched and places his hand on Keyson's chest, his back to Patty and Jim.

'Marcus, I think this has gone on long enough.'

'Mr and Mrs Lancing...' Keyson begins, ignoring Tom.

'Don't, Marcus.' Tom is insistent.

'...your daughter Danielle was murdered...'

'Please, Marcus,' Tom says in a whisper, pleading with his old friend.

'...by Police Constable Tom Bevans,' Keyson steps back. 'Now Detective Superintendent Tom Bevans, of course.'

'Tom?' Jim shakes his head. It is unthinkable.

'Tom?' Patty barely manages to get the word out, her face contorting with effort.

From the shadows Dani walks forward and circles Keyson, until she can see into the face of her best friend.

'Tom?' she breathes.

Tom Bevans looks through Dani, and slowly turns to face the parents of the woman he has loved almost his whole life. Tears coat his face. Dani walks over to stand between her parents. The Lancing family wait.

'Did you?' Patty asks.

Tom cannot speak. He nods slowly.

Dani seems to crack, like fine porcelain in a fire – hairline cracks that twist throughout her entire form.

'Oh my God,' Jim steps back, lurching sideways. He walks away, into the shadows and sits on the floor, lost in thought. He recalls the look on Tom's face when he saw him that morning, over twenty years ago. The look of total distress as they faced each other on the street – how is it possible that he... that he...

'Dani.' Jim holds his head in his hands. He can't bear it.

Patty watches Tom's face, sees the tears and the pain that eats him. It's genuine – she knows the purity of his anguish; he is, after all, the Sad Man. He was transformed by Dani's death but for the first time she wonders what caused that pain? Is it something more than grief? Is it guilt? Her face hardens – like her heart. Her eyes are ice.

Keyson watches her and licks his lips. From his pocket Keyson takes a knife, sharp like the blade Patty used on Duncan Cobhurn. He walks over to her and bends his lips to her ear and whispers, 'Twenty lost years. A life snuffed out. Jim lost to you – your whole life ruined and you yourself, turned into a murderer. Responsible not only for the death of Duncan Cobhurn but Audrey Cobhurn too. And the broken heart of Lorraine Cobhurn. Tom Bevans has done that to you. He made you trust him, he wormed his way into your family and then...' He takes her hands and uncurls the fingers, wrapping them around the knife handle. 'He kills the thing you hold most dear, he killed your daughter Dani.'

Keyson takes a step back. Patty stands there holding the knife before her. Keyson moves to her side and takes her softly and walks her forwards.

'He said he loved her but he killed her and left you in anguish for more than twenty years.' Keyson's voice is seductive as he leads Patty, knife in hand, to face Tom.

'Is it true, Tom? Did you kill her?'

Tom stands his ground, his eyes red and his mouth in constant motion, yet no words come.

'Tell me, Tom!' she hisses at him.

He closes his eyes and breathes. 'I did.'

Patty's jaw clenches; it looks like it could shatter. She steps forward to bring the knife up to his chest, level with his heart. The tip cuts into his clothing and, through them, to his skin. He cries in pain but does not move.

'Do it, Patricia. Do it,' Keyson urges.

'You killed Dani?'

Tom doesn't answer. His head is bowed to the floor.

'Jesus, Tom.' She pushes forwards, feels flesh split, and sees red pool on the knife and start to soak into the cloth. Tom sobs with pain. She moves a hand up to his chin and forces his head up; she wants to see his eyes. The blood pools on the hilt and three drops of blood fall to the ground. Patty looks into his eyes and yells into his face – the sound of deep pain.

Jim looks up, hearing his wife's anguish, his own pain broken for a second as he watches her hold a knife to the heart of the man who killed their daughter.

Jim sees Dani walk forwards, She seems to flare bright like the sun, filling the chapel with daylight. Tears drop from her cheeks, three perfect teardrops that fade into nothing before they hit the stone ground.

'No, Mum,' she whispers, and her light seems to shimmer around Patty for a second.

Patty howls, and throws the knife away. It bounces on the hard stone and skittles along the floor, coming to rest by stone steps close to Jim.

'You didn't kill her.'

Patty wraps her arms around him and he sags into her – his sobs loud like screams. 'Tom, Tom... poor pup.' She strokes his hair.

Dani turns and walks away, the brightness fading once again until she is normal. Normal for a ghost.

Keyson looks like he will spit blood. 'What the— you stupid woman. He killed your daughter. What the hell is wrong with you – what are you?'

Patty looks up at Keyson. 'A parent. That's all.' She turns back to Tom, who has calmed a little. 'Tom, tell the truth. What happened?'

He whispers so softly that only Patty can hear him.

'I wish you had done it, Patty.' He kisses her lightly on the cheek. Then he begins.

'Dani was pregnant with Duncan Cobhurn. She told me and Izzy that Christmas she came home. She said she couldn't tell you, didn't know how you'd react as he was married.'

Patty nods her head, knowing she would have exploded.

'She planned to take a year out – have the baby and then go back to uni. They were going to live together, he was leaving his wife and everything. I couldn't...' Tom closes his eyes and lets the memories flood back.

Duncan Cobhurn hurries, his heart beats fast, she is not chasing him – that's good. It's hard to rush with the case. He feels so ashamed. Telling Audrey was the hardest thing he has ever done. He loves Dani, will do anything to be with her – but... no, he has made his choices. Audrey will find it tough but eventually she'll get over it. It will work out for the best, he knows it will. He just needs to get to Danielle, hold her and tell her it will be all right. They can have another baby.

Up ahead in the shadows there is a movement. A policeman who...

'Mr Cobhurn, Duncan Cobhurn?' He steps directly in Duncan's way, stopping him dead.

'Yes, that's me. Do I know you, officer? How do you know my name?'

'Duncan Cobhurn. Husband of Audrey and father of Lorraine.'

Duncan feels something's wrong. 'I'm on my way to something important, if you'd just let me pass.' He tries to get past the policeman, but he bars his way.

'Sweet kid, your Lorraine. Awful if something happened to her.'

'What the hell are you—'

Tom is quick, he swings his arm and from nowhere a truncheon slides into it. He catches Duncan Cobhurn on the leg just below the knee. An inch higher and the blow would have shattered his kneecap.

'Christ.' Cobhurn falls, grabbing at his leg and rolling on the ground in pain.

'This is no idle threat, Duncan. You are not going to see Dani Lancing again. You are going back to your wife and daughter and you're going to keep your dick in your pants. If you don't, Lorraine is going to get a visit from some lads I know and they will fuck her up – do you understand what I'm saying? She will wish they'd killed her by the time they finish.'

Duncan grabs at Tom, but he's quicker. The truncheon catches him hard on the shoulder.

'Jesus. Why are you doing this?'

'Because Dani Lancing is owned by someone else and they will destroy anyone who hurts her.'

'I love her.'

'You have caused her nothing but pain. Leave her alone you bastard. In fact—'

Tom grabs him by the collar and pulls him up on his injured leg – Duncan screams with the pain.

'Come here.' Tom drags him towards a phone box close by and throws him inside. 'Where are you meeting her?'

'Her home. She's going there by cab…'

Tom dials the number. 'You are gonna tell her you're finished

with her, that she means nothing to you. That you can't imagine
having a baby with her – she's just a kid.'

Tom pushes the swing and sees the child flash in the air – weeeeeeeeee
it cries. Dani waves at them both. 'I don't care that he isn't mine – I
will love you both forever,' he hears himself say. This is my family.

'The baby... she lost the baby.'

'You fucker.' Tom's truncheon is in his hand again and he
smashes into Duncan's thigh. The older man screams and drops to
the bottom of the phone box.

'You will never see Dani again.'

'Please no...'

'Say it or your wife and daughter will wish they were dead.'

Tom hands him the phone.

In the cathedral, Patty and Jim feel their hearts break. For Dani,
for Tom, for the baby... even for Duncan Cobhurn. And in the
shadows Dani remembers the emptiness – the pain rushes back into
her. She remembers the pit opening inside her soul when she heard
Duncan on the phone that night.

'I hate you. You won't trap me again with your brat – I'm glad
it's dead,' he had told her. Tom had made him say that – how could
he? He was supposed to be her friend – he had been her protector
and confidant. How could he? And Duncan, her poor Duncan.

She looks to Tom. His head is bowed. She fades from where she
is and reappears, floating in mid-air below him, looking directly

into his face. Tears drop from his cheek and fall towards her... flaring slightly as they pass through before striking the flagstones. She sees his pain and yet cannot understand how the gentle boy she once knew beat a man and left him broken in the bottom of a phone box. Forced him to break a woman's heart. How can this man be her Tom?

'Tom?' she whispers.

He looks right through her – there are no answers from him. He stands up and looks back to Patty.

'My plan had been to make him dump her on the phone and then I'd turn up an hour later. I had a cake and flowers. It was just gonna be by chance – on her birthday...'

Dani understands.

'...and she'd be all sad from Cobhurn – but all happy to see me. She'd fall into my arms and realise we were meant to be together. I just wanted her to love me like I loved her. I even wanted to... I thought we could raise the baby. Our baby. I didn't care that it was his.'

'But?' Patty asks.

'When I heard she had lost the baby I thought she'd need time. I decided to wait for twenty-four hours. Go back the next day. I still thought she'd be so happy to see me that...'

'Tom, I loved you but I was never in love with you,' Dani tells the air.

'I just loved her so much,' Tom repeats.

'I know you did, Tom. I know you did,' Patty says in a tired voice.

'But when I got to her flat the next day – the... the door was open. The place was empty. I sat down and waited. I stayed in her flat all that day and night but she never came back. She never came back. I killed her, Patty. I killed her because I couldn't let her be with him.'

Patty takes his hand. 'Christ, what a mess.'

'Oh Jesus this is desperate,' sneers Keyson. 'Then what are you telling us? That while she was walking around she was taken by a gang and killed a month later? Is that the shit you're pedalling?'

'No. No, you aren't saying that are you, Tom?' Jim asks. He has walked out of the shadows. 'She went back to him, didn't she?'

'Who?' asks Patty.

'Seb Merchant.' Jim looks at his wife with, sad, soulful eyes. 'In that first year at university, she got involved with drugs. Merchant was the bastard who dragged her into it. She kicked it, though, she was so strong – and I was so proud of her. She promised me she would never go back to him – she promised me.'

'Dad, I am so sorry,' Dani calls to him.

Patty shakes her head. 'But Seb Merchant wasn't in the country when Dani went missing – he'd gone to Australia months before. I found him when he came back to England. I interviewed him and he wasn't involved.'

Tom shakes his head. 'It wasn't Seb Merchant; I wish it had been. I looked for her for days after that night, but there was no trace. I thought she'd just gone away to think, I was sure she'd call me or Izzy soon. Come home and cry on our shoulders… but nothing. I didn't know about the trouble she'd been in that first year, she never told me. I kept waiting to hear… then you reported her missing and I just couldn't believe it.'

'No.' Dani feels so cold.

'I went straight round to you but you didn't know anything. I couldn't tell you what I'd done – couldn't tell anyone. So I carried on searching, kept calling the Durham police – drove up there any time I had off work. Then Ben Bradman's piece came out in the

News of the World – I was so angry I had to confront him. He told me he'd heard rumours about Dani from a jazz musician but he had no name. It took days to track him down.'

⁂

Tom finds him in a rehearsal room, alone. Trumpet player, big with a thick neck that oozed gold chains and an enormous crucifix that hung over his heart and danced as he played. In his mid-thirties, shaved head – a large man, but slow, no muscle. Clyde Trent.

Tom pulls the heavy door closed as he goes through. The room had once been an old bank vault, now it's used for cheap bands to rehearse and make tinny recordings. Dead acoustics.

'I done nothing…' are his first words as soon as he sees the uniform.

Tom pulls Dani's photo out from his jacket and he holds it out with one hand. In his pocket his other hand slips inside his knuckleduster. Violence is coming so easily to him now.

'Dani Lancing. Remember her? You told a reporter that you knew her, that she was involved with drugs in a big way.'

'Oh Christ, man.' He makes a break for the door to the outside, but Tom is quicker and bars the way.

'I need to know just what you told him.'

'You got the wrong m—'

'Bradman was very clear. Now we can do this messily, which ends badly for you, or you can tell me what you know and I leave you alone and go back to London. That way nobody but you and me know we had this conversation. Which option do you like?'

Clyde is impassive, but Tom can see that inside the large man the cogs are starting to shift.

'The newspaper paid me,' he says finally.

'Lucky you. I hope you got at least thirty pieces of silver. I am offering you something far more rewarding than money.'

'Shiiiit,' he grinds his teeth and shakes his head. 'These are bad men.'

'Then help me save her from them.'

Clyde looks incredulous for a second and then laughs a deep braying laugh. 'She don't want no saving. Man, she chose the gig.'

'What?'

'I know her a while back. She was with some small-time pusher, worked the university – some spliff then on to H, but she could afford it. She didn't turn no trick. Not then.'

Tom begins to feel everything start to unravel. 'Now?'

Clyde hesitates, before he leans forward and speaks softly. 'A few weeks back I were at a party, she came looking for her ex but no one seen him. She seem desperate for somewhere to crash and get lost, she make an offer. She was pretty, so she got owned,' he shrugs. 'She knew what she were doing.'

Tom feels bile rise in his throat. 'Owned,' he repeats slowly. He knows what that means. He thinks of the branded girl at Franco's.

'One man?'

'A gang.'

Tom wants to be sick but has to keep it all inside. 'I need a name.'

'Come on, I can't...'

'If you don't, I will list you as an informant and have it leaked to every scumbag in this city. They will nail you to a fucking cross.'

Clyde shakes his head. Tom feels his fingers tighten inside the cold metal in his pocket. He has come too far, he will do anything now.

Clyde is quiet for quite some time, before he finally speaks. 'Jackson. They known as the Jackson Five. Big joke.'

'Address?'

'Ain't got.'

Tom nods, he can see the big man has given him all he knows.

'Thank you,' he says in what must sound so hollow to the other man – then he's gone.

Tom runs back into the early evening gloom and heads towards the centre of town. He finds a phone box and places a call to Franco. It takes some time to make his way through the entourage surrounding him, but finally he gets to speak to the man himself and ask his favour. Franco listens to Tom's story.

'I see how you love this girl, Mr Policeman. I hope there is a sweet outcome here… so I will help, but you owe me. You owe me personally, and you owe me big. I will collect on this debt, you can be sure of that. One day you will return these favours.'

'I will, Franco. You have my word.'

'Your word is your heart and your soul, PC Bevans. You understand that?'

'I do.'

He pauses for a moment. 'Okay, give me an hour.'

It takes twenty minutes. Twenty minutes where Tom stands in the phone box and tries to keep all thoughts out of his head, all thoughts of what *being owned* by a gang might mean. But that is impossible as the image of the beautiful girl in the sarong forces itself into his mind. She was owned, kept junked up, oblivious to the world and whatever she was trying to escape from. And in return she was used whenever the gang wanted, for whatever the gang wanted. He sees again the carved F on her shoulder, her brand.

'Dani,' he moans.

Two people come to use the phone box but he makes them move on, growling at them like he's a madman.

After twenty minutes the phone rings and he rips it from its cradle.

Franco has an address in the Gilesgate district.

'This is a heavy scene here, PC Romeo. I tell you this not so you can call in a raid but go there yourself. You okay with that?'

'Fine, Franco.'

Tom pulls out his Durham A to Z and finds the address. Not too far. He starts to run. It takes maybe fifteen minutes; he runs like a fox chased down by hounds. He has no plan, he just wants to find her – he'll threaten, barter and pay for her release from them. Anything. He will sell his soul to the devil to get her back.

'Even if she goes straight back to Duncan Cobhurn?' The devil hisses in his ear.

FORTY-ONE

Wednesday 29 December 2010

In the guttering candle-light of the cathedral, Tom sways, his face drained of all colour; contrasted to the bloom of blood on his shirt he looks like a dead man.

'I found her. Patty I found her and—'

He sees her again, as she was that night. Lying naked, alone... already dead.

He finds it; a squalid house in a dirty street of student digs and squats. Its windows have boards nailed across them, the small front garden a tumble of weeds with the detritus of a washing machine lying tangled and twisted across the path leading to the door. Inside, the house seems dark and noiseless.

Tom strides up to the front door and hammers with authority, an authority he no longer feels. There is no answer. He drags a large piece of metal over to the window and stands on it, trying to look inside, but he can see nothing. He makes his way around to the back door. Again it's locked. He lifts some metal, a battering ram of sorts, and begins to swing. It takes seven attempts to shatter the wood and push it through into the kitchen. Then he climbs through the hole he's made, and falls into the darkness. He takes a torch from his belt and...

'Christ.'

In the beam a sea of cockroaches scuttle away. The smell of rotting food takes his breath away. The floor is sticky, there are empty take-away boxes everywhere, and they undulate with the movement of small insects. Tom pushes on, torch shining the way. He checks the downstairs and then up, up...

The first two rooms are empty, abandoned in a hurry. Tom shines his torch around and can see powder residue and empty phials. This had been a factory for the gang – probably where they cut the pure drugs for sale on the street. But they'd moved on – and in a hurry. Tom feels anxiety building in him as he goes room to room. Finally there is only one room left on the second floor. The moment he opens the door he knows something is wrong; an over-powering smell of bleach hits him. He shines the torch inside and it catches the edge of a mattress in the centre of the room. He walks in, his boots crunching on shattered glass, bleach lies pooled at the base of the mattress. And there lies Dani.

She is naked – more than naked, if there can be such a thing. And she is dead. A syringe sticks out of her arm. Pushed in but never pulled out. Her hair is greasy, there is semen in it. The mattress is stained with sick and blood. Her legs and arms are heavily bruised, the paleness of the body makes them all the more livid as the blood has settled. Her hip looks swollen.

On her shoulder there is a dark scrawl that looks like a marker pen – but he knows is a primitive tattoo – a brand: J5. He touches her, she is a little stiff with rigor that is fading. Two days – probably two days dead. If only he could have... but what is the use of think-ing like that? The room is cold, that has kept her looking fresher, but he knows that within a day or two she will start to bloat and insects will come. The bleach has been splashed around to keep anything off of her for a while. He is grateful for that, at least.

Tom kneels down to her and strokes her arm, up to her shoulder and then her hair. He sits there looking at her in the harsh light of his torch beam until he cannot bear it and turns it off. In the dark he does something he has not done since primary school. He prays.

In the cathedral the memories scorch his eyes from the inside.

'They just left her there; they just left her there with the cockroaches,' he howls like a wild animal.

Jim looks across from Tom, to his daughter as she stands tall, listening to the story of her own death. He cannot tell what she feels, or if she knows this part of the story at all. Maybe she had watched Tom find her that day, and sit with her lifeless form. Jim feels such sorrow for her.

Tom snorts away tears and snot before he continues.

'I didn't have any plan. There was no power in the house but I found a candle and lit that. She looked so... I ran a bath and washed her. She was stiff, hard to manoeuvre at first but it was lessening and the bath helped. She looked so beautiful when I'd cleaned her up. I cut her nails and her hair a little. Then I wrapped her in a sheet I found – it wasn't totally clean but it was better than nothing.'

Tom closes his eyes and remembers how she looked as she lay before him that night so long ago – pale but radiant in death. That night he cradled her head in his arms and spoke to her, told her all the things he'd always wanted to say but was too shy. He told her how much he loved her. He remembers kissing her one last time.

'As I sat there with her I realised I couldn't let anyone else see her and think she'd chosen that awful death. I thought about taking her body away and burying her – but I knew I couldn't do that to you two,' he looks to Jim and Patty. 'I had to let her be found, but not like that. I knew there was no way I could fool any pathologist or coroner; toxicology reports would show she was a chronic user and... and that would have been it. I didn't know what to do but knew I couldn't let the world think she—' He can't finish the sentence.

'What did you do?' Jim asks.

'I made her comfortable and then I left her – just for a little while. I called Franco again. I told him what I'd found.'

'I am so profoundly sorry, my friend,' Franco had said, then he paused. Possibly realising he had used the word 'friend'. 'You are a worry to me.'

'I can't let her be seen like that, Franco. I can't let the world know her like that.'

'You want history to remember her as a victim?'

'I want... those who loved her to remember the wonderful woman she would have become. Not the girl who lost her way and couldn't get back.'

'You love her?'

'With all my heart.'

Franco had sighed. 'This all very *Romeo and Juliet*. You are lucky I am a big romantic. Go back to your sweetheart and sit with her for a while. A man will be with you soon. Do as he tells you.'

'Thank you, Franco.'

'I am not doing this for you, Policeman', Franco tells him and then rings off.

Tom goes back to the house and sits with Dani.

'I'm sorry', he tells her, stroking her face.

Then he begins to recite poetry to her. He had spent hours

learning dozens of love poems for her – for the night he hoped they would be lovers. This is the closest he will ever come.

Finally, at around 10.30p.m., there is a pummelling on the door and Tom goes down to answer it. Before him stands a tall, thin man with a long face. He has a pencil moustache that sits on his upper lip as if it's been inked there. He's dressed in the uniform of a Detective Inspector.

'You PC Fucking Romeo?' He asks.

Tom can only nod slowly.

'DI Dent.' He pushes inside. 'Where's Juliet?'

Tom treads up the stairs with Dent following, into the room with Dani.

When he sees her Dent gives a little wolf-whistle. 'She's a looker.' He moves her head from side to side. 'Dead thirty-six to forty-eight hours.' He touches her shoulder. 'Branded – she was their Snow White, for any hard-working dwarf that wanted his wick dipped.'

Tom feels bile rise.

Dent touches her leg and swollen hip.

'And they fucked her bandy.'

Tom screams and swings a punch at Dent – but the older man is pistol quick. He feints to the side and drops Tom with a fist into the kidney. Tom falls and Dent grabs his arm and twists. Tom yells in pain.

'This is no fucking pantomime, you idiot. If you want your girlfriend to come out of this without looking like a whore you need to think like the shits that put her here. We need to lose the brand – the hip works for us. Makes it look like she was forced.' He lets Tom go.

'How do we lose the brand?'

'We cut it or burn—'

'No!'

'She's dead. The dead don't feel pain.'

With a look of contempt, Dent walks out the door and down the stairs. Tom sits there, at Dani's feet, lost.

'Are you fucking coming?' Dent calls up the stairs. With a last look at Dani, Tom leaves and heads down. The front door is open. Through it Tom can just about see the disappearing form of DI Dent. Tom bounds after him, catching up with him as he climbs into a squad car.

'Where are we going?'

Dent looks up at him from the driver's seat.

'Just get in the fucking car, lover boy.'

Tom holds his anger in check and gets into the passenger seat. Dent pulls away from the kerb. Tom turns to see the house disappear from view.

'Can you—' Tom starts.

'Button it. Look I don't know how but you've got some seriously fucking important friends and I have been told to do whatever I can to make your lady friend smell sweet as a newborn.'

'I—'

'I said, button it. I don't want to hear your stories. We need two things to make this work. Number one – we need some clean samples. Blood sample, piss and cotton swabs from a clean mouth.'

They drive in silence for another ten minutes and pull up in front of a regular residential house.

'Come on.'

Dent gets out and walks up to the house, Tom follows. Dent

pulls keys out of his pocket and opens the door. Tom stops on the threshold.

'Is this your house?'

'Yes – get in.'

Dent walks in and heads upstairs, turning the lights on as he goes. Inside the house is really nice. Tom can see the quality of the carpets and the wallpaper. All the way up the stairs are paintings.

'Is that a—'

'Francis Bacon. Just a little one, for me old age,' Dent winks. At the top of the stairs he walks into the bathroom and opens a cabinet, taking out a sponge bag. Then he goes back onto the landing and knocks on one of the doors.

'Julie.' He waits a moment. 'Julie.'

'I heard ya.'

A minute or so later the door opens. Standing there, in a stripey nightgown is a girl, maybe thirteen or fourteen. Blonde and thin, her skin a little acned.

'Dad.'

He stretches out a hand and gives her a test tube, a small pot and a bag of swabs.

'Not again, Dad.'

'Come on, darling. I'll buy you something nice.'

'You bloody better,' she says and walks into the bathroom, closing the door behind her.

Tom feels like he's in a dream. 'Is that your…?'

'Eldest. She's a good girl.'

They stand in silence for a while and then the door reopens and Julie steps out. She hands the samples back to her dad.

'Thanks, darling.'

'Nice, you promised.'

'Got it, love.'

'Expensive, too?'

'Within reason. Goodnight, sweetheart.' He kisses her and she goes back to bed.

'Romeo – you need to get out of that uniform.' He leads Tom into a bedroom. It's stylish, like a fancy hotel. Dent opens a drawer and pulls out jeans and a fisherman's sweater. He throws them at Tom. 'Change – then come down. I'll find a holdall for the uniform.'

Dent heads back downstairs. Tom puts on the change of clothes, then heads down. The front door is open and Dent is outside smoking. He hands a bag to Tom.

'How did you get here?' Dent asks him.

'What do you mean?'

'From London – I mean, you are from fucking London, aren't you?'

'Yes.'

'So?'

'Train.'

'Well, it's too late for that now. I'm gonna drop you at an all-night cafe – there you can cadge a ride with a truck. There's loads heading down at this time of night.'

'I need to go back to the house.'

'No you don't. You need to get the fuck out of Dodge.'

'I have to say goodbye.'

'Who...' Dent looks lost for a second – then he understands. 'To your girlfriend.'

'Dani.'

'She's fucking dead.'

'She—'

'Christ, Romeo, let me tell you how this works. You are gonna get a truck down south. If you're lucky you won't have to suck his cock for the ride. Before you leave you are gonna make a phone call from a public phone to say the police will find Dani Lancing at that house and that she was abducted. Abducted. That will get them looking for signs of a struggle and of forced captivity. You understand?'

'Yes,' though Tom doesn't sound sure.

'That house is a known drugs den. If you just call in a tip-off they will send a drugs team in. That isn't what we want – we need a serious crime team to be called in.'

'Why?'

'Cos it'll be my fucking team, that's why.' Dent shakes his head. 'They'll take photos and collect samples – clean samples, from my fucking pocket.'

Tom nods. 'The samples from Julie.'

'A prize to the shithead for getting it right. My team will write the report up as abduction and multiple rape. Then the body will get transferred to the morgue – and the coroner.'

'But he won't—'

'That's the second thing to do. Remember I said there were two things we had to do to make this right?'

'Bribe the coroner.'

'Are you fucked? Coroners make too much bloody money and they think they're above all this shit – like they're doctors or something. No, we don't bribe him.'

'Then what?'

'Blackmail the fucker.'

'How?'

Dent sucks the last of the cigarette into his lungs and flicks the butt into the darkness.

'His son.' He walks quickly to the car, Tom follows. They get in the car and Dent drives.

'What's the son done?'

'Took his dad's car when he was fourteen. Thought he was Sterling fucking Moss. Did a shitload of damage and put two people in hospital. One was serious – the kid begged us to hush it up. He's eighteen now – university boy whose life would be totally fucked by this. Pretty sure the old man doesn't know. Well, he will tonight.'

'And he'll alter his report.'

'Oh yeah – I'll make sure he does. He doesn't want his son going down. He's far too pretty to do well inside. The coroner's a family man.'

'So his report won't mention drugs in Dani's system.'

'Nothing.' Dent pulls onto a stretch of motorway. The car moves through dark to sodium orange and back to dark. Ahead is a transport cafe. Dent pulls into it and up to a phone box. They sit in silence.

'You are gonna get a ride set up for about an hour and make that call just before you leave. That will give me plenty of time.'

'You don't want me back at the house.'

'You know what I'm gonna do.'

'The brand, you'll remove it.'

'Yes. And then I am gonna take your girlfriend's hand and scratch the wall. I'm gonna make twenty-one lines on the floor and then the words "Help me!". Then I'll tie her wrists and ankles together.'

Tom nods his head with the smallest of gestures. He realises what must be done – is even grateful in a way to be saved from seeing that room again.

'Then I'm gonna go and visit the coroner.'

FORTY-TWO

Some of the candles have already burnt themselves out, leaving the driftwood sculptures darkened in places. The chapel is quiet and cold while everyone takes in what Tom has told them. Suddenly Tom snorts with nervous laughter.

'Then a couple of days later, when we went to see her, you and me,' he looks directly at Jim, 'I thought the game would be up. The report said no drugs – but you had to look at her arms because you knew about Seb Merchant. I thought I was going to die. I thought you were going to be the one to question why it was a murder inquiry, ask about the drugs... but you didn't.' Tom stops for a second. 'I thought someone, somewhere, would work out what had happened – the coroner would stand up to Dent. But no.' Tom looks directly at Patty 'I thought you would sink it – make the house of cards tumble down with your questions... but it didn't. Everybody assumed she'd been killed. You were looking for a killer, Patty – but there wasn't one to find. There wasn't a murder, but a dead girl. Just a dead girl.'

'Tom,' Patty's voice is barely audible. Her eyes closed. 'Was it an accident?'

Dani hits her head with her palm. Jim hears it but nobody else. He sees the pain in his daughter's face.

Tom shakes his head. 'There was no note.'

It is not an answer to the question.

Jim remembers the church packed full of people on the day of her funeral, so much love for Dani, for the good girl who had been taken from them. How different would it have been if the truth were known?

Patty nods. 'I unders—'

'Bastard.' A fist lands on Tom's chin and sends him sprawling. Marcus Keyson stands there glowering, shaking with anger. 'You fucking hypocrite. You sad little man. All you've done, lives ruined by you and because of you. Yet you swan around like a saint, dishing out your moral code and judging others like an Old Testament, petty god. You don't have the right.'

'Marcus, I—'

'Don't you dare act like we're friends. You let that animal Dent loose on a kind and great man.'

Tom is lost for a second and then – the pieces tumble into place; he understands Keyson's anger. 'The coroner?'

'Gerald Spurling was his name. He was the greatest man I knew – the smartest man I will ever know. He was like a father to me and…' He chokes on the words, a tear falls.

'Marcus.'

'For the sake of your fucking dead girlfriend's reputation – you destroyed him.'

'I did nothing—'

'Your weapon of destruction – DI Dent. He went to an honourable man and he stuck the knife into his guts and twisted it until he broke.'

'I didn't ask him to…'

'Oh, Tom, take some fucking responsibility. Whatever it took to make your girl look clean. You ruined Ben Bradman's life and you let Dent pressure an old man into fabricating a report.'

'It was only changing evidence.'

'Only.' Keyson's eyes flash violence. 'Only. What the hell did I lose my career for? Lose my reputation for?'

'That was different.'

'How different? You made a man who was proud of a life-time of honesty and service to this country lie – and you did it by threatening his family and his way of life. Do you know, he was so ashamed of what he'd done he took an overdose – it didn't kill him, probably would have been better if it had – it gave him a massive stroke. He took more than ten years to die – ten years of misery. His son Paul nursed him all those years. He felt so guilty that a reckless moment as a teenager had been used to destroy his father. When Gerald finally died do you...' Keyson closes his eyes, unable to go on for a second. 'Paul hanged himself. Both gone, what a fucking waste.'

'Marcus, I had no idea—'

'No, of course you didn't. You high and mighty bastard. You use people. Knock down anyone that gets in your way and don't care what happens to them.'

'Back then—'

'But if anyone else deviates, even slightly from the Bevans code, then you judge them. You are judge, jury and executioner – you judged me and had me thrown out with the rubbish. Yet you—'

'You're right. I have done awful things, I should pay for it all and I've tried. For twenty years I've tried to pay for what I did, tried to do right by women like Dani.'

'Like Dani... like Dani.'

'Damn you, Marcus.'

'You already have – you damned me. You sold me out.'

'You slept with women and took bribes to change evidence.'

'No. No, I did not. People came to me to help right wrongs, men and women who were being failed by the system. I altered evidence to highlight the truth – show it had been presented by liars and cheats. Men with ulterior motives, men like you and DI Dent. I was wronged, I am the victim.'

'Oh, come on. I saw your bank records – I saw the women visiting you.'

'They wanted to say thank you. Who was I to deny them that? It was never about the money – I accepted their gratitude as I had saved them from wrong.'

'You are crazy.'

'And you, DS Bevans, are ruthless. You know nothing about true friendship or real loyalty. You would betray everyone for the sake of the memory of a long-dead girl. How do you sleep at night?'

'Me? What about you, Marcus – you're here to blackmail us.'

'Blackmail?' Keyson spits. 'I need money to keep fighting for truth and justice, to protect society from men like you. You don't keep the girls safe.'

'That's not true,' Tom says sadly.

'Oh my melancholy friend – you need to learn a lesson. I don't want money any more. You have destroyed so many lives. I am going to destroy yours.' He turns to Patty. 'And you, Mrs Lancing. Mr Cobhurn was weak, his wife vicious, but you cannot take the law into your own hands. You can't take a life – you are not God. I've asked Mr Ronson to deliver your confession to someone who can make good use of it.' Keyson stands above them all – looking down with triumph.

'I deserve it.' Patty starts to shake. The end will be soon.

Tom puts his hand on her shoulder softly, kindly. 'There's no need to bring Patty into it. She didn't kill Duncan Cobhurn. I did.'

'What?' Patty feels everything shift below her, she almost falls.

'And it's your fault, Marcus. You came to see me too soon after Patty hired you.' Tom turns to Patty now. 'He'd already talked to the journalist who wrote the *News of the World* piece all those years ago, Ben Bradman, and had sniffed out where I'd altered evidence. He had the case notes from that first night– showed them to you. Even though Dent was good, there were inconsistencies. I knew he could find the truth – that didn't worry me so much as you digging deeper. I...' He snorts back some tears. 'I didn't want you to know about her death, or my lies. I'm sorry... that's why I wanted it to be me that told you about the case review. I hoped I could do it in such a way that you wouldn't get worked up about it...' he smiles a tight smile. 'Fat chance of that happening. You immediately got roused, a dog with a bone. I could see it that day,' he looks directly into Patty's eyes. 'Then, after Keyson came to see me, I knew you'd have to follow it up and that Cobhurn was at some kind of risk. I put him on an alert, you and Jim too. Then I decided to visit you again and this time I intended to tell you the whole truth. But, as I got there you came out – in disguise. I followed you to a Heathrow hotel.'

'That was a reconnaissance trip.' Patty sighed.

'When Duncan Cobhurn went missing I guessed what had happened and figured out why you'd gone to the hotel before. So I went to the same hotel; I thought I would find you there with him. Instead, I found him trussed up – he was unconscious, but alive. There was a syringe on a table with phials of Ketamine. I saw red. I remembered what he'd done to Dani. Got her pregnant and... I pumped him up with another two phials, enough to kill him, and then I left.'

'Oh, Tom.'

'I would never have let you take the blame. I tried to find you after – but you just disappeared.'

She nods.

'He destroyed Dani – he should have loved her enough to stand up to me. He should have loved her as much as I did. I would never really have hurt his wife or daughter, it was just a threat, but he didn't love her enough.'

'Tom.' Patty folds over and begins to sob and sob with relief. The pressure of believing herself to be a killer had been too much. She had been so close to the edge.

'Oh thank God. I didn't… thank you thank you.'

Jim watches his wife cry tears of happiness – joy that she isn't a murderer, and then looks to Tom. Jim sees the lie. He didn't find Cobhurn – he is taking Patty's crime onto his own shoulders. He can cope with it, whereas it would crush Patty eventually. In that moment Jim loves Tom, sees the hero in him. Not the villain.

Tom looks up to Keyson. 'Marcus, stop torturing us, turn me in. For everything – for the cover-up of Dani's death, for Spurling and his son, for Cobhurn, for you. End all this.'

Keyson grins. 'Tom. It will be a pleasure.'

Jim watches Keyson open his phone and start to dial.

'Dad.' Dani's voice is all around him. With a smile he looks into her beautiful face again.

'Oh, sweetheart, I am so sorry.'

'You need to help me, I can't do it alone,' she pleads.

'Anything.'

She takes his hand in hers – and for the first time he can feel something, a real physical presence. He stands up and she leads him over to the wall. By the steps is the knife Patty almost killed Tom with.

'Pick it up, Dad.'

He does so, and she points to a brass censer tied to the wall.

'Cut it for me, please.'

He cuts the censer free from the wall. It is made of brass and incredibly heavy. It hangs from one end of a very long leather strap that extends down, out of the gloom above them. As soon as he cuts it free, it begins to arc into the centre of the room and he grabs at it to keep it steady.

'Hold it for me, Dad.' She slowly rotates her hands, showing him how to aim it.

Keyson stands with his telephone in hand.

'What service do you require?' The 999 operator asks him.

'Police.' Keyson smiles.

'Thank you,' Dani says to her father as he holds the brass globe. She moves her hand close to it, as if she could almost touch it herself.

'You can let go now,' she tells him and he opens his hands. It swings – a pendulum building up speed as it flies through the air.

'I love you, Dad,' she vanishes and appears next to her mother. 'I love you, Mum.' She blows a kiss to Patty, who for a second feels a shiver deep in her heart. Then she is next to Tom.

'My white knight, be safe,' she tells him.

Dani waves to Jim. He watches her float up from them, into the shadows above their heads. Gone.

❄

The sound is like a watermelon hit with a hammer, brass on skull. Keyson's eyes flare as his brain shifts to the left and countless blood vessels burst. His right eye pools with blood and he falls to the ground.

'What?' Tom is up first. He thinks Keyson has been shot, it was so quick.

'The censer.' Jim points to it as it sways on the rope like a punch drunk boxer. There is a slight dent on one side.

'How the hell did that happen?' Tom asks.

Jim would like to tell but... what would he say?

'The phone,' hisses Patty and she drops down to it. From a long way off she hears: '... do you need emergency assistance?'

'Help me,' Patty croaks into the phone, then kicks it a long way.

'They'll trace it,' Tom warns.

'He needs help.'

'What about the other man?' Jim asks.

'Ronson. He probably ran.' Tom indicates the prone form of Keyson. 'Is he alive?'

Patty reaches out to his neck and lays her fingers over his throat. It's barely there – but there is a pulse.

'Yes, just,' she tells him.

Tom looks helpless. A part of him wants to finish Keyson off. Patty sees that run through his mind.

'There's been enough killing, Tom. Enough people hurt. Let's go.'

'The knife.' Jim goes and picks up the knife.

'Try and clean anything you might have touched. Use a sleeve,' Tom warns.

The three of them retrace their steps, picking up anything they see – wiping and cleaning as they go. They walk away from the driftwood Mary and Jesus. Now the ancient woman of wood has two sons at her feet. Cain and Abel?

There is no sign of any other living soul as they leave the cathedral. It is still night but from somewhere they hear the bark of a dog. They pull their coats up to cover their faces and run to the path down by the graveyard.

As they get to the main road, they see their little car is still there. The accident has still not been cleaned up, the police barrier still in place – no vehicle has moved. The three of them get into the car, Tom in the driver's seat and Jim and Patty in the back. Each is silent as the events of the night re-run in their heads. Patty looks out and sees Audrey Cobhurn's blood shine in the light of the emergency vehicle's headlights.

Jim feels Patty place her head in his lap and he strokes her hair as she falls asleep. He looks out of the window and wonders where Dani is. Is she released from her stay on earth?

He wants to call to her – he feels an ache in his heart already. But he looks down and nestled in his lap is his wife who is asleep. That feels like a miracle to him.

Together the two men and sleeping woman wait in the car, to be released. From somewhere far-off they hear a siren. Maybe heading to the cathedral to find Marcus Keyson. Maybe.

As the first light of dawn strikes the city – the emergency vehicles are finally done, and the cars and truck in front of them start to move, limping away from the scene of such awful events. They all have stories to tell. Tom drives them all the way round the ring road, and then second star on the right and straight on till London.

EPILOGUE

Monday 7 February 2011

The three of them meet at 11 a.m. They go to the garden of remembrance where Jim and Tom have gone, both together and alone for so many years. This is Patty's first visit. Together they read the words on the plaque: DANI, LOVED DEARLY AND MISSED DEEPLY. They lay flowers alongside and Tom reads from Keats.

Then the three of them go to Patty's place of remembrance, the park by the hospital where she planted a tree for Dani. They even go into the supermarket and stand in the deli aisle, on the spot where Dani was born. They all agree it's too cold to stay long. They buy a bottle of champagne and some cheese and bread. They go back to the park and open the fizz. They've forgotten cups so they drink from the bottle, like students.

They toast Dani. She has been dead longer than she lived, but each of them still loves her so fiercely. They toast Jim and Patty – about to renew their vows once again. Tom's phone beeps. He looks at the message and his face clouds over.

'What?' Both Jim and Patty ask.

'It's Keyson. He just woke up from his coma.'

Dani stands and watches the watery sun ebb away. Behind her, in a shadowy corner of the room, the young woman sobs quietly. Dani would love to help her, but how – it's impossible.

'Please stop crying Sarah. It doesn't help.'

But the tears continue. Dani sighs. She knows what Sarah Penn needs – to tell her story to the Sad Man. That's what the three of them need, because somehow they know there will be another victim. Soon. But what can she do, apart from listen to the tears fall?

'I'm sorry Sarah. It's lonely being dead.'

ACKNOWLEDGEMENTS

I owe a great debt of gratitude to many people who helped me in the planning and writing of this book. My biggest thanks goes to Catherine Smith who pushed me right at the start and nurtured the first shoots of the story. Sophie Hannah gave me support and advice at a crucial time and connected me with my agent, Simon Trewin, who helped me to craft all those pages into something that felt like a book. I am also incredibly lucky to have Gillian Green and Zachary Wagman, two wonderfully creative editors; Emily Yau, at Ebury Press; and Justine Taylor, my copyeditor. Plus everyone at WME, Ebury and Crown – what a team.

I also want to thank for their insight and advice on technical aspects of this novel – Durham Coroner Andrew Tweddle and DI Vicki Harris. For medical expertise – Kellie and Kim Cronin. Thanks also to Dominic Parker for his knowledge of Durham.

Many people read early drafts and gave me wonderful feedback and support. I especially want to thank Rebecca Ball, Sylvia Cooke, Rachel Donoughue, Annie Fletcher, Melanie Green, Vikki Logan, Lynne Murphy, Mark Slater, Sam Shorter, Charlie Turner, Jools Wood, Jane Viner, Michael Viner and all at CCE.

And for inspiring me – Arden Murphy-Viner.

An exclusive interview with P. D. Viner:

What was your inspiration for *The Last Winter of Dani Lancing*?

The moment the initial plot idea came to me is very easy to pinpoint. It was mid-December and I was attending a writing class with the poet and short story writer Catherine Smith. She suggested we look at some of Grimm's fairy tales and try to re-imagine one of them for the modern day. I read a few of the tales and there was an idea that cropped up in two of the stories. Somebody was murdered and their bodies disposed of… but as they were hidden, three drops of blood fell to the floor. These drops of blood screamed bloody murder, raising the alarm and leading to the murderer being caught… and it set me thinking. It reminded me of modern DNA profiling, the fact that each drop of our blood carries our signature, in the same way that our fingerprints do. I remember taking the train home that night – a very dark and cold evening – and as I watched the world whip by I had a 'Eureka' moment. When I got home, I wrote a short story about a woman who kidnaps a man to take a blood sample from him, to discover if he killed her daughter. The story was only 500 words and it was titled 'Three Drops of Blood'. At that point it was Patty's story, and I became absolutely enmeshed in the idea of a mother desperate for both closure and revenge. I felt her pain very deeply and wanted to help her find the truth. There is a lot of my own mother in Patty. Whenever my sister or I were hurt she would become a demon – wanting to fight for us and avenge us. She once punched her fist through a door in rage as I had been hit at a party. I know if I were trapped under a burning truck she would be able to lift it.

So I began to write Patty's story... but I found that she is so full of rage and guilt and the pain of loss that I couldn't be in her head all the time. More than twenty years of having anger bubble inside her has eaten her away, like acid burning the hope from her. So I looked to the family, to allow me greater access to the story – and I created Jim and Dani. I must admit I fell in love with Dani a bit, and with her relationship to Jim. And I think that is the other part of the inspiration jigsaw. I have a daughter. She will be six years old this Christmas (I am writing this in October 2013) and by the time she is twenty-one (Dani's age) I will be sixty-three (close to Jim's age). Except for the being dead bit, I would love to have such a funny and close relationship with my daughter when she is grown.

I started writing the book when my daughter was two years old and I was both full of awe at how wonderful having a child was and fearful that I could lose her at any moment – that some terrible tragedy could occur. I think the double-edged sword that accompanies parenthood (especially a little later in life) really drew me forward with the parents' story of loss because it made me ask questions, like *how would I cope if I lost her?* I found myself (and I am pretty much the poster boy for the new/modern/pacifist/muesli-loving man) thinking about how I would hurt anyone that threatened my child. I wondered if I would kill to save her… to revenge her. I decided I would. But I also knew that even worse was the chance of not being able to have closure; how does a parent cope with a child that just goes missing? Faced with that, I thought I would crumble, collapse in on myself and live in the past. I would go crazy. And with both those possibilities for characters in my mind, I wrote Jim and Patty. They are in equal measure the bravest and the weakest of characters – they are parents pushed to the limit. I hope they ring true. It is hard to be a parent even without tragedy layered upon that.

This debut novel centres on Dani Lancing, a girl who has a ghostly presence. Tell us more about her. And if you were to come back as a ghost what would be your first choice of residence?

First of all, Dani is alive. She lives in the hearts and memories of Jim, Patty and Tom (the trinity of the pained) and they continue to talk to her and live with her. I write her as the cool and interesting girl she is: in part she is still a twenty-one-year-old university student, experimenting with life and love, but she is also a wise spirit who is aged far beyond her years. I love writing about her and so far she has not explored what she can do as a spirit. That will change next year as I have spent some time at the Greenwich observatory in the last few months. It is a fascinating place and is pivotal to the story of Dani. It is amazing – of course it is the very centre of our planet's timeline and has a fascinating history of discovery and adventure. I was shown around the secret places by a young astronomer and have found a ghost there. A woman who used to sell time (I will explain all) in the streets of London until she was murdered at the Royal Observatory... and the killing was never investigated. So there will be a special Dani Lancing story next year where she investigates the death and unmasks the killer.

So that's where I would choose to be a ghost, the Royal Observatory, and I could investigate hundreds of years of intrigue. Hmmmm... maybe next I will try the British Museum. The place must be full of ghosts.

And what would be your signature 'scare tactic'?

As a ghost? That is a tough question. I don't like the thought of being really scary, because I would like my daughter to be able to visit me and she gets scared easily – but if I must, then I would like to be able to melt... have my skin burn away and just leave a skeleton. Except, the thought of it makes me feel a little queasy. Maybe I could just float through walls in a traditional manner, or be more like Casper the friendly ghost.

The Last Winter of Dani Lancing **is set in London and Durham. What other destinations would you like to write about?**

I have already shared that important scenes in future stories will be set in the Royal Observatory. And I have been really lucky that I have been given two tours of Brighton's Royal Pavilion, a palace built by George IV (when he was Prince Regent) which is modelled on India's Taj Mahal and was created in the late 18th Century/early 19th and almost bankrupted Britain. I was able to go into secret passages between rooms and even an escape tunnel below the building. Finally I entered the saloon bubble, a secret room in one of the domes above the main palace, where the Prince would make his romantic conquests. Look out for it in my second novel, *The Summer of Ghosts*, as a murder takes place there; guess who dies? (Spoiler alert... you will have to read it).

Apart from that I have been researching the bush-wars of independence in Zimbabwe and modern-day South Africa as both of these places will feature in future novels. I am thinking about sending DS Tom Bevans, The Sad Man, to the American Deep South.

Also I lived in Moscow for a year and certainly want to write a Russian-set novel. We will have to see.

What do you like about being a writer?

I dream and think... I sit around (or walk around) and imagine what a twenty-one-year-old ghost is thinking about, or a lonely police detective, and then I write it down. I make connections and solve puzzles... I love it. It is amazing to think that something I develop in my imagination will eventually be out in the world, and maybe someone will be entertained by it and possibly realise something about the world or human interaction they didn't know before. That is fantastic. And sometimes I do this – write about myself and answer questions... and people might even read the answers and care.

Describe your working day.

The alarm goes off at 7.10am. I get dressed and my wife wakes our daughter. I make breakfast. Daughter is taken to school and then I make my way to a coffee shop. My favourite place is The Emporium Theatre in Brighton. It is a converted church and has great coffee and a good atmosphere. Other coffee shops are available.

I write from 9.30 to 12.30. Then I walk home and have some lunch. I read what I have written or deal with emails and then collect my daughter from school. One day a week my wife collects her so I have a longer writing session. In the evening I do some social media things and try to read. At the weekend I try not to write as that is family time.

What drew you to the crime genre? Have you ever written anything outside of this?

I think the truthful answer is that I wasn't drawn to crime, I was drawn to this story and these characters. I think the reason the book works (I say this trying not to display my big head, but echoing what so many people have told me about being gripped and moved by the book) is that it isn't by someone trying to write a genre novel. I didn't think 'oh yes crime sells'; it was more that I fell into crime due to the story unfolding in my head. I wrote unfettered by tags, or trying to slot it into existing tropes and ideas about crime writing. There is something really special about a mystery, the way (as a reader) we love to be drawn in and are asked to work a bit, to orient ourselves in a morally ambiguous world, and start to unravel the puzzle ourselves. I am really happy to call myself a crime writer now and love working on the continuing adventures of Dani Lancing and *The Sad Man*.

I started writing comedy sketches at fifteen and produced two shows – *Fun with Neville* and *Santa's Chainsaw Massacre* (juvenile but fun). In my twenties I tried to be a stand-up comedian (I was horrible). Under the bed, covered in mildew and dust are two unpublished novels: one is a comedy about an American cult and the other is a love story. I have had two plays produced: a dystopian comedy about the world after a financial crash called *Chasing the Hypnotist* and the second was performed at the International Shakespeare festival in Verona. I hope none of these see the light of day again.

Who, in your opinion, is the greatest writer of all time?

What? How can anyone answer a question like this? I have different favourite writers for different moods and over the years my tastes have changed. When I was twelve I would have said it was Terrance Dicks for the target novelisations of *Doctor Who*. Now, I would point to Kurt Vonnegut Jr and Graham Greene... and Mo Willems who writes the pigeon books. My daughter and I love them.

Which classic novel have you always meant to read and never got round to?

Bleak House. I love Dickens but have never read this. It's probably free on kindle. Oh and I have meant to read Stephen King's *The Stand* for ages. Does that count as a classic yet?

Which fictional character would you most like to meet?

Jesus. At least the Jesus who has been created over the past two thousand years (there may be a true historical figure, but he is not the man such bestsellers as The Bible, or guest slots on *South Park*, paint him).

Otherwise it would be Harry Lime. He is such a morally ambiguous character that a chat with him would be fascinating.

What's your favourite crime/thriller film?

Oh this is mean – how can anyone pick one choice when there are so many different crime genres and times and tastes change so much. OK... I am going to pick *The Night of The Hunter*. It has an amazing chase and such a nuanced villain. My list of honourable mentions: *The Third Man* (of course Harry Lime is a truly great baddie), *The Silence of the Lambs* (another great villain), *Get Carter* (an anti-hero) and the TV adaptation of *Tinker, Tailor, Soldier, Spy* (I know it isn't a film but it is fabulous). There is a definite theme of loving interesting bad guys... hmmm.

Other than your writing career, what other jobs or professions have you ever undertaken or considered?

I started working after school when I was twelve; it was a hardware store and I did two hours three days a week. Later I had a Saturday job in a shoe shop and worked there in the holidays.

I have been a manager at Oddbins, worked for WHSmith and been a bookbuyer and store manager for Whitcoulls in New Zealand (went there to marry but she dumped me – long story). I have been a stand-up comedian (short lived) and head of production at the world's largest Holistic health centre. I have made an award-winning film and productions for Japanese TV. I have made a few short films, a couple of documentaries and lots of audiobooks. I started an audio publishing company with my sister and, for ten years, we made a series of educational guides to Shakespeare and the classics – and then the financial crisis happened and the company crashed. That was what led to me writing *The Last Winter of Dani Lancing*.

In terms of jobs I would like... I dreamed from the age of five about being a film director. I did get to dip my toe in, but I would love to direct a film. My wife's father is a funeral director in America and the family lives above the funeral home. I don't want to be one – but I am fascinated by the job. Look out for a novel based around a funeral home.

What are you working on at the moment?

I am still living with Dani, Patty and Jim Lancing and DS Tom Bevans. I have written two novellas (of a planned five), the first of which is already available, titled *The Sad Man*, and set in 1999; it tells the story of Tom's breakthrough case. All five novellas will be free downloads (check them out). And the big project is to continue with (what I am calling) The Dani Lancing trilogy. *The Summer of Ghosts* brings one of the supporting characters from the first book to the fore: Franco. In the first book we meet him as an eighteen-year-old ganglord, a man who has killed and runs rugs and prostitution rings with violence and intimidation. He helps Tom find Dani and he tells the policeman that one day he will ask him to repay the debt. Twenty years later that debt must be repaid... and what he wants is for Tom to solve four murders. The last of which is Franco's own daughter.

I am loving writing about Tom and Franco and learning

more about this man who lives in the shadow of violence and lawlessness, and asking: can a man who lives in this world have a good heart? Tom, Jim and Patty are drawn into the turmoil of his life and along the way, even more is revealed about the truth of Dani's life and death.

There are more secrets, lies and reveals for poor Dani.

Also available from P. D. Viner:

THE SAD MAN

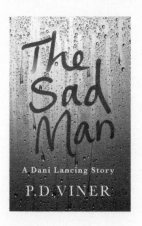

available for free by download now

Police officer Tom Bevans is nicknamed the Sad Man by his colleagues. As a Family Liaison Officer he is always the bearer of bad news – it is his job to tell the friends and family of victims the fate of their loved ones.

But Tom is weighted down by crimes both old and new – haunted by the death of his best friend Dani, whose murder has never been solved.

When a rare opportunity emerges for Tom to take the lead in a horrific murder investigation, he is determined to get justice for the victim. A young girl has been found in her own home, cut so badly – and so carefully – that she has bled to death, leaving a deliberate pool of blood in the shape of angel wings....

THE STRANGER YOU KNOW
by Jane Casey

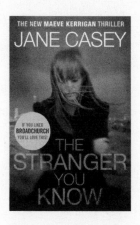

He meets women.
He gains their trust.
He kills them.

That's all Maeve Kerrigan knows about the man she is hunting. Three women have been strangled in their homes by the same sadistic killer. With no sign of a break-in, every indication shows that they let him in.

But the evidence is pointing at a shocking suspect: DI Josh Derwent, Maeve's colleague.

Maeve refuses to believe he could be involved, but how well does she really know him? Because this isn't the first time Derwent's been accused of murder...